The God Makers

By

Scott Alward

The characters and events portrayed in this book are fictitious. Any similarity to real persons, living or dead, is coincidental and not intended by the author.

ISBN: 9798328771979

Cover design by: Jessica Alward

Library of Congress Control Number: 2018675309

Printed in the United States of America

For my lovely wife, Jessica. Thank you for the many years of patience, support, and encouragement. Not to mention your unabashed critiques. As with all things in life, I couldn't have done this without you. I love you.

Some think there is something wrong about enhancing people.

-James D. Watson

1

Alex Carter screamed and bolted upright in bed; his cry cut off by the sudden shift from sleep to waking, reality slowly taking over the fading details of the dream he had just escaped. His muscles tensed as the dream slowly receded from his consciousness, just enough of it remaining to keep him on edge. He stretched his arms up and out, forcing his muscles to relax. A knot persisted in his back and he twisted, a small moan of pain escaping him.

A form in the bed next to him moved and his stomach tightened suddenly as a flood of anxiety washed over him again. His stomach was hot with fear as the shadowy form rose slightly next to him, reaching out into the night, black against black. The heat in his stomach rose, his muscles tense, as a chill in his spine grew. He choked back the urge to scream and run as the shadow beside him reached deeper into the darkness, flailing as if grasping for something. Someone.

There was a small click and a pool of amber light sprang into existence around his bed. The darkness retreated, chasing out the dream world. Next to him was his wife, Rachel, replacing the shadow beast from moments before. Her eyelids fluttered, desperately trying to batter sleep from her eyes. She yawned and stretched, propping up on an elbow. Brushing an errant strand of red hair from her face, she pushed herself up the headboard, giving up halfway and taking up an awkward half-sitting position.

"What was that?" she asked, stifling another yawn.

"It's okay. Just a bad dream. That's all." He avoided looking straight at her. The question was a courtesy, she knew what was going on. This had happened to her before, being awakened like this. Outside the window, trees danced to the howl of sharp autumn winds, awash in the glowing streetlights, casting darting shadows across the room. His stomach tightened at each shadowy movement.

Rachel rubbed at her eyes with the heels of her hands. "Was it another one of those dreams?" Her voice was soft, like she was trying to convince a frightened child there were no monsters under the bed. An edge of frustration accompanied it because she wasn't dealing with a child, but a grown man who refused to accept there were no monsters.

He started to say something to her and stopped before any words came. He wanted to talk to her about the fear. About the dark cold that filled him when the dreams came. But all he had were random images that slowly faded from his mind the further he got from sleep. The icy darkness in his belly was slipping away, the terror of moments ago slipping away with it. The memories of the dream, without the iron grip of terror that accompanied them, were just a series of random images with no substance. It was like talking about a good meal; the idea was there, but it lacked the intensity of the experience.

She slid across the bed to him, slipping her arms around him. Cold sweat covered his body, and he quivered at her touch, his muscles tensing beneath her arms. More shadows danced in the corner. His heart beat faster.

"It's okay, sweetheart. I'm here." Her voice was like a lullaby, any trace of bitterness gone as she snuggled in beside him. Her body was warm against his, melting his anxiety. He sighed, releasing the last of the tension that gripped him in one great rush and melted into her arms. The furious ball of fear in his stomach cooled, warming the chill in his spine as the dream dissipated.

"Yes," he answered, his mouth suddenly dry. He sucked on his tongue to relieve the dryness. "It was one of those dreams."

"Do you remember any more of it?" she asked, running her index finger through his dark hair while she stifled another yawn.

"Just images. Brief flashes of pictures. Like a movie skipping the reel."

"What kinds of images?" Her hand slid from the side of head to rest at the nape of his neck, rubbing gently. He leaned into it; his neck still knotted.

"I'm in a desert, I think," he started, grasping at the fleeing pictures in his head. "I can see a bunch of small, weird buildings just beyond a rusted chain-link fence. Like the bunkers you see in war movies. I want to climb the fence, to get to those buildings. Like there's something there I have to see. That I'm desperate to see. But every time I start to climb the fence, a storm comes up on the horizon, closing in fast. A storm that scares the living hell out of me. Even though it's still miles away, I have to get away from it as fast as I can. And then..."

His voice dropped off, the chill in his spine returning like a jolt of electricity. His breath caught in his throat and he had to pause, unable to speak. Rachel hugged him close.

"Then he's there. It's night all around us, but the darkness around him is different. It's not exactly the lack of light, but more of a living entity. He is being clung to by it, as if the darkness is a part of him. Like he's its master, somehow. And his eyes." Alex paused again, the familiar knot of fear returning to grasp his belly. "His eyes are so cold. Icy. Not just because of the color of them. The way he stares at me, it's like there's nothing human behind those eyes. Like staring into the eyes of a predator...."

Rachel felt him shiver. "Well, I'm here and I'm not going anywhere." She took his hand gently and placed it on her belly. A slight swell had started to develop, the first sign of the baby growing inside. "Neither of us are."

Alex thought he felt the baby kick to echo its mother's sentiments, but he knew that was his imagination. It was far too early for that. Still, imagined or not, he took comfort at the thought and focused on the warmth it brought him to drive back the cold pall of fear. Patting his wife's stomach, he silently thanked his son or daughter for their unspoken support.

Rachel squeezed his hand and smiled a warm, contented smile at him. She is beautiful, Alex thought. When he first saw her all those years ago from across the quad, he had thought she was the most beautiful woman he had ever seen. Her fiery red hair. Emerald eyes. Skin like fragile porcelain. From the moment he saw her, he knew she was the only one for him. If it wasn't going to be her, it wasn't going to be anyone. When she said yes to his proposal, it became the happiest day of his life. The second was when she had told him they were expecting a baby. The chill in his soul completely evaporated under the radiance of her smile.

"Are you going to be all right?" she asked, resting her forehead against his and caressing his stubbled cheek.

"As long as I have you, all is right with the world, my darling," he replied, quickly kissing her before she could remark how cliché he sounded. "You know how I get about these dreams."

She sighed lightly. "Yeah. They scare the beejeezus out of you."

He grinned at the word 'beejeezus'. As long as he'd known her, she'd had an aversion to swearing. She had always considered it 'base' and 'crass', so she spiced up her language with nonsense words instead. He found it adorable and hoped it would never change.

"Yes, they do," he answered, returning to stare out the window. The trees continued their dance and shadows jumped and lunged around the room. For each dark twist and turn, his mind conjured up an infinite number of monsters. "They do scare the beejeezus out of me."

Rachel chewed thoughtfully on her bottom lip as she riveted her eyes to some invisible spot on the far wall. Alex knew that look well. It was the same look she gave him the night he proposed in the moments between the question and her answer. The look she gave him when he wanted to quit his job in Boston and move to Pine Haven in New Hampshire. The look she gave him when he and his friend Rick decided to open their own architectural firm. The same look of tentative introspection she had when he insisted they could afford to buy their house, just before she announced she was pregnant. Every time her bottom lip disappeared and her eyes became vacant, Alex knew they were in for a serious talk.

"What is it?" Alex asked, brushing an errant strand of red hair from her face.

Rachel forced her bottom lip from its hiding place. "You said once that these dreams, these nightmares, might be a part of your past. That somewhere in your mind there are memories of your life before..." She paused, searching for a different word. None would come, so she continued. "Before the accident. Do you still think that? That these dreams are your subconscious trying to tell you about your past?"

Alex shrugged as the chill returned to his spine. The possibility had been in the back of his mind. The possibility that his dreams were more than some heartburn induced terror. That they were a window into his past. A way of coping with some past terror he couldn't recall. And there was a lot he couldn't recall.

Fifteen years. That was all he could remember. He could only remember the fifteen years that had passed since a few early morning runners found him on a beach, soaked to the bone, suffering from hypothermia and exhaustion, and inexplicably at the point of starvation. For three days he had drifted in and out of consciousness, finally lucid enough on the fourth day that to be questioned by the police.

Over the next few days he was visited by police officers and social workers, all with questions. What was his name? Where had he come from? How had he ended up on the beach like that? Had there been an accident? Did someone attack him? Was there anyone they could contact? The questions were like a tsunami, drowning him in confusion and frustration. He wanted to answer. To help. To know. But he couldn't. There simply wasn't anything there.

The police concluded he had been the victim of a boating accident. Happens all the time, they said. Boats capsize. Boats sink. People have washed up on shore after storms before. It happens. He should consider himself lucky to be alive. Except that they found him in mid-October. There hadn't been a powerful storm since June. And the day prior to him washing up on the beach, the weather had been unseasonably calm. Yup, quite the mystery, he was told. No doubt they'd get to the bottom of it when his memory returned, as the doctors assured him it would in a few days. Weeks went by and his body healed, but his memory remained a void. The police had found no evidence of an accident, no other victims, no debris or other bodies had washed ashore along the coastline and no one had come forward with knowledge of a boy approximately fifteen years old who had disappeared. His fingerprints and DNA were not on record anywhere and any missing persons reports that matched his description turned out to be dead ends. It was as if he hadn't existed before that day. As if he had materialized on that beach.

He shrugged, shaking off his brief reverie. "I suppose it's possible that these are long buried memories. Images of the past bubbling up to the surface. I just don't know."

Rachel shivered, pulling her knees up close to her chest and hugging herself tight. "If these are your memories. If these dreams are snippets of your past, then who is the guy at the end of the dream? And what does he want from us?" Her voice caught a bit as she finished speaking.

He had no idea how to answer that. He had lived for fifteen years with no knowledge of who he was and where he came from. Even his name, Alex Carter, had come from one of the foster homes he had been relegated to. One of the nicer ones, where at least someone thought he should have a name. He was a mystery even to himself. The only link he had to his past was vague images, darkness, and shadows.

And the cold, blue eyes of a stranger.

And the fear. The fear was genuine. It was the one thing that stayed with him after the dreams faded, holding him in a paralyzing grip well after he escaped into awareness. He knew it was irrational to fear something he couldn't remember, but that didn't make the fear any less of a palpable and crippling thing. No matter how hard he tried to shake it, it was always there in the back of his mind.

If these dreams were the breadcrumbs that marked a path to his forgotten life, was it a past he wanted to remember? What if the reality was far worse than anything his dreaming mind could conjure up? Was knowing the truth worth the price? What if Rachel was right and the blue-eyed stranger wasn't just a construct of his subconscious? What if he was real? Again, icy fingers gripped his spine....

Rachel threw back the blankets, revealing legs Alex had always considered to be flawless. She had always been a bit of a fitness fanatic, working out five days a week and watching what she ate. It was a philosophy Alex had never ascribed to, and it drove her crazy that he ate every meal like it was his last, didn't exercise more than taking out the trash or mowing the lawn and yet remained thin and infuriatingly healthy. That bit of animosity had blossomed of late as, happy as she was about expecting a baby, she had in the last month become rather self-conscious of her condition. She referred to herself as 'bloated as a whale' or 'inflated as the national deficit', even though she was just approaching the end of her first trimester. Through all the self-deprecating jokes and anxious sighs, Alex thought she was as beautiful as she had ever been. There was something about her since the baby. A glow, as cliché as that sounded.

"Where are you going?" he asked as she slipped on her robe, her shapely form disappearing amidst an avalanche of terry cloth.

"Not that it's any of your business," she said, shooting him a playful smirk, "but Shamu has to potty." She dramatically and playfully pulled the folds of her robe closed.

"Why the robe? The bathroom is just down the hall, and you poor deprived husband likes a few cheap thrills now and then. Watching you sashay around in that little silk number you've got on is at the top of the list." He smiled wryly from one corner of his mouth.

"Maybe I'm just a little self-conscious right now, you know? I have a whole human being growing inside me, it can affect a girl's body image. And as far as cheap thrills go...." She opened the robe again, letting it fall slightly and expose her porcelain white shoulder as she ran her hand down her midsection and across her buttock, bringing it to rest gently on her thigh. "This is most certainly not cheap."

His wry smile slipped into a full smirk. "I'll say. So far, lusting after that has cost me my freedom and youthful innocence. Who knows what comes next?"

"Any future possibility of a sex life with cracks like that," Rachel retorted, snapping her rope closed and tying the sash loosely around her waist in a dramatic display. "And to think, this loving and devoted wife was about to go downstairs and get you a glass or orange juice to soothe your ills."

Alex smiled. For some reason, whenever he had a dream like the one tonight, he always craved orange juice after. On the worst nights Rachel would bring him juice and sit with him, singing softly and stroking his thick black hair. It was like a magic spell that would put him right back to sleep.

But not tonight. Tonight felt different. Like the danger was closer. More real.

He stripped the blankets off and pulled himself to his feet. "I appreciate the gesture," he said, slipping an arm around her waist and kissing her gently on the forehead, "but I don't think I'll be getting back to sleep anytime soon. I think I'll head downstairs and get some juice myself. Maybe see if there's anything interesting on Disney+ or HBO Max."

"So another night of Robot Chicken, then?" she said, a sly smile spreading across her face.

Her smile was infectious and he couldn't keep his own grin at bay. "You know me so well."

"You want some company?" she asked, concern edging out sarcasm in her tone.

He shook his head. "I don't want to keep you up. Just because I can't sleep doesn't mean you should go without. Besides, you despise Robot Chicken."

"That is true, it is mindless drivel. Which is why I'm sure it appeals to you so much." She tilted her head up and kissed his cheek. "And you are very sweet. I love you."

"That's me, sweet and dumb. Besides, we both know how you get when you don't get enough sleep."

"And how would that be?"

"I believe the common term is 'bitchy'."

"I do not get bitchy," she replied, dramatically planting her hands on her hips in a stance of mock indignation.

He grinned at her as she stood defiantly before him, all five feet three inches of her. "Sure you don't."

"Screw you, Carter."

"If only, Mrs. Carter." He bowed a deeply sarcastic bow and quickly backed out of the room.

"Don't be gone too long," Rachel called after him, "the Queen Bitch gets lonely up here by herself."

He watched her guide across the hall to the bathroom and close the door, snuffing out the light. Alex was alone in the hallway with only the green glow of the night light for illumination. He fumbled his way down the hall, his mind flashing back to every horror movie he had ever seen, his recently subsided fear slowly creeping back into his stomach. Alone in a dark and foreboding place with just enough light to see the gore as the monster leaped from the shadows and eviscerated him. The newly returned chill in his spine slogged its way up his back and across his shoulders, leaving goosebumps on his arms.

He had never been much of a horror movie fan. It would be accurate to say that he despised them, usually choosing a good science fiction or superhero movie instead. Or a Marx Brothers movie, those were always fun to watch. But Rachel was an avid fan of horror movies, particularly of the gore filled splatter fests of the '70s and '80s. He didn't get the fascination, to him they were all the same. Horny, half-dressed teenagers filled each movie, always making the same stupid mistakes and ending up hacked, chopped or slashed to death by the end credits. Except for that one girl who always got away somehow, rescued by the authorities at the last minute. The girl who no one believed. At least until it was time for a sequel. He was not a fan, but he had capitulated for Rachel's sake, sitting through countless of these Mad Lib inspired stories. Name a location. Pick a fetish for your killer. Choose a weapon. Cut, print, kill. The same movie, over and over again. But she loved them and he loved her, so he watched.

And now it was coming back to haunt him. As he fumbled through the muted green light of the hallway, he thought of all the myriad of horror movie killers he had been subjected to over the years, and he envisioned himself being pulled down and disemboweled by each one lurking in the deep darkness. He knew it was irrational, but that didn't make it any less real in his mind.

He found the light switch at the end of the hall, which was a dimmer. Sliding his finger halfway up the dimmer panel, he aimed to improve his visibility without risking being momentarily blinded by a sudden flood of light. The room filled with a warm glow, like an early sunrise.

He stopped on the mezzanine at the end of the hallway and took a moment to survey the space below. Satisfied there were no shadowy strangers with cold, dead eyes waiting below, he descended the spiral staircase to the living room. He crossed the room to the kitchen beyond, the dim light above the room extending into the open concept kitchen. Unlike the shadows coming into his bedroom from the street outside, the light in the kitchen was stationary and familiar. He was wary of each pool of shadow, eyes alight for any unusual or irregular movement. He shook his head at the stupidity of it. It was a dream. This is his kitchen. There was nothing here that was waiting to leap out at him from the darkness.

Shaking his head to shed the irrational fear, he reached for the light switch he knew was on the wall next to him. Unlike the light in the living room, the kitchen light was not on a dimmer. When he turned on the light, a burning white light assailed his eyes. He squinted and blinked rapidly against the ocular assault until his eyes adjusted enough to allow him to move to the refrigerator without fear of attack by an ethereal shadow creature or an errant piece of furniture.

At the back of the refrigerator was what he had come for, a half empty gallon of orange juice. He didn't bother with a glass, instead lifting the gallon jug to his lips and intensely gulping the juice. The juice splashed down his throat, acidic and sweet, and he gulped harder at it. It wasn't a matter of thirst; it was a deeper need. The juice was a drug, and he desperately needed a fix.

He drained the jug, staring at the empty container in his hand. The cold juice was still settling in his stomach, and he took a moment to savor the feeling. Deep inside, he felt a slight satiation of the intense gnawing need he didn't know he had until he drank the juice. His stomach gurgled at him, crying for more. In a moment it intensified into a pain, screaming at him to be satisfied. It was like nothing he had ever experienced before. After dreams like this orange juice had always soothed him, but usually a glass was enough to do the trick. He had just drunk a little over a half gallon of juice, and the craving still existed.

Dropping the empty container on the floor, he looked through the refrigerator for something that would satisfy the craving in him. He passed by soda, milk, beer; none of those would take away the need within him. He wasn't sure exactly what he was searching for, but he knew what he wouldn't do it.

On the second shelf, behind a six-pack of Samuel Adams, he found it. He snatched up the full bottle of grapefruit juice and tore at the lid, the unrest in his gut intensifying. Freeing the lid from the bottle, he shoved it against his lips so hard it clicked against his teeth. He gulped greedily at the cold juice, swallowing hard repeatedly as the bitter fluid flowed along his tongue and down his throat. Each gulp elicited a grimace, but he finished the bottle, dropping it on the floor next to the empty orange juice container. Nothing remained in the previously full bottle but a few pale yellow drops.

The deeply intense craving in him subsided and the aftertaste of the juice exploded bitterly in his mouth. He went back to the refrigerator to find something to vanquish the awful taste. He grasped the gallon of milk first but stopped, thinking of the amount of acidic fluid he had just put in his stomach. Next to that was a bottle of Cherry Pepsi and he grabbed that instead and drank straight from the bottle, this time without the consuming sense of need he had felt just a moment ago.

Swishing the soda around in his mouth to kill the grapefruit taste, he replaced the cap on the soda bottle and returned it to its place beside the milk. Both the awful taste in his mouth and the craving in his belly were subsiding and as sense returned to him he wondered what could have possessed him to drink the grapefruit juice. He hated grapefruit. Hated it with a burning passion. Always had. The only reason it was even in the house was on the orders of Rachel's obstetrician, who recommended it because of the high concentration of folic acid. That, and because it was a diuretic which would help to further flush toxins from her body and away from the baby. The juice had always repulsed him. So why had he just gulped down an entire bottle of it?

Not finding any answers in the refrigerator, he placed the two empty juice containers into the recycling bin and headed back toward the living room, snapping off the kitchen light as he left. Enveloped once again in artificial twilight, he made his way to the street side bay window and peered out into the street. Deep purple and black shadows shrouded the street, broken only by the glow of the streetlamps fashioned to resemble turn of the century gas lamps. It was a scene from a postcard with colonial style houses lining both sides of the street, some as old as two hundred and fifty years, the rest designed to mimic that look. The 'old world charm' kept the tourists coming in droves and the local businesses thriving, providing a healthy economy for the small lakeside town of Pine Haven. That was what had drawn him and Rachel to New Hampshire. It was a slow, more sedate pace of life, and he loved it. Even at the height of tourist season, when the town's population tripled, there was still plenty of peace and solitude to be found.

The streets were devoid of tourists now. Aside from the fact that it was three o'clock in the morning, it was early autumn, a few weeks after Labor Day. All the summer residents were gone, their camps and cottages closed up for another year, and the leaf-peepers wouldn't start coming in for at least another week. The streets were silent and still in the in the hazy glow of the streetlights and Alex felt as if he were the only person in the world.

He shivered again as a sudden chill came over him. A wind picked up outside, sounding like the mournful wail of a lost and lonely animal, mirroring his feelings. He thought of Rachel, sleeping peacefully upstairs, and how much he loved her. Not just loved her, but needed her. How much he needed to be with her right now.

With that thought firmly at the forefront of his mind, he ascended the spiral staircase, coming once more to the green light of the dimly lit hall. The previous feelings of dread were still with him as he peered into the gloom, but he thought of Rachel and the thought of her pushed back the fear of monstrous shadows and icy-eyed strangers. He clicked the living room light off behind him and plunged once more into the dark, claustrophobic tunnel. With his mind occupied by happy thoughts of his wife, the darkness wasn't nearly as frightening as it had been before and he strode down the hall, thinking of a few hours of peaceful sleep beside her.

2

The frigid autumn air clung to him, chilling his fingers and toes. The stone wall he had been leaning against felt like a mortician's slab, leeching his body of warmth even through his wool overcoat. He pulled the coat tight around him, cursing silently at the need to be out on an icy night like this.

He cupped his hands and blew into them, his breath a white smoke that danced and played around his fingers in the soft glow of the streetlights. The strange ballet held a particular fascination, and he blew again, harder this time. The breath shot from his mouth in a cone of pure white before again becoming the dancing fog and then dissipating into the darkness beyond the reach of the streetlight.

He had been on this same street corner for the past six hours, watching as the yuppie city dwellers went about the daily routines of their mundane lives. They walked or jogged by him, some with their dogs, and smiled while offering a cheerful hello. He smiled and offered a friendly greeting in return, not wanting to arouse suspicion about his being in their neighborhood. All the while, he thought about the various ways he wanted to kill each of them. And their dogs.

He returned his gaze to the house across the street he had been watching for hours now. It was one of many townhouses that lined both sides of the street, indistinguishable from one another. The project had been part of a neighborhood revitalization a few decades earlier to bring a more monied element to the neighborhood, to create a desirable destination for young status seekers. Judging by the lines of BMWs and Teslas on the street, as well as the designer active wear he had seen earlier, it seemed like the project had been a success.

Most of the homes were dark at this time of night, with only a few points of light gracing select windows. He thought of all of those yuppies curled up in their warm yuppie beds dreaming happy yuppie dreams, visions of Ikea dancing in their heads. He wondered if they would feel that safe and comfortable if they knew he was in their neighborhood. If they were aware of what he intended to do that night. If they knew what he was capable of. He smiled as he thought of the fear and terror his presence would create, thoughts of comfortable sleeping yuppies fading like the fog of his crystallized breath.

One point of light in the houses across the street blinked out and a sudden charge of excitement filled him. Finally, he could do the job he was here to do. Blood rushed through him at the thought of it, warming his frigid fingers and toes.

He hurried across the street to the front steps of the house, careful not to stand directly in sight of the front door. He had observed doorbell cameras up and down the street and wanted to avoid being caught by one of them. The proliferation of cameras in society had made his work so much more difficult. Remaining anonymous was a chore in modern society. He sighed as he hugged the line of shrubbery separating the lawns of the homes.

From his pocket, he produced a small device, like a foldable cell phone. Modern society had made it more difficult to remain anonymous, but modern technology could help gain back a measure of that anonymity. Opening the device, he found a blank screen with a blinking green cursor staring back at him, awaiting his command. The interface was old school, but it was also almost completely immune to outside hacks or interference, which made the inconvenience worth the hassle. On the tiny keyboard, he typed, GENIE-AWAKEN. The cursor flashed at him for a moment before a reply appeared. HOW MAY I SERVE YOU, MASTER?

Adam grinned slightly. Genie was always so eager to please. He wished humans were as accommodating as the artificial intelligence was. They might be more tolerable if they were. Some of them might even live longer.

He typed, INITIATE SCRAMBLER>ALL FREQUENCIES.

AUTHORIZATION? Genie's reply was cold and calculating, but the interaction comforted him.

He typed his response. ADAM NINE> CODE ALPHA-B-9.

The floating cursor blinked, deciding whether to grant him access. Even though Genie was a machine, the idea that she was thinking about granting him access was close to the truth. At that moment, she was combing through databases, collecting information about him, his security profile, personality evaluations, and more. Once she had collected that information, she would match it against his current mission parameters and risk profile, and weigh his requests for assistance against the data on file before determining whether to proceed. Based on the outcome of that data, she would determine whether his request was valid and either proceed with it or deny him. He figured that was about as close to thinking as a machine could get.

A second later, the screen flashed. SCRAMBLER INITIATED> PROCEED WITH OPERATION.

He snapped the cover closed, still and listening for a moment. He expected that most of the neighborhood would be asleep at this time of night, but he believed there might be someone, such as an angry gamer or a late-night movie streamer, who would be unhappy about their interrupted internet service. Despite the temporary disablement of cell service and the internet, it was possible that someone still possessed a landline. An errant call to the internet service provider could cut his timetable short, increasing the odds of mission failure. The Eden Project did not tolerate failure and dealt with it severely.

The world was quiet, and he decided to proceed. He had a fifteen-minute window and there were still other variables ahead that could affect his mission. He closed the cover of the computer and moved warily up the step. Even though there wasn't a threat of being caught on a camera, either wirelessly connected doorbell camera or standard security camera, there was always the chance of being spotted by an insomniac neighbor. He hugged the shadows, slipping up to the front door.

Adam kneeled to check the locks on the door. There were two, the first being a standard key operated deadbolt and the second consisting of an electronic keypad requiring a numerical code. The first one would be simple to bypass, the second would require some help.

He reopened the device in his hand, greeted by the flashing green cursor of Genie awaiting his request. He typed, REQUEST ELECTRONIC LOCK OVERRIDE> CODE JERICHO.

Genie came back instantly. COMPANY NAME?

A small reflective sticker on the door read, Protected by Samson Security. He typed in the name, watching the cursor blink as Genie searched for an answer. A second later, an answer trailed across the screen.

ACCESS CODE: 470-374-09.

Adam tapped out the numbers on the panel. Almost immediately, the status indicator on the panel went from red to green. Closing the uplink device, he placed it in his jacket pocket and dug the lock pick gun from his other pocket. As its name suggested, the device resembled a tiny handgun that someone had sawn in half and jammed two thin pieces of wiring into the barrel. He placed the two pieces of wire in the keyhole, pushing until they met resistance. Pulling the trigger sharply, there was a small click as the thin but strong wires manipulated the mechanism inside the door.

He tested the door to be sure the lock pick gun had done its job, slowly turning the knob and pushing the door open. There was a dull creak when the door was half open and he stopped suddenly to silence it. He held his breath, listening for any activity in the darkened house, waiting to hear if any of the home's residents had noticed his presence. After a few moments of continued silence, he felt confident enough to slip carefully through the half-open door and into the darkness of the foyer before slowly closing the door again as quietly as he could, locking the door behind him once again.

His eyes adjusted to the darkness quickly, and he took in the house's layout. To his left was a rather intricately carved archway, through which he could see a large wooden table and a set of eight rather ornately crafted chairs. At the back of that room, there was a door that led to the kitchen. According to the schematics for the house he had looked at earlier, there would be a door to the backyard in the kitchen. He made a mental note of it in case he needed an exit other than the front door.

To his right was the living room, which had all the warmth and taste of an Ikea show room. In contrast to the traditional furnishings of the dining room, the living room showcased sloping, curved furniture that resembled a dentist's chair in terms of comfort, along with angular coffee and end tables and two lamps that adorned the room. A bar made from a single slab of rough-cut wood was at the far end of the room, accompanied by the ugliest barstools he had ever seen. It was like the far end of the bar had come from some posh hunting lodge. A dim light behind the bar illuminated the bottles on the shelves, revealing the colored liquids within. It was beautiful in a surreal way, adding an ethereal color to the otherwise drab and lifeless room.

Putting the living room behind him, he approached the stairs at the end of the hallway. The landing above was covered in a shroud of darkness, but there was no sign that anyone had detected him yet. He produced a SIG Sauer P229 handgun fitted with a silencer from under his jacket and climbed the steps into the waiting darkness above.

His eyes once again adjusted almost instantly to the change in lighting and he surveyed the hallway ahead. To his right was a window that ran the entire length of the hall, looking out over the small backyard. It was a dark night; the moon shrouded by cloud cover, but he could make out a swing set and a treehouse. No one had used either in quite some time. That made sense. According to the mission brief there hadn't been children in the house for a long time. He wondered if they left the swing set and treehouse up in hopes of someday having grandchildren play there or in some misguided fog of nostalgia.

He shrugged. It wouldn't matter anymore after tonight.

Of the two doors on the left side of the hallway, only the door at the far end was open. That was where he would find the target. He readied the SIG Sauer and approached the door, quieting his breathing and footsteps as much as he could. The soft and no doubt expensive carpet in the house fortunately helped deaden the sound of his footsteps. Small favors, he mused.

As he had with the front door, Adam slipped into the room through the half-open bedroom door. By now, his eyes had adjusted well to the darkness, and he took in the bedroom. Unlike the living room, someone had decorated the bedroom tastefully. Heavy curtains of forest green adorned the windows to his right, complementing the stock beige carpet. The bed was king sized, but given the room, it didn't appear overly large and the two nightstands helped to reign in the appearance of size. A modest television occupied the corner, and family pictures adorned the walls. Wedding pictures of the happy couple. Baby pictures. Pictures of children playing on the same swing set and in the same treehouse he had seen in the small backyard a moment ago. Pictures of children graduating from college. A lifetime condensed into a single wall.

He turned his attention to the bed again and found his reason for being here. Laying on the bed were a man and a woman, both in their early fifties. Lying flat on his back, the man's chest heaved up and down with each hard breath, his lungs fighting to expand against the oppressive heaviness of his abdomen. The woman was curled up tightly beside him, her head nestled against his arm, her breathing quiet and shallow. The scene was decidedly peaceful. Adam wondered if they were dreaming and if their dreams were pleasant.

With that thought still on his mind, he raised the SIG Sauer toward the man and squeezed the trigger twice in quick succession. The weapon chuffed with each pull of the trigger, its report only a whisper. The bullets struck the man in the center of his exposed chest, sending up a spray of blood as they tore through him. His body convulsed once and then lay still. If not for the wounds in his chest, he looked as if he were still sleeping peacefully.

The woman was no longer peacefully sleeping, having been jolted awake by the spray of warm liquid spattering her face. She bolted upright, almost immediately awake from the jolt of adrenaline that no doubt filled her at the sight of a stranger with a gun at the end of her bed. She wiped at the spatter on her face, smearing the red fluid across her cheek. It was then she realized where the warm, red, metallic smelling fluid had come from and she froze, caught between crying and screaming.

Adam said nothing. He didn't move. A tsunami of emotions flowed from the startled woman and washed over him. Fear, surprise, anger, despair; everything she was feeling bombarded him in that moment. He took it all in, devouring everything, feeling the intoxication as it flowed over him. It was delicious. Pure ecstasy.

And then it changed. The fear and surprise subsided as something else grew in its place. Anger. No, it was rage. Blinding, unfeeling rage accompanied by a tinge of desperation. Adam pushed back on the tide of emotion, refocusing on the woman at the center. As he pushed back on the newfound emotions of rage and determination, he raised the SIG Sauer as the room came back into view. Before he could get a position on her he a heavy impact slam into his chest, pushing him back. His back hit the wall, snapping his head against the television mounted on the wall there with a snap of acrylic. She was a slight woman, but at the moment driven by anger and desperation. It didn't help that he was still shaking off the effects of the emotion wave that had been consuming him a moment earlier.

There was a flash of movement to his left as she jumped past him and dashed into the hallway. Adam pushed himself up from the floor and chased after her, but she was remarkably quick. He reached the top of the stairs just as she leaped off the bottom step. Raising the pistol, he snapped off a shot. Still reeling from her emotional onslaught, the shot went wide as chunks of wood and sheetrock exploded from the wall.

He shook his head to clear the last remnants of the woman's emotions from his head and bounded down the stairs two at a time. At the bottom of the steps, he turned into the living room, the quickest place for her to go to escape him. Standing perfectly still, he surveyed the room, catching no movement. The gaudy bar was just ahead of him. In her panicked state, watching her husband killed and then fleeing for her own life, she may have boxed herself in while trying to escape.

But no. She couldn't be that panicked. Not that stupid. Not based on the rush of rage and determination that had come off of her a few moments ago. No, she was determined to survive. To escape. Her best chance of doing that would be through the front door. If she could get out that door, she stood a better chance of alerting her neighbors and the police before he could stop her. He couldn't let that happen. Failure was never an option in his profession, and he had never been so close to failure in an assignment as he was right at this moment.

As he turned to approach the entryway, a flutter of movement at the bar caught his eye. He spun and let off another round. A small mirror advertising Finnegan's Whiskey exploded in a shower of glass. At the same time he heard a small sound to his left, he felt a small burst of rage and anger tinged with hope. He turned to his left to see a small shadow racing across the dining room toward the front door. He bolted across the living room in pursuit, clumsily knocking over one of the ugly end tables by the couch, sending the equally ugly lamp resting on it crashing to the floor. As he rounded the corner of the foyer, he saw her. She bolted recklessly toward the front door, her ragged breath and gait showing her desperation, frantically trying to make it to the street and find help. She screamed desperately for help, not looking behind her to confirm if her attacker was even still there. It was as if she could sense him as much as he could her. She slammed hard into the door, a sound somewhere between a grunt and a squeal escaping her, and clawed at the doorknob. Realizing the door was locked, she fumbled with the bolt latch just above the doorknob, leaving crimson smears on the brass.

Adam raised the pistol and fired. The woman screamed as the bullet tore through her left thigh, driving her hard onto the tile floor. She grasped the wound with both hands, blood flowing freely and already forming a warm puddle beneath her. From where he stood, Adam smelled the metallic salty essence of the blood. It invigorated him, sharpening his mind and snapping him back to his professional self, eliminating all traces of the earlier emotional intoxication.

When she looked up at him, her face transformed into a mosaic of color as soft light filtered through the stained glass of the front door. She sobbed; her tears transformed into a dazzling spectacle. She looked beautiful at that moment. Possibly as beautiful as she had ever been, here in the moment before her death.

He had always thought that people were so much more beautiful in the moments just before they died. More honest. Truer. More whole. As if they finally could allow their genuine spirit to reveal itself through the façade they had spent a lifetime building. On some deep inner level, he was certain they thanked him for his actions. He appreciated that.

With that, he pulled the trigger again. There was a wet slapping sound on the wall behind her, splattered with red, as a small hole appeared in her forehead. Her body slumped to the floor and spasmed twice, then remained still among the artificial rainbows.

Slipping out the back door, Adam made his way to where he had left his car earlier in the day, a few blocks away in the parking lot of a 7-11. He had selected an older model Ford Escort in blue for this assignment, given that it would allow him to keep the lowest of profiles. From the trunk he retrieved a small backpack and removed a pair of khaki pants, a powder blue Polo shirt, a pair of leather loafers and a windbreaker. The perfect suburban camouflage.

Concealed in shadows, he removed the clothes he had been wearing and slipped into his new attire. Stuffing the jeans, black sweatshirt and overcoat into the backpack, he replaced it in the trunk, quietly closing the hatch. He glanced around the parking lot to check if anyone had noticed his actions, though he was confident that he had made himself inconspicuous enough not to raise any undue suspicion.

Confident that he was not in danger of being recognized, he turned his attention to more immediate matters. His stomach churned and loudly cursed him. He knew he would be hungry after the job, that was one reason he left the car in the store's parking lot, but he was unprepared for the voracity of his appetite. His body burned through calories at a phenomenal rate, which was a drawback to the gift given to him. He needed three times the caloric intake of the average grown man just to get through his normal routine. And tonight's routine had been anything but normal.

His stomach chided him again, and he went inside the store where a rotund man, whose face naturally appeared rather jolly but was stuck in a scowl, greeted him. He was like some strange, sad clown. He should be happy, but he just wasn't. Adam smiled a half smile at the sad clown and slipped down the first aisle, avoiding any potential attempts at small talk. That was something he couldn't make time for. To have prolonged conversations with someone enables them to subconsciously examine and memorize a face, and Adam desired to be gone and forgotten.

His stomach screamed at him, this time urgently. A sharp pain jabbed him, a hunger pang like he had never felt before. He cursed himself for not eating more during the day when he had been surveilling the house from the street corner all day. But he had not expected the chase with the woman, nor the exquisite flood of emotions he had absorbed from her. Both had drained him considerably.

His hunger clawed at him as he searched the store. It was well stocked and offered a variety of snacks, enough to appease the late-night cravings of most nocturnal patrons in need of a Twinkie fix. Quickly he selected a bag of kettle cooked jalapeño potato chips, a box of chocolate frosted mini donuts, two Italian cold cut sandwiches, three packages of beef jerky, a Snickers bar, two quarts of orange juice and two quarts of ruby red grapefruit juice.

"Dude, you need to lay off the weed," the clerk said, wide-eyed, as Adam piled the food on the counter. "I get a lot of stoners in here, but this is way off the scale. What are you smoking? Is it good stuff?"

The clerk looked up from Adam's late-night feast and saw the pained expression on the other man's face. His skin had gone white and clammy and pain was visible on his face, his arm grasping his stomach. He looked like he was ready to keel over.

"Guess that's a no."

Adam's head spun and pangs of hunger tore at his insides as the clerk rambled on about the health ramifications of eating beef jerky and chocolate donuts together after midnight. Like this guy would know. He was one cheeseburger away from a heart attack himself. His anger was growing along with the pangs of hunger now tearing at him like a thing alive, and his thoughts turned to the gun under his jacket. Fantasies of jamming the pistol into the clerk's mouth and spattering his brains out of the back of his head gave him some momentary pleasure and relief from the pain in his gut. But the authorities would definitely not view a murder this close to the other two as a coincidence. He was certain he had avoided the video surveillance cameras in the store, but it might spark some witnesses who had seen him earlier in the day to come forward and give a description of him. That would create a situation that would be difficult to clean up. The Eden Project did not like messes. And the cleaners could be... difficult.

He pushed that unpleasant thought from his head as the irritating clerk spoke. "Twenty-six forty-two," he said, carelessly stuffing the smaller items into a small plastic bag.

Adam reached into his pocket and dropped a twenty and a ten-dollar bill on the counter. "Keep the change."

The clerk looked back at him apathetically, despite the tip. "Thanks man. Come in any time for your after-smoke munchies."

A deep feeling of satisfaction rose in Adam's gut as he thought about risking possible recognition and killing this idiot anyway. Pushing the thought aside, he grabbed the plastic bag and headed for the door as his stomach clawed and roared at him again. All that mattered now was the food.

Back in the car, he savagely tore into the bag, spilling the contents onto the passenger's seat. The bag of potato chips was first as he ripped the bag open and shoved chip after chip into his mouth, faster than he could chew and swallow. Forcing himself to slow down, he forced the thick paste in his mouth down his throat. The donuts went next in the same fashion, again forcing him to slow his pace before he could continue. With the recklessness of a wild animal, he tore into his kill, biting and tearing without restraint.

Gulping down the contents of one of the orange juice quarts, he hastened to drink one of the ruby red grapefruit bottles. He closed his eyes as the juice filled his stomach, a renewed sense of ease and comfort filling him. He didn't understand the science behind it, he simply knew that an acidic juice was the best restorative he could ask for after a mission like the one he had just completed.

His desperate hunger was passing, and he slowed his voracious binge, allowing himself to taste and savor some of the food. He ate until nothing but the beef jerky and two candy bars remained, which he tucked into the glove compartment for later. Just in case.

His hunger satisfied, he leaned back in the driver's seat of the Escort and closed his eyes. This was not a good place to sleep, he knew that, but needed a few minutes of rest just the same. Just a few moments to revel in the satisfaction brought on by a full stomach and a satisfying night's work.

As he drifted into sleep, his mind filled with images. A desert landscape. There is a complex that resembles a military facility. A man in a leather jacket and jeans, alone in the desert, lost and searching for something. No, searching for some*one*.

A woman's name. He was shouting a woman's name. Adam felt something in this moment. A connection. A connection to this man that he could not deny. More than that, though. There was so much more.

Hatred.

He hated this man. This man alone in the desert, searching. Searching for someone. Not just someone. A woman. It was a woman's name he was screaming.

Rachel.

The image of a woman, flowing red hair and bright green eyes, filled his mind. It was her. The woman this man was searching for. It was her he was so desperately searching for. The image flooded him, permeating every corner of his soul. He had never seen this woman before, but somehow he knew her. And somehow, he knew he had to have her.

The man in his dreams turned to him, terror in his eyes. Adam laughed. And suddenly there was a connection. It wasn't something he could explain. It was an immediate kinship, like he had known this man his entire life. And hated him for all that time.

Adam was awake with a start, the images of Rachel and the man searching or her burned into his mind. It was haunting her green eyes. His desperation and passion. The hatred he felt for the man. The desire he felt for the woman.

He did not know who they were, but the connection was palpable. Tangible. He had to find them. No matter the cost, he had to find them. Rachel, the woman, he had to possess.

And the man. Alex. The man had to die.

3

A shrill sound shot through Alex's skull and he bolted upright, desperately flinging blankets from him. Still tangled in a web of sleep, he found his iPhone on the nightstand, the source of the noise that woke him, his alarm clock blaring a European siren. Whether or not he was ready, it was time to get up. And after last night, he was most decidedly not ready.

Pulling himself out of bed he noticed Rachel's side was empty. He glanced at the face of his iPhone again. 7:05. That was odd. She wasn't normally a morning person and rarely even woke before 8:00, much less got out of bed. Since her pregnancy she had slept in even longer, sometimes not getting out of bed before 9:00. It was unusual, but last night had been unusual for all of them.

He slid into a pair of sweatpants and a t-shirt; the question rattling around his head. Sunlight filtered through the bedroom windows, bathing the room in a morning light that seemed somehow magical, a mystical luminescence that had driven the monsters of the night back into their daytime lairs. He thought about last night; his dreams, the shadowy blue-eyed man. He remembered the fear that had gripped him, the helplessness that had paralyzed him. It had all been so real.

Now here he was in that same room, the purifying light of day burning away the shadows of night. The crippling, gnawing fear of last night was fading into the back of his mind, like the shadows of night retreated into the corners in the onslaught of daylight. He could hardly remember the icy grip of it the previous night. Now all he could feel was a deep weight of embarrassment and foolishness.

Thoughts of coffee filled his head, and he headed for the kitchen. At the landing overlooking the living room, the smell of bacon greeted him. Not only was Rachel up, she was already making breakfast. Either that or some psychopath was in his kitchen making himself bacon, eggs and coffee while deciding what sort of mayhem he would carry out today. He smiled a crooked smile. Considering the events of last night, he almost wouldn't have been surprised to find the psychopath cooking at his stove instead of his wife.

But no, the only person in the kitchen was his lovely wife. She was at the stove, poking at a few pieces of bacon with a spatula as they sizzled and popped. The frying pan next to the bacon held three fried eggs, just turned and ready to be served. The coffee maker had just dripped its last drop, ready to be poured and enjoyed. His stomach grumbled at the sight and smell of the food.

He padded up behind Rachel and slipped his arms around her waist, kissing her softly on the back of the neck. "Good morning, gorgeous," he whispered lightly.

"Good morning to you," she replied, continuing to focus on breakfast. "Did you sleep well after you came to bed last night?"

Alex grabbed a coffee mug from the cabinet and filled it with the pot on the counter. "Like a baby."

"Liar," she said, scooping the eggs from the frying pan and placing them on plates beside her. "You were up every couple of hours."

"That's how babies sleep, up every few hours. So I slept like a baby."

She shot him a sideways glance and a half grin. "Don't remind me. Bad enough I already have his one," she lightly patted her stomach with her free hand, "keeping me awake with heartburn, indigestion, and weird cravings. Now it's Dad keeping me up, too." She took the bacon from the second frying pan and placing it alongside the eggs. She lifted a plate to her husband, who grasped it eagerly.

"Is that why you're up so early?" Alex grabbed his coffee mug and some silverware for the two of them and sat at the small kitchen table.

"I woke up about forty-five minutes ago and just couldn't fall back to sleep. So I came down here and make you a decent breakfast. Get you away from cold cereal for a change."

"Thank you. I appreciate it greatly." He nabbed a napkin from the center of the table and spread it over one knee. "But Count Chocula may get jealous if he thinks I'm cheating on him."

"Count Chocula can bite me."

"Yeah, that's kinda what he does. I guess. I mean, he's a vampire, I think. But he doesn't drink blood. He just shills sugary cereal to kids."

"And emotionally stunted adults," Rachel replied, a slight grin forming on her face.

"And emotionally stunted adults," he echoed in agreement.

Her grin faded as she opened the refrigerator. "Did you drink all that orange juice *and* the grapefruit juice last night?"

Alex flashed back to last night's binge. The desperate need he had felt for the juice. The intense gnawing at him. Just like the dark fear burned away by the light of morning, that feeling was fading as well, becoming just an inexplicable memory.

"I did. And I honestly have no idea why. You know that orange juice has always been my go-to after a night like that, but I just couldn't help myself. Not that I wanted it. Especially the grapefruit juice, you know how I feel about that. It was more like I needed it. Desperately.

Like my body would just, I don't know, stop if I didn't have it. Like some kind of super-charged craving. Maybe you're wearing off on me."

He looked up at his wife. She wasn't smiling. "I'm sorry. I'll pick up some more today."

She sighed. "That's okay. I get it. Last night was unusual." She closed the refrigerator and moved to the sink, taking a glass from the cabinet above. "Water will do this morning. Doctor says I should drink more of it, anyway."

Gathering her plate and glass, she joined Alex at the table, spreading a napkin of her own across her knee. "I'm a little worried about you."

Alex lowered the bacon he was about to eat, placing it back on his plate. He was afraid this would come up this morning. "Why? It was just a dream. Yes, it was a bit more intense than what I usually have, but still just a dream. I know it was a rough night, but everything's fine now. No need to worry."

"I think you should go see Dr. Carlton again."

And there it was. "The shrink? Come on, honey. It's a few nightmares. It happens sometimes. Maybe I should just change my diet. Or get more exercise..."

"Or get *some* exercise," she interjected.

He ignored her jab. "What I'm saying is, I don't think this justifies me spending an hour on her couch pretending to share my deepest feelings."

"One," Rachel said, "you sit in a chair in her office. Two, maybe if you *actually* shared your deepest feelings, you wouldn't feel like it was such a waste of time."

"It'll be the same as always. I'll sit across from her for an hour and talk about nothing while she nods and writes in that little pad of hers. Then she'll sum up the entire conversation like I'm supposed to have some sort of life-altering revelation by hearing my words coming from her. Then she'll charge me three hundred bucks and send me on my way. A waste of time."

Rachel took a sip from her glass and set it back on the table, reaching over and taking his hand in hers. "I get you don't feel as if this is important. But things are changing. Pretty soon it isn't going to just you and me. We're going to have someone else in our lives. Someone who is going to need us both to be as stable as we can be for her."

"Her?" Alex asked, raising an eyebrow.

"Just a guess. What I'm saying is, these dreams have been an issue since the day we met. I've learned to deal with them, even though they still scare me half to death, but now we have to think about someone else. Someone who may not react so well to their father screaming in terror in the middle of the night. That doesn't exactly make for the most emotionally stable environment for a child, you know?" She squeezed his hand slightly to punctuate her request.

Alex's resolve vanished like wisps of fog. Her eyes were pleading, her mouth a thin line of concern. She never asked for much in their time together, and he had never denied her when she did. He heaved a heavy sigh and met her worried gaze. "Okay, I'll go. But don't expect me to enjoy it. I'm doing this for you." He glanced down at her belly. "For the two of you. For your peace of mind."

He reached for his cell phone. "Guess I better call for an appointment."

Rachel stood, clearing plates from the table. "Don't bother. You have a 9:15 this morning, so you better get a move on."

"Should I call work?" he asked, a feeling of being conned coming over him.

"All taken care of. They said not to worry and everything was under control."

"Unbelievable."

"Yeah, I really am. Now go take a shower and get dressed or you'll be late."

He took her by the waist and pulled her close, kissing her lightly. He lingered a moment longer than he intended, enjoying her being so close. "I love you. Even if you are a scheming witch."

"Whatever it takes to motivate a basket case like you," she answered. She gave him a playful shove. "Now move!"

He did, heading back upstairs, thinking about how lucky he was to have her.

4

Adam maneuvered the blue Escort down the street in a neighborhood that looked like a Norman Rockwell print brought to life. The houses on either side of the street were of almost identical design, differentiated only by blue-gray or beige siding. Children played in yards while their parents raked leaves or fired up the barbeque. Dogs were being walked. Neighbors stopped to talk, no doubt with tidbits of gossip about the goings on in the cul-de-sac. It was the perfect scene of suburban tranquility.

Adam felt out of place here, uncomfortable with the surrounding scene. He didn't fit in here with these people living their normal, mundane lives. He wasn't like them. His life, his existence, had been anything but normal and he didn't understand their lives or way of thinking. But that was necessary. Without him and what he did in the service of The Eden Project, none of their suburban happiness would be possible.

He pulled up to the curb in front of one of the nearly indistinguishable homes at the end of the cul-de-sac, this one sporting blue-gray siding. He got out of the car, his attention shifting to a pair of young boys tossing a football on the adjacent lawn. The two ran and dodged imaginary rival players, engaged in a tense game only they were completely privy to. The smaller of the two boys reached an invisible line and stopped, spiking the ball and performing an end-zone dance to celebrate his victory. Undeterred, the other boy plowed into him and tackled him to the ground, both boys a flailing heap of limbs and laughter.

As he watched the boys move from football to wrestling, his mind wandered back to the odd contact he had felt the previous night. The long drive had dulled several of the details. All that remained were broken images and unexplained emotions. The man in his vision appeared to be in pain. In anguish. He had been afraid. Somehow Adam knew he was the center of that fear, was causing the man's desperation and pain. But he had no idea who the other man was or what connection they may share. But there was a connection. It was subtle and but it was there, a tenuous thread linking the two. They shared some common bond, but what it was exactly had eluded him so far.

Alex. That was the man's name. Adam did not know who he was or why he felt such a deep connection with this man. It was something he had never encountered, something that tapped into his own emotions. He had become accustomed to feeling the emotions of others, an ability that The Eden Project had granted him, or maybe cursed him with. But he didn't understand emotions. Didn't understand how they drove people. How they affected people. In his life, he had received training that taught him to suppress his emotions. To make his life's mission easier, he had been told. To do what needed to be done with no regret or remorse clouding his judgement. But someone had given him the ability to feel the emotions of the surrounding people, to experience their feelings, turning him into a voyeur of their psyche. He could feel their happiness and their sadness. Their pain and their fear. Especially their fear. Fear was always particularly strong, and he had reveled in it, as he did with the woman last night. Fear was the least complicated of all emotions, bringing out the basest instincts of humanity. It was the easiest for him to comprehend, as much as he could comprehend emotions at all. And this man, this Alex, had been rife with it. And it had all been directed at Adam.

For the first time in his memory, Adam had experienced something himself.

Hatred.

Loathing.

Jealousy.

Breathing deeply, he let this new experience envelop him. His chest tightened, his fingers involuntarily balling into tight fists. His fingernails dug into the flesh of his palms as he thought about Alex. A ball of explosive force formed within him at the thought of the man, his fear becoming the catalyst of Adam's rage. He didn't know the man, had never seen him before the previous night and wasn't even sure he actually existed, but he still evoked an emotional response powerful enough to override a lifetime of mental conditioning. He wanted to kill him. No, not just kill him; he wanted to hurt him. Wanted him to suffer. The desire to ruin him was nearly all-consuming.

And then something new came over him. A gnawing in his chest. It wasn't hunger or rage; it was something else entirely. Something that rolled over him uniquely, focusing his rage more clearly with purpose. It was the woman. Rachel. Her name was Rachel.

Rachel Carter.

It was jealousy he was feeling now. The thought of the woman, Rachel, being with Alex enraged him. Enraged him because it wasn't him who had her, it was Alex. And again, he wanted Alex to hurt. To suffer.

He took another deep, cleansing breath and pushed all of those feelings together, forcing them into a cage in the back of his mind. When the time was right, he could access those memories, those emotions, and use them to complete his mission.

Alex and Rachel Carter. Now he had a place to start.

"Hey mister, you okay?"

Adam opened his eyes, the soft light of twilight pulling him back to the present. The two football players stood in front of him, their faces scrunched up in looks of puzzlement. The events of the last twenty-four hours must have taken a toll on him if these two could take him by surprise. He had to be more careful. Tamping down the last vestiges of his precious emotions, he stored them with the rest where they would be of the most use to him later. He couldn't afford the distraction the emotions caused him right now.

"I'm fine, thank you," Adam replied to the boys, flashing them an awkward smile. "Just daydreaming. Thanks for asking."

The bigger of the boys looked him up and down, sizing him up. Adam's fists clenched again at his sides, his hands trembling slightly. He widened his already awkward smile, regretting it immediately. He wasn't good at interacting with others, it wasn't his strength. Most of the time, he avoided any such interactions at all costs to protect his cover identity. Awkward interactions were always more memorable, and he was awkward around people.

The boy looked up at him, their eyes locking. An odd lump formed in Adam's throat. Tension hung between them and Adam considered extreme options should these boys decide he was a risk.

The tension broke when the boy spoke. "Just wanted to make sure. You were kinda freaking us out. Catch you later, man!"

The boys ran back to their yard, engrossing themselves in their invisible football game again. Adam unclenched his fists, leaving sharp red welts on the palms of his hands where his fingernails had dug in. That was odd. He normally didn't get tense. No matter the pressure or the situation, he always maintained a level head. His mission called for it. His training supported it. Yet something as simple as a chance encounter with two children had shaken him. It rattled him that the boys had got that close to him without him noticing, something that would prove deadly in other circumstances. Or worse, it could lead to failure, which would also be deadly for him. He would have to be more careful.

Adam signed, the sharp chill of the fall air filling his lungs. His eyes watered a bit from the cold as he exhaled a white puff of crystalized breath. Winter would be here soon. Not that it mattered to him. One season was like any other. He would always have new assignments. New people needing to be 'sanctioned', the official term for his work used by his superiors. The cycle would continue unabated. One would be killed so another one could further their agenda. Then another person would request the killing of that one to advance a new agenda. Then that one at yet another request, and so on. As long as there were greedy and ambitious people in the world, the cycle of power and death would never end. It would go on and on forever, like the changing of the seasons.

He drifted up the front steps of the house to the front door. A doorbell camera sat to the right of the door, staring out at the neighborhood with its cycloptic gaze. He shifted his feet, feeling the weight of surveillance not only from the doorbell camera but from the many cameras he couldn't see but knew were there watching him. They would examine his every move, considering his biometric signatures, measuring his every response and movement from skin temperature to stance to respiratory reaction. The moment he set foot on the front porch, they scanned his retinal patterns, and they would scan his fingerprints the moment he pressed the doorbell. The Eden Project didn't like uninvited guests, and they were very good at making sure they didn't have any.

He couldn't delay an interaction any longer without arousing suspicion. He reached out and pressed his doorbell. It buzzed under his fingertip as the company took his fingerprint and ran it through their database, along with all the other information they had collected. Seconds after pushing the doorbell, a voice came from the camera. A kindly and frail old voice.

"Is that you, Joseph?" The voice was pleasant and grandmotherly.

Adam started to speak, to give the coded response that would gain him access, but paused. He could give an incorrect response. If that happened, the 'old woman' inside would send him away under the guise of fearing for her safety. He could turn around and walk away from this place, begin his search for Alex and Rachel Carter and get the answers to his questions. He could start his life anew and pursue his own happiness.

But that would be futile. There was no way the Project would simply let him walk away. He was a valuable asset with secrets they most certainly did not want getting out into the world. They would find him and either reprogram him if possible or simply 'liquidate' him as an uncooperative asset. This was not his opportunity. He would have to bide his time and wait for a better one to come along.

"Yes, Mom," he answered the faux frail old lady on the intercom. "I was able to catch the 12:45 instead of the 3:15 out of Los Angeles so I could get here early." He carefully enunciated the times and place, speaking loudly and slowly so as not to be misunderstood. Those numbers and letters contained his passcode. He had only one opportunity to ensure effective communication; if he didn't succeed, he would be sent away. And then the Project would come after him. So now he waited as they scanned and analyzed his passcode, voice print, fingerprint, and other biometrics to confirm his claimed identity.

Seconds ticked by with no response. It was unusual for the process to take so long. He wondered if maybe something in his biometric profile was off, maybe because of the newly awakened emotional response he'd had. His chest tightened, his leg muscles tensing as he readied to run.

The door emitted a click, signaling the release of the lock. The old woman's voice came again from the doorbell camera. "Please come in, Joseph. Your father is downstairs, and he's looking forward to hearing what you've been up to."

The doorknob felt hot in his hand despite the chill of the day. Bracing himself, he turned the knob and pushed the door open slowly, pushing one shoulder against it and peering around for a look into the house.

What he saw was unimpressive. A small entryway leading into a living room, which melded with the kitchen and dining room further out. He slid his body completely in past the door and allowed it to close behind him, a slight click indicating the lock had reengaged. A pang of something sprang up in his gut at the sound. Fear, maybe? Apprehension? It wasn't anything he was familiar with, but he didn't like the tight knot in his stomach. He closed his eyes and breathed deeply, following the techniques he had been taught, inhaling and exhaling. Slowly, the knot in his stomach unraveled itself and he pushed it down, regaining control.

Gathering himself up, he continued into the house, moving into the living room. To his left was a hallway, two doors on either side. Fading daylight filtered in through the window at the end of the hall, casting an eerie pall over the space. As he passed, he looked into each of the three doors that were left ajar. The first door on his left was a bedroom. The bed appeared small, possibly a twin size, and someone had made it neatly. Across the hall was a slightly larger bedroom with a larger bed, most likely the primary bedroom. The door after that on the left was a bathroom, clean and almost obsessively organized.

Unlike the other three, the last door was securely closed. This was where he needed to be. He placed his hand on the doorknob and waited while it vibrated almost imperceptibly. Similar to the doorbell at the front of the house, the doorknob here was scanning his fingerprints. In a moment, the door clicked and he turned the knob, entering the small room.

There were no windows in the small space, only a single light overhead in the middle of the room. It glowed with a soft bluish light, illuminating the space with a glow Adam found eerie. Again tamping down his discomfort, he moved into the center of the room, directly under the light. A small door adorned the wall on the other side of the space, but unlike the rest of the house, this door had no doorknob. No handle. No apparent mechanism for opening it. If it weren't for his superior eyesight, he wasn't sure he would have noticed its outline in the gloom beyond the cone of bluish light.

"State your designation." The voice was emotionless and cold, with no discernable gender to it.

"Adam Nine," he replied, slowly and with great enunciation.

Silence filled the room for a moment, and then the door slid back and disappeared into the wall, revealing yet another small room inside. The house was like a matryoshka doll, housing rooms inside rooms inside rooms. He stepped inside and moved to the center of the tiny space as the door slid closed behind him. The room shook slightly around him and felt it move, descending to the lower levels of the complex.

The room stopped shaking, and the door reopened. Standing just outside the elevator door was a man in a precision tailored suit and sporting a military issue crew cut. He was a beast of a man, standing at six feet and six inches, at least yet looking squat because of his bulk. His head tilted down slightly to examine Adam; his face set like chiseled granite.

"This way sir, please. The Director is waiting." The mountain of a man turned and walked down the corridor, astounding Adam with the grace and ease with which he carried himself, considering his size. Adam had to pick up his pace significantly just to keep up with the man. He stopped in front of a rather innocuous looking door at the far end of the corridor and addressed the intercom.

"He's here, sir." The enormous man's voice pitched up ever so slightly, less the imposing bully and more the child explaining a bad report card to a disappointed father.

"Send him in." The voice on the other end of the intercom was confident and self-assured. Even though he had only heard the man speak three words, Adam knew he was a man of power and influence who not only was aware of the power he wielded, but enjoyed exercising it as well.

The door slid open, almost as if it were eager to follow the whims of the man inside. Adam stepped inside, the room dark. He couldn't make out any shape or form outside of the stretch of light that reached in from the hallway. He squinted into the shadow, waiting for his eyes to adjust, when the door slid closed behind him and plunged him into total darkness.

The darkness receded slowly as his eyes adjusted, allowing him to make out a few details of the room. The room contained minimal furniture, including a desk, a high-backed chair behind it, and two noticeably smaller chairs positioned in front. He couldn't make out anything on the desk aside from a laptop computer and a lamp. He felt secure that there were no pictures, paintings, diplomas, certificates of achievement, or anything like that adorning the walls, even though he couldn't see them in the gloom. This office presented the highest level of efficiency and functionality. Someone could easily settle into the space and, without personalizing it, would not develop any emotional attachments. They could move in and out easily, with little to no evidence they had ever been there. The Eden Project designed this to keep their people on the move. To keep them focused solely on the task on hand by not allowing personal connections to take root, whether it be to an office or a co-worker. There could be no distractions from the work.

"Come in, please. Have a seat." The invitation was strangely warm, like a father inviting his grown son in for coffee and a chat. Adam moved forward and sat in one of the smaller chairs facing the desk. The high-backed chair was still turned away from him. "I take it your mission as successful?"

"Yes, sir," Adam replied, fully aware that the Director had received a briefing on every detail of his mission immediately after he completed it. The question was a formality.

"Did everything go as planned? No complications?"

"Yes sir," Adam answered, being cautious to answer quickly and keep his replies brief. "No witnesses."

Adam's stomach tightened as the statement hung in the air. It seemed like an eternity before the high-backed chair slowly swung around, bringing him face to face with the Director. A slightly overweight, balding, middle-aged man sat there, his face kindly and looking as if he had never harbored a malicious thought in his life. His big, blue eyes were disarming, his face round and pleasant. It was not what Adam had expected.

"Good. That will advance our plans considerably," the Director answered, leaning back and smiling widely. The smile was warm and inviting and seemed genuine. "You've done well, Nine."

The clench in Adam's stomach released slightly at the other man's smile. "Thank you, sir."

"Except for one thing."

The clench returned almost as soon as it had left. "What would that be, sir?"

The Director leaned forward, lacing his fingers together and placing them on the desk. "The woman was found by the front door, not in the bedroom where the husband was. Why is that?"

The man's blue eyes stared unwaveringly at Adam, waiting for his answer. There wasn't a good one to give. The man would detect a lie. He had been taking measure of Adam's responses since he entered the room. He could sniff out any fabrications on Adam's part. But the truth would be perceived as a weakness, if not an outright failure, and neither of those would be looked upon kindly by The Eden Project.

Steeling himself, Adam decided on the truth. "She slipped by me, sir. I was....." he paused, wanting to select exactly the right word. "Distracted. She slipped past me and almost made it to the front door before I could eliminate her." His voice was steady and his eyes never left the Director's gaze.

"Distracted. I see." He leaned back again, running a hand through thinning wisps of silver hair, and sighed heavily. The wrinkles surrounding his blue eyes deepened, his face suddenly seeming far less kind. He pulled open a desk drawer and reached inside. Adam flinched and instinctively reached for his weapon, stopping himself when he saw the Director produced a small stack of papers.

"These are the preliminary reports filed by our people in the local police department. These reports indicate that someone killed the man first while he was sleeping. But the woman managed to escape from you long enough to make it out of the bedroom, down the stairs, and almost reach the front door before you shot her." He rifled through the papers, taking the third one down from the stack and placing it at the top. "This report states she was killed by a gunshot to the head. It was quick, clean and efficient. She would never have had the opportunity to scream, much less cry for help. But if you look here," he pointed to a section halfway down the report, "it states that someone shot her in the leg before delivering the final shot." He lifted the stack of papers, tapped them into a neat order on the desktop and returned them to the drawer they had come from before turning his gaze to Adam. "Why?"

Adam didn't answer, instead going back to the previous night's events. The woman's emotions, her fear and anger and rage, had been exquisite. He hadn't expected such a powerful response. He had encountered intense emotions before, but never quite to the same extent as he experienced last night. It was an awakening for him, bringing something to life inside of him he had never felt, not in the dozens of liquidation missions he had carried out previously. He did not know why last night had been so different, why it had touched him so much. Maybe it was the contact with Alex Carter that had awakened something in him. Something subconscious that had opened him up in a way that had never been before.

More than that, he didn't care. The Eden Project had created him, made him into what he was. It had suited their purposes for years. They had a good little soldier who had followed orders unquestioningly and carried out assignments with no reward for his efforts. He had been the perfect weapon, the ideal soldier, and they had reaped vast benefit from his efforts without sharing any of the spoils. They had no right to question him. They had made him this way and now they were judging him?

Anger rushed over him like a hot tide, washing away all traces of fear in a flood of fiery rage. It was time to take something for himself; the consequences be damned.

"Who is Rachel Carter?" The question spilled from him through gritted teeth, his fists balled tightly, the fingernails digging into his palms.

The Director's blue eyes widened slightly, smoothing the creases at the corners while deepening the wrinkles on his vast forehead. He reached up and absently straightened his tie. "Excuse me?"

"Who is Rachel Carter?" Adam repeated the question more slowly, his tone low and drawn out, nearly a growl. He didn't avert his gaze from the other man's cold eyes.

"Where did you hear that name?" His voice trembled slightly, almost imperceptibly. To anyone else, it would seem as if the Director was still in complete control, but Adam knew differently. The bravado the man had extruded earlier was falling away, replaced by something Adam had become increasingly familiar with lately. Something he savored.

Fear. It was there, at the edge of the man's psyche. Small, but growing. Adam breathed deep, as if he could actually smell the other man's growing sense of dread, and he reveled in it.

The balance of power in the room had shifted, and Adam pressed forward. "Where I heard it isn't important. Who is she? Who is Rachel Carter?"

"That is of no consequence to you," the Director said as he stood to assert his dominance, which was dwindling by the moment. "Do I need to remind you who is in charge here, *Nine*?"

The name shot through him like a dagger of ice. Nine was the designation he had been known by all of his life, the only form of individual recognition he had ever had. Even the name Adam hadn't been his alone. He had shared it with the other subjects of The Project's programs. Now that nameless past was being used as a weapon against him. An effort to dehumanize him. His entire life reduced to one uttered threat.

Fists clenched tightly, he rose slowly from his chair, his gaze tightly fixed on the Director. His fists tightened further, his knuckles crackling with the slight motion. A ball of heat gathered in his chest and slowly spread throughout his body, fueling his resolve.

"Who is Rachel Carter?"

The Director took a step back, falling back into the high-backed chair. "You'll never walk out of here alive, Nine!" Sweat beaded on his forehead as he sank back into the chair.

"That may be true," Adam said, rounding the desk and grabbing the other man by the throat, "but at least I'll have the satisfaction of knowing that you didn't, either."

The Director thrust his hand under his coat, reaching desperately for something there, but he wasn't quick enough. With a fierce grip, Adam grabbed the smaller man's wrist and twisted, causing a sickening crack to fill the room. Adam's grip on his throat tightened, and the Director issued a choked scream, his eyes wide with shock and pain.

Releasing his grip on the man's throat just enough, Adam allowed him to breathe. The Director drew in a few sharp breaths and coughed weakly. The shattered bones of his wrist were grinding together under the pressure of Adam's grip and a ragged gasp of pain escaped him. Adam reached under the man's coat and removed the handgun he had been reaching for, releasing his throat and wrist simultaneously. The Director fell to the floor in a heap.

"You're a dead man," the Director choked out between ragged breaths, cradling his broken wrist. "This is the end for you, you worthless piece of shit."

Adam's knee crashed into the other man's face, crushing his nose in a spray of crimson. The man fell back, crashing into the high-backed chair and sending it rolling against the back wall with a thud. He held his shattered nose with his good hand, blood running freely between his fingers.

Adam grabbed the Director by the thicker hair at the back of his head and forced the man to look up at him. The injured man coughed and wheezed as his face contorted in pain. Adam ignored the man's agony. He had a singular focus, and he needed to see it through.

"Who is Rachel Carter?"

Blood dripped from the tip of the Director's nose onto his pristine white shirt. "I'll see you dead."

"Rachel. Carter."

"Fuck you."

A vicious kick to the older man's midsection elicited a sharp snapping sound and a cry of pain. The Director tried to stand but couldn't, falling back to the floor in a heap, coughing and spitting blood. Giving up on the idea of standing, he leaned back against the wall, pulling himself into a sitting position despite the grinding pain in his wrist and ribs.

"You're running out of time, old man," Adam said, leaning down and bringing his face close to the other man's. "I broke your nose," Adam said, leaning down and bringing his face close to the other man's. "I bet that hurts. Not to mention that wrist, it looks a little floppity. And those ribs." He pressed the Director's midsection where his kick had connected and pushed. The man writhed and screamed in pain. "Definitely broken. And possibly puncturing some organs there. Probably a lung, based on the amount of blood you're coughing up. Tell me what I need to know and we can make all of this go away."

"You won't kill me. You won't get the answers you want," the injured man rasped, a string of crimson falling from his lip. His voice was ragged and wet, but even weakened as it was it still carried a particular strength. A sense of defiance. Pain alone wouldn't break him. Adam felt confident he could break the man, but it would take time. And time was in short supply at the moment.

A loud banging on the office door stressed that thought. He scooped up the Director's limp form; the man screaming in agony at the sudden movement, just as the door exploded inward. Almost immediately an enormous figure filled the doorway and Adam recognized the agent that had escorted him to the Director's office, his suit still perfectly in place, crew cut framing his massive head. He scanned the room, weapon raised, and ambled into the room. His gaze fell on Adam almost immediately and he stopped, his handgun pointed straight at the other man's chest. Adam recognized the weapon as a Desert Eagle, an enormous weapon that still somehow looked like a child's toy in the man's hands.

Knowing the damage the gun could do to him, Adam held the Director in front of him as a shield, banking on the fact that Crew Cut wouldn't fire with his boss in the way. Not that it would make much different if the big man decided to shoot. With that gun, the bullets would cut through the Director and shred him as well. His only hope was that Crew Cut was a man who prized loyalty.

A second later, his hope was confirmed. "Give up the Director, Nine," Crew Cut growled. "You know that I can't allow you to leave this facility, no matter who you're hiding behind. I'll shoot through him if I have to."

Adam edged himself and the whimpering heap of meat that used to be the Director over to the desk. As he did, Crew Cut took a step into the room to clear the way for two other, significantly smaller, security personnel to enter the room. They fanned out to either side of the bigger man, weapons raised and ready.

This complicated matters. Adam was already at a disadvantage being backed into the room. The only exit was the door now blocked by Crew Cut's bulk. It was going to be hard enough getting past the big man, the additional security forces were an extra annoyance he didn't need right now.

Adam kneeled behind the immense desk, dropping the limp form of the Director into his chair. The man fell like a rag doll, the only indication he was even still alive being a few pitiful moans and ragged breaths that escaped him. Blood continued to drain from his mouth and nose, a good indication that his broken ribs had indeed punctured a lung. Being tossed around as he had been had most likely caused it to shred. Without medical attention the man would surely be dead soon. Even with medical attention, his odds weren't good. But Adam only needed him for a bit longer.

He snatched the Director's interface device from the desk. It was a small device, larger than a cell phone but smaller than a tablet, with access to a wealth of knowledge. Knowledge he would need to start his search for Alex and Rachel Carter. More than that, it could also offer him an escape route. The small devices allowed the directors to move from safe house to safe house to conduct operations while being able to access the wealth of information and use the array of operatives and resources The Project maintained. To do this, the devices would link to the operating system of the safe house they were using, increasing their already considerable computing power a thousandfold. That was useful to Adam, as he could access the data he needed. It was also useful to Adam as it gave the user of the device complete control over the operations and systems of the safe house. That was the function that would pave the way for his escape.

"What's it going to be, Adam?" Crew Cut's voice filled the room, low and commanded. "If you make it difficult for us, I can guarantee it will be excruciating for you. If you give up now, hand over the Director, I'll make it quick and painless for you."

Crew Cut was pushing the timetable up. Adam couldn't have that. He needed to slow things down a bit.

He caught movement to his left, one of the security offers that had come in after Crew Cut. The man moved slowly, weapon raised, trying to position himself for a good shot at Adam. His dark suit and brown skin blended well with the darkness, almost concealing him in the peripheral gloom of the room. He would make an excellent distraction.

Adam snatched up the pistol he had taken from the Director and leaned out from behind the desk. The man's eyes went wide and he raised his weapon to take a shot, but he was too slow. Adam squeezed off a shot, the report booming in the enclosed space, hitting the man in the throat just above where his Kevlar vest would sit. His head snapped forward with the impact and he fell to the floor in a heap of flailing limbs that reminded Adam of the boys playing football in the yard above. Only this player wouldn't get up and laugh it off.

"There's my answer. You want to keep your people alive? Keep them away." But Crew Cut wouldn't stay away. It was his job to protect the integrity of The Eden Project, a job he would do with the most extreme of prejudice. But he may have bought himself the few minutes he needed.

From his jacket pocket he produced his own link device, snapping it open to the same dark screen and flashing green cursor from earlier. He set it aside and opened the Director's device, encountering another black screen with green lettering that read: DIRECTOR 4> PLEASE INITIATE VERIFICATION. A small red pad glowed dimly at the edge of the screen, a feature missing from Adam's device. He turned to the Director. The man's face was ashen, the color drained. A sheen of sweat covered his face, his lips and chin wet with blood that dripped onto his chest, soaking into his white shirt. His chest rose and fell slightly, but it was shallow at best. He wouldn't survive much longer.

Adam reached out and grabbed the man's arm, the one without the shattered wrist, and wrapped his hand around his thumb, exposing the pad but controlling the hand. Adam contorted the Director's broken body once again against his will, eliciting only a slight moan and a sharp but shallow gasp as a reaction. He pressed the man's thumb against the glowing red pad and almost instantly it turned green and the screen came alive with a new message.

GOOD AFTERNOON, DIRECTOR. HOW MAY I SERVE YOU?

Adam smiled slightly and dropped the Director's hand, which fell limply to his side. The hand twitched slightly, showing he was still alive. Adam was relieved. He didn't want the man to miss what was coming next.

Adam tapped out a command. LINK TO NEAREST DEVICE. As if in response, Adam's device sprang to life, the screen filling with numerical code. He peered around the corner of the desk to check on Crew Cut's position. The large man was still standing just inside the doorway, his massive frame blocking the exit. He hadn't moved, standing like a statue, watching the room and waiting. Even the death of the other agent hadn't fazed him. The man was a true professional.

He tapped furiously on the small keyboard. ACCESS FILES> ALEX AND RACHEL CARTER. The screen filled with numerical code as it searched the main database for information, just as Adam's device had been a second ago. Within another second, the screen flashed COMPLETE.

TRANSFER TO LINKED DEVICE. Both screens came to life again with a flurry of green code. Within a second, both devices exhibited the word "COMPLETE" in vibrant green letters.

Adam snapped shut his device and dropped it back into his pocket. He had the information he needed. Now it was time for the escape.

He peered carefully around the edge of the desk once again. Crew Cut was standing motionless exactly where he had been since he had entered the room. To his right stood the second security agent, scanning the room with his weapon raised, waiting for his next orders. Standing next to Crew Cut, the man seemed almost cartoonishly small, but he was still rather imposing in his own right.

It would not be easy to get past both men. Aside from their size, they were highly trained and extremely capable, the fact that they were here was evidence of that. They wouldn't be with The Eden Project if they weren't amongst the best in their field. And they would exercise the utmost of caution after the death of their compatriot, as well as the fact that the Director was still a hostage. Their fierce loyalty to The Project was another problem. It would require a unique solution, something that would test them by dividing their loyalties.

As if on cue, Crew Cut's voice boomed through the room. "My patience is getting thin, Adam. You know how this ends. Give us the Director and let me make it quick and easy for you. Please."

Adam leaned out slightly from behind the desk with his gun and snapped off a random shot. He wasn't aiming at anything in particular, he just wanted to make some noise and hoped it would give him an extra few seconds. The bullet pinged off of the metal door frame to the right of the smaller man, a small burst of sparks appearing under the impact. The man flinched at the close impact, falling into a crouch, his weapon still at the ready. Crew Cut hadn't wavered, standing stone still.

"Shit," Adam muttered under his breath. Distracting them was going to be far more difficult than he thought. And then he noticed the emergency lighting in the two corners of the room. There was the distraction he needed.

He snatched up the Director's link device again and typed in a command. INITIATE CLEANSING PROTOCOLS. The device sprang to life again with a question. WHAT IS TO BE CLEANSED?

Adam responded, CURRENT SAFE HOUSE.

COUNTDOWN?

His plan flashed through his mind as he considered the question. TWO MINUTES, he answered.

COUNTDOWN INTIATED. The screen was taken up by a countdown clock starting at two minutes. He dropped the link device and gripped the pistol in his hand, squeezing his eyes shut as tightly as he could, and waited for what he knew was coming.

The darkness behind his eyelids lit up in an explosion of light as the floodlights filled the small room with radiance. Part of the cleansing protocols was to activate the emergency lighting to assist in evacuation, creating a well-lit path for staff to follow to safety. For him, it served another purpose. The formerly dim room was now flooded with a white brilliance. At first, his eyes stung from the sudden change, and he had prepared, but someone who was not as prepared would experience a devastating effect. Exactly what Adam was counting on.

Keeping his eyes closed, he turned his back to the floodlights. Still crouched behind the desk, he opened his eyes slowly, allowing the light to filter in. A field of white filled his vision, but shapes developed in less than a second as his eyes adjusted. Bolting upright from his position behind the desk, he saw Crew Cut and the other guard. Both were standing with their arms raised up against the luminous assault, blinking wildly, trying desperately to regain their vision and advantage.

Adam raised his pistol and fired, a red blossom erupting from the smaller man's forehead as his body trembled, shook and fell to the floor. Before the smaller man hit the floor, Adam adjusted to fire at Crew Cut, squeezing off two more shots. The big man was already on the move, falling back out of the small room and into the hallway. One of Adam's bullets tore into his chest, his expensive and well-tailored suit shirt bursting at the impact. This time there was no accompanying red spray as the man disappeared from sight.

"Damn Kevlar," Adam muttered. With Crew Cut still in play, he'd have to amend his plan, and time was running out. From behind him, Adam pulled the limp, gray and nearly lifeless form of the Director from a heap on the floor to his feet, throwing the man over his shoulder. He hardly made a sound, even though all the movement must have been excruciating with his injuries. He wouldn't last long, but Adam needed him for one last task.

Hefting the dead weight of the man, he made his way to the office door. Weapon ready, he peered into the hallway. The emergency lighting had come on there as well, the hallway awash in bright light. He scanned the length of the space and saw no movement. There were several doors on either side of the hallway leading to the elevator, and freedom, and Crew Cut could hide in any of them.

He estimated he had a little over a minute to escape before fire would obliterate the safe house. Shifting the Director's weight slightly, he picked up his pace. Caution would have to take a back seat to expedience. He hadn't seen a sign of Crew Cut. Maybe his bullet had hurt the big man more that he thought. Maybe he had tucked himself away somewhere, tending to his wounds. Whatever it was, it didn't matter at this point. Only escape mattered.

Reaching the elevator, he allowed himself a slight sigh of relief. He pushed the button to request the car and a small red square lit up. It was time for the Director to perform his final service. Dropping him to the floor, Adam once again guided the injured man's thumb, placing it firmly over the red square. The light changed to green and with a cheerful ding; the doors slid open. Adam released the breath he hadn't been aware he was holding and moved to enter the elevator. A familiar voice froze him in his tracks, the last voice he wanted to hear right now.

"Stop right there, Adam!"

Crew Cut was there. A sheen of sweat and pain contorted his face, melding with the look of rage that tore into Adam like a bullet. His Desert Eagle was trained on Adam, finger firmly on the trigger.

He had lost any sense of the time remaining before the cleansing protocol began, but he knew there wasn't much left. The Director still clung limply at his side, barely hanging on to life. Adam forcefully slid his arms under the other man's armpits, exerting all his strength to propel him towards Crew Cut. With a swift leap, Adam jumped backwards into the elevator car. He pulled himself in as far as he could, trying to find some cover in the shallow space. The Desert Eagle boomed and the Director's body lurched as the bullet ripped through him, tearing through his back and striking the wall just to the right of the elevator in a shower of drywall. The man's body fell to the floor, the bullet finally putting all of his recent suffering to a definitive end.

Ignoring the body of the man he had been charged with protecting, Crew Cut fired again. Adam's left side exploded with pain, driving him to the floor in agony. He scrambled to get off a shot, but the intense pain in his side clouded his vision. Another boom from the Desert Eagle and his face erupted in countless stings as the wall next to him exploded on impact.

His one eye was completely blinded, and his other eye was nothing but a haze of pain as his body reacted to the trauma it had just experienced. There was a blur of motion just ahead of him and he fired blindly at it, snapping off three shots in quick succession. There was no immediate return of gunfire. Taking advantage of that momentary respite, he pulled himself to his feet, stepping up to the elevator controls. To his right were two blurred points of light, their purpose completely obscured by blood and pain. Hazarding a guess, he pushed the topmost button just as another thunderous shot rang out and the wall behind him exploded into a swarm of tiny projectiles that sprayed his back with piercing splinters.

There was another cheerful ping and the elevator doors slid closed. From the other side of the closed doors came two muffled explosions, with corresponding dents appearing on the door. The elevator car moved with a start, and Adam hoped he had hit the right button to take him to the house above.

The elevator stopped and the doors opened. Even with his diminished vision, he recognized the hidden room where the elevator had been housed. He had almost made it.

A low, guttural tremor shook the elevator car. The cleansing protocol was starting. Another blast, this one closer. The installation was being destroyed from the ground up, the last section being the house that had served as cover.

The house he was now standing in.

More explosions rocked the elevator car. The floor was feeling hot beneath his feet. Breaking into a run, he made for the front door of the house. It seemed like such a long distance, like the hallway had grown since the last time he was in it. He passed the bathroom, the guest bedroom, the main bedroom, before making it to the kitchen. His entire body throbbed in pain, but he kept running for the door. Only a few more feet.

Reaching the front door he yanked it open, the house shaking on its frame. As a searing pain shot through the wound in his side, he stumbled. He took a sharp breath and pushed the pain down, continuing out the front door and racing for the street to put as much distance as possible between himself and the coming explosion.

As he was crossing the street, the house erupted into a magnificent ball of yellow and orange fire. The heat from the blast washed over him, searing his skin and filling his lungs with in a searing flash. Less than a second later the shockwave hit him, driving him down onto the pavement, pushing him across the unforgiving surface. He ended up sprawled across the road, his already wounded face torn apart by the pavement.

Another smaller explosion, bright flames leaping upward into the night sky, releasing plumes of dark smoke. The intense heat washed over him, his wounds feeling as if they were on fire from the onslaught. He risked a look at the gunshot wound on his side. Blood flowed freely, a puddle already forming beneath him.

He pulled himself into a sitting position, his entire body protesting the movement. He pulled himself out of his jacket and pressed it against the gunshot wound to staunch the flow of blood. Each movement screamed with agony and it occurred to him he might pass out. He had to get away from here before that happened. Emergency crews would arrive soon. Neighbors were already rushing from their homes to investigate. He couldn't risk any good Samaritans trying to help him. He had to go. His car was parked at the curb where he had left it, directly in front of the little house. Pressing a hand firmly against the gaping wound in his side, he stood shakily on his feet and stumbled toward the vehicle, fishing through his pocket for the keys with his other hand. In the fire's light he could see the paint bubbling and churning on the passenger's side, the side facing the inferno, as waves of heat assaulted the car. All the windows on that side of the vehicle were gone, blown out by the blast, but otherwise the vehicle appeared to be in good shape.

Neighbors had come out from their homes to investigate the explosion and fire. Adam could see the jagged remains of windows that had also fallen victim to the explosion, the homeowners stunned as they spilled out onto their lawns, trying to deduce what had disrupted their idyllic suburban life.

The driver's side door creaked loudly as he pulled it open, the noise drown out by the roar of the blaze. Sliding into the car, he pushed the start button. The engine sputtered lightly as if it were still in shock itself before roaring to life. He put the car in gear and stepped on the accelerator; the car lurching forward as he yanked the steering wheel hard to the right, skidding into the street. A glance in the rearview mirror showed a few faces in the crowd turning toward the new commotion, but he didn't let up on the accelerator and the car raced down the street, away from the crowd and past the arriving emergency vehicles.

Another quick glance in the rearview mirror showed he was not being pursued. The overcast night sky was brightly lit, aglow with the flames of the burning safe house and the whirling, colored lights of the emergency vehicles. Rounding a sharp corner, the scene disappeared from view behind a grove of pine trees, the sky still alight with a cacophony of red, blue, yellow and orange mingling like a painter's palette. Another time, he would have stopped to savor the beauty in that dark autumn sky, but not today. He couldn't afford to stop now. He needed to get far away, take some time to deal with his wounds, and procure a new car. First, he needed to find some place quiet. Somewhere he wouldn't be disturbed. Healing took time and energy and no disruptions.

For the moment, he continued driving. Moving forward. He had to get away from this life. He had someone to find. Someone special was waiting for him, and once he found her, his life could begin anew.

5

Alex shifted uncomfortably in the waiting room chair, shuffling his feet on the deep blue carpet. As an architect, he had once been told that the color of the carpet in a psychiatrist's should be something calming. Soothing. Like the ocean blue in this office. It relaxed patients waiting to see the doctor so they might be more open and expressive during their sessions. Given the tense hunch in his shoulders and lump in his throat, Alex surmised it didn't work on all patients.

He leaned back in the chair, let out a deep sigh, and closed his eyes. In that darkness, he tried to focus on something that would calm him, allow him to relax a bit, but the events of the last twenty-four hours kept running roughshod through his mind. The icy ball in his stomach had returned with a vengeance as the cold-eyed man from last night dominated his thoughts. Even fully awake, he couldn't shake the feelings the memories brought out in him. He was like a child that had a bad dream and refused to go back to their own room because they were sure a monster was still lurking under their bed. Only in his case, the monster firmly entrenched in his mind, he couldn't escape it simply by moving to another bed. As much as he hated to admit it to himself, Rachel was right. He needed to do this. For him. For her. For them.

He opened his eyes, the icy knot in his stomach loosening, even if it wasn't completely going away. He didn't feel any better about being here, but if it lead him to answers it would be worth it.

The intercom at the receptionist's desk buzzed. He jumped a bit at the sound, a touch of dread joining the icy ball of fear in him. He worked to quiet it as the young woman at the receptionist's desk answered the call.

"Yes, doctor?" She sounded pleasant, but hollow. Polite with no personality.

"Would you please send in Mr. Carter, Denise?"

The voice on the other end of the intercom was pleasant, warm, and friendly. The gnarled ball of fear and anxiety Alex had been working so hard to keep in check suddenly exploded inside him at the sound of her. Dr. Simone Carlton. All of his long-suppressed anxieties rushed to the surface as she spoke, nervous uncertainty enveloping him. Suddenly, his palms were moist, his hands shaking. Perspiration dotted his forehead. Even though quite a few years had gone by since he'd last spoken with her, the sound of her voice triggered panic in him. He tried to tamp the memories down, but they flooded over him....

He was in her office. Dr. Carlton. She was seated directly across from him, looking every bit the psychiatrist: legs crossed, hair tied back in a tight bun, notepad and pen at the ready, glasses resting firmly on the bridge of her nose. He remembered thinking she couldn't be any more of a stereotype if she tried.

"Are you still having the dreams, Alex?" Her voice drifted around him like smoke, stern yet ephemeral. He wanted to open his eyes, to look at her when he talked to her, but he had been instructed to stay on the couch with his eyes closed. He didn't know why, but he did as he was told.

"Yes, ma'am."

"Every night?"

"Yes, Ma'am."

"And they are always the same?"

"Yes ma'am, always the same."

"Tell me about them again."

"Do.... do I have to?"

"Are you afraid to?"

"Sort of."

Actually, he had been terrified, even though he didn't want to say it. As if to admit his fears would only make them worse. Like this woman trying to help him actually preyed on fear. It was ridiculous, but it was real enough to him that he clung to his fears.

"Alex, we've been over this before. If you want to remember and understand your past, you have to be ready to face and accept it. To open yourself up to it. The only way to do that is to talk about it."

"Yes, ma'am." He swallowed hard as he brought to mind the images that had haunted his dreams for weeks. A strange, desolate place. A dangerous stranger with deep blue eyes. Feelings of pain, fear, anger and bitter hatred...

"Mr. Carter? Are you all right?"

Suddenly he was back in the present, snapped back by the receptionist's voice, his memories falling away from that afternoon so many years ago. He was surprised by how deeply he had lost himself in his past. That never happened to him, mostly because he had little past to remember.

"Mr. Carter?" the young woman repeated, sliding out from behind her desk and cautiously approaching him.

He gave her an awkward smile. "I'm fine. Daydreaming, I guess."

She returned his smile with an uneasy one of her own. "Dr. Carlton is ready for you."

He nodded and smiled awkwardly again, heading for the door to Dr. Carlton's office. *Great,* he thought, *now even the fruitcake experts think I'm nuts.*

As he reached for the door handle he realized how clammy his hands were. He realized how clammy his hands were as he reached for the door handle, with his breath slightly ragged and his heart pounding, trying to crash its way out of his chest. Dizziness and a slight feeling of nausea hit him. He pulled his hand away from the door handle and took a step back.

Stop! He yelled at himself. *She's not a monster. She's a doctor, and she's trying to help you, for Christ's sake!* Taking a deep breath he reached out for the door handle again; this time rallying the courage to open the door and take a step inside.

The office looked exactly as he remembered it, as if it had remained untouched in the years since he had last been there. To his left was the shelf of books, volume after volume on the human mind and psychological condition. Each one showed wear and tear, suggesting that they had been read and referred to multiple times over the years. To his right were two small chairs that faced each other, along with a small sofa that was just large enough for an average person to comfortably lie down on. Directly across from him sat her desk, the desk that he had found so intimidating so many years ago. It was large and intricately carved with a Gaelic design. Dr. Carlton had once told him the story about the desk, what it meant and how it had come to be in her office, but he had forgotten its history. The desk seemed somehow smaller now. Less intimidating.

Behind the desk was a window that encompassed almost the entire wall and looked out over the main street. He had spent quite a bit of time at that window, watching the people scurrying about below as they went to work or school or shopping or wherever. He used to imagine what each person was doing and where they were going, envying their normal lives. He loved the view from that window. It was just high enough off the street that he could clearly make out everyone's faces, to see their expressions, but still far enough away to maintain a sense of distance from the world. Looking down from that perch had often helped to add some perspective to his life, chaotic as it had been. He watched as all the problems of the people on the street faded into the rhythm of life, and he imagined his own troubles doing the same thing. It had made his life seem so much less daunting back then. Like he might actually make sense of it all. And in a way, he had. At the very least, he had put it all behind him and build a life for himself. Loving wife, successful business, friends, and now a baby on the way. It took time, but he had pulled it together.

And now it was all coming apart again, and he had been powerless to stop it. Maybe he needed Dr. Carlton again after all. If nothing else, he owed it to Rachel and the baby to at least try.

"Remembering old times?"

That voice. This time not through a tinny speaker but right behind him. Just as he remembered it. Her voice. Still imposing, but somehow not nearly as frightening as it had been years, or even a few minutes, ago. In fact, it sounded weak. Almost frail. Curiosity nibbled at him as he turned to face her.

Equally gray eyes and hair greeted him as she looked up at him from her wheelchair. She smiled, which was dampened somewhat by her pale, drawn face. Slumped against the cushioned back of the wheelchair, she appeared unable to support herself. She had always been slight, but now she appeared to be wasting away. Emaciated, as if her body were consuming itself. He pulled an image from his memory of the woman he knew all those years ago and compared it to the woman before him. They couldn't be the same person. And yet the smile, the glint in her steely gray eyes, that had remained the same. It was most certainly Dr. Simone Carlton in front of him.

"Dr. Carlton?" His voice was barely a whisper.

She replied in a voice not much stronger than his. "Yes Alex, it's me."

"Ma'am, what..... I mean, how...." The words tumbled from him before he had a chance to form them into coherent sentences.

"The wheelchair?" She looked down at the device. "I'm sorry. I didn't know you weren't aware of my condition. I should have informed your wife this morning when I spoke to her." She looked back up at him, concern on her face. "Are you all right, Alex?"

"Me?" He suddenly realized he had been staring. "I'm fine." He wanted to look away, to not gawk like an idiot, but at this point that would be even more conspicuous than the staring.

The doctor bobbed her head slightly in a nod. "Good. Shall we get started, then?" Manipulating a lever on the arm of the chair, she moved around him. "A chair? Or the couch?"

Averting his stare, he fixed his eyes on one chair on the left side of the room by the couch. "A chair would be fine, thank you."

She continued across the room to position herself next to one of the small chairs. "Excellent. I've never really been a fan of the whole 'lie on the couch' thing, to be honest." She flipped open a laptop and tapped a few keys, staring intently at the screen. Alex slid into the chair opposite her. After a few seconds, she rolled her head around to look at him.

"Aren't you going to ask me?"

"About what?" He felt like an idiot the moment he asked the question. He knew what she was talking about, and he wanted to know, but he didn't want to ask awkwardly about it. It was like asking a blind man to describe how the world looks.

She continued, undeterred. "About my condition. You haven't stopped staring since I came into the room. I know it can be disconcerting at first, so if it will make you feel more comfortable, ask me about it."

Alex squirmed in his chair, the leather creaking beneath him. "Okay," he breathed, "what happened?"

"Nothing." Dr. Carlton smiled a sideways half-smile. "It's entirely genetic. A degenerative nerve disease. I won't bore you with the details, but I started showing symptoms about a year after your last visit. It will not get any better, quite the opposite actually, but I've learned to live with it. As has everyone around me. I don't get around as easily as I used to, but I'm still a damned good psychiatrist and I don't intend to give that up until I absolutely have to. Are you all right with that?"

A sense of warmth Alex hadn't felt in days spread through him. This was the Dr. Carlton he remembered. Determined and inquisitive with a will to help in any way she could. Her body might be betraying her, but her mind was as sharp as ever. If anyone was going to help him sort through the mess that was his mind, it would be her.

He smiled again, less awkwardly this time. "I'm fine with that, ma'am. It's good to see you again."

"It's good to see you again too, Alex." Her expression softened, her tone going from psychiatrist to concerned mother. "I had almost given up on you. That's difficult for me to say, not the right thing to say, but I felt so helpless. After four years of therapy we should have uncovered something, anything, about you. I have no idea where I went wrong." She sighed and lolled her head away from him, unable to look at him.

The warm feeling Alex had faded slightly at the defeated look on the doctor's face. "I'm not sure it was anything you did wrong, Doctor." He leaned forward, moving slightly closer to her. "I've been thinking about something you said to me during one of my earliest visits. During one of my earliest visits, you said something that stuck with me - you believed that the truth was present and that certain fragments or memories were still deeply rooted in my mind, but some trauma had suppressed them."

"I remember," she replied, her face still positioned away from him. "I posited your dreams were actually memories trying to break through. Fragmented images from a traumatic past occasionally coming to the surface." She sighed heavily and pulled her head back around to face him. "We got nowhere."

"Not then, no. But now? Now I'm not so sure you weren't on to something. The dreams are different this time, Doctor. I mean, the imagery is much the same, but the dreams themselves are more distinct. Sharper. More real. It's almost as if...." He trailed off before he could finish, a strong chill in his gut. His fears of years ago, of being dismissed as some kind of schizophrenic crackpot, slowly crept back into his subconscious. Doctor Carlton had an open mind, but she firmly grounded herself in science and was not prone to believe talks of psychic experiences. He sat back again and sighed heavily, pinching the bridge of his nose between his eyes.

"Alex, if you want me to help you, I need to know everything. What is it?" The electric motor in her chair whirred as she moved closer to him. "I'm here to help."

He opened his eyes, blew out a breath he hadn't realized he had been holding, and sat up again. "I almost feel as if there's someone else with me."

"In your dream?" There wasn't a hint of shock or surprise in the doctor's voice.

"Yes."

"As if someone were living the dream with you?" Again, no doubt or disbelief in her voice.

"Exactly."

"A dream shadow," she stated flatly.

"Excuse me?"

The chair whirred again as she altered her position once more. "A dream shadow. It's a well-documented phenomenon. Sometimes we get a guide for our dreams. Someone to show us around our dreamscape. They may appear so frequently that the dreamer feels as if the shadow were another person. Another entity sharing the dream with them. That's obviously not the case. The dream shadow is merely a manifestation of our subconscious. But if the dreams are strong enough, turbulent enough, the dreamer may feel as if their dreams are being invaded by someone."

Alex shifted in his seat, a slight lump forming in his throat. "Can the dreamer interact with the dream shadow? Or, more importantly, can the dream shadow interact with the dreamer? Or maybe even... hurt the dreamer?"

She paused, her eyes glancing upward in thought. "Not in any of the cases I've ever read. And certainly not physically. While they may represent people or things in our lives being brought to life by our subconscious, they aren't physical beings, of course. They're normally passive. They may offer information or directions or even suggestions sometimes, but typically they don't interfere with the events of the dream or the dreamer. I've heard some rare cases of a dream shadow arguing with the dreamer, but never inflicting harm." She turned her eyes back to Alex. He felt like they were boring into him. "Why? What happens in your dream?"

She sat quietly and listened as Alex told her about the stormy skies, the squat military style buildings in the desert, the rusty chain-link fence and finally about the dark man with the cold, blue eyes. Especially the dark man and his cold blue eyes. Most of all, he told her about the fear. The mind-numbing, bone-chilling terror that gripped him and held tight, staying with him even after he woke up. And the feeling that the dark man with the ice-blue eyes had followed him into the waking world and was stalking him, waiting to destroy him and take his family.

When he finished he leaned back hard in the chair, letting it take all his weight. His hands were clammy again, his brow damp with sweat. The familiar chill from last night had once again formed in his gut, and he fought back the urge to vomit it up. Taking a few deep breaths, he closed his eyes and firmly pressed his palms against the eyelids, so much so that dark purple spots appeared and danced in his dark field of vision. He sat like that for a moment in silence, waiting for Dr. Carlton to respond. Even after all these years, the woman's opinion mattered to him greatly. If he were sick, if he needed serious mental help, she would know. And that opinion, while valued, also scared him.

Her voice came out of his self-imposed darkness. "This fear you feel? It's so strong in your dream state it lingers even after you come out of the dream?"

The calmness of her voice was in direct contrast with the roiling in his stomach and the tumult in his head. He was having trouble with the contrast between them. Taking a second, he focused on her words, her questions, actively trying to suppress the noise in his head.

"Yes, Ma'am." It was all he could muster at the moment.

"How long would you say these feelings last?" Again, she was infuriatingly calm.

He exhaled heavily, removed his palms from his eyelids, and opened his eyes. The muted autumn daylight stung his eyes, and he squinted, allowing them a second to adjust. "It's different every time. Last night was the worst. I didn't think I was going to make it out of the bedroom, much less downstairs. I felt so shaken. So scared. So..... violated."

She absently tapped the keyboard on her tablet. "How long would you estimate?"

Her calm demeanor was infectious. He felt his tension receding, his cognitive abilities making a slow comeback. "Maybe ten minutes?"

"And that's the longest, you said?"

"Yes, ma'am," he replied.

The typing stopped and she lolled her head to the side again to meet his eyes. "Alex, please do me a favor?"

He swallowed, wondering what he may have done wrong. "Yes, ma'am."

A slight smile creased her face. "Would you please stop calling me ma'am? When you were younger it was cute, but now I just feel like an old lady. You may call me Doctor Carlton or

Simone. Hell, even Doc is better that ma'am, and I hate being called Doc. Anything but ma'am. Okay?"

He hesitated, an odd fog in his brain at that request. "Okay.... Dr. Carlton."

"Not Simone?"

"I'm sorry," he replied, the fog in his brain increasing and darkening as he thought about how to address her. "I just don't feel comfortable with that."

"Why?"

"I....." He trailed off, reaching for an answer. He reached for an answer, but if there was one in his brain, it was concealed in the fog there. He had no idea why he was so uncomfortable with the thought of addressing her in a more informal manner, he just felt it wasn't right. He felt as though someone had instructed him to address women in authority respectfully. No, not just women. Every figure in authority. But it was more than good manners, more than teaching. It was as if he had been trained to give a response like that. Conditioned.

"Alex?" Dr. Carlton's voice broke through the fog.

"I don't know, Doctor. I guess I just.....am, is all." He sighed and met her gaze, a look of concern on her face. Shrugging, he replied, "Just another mystery to add to the pile, I suppose."

"That pile of mysteries is getting far too high, Alex. We need to do something before it crushes you." Hesitant to continue, she paused. She tapped on the keyboard in front of her again, more to fill the silence than anything else. She stopped typing and pulled her head upright, exhaling loudly before continuing.

"I'd like to try hypnosis again."

Alex's already clammy hands went even slicker with sweat at her words. His mind drifted back through the years to his last visit with Dr. Carlton, the last time they had tried hypnosis. It had not gone well. More than that, it had somehow intensified his nightmares; the terror becoming crippling. The harder Dr. Carlton tried to push through, the worse the dreams became until he felt he was on the verge of insanity. He was in danger of losing his mind completely, the terror of the dreams beginning to follow him into his waking hours. Shadows and terrors followed him everywhere, haunting and hunting him until he couldn't tell dream from reality. He had almost completely lost himself and was no closer to discovering who he was.

It was then that Alex decided to stop. To stop searching for his missing past. To create a future for himself. He stopped seeing Dr. Carlton, and the nightmares subsided, returning only periodically and without the prior intensity. Deciding that was acceptable, he turned his back on Dr. Carlton and moved on with his life. He had gone to school, made friends and moved ahead without looking back. He had put it all behind him and forged a good life.

Until now. The nightmares had returned. They were different, but they were just as intense and frightening as before. And now Rachel was involved.

Rachel. His heart sank at the thought of dragging her into this. She hadn't been there the first time around, hadn't seen what he had become. What would she think if he sank back into that madness again?

No. He couldn't think that way. These dreams, and the cause behind them, were disrupting their lives. All the fear and uncertainty couldn't be allowed to upend everything they had built. He would not let that happen. He wouldn't be the catalyst that broke his happy life and family apart.

Wiping his damp palms on his jeans, he sighed once more. "Do you think it will do any good this time? If you remember last time," he stifled a shudder, "things got pretty hairy there for a while. Why would now be any different?"

She picked up on the quaver in his voice and the very palpable fear behind it. Considering her words, she said, "Well, you're older, for one thing. There are some things the human mind simply isn't capable of comprehending until it reaches a certain level of development. That was most likely a part of the problem back then, you weren't ready for what hid in your subconscious. As such, your mind reacted in the only way it could, by making your nightmares so unbearable you had to stop trying. You're more mature psychologically now. I think we can break that barrier."

"And you think things will be different now? Why?" He tried to disguise the hesitance in his voice, pushing down his fears and concerns.

"I think you're ready to discover the truth now. Despite what you expressed when you were younger, I don't think you wanted to know what was lurking in the darker recesses of your mind. Maybe you were afraid of what you might find there, so it was just better not to know. Now you have a wife and are expecting a child. You have something more than just you in your life, something in need of preserving. Protecting." She moved her wheelchair closer to him in a show of support. "I think that will get us results."

Alex considered what she said. He had stashed everything away in the back of his mind, and it had gone on long enough. He was ready now.

"When do we start?" His voice became emboldened and impassioned. The fog of doubt in his mind cleared a bit with his confidence.

Dr. Carlton glanced down at her tablet and tapped a few keys again. "Soon. I need to arrange a few things first. I'll call you in a day or two and we can set up a time."

"I'll be here," he said, standing and closing the slight distance between him and the doctor. As he got within sight of her tablet screen she reached up and closed the cover, blocking his view. He found that odd, but they were her notes. Even if they pertained to him.

Ignoring her mysterious action, he said, "Thank you for everything, Doctor. I'm sorry it took me so long to come back."

She looked up at him and smiled. The look of her smile struck him as unusual. Not in any way he could identify, it just seemed strange to him.

"That's nice of you to say," she said, the odd smile playing across her face. "I look forward to our next visit."

Alex countered with an awkward grin of his own. "I wish I could say the same. No offense."

She nodded slightly at him. "Of course."

"See you soon," he said, turning to exit the office, the strange feeling following him persistently.

Left alone in her office, Dr. Carlton resumed typing.

6

Adam pulled off the interstate into the rest area, bypassing the fast-food restaurants, convenience store and gas station, and opting for a secluded back corner of the parking lot. He parked in a spot at the very end of the lot under the shade of one of the few trees in the paved oasis. It was almost noon and the rest area was filling with tired and hungry travelers, clad in light jackets and sweatshirts, and enjoying the unseasonably warm and sunny fall day. Adam himself couldn't seem to get warm even with the heater in the car at maximum output and him being tightly wrapped in his overcoat, he was still shivering, his body consumed by a chill.

Except for one warm spot at his side.

He had been bleeding from the gunshot wound Crew Cut had inflicted on him almost continually since fleeing the safe house this morning. A few hours ago he had stopped and created a makeshift bandage from a shirt he found in the car's trunk. It had gotten him this far, but a few miles back he had nodded off, no doubt from the loss of blood. The need for attention to his wounds was urgent now.

At least he should be able to accomplish what he needed without drawing attention to himself. One of the good things about rest areas like this one was that people who came through were usually consumed with their own business, enabling him to accomplish what he needed without drawing attention to himself. With all the traffic flowing through in a day, one more commuter pulling off to catch forty winks would most likely go unnoticed.

Before caring for his wounds, there was one other pressing issue. The data link device and all the data he had downloaded at the safe house from the Director's computer. He needed to make sure the data was still intact and viable and that all of this hadn't been for nothing. That he hadn't thrown away his life while trying to gain one.

His stomach turned as he reached over to the passenger's seat and grabbed the small device from his jacket pocket. His side screamed in fiery agony as he did so, but he was so consumed by checking the data that he barely noticed. The feeling in his gut was new to him, as so many things had been in the last twenty-four hours, and he recognized it as anxiety. He was fearful of the uncertainty that awaited him. He stopped for a moment, savoring the feeling, letting it run through him. It didn't feel good, and it peaked as he opened the small device.

The turning of his stomach turned to something altogether different a moment later. The gnarled entanglement of anxiety gave way to something warm and comfortable. Possibly even pleasant. Relief, he thought it was. The data was all there, intact and ready for him to review. He happily basked in this unfamiliar warmth, grateful that his quest for a new life hadn't become unduly complicated.

His side throbbed, pulling him away from his newfound feeling of relief. He shifted his attention from the kink device for a moment and gently pulled at the makeshift bandage on the wound. A trickle of crimson fluid escaped from beneath the shirt and ran down his leg into the floor of the car, joining the widening pool of blood gathered there over the course of his drive. Feeling himself fade into unconsciousness again, he yanked the bandage roughly against his wound. A sharp pain jolted through him, eliciting a sharp gasp, and jolted him back to consciousness. It was, at best, a temporary measure, but he couldn't allow himself to lose consciousness. If that happened he would either bleed to death or The Project would find him. Either of those options would end in his death. With that thought at the forefront of his mind, he edged the bandage up again and sent another shockwave of pain through him like a jolt of electricity.

He shut off the link device and slumped back into the driver's seat, exhausted. The strain of his escape and the severity of his injuries had finally taken their toll. It wouldn't be long before he would succumb to them. He needed to heal..

Drawing his jacket around him, he leaned the driver's seat as far back as he could into a reclining position. The jacket would keep his injuries out of the sight of any curious passersby with a streak of Samaritanism while also maintaining the image that he was just another weary businessman who stopped for a catnap.

Adam closed his eyes, but not to sleep. The darkness was enveloping him, taking him into itself, making him a part of it. Slowly, the outside world faded. The thrumming traffic of the highway, families laughing or bickering, car doors opening and closing, the smells wafting from the fast-food joints, all falling away as he slid deeper into the comforting darkness. He didn't fear the darkness; he had no reason to. He commanded this darkness and it would help to heal him. To restore him. He had nothing to fear from it and he would emerge from it whole and strong again.

But there would be the dreams.

The dreams were always there. All the subtle terrors his conscious mind would never acknowledge would be revealed by the darkness. The dreams would be there. The terrors would be there. Always there, waiting in the back of his mind. Waiting for him to allow them to escape, to reign free in his mind, even for a short while.

Soon, the darkness would take him completely. The dreams would come and he would know terror again. But he could control the terror. He was the master of the darkness. It would not take him.

In the deep darkness, he screamed.

7

Alex checked his watch: 12:15. He was late. He hated being late. However, if anyone understood the concept of being late, it was Rick Banning, Alex's longtime best friend and current business partner. In their twelve years of friendship, Alex felt secure in estimating that he had probably spent at least one year waiting for Rick. The man was late to everything, including Alex and Rachel's wedding. That by itself had been bad enough, but Rick had been Alex's best man and his transportation to the wedding. So when Rick was late, Alex was late. When greeted at the church by a fuming bride, Rick, always the charmer, explained to her they were 'making an entrance'. Alex was certain that the explanation hadn't satisfied Rachel, but it ended there, never to be spoken of again. Since then, Rick's tardiness at everything in life had become the stuff of legend, so much so that everyone who knew him simply pushed back meetings with him by thirty minutes without telling him.

Alex pulled up in front of Antonio's, relieved to find an empty parking spot right at the front of the restaurant's entrance. It was a lucky find. Antonio's was located right at the heart of the business district and was the best game in town for a great meal. Lunchtime could be packed, and finding a table could be challenging, but he and Rick would never consider going anywhere else. They had both worked at Antonio's during college, waiting tables, washing dishes, bussing tables, and studying during breaks. During that time Antonio and Isabella DiArona, the owners, had practically adopted them as their own. It had been like working for family. And family was something Alex had never really known. Isabella introduced him and Rick as 'her boys', regaling customers with stories of their accomplishments like any proud parent would. The DiArona's fed them. Meted out advice when needed and even occasionally slipped them a few bucks when they were short. When Alex and Rick set out to establish their own architectural firm, it had been Antonio and Isabella who had initially bankrolled them. To Alex, they were the family he had never had and he loved them dearly. Now he and Rick had a business and lives of their own, but they still stopped in almost every day at noon for one of Antonio's specials. And when they walked through the door, Antonio and Isabella still treated them as sons.

He crossed the patio dining area. Not that long ago, the patio was full of people talking and laughing and enjoying their meals. The only sounds that could be heard now were the noises from the street and the occasional dried leaf skittering across the concrete, pushed along by the chilly autumn winds. Pulling up the collar of his jacket, he jogged to the front door, pushing it open and moving in out of the cold. As usual, there was a line in the entry. He made his way to the front of the crowd until he saw Isabella, who was stationed at the hostess stand as always. She motioned him over, and he nudged his way through the crowd to reach her.

"Rick's already here, in the back. You know the one." Her voice had always had a wonderful melodious sound that made Alex think of an opera singer. The thick Italian accent she and Antonio both had certainly helped with that association. "How did he get here before you? That never happens!" She waved her hand wildly, as if waving off the thought. "Never mind. He's waiting for you now. And don't even think about looking at a menu. I have Antonio cooking up something special for my boys!" A tingle ran up his spine as she said 'my boys'. No matter how many times he heard it, it still hit him. Family.

"You're too good to us," he replied, kissing her lightly on the cheek.

"Nothing's too good for you two. Now go!" She shoved him lightly toward the dining room, smiled a motherly smile at him before returning to the waiting crowd of eager diners in search of a table.

In the dining room he paused, taking in the place. The stucco walls, the bright red carpeting, paintings of Italian landscapes on the walls, all almost exactly as it had been the day he first set foot through that door. Waitstaff dashed around tables, placing plates full of Antonio's steaming specialties in front of eager diners. Glasses tinkled and silverware rattled. The sounds of conversation filled the air, all melding together to form an indistinguishable yet oddly comforting drone. Rich, delectable smells wafted around him. A warm feeling washed over him, like a comfortable blanket on a chilly night. To him, this place would always be home, and it was good to be home.

He found his way to a secluded booth in the back, out of sight of most of the other tables in the dining room. Local celebrities prized it for its privacy, of which Pine Haven, New Hampshire, had relatively few. But in the summer and early fall it was a bustling tourist town and there had been quite a few celebrities over the years that had come through. Antonio's reputation had made the restaurant a favorite for more than a few famous faces over the years. So much so that Antonio and Isabella kept a wall of autographed eight by ten photos by the booth as a shrine to those who had sat there in the past. There were four governors, two presidents, several senators, dozens of film and televisions stars and one local author. Antonio took great pride in showing off this wall, his collection of celebrities. It was the pride of his restaurant.

Rick sat under the photo of Robin Williams, which bore some unreadable scribblings, poking at a plate of fresh cut vegetables with an uninterested look on his face. No doubt he was humoring Isabella, who had always tried to instill in them some sense of proper nutrition. Rick perked up as Alex came around the corner, dropping the celery stick he had been toying with.

"Is that the special lunch Antonio was cooking up for us?" Alex asked, indicating the plate of vegetables. He slipped out of his jacket and slid into the booth opposite Rick.

"God, I hope not," Rick answered with a sarcastic tone as he pushed the plate away. "Just Isabella's idea of an appetizer."

Alex looked at the plate of vegetables and his stomach rumbled, a reminder of the uneaten breakfast Rachel had prepared for him that morning. He snatched up a few cucumber slices and popped one in his mouth.

"So, what happened this morning?" Rick asked as he set aside the carrot stick he had been playing with and reached for his water glass.

"What do you mean?"

Rick glowered at him over the rim of the glass. "I meant at Dr. Carlton's? Your appointment this morning. The reason you left me neck deep in work. Remember? Or was it that traumatic?"

"I knew what you meant," Alex replied. "I was just trying to avoid it. And for the record, Rachel told me you said you had everything under control at work and not to worry."

"Of course I told her that. She's a pregnant redhead. That's scary, man. You think I'm going to cross her?" A smile creased Rick's face, mischievous yet disarming all at the same time. A look only he could manage successfully.

Alex tipped his water glass at his friend. "Smart man."

Rick's smile faded. "Seriously though, man, why are you avoiding it with me? Is it that bad?"

Alex averted his eyes from his friend's gaze. "I'd rather not say just yet."

Rick's expression turned completely dour. "Is it the dreams again?"

Alex didn't know what to say. Aside from Rachel, Rick was the closest person in the world to him. Rick had been there for him when they were roommates in college, when the dreams took him almost nightly for a while and he had to be brought back to reality kicking and screaming. Rachel and Rick were the only two people in his life who had witnessed him going through what he had. And the two people that cared the most. If anyone were going to understand and support Alex, it was going to be Rick. And Rick deserved to know. If for no other reason than he had gone through it with Alex all those years ago and had stood by him ever since.

Alex swallowed hard, his mouth dry. "Dr. Carlton wants to try hypnotherapy again."

Rick's eyes widened, the corners of his mouth tensing. "You said no, right?"

Alex still couldn't look Rick in the eyes. "Not exactly."

Silence hung between them, interrupted only by the background noise of the restaurant. Rick spun his water glass in his hands, watching intently as the water bounced and splashed inside. Without looking up, he said, "Define 'not exactly' for me, please."

Alex absently played with his silverware. "I, uh, I told her I'd call her about it."

The water glass stopped its rotations. "Then you're considering it?"

"If she thinks it'll help, yes, I'll consider it."

Rick's tone remained completely unchanged. "Are you completely fucking insane?"

Again, silence between them. The tension between them was palpable. Like it had weight and mass. Alex was at a loss to form a thought, so he just started speaking. "No, I am not fucking insane. I have a family now. This thing, it's eating me alive. I need to get rid of it. I just can't carry it around with me anymore, especially with the baby on the way. It needs to end, and it needs to end now."

"Have you forgotten what happened last time? Because I sure as shit haven't." Rick's voice deepened and quavered, hands shaking ever so slightly.

"No, I haven't forgotten. I just....." Alex paused, his mind racing. "I just need to know. I can't explain it. Maybe it's to give the baby some sort of history, some lineage. Or maybe it's because I don't want my child to be afraid of me because I can't stop screaming at night. Maybe I just need some peace of mind. I don't know. I just have to do it."

Rick returned to rolling his water glass around and studying the disruptions to the liquid within. The din of the restaurant seemed to grow louder in the quiet of their table. After a few moments, Rick spoke, his voice almost a whisper. "Last time, you were a complete basket case. You were almost completely gone, lost in whatever it is you keep locked up in there. You would fade out for days at a time, then come back in a crazy burst from a flashback. When you would fade away I was so afraid you would get lost in your mind and just never come back."

"Rick, I...."

Rick's hand went up. "Let me finish, please." He took a drink from his water glass, cleared his throat, and continued. "I hated when you had those dreams. You would scream and cry and thrash around and there wasn't anything I could do about it. I knew you were hurting, that you were scared, and there was nothing I could do to put an end to it. Do you know what it's like to watch someone you care about suffer? I mean really suffer? I don't want to see you go through that again. I'm not strong enough for you to go through that again. I know I'm not strong enough for Rachel, too."

Rick stopped, looking up at Alex for the first time since he started his speech. Tears welled up in his eyes, threatening to spill down his cheeks. Alex could feel tears forming in his own eyes.

Alex managed a slight smile, pushing back the tears in his eyes. "I'll be fine. Count on it. Besides, you don't really think I want my baby raised by you, do you?"

Rick shrugged an exaggerated shrug. "True enough. Kid's got enough challenges ahead as it is. I mean, look at who the father is. Maybe this kid will be lucky enough to take after their mother. Be a shame to be ugly as well as emotionally disturbed."

They laughed, both discreetly wiping tears from their eyes with their napkins. For once, Alex appreciated the appeal of the privacy the booth offered.

The rest of the meal passed by with hardly a mention of the issue. They ate heaping plates full of Antonio's special seafood marinara over angel hair pasta along with garlic bread and their usual wine, one glass each. They laughed and joked, but Alex couldn't shake the feeling of doubt Rick's speech had stirred in him. Despite the dangers, he needed answers. For him, for Rachel, for the baby. He would do anything to get them, no matter the sacrifice.

But the feeling of doom still gnawed at his gut, screaming that his time would soon be up. Swallowing hard, he tried to forget about the storm that was coming.

8

Burke Darnell burst into the laboratory like an angry dervish, shoving aside technicians who were too slow or not smart enough to get out of his way. He bullied his way to the far end of the room, stopping before a gnomish man stooped over a laptop. The little man continued to review the data in front of him, mumbling incoherently, completely oblivious to Burke's boisterous arrival. A hush fell across the room like a killing frost.

Burke stood, arms crossed and foot tapping furiously, waiting for the other man to notice him. Burke was not accustomed to waiting. Given that he was the Chief Executive Assistant to one of the most powerful and influential people on the planet, he was used to having his every whim met almost as soon as he uttered it. And he savored it. The attention, the envy, the fear, the power that came with his position. Especially the fear. He had achieved a position in life that earned him respect and he truly enjoyed the fear in people's eyes as he passed. The fixed stares, the hushed whispers, the tangible anxiety whenever he entered a room. The relief when people realized he wasn't there for them. He had total control of the lives of those around him, and they knew it. Pity on anyone who didn't realize it, because the only thing Burke Darnell enjoyed more than the fear he inspired in people was finding reasons for them to fear him.

His almost non-existent patience was dwindling regarding the hunched scientist before him. He cleared his throat loudly, but the man didn't budge from his work. Burke grunted again, considerably louder this time. Still nothing. Impatience was becoming intolerance. He could hear the murmurs of the gathered technicians behind him, watching as their boss continued to defy him. A fiery streak of anger filled him, his vision going red with a growing rage. If this were anyone else.....

But it wasn't. The little scientist in front of him was a member of a very exclusive club, one of the few people on the planet out of Burke's reach. That rankled him, the thought that anyone was out of his reach. Beyond his power. He enjoyed control. He enjoyed exerting control over others. That he had no control over this pathetic lump in front of him filled him with an anger that made his chest hurt. His hands became fists at his side, clenched so tightly they may have been able to turn coal into diamond. Clearing his throat a third time, he was uncertain of what he would do if he were ignored again.

It was a question that would remain unanswered as the small man turned his attention away from his project, clearly irritated by the interruption. "Yes, Mr. Darnell, what can I do for you?"

Seething, Burke thrust a sheet of paper at the man. "This just came in, Dr. Forrester. I thought you might find it interesting."

Forrester took the paper, reading through it. His normally narrowed eyes widened so much that for a moment Burke thought they might simply tumble from their sockets. He smiled. If he couldn't deal with the scientist like he did everyone else, he could still shake him up a bit.

Dr. Forrester's hands shook as they drew the thick glasses from his round face. Taking a handkerchief from the breast pocket of his lab coat, he furiously wiped his brow.

"How could this have happened?" Dr. Forrester asked, the question not directed at anyone in particular.

"That's what Mr. Penders would like to know," Burke replied, a tinge of excitement running through him as Forrester visibly flinched at the name.

Dr. Forrester absently wiped his glasses and returned them to their perch atop his nose. Sighing, he stood. "Yes, I suppose he does. Now?"

"Now," Burke stated, stepping aside to allow the scientist to precede him. As the older man passed, Burke noticed how he seemed smaller somehow. Less proud. Less confident. Like a man who knows he's guilty, walking to the gallows. Despite himself, a smile creased Burke's face. Maybe the good doctor wouldn't be out of his reach much longer.

****

Robert Penders' office was in the penthouse of his corporate headquarters. It was simple in its décor; a large mahogany desk with a high-backed leather chair, three smaller visitor chairs on the other side of the desk and a small hospitality center with a fully stocked bar and more comfortable looking chairs by the window overlooking the city. It was comfortable but spartan for the space it inhabited. The centerpiece was really the view of the city itself, which was breathtaking, and why Robert Penders held his business meetings by the bar instead of at his desk.

Today, however, he sat behind the enormous desk and engaged in what sounded like a heated phone conversation. He waved the two men in and gestured for them to sit opposite the desk. Burke recognized the phone conversation was being conducted in Japanese, which he was fluent in, along with a dozen other languages he has mastered to make himself indispensable to Robert Penders and PenTech. While he was only privy to one side of the conversation, he could tell it was not going well for the man seated in front of him.

Penders finished the conversation with a definitive push of a button on his cell phone, leaned back in his chair and sighed a heavy sigh. Closing his eyes, he let his head rest against the chair back; the room entombed by an interminable silence.

Burke was accustomed to this silence, but Forrester was a wreck. He fidgeted in his seat, uncertain what to do with his hands before finally thrusting them into the pockets of his lab coat. Unlike Burke, who sat comfortably with his legs crossed in the comfortable chair, Forrester sat at the edge of the seat. His knees danced nervously, bouncing up and down ever so slightly. Burke's sense of satisfaction at the scientist's discomfort felt like a warm embrace.

Robert Penders rose from behind his desk and made his way to the bar, not acknowledging either man. He pulled a glass from beneath the bar and grabbed a crystal decanter, filling the glass about a quarter full with an amber liquid. He swallowed it hard, some of the tension draining from his face, and poured another before turning to face the other men.

"That was Yahama in Tokyo," he announced, swirling the amber fluid around in the glass. His voice was deep and commanding, resonating throughout the room. "He's extremely distressed by recent developments that have occurred with our mutual interests. I assured him we have it under control." His gaze shifted from the glass to the two men, the look cutting through them like a hot blade. "Do we?"

"No sir, not yet," Burke shot out before the scientist could speak. Burke was a negotiator; he knew how to speak the language his boss would want to hear. He was certain Forrester would only irritate Penders, which would be fine if the scientist were here on his own. Burke would have been happy to let the little man take the brunt of this himself, but there might be blowback on Burke and that was something he couldn't have.

"I see," Mr. Penders continued, his voice remaining calm and even. "And when do we anticipate regaining control?"

"Soon, sir. Within a day." That was a lie. Burke had no idea how long it would take to find Adam and either recover or redact him, but the lie was better than the truth at this point. It might at least buy them some time to clean up the mess.

Penders nodded slowly, downing the second glass and refilling it again before turning his attention to Forrester. He shook his head slowly and let out a long, uneasy breath. "What happened, Elliot? After what happened with the others, you assured me he would remain in our control. That there would be no more screw-ups. What went wrong? How did he go rogue?"

Forrester said nothing, his eyes locked and frozen on the silver-haired man before him. He seemed entirely frozen in that moment of time, his mind racing to find an acceptable answer as his body seized. Even his knees had stopped their dance.

Penders did not relent. "Well, Elliot? What happened?"

Forrester finally broke out of his trance. He took his glasses from his face and absently rubbed at the lenses with his lab coat, the familiar routine allowing him to regain his composure. After a few seconds, he replaced his glasses once again and looked up at Robert

Penders. "I'm uncertain. As you know, they were highly unstable to begin with. The levels of violence they displayed, turning on each other like they did. Tearing into each other like...."

"Like animals," Burke finished for him.

"Yes, animals. That's what they were, all of them. All except the two. They were the only ones we had any control over. I still can't explain to you why those two out of all the others were the only ones able to contain and control themselves, to keep their primal instincts in check. Without knowing that, I'm afraid I can't give you any indication as to what went wrong with Adam Nine." He fiddled with the thick glasses on his face, his eyes like a mutant insect in search of prey.

Penders stared into his glass, the amber fluid slowly rocking like a wave in a storm. He gulped it down and poured yet another before once more retaking the seat behind his desk. "I'm afraid that answer just won't do, Elliot. You were the one who created them, you need to fix this. Now. Bring him back into the fold or destroy him, I don't care which, but get this situation under control before he does any more damage to this organization."

"Destroy him, sir?" Burke started; a bit taken aback by Penders' pronouncement. "Do you think that's a good idea? I mean, the money we have tied up in research and development alone....."

A wave of Penders hand cut him off. "Take care of these things before they can be traced back to me or to PenTech," Penders said. We've already had one very public fuck up, Burke. We can't risk anymore." He turned his attention back to Forrester. "You have your instructions, Elliot. Bring him back under our influence, securely this time, or destroy him. Are we clear?"

"Yes, sir," Forrester answered, his bug-eyed gaze riveted to the floor. His feet shifted uncomfortably, lightly scuffing the carpet. He stared down intently, his attention focused on feet to avoid meeting the stare of either Burke or Penders.

"I hope so, Elliot. We need to be on the same page here." He placed his now half empty glass on the desk, leaning forward toward the scientist. The older man didn't move, wouldn't meet Penders' stare. "We are on the same page here, aren't we, Elliot?"

Forrester nodded slightly, his heavy glasses bouncing on the bridge of his nose. "Yes, sir. Same page."

Burke noticed the slight quiver in the man's voice. It wasn't fear, as he would have expected. No, it was something else. Something different. The fidgeting. The lack of eye contact. Brief answers given in short bursts.

Forrester was lying. He had no intention of destroying Adam, as he had just promised Penders he would. No, Adam was his life's work. His greatest creation. There was no way he would destroy that. He was defying Penders directly to his face. But Burke saw no reason to cue Penders in on that, not yet at least. It could come in handy later.

Penders nodded and sat back again. "Good. Go on, make any preparations you may need to. I'd like this taken care of as soon as possible."

"Of course," Forrester replied, absently pushing his glasses up the bridge of his nose. He rose from his seat and headed for the door, feet shuffling on the carpet, hands still firmly in the pockets of his lab coat. He exited without another word, or even so much as a glance at either of the other men in the room.

"I don't trust him," Burke stated.

"Neither do I," Penders agreed. "Which is why you're going with him."

Burke's throat suddenly went dry, his stomach dropping. "Me, sir? Why? We have a dozen field agents who are far more capable of handling a watchdog assignment like this. Wouldn't it be wiser to send them?"

"Oh, I'm sending along another operative as well. Don't worry about that. I wouldn't want you to have to deal with something messy or unpleasant. Burke bristled visibly at that remark, which brought a smile to Penders' face. Burke was a highly effective and valuable member of the organization, but he could be a little pissant and needed to be reminded of that from time to time. Something Penders was more than happy to do when the occasion called for it. "I need someone I can trust. Someone I know who will make sure the good doctor does as he's told. You're my right-hand man, who else would I send?"

Burke stammered, "I understand that, but fieldwork is..."

Penders looked up from his glass and Burke's words froze in his throat. Penders' icy blue eyes bore into Burke and he felt his insides go cold. Burke had seen the look before. It had never been directed at him, but from past experience, Burke knew better than to press his luck when he saw that look.

"When do we leave?"

Penders leaned back slightly in his chair, his face softening a touch. "Right away. I have a helicopter coming in as we speak. One of our search teams has a lead on him, they'll take you directly to the sight they believe he's at."

Burke thought Penders seemed unusually calm for a man in the process of throwing away hundreds of millions of dollars in research, development and deployment in the destruction of Adam Nine. His face didn't betray any of the inner turmoil he must have been feeling as he considered his losses. There was an almost preternatural calm about him, but Burke had been around the man long enough to notice the glint of excitement in his eyes. Yes, he would lose a fortune, but he would recover that money in no time. Robert Penders had an uncanny knack for bouncing back from financial loss. No, there was something deeper about the Adam Nine situation. Something he hadn't felt in a long time.

The thrill of the hunt.

Penders received a unique opportunity, which rarely came across a man in his position. He had been granted a spiritual experience. He had the opportunity to chase down a quarry that was as ruthless as he was.

"I'll get ready then, sir," Burke said, turning to head for the door. He stopped, turning back to Penders. There was one more issue they had to discuss, something he was certain had been on Penders' mind and was absolutely on Dr. Forrester's.

He swallowed hard. "Sir? What about the other one? What are the plans for him?"

Penders waved his hand dismissively. "It's been taken care of, Mr. Darnell."

"Yes sir," Burke replied, hurrying out the door to meet the helicopter and leaving Robert Penders to his machinations.

9

Alex and Rick stood on the empty patio outside Antonio's, taking in the cool fall air. This was part of their longstanding lunchtime tradition, the digestion session. After eating, they always took a few moments to let their lunches settle while they traded light conversation. That was the only rule of the digestion session, no heavy conversation. It was intended to lighten the mood if the conversation had been somber during lunch, or to keep it light so they would be in good spirits going back to the office. Either way, both felt it to be a beneficial and crucial part of their daily ritual.

"Want one?" Risk asked, holding out a roll of Tums to Alex.

"No thanks, I'm good." He glanced back at the restaurant entrance. "Don't let Antonio catch you with those. He'll never recover from the trauma."

"I wouldn't need it if you didn't keep giving me ulcers. If he sees me, I'll just blame it on you. What goes around comes around, after all." He popped two tablets into his mouth and crunched loudly, grimacing at the taste, and replaced the roll in his pocket. "Why is it you get an iron stomach and I get a passion for Antonio's spicy seafood marinara?"

Alex shrugged. "Who knows? Fate? Karma? Maybe a little of both? Maybe I'm just blessed by the patron saint of Italian Food."

"Hilarious. Make light of my handicap. You know this is an addiction that will kill me someday, right?" Rick fished his car keys from his pocket and pushed a button on the fob. A few spaces down, his car started. "What are you going to do now?"

"I thought I'd head back to the office," Alex answered. "I've already last half a day's work, maybe I can still get something done."

Rick held up his hand like a cop stopping traffic. "Like hell you will. Rachel will skin me alive if I let you go back to the office. And no, I am not exaggerating, she will *actually* skin me alive. I'm sure she's a wreck at home waiting to hear about your visit with Dr. Headshrinker. It's bad enough you stopped for lunch, my ass is grass if you go back to work."

"But I should..." Alex started.

Rick cut him off again. "Don't give me any of that bullshit. You have been a lousy husband and I would be remiss in my duties as your best friend if I allowed it to continue. How would that make me look? Honestly, I don't know how Rachel puts up with you sometimes. I know I wouldn't."

Alex smiled. "You wouldn't have to."

"And why is that?"

"Because I wouldn't have married you."

Rick's face turned to a deep look of mock indignation. "And why not?"

"Because you snore. And your back's too hairy."

Rick snorted and a laugh tumbled from his mouth before he could get another shot at his friend. Alex joined in the laughter, the sound of it seeming to warm the otherwise damp and cold afternoon.

"Okay, you win," Alex chortled. "I'll go home. If for no other reason than to save you from Rachel's wrath."

"Thank you," Rick replied. "Because you know that woman scares the living snot out of me, right? I mean, I love her and all, but she can be frightening sometimes."

"You don't have to tell me about it," Alex replied. He turned away, his gaze dropping to the patio floor. "Rick, I just want to say thanks. For everything."

"No problem, man," Rick replied, lightly patting Alex's shoulder. "You know I'm here for whatever you need."

"Yeah, but thanks all the same." Alex turned back, a slight smile on his face. "See you tomorrow morning?"

Rick gave a mock salute. "Aye, aye Cap'n."

Alex left Rick, making his way to his Pathfinder. As much as he dreaded it, it was time to tell Rachel about Dr. Carlton's suggestion. It was not something he was looking forward to.

****

Alex hardly noticed the drive home as he tried to think of a way to tell Rachel about his session with Dr. Carlton. She would be against hypnotherapy. Adamantly against hypnotherapy, but he would have to convince her it was for the best. Not only for him, but for her and the baby as well.

He pulled into the driveway and turned off the car, sinking back into the seat. He opened the car door as the rush of cold air shocked him out of his speculative trance. No more planning or thinking. It was now or never.

He got out of the Pathfinder and headed down the stone path to the front door, still contemplating the upcoming conversation, when a screaming pain in his skull drove him to his knees. The pain shot through his body, filling every nerve with a sudden fire. He tried to scream, and maybe he did, but the pain running through him devoured him completely and the world went away.

Flash! Light filled his eyes and the pain spread through his body as a thousand thoughts and images not his own wormed their way into his mind. Gruesome and frightening scenes filled his head.

Flash! People in lab coats watched over glass coffins, each one containing a human form bobbing in liquid.

Flash! Those same people in lab coats standing in a mass of mutilated corpses. The floor was awash in blood and gore, the wounds on the bodies ragged and torn as if by some animal. Two men stood in the center of the carnage, covered in a sheen of viscera. Shadow concealed their faces, but they seemed unmoved by the gruesome destruction around them. Stoic. Uncaring.

Flash! One doctor moved to the two men slowly and carefully. He spoke, but the words were lost in the din of pain still ringing through his skull. At the words, the two men moved forward slowly, the shadows peeling away from them. Despite the intense pain he was in, Alex was riveted to the face of the first man who emerged from the shadows and revealed his face.

Shock and fear gripped him as the man stepped into the light. He wanted to run, to get away, to escape this horrifying carousel, but he couldn't. the terror wouldn't let him.

It was the face of the stranger with the ice-blue eyes from his dream. The shadow that had gripped him in terror all these years. Here. Now.

The other man moved forward, shadows melting from him. Alex wanted to turn away, wanted to run, but he couldn't. He needed to know who the other monster was. Needed to know who else was capable of such horrible carnage. He pushed back on the pain in his skull, his breath caught in his throat as the darkness slid away from the other man's face.

It was him. His own face, covered in blood and God only knows what else, staring blankly ahead.

His stomach tightened, violently expelling his lunch onto the walkway. The pain in his head exploded like a nova. Finally, he found his voice and screamed.

"Alex!"

A voice calling his name. Someone's hands on him. He lashed out, fighting against the clinging darkness and the image of his own uncaring face framed in blood, unrepentant for the killing around him. He screamed, fighting the encroaching darkness.

"Alex!"

The voice again, shouting his name. But not just one voice, he could make out two distinct voices. A man and a woman. The woman's voice, while panicked, was warm and comforting and helped to push back some of the darkness and terror that gripped him so tightly. But the man's voice, the man's voice was dark and cold and hungry and filled with venom. It was a voice he recognized. A voice he knew.

The voice of the dark stranger from his nightmares.

He tried to pull back from the stranger's voice and find the woman again, but he couldn't. Her voice was nowhere to be heard. But the stranger's voice was everywhere, filling his world.

I'm coming for you, Alex, it said, the sound like the hinges on the gates of Hell opening wide. *For you and your lovely Rachel. She will be mine. There's no place you can go to escape me. I will have your life. Your wife. And when I do, when she is finally mine, that's when I will end you. You should have killed me when you had the chance....*

..... brother.

Suddenly there was a sharp crack and a hard pain on his face. The world flooded in around him, reality once more taking hold. He saw Rachel, her beautiful yet anguished face replacing the horrible image of him soaked in blood. He glanced furtively around, looking for the dark stranger, but there was no sign of him. No trace of him ever having been there. A sigh of relief escaped him and he slumped into Rachel's arms, the pain and terror slowly receding.

"Alex! My God, are you all right? What happened? What's going on?" She hugged him fiercely, tears streaming down her cheeks as she rocked him in her arms. "Please tell me what's happening to us?"

He put a hand on her cheek and felt the moist warmth of a tear. When he spoke, his voice was raspy and weak from the vomit and the screaming. "I don't know, Ray. I wish to God I did, but I have no clue." That wasn't entirely true. He had one hypothesis, but it was one he was not about to share with her at that moment. A simple theory.

He was going insane.

10

Adam bolted upright in the front seat of his car, trying to wrench himself free of the images that engulfed his sleeping mind. Images from his past, doctors in white coats and the dismembered bodies of the unworthy at his feet had assailed his unconscious mind. Blood and entrails soaked him and he knew he had been the architect of the surrounding destruction. The culling of the weak. He remembered it well, and he remembered the sense of pride and accomplishment that had come with it. The broken, twisted corpses around him would never have lived up to the expectations of the Project. They hadn't been able to adapt to the conditioning and care the program offered. Their deaths had been a gift, a release from a life of consistent trial and failure. It had been a gift he had been all too happy to bestow.

But this was different. It wasn't just a memory of his time in The Eden Project, this was something else. Like experiencing a familiar memory through someone else's eyes. As if he were not only a participant in the action, but an observer as well. Even now, the images clung to the edges of his memory and he felt despair, hopelessness and fear building in him. But these weren't his feelings. He had long ago reconciled what had happened that day. What had to be done. No, this was something else entirely. Someone else in his mind with him, watching the events with fresh eyes. Fresh eyes that were terrified and horrified at what they were seeing.

He closed his eyes and lay back in the reclined driver's seat. He needed to pull himself away from this intrusion and back into the real world. To get away from the false sense of terror he was feeling. Breathing deeply, he closed his eyes, opening his other senses to the physical world around him. A car door slammed shut. The murmur of conversation in the distance. The scent of the tree-shaped jasmine air freshener that hung from the rear-view mirror mixed with the coppery smell of blood. As the daylight faded, the sodium vapor lamps emitted a humming sound as they clicked on. A slight pattering of rain on the roof. He focused on these things, moving his mind further away from the memories of his past and the inexplicable terrors they were inflicting on him. The panic melted, lifting the haze of fear from his mind and allowing him to think clearly again.

As the memories and the emotions faded away, while they remained a harmless fog of half-images in his mind, he explored them from a distance like some odd voyeur into his own thoughts. The doctors from the Project were there, as they always were, applying their tortures. The usual sight of the unworthy lying broken around him. All of that was familiar to him. But there was something else present there as well. Something that had not existed in his memory before. A wisp of a thought lingering in the back of his mind that, when he reached for it, was as elusive as a fog retreating once more to the one place he was unwilling to pursue it: his own mind.

At that point, his stomach grumbled loudly and pain gripped him. He doubled over as hot agony tore through his midsection, a rippling pain that wracked him. The wispy fog of memory was gone, driven back into hiding by the very real pain he was in. He grabbed the rear-view mirror and adjusted it so he could see himself, knowing what he would find. Even though he expected it, the sight still sickened him. The regenerative coma he had been in had saved him, healing his wounds and making his body whole again, but once again it had exacted a price. The eerie blue light of the parking lot's overhead lamps washed over him, his cheeks and eyes sunken deep into his face. His skin was like a corpse's fresh out of the mortuary, pale and ashen. To heal him, his body had cannibalized itself, stripping him of fat and muscle and leaving him weak and emaciated.

White hot daggers shot through him again, accompanied by more urgent growling from his stomach. It was reminiscent of the previous night when he encountered the powerful emotions of the woman he had killed, but much more intense. Much more intense. Much more immediate. He needed to replenish what his body had taken to make him whole again.

As his stomach roared ravenously once again, he remembered the food he had left in the glove compartment. He slid over to the passenger's side and popped the compartment open, grabbing the bag of beef jerky and furiously tearing into the bag before shoving the salty pieces of dried meat into his mouth and chewing furiously, swallowing hard to push them down his throat. The bag was half empty when he remembered the candy bars, taking one up and devouring it in three bites before returning to the beef jerky. In no time he had eaten all the jerky and the two candy bars and the terrible pain and rumbling in his stomach subsided somewhat. It wasn't nearly enough to nourish his ravaged and emaciated body, but it would buy him enough time to formulate a plan.

His side itched terribly where Crew Cut had hit him with the Desert Eagle. The wound had been severe, taking a sizeable chunk of flesh out of him. Now, where the gaping wound had once been, there was only smooth new skin. He ran his hand over the spot where the injury had been previously, scratching at it to ease the last few irritations as the final nerves grew into place. The more minor injuries left behind only dried blood and a few splinters of wood and flakes of metal that had been ejected during the healing process. Even his eye, which had been ravaged by flying debris, was completely intact once more.

He brushed the splinters and metal flakes away before realizing it was futile. His clothes were completely ruined; ripped, torn, and soaked in dried blood. There was no way he could move about unnoticed in a crowd looking like he did. Even the most apathetic of passerby would notice and, even if they didn't try to help, it would draw unwanted attention. He needed to find something to cover his battered and bloodied appearance.

A search of the car turned up nothing but a navy-blue windbreaker. It wasn't much, but it covered the gaping hole in his shirt left by Crew Cut's Desert Eagle. Zipping it up to his neck, it covered the bloodied clothes above his waist, at the very least. It would have to do.

Hopefully between that, the waning daylight and the uncaring attitudes of most people, he could avoid calling any unwanted attention to himself. At least until he could procure some food, new clothes and another car.

Food was the priority. The credit cards he carried, in a variety of false identities, were useless to him. Even though they carried impressive credit limits, any attempt to use them would alert the Project of his whereabouts almost immediately. He still had around six hundred dollars in cash from what they had given him at the start of his mission yesterday. It would have to suffice. Besides, it wasn't hard to get more.

Taking the credit cards from his wallet, he dropped one near the car. He would spread the others around the rest area in the hopes that they would be picked up by thieves and frauds who would try to use them, drawing the Project's attention from him. Given his experience with human nature, he felt positive that at least one of the cards would be picked up and used.

He was lucky enough to uncover a few wet wipes in the glove compartment and was able to clean the blood from his face. Another step in making himself more presentable.

Since he would abandon the car, he needed to strip it of anything useful to him. He placed the uplink device into one of the windbreaker's pockets and slid the SIG Sauer into the waistband of his pants at the small of his back. The regeneration of his wounds had cost him so much body mass that the weapon slid into his pants, forcing him to tighten his belt as far as it would go. He needed to eat quickly. He picked up the silencer and dropped it into the jacket pocket opposite the uplink. The baffles would completely compress in four or five more shots, rendering it useless soon, but he might find it handy again before he had to discard it.

A sharp, stabbing pain shot through his midsection and forced him to his knees. The world threatened to go black for a moment, but he fought back unconsciousness and staggered to his feet. His body felt as if it were on fire. Touching his face, he recoiled in shock. An intense, feverish heat radiated from him despite the chilly dampness of the autumn rain. His metabolism was continually trying to repair his devastated body. It had already used up the beef jerky and candy bars and now, with no other fuel to maintain the effort, it turned to the only source available to sustain the process, his own body. As if caught in some unyielding fire, he thought he could feel the muscle melting away. He needed to provide more fuel for the process.

Across the parking lot stood the building that housed the fast-food restaurants, convenience store and gift shop. The rain was falling more heavily now, cascading down in a near continuous sheet of water. The lighted signs on the side of the building seemed to glow through the rain, transforming into something more than simple advertisements for quick, cheap food. It was the sign of salvation beckoning.

Once inside, he headed to the nearest food he could find, a Taco Bell. It wasn't his favorite, but at the moments he wasn't exactly in a position to be selective. Before approaching the counter, he checked to ensure that the SIG Sauer was still tucked in the small of his back and covered by his jacket, and that the jacket adequately concealed the remnants of his injuries. With everything in place, he walked over to the counter, trying to be as inconspicuous as possible. The last thing he could afford was to draw attention to himself.

At the counter he was met by the blank stare of a girl who was, at most, seventeen. Her eyes remained fixed on the screen of her cell phone, ignoring the customer standing directly in front of her, ready to order. It wasn't until he loudly put his hands on the counter that she snapped to attention like an animatronic brought to life by his presence. She smiled a rehearsed and obviously forced smile.

"May I help you?" Her voice was flat, with no enthusiasm; her smile betrayed by her flat eyes.

"Probably," Adam replied, focusing on the menu overhead and avoiding eye contact with the girl. "I'll have three value packs of regular tacos, three bean burritos, an order of nachos, three soft chicken tacos and a Pepsi."

A sound much like a sigh escaped her. "I take it that'll be to go?"

"No, I'll eat it here."

There was a slight pause as she punched in his order. "Your funeral," she replied. "That'll be thirty-one seventy-four."

He slid two twenty-dollar bills across the counter, which she snatched up without a sound, dumping his change into his palm. She turned to the small window that opened into the kitchen beyond, tossing small paper packages onto a tray before returning and sliding the tray across the counter toward him. Without another word, she returned to her place by the cash register, once more pulling her phone from her pocket and staring blankly into the small screen.

Finding a secluded table in the far corner of the combined dining area, Adam immediately tore into his food, swallowing two bean burritos and a chicken taco almost without chewing. He was still radiating heat, and he thought he could feel his body absorbing the food directly. He ate the nachos and a value pack of tacos next, pausing only for some Pepsi, before ripping into the third bean burrito and another value pack of tacos. The food was going down so fast he could hardly taste it, but the taste wasn't the biggest concern at the moment. Getting the food into him to replace the fuel he lost in regeneration was.

Fifteen minutes later, he had eaten every bit of the food he had just purchased. Sitting back, he closed his eyes while his body absorbed the caloric energy, feeling stronger by the second. Reveling in his newly recovered strength, he gathered his trash, piled it high on his tray and dumped it in the nearest trash can on his way to the men's room.

The mirror in the men's room was filthy and smeared, but it still showed Adam exactly what he had hoped to see. His face had filled out once more, his body filling his clothes the way it was supposed to. The handgun at his back now dug uncomfortably into him and he loosened his belt again to ease the pressure. His wounds were gone, he was back to full strength. However, his clothes remained shredded and bloody. Some new clothes were the new top priority.

And just at that moment, company walked into the room.

11

From the window of the helicopter, Burke watched the Connecticut landscape race past beneath him. At the speed they were traveling the rain smashed against the windows more like a hard slap than a gentle patter, creating a noise that rivaled the rotors keeping the helicopter in the air. Normally he hated flying, but flying through weather like this at the far end of twilight, he absolutely loathed it.

Next to him sat Dr. Forrester, a look of child-like delight on his face as he stared out the window and loudly hummed Wagner's *Ride of the Valkyries*. Burke suspected it had been a while since he had been out of the lab. A twinge of what might have been pity quickly dissipated as he reminded himself he wouldn't be here in the first place if not for the aging scientist's screw-up. Silently he cursed the other man, turning back to the rain slicked window.

"How much longer?" Burke asked the pilot through the intercom.

"Roughly ten minutes, sir," came the reply, the pilot's tinny voice almost inaudible above the din of the rotors.

"Did you get that, doctor?" Burke asked. He didn't really want to engage Forrester in conversation, but at this point anything was preferable than listening to him hum Wagner.

"I did, Mr. Darnell. Thank you." He straightened up in his seat, a look of disappointment on his face from having his fantasies interrupted. "What is our course of action, if I may inquire?"

The doctor seemed entirely focused on the present now, his previous distraction completely forgotten. It was the one thing to admire about the man, his 'live in the moment' way of life. Burke wasn't sure if that was a conscious choice by Dr. Forrester or just another example of him as the absent-minded professor.

"You're up first, Doc," Burke replied. "If you can't reason with our boy, you have to at least get close enough to him to use this." He held up an air-compression hypodermic gun, a reddish-orange fluid swishing around in the attached vial. "I'm sure you recognize it. It was your invention, after all."

Forrester's face twisted into a mix of surprise and shock at the sight of the fluid filled vial. Swallowing hard, he said, "How did you get that? How did you even know about it?"

A grin spread across Burke's face, his satisfaction at Dr. Forrester's discomfort evident. "Doc, I know everything that goes on at PenTech. It was a little crazy, not to mention futile, of you to try to hide it from us, but that's something we can discuss late. The fact is, you are the only one who has even a remote chance of getting near enough to Adam to use this. I need to be sure you'll do it."

The grin melted from Burke's face, his eyes turning cold. "Please tell me you'll do it."

A wild look filled Dr. Forrester's eyes, the look of desperation that comes with being cornered. Animals who had been hunted and trapped would exhibit that look just before they turned on their captors. Burke moved his free hand to the Glock 17 at his hip, observing the doctor for any signs of rebellion. Silence rested in the air as the question hung between them.

Dr. Forrester finally broke the silence, his voice low. "Do you know what you're asking me to do?"

Burke's face was like stone. "I'm asking you to clean up a mistake."

"No, you are asking me to destroy my greatest achievement! My child!"

Burke tightened his grip on his pistol at the doctor's raised voice. "You remember what you told Mr. Penders? That you would do what had to be done? There's no going back now. Adam is a lost cause. You have a commitment, doctor, and I am here to see that you go through with it. Besides, he isn't your greatest achievement. Remember the Sleeper."

Forrester's face softened at the mention of the other. His shoulders relaxed slightly, and he sank back into his seat. Not contentedly, but not upset any longer, either. "Yes, the Sleeper. How could I forget?" His voice was a whisper, barely audible even over the helicopter's comm system. He appeared distant, as if he were lost in a daydream.

Without warning, he snapped back from the dream world. "What if I can't get through to him?" There was hesitation tinged with hope in his voice.

Burke was more than happy to shatter that hope. "I'll have no choice but to activate Phase Two." Burke jerked his thumb at the rain slick window to punctuate his statement.

In the driving rain and fading twilight, Dr. Forrester could barely make out the other helicopter cruising alongside them. A chill ran through him as his mind raced, filling in the blanks to what Burke had meant by 'Phase Two'. The more scenarios that flipped through his mind, the more ominous the feeling became.

"And what, may I ask, is phase Two?"

Burke's lips pulled back in a smile, revealing gleaming white teeth. It reminded Dr. Forrester of a shark, just before it ripped into its prey. He repressed a shudder, but his mind raced with thoughts of what Burke Darnell might be capable of.

"A surprise from Mr. Penders. One you won't have to find out about if you're successful."

The pilot broke in. “We’ll be landing in about three minutes.”

Burke’s smile widened. It looked to Forrester as if the man had just picked up the scent of blood.

12

"Not bad. Not bad at all."

Adam adjusted the collar of his new shirt as he checked out the look in the mirror. It was silk, a material he had never worn before. He had felt silk before, had experienced how it felt. Several people he had been sent to dispatch over the years were wearing silk when he helped them move on to their destiny, but he had never actually worn it. Had never felt it against his skin. He ran his hands down his chest, pressing the fabric against him. It was cool and smooth and luxurious, everything he imagined it might be. He had been lucky to find it. He just wished he'd thanked the person who had given him the opportunity to experience it like that.

Howard Orosco was a computer systems consultant out of Waterbury. He had been wearing the slick red shirt and black chinos when he burst into the restroom, talking at anyone within earshot about his plans for that night, which included a woman from his office, drinks and 'a whole lot of banging'. Howard's evening had not gone as he had originally planned, however. Within a few seconds of entering the restroom, his neck had been snapped and he had been stripped of his clothes, wallet and car keys and stuffed into the suspended ceiling, where he would no doubt go undiscovered for a few days. At least until he started to smell. Or putrefy. Whichever, it still gave Adam enough lead time to get ahead of the Project and find Rachel Carter.

Checking himself in the mirror again and satisfied with his appearance, he slid the SIG Sauer back into his belt at the small of his back. The gun stuck uncomfortably into him, but Adam looked at that as a positive sign. It meant that he had regained most, of not all, of the muscle mass he had lost during the regeneration. He was in peak form again. With a slight adjustment of the gun, he felt the discomfort in his back ease.

He slid the blue windbreaker on to cover the weapon, hating that he had to cover the beautiful silk shirt with such a mundane accessory. To him, it was like painting over a Picasso with a picture of dogs playing pool. But since Howard had not been wearing a jacket to complement his otherwise tasteful ensemble, he had no choice. He couldn't just waltz back into the food court with a handgun jutting out from his waistband. That would be sure to draw unwanted attention. For now, the tasteless nylon jacket would have to suffice. He made a quick mental note to remedy that as soon as possible.

With a last glance at the resting place of Howard Orosco, Adam stepped out of the restroom and back into the main lobby of the rest area. The food court was abuzz with people filling up on cheap fast-food and he melted into the crowd, losing himself in the flow.

He was almost at the exit when he noticed a peculiar buzzing just behind his right ear. It was more of a tingling sensation than a noise, like a mosquito routing around in search of a vein to tap. Scratching at the area did nothing, the sensation persisted. It's possible it was an aftereffect of the regeneration, some wound that hadn't fully healed itself yet. Or perhaps his body was still craving something. The events of the last twenty-four hours had stretched his abilities, both physical and metaphysical, further than ever before. And while he had given his body plenty of fuel to recover from the damage and subsequent repair of that damage, he had still not yet replaced the acids that were vital to the operation of his stepped-up metabolism. Maybe the buzzing sensation was just a side effect of having pushed himself too far without having the rest and recuperation to get back to full strength. Maybe he just needed to get some citrus and replace some acids he had depleted.

Across the hall was an extraordinarily well-stocked travel mart. While they had no gallon containers of orange juice, he could find three quarts as well as two quarts of grapefruit juice. He despised grapefruit juice but given the situation he felt secure he could choke some down, especially if it helped with the incessant buzzing in his head. It was getting more intense, having graduated from a mildly annoying buzzing to a seriously annoying itch.

After finding a table, this time in a less remote corner of the dining area, he opened up one bottle of orange juice. As he drank, he checked the contents of Howard Orosco's pockets. From the back pocket of the pants he produced a leather wallet, expensive by the look of it. Inside was a driver's license, several major credit cards of the gold and platinum variety, and two condoms tucked into a middle pocket to avoid creating unsightly rings on the leather. Nothing there he could use. The credit cards were too easy to trace and the driver's license was undoubtedly Howard with his balding head and out of style mustache. The front left pocket yielded a set of car keys and a small bottle of Binaca peppermint breath spray. Spritzing a bit of the Binaca into his mouth, he searched the right front pocket, finding four hundred dollars in cash and a tiny plastic bag that contained three small white pills. The pills had the look of aspirin but didn't bear the imprint of any drug company, leading Adam to suspect these pills were anything but aspirin. He didn't know what they might be, but they might come in handy at some point.

Most of the keys on the keyring were simple house or office keys, undistinguishable and unidentifiable. One item caught his attention, though. A small black plastic key fob with the name Porche emblazoned across it. Silk shirt, wad of cash and now a Porche. Howard had done very well for himself. And now so had Adam. Not only had he secured new transportation, but he was also traveling in style. A smile crept across his face that he didn't even try to repress.

Gathering up the cash, Binaca, pills, and key fob, he stuffed them all back into the various pockets they had come from before gathering up the bag that contained the remaining bottles of juice. In doing so, he nudged Howard's wallet, complete with identification and credit cards, onto the floor toward the back of the table. He wanted it out of sight, but difficult to find. As with his own credit cards he had seeded the parking lot with earlier, he was hoping someone with questionable morals would find the wallet and use the highly traceable cards. After discovering Howard's body, the investigation would follow the trail of credit card purchases, leading them away from Adam and his involvement in the murder. It wouldn't sidetrack the Project, but it would keep local law enforcement off of his trail.

The itch behind his ear was becoming more and more unbearable, almost to the point of being painful. The cause was still an irritating mystery, but one he didn't have time to ponder at the moment. He had to locate his new Porche and put as much distance as possible between him and Howard's corpse. Not that he couldn't handle any local cops who came sniffing around him, it would just be very time consuming and time was something that was in very short supply at the moment.

As he stepped into the rain and wind-swept night to locate the Porche, he noticed a particular thrumming sound. At first he thought it was just the odd sensation behind his ear getting worse, but the sound wasn't coming from inside him. It was a faint noise off in the distance, getting louder with each passing second. It was familiar, the sound. He strained to hear through the downpour and wind, trying to ignore the itch and now audible buzzing coming from behind his ear.

It hit him suddenly, a cold steel hand grabbing his guts and squeezing hard. He knew what the sound was. The rain and wind and sounds of the highway had muffled it, but it was completely clear to him now.

Helicopters. Two of them. The Project had found him. He had no idea how they had caught up to him so quickly. His escape from the safe house hadn't been the cleanest get away but he should have had more time. How had they found him so soon? He needed to think, to formulate a plan of escape, but it was so hard with that incessant buzzing and itching in his head. It was driving him mad.

The cold steel hand in his guts squeezed tighter. The itch. That was how they had found him. He raced back to the men's room where Mr. Orosco had so recently taken up residence, the ceiling tile still slightly askew. His reflection in the mirror looked harried, despite the fine silk shirt. Gently he touched the area on the back of his head where the buzzing was coming from, just above where his spine met his skull, pressing hard into the flesh and feeling out the area. There it was, a slight lump resting just under the skin. Making a mental note of the lump's location, he headed back out of the men's room at a run.

Outside, he could see the running lights of the helicopters as they approached the parking lot of the service area. They were dangerously close now, landing in just a few minutes. He was out of time.

In the travel mart, he ran past the snacks, soda and overpriced souvenirs to the small area in the back where the toiletries were. Grabbing a nail file, he ran to the counter and, before the heavyset woman behind the counter could say anything, he dropped a five-dollar bill on the counter. "Keep the change," he exclaimed, running from the travel mart and back to the men's room again. He had no time for change or niceties.

In the men's room he stripped off the windbreaker and the silk shirt, setting them off to one side of the sink. What came next was going to be messy, and he didn't have time to search for new clothes again. He tore open the nail file package. The file was far less sharp than he would have preferred, which would slow him down considerably, but it was all he had. Finding the tiny bump that was the source of the vibrating itch in his skull, he positioned the nail file just above it. Taking a deep breath to steel himself, he jabbed the tip of the nail file under his skin. Pain erupted from the spot as a small trickle of hot blood ran down his back. He pushed through the pain, twisting the file in a search for what he knew was there. He probed the wound, each movement of the mail file sending spikes of pain through his head, until he felt the tip of the file hit something. Something inorganic. Something metallic. Turning the file gently, he nudged the small object toward the open wound, feeling it scrape and slide through the meat of his neck. After what seemed like a lifetime of pain, he felt the chip pop loose of his head and, with a metallic ping, it hit the floor.

A subdermal tracking chip, no larger than half a grain of rice. That was how they knew where he was. Why there wasn't immediate pursuit after he fled the safe house. They could find him whenever they wanted, all they had to do was activate the chip. Damn it, he had been so stupid. After all of his years with the Project, how had he not expected this? Of course they would have a way to track him. Aside from the fact that he himself was a valuable asset, the knowledge he had was incriminating enough to bring down governments. They couldn't let him escape.

Pressing a handful of paper towels against the wound in his head, he dropped to his knees to recover the small chip. Outside the thrumming of the helicopter's massive whirling blades grew louder, overtaking the even the slapping of wind-driven rain against the side of the building.

It was too late. They were here. Soon they would have him.

13

Burke was out of the helicopter as soon as it touched down, anger rising at the sudden onslaught of the storm. He peered around the parking lot frantically trying to catch a glimpse of Adam, the rain and wind pelting him mercilessly, the noise of the storm exacerbated by the rotors of the helicopter still spinning wildly above him. An angry flush ran through him as he wiped the collected rain from his eyes and cursed the sudden onset of the storm. It was another impediment he didn't need right now.

The second helicopter touched down a few hundred yards from the first and Burke's anger subsided a bit as the door swung open and a half-dozen other people, dressed in black military fatigues and body armor, joined him on the rain-swept pavement. Each of them carried an AR-15 assault rifle and a holstered pistol. They moved precisely, each step a measured and practiced maneuver. This was Robert Penders' personal commando team, assembled exclusively by Penders himself to be at his beck and call whenever needed, and paid to follow orders without question. Tonight, that power had been extended to Burke, and he felt an almost sexual arousal from having this much raw power at his command.

One soldier approached Burke, a small device in hand. "We've got his location tagged, sir. He's definitely inside. What are your orders?"

The feeling of power rose in Burke at the question, a slight tingle in his crotch. Burke turned to face William Harriman, former Army Colonel and now the leader of Penders' mercenary squad. Harriman was in excellent shape for a man of fifty-six, a commanding figure even at an unimpressive height of five feet six inches. White hair stood in direct contrast with his ebony skin, his squat body a mass of muscle and strength. He turned his attention once again to the device grasped in the thick fingers of his left hand and consulted the readings. The steady stream of blinking light and beeps on the simulated map confirmed to Burke that the subdermal tracker in the back of Adam's head was working as intended. He was here, and it was time to bring him home.

"Have your men surround the building and cover every escape route," Burke ordered. "I'm going to let Forrester try to talk to him first, but if that fails I don't want that son of a bitch slipping by us." Burke wiped at the rain on his face but it was no use. The rain already soaked his suit coat, and he could feel his shirt becoming waterlogged as well. He shivered as the chill grew. He hated being cold. If Adam was going to make a run for it, why didn't he at least have the courtesy of running to the Bahamas or some place else warm and tropical? This shit was ridiculous. "And get me a poncho or something," he added to Harriman.

Harriman reached under his own poncho and produced a nylon square the size of a wallet. "I already took the liberty, sir. I figured you wouldn't have been field ready with the time crunch."

Burke snatched the poncho from Harriman, annoyed with his presumption that Burke wouldn't be prepared for the field and yet equally impressed with the fact that Harriman had planned for the fact. He stripped out of his sodden suit coat and slipped the poncho over his head, relieved to have something on that would help fend off the rain. He turned back to the helicopter cabin in time to see Dr. Forrester tumbling out, stumbling as he hit the wet pavement. The scientist wore a black poncho that seemed to swallow him whole. While he and Harriman shared the same height, Forrester had none of the soldier's bulk to help him fill out the bulky poncho, which still dragged on the ground under him despite being pulled up tight over his head. It didn't help that he stooped over trying to avoid the helicopter's rotors, which were well above him and posed no danger. Dr. Forrester kept his hands over his head and ducked down, moving forward as quickly as he could to get out from under the spinning blades. Burke had to work to keep from laughing as Forrester shuffled forward, nearly tripping over himself twice.

Forrester made his way to Burke's side and stopped, wiping the rain from his thick glasses. Burke leaned into the older man. "You're on, Doc. You know what to do?"

"Talk him into coming back with us." There was a strain in the scientist's voice that was audible even through the incessant pounding of the rain.

"And if he refuses?"

Forrester paused, his body tensing noticeably even under the bulk of the poncho that covered his slight frame. "Then I use this," he said, producing the hypodermic gun from an oversized sleeve.

Burke nodded firmly. "Good. As long as we understand each other, everything will work out just fine. Remember, I'll be watching you. I'll know what's going on in there, so don't start thinking you can find another way out for your boy. He's PenTech property, and he's going back there. Whether he goes in shackles or a body bag is your call. Understand?"

Forrester offered no reply, just stared at the hypodermic in his hand. Burke waited a few more seconds for a response before grabbing the doctor by his shoulders and shaking him gently. "Doc? Do we have an understanding?"

"Yes," replied the older man, his voice little more than a whisper. "I'll do what needs to be done. Just be sure to have my thirty pieces of silver ready for me when it's finished."

Forrester lifted his head and made eye contact with Burke for the first time since learning what was expected of him. The old man's eyes held a fire Burke had never seen in them before. A passion he hadn't expected. He wasn't sure how he felt about that. When passive, the doctor could be controlled and manipulated, but if were to rebel he could become a liability. That was something Burke could not allow to happen.

Burke squinted against the rain, locking his gaze with the scientist's. He held the doctor's stare, never averting his eyes for a moment. Unblinking, unwavering. In a moment, the passion behind the doctor's eyes faded as quickly as it had appeared, leaving only the absent-minded oaf that Burke had grown to loathe.

"I'm sure you'll get everything you're due, Doc. Now get in there and snag our boy." As if to punctuate the order, Burke thrust his finger toward the entrance of the visitor center. Forrester's gaze lingered on the younger man for just a moment before he turned without another word and headed for the door.

****

Just inside the door, Dr. Forrester stopped in the now deserted food court of the rest area. Harriman and his team had cleared the lobby a few minutes ago, leaving the enormous room in an eerie silence. The only noise he heard was the patter of rain on the roof high above him that echoed through the chamber, becoming a nerve scathing timpani. As the chill in his stomach grew, slowly ascending his spine, he attempted to block it out. He tried his best to push down the fear, not understanding why he was overwhelmed with dread. He was here to help Adam. He had always tried to help him, certainly Adam would know his intentions this time. In his rational mind, he was certain he had nothing to fear, but his heart was apparently unaware as it beat furiously in his chest.

To his right, a screeching, grating noise erupted, the sound racing through his body like a bolt of lightning. He turned to face whatever was there, fumbling for the hypodermic gun in the pocket of his coat. He clenched his eyes shut, afraid to see what was coming for him, unable to grasp a weapon to defend himself. When no attack came, he opened his eyes. There was no sign of Adam in a homicidal rage, instead there was only an ice cream chest freezer in need of service. The machine continued to rattle and hiss as the electric jolt of fear and adrenaline slowly left his body. His shoulders slumped once more, the tension of fear subsiding. He slumped down in the nearest seat he could find, a molded, hard plastic chair that serviced the fast-food restaurants, his heart racing furiously. He needed a moment to calm himself, and to make certain he hadn't wet himself. His heartbeat slowly returned to normal and a slight smile crossed his face, despite the fact that terror still sat in his gut. He shook his head, chuckling slightly to himself.

As he sat gathering himself, he watched outside as the lights of the two helicopters shone on the rain slicked windows like psychedelic stained glass. Shadows wavered and twisted as Harriman's people scurried about to lock down the building. They were like dark wraiths, figures of impending doom who would come and drag Adam into the darkness, into a place of unyielding pain and torment. His gut tightened again, not from fear this time. This time, it was guilt that wracked him. Adam never had an opportunity to direct the course of his own life. His path had been predetermined well before his 'birth'. The Eden Project had fed him information and training in vitro, conditioning him to be the perfect obedient soldier before his life even began. He never had the chance to make a choice about his own destiny, belonging body and soul to the Project and the machinations of Robert Penders and his ilk.

Until now. It appeared Adam had had enough of the Project and their demands and was ready to take charge of his life, to decide his own destiny. There was a swell of pride in Forrester's chest at the thought of that. Perhaps he had accomplished more than he had set out to do after being approached by Robert Penders regarding his theories concerning cloning and genetic engineering. Robert Penders provided resources and funding that Forrester had never encountered before, and with those resources had created one hundred viable life-forms never before imagined by humanity. It was then, at the time of his greatest success, that he made his biggest mistake. He allowed the Project to take over the education of his subjects. He watched as all one hundred of them underwent training to become engines of destruction. Trained in espionage and military tactics. Trained to kill without question or remorse. Their minds were still fragile, however, being that they were not much more than newborns mentally and emotionally. Adding to the challenge was the fact that they had been physically aged up to pre-adolescence, going through all the typical hormonal shifts experienced at that stage of life. All of those things combined were more than their delicate systems could handle. In one fell swoop, they turned on one another, attacking and killing with the brutal efficiency they had been trained with. In the end, when they cleared the blood and broken bodies, only two remained. Two survivors. Two successes.

Now one of those successes was under threat again. The Project would have their property back or they would destroy him if they couldn't bring him back under their control. To them, he was nothing more than a tool, another weapon in their arsenal, a piece of technology to be possessed and used before being disposed of when it no longer suited their needs. He couldn't let that happen. He couldn't allow Adam to be destroyed. No matter the personal cost, he would see that Adam left here alive.

The restaurant gallery was strangely still without the constant rush of travelers. An eerie sense of dread washed over Forrester, his stomach seizing up in an icy ball. He suddenly felt alone in the world. Vulnerable. Even though he could still see Harriman's mercenaries moving around through the rain-slicked windows, he felt a cold numbness, a loneliness. His work had left him very little time for a social life and he had no family to speak of. All he had in the way of company, of a continuation of his legacy, was his 'children'. The accomplishments he had seen through his research. It was the only legacy he had to leave the world. And now that legacy was under threat. He would not allow Burke to force him to destroy his creation. His progeny.

"Dr. Forrester."

His name boomed across the empty room, low and loud, echoing from wall to wall. It was like the rolling thunder that came in with the storm outside, coming from everywhere and nowhere all at once. The doctor felt a startle, and his heart seemed to threaten to leap from his chest. Glancing around the vast space, he saw no one, but he knew he was being watched. Being judged. The grip of fear was on him again, its hands cold.

He swallowed hard, forcing the fear down so he could speak. "Adam," he squeaked out, "is that you?" His eyes darted around the cavernous chamber to find where the voice had originated from. He found nothing.

The voice returned, once more filling the room. "Yes Doctor, it's me. I know why you're here, and I think it's only fair to tell you I won't go back. I can't go back. There's nothing you can say, nothing you can do, that will change my mind. I will die before I go back to the Project. And I will take as many of you with me as I can."

Forrester's throat went dry at that. He had to clear it loudly before continuing. "I know that, son. And I'm not here to take you back. I don't want to see you.... like that ever again. I'm here to help you, Adam. Together, we can work to find a way to get you what you want. What you need."

"What I want? What *I* want?" Adam's disembodied voice exploded in anger in a way Forrester had never experienced. "You don't care about what I want! To you, I'm just another rat in a maze. Scurrying around to prove what a great scientific mind you are. But if we break from the parameters of the grand experiment, if we stray from the scientific path, we're no longer of any use. We are contaminated. And for the good of the experiment, we must destroy any lab animal that has been contaminated! Am I right, Doctor?"

Forrester froze, uncertain how to respond. This was something new. Something unprecedented. He had never heard this kind of rage from Adam before. He had always controlled his emotional responses. Now they were out, raw and angry. This was not what he was expecting, and he wasn't sure how to best address it. Fear creeped in, boxing in the corners of his rational mind. The scientific method became a hazy fog.

"It's not like that," he stammered, unsure of how to proceed. Allowing raw emotion to carry him forward. "I *do* care. I wouldn't be here if..."

"Isn't that right, Doctor?" Adam's booming voice cut him off.

The voice had gone from awe-inspiring to chilling with that last sentence. The fear returned to the pit of the Doctor's stomach and slowly crept up his spine, leaving a chilling trail as it went. Whatever confidence he had in his ability to talk Adam down was slowly fading away.

"Adam, please, listen to me. I'm here to help you." Forrester's eyes scanned the room in earnest now, peering into every darkened corner and listening for any minute sound that might tell him where Adam was hiding. His extremities became frozen, gripped by the same icy fear that had traveled the length of his spine. That same icy terror rooted his feet to the floor, stopping him in place. His hand once again clenched the hypodermic gun in his pocket. He wanted to release it, to show Adam the good faith he had just promised him, but he couldn't. The weapon was his only protection, and his grip was like concrete. His fingers were numb and disobeyed any commands his rational mind tried to give. He couldn't move. He could barely breathe. The blood rushing through his ears was like thunder, shattering the previously eerie quiet of the room.

"You're here to help me? Help me do what? Return to the Project? Go back to being a mindless slave to them again? Killing on command and then going back to my little box every night, neglected and ignored until I'm needed again? No, Doctor. It's too late for that. I am contaminated. Contaminated by free thought. Contaminated by free will. And I've gotten used to it. I won't let anyone else control my life ever again. Adam's voice calmed, softened, but remained focused. His tone was one of dedication. Of resolution.

"I have a life waiting for me, Doctor. A life I should have had a long time ago. A life that you denied me. That you callously gave away to someone less deserving."

Forrester's sense of fear was becoming panic. He tried to interpret what Adam was telling him, but his mind raced with the possibilities of what Adam was capable of. He had been witness to some of the horrible things that had been done, and he had no desire to be on the receiving end.

And then it hit him, what Adam was referring to. A life waiting for him. A life denied to him. But it couldn't be that. He couldn't know about that. Those memories were gone, buried by intensive training and psychological conditioning. He couldn't be aware of the other one. It just wasn't possible.

Adam's voice shattered the quiet of the room again. "You're afraid, Doctor. I can tell. I can feel it from here. Do you have any idea how exhilarating someone else's fear is? The feel, the taste of it, it's exquisite. I can practically taste your fear. But you knew that, didn't you? After all, you created me. You designed me. Just like that other doctor you had me read about. What was his name? Oh yes, Frankenstein."

Despite its playful edge, Adam's voice still contained venom. Forrester said nothing, choosing instead to listen. Maybe if he could keep Adam talking, he could learn more about what had caused his break. Maybe talk him down. Pushing his fear aside as best he could, he listened to what the other man had to say, waiting for the right opportunity to interject. Provided he wasn't dead before that happened.

Adam continued. "Dr. Frankenstein also created life. He also threw out all morals and ethics and scientific responsibility and brought a creature to life. You should feel a great kinship. Except Frankenstein's creation was not as perfect as yours, was it? But what did he have to work with? Old body parts and second-rate brains. No, you had it much better, didn't you, Doctor? You had unlimited funding, state-of-the-art laboratories, and access to the best building blocks imaginable. You could choose DNA from professional athletes and Nobel Prize-winning scientists and great military leaders and cook them all up in a great big vat to create the most perfect human being the world has ever seen. And you did. In fact, being the over-achiever that you are, you created a hundred of these perfect human being. What a proud papa you must have been! But, like all children, they didn't quite turn out the way you had hoped, did they?"

Forrester was being baited. Adam was trying to get him to defend himself, to justify his actions. To admit that he was wrong. But he wasn't wrong. Adam and the others were the culmination of a lifetime of work and they still had great potential to change the world, to make it a better place. He had nothing to hide, no reason to be afraid. And if he were going to die today, it seemed poetic that it be at the hands of his own creation.

Forrester stood from the hard molded plastic chair and took a deep breath, straightening his spine and squaring up his shoulders. The icy cold in his gut was replaced by a warm confidence in his actions, in his past. "Yes, I was proud. Proud of the marvels I had created. Proud of my scientific accomplishments. But like everything else in this world, pride exacts a price. And sometimes it can be a very expensive proposition."

He paused, his words caught in his throat. He no longer scanned the room for signs of Adam, he simply didn't care anymore. If his errant creation wanted to kill him, let him. But he would speak his mind, his heart, and maybe even purge his conscience before then.

"Sometimes it can cost you your very soul."

Quiet overtook the room again, the only sound the consistent beat of the rain on the windows. Apparently, Adam had decided not to speak, so Forrester continued. "You and the others, you were going to be the apex of my scientific career. Finally, I could prove to the world that my theories had been right all along and that the wonders of genetic engineering could propel human evolution forward. That we could force evolution."

He paused, a lump in his throat as memories flooded back to him. Painful memories. "The scientific community spurned me. Considered a crackpot. It's an unkind term and one that was never used officially, although I'm certain it came up a few times at scientific conferences and cocktail parties. I can't be sure, as they never invited me to those functions after I revealed my beliefs. You see, genetic engineering was a relatively new science. The first attempt at cloning was still years away. But my work, my work was so far beyond that. I wasn't proposing cloning at all. No, what I was proposing was the actual creation of a human life by gathering, structuring, and assembling all the components for that life to take shape. I knew that with the proper genetic materials we could create life that was as close to perfect as humankind was likely to get. Physically perfect. Immune to every known disease. The ability to accelerate the healing process, allowing recovery from even the most horrific and life-threatening injuries. Strong. Fast. Indominable. I knew it could be done; I just needed the opportunity to try. I needed someone to believe in my research and give me the tools and funding I needed to see it through." Forrester paused again, his stomach sinking. "But that would not happen. My reputation preceded me everywhere I went. I was an outcast, a bizarre eccentric, the 'mad scientist'. No legitimate research firms were willing to take a risk on my work. I was on the verge of giving up when Robert Penders approached me. Not by a subordinate vice president at PenTech, but by the founder of the world's largest firm that focuses on pioneering scientific research. He offered me a research position on the spot, with unlimited funding and resources. It wasn't until later that I realized the mistake I had made. That I had made a deal with the Devil himself, and that he now owned not just me but my creations as well." He hung his head as if the weight of his confession was too much to bear.

Slumping back into the hard plastic chair, he continued. "Do I regret my decision? Yes. Every day. What they did to you and the others fills my soul with sorrow, and the thought of the ones we lost breaks my heart. And I despair when I think about what you have suffered through. I wish I could change that. So desperately I wish I could change that. But I can't. So now I am asking you, begging you, to listen to what I'm saying. To accept what happened and forgive me, at least long enough so we can save you."

He waited, breath shallow, for a response. Any response. Nothing came. He wondered if Adam hadn't already found his way past Harriman and his men and if he had been here confessing to himself. If that were the case, there would be no absolution for him today.

Once again, he hauled himself out of the uncomfortable plastic chair, shaking out his legs and trying to get the blood flowing to his numb buttocks and legs. He started for the front door, his gait slow and drooped. He had failed. Now he would have to report that to Burke. At that point, Burke would give Harriman the okay to send in his troops. His heart fell even further at the thought of Adam being lost this way. He was so lost in his remorse he didn't see the figure standing in the shadows of the alcove that housed the men's room door.

"Dr. Forrester."

His breath caught in his throat and his body spasmed with a nervous jolt as the figure spoke. Forrester turned sharply toward the voice, his thick glasses dislodging from his face with the momentum. He caught them at the end of his nose and slid them back up to the bridge as the figure before him came into view. It was Adam, of that much he was certain. But there was something different about the man who stood before him. Something unsettling.

His eyes.

His face hid in darkness, but the eyes stood out from the shadows, catching the light in the backwash of the harsh fluorescents. They were the same cool blue, radiating icy efficiency as always, but there was something more now. Something dangerous and unpredictable. Something savage. They were still cold and unforgiving like a predator, but beneath that was a passion. The man possessed a desire that Forrester had never witnessed before. A human need that drove the animal. A focus.

Forrester's breath caught in his throat, his heart hammering in his chest again. It wasn't good for a man his age to have these swings in cardiovascular activity, and he felt a twinge of discomfort in his chest. Unconsciously, he stumbled back away from Adam, coming up against a cold, unyielding wall. An exit sign burned brightly no less than a dozen feet to his right, but he knew he was trapped. Adam's cool eyes told him that as they froze him in place with their gaze, stripping away the façade of human dominance and revealing the small, frightened animal that existed beneath. Forrester's mortality suddenly became a palpable thing, and he realized that, his previous bravado aside, he was terrified of dying.

Adam spoke again, his voice like a predator's growl. "You asked if I could forgive you? I believe I can. But I need to know one thing before I can. Why him? Why was he chosen over me?"

Terror exploded in Forrester's chest. Adam *did* know about the other subject. Knew he was out there. Knew his life was different. That explained the passion in his eyes. The subdued rage in his voice. He was angry and jealous, and like a child, had no idea how to handle these emotions except by lashing out. But he wasn't a child, and when he lashed out, people would die. People had died.

Adam continued. "Why was he allowed to live free of the Project? He has a wife. He has friends. People who care about him. All the things I was told I could never have. That someone created me for a different purpose. That I was unique. Now I know that was nothing but lies. Lies to control me. To condition me. To keep me in line and continue to do the Project's work. But that aside, I still need to know. Why him? Why was he the favored son?"

Forrester didn't answer. Couldn't answer. He wanted to speak, to defend his actions, but he couldn't get his chest to take in breath or his mind to form the words. Fear had paralyzed him.

A few moments of silence hung between them before Adam spoke. "Never mind, it doesn't matter. We will rectify it soon enough. Besides, your concerns in this matter are coming to a close right now."

Adam stepped forward, and Forrester felt his heart explode in the grip of terror. He couldn't even manage a scream as Adam emerged from the darkness and advanced toward him. A quick glance at the exit again, the red letters glowing like a beacon. It was so close, but it may as well have been miles away. When he looked back, Adam's eyes filled his view.

"I appreciate your efforts on my behalf, Doctor. But I'm quite capable of saving myself."

As Adam reached out for him, Forrester finally succumbed to his fright. Darkness caved in around him, the world going black and silent.

****

Burke looked at his watch again, surprised that only twenty-two minutes had gone by since Dr. Forrester had entered the hospitality building of the rest area. It seemed like the little man had gone in an eternity ago.

Even at only twenty-two minutes, he had been in there too long and now Burke's mind was reeling from the possibilities of what was going on inside. Did Forrester underestimate the strength of his relationship with Adam? Had Adam already killed the little scientist and escaped? Had Forrester found his balls and killed Adam? Bile rose in his throat as he considered the ramifications of each scenario and how it might blow back on him. This is why he hated field work, too many variables and too many opportunities for things to tits-fucking-up. He had to figure out what was going on in there, if for no other reason than figuring out how to spin it in his favor.

"Harriman!" Burke shouted over the din of the rain smacking the pavement. He wiped at his face and squeegeed a sheet of water off, splashing it to his feet. His shoes were soaked through. No doubt he would develop a case of pneumonia soon. Oh yes, Forrester was going to pay for this night.

Harriman dismissed the two operatives he had been briefing and sloshed across the rain-slicked parking lot to Burke. Even though the rain clung to him as it did Burke, somehow the older man seemed to ignore it without squinting, wiping, or sputtering. Burke sighed sharply, a droplet flying from his upper lip. He wiped angrily at his face again.

Harriman snapped to attention. "Yes, sir."

Burke ignored the enthusiastic display of military decorum. "Any idea what's going on in there?"

"Nothing, sir."

The bile in his throat sank back to his stomach, hitting like molten metal. He turned to face Harriman directly, his shoes squishing and squeaking. His socks were drenched and he could feel what little patience he had dissipate. "Do you think you could elaborate a bit on this 'nothing', Colonel?"

Harriman cleared his throat. "Of course, sir. It looks like he's in there talking to himself. We can't see anyone else in there. We have solid coverage between the security cameras on site and the flex cams we snaked in through the roof. Dr. Forrester is at a booth in front of Burger King, just rambling on. Talking to..... nothing. It appears he may have had some sort of psychotic break, sir."

Burke had been thinking the same thing, that the pressure had finally gotten to the old man and he had lost it. "What's he doing now? Still rambling?"

Harriman spoke into his headset, staring vacantly into the night as the reply came in. "He's heading for the front door now, sir. It looks like he's aborting the mission. Wait, we've lost visual, but he should be in sight in a second."

Burke sloshed around to get a look at the main doors, squinting against the light of the restaurant signs enhanced by the rain. It was difficult to see, but he was certain no one was coming out of the doors. "Where is he? Where the fuck is he?"

"I don't know, sir." Harriman began shouted orders into his headset. "Position Delta, I need a reading! Alpha, move in with Gamma on the main entry. Beta, spread out and cover Gamma's previous position. No one fires without my command! Delta, position!"

Static crackled for a few seconds before Delta replied, each second unsettling Burke's stomach even further. When it finally came, Harriman relayed the response. "They can't see him, sir. I'm sending in a few men for a closer look."

"Fine," Burke snarled. "Just don't scare our rabbit."

Harriman nodded. "Understood, sir." He returned to his headset. "Gamma, Beta, move in closer and try to establish a visual!"

Through the downpour, Burke could make out two shapes as they converged on the front entrance. They hovered there for a moment, two almost indistinguishable shadows against the backdrop of a gloom filled rainy night. He was about to instruct Harriman to have them converge when the door suddenly burst open and another vaguely human shaped joined the group. This figure wasn't as graceful or stealthy as the other two, moving in an unsteady lope. The operatives designated as Beta and Gamma were at his side immediately, leading him away from the door and toward the helicopter. They reached Burke's position in seconds, but his temper flared exponentially in that time. Enough was enough.

"You had your chance, Forrester." Burke turned to Harriman, angrily wiping water from his face again. "Do it. Take that place apart brick by brick if you have to, but find that son of a bitch and bring him to me!"

"Alive?" Harriman inquired.

Burke's rage reached its limits and finally boiled over. "I don't give a shit anymore! Alive, dead, crippled or with an apple stuffed in his mouth, I don't give a fuck! Just make damned sure he doesn't get away!"

"Understood, sir." Harriman rushed off to organize his men, disappearing into the rain.

Once Harriman was gone, Burke turned to the man tightly wrapped in a poncho, hunched over to avoid the rain and wind. Despite the events of the last day, Forrester seemed somehow taller. More in control. Burke felt his rage rising again at the thought of a confident Forrester. His life's work was on the verge of being destroyed. Hell, he'd be lucky to survive once Penders heard about the fiasco this night had been. He had no right to be proud of himself. He should be broken, not gloating. Burke's vision went red, his anger finally reaching the tipping point. Rushing the other man, he grasped him by the shoulder and spun him around.....

.... and felt the barrel of a SIG Sauer P229 pressed firmly against his left nostril. His anger fell away, replaced by a sudden onslaught of fear. Shifting his gaze slightly, he moved his eyes away from the barrel of the weapon and onto the face of the person wielding it. He saw the coldest, iciest pair of blue eyes he had ever seen. The eyes of a remorseless killer, boring into Burke like a thousand icy needles. Beneath that was a wide grin, like the jaws of a shark that had just found its next meal. A mixed groan of fear and despair escaped him.

Adam pulled him closer, bringing that shark's smile up to Burke's ear. "Not a sound. Not a word. Not a whisper. You know me, Mr. Darnell. You know I would have no qualms blowing your brains all over this pavement. In fact, it's something I'd really like to see. So don't piss me off. Do we have an understanding?"

The voice behind the grin was not at all what Burke expected. It was warm and calm, perhaps even soothing despite the sinister words behind it. In another time and place, it may have even been pleasant. All it did at the moment was make Burke want to wet his pants.

Adam pressed him. "I asked you a question, Mr. Darnell."

Burke could only manage a slight nod that drove the barrel of the pistol further into his nose.

"Good. Now get inside, we're getting out of here. Things have become a bit too hot for me around here." Adam casually motioned toward the door of the helicopter with his free hand, asking Burke to step inside as if they were going to a bar for a drink. The barrel of the gun pulled away from his face and Burke climbed into the vehicle, still shaking from the sudden rush of adrenaline.

Once inside, with a pistol no longer exploring his nasal cavity, some of Burke's courage crept back. Remembering the Glock that rested on his hip, he slid quickly into one of the plush seats that adorned the sound-shielded walls of the executive helicopter.

Adam made his way to the cockpit door and slid it open. The pilot and co-pilot were both staring into their smartphones, one playing a game of some sort and the other swiping through pictures on a dating website despite the band of gold around his left ring finger. The younger man, the co-pilot, was the first to acknowledge him by looking up from his game. His eyes went wide with surprise and he reached across the cabin to slap the arm of the pilot, who finally took his eyes away from the parade of women sliding across his phone. His jaw dropped at the sight of the intruder with the gun in his hand, and he let his phone clatter to the floor. From their reactions, Adam surmised they were most likely civilian pilots and not soldiers like the operatives currently scurrying around outside in search of him. Good, that would make this much easier.

Without missing a beat, Adam laid out their options for them in a calm, warm, and persuasive voice. "This can play out one of two ways. The first is that you get this bird in the air when I tell you to and take me where I want to go, where you will leave me and forget I ever existed. The second, far less pleasant, option is that you refuse my request and I kill you both right now. I know I'm not you, but if I were, I would certainly lean more towards option number one." He paused, a slight yet menacing grin sliding across his face. "What will it be, gentlemen?"

Adam expected the younger of the two, the co-pilot, to crack first. Instead, the pilot spoke up almost immediately. "N-number one, sir," he stammered. "Without a doubt, number one." With a quick glance between them, they prepared the helicopter for take-off.

"I'm so glad you see things my way. Now Mr. Darnell and I can continue our conversation, since I see he's getting his balls back." Adam turned back to Burke and left the pilots to their work, unconcerned that they would fail to live up to their obligations. He had that effect on people.

Adam turned back to Burke, whose face had turned an almost unnatural shade of white. Like a cartoon ghost. Adam slid into the seat next to him, lowering the SIG Sauer. The tension in Burke's shoulders eased slightly, but his breath was still coming in brief clips as adrenaline raced through him. Like the pilot and the co-pilot, he was a civilian. A desk jockey. The excitement of the day was wearing on him.

Adam faced him directly and smiled. "Relax, Burke. I'm not going to kill you. Not unless you give me reason to. There's no reason to be afraid." Burke stayed silent, eyeing him cautiously. "You're scared, I get it. How can I tell what's going on in your mind? I'll let you in on a little secret." He leaned in close to Burke, who shrank back until he hit the back wall of the helicopter's cabin. "I can't. You know that telepathy thing they were supposed to have worked out in us? Yeah, it didn't work. Sure, I can detect powerful emotions. Like the pants-shitting fear you're experiencing right now. But actually reading someone else's thoughts? Nope. I can't see inside your head, which is a pity. But with a man like you, filled with such hatred and passion, being able to see into your heart is so much more gratifying. So much more revealing."

Adam lifted his face, coming eye to eye with Burke, a smug grin on his face. "It lets me know exactly the weaselly coward you really are."

The rotors above whirred harder as the helicopter readied to take off into the storm. Burke's shoulders tensed again, his brow creasing, his hands balling into tight fists. Inside him, Adam could feel the other man's fear turning over and becoming a white-hot rage. Adam's smile deepened, and he gave Burke a look that said, *I know what's going on inside you*, which only infuriated Burke and ratcheted up his anger.

The copter left the ground with a lurch, taking Adam by surprise. Burke took advantage of the split-second distraction and drew the Glock, taking aim at Adam just as he turned back. Burke squeezed off a shot that boomed through the soundproofed cabin just as the airship lurched in the buffeting winds. The shot went wide and a window behind Adam disintegrated, wind and rain pouring in from the night. The helicopter bucked like a ship in a hurricane and threw Adam back onto the deck. He got his feet under him just in time to witness Burke reaching behind where he was seated and grab the handle to the cabin door. With a hard upward tug, the door slid open; and the storm ripped through the cabin.

They were already fifteen or twenty feet off the ground. Burke glanced back at Adam, who was just recovering the SIG Sauer, and decided the risk was worth it. Without hesitation, he threw himself into the cold embrace of the stormy night. A second later, he impacted on the wet pavement with a sickening thud, all the oxygen forced from his lungs. Before he blacked out, he watched the helicopter rise shakily into the stormy night sky. Adam was at the open hatch.

The son of a bitch was still grinning.

"I'll kill you, you motherless piece of shit," was all Burke could rasp out before being swallowed by darkness.

14

It was past midnight and Alex found himself once again staring out his front window, watching the dead leaves blow through the amber lit streets. The stillness outside wasn't as peaceful as it had seemed the night before. It was more unnerving now, more unsettling. Like the shadows and darkness were closing in him, ready to entomb him.

Not finding any peace in the scene outside, he drew the curtains closed and wandered the living room to unwind the knot in his stomach. When that proved unsuccessful, he staked out a typically comfortable place on the loveseat facing the fireplace, even though comfort was elusive tonight. He had started a fire right after Rachel had gone upstairs to bed. Under normal circumstances, he would never start a fire anywhere close to bedtime, but he knew there wouldn't be much sleep for him tonight. So he had built the fire, kept it stoked and burning strong, trying to find solace as he normally would in the warmth and light of the fire. He sat transfixed by the dancing flames as they leaped and played around the logs, longing for them to burn away his troubles.

The events of the afternoon played over and over in his mind. He couldn't imagine why he had collapsed like that. His dreams had always been dreams, staying within the confines of his unconscious mind. They had never accosted him while he was awake. That was completely new. And frightening. His condition seemed to be worsening and there was still no explanation for what caused it. It was bad enough before when the dreams would take him at night, but if they invaded his waking hours...

His mind drifted to Rachel upstairs in bed, most likely lying awake as her mind raced through the events of the day as well. She had gone up hours ago, no doubt for his benefit, as he pondered the situation. He had a habit of losing himself in important issues and needing time to consider them. Rachel had always picked up on that and was happy to give him space and time to think about his problems, yet always close enough to help him if he wanted help. They had always been in synch like that, knowing what was best for the other without having to voice it. It was the thing he had found most attractive about her, the way she could read him. That and the fact that she was willing to leave him to work out these issues by himself. Even though she wasn't a direct participant in his process, it didn't keep her from losing sleep over him and he consistently felt guilty about that.

As much as he loved her for her dedication to his thought processes, love alone would not solve the problem. He needed to figure out where these dreams were coming from. No, more than dreams now. Attacks. He was being assaulted in his waking hours now. These were attacks. But what were they? And where were they coming from? The answer to that would seem to lie in his hidden past, which brought him back to Dr. Carlton and her hypnotherapy proposal. He still hated the thought of it, especially after this afternoon's escalation of the issue with his waking dream, but more and more it seemed like the only option. He hadn't wanted to say it openly to either Rachel or Rick, but he was afraid. Though he wasn't sure what scared him more; finding out about his past and not being able to live with what he discovered or not finding out and being driven mad by escalating dreams and waking visions. Neither option was particularly pleasant.

He had been trying to avoid thinking about the dreams themselves, but those images kept flashing through his head as the fire crackled and danced. They had always been dark and violent, but he had never been a participant in the carnage before. All that blood, broken bodies and gore and he had been standing in the middle of it, completely oblivious to all that slaughter. Bodies beaten to the point of no longer being recognizable as human, and he didn't seem to even notice. It was terrifying enough before, but then he had written it off as just a bad dream. A fevered response to the uncertainty of his past. Now he wasn't so sure. Now he had been awake, and he had lived it. Felt it. Smelled the blood. Tasted a coppery tang in the air. Felt the warm liquid on his hands. All without care.

He squeezed his eyes shut, trying to smother the image in the inky black. All that did was strengthen the memories, and he snapped his eyes open again, blinded for a moment by the flames in the fireplace. He found some comfort in their hot, sultry dance and his shoulders dropped a bit, muscles relaxing, as the fire succeeded in momentarily burning the violent memories from his mind.

His eyes were half closed in much needed sleep when his cell phone rang. Pulling himself out of his half-slumber, he frantically reached for the phone to answer, not wanting the noise to wake Rachel if she had fallen asleep. As he put the phone to his ear, he was almost afraid to speak. Phone calls at this time of night were never good news.

"Hello?"

"Alex? Is that you?" The voice on the other end of the phone was weak, but Alex was almost certain it was Dr. Carlton.

"Yes, this is Alex. Dr. Carlton, is that you? What's going on?"

The woman on the other end of the line took a deep, raspy breath. "I need to see you."

"Why?"

"I can't say over the phone, but it's vitally important to you. And your family."

Alex's stomach clenched at *and your family*. "I can come by your office first thing in the morning."

"No," Dr. Carlton stated emphatically, "this won't wait until tomorrow. You have to come now. I'm not sure how much time we have as it is."

"Dr. Carlton, it's after midnight. Are you sure this can't wait until tomorrow?"

"I know it can't. I have information you need, Alex. Information about you and your past. Information that will have a dire effect on you and your family. Do you want to know about your past? About who you are?"

"You know I do." His voice was strained.

"Then come to my house now. 246 Maple Tree Drive. And Alex?"

"Yes?"

Her voice, still light and raspy, took on a darker tone. "Don't leave Rachel home by herself. Whatever you do, don't leave her alone."

"What do you mean, don't leave her....." She disconnected the call, cutting his reply short. Staring into the picture of Rachel on his phone's screen, he replayed the conversation in his mind. Why did she need to see him now? What was so important it couldn't wait until morning? And most importantly, why couldn't he leave Rachel at home?

"Alex, who was that on the phone?" Startled at the sound of her voice, Alex turned sharply to see Rachel at the top of the spiral staircase. She was wearing a diaphanous silken green nightdress, the flickering light of the fireplace glinting off of her hair and eyes. For a moment he was stunned into silence by how beautiful she looked, even freshly rousted from bed.

"Alex?"

"What? Oh, the phone call." He shook off his trance, bringing himself back to the moment at hand. "That was Dr. Carlton. She wants to meet with me. She said she has some information for me."

"Information?" Alex detected an undertone of concern in Rachel's voice. "What kind of information?"

He shrugged lightly. "She didn't say. Just that it was very important."

"So you're going to see her in the morning?"

"Actually, she wants me to meet her at her house. Tonight. Right now, in fact. She even sounded almost..." He couldn't think of the proper word to describe how she had sounded. *Desperate* was what he settled on, even though he wasn't sure it was quite right.

"Alex, it's nearly one in the morning. Are you sure it can't wait until later?" She had that look on her face, the look that said he was about to do something she didn't approve of.

Vehemently. He hated that look, mostly because when she brought it out, he knew he had lost the battle.

This time was different. The urgency in Dr. Carlton's voice was something he could just ignore. She may have information that was vital to the safety of his family. He decided and decided to see Dr. Carlton now, no matter how many looks Rachel gave him.

He squared up to her with a look of his own. A look of determination. "I know it's late, but I have to go. And hon.....?"

"Yes?" Her eyes narrowed as she said it, becoming nothing more than slivers of jade set against her face. She always narrowed her eyes when she was expecting bad news. Narrow for bad, wide for good. It had taken him all the time he had known her, but he had finally devised that system. Not that knowing that minor fact made it any easier to continue.

Bracing himself for the resistance he was sure would come, he continued. "You need to come, too."

Her narrowed eyes widened slightly, and she gave him a side-eye. "Do you think it's necessary?"

Her voice was so calm, it was unnerving. "I'm not sure, but Dr. Carlton seemed to think so. Are you OK with that?"

"I'm fine with it. Just give me a second to change, OK?" He wasn't able to reply before she turned and headed back to the bedroom in a flurry of light silk.

Rachel returned a few minutes later dressed in jeans and a sweatshirt, her hair pulled harshly back from her face and bound into a tight ponytail with a simply elastic band. She was the epitome of feminine functionality, but Alex could still see nothing but the beautiful Irish girl who met him at the altar. She could have worn an old canvas sack tied around her waist with a rope, and he still would have thought she was the most beautiful woman he had ever seen.

"Ready?" She pulled the laces on her shoe tight and headed for the front closet to get her coat. He reached out and grabbed her arm, gently turning her towards him.

"Rach, I just want to say thanks for supporting me and believing in me, especially when you don't really have much reason to right now."

"That's what marriage is all about. I may not always know why you do things, like tonight, but I trust you. I'm with you every step of the way." She took his hands in hers. "I love you, Alex Carter. No matter how many times you send me into a panic by collapsing in the front yard or drag me out in the middle of the night, I'll always love you."

He kissed her forehead lightly. "I love you, too. And I appreciate everything you do for me."

"No problem. But when considering gratitude, think diamonds." She smiled and let go his hands, lightly patting his chest. Taking their coats from the closet, she handed Alex his. "Now, are you ready to get this over with?"

"I think so. Hope so. I just wish I had a better idea of what she wants to talk about. I can't seem to shake this feeling, like we're in for a rough time."

"So now you're a fortune teller?" She flashed him a grin.

"No, wiseass. But I am serious. I think we should be careful."

She shrugged. "If you say so. I mean, hey, it's no stranger than going to see your psychiatrist at one in the morning."

"Are you ready, or do you want to make fun of me some more?"

"No, I think I'm all set for now. But wait until I really wake up, then you're in for it." She turned, sliding into her coat.

"Great. I can hardly wait." He held the door open, and she slipped past him into the frosty fall night. He glanced back into the living room one last time, a strange feeling that he wasn't alone suddenly coming over him. The room was empty, with only shadows dancing across the walls in the fading light of the fire. Shaking his head, he stepped into the chilly night air and swung the door shut behind him.

In the empty living room, the shadows continued to dance.

15

The house was completely dark, eliciting a sharp pang of anxiety in Alex. Not that having the lights off in a home at one o'clock in the morning was unusual, especially for a working person in a small town, but if they were expecting someone, the accepted etiquette was to leave a light on for them. It was common courtesy and in all the time he had known her, Dr. Simone Carlton had been eminently courteous. That not a single light was on meant one of two things; that she was expecting trouble...

... or she was already in trouble.

"She *did* say 'right away', didn't she?" Rachel said as she peered at the house for any signs of activity inside. She shivered from the cold of the bitter fall air, tightly wrapping her arms around herself.

"That's what she said," Alex replied, realizing he was shivering as well.

"As in 'immediately'?"

"Yes."

"As in 'right this very moment'?"

"Yes."

"Not as in 'first thing in the morning so as not to interrupt your lovely wife's sleep in her warm, warm bed?"

He glanced at her and sighed, his breath a puff of white. Guilt was settling in for dragging her out of bed based on a panicked phone call. Dr. Carlton had sounded so incisive. She wouldn't drag the two of them out here in the middle of the night, especially considering Rachel's condition, on a whim and without good reason.

"C'mon," he said, taking Rachel's arm and leading her up the steps to the front door.

"What are we doing?" she asked, pulling slightly against him.

"Knocking."

"And what if she's asleep?"

"Then we'll wake her up," he replied. "She asked us to come here, remember?"

"I remember you telling me she asked us to come here..."

The tone of uncertainty in her voice chafed at Alex a bit. While it was true he hadn't been the most mentally stable individual in the last twenty-four hours, he certainly felt well enough to know if a phone call was real and whether it was important enough to take his pregnant wife from a warm bed and into the icy cold of a New England fall night. But seeing her now, cold and shivering but still standing there with him, made his heart hurt a bit. With everything that had gone on lately, maybe he wasn't the best judge of circumstances.

"What if she's in trouble?" Alex asked, his voice thick with concern.

Rachel sighed, relenting. "Then I guess we should do what we can to help. Go ahead and knock. But if she wasn't expecting us, you are on your own trying to explain why we're here."

Alex turned away from her and faced the front door, reaching out and knocking lightly. The door swung inward slightly with the first impact.

It was open.

At first he didn't move, unsure of what to do. Finding the door unlocked didn't surprise him. They live in a small town; many people don't lock their doors. But finding this particular door standing open at this particular moment did not set well with him.

"Alex, what's the matter?"

"The door, it's open."

"Well, that'll make it a lot easier to get in."

He was about to say she should wait out here for him while he checked inside, but something Dr. Carlton said earlier kept flashing through his mind. "Don't leave Rachel alone." He didn't know if that meant not to leave her at home by herself or to not leave her by herself at all. He erred on the side of caution.

"Come on, let's see what's going on."

Rachel reached out and grabbed his arm, pulling him back from the door. "Wait a minute, you're just going to barge right into her house?"

"No," he replied, "I'm going to enter her house quietly. Do you have a better idea?"

"How about knocking again? Or going home and calling her in the morning? Or calling the police to come check on her if you're worried? All of those sound like better suggestions to me."

Alex nodded lightly. "Agreed. But you didn't talk to her earlier. I did. Whatever she wants us here for is important, and I intend to find out what it is. Now, are you coming or not?"

She smiled at him for the first time since they stepped into the icy night. "You know, you're awfully sexy when you get all decisive like that."

"I thought I was awfully sexy anytime."

She shrugged. "Meh, I just let you think that to keep your ego up."

"Am I sexy most of the time?"

She wagged her hand in a 'so-so' motion. "I'd give you a good majority of the time. But then again, I'm not really a great judge of character. I mean, here I am at one o'clock in the morning, standing at the open front door of my husband's psychiatrist's house in the freezing cold, about to make an illegal entry. So who knows if you can really trust what I say?"

He smiled a wide smile at her. She was scared right now, that much he could tell. Humor and sarcasm were her coping mechanism for stress. He had always found that unnerving about her, that she could joke at times like this, but he supposed it was better she had that release than to crack under pressure. It seemed to work for her. To most people who knew her, she always seemed calm and under total control. Alex knew better. He knew when she was scared and nervous, and right now she was feeling plenty of both.

"As long as I'm sexy most of the time I can live with your questionable state of mind." He gestured to the door. "Shall we?"

"I suppose," she replied, but as he started forward, she grasped his arm again. "Alex, what if you're right and there is something wrong in there? Something very wrong?"

"What do you mean?"

"Please don't take this the wrong way," she continued, "but will you be all right? I mean, normally I wouldn't think twice about your mental state, but with all the attacks you've been having lately I don't want you to freeze up at when I really need you."

He wanted to be hurt, but her point had merit. What if they encountered some threat and he went catatonic again? Under normal circumstances he was certain Rachel could handle herself, she was the strongest and most self-sufficient person he had ever met, but these were far from normal circumstances. The most important thing was to ensure that she and the baby were protected. He didn't want to have another episode and leave them defenseless.

"Promise me something?" he asked, trying to add a tinge of optimism to his voice.

"What is it?" Her reply was tentative, recognizing his tone as one usually reserved for questions he didn't want to ask.

"If we run into..." He paused, searching for the right word. "...a situation, promise me you will get out of there as fast you can."

"Only if you do, too."

"No problem. I feel better now."

"Because I said I'd stay out of harm's way?"

"No, because now I can act like the coward I really am." He gestured to the door again. "Ready?"

"Not really." She shivered again, pulling her arms tighter around her. "I hope it's warmer inside, at least."

Alex pushed the door open and peered into the inky gloom beyond. The streetlights cast an eerie, warm glow a few feet into the front hall, but that was all the light he had. He took a step inside, hoping his eyes would adjust enough so that he could ferret out a light switch. Running his hand along the wall, he found nothing.

"What I wouldn't give for a flashlight right now," he muttered.

Behind him there was the sound of a zipper opening and the rustling of nylon before a narrow beam of light stabbed into the obsidian darkness. Turning, he saw Rachel's smiling face aglow in the backwash from the pocket flashlight she held in her hand.

"Ask and ye shall receive," she said, handing the light to him.

He grinned. "You weren't a boy scout by any chance, were you?"

"I wanted to be. Couldn't pass the physical."

"Their loss."

"Yeah, that's what all the boys said, too."

He waved the light across the entryway. The house was a colonial, as were most of the homes in town, and there had been virtually no change in the layout in the past hundred years. To his right was the living room, which was as good a place as any to begin the search for Dr. Carlton.

Despite being sparsely furnished, the room displayed a layout of furniture that was logical and sensible. A television sat in the far-left corner of the nearly perfectly square room, opposite a sofa that looked designed more for aesthetic than comfort. A single end table stood beside the sofa with a single coaster on it. Other than that, the room was empty. There were no decorations at all; no pictures or paintings on the walls, no plants, no bookshelves, nothing but drab room darkening curtains hanging over the windows. Even the coaster on the end table was nothing but a beige square of cork. The room was the height of efficiency but void of any character, any feeling whatsoever.

And Dr. Carlton wasn't there.

He searched the walls for a light switch, finding one just inside the door. As he reached for the switch, Rachel grabbed his wrist.

"Do you think that's a good idea? What if there is an intruder here? We turn on a light and lead them right to us?" she whispered.

"Rach, I've been waving a flashlight around here like a lighthouse on steroids for the last five minutes. If there's an intruder here, I can almost guarantee you they know we're here."

She relaxed her grip on his arm. "You make a good point. A scary one, but a good point. Carry on."

Alex gave her a warm smile. "It's okay, I'm scared too."

He flipped the light switch and a harsh white light filled the room, spilling out into the entryway and dissolving a few feet of shadow there. Alex moved out into the entryway with Rachel close behind. In the spillover light from the living room, Alex came across another switch and illuminated the entry, exposing the central welcoming annex of the house. Straight ahead was an entry to the kitchen, the clock of the microwave staring back at him from the dark like demonic green eyes. To his left was a small bathroom, still mostly bathed in shadow. To his right was a staircase leading to the second floor. Leading up the stairs was a small metal rail which he recognized as a lift chair Dr. Carlton could use to access the top floor of her home.

He moved forward toward the kitchen when Rachel stopped him. "She's upstairs."

"How do you know?"

"The lift, it's at the top of the stairs. She must be upstairs."

It was a good assumption. He was embarrassed he hadn't thought of it first. "Makes sense," he replied.

"No problem." She gestured to the stairs. "Lead on, intrepid adventurer."

He took Rachel's hand and moved cautiously up the stairs. The house was enveloped in an eerie quiet, the only noise he could hear was the humming of the furnace through the ventilation ducts. At the top of the steps he stopped, watching and listening for any sign of Dr. Carlton or, worse, an intruder. The only thing he saw were four identical doors standing in a row along the wall to his left. A fifth door, sturdier than the others, sat at the far end of the hall. All were closed, which struck him as odd. Given Dr. Carlton's condition and her limited mobility, wouldn't she be smarter to leave the doors open for easier access? As far as he knew, she lived alone. Given her withered hands he had witnessed earlier in the day, it would be exceedingly difficult for her to open and close doors all the time. So why would they all be closed?

Unless she wasn't the one who closed them.

The thought fell to the back of his head as Rachel spoke. "Where do we start?" Her hand tightened around his a bit, mirroring the tension in her voice. The lack of jokes to accompany it meant her fear was becoming very real.

"At the beginning, I guess." He reached for the knob of the nearest door, his stomach tightening as he moved closer. His heart hammered in his chest as he felt the cold metal of the doorknob hit his hand and he turned, pushing the door in slightly.

After pushing the door open about six inches, he stood still and waited. There was no light in the room, which didn't make him feel any more at ease, but also no sound or motion he could detect either. His hammering heart slowed a bit at that, and he swung his torso around the opening to scan the room with the flashlight. He saw a toilet, sink and bathtub, all specially equipped for Dr. Carlton's needs, but no sign of the doctor herself. The ball of tension in his stomach eased somewhat as he pulled the door closed again. He turned back to Rachel and shrugged. "She's not there. Should we try door number two?"

Rachel didn't answer. Instead, she stood perfectly still, her eyes wide and breathing stilled. She stared into the shadows ahead, furtively searching the darkness for something.

"Rach, honey, what's....."

"Shhhh!" she hissed, raising her finger at him. "I thought I just heard something."

Alex froze in place and listened. All he could make out was the constant rush of heated air through the ventilation ducts and the soft rumble of the furnace from two floors below.

Then he heard it. So low as to be almost imperceptible. A slight thump followed by a sob. He strained to hear it again, to pin down where it was coming from, but there was nothing.

"Did you hear that?" Rachel asked. Her hand was practically crushing his now.

"Where do you think it came from?" Alex asked, scanning the remaining doors with the flashlight.

Rachel didn't answer immediately, still straining to hear. "I'm not sure, but I think it might have been the last door."

The thumping in Alex's chest continued to hammer away as he focused the flashlight's small circle of light on the last door in the hall. He pulled in a deep breath and slowly exhaled. "I guess there's only one way to find out." He extricated his hand from hers. "Wait here."

"Wait here? Are you out of your mind?" she whisper-yelled at him, grabbing his wrist and pulling him sharply around to face her. "Alex Carter, if you think you can leave me alone here right at this moment, you had best think again!"

He sighed at her, the noise sounding thunderous in the pressing darkness. "Fine. But will you please stay behind me at least?"

She nodded vigorously. "No problem."

They moved together, slowly and quietly, inching toward the door at the end of the hall. The house had fallen silent again. Even the furnace had stopped heating and forcing air through the ducts for the moment. The only sounds heard were the light shuffling of their feet and their shallow breaths. When they reached the door, Alex motioned for Rachel to stay behind him and grasped the doorknob, feeling the cool metal. There was a touch of slickness to it as well and he realized his palms were sweaty, despite the chill outside and coolness of the house. His heart was beating furiously, the pounding in his head deafening. Bracing himself, he turned the doorknob and pushed the door open. There was nothing but darkness on the other side. Carefully, he stepped past the threshold and into the inky black of the room...

... and froze. The sound that Rachel had alerted him to earlier came from out of the darkness. Louder and more defined, but definitely the same noise. A low moan. A sound of pain.

And it was close by.

"Dr. Carlton?" His voice was nothing more than a whisper, his throat swollen and tight. Pausing, he listened again, drifting the beam of the flashlight around the large room. Everything was quiet, save for his pounding heart.

"A... Alex? Is.... is that you?"

He started at the sound of another voice in the room and jumped; the flashlight darting in a mad spiral. Pulling himself together, he realized he recognized the voice.

"Dr. Carlson? Is that you?" With the flashlight, he scanned the wall by the door for a switch. Finding one, Rachel reached out and flicked it on.

Alex's eyes flooded with white light and he shielded them against the glare, allowing them to adjust. As his vision cleared, he took in what had once been Dr. Carlton's home office, although right now it looked like a tornado had torn through it. The file cabinets had been overturned and rifled through, a smashed laptop was in the center of the room, and papers were strewn all over. A sense of dread crept over Alex as he examined the room, the final wave of fear crashing over him as his eyes came on the crumpled pile in the far corner of the room.

It was Dr. Carlton, lying in a heap next to her overturned wheelchair, positioned with her face half toward the ceiling and the other side pressed firmly into the carpet. Her body was twisted and appeared broken and distorted, her eyes straining toward the door to find him. She was lying on one arm, the other flayed out to her side. Her index finger moved slowly and erratically, like she was calling him to her.

"Doc! Are you all right?" Alex raced across the room and kneeled by her, looking her over for injury. Given her condition and the obvious impact of her chair being overturned, it was hard to tell if she was alright, but he didn't want to risk exacerbating her injuries by moving her if he could avoid it. She strained her eyes up toward him.

With her voice muffled from her face being half buried in the floor, she pleaded, "Alex, please, help me up."

Panic rose in his gut, his mind racing through the possibilities of moving the doctor versus not moving her. Moving her might make her worse. Might even kill her. But leaving her there and waiting for an ambulance to arrive might kill her as well. He didn't know what to do, how to help, and did the only thing he could think of which was place a comforting hand on her back...

It happened as soon as he touched her. A sense of calm came over him, quieting the panic in his mind, all of his doubts disappearing like fog at sunrise. A preternatural sense of confidence filled him, as if he knew exactly what Dr. Carlton needed from him at that moment. He didn't know where this came from, but he didn't waste it. Lifting her wheelchair to an upright position, he moved to lift her from the floor and help her into it.

"Alex, wait!" Rachel said, her voice high-pitched and edging on panic. "She might be hurt." Instinctively, she reached out to stop him from lifting the doctor off the floor as Alex touched her hand in response. As he closed the circuit between the three of them, she felt her tension and panic fall away and a sense of confidence and purpose take their place.

"Help me," Alex said, pulling away from Rachel and the doctor. Once they broke the circuit, the feelings of calm and confidence faded, but the memory of them stayed strong and guided their actions. Each of them grabbed one of Dr. Carlton's arms and placed their own arms around her waist, gently lifting her from the floor and setting her to rest in her wheelchair.

Alex pulled his cell phone from his pocket. "I'm calling an ambulance."

"No, there's no time for that," Dr. Carlton said, so weak her voice was practically imperceptible. "I'm afraid it.... wouldn't be of much use to me, anyway. And there are.... things...you need to know." Coughing weakly, spittle ran from her mouth down the front of her nightshirt. Alex noticed a pinkish tinge in color and while he didn't know what it meant, he felt certain it couldn't be good.

Dropping his phone back in his pocket, he kneeled beside her wheelchair, bringing himself eye to eye with her. Her pupils dilated randomly, unable to focus on anything in front of her. "That's what you said. What things? What do we need to know?"

Dr. Carlton coughed again, harder, expelling more spittle. This time it was redder, the blood it contained evident, and she had more trouble recovering her breath. Alex motioned for Rachel to call an ambulance. She stepped quietly away so as not to upset Dr. Carlton any further.

The doctor breathed in a deep, raspy breath. "On my desk, underneath my computer, there's a thumb drive." Another deep breath, this one rattling around in her lungs before settling. "Take it. It will...help to explain some of this to you. To help you discover who.... what you are."

Despite his sudden wave of certainty and confidence, those words hit him in the gut like a fist. *What* he really was. What could that mean?

She continued as best she could, taking in another shallow breath to fuel her speech. "The password to... get into the protected files is Zeus. Once you get in, you should have no tr..." A sudden cough rattled her. She steadied herself and struggled to continue. "No trouble figuring out what to do next. Do you understand?"

"Dr. Carlton, I..." Alex stammered.

She cut him off hard, forcefully. More forcefully that it seemed her body might allow at the moment. *"Do you understand?"*

His face fell away from hers. "Yes ma'am. Zeus."

A weak laugh escaped the frail woman. It surprised Alex that she had the strength for it. "Zeus, the father of the gods. What a joke." The slight smile faded from her face, becoming somber. Her eyes, still unfocused, somehow came to rest on Alex with a piercing glare. He felt uncomfortable by it but didn't turn away. Rachel came back into the room just then, signaling that an ambulance was on the way. It wouldn't matter.

"You have to stop them, Alex. You're the only one who can." Dr. Carlton's voice was barely audible now, her body falling limply in her chair. "I tried it once. All it got me was a wheelchair for the rest of my life. That's what they do: remove obstacles. However they can. They did this to me, and I wasn't strong enough to keep fighting after that. They manipulated me, and you, and all I did was sit back and watch."

Alex reached out to touch her arm, to comfort her. As soon as he touched her, remorse and regret engulfed him. Shame and anger. He felt a tear well up and run down his cheek. It was almost more than he could bear.

"You feel it too, now, don't you? All my regrets. I'm so very sorry. Not for what I did, although there's plenty of shame in that, but for what I didn't do. It was bad enough what happened to you, but when Rachel came into the picture, I knew I had to do something. But...." She coughed suddenly, a slight noise but it wracked her body. She took another rattling breath to steady herself. "I should have stopped them then, with Rachel. But I would not let them destroy life at its most innocent."

"The baby?" Alex gasped out, his heart turning to ice. "What does this have to do with the baby?"

Dr. Carlton either didn't hear Alex or simply ignored him and continued her dialogue. "Stop them, Alex. Not for what they did to me, or to you, or to countless others." Her head fell to one side, thick blood falling away from her lips. Helplessness had him again, knowing she was dying, and there was nothing he could do to help her.

"Stop them for what they want to do to your baby."

His heart turned to ice. The baby. He had been so focused on what was happening to him and how it affected his and Rachel's life he had never considered a threat to his unborn child. But there it was, laid bare in the utterance of a frail, dying woman.

He turned back to Dr. Carlton again to ask another question, but before he could speak, she went into convulsions. Her body shook violently, her limbs spasmed uncontrollably, she gasped for air and when she could take some in, she choked on it. Alex fell away from her as she thrashed, helpless.

The doctor gasped, her body jerked, and a low gurgle issued from somewhere deep within her. Then she slumped in her chair and was still. For a moment, neither Alex nor Rachel moved, unsure of what to do next. After a few excruciating seconds of stillness, Rachel reached out and touched the doctor's throat, searching for a pulse. She couldn't detect anything. Placing her ear to the older woman's chest, she strained to hear, but there were no sounds within indicating a heartbeat or breathing. She was completely still.

"Is she..." Alex croaked out, unable to bring himself to finish the sentence.

"I can't find a pulse. I can't hear her breathing. I think she's gone." Rachel replied, her voice barely audible even in the quiet stillness that gripped the room.

Dr. Carlton's empty eyes still stared at Alex as if she had more to say. More to tell him. Her eyes still seemed to gleam with knowledge even now. Even after the light of life had left them. He reached out and gently closed them, allowing her to rest.

Standing on shaky legs, he almost fell to the floor again as his knees wobbled and threatened to buckle beneath him. He stared at the now lifeless body of the woman they had come to see. The woman who had told him she had answers. Now she lay dead, leaving them with a bigger mystery than before.

She was dead. The thought rattled around his brain, finally sinking in. He had spoken to her only an hour ago, and now she was dead. Why? What did it have to do with him and Rachel? More importantly, what did it have to do with their baby? Why did someone ransack her office? The questions flooded into his mind all at once and he felt dizzy, closing his eyes to keep from passing out as a wave of nausea gripped him.

"Alex, are you all right?"

Opening his eyes, he saw Rachel standing close to him, gently touching his shoulder. A feeling of concern flooded over him, intermingling with and expanding on the roiling emotions already there. Startled, he pulled away from Rachel. The emotion storm subsided a bit, and he stood straight.

"I'm sorry," he said to his startled wife, who stood in front of him with her arm still outstretched. "I just don't know what to think right now. I feel.... numb."

The faint wail of sirens in the distance cut through the night. Outside, he could see nothing but the smothering darkness of night and he felt as if it were closing in on him, like a trap set for unsuspecting prey. For the first time since the nightmares returned, a real, deep, gnawing fear burned inside his gut. The danger that he had perceived, had hoped, was only in his mind, had proven to be real. And now it had been unleashed. What scared him most of all wasn't that the terror was free and coming for him. It was the fact that it wasn't coming just for him; it was coming for Rachel. And the baby.

It was coming for his family.

He felt helpless. Alone. In the darkness beyond the window, he thought he could see the face of the dark stranger materialize. Grinning at him. Taunting him. Then, the night became splashed with a blood red flash of emergency lights, and the wail of the siren resonated like the cries of the damned.

16

Burke winced as the field medic pulled the bandage tight around his midsection. Despite his ribs being only bruised and not broken, Burke still felt excruciating pain. Even with the agony he was in at the moment, he hadn't allowed them to give him any painkillers. They would dull his senses and right now, he needed to stay sharp.

"What's his status?" he asked through gritted teeth, throwing the question at Colonel Harriman. As bad as the pain was, he had been lucky. There aren't many people who could say they fell out of a helicopter and lived to tell about it.

"We've been tracking him since take-off, sir," Harriman replied, his gaze held steadfast by the palm sized computer uplink in his hand. Right now the small module was accessing Genie, the Project's central computer, and using those resources to home in on Adam's subdermal transmitter. Even in the face of such remarkable technology, Harriman remained as cool and unemotional as ever.

"Where is he?" Burke asked as the medic finished dressing his wounds. He had suffered cuts and bruises, some already becoming deep purplish-black splotches, but nothing more. He really had been fortunate. Another twenty feet and the drop may well have killed him. He had managed to walk away with little more than some uncomfortable bruises and wounded pride. Although it was the wounded pride that hurt him more than anything else.

But now he could focus on revenge.

Harriman answered without taking his eyes from the screen. "The helicopter landed just outside Boston. From there, we've been tracking him at a steady pace heading toward Providence, Rhode Island."

Burke carefully threaded an arm into a clean shirt, his ribs exploding at the effort. "Have we heard anything from the pilot or co-pilot?"

"No sir. We assume he eliminated them as soon as they touched down."

Burke nodded, slipping his other arm into a sleeve and pulling the shirt closed around him. He winced as he did it, the bruises making themselves known with each movement. "I'd say that's a certainty. Providence?"

Harriman nodded. "Yes, sir. That's what the tracking computers show."

"Why would he go there?" Burke asked, as much to himself as the other man.

Harriman's reply was as static as usual. "I'm certain I don't know, sir."

Burke buttoned the shirt carefully, avoiding scraping even the light fabric across his injuries. "It's exactly the opposite of what we would expect him to do."

Harriman looked up from his screen for the first time since he started tracking Adam. "Maybe that's his plan, sir. Do exactly the opposite of what we'd expect to throw us off."

Burke shook his head slowly. No, that wasn't Adam's style. He was up to something, something entirely different from anything they had yet considered. Adam was a man on the run with nowhere to go. He was as alone in the world as any person could be, with no ties to anywhere or anyone except the people he was running from. He wasn't nearly stupid enough to go back there. Where would he go? Who did he know, or even know of, that he might use to hide from the Project? Who would he go after?

It hit him in a flash; the name screaming into his brain: Alex Carter. Burke cursed himself for not thinking of it sooner. The fall must have shaken him more than he thought. He must be heading there. It's the only other place he has any connection to. But how could he even know about it? Was there something Burke had missed? Some piece of crucial information that had been left out? He had come to the Project after 'the incident', the event that had left all of Forrester's subjects except Adam and Alex dead. Not just dead, murdered. Murdered at the hands of their siblings. While he hadn't been there to experience the massacre firsthand, he had read every written report and viewed every video record of the event. The Project had covered their tracks. There was no way Adam could know about the existence of his 'brother', much less know where to find him.

Another epiphany hit him like a Mack truck. The files he had taken with him during his impromptu 'retirement' from the company. It was possible the records he had obtained had given him a record of the events that had occurred, including the plans for him and his 'sibling'. That was bad. Very bad. Depending on how stupid and vindictive Adam was willing to be, it could pose a great threat to the Project and its agenda. An agenda Burke was personally responsible for executing.

Another thought suddenly jolted through Burke's mind and sat in his stomach like a cold stone. What if Adam made the information public? The Project's agenda required secrecy. If that were gone, it would be disastrous. The Project revolved around genetic engineering, a science that created elicited powerful feelings from all facets of the public. PenTech was far ahead of anything else being done in the field, which mostly revolved around ways to make a tomato stay fresher longer or to raise meatier beef and poultry animals. Or to make plants taste like meat, which Burke found to be an affront to carnivores everywhere. The idea of creating a better human being, however, had been taboo since the discovery of the human genome. The media branded anyone who discussed experimenting with human genetics as a 'monster' who was 'playing God', feeding on the irrational fears of the masses that some modern-day Dr. Frankenstein would create a monstrous cow or tomato that would destroy the planet. Idiots. Most people on the planet were oblivious to the fact that the food they ate daily had been genetically modified at some point in history, and that there was no such thing as 'non-GMO' anything. That was why the science remained in its infancy. Everyone was afraid of what it would be when it grew up.

Everyone except Robert Penders. He wasn't cowed by the fears of others, which had allowed him to build the business empire he had. Seeing the potential in genetic engineering, he had hired the finest scientific minds in the field (regardless of their standing or reputation in their field), assembled the largest storehouse of DNA to ever exist and enlisted investors to help bankroll it all, thus creating the Eden Project. The mission of this secret arm of PenTech was simple; to create the most marketable commodity to come along in this century and perhaps even the next: Designer human beings.

That dream was teetering on a deep precipice at the moment, brought to the brink by the ineptitude of one scientist who lacked the foresight to rein in the rebellious tendencies of his creations. Because of Forrester's failure to keep them on a tight enough leash, the Project was compromised. Unless Burke could clean it up.

First, he had to figure Adam out. The bastard had been two steps ahead of them the whole way. Burke needed to close that gap. He knew where he was heading now, Burke needed to decipher why. Or how Adam could even know his 'kin' existed. He needed more pieces to the puzzle.

"Forrester," Burke barked. "Where is he?"

"Waiting for you at the helicopter, sir," Harriman replied. "He said he had some work to do while you were being tended to."

"Have him brought here," Burke answered. "I have a few things to discuss with our resident mad doctor."

"Yes, sir." Without wasting a word, Harriman gestured to one of his people stationed at the entrance to the tent. The man nodded his acknowledgement and moved out into the rain to carry out the unspoken order.

Burke slid uncomfortably off the medical cot. "And get me a phone. Get me a phone. My cell got smashed in the fall."

Harriman reached into his jacket pocket, pulled out a new cell phone, and held it out to Burke. "It's already programmed with your number. Your contacts, texts and e-mails are all intact."

Burke took the phone from the squat, older man and smiled. "Is there anything you aren't prepared for, Colonel?"

"Failure," Harriman replied, his expression unchanging. Burke wasn't sure if he was kidding or not, given his stoic expression. Most likely not.

"Should I prepare to move out, sir?" Harriman firmly focused his attention on Burke as he awaited his orders.

"An excellent idea, Colonel."

"To Providence, sir?"

Burke paused. This was the make it or break it moment in his pursuit of Adam. A wrong decision here could be catastrophic to the Project, not to mention his career. Caution was warranted. "I want you to send a few of your people to Providence to follow up on that lead, but I don't believe that's where he's going."

"Where are we going then, sir?"

"North," Burke replied. "I hear New Hampshire is lovely this time of year."

17

Alex watched as the paramedics carried the stretcher down the stairs, a simple white sheet pulled over the still form. One of them, he knew. Jack Devane was a long-time patron of Antonio's and spent many evenings there devouring the daily specials. He was the quiet type, keeping to himself most of the time, but if he warmed up to you, Jack was exactly the kind of person anyone would want in their corner. He would be the first person to step up and help if you needed it and expect nothing in return.

Jack caught Alex staring at the gurney and quickened his pace. That caught the younger man at the back of the gurney by surprise and he nearly lost his grip, the gurney tilting precariously to one side. They recovered, but not in time to keep a thin, frail arm from flopping out of the sheet. The younger man said something under his breath that Alex couldn't quite hear, but he felt it was something he shouldn't have said based on the harsh look Jack gave him. Gently, Jack picked up the almost skeletal arm and tucked it under the sheet. As he returned to take up his end of the gurney, he threw Alex a look that seemed to say, "I'm sorry," and hurried out the front door.

Alex watched until they were gone, his stare lingering on the vacant space. He still couldn't believe she was gone. He had been with her just that afternoon, had spoken to her on the phone less than an hour before she died. His mind had been racing with possibilities surrounding her death, each one seemingly more frightening and unrealistic than the last. But given how the past few days had gone, he wasn't sure what he could discount as unrealistic anymore and what he couldn't. But even amongst all the noise in his head, he couldn't shake what Dr. Carlton had said about someone coming for him. And the baby. And the secret she had tried to deliver to them before she died.

"Mr. Carter?"

As Alex turned from the door, the stubbled, round face of Lieutenant Ernest Babcock greeted him. Lieutenant Babcock was a detective of the Pine Haven Police Department, a man he and Rachel had spent the better part of the last hour getting acquainted with as they ran through the night's events. Over and over. He would ask questions and nod as they spoke while making notes in the small notebook he clutched in his thick, stubby fingers, never looking directly at either of them. When they finished recounting their story, he would look up and inevitably say, "Now let me just get this one detail clear...." And they would begin the process all over again. Alex was starting to think of him as a demonic version of Columbo, and his patience was wearing thin.

"Yes, Lieutenant?" The reply escaped him as more of an exasperated sigh than he intended.

"My apologies for keeping you and your lovely wife here, but I'm sure you can understand the need. Given the circumstances." He scratched at the dark stubble on his chin before running a thick thumb through his notebook. He squinted at his handwriting, his eyes appearing tiny against his meaty face. "Forgive me if I'm not getting this right, but you came to Dr. Carlson's home tonight because of a phone call?"

Alex nodded. "That's correct."

Babcock absently tugged at his belt in an effort to keep his pants from slipping any further down past his ample waist. "And it was Dr. Carlton who placed this call?"

"Again, correct." Alex tried to keep the exasperation from his voice. He wasn't successful.

Babcock cleared his throat as he continued to thumb through the notebook. "And what was it she said to you?"

"She said she needed to see me right away."

More rustling of paper. "And why was that?"

"Because she had some information for me."

"About your amnesia."

Alex squeezed his eyes shut, his fingers involuntarily balling up into loose fists. "That's right. About my amnesia."

Babcock looked up from his notes, the bridge of his nose scrunched up quizzically. "You have amnesia?"

Alex felt the muscles in his shoulders tense. "Yes. I suffer from amnesia."

"But you remember your name. Your wife. Your address."

An exasperated sigh escaped before Alex could stop it. "It doesn't always work like that."

Babcock took a few steps closer, closing the space between them. "How does it work in this case?"

"I don't remember anything from before I was maybe fifteen. Everything before that is a blank. Dr. Carlton was helping me try to recover some of those lost memories."

"That's rough." Babcock's gaze returned to his notebook, his stubby fingers dragging his pen across the page. "And that's why she called you? At midnight?"

Alex nodded. "Yes."

"And that didn't strike you as unusual?"

Alex couldn't tell if the accusatory tone in Babcock's voice was there or just the product of his growing fatigue and impatience, but his frustration was growing. "At the time it did, of course. But Dr. Carlton isn't...." He paused, a flash of her frail form on the gurney striking him. "Dr. Carlton wasn't the type of person to make a request like that lightly. If she wanted to see me right away, it was important." He glanced up the stairs, remembering the office that had been ransacked in a desperate search. "Looks like it was."

Babcock continued unabated. "Important enough to get your pretty wife out of bed in the middle of the night and drag her down here, too?"

"Dr. Carlton told me not to leave Rachel alone, so I didn't. Besides, whatever she had to say concerns Rachel just as much as it does me. She had a right to be here." Alex noticed the tone of indignation in his voice, but he had moved beyond caring. He was tired. The adrenaline from the excitement of the night was wearing off and the fatigue it kept at bay was hitting him hard. His legs wobbled as he moved, his hands shaking from the shock. He could only image how bad Rachel was feeling right now. He wanted to get Rachel home so she could rest. He wanted to be out of Dr. Carlton's house and away from Lieutenant Babcock. Maybe it was the shock of the night's events or just his growing impatience, but Babcock's tone seemed to become more and more suspicious of Alex's answers.

"So what was it?" asked Babcock, scribbling in his notebook.

"What was what?" Alex pushed his hands into his pockets to hide the adrenaline withdrawal.

"What was it she had to tell you?"

Alex thought back to Dr. Carlton's last moments. Her last words had been a warning to Alex. A warning to protect his family from something that was coming. Thinking back on it now, it wasn't any clearer than it had been earlier that night. The fatigue fog in his brain wasn't helping any, either. But at this moment, he didn't think it was a good idea to share what she had said with the local police.

And then there was the mysterious thumb drive.

"I don't know," he lied. "She was gone before she could say anything."

Babcock's head popped up again, his beady eyes locking on Alex's. "She was still alive when you found her?"

A lump formed in Alex's throat as he returned the cop's stare. He was suddenly flush with adrenaline again, his mind racing at what he had just said. Had Babcock somehow picked up on his lie? Did he contradict something he had said to the cop earlier in the evening? A sinking feeling hit him as his mind raced for an answer.

"Yes, she was still alive. What does that have to do with anything?" He had decided on confrontation to mask his uncertainty. Belligerence to cover his lie.

Babcock shrugged. "Maybe nothing. Maybe everything. In my years of experience, Mr. Carter, I've discovered that the slightest detail can make or break a case." He peeled his gaze away from Alex and moved back to his notebook. "Did she say anything before she died? Anything at all?"

Alex started to answer, but stopped himself. He had backed himself into a corner already with one lie, and he felt fairly certain he wouldn't be able to mask another with feigned anger. He had no clue what Dr. Carlton meant to tell him with her last words, but he was still certain he wasn't ready to share them with Babcock.

"Just some gibberish. Nothing I could make out."

"Nothing about who had ransacked her office?"

"No, nothing like that." Alex's patience had reached an end at this point. That, and he didn't want to risk engaging Babcock in further conversation in the event he might inadvertently say something the cop would interpret as suspicious. "Look, Lieutenant Babcock, my wife and I have had a hard night. Traumatic, really. Do you think we could continue this some other time? I'd really like to get her home so she can rest."

"Just one more thing." Babcock shifted between pages of his notebook, fumbling for a note from earlier. "You said you didn't see anyone leaving here when you arrived and that, to your knowledge, there was no one in the house when you entered?"

Alex nodded. "That's correct."

"No one at all?" Babcock continued. "Nothing even remotely suspicious?"

"Not until we got to the front door and discovered it was open," Alex replied. "Until then, everything looked exactly as it should have at one o'clock in the morning."

Babcock scribbled a few more notes in his notebook, then flipped it closed. Looking up, he locked eyes with the other man. The cop's eyes were a deep brown, almost black throughout, and his fixed stare never wavered. Alex's stomach tightened. Looking into those black, bottomless eyes, he saw for the first time what was going on. They were being interrogated. Babcock thought of them as suspects and had been trying to find some gap, some discrepancy in their story. He knew Alex had lied. Knew there was more to the story than he had been told. That was why he had them repeat their story over and over. He wasn't absent-minded; he was thorough. And suspicious. Very suspicious. He didn't hide it well, either. Alex could feel the suspicion, the mistrust, coming off the man. Waves and waves of it, directed at Alex and Rachel. It was palpable. It was intense.

The feeling was overwhelming. Wave after wave of intense emotion cascaded off of the detective and washed over Alex in a deluge. They poured over him. Covered him. Smothered him. He tried to break his gaze with Babcock, but found he couldn't. He froze, unable to so much as blink, completely locked with the cop by an invisible force. He was falling in deeper, past the suspicion to deeper, darker emotions that lay just past the surface, ready to boil over at any moment but held in check by the sheer force of the Lieutenant's will and restraint. They were powerful feelings, a mix of fear and anger and hatred, blending with an intense compassion for the people he felt were under his protection. Ernest Babcock was an honorable man, a protector, but beneath his calm veneer was a beast ready to be unleashed. It was the lair of that beast Alex was entering now, a miasma of base emotional responses. He tried to pull back, but the irresistible tidal pull of Babcock's conflicting emotions carried him deeper. Love. Hate. Love. Hate. Love. Hate. Alex felt himself coming apart at the seams, his consciousness being pulled in a thousand different directions by the storm force of Babcock's emotional maelstrom.

He screamed and pulled himself out of the swirling contradiction that was Babcock's mind, falling away from the officer and landing hard on the living room floor. The pain of the impact shot up his spine like an arrow, slinging through his brain and completely severing any connection with Babcock. He was alone again in his own mind, the world once again quiet. Relief washed over him, made more palpable because the emotion was his and his alone.

"Alex! Are you all right?" Rachel jumped up off the couch and kneeled beside him, throwing her arms around his shoulder. She pulled him tight into her, his face pressed against her chest, and held him. Tears streamed from her cheeks, accompanied by a barely contained sob. He suddenly felt crushed and smothered and pushed her gently away, breathing deeply from the empty space around him.

"I'm okay.... I think." There was something warm and wet on his face and he wiped at it. Blood smeared the back of his hand.

"What the hell just happened?" Babcock was pulling himself up into a kneel from where he had fallen. A fat trickle of blood issued from his nose as well.

"You're bleeding," Rachel said, reaching into her coat pocket and producing a travel pack of tissues. She handed one to Babcock, then turned back to Alex and swabbed at the blood beneath his nose.

Babcock pulled himself up off the floor as two officers came running from the kitchen in response to Alex's scream. They relaxed when they saw it was Alex on the floor bleeding instead of Babcock.

"What happened, Lieutenant?" asked one of the men, indicating their bloody noses.

"I…." Babcock started to answer. But he had no idea what had happened. No way to explain it to the two men. At least not yet. He needed answers himself, first. "It's nothing. Don't worry about it."

"You sure?" the taller man, a sergeant, asked, casting a wary glance at Alex as he struggled to his feet with Rachel's help. Babcock nodded, dabbing more blood from his nose. "We'll be right down the hall if you need us, Ernie."

"I appreciate that, Jeff, but I think I can handle things here. Why don't you guys get back to what you were doing so we can all get home before noon, okay?" Babcock wiped at the blood under his nose as he spoke, never taking his eyes off Alex.

When the two uniformed officers left the room, Babcock stepped in close to Alex. When he spoke, it was in a whisper, but there was anger in it. "What was that? What did you just do to me?"

Alex expected the anger in Babcock's voice, but there was something else there as well, something he had become intimately familiar with himself over the last few days. Fear. And it was something Babcock was most certainly not accustomed to. Alex could feel it in the bigger man, swirling around him like a wisp of smoke. He squeezed his eyes shut, pushing against it. Forcing it away from him. He didn't want to be sucked back into that frenzy.

Babcock's voice turned from a low whisper to a guttural snarl. "I'm going to ask one more time, Carter. What was that?"

The fear and anger were so tightly intertwined now that Alex could no longer distinguish the two within the other man. But he seemed to be keeping the forces of Babcock's emotions at bay, at least enough to give him the time he needed to regain his strength. He pushed himself up to his full height and away from Rachel, standing alone against the cop. Tentatively, he looked into Babcock's eyes again, preparing for a swirling eddy to take him away. The pull was there, but he was able to resist it. The detective's eyes didn't seem quite as dark as they had before, either.

Steadying himself further, Alex replied, "I don't know what just happened. I'm as surprised as you are."

Babcock's cool eroded further, his guttural snarl creeping up in tone and intensity. "What the fuck do you mean, you don't know? One minute I'm interrogating a suspect, the next thing I know we're both flat on our asses with bloody fucking noses! How the hell did that happen? What did you do?"

Alex put up his hands, palms up, in a submissive gesture. "Lieutenant, I wish I knew, but I don't. Believe me, this scares the hell out of me a lot more than it does you. Maybe….." He trailed off, not wanting to share too much.

Babcock wasn't willing to let the issue slide that easily. "Maybe what?"

Alex wasn't sure how much he wanted to trust the detective. It wasn't just a matter of his own safety any longer, Rachel and the baby were in danger now as well. The situation had already outgrown his and Rachel's ability to handle it; they needed someone else on their side. Someone in Babcock's position might be able to offer them help and protection. Eventually he was going to have to trust someone, and he had just experienced firsthand how seriously Ernest Babcock took the responsibilities that came with his profession. Maybe he could help them. Even if it couldn't help, it wasn't likely he could make things any worse.

Alex breathed deeply, drawing in courage. "I think it has something to do with why we were here to see Dr. Carlton tonight. She said she had something vital to tell us, that our lives depended on it. I have no idea what it was."

"And when did she say this?" The mixture of anger and fear was fading from Babcock's voice, replaced by curiosity. He was a true investigator through and through, more concerned with divining the truth than with his own fears and concerns.

"Tonight, after we found her. Before she... before she died." Alex tensed, knowing he was taking a chance by admitting to Babcock he had lied before, but he had already taken the plunge and was in it now. He would tell the cop the complete story and let him decide for himself what he wanted to do with it.

"And what exactly did she say?" Babcock dabbed absently at the blood on his upper lip, already crusting around the stubble on his face. He didn't acknowledge Alex's lie at all.

Alex went on, his stomach churning at what he was about to say next. "That I had to stop 'them'. For what they had done to me, for what they had done to her and for what they were planning to do to Rachel and the baby."

Babcock shoved the bloodied tissue into his pocket, his face still carrying some dark smears. "And just who are 'they'?"

"I don't know."

Babcock threw his hands up in frustration. "Well, that's just fucking great! Who the hell gave her that information, Oliver Stone? What the fuck kind of shadow conspiracy is going on here?" Stopping his rant, he turned his gaze on Alex like a laser. "Kid, unless you want to find your ass in a holding cell, you'll come clean with me. Right fucking now."

Alex shrank back, trying to put some comfortable space between them. "I'm trying to, Lieutenant."

"I'm going to need something more substantial than your crackpot theories," Babcock replied, roughly running his fingers through his salt and pepper hair. "I need some proof."

Alex looked at Rachel, who reached into the inner pocket of her coat and took out the thumb drive Dr. Carlton had led them to just before she died. She held it up for Babcock to see before gently slipping it back into her coat pocket.

Babcock looked at the device and then back to Alex. "What the hell is that?"

Alex returned his stare. "Proof."

18

Adam sat on the apartment's balcony, taking in the city. Above him, the night sky was a velvety blue, the stars muted or blocked by the lights of the city. Three stories beneath the balcony, the city was alive with the sounds of the night. Car horns were honking, being met with angry retorts. People were laughing and talking, sometimes arguing. A siren off in the distance was growing steadily closer, its wail piercing the night. He could feel the energy swirling around him, as if the night itself were a living thing, breathing its sweet breath and whispering the promises of a lover.

He loved the city. It didn't matter which one. In the end, when reduced to their primal elements, they were all the same. They held the same throng of excitement, the same promise of adventure. The only difference was the people. But people were inherently different. He had never encountered two people alike in every way. On the surface, they may appear to have similar views and feelings. Similar dreams and aspirations. But unlike the city, people were very different when reduced to their primal elements. No two loved, feared, or hated in exactly the same way. That was what he found so enticing about them, why he felt drawn to them like a moth to a flame. It was why he loved cities so much; they were absolutely full of the diversity of humanity in all its glory. But like the moth and the flame, he knew that someday his obsession would bring about his downfall. But what a glorious end it would be, going down in a spiral of flaming beauty.

He sipped lightly at the Zinfandel he had picked up at the corner liquor store. It wasn't an expensive brand, but he didn't have expensive tastes. Until recently, he hadn't had any tastes that weren't dictated to him, so the freedom to make his own choice made the cheap wine as sweet to him as the most expensive champagne. Taking one more deep breath of the frigid night air, he retreated into the apartment, leaving the French doors wide open behind him. It was cold, but he didn't mind. He wanted to enjoy the city for as long as possible.

The apartment was small and sparsely furnished. This was only the third time he had been in it since renting it four years ago. Renting this space without their knowledge was when he first experienced his true independence from PenTech and the Project. Right from the start, he had always intended it to be the first steppingstone in his 'retirement plan', renting it under a false identity and paying the rent by channeling resources through an obscure branch of PenTech. He hadn't been expecting to be using it so soon, however.

He wouldn't be able to use it for long. It wouldn't take the people at the Project long to discover what he had done and trace him to this place. He needed to be long gone by the time they figured it out. But he was ahead of them already.

Other than the table in the middle of the floor, there was a futon and a desk lamp that had been placed unceremoniously in one corner of the room. Beyond that, the small room was completely devoid of furnishings. Adam didn't mind, he didn't need much. Besides, he would not be here for long. No sense cluttering things up now.

On the table sat the uplink and a laptop he had acquired from the helicopter after landing and liberating the pilot and co-pilot of their earthly concerns. Currently, he was downloading all the files he had acquired from the safe house to the laptop so he could access the information. It was slow work. The uplink wasn't designed to handle that much data without the backup of a larger system like Genie. But so far, it seemed to work. Soon he could access all the files he needed on Rachel Carter. He would finally know who this woman was and what it was about her that drove him to such extremes.

Next to the computer sat the hypogun with the vial containing the odd amber liquid. He had discovered it in the pocket of the good Dr. Forrester's poncho after borrowing it during his escape from Burke and his people. So far, he hadn't been able to figure out what it was and what the doctor intended to do with it. Was it meant to kill him? Incapacitate him? Something else? There was no way for him to know right now. He decided it was something worth holding onto, though. It might prove useful. Even if it didn't, it was almost certainly better off in his hands than in theirs.

The laptop emitted a tone, signaling that it had finished loading the files. Smiling, he took another sip of the wine and savored the fruity sweet flavor of it. The taste of the wine seemed different somehow. Sweeter. More intense. Like his success enhanced it.

Picking up the computer, he made his way to the futon to make himself comfortable. It wasn't an easy task, but eventually he was able to find a position that suited him for the work he had to do. Swallowing the last sips of the wine, he placed the glass on the floor and balanced the computer on his lap. The screen was an electric blue that faded into black at the bottom, the PenTech logo overlaid on the field of colors. At the bottom was a small box that simply said, 'Continue?'. Clicking on the box brought up a menu of files, all of which looked like they contained the mundane business of PenTech. But one file jumped out at him, drawing in his attention: Eden. He clicked it.

The screen went black and panic set in, his mind immediately going to the worst possible scenario: the loss of the files. Involuntarily, he held his breath as the internal drive whirred and whispered until a few seconds later the familiar blue and black screen returned with a new message. **Connection to Genie not established. Continue?**

Again, doubt bored into him. Without the larger system to draw from, would the files still be intact? And would he still be able to access them? He had no idea what security measures the technicians at the Project had in place for an incursion like this. Would the security clearance still be in place? He no longer had access to the Director's thumbprint, and who knows how long it would take for him to procure another one. But he had to try. He had to know. Steeling himself against the worst outcome, he clicked 'Continue'.

Almost immediately, the screen went black and his stomach dropped. The files hadn't held up. He had lost everything. All that effort. All that pain. All for nothing. Yes, he could still track down Rachel Carter. He could still find her. He could still accomplish his goals. But it was going to take time, and time was the one thing he was running out of.

His vision went red as a violent need to destroy consumed him. Slamming the screen closed, he lifted the worthless laptop and was about to smash it on the hardwood floor when a small ping emitted from the machine. He could hear the drive whirring, the heartbeat of the machine, as it worked. Rage turned to hope, and he gently replaced the computer on his lap and lifted the cover. The screen underneath was once again lit up with the familiar blue/black pattern, and a new message awaited him.

==TRANSFER COMPLETE==

<==SECURITY AUTHORIZATION APPROVED==>

Your files are ready.

Would you like to continue?

The roiling ball of rage and uncertainty in him dissipated at the message. The files he had downloaded to the uplink had remained intact. His mission would not be impacted, he could still fulfill his destiny. All he needed to do was click 'Continue'.

He did, and the screen once again went black. This time, however, the drives were working as they accessed the files. He took comfort in that sound, like a swarm of worker bees working to see his vision to fruition. A few seconds later, the screen came to life with an image of the PenTech tower superimposed with another option box. Inside the box it read:

Welcome to PenTech.

Please input a keyword to start a search of the files, or simply click 'Continue' to view all files.

A keyword search. This was going to be far easier than he thought. In the box provided, he carefully typed **Rachel Carter**.

The drive whirred again, searching the files for that name. Adam smiled and retrieved his glass, emptying the bottle into it. He sipped lightly, savoring the wine and listening to the computer do its work. A second later, there was a ping and a new message appeared.

36 files found.

Beneath that were two boxes offering two distinct choices. **Review All** or **Redefine Search Parameters**.

Thirty-six files. Excitement swelled up in him at the thought of it, ready to burst. He wanted to savor it, the excitement of discovery. Wanted to carefully and methodically pour over each file, absorbing every minute detail. To drink in every piece of the person who is Rachel Carter. To feel her presence and make her more than a ghost that lingered just out of reach in the back of his mind.

But that wasn't possible. He had escaped Burke Darnell and his cronies last time, but they would learn from the experience. As much as he despised the little weasel, Adam had to admit that Burke was crafty. The outcome could be decidedly different next time if he wasn't careful. The light feeling of excitement and anticipation from a moment ago became a dark and heavy mix of anger and frustration. He should have killed Burke when he had the chance.

Sighing, he clicked **Redefine Search Parameters** and typed **Current Status** into the search box. The screen shifted to display the information he requested. All of her immediate vital statistics flashed in front of him: her name, age, sex, height and weight, eye and hair color, phone number and e-mail address, physical address. All the mundane yet necessary details he would need. The information was good, but it still lacked substance. It lacked soul.

One thing that popped up caught his eye. **Status: Active Surveillance**. Next to that was the number for another associated file: **Subject Serial Number 20-00**. Why was she under active surveillance by the Project? What could their interest in her possibly be? He brought up the companion file. The companion file was considerably larger than her file and had been flagged with several warnings and security alerts. Still pondering Rachel's connection to the Project, he clicked on the file.

And froze. The first thing to pop up on his screen was a picture. A picture of *him*. The one from his nightmares. The mysterious stranger that had haunted him for as long as he could remember, right there in front of him. In a computer file associated with Rachel Carter.

Alex.

The name crept into his head like a snake, as it had in his dream. He didn't know how he knew it; he just did. But the file gave him something he hadn't ever had before, a last name. Carter.

Alex Carter.

Rachel's husband. She was married. To him. To the shadow figure that had haunted him for as far back as he could remember. Anger seethed inside him, just beneath the surface. It consumed all rational thought and feelings in a fire of rage and jealousy.

Once again, someone had betrayed him.

His hands shook violently as they hovered over the keyboard as he fought the urge to smash the computer. He still needed it, even though he couldn't stand being taunted by the face on the screen. Slowly, he calmed himself, pushing back the anger and allowing his rational mind to take over. It wasn't a betrayal; it was just a slight diversion from the path his life was fated to take. A minor inconvenience that he could rectify in order to claim the life he should have had years ago. The life Alex Carter had been given in his place. He could correct that oversight and begin anew.

His hands stopped shaking as he gradually suppressed his rage and anger with determination. What had happened to him wasn't Rachel's fault. She was an innocent, caught in the machinations of the ones responsible for his situation. Elliot Forrester. Burke Darnell. Robert Penders.

And Alex Carter. For his offenses, his punishment would be the worst of all. Simple motivations guided the others: ego, power, money. They committed their grievous acts to achieve their own greedy ends. But with Carter, it was different. He was a thief, a thief who had stolen something precious. He had stolen a life of peace and happiness to avoid the hell that was the Project, and in doing so had condemned Adam to remain in that same hell. More than greedy, his actions were evil. Malicious. And he would pay.

Looking at the picture on the screen, Adam couldn't suppress a smile. Soon, this pretender would be gone. He would receive the justice he deserved. Adam would be with Rachel, and everything would be the way it was supposed to have been from the beginning. Warmth filled him with the thought. Not only of being able to be with Rachel, but of seeing Alex completely and utterly destroyed by his betrayal. Satisfied for the moment, he set the computer aside, picked up his glass and retrieved another bottle of wine before returning to the balcony to enjoy the spirit of the city night once again.

19

Alex plugged the thumb drive into the laptop and it whirred and hummed softly as it accepted the device and the information it contained. He clicked on the icon for the newly accepted drive and it opened to a few digital envelops showing the files on the drive. There was a rather large video file titled 'Carter, Alex' on the drive. He clicked on it and watched as the data extraction started and the download began. The file was huge and was going to take some time. He pushed back in his chair, away from the laptop, and sighed. It had been a long night. He wanted answers. But now he would have to wait again.

Alex's attention was diverted from the slow-loading file to Lieutenant Babcock, who paced in front of the fireplace mumbling something to himself that Alex couldn't quite make out. The tone of it was decidedly unpleasant, though, so Alex decided not to ask. He and Rachel had been lucky in that the detective had been willing to go back to their house to review the data on the thumb drive firsthand with them and hadn't instead just confiscated the device and thrown them both in jail. He had cited something about police procedures and the chain of evidence, but Alex was sure it had more to do with the man's innate curiosity.

The aroma of coffee drifted from the kitchen where Rachel was preparing breakfast. The coffee smelled great to Alex's sleep-starved self, but more than that, his stomach rumbled intensely at the thought of food. He had been ravenous since they had left Dr. Carlton's and nothing seemed to sate him. Since coming home, he had eaten four donuts and a couple of Pop Tarts, not to mention two-thirds of a new gallon of orange juice, and he was still starving. He had always been a big eater, but this new appetite was tremendous. Most likely a result of stress, he thought.

"Can't that thing go any faster?" Babcock asked as he absently chewed on an unlit cigar. There was no way Rachel would have ever allowed him to light it up in the house, but she had welcomed him to enjoy it outside. He declined, muttering under his breath about the cold, but made do by chomping on the end of it as he paced. Alex thought that was only slightly less pleasant than actually smoking it, but it was the detective's choice and he appeared moderately happy with the idea. As happy as he could get, based on Alex's observations of him. The man seemed to be in a constant state of tension, his entire life spent in a defensive posture. Alex wondered if the man ever really relaxed. If he even knew how. If he did, he hid it well.

"It's going as fast as it can, Lieutenant. Why don't you sit down and relax? This could take a few more minutes." Alex gestured to the sofa and loveseat arranged in an L-shaped configuration facing the fireplace.

"Thanks, but I'll stand." He continued to wander around the room, taking it all in. To the average observer, it would seem as if he were just exploring the room and admiring the décor, but Alex knew better. He knew what Babcock did for a living, and he knew the man was searching for something. Alex didn't know what the detective was searching for, and he wasn't certain if Babcock himself knew what he was looking for, just that he felt compelled to look. That he had a deep need to familiarize himself with his surroundings.

Rachel came in from the kitchen as Babcock was examining the bookshelf at the far end of the room. There was nothing there but the science fiction novels he liked and the horror novels Rachel enjoyed, as well as a few romance novels neither of them would own up to having brought into the house, but Babcock still found it necessary to peruse them.

Rachel set the tray on the small table by the couch, the smells of the meal wafting through the room. On the tray was a pot of coffee, a decanter of orange juice, a half dozen uncut bagels accompanied by butter and cream cheese, and three plates that each contained a decent pile of scrambled eggs and bacon. Alex's stomach roared back to life at the smell and sight of the food, his animal brain reminding him he needed to eat.

"Hungry, Lieutenant?" Rachel asked, taking up a place on the loveseat. "I hope you don't mind eating in the living room. Alex's computer has sort of co-opted the dining room table." She poured herself a glass of orange juice.

"I don't mind," Babcock replied, replacing a copy of Stephen King's *Carrie* back on the bookshelf. "And I'm starved. Thank you." He sat on an end of the couch and grabbed the coffeepot to pour himself a cup.

Alex picked up a plate of bacon and eggs and sat across from them on the fireplace hearth. He wasted no time in feeding himself, shoveling a mountainous pile of eggs into his mouth. It proved to be more than he could handle as some egg fell away from the sides of his mouth and tumbled into his lap or onto the carpet. He hardly noticed. It didn't matter, as long as he finally got to eat.

Rachel, however, cared. "Alex Carter!" she snapped in a low but commanding voice. "What is the matter with you? I don't care how hungry you are, observe a few basic manners, would you?" She turned to Babcock, her face red. "I apologize for that. He's not usually such a slob."

Babcock smiled slightly, which surprised Alex. Until now, he hadn't been certain that Babcock was even capable of the expression. The man was just full of surprises.

"That's all right, Mrs. Carter. I'm used to it. You should see how some of the guys at the station house eat. It's downright disgusting." He dropped a few cubes of sugar into his coffee and stirred vigorously, never once hitting the inside of the cup with his spoon. When he finished he tapped the spoon lightly on the rim of the cup and set the spoon on his saucer. His table manners were impeccable, not at all what someone might expect upon their first meeting with the man.

Babcock's table manners aside, Alex needed to eat. His stomach felt like it was collapsing in on itself like a dying star. He kept at the eggs on his plate, mindful of his pace so as not to further upset Rachel. He was absolutely ravenous, as if he hadn't eaten in days.

Rachel sighed as she watched her husband eat. "I'm afraid when this one comes," she patted her stomach lightly, "I'll have two children on my hands."

"You're expecting?" Babcock asked, seemingly at ease with the conversation now. It had been like that since Rachel came into the room. She seemed to have a humanizing effect on the bearish detective.

"Yes," she replied, a smile spreading across her face. "In March."

"That's fantastic," Babcock stated. "I have three myself, a boy and twin girls." Fishing his wallet from his back pocket, he retrieved two small photos. "Zack is seventeen now and the girls.... pardon me, Lucie and Tina, they hate when I refer to them as 'the girls', just turned fourteen."

They were beautiful children, Alex thought as he looked at the pictures. The boy, Zack, had the same sharp features as his father, but without the edge that age and experience gave the detective. In another twenty-five years or so, Alex could picture him looking almost exactly like his father. The girls were a different story. They were more delicate than their brother, with an air of innocence that struck him even from the simple picture. It was more than the way they looked, although the soft complexions and light auburn hair of the identical girls added to the overall perception, it was in their deep brown eyes. There was innocence in their eyes. They hadn't yet seen the world and all it offered, both good and bad. They were still full of life, joy, and hope. Their eyes must have come from their mother. While they shared their father's deep brown eyes, his were colder. He had seen the world, experienced the worst it offered, and the innocence had faded from his. Alex silently hoped that the girls could hold on to the light of innocence for a while longer. Innocence was a rare commodity these days, used up far too quickly. It would be a shame to see it vanish altogether.

Alex handed the pictures back to Babcock. "You've got a great-looking family, Lieutenant. In a lot of ways, I envy you."

Babcock replaced the pictures in his wallet and the wallet in his pocket. "How's that? Seems to me you aren't doing too badly. Lovely wife, baby on the way, successful business, nice house. What more could you want?"

Alex paused, considering the question. What more did he want? What more was there? The answers that had been so clear yesterday were now obscured. Still, one thing stood out.

"Lieutenant, do you know your mother?"

Babcock's face was dull, like Alex had asked in a foreign language. Alex knew the look; it was one he had become accustomed to. The question was so completely alien to most people, something they took for granted, that they never really knew how to react. Yet for Alex, it was a fact of life.

Babcock finally came to life, the question seeming to settle in his mind. "Yeah, I knew my mother. She passed away three years ago. Why?" The sharp, suspicious tone reappeared in his voice.

Alex set down his plate and poured himself a glass of orange juice, taking the time to frame a reply. "I never knew my mother. At least, not that I can remember. I don't even know who she is. The only thing I know about her is when I think about her or try to remember her, all I get is a deep, empty aching feeling in the bottom of my gut. Not a depressed or angry feeling, nothing like that. Just..... empty. It's as if there's nothing there. Like there never was. Like all that ever existed of her was some dark void, as if I never had a mother at all. I know how crazy that sounds, everyone has a mother, but that same feeling hits me whenever I try to picture mine. It's unnerving at the best of times, maddening at the worst."

"What about your father?" Babcock asked, leaning into the conversation as his natural curiosity overcame him. "Brother or sister? Aunt? Uncle? Grandparent?"

Alex shook his head in response to each suggestion. "As far as I know, I have no family anywhere. Until I met Rachel, I was entirely alone."

"For your whole life? No one has ever tried to contact you?" Babcock sipped lightly at his coffee; his gaze fixed on the cup as if he could uncover the answers within. Apparently, there were no answers to be found there because he continued. "That seems odd, if you don't mind me saying. Every missing persons case I've ever seen, someone comes looking."

"No one," Alex replied quietly. "Never."

"But you've tried to find them?" Babcock continued.

Alex sighed. "Yes, but with no success. It's like I never existed until the day I washed up on the beach...."

Babcock's head snapped up, his expression one of puzzlement and recognition all at the same time. After a few moments of those struggling reactions, he exclaimed, "You're him! That kid that washed up on the beach all those years ago! The amnesiac! I remember that story, came down the wire when I was a uniform in town. I wondered what happened to you after the media blitz died. How'd you end up here?"

Alex shrugged. "Chance, mostly. After the hospital released me, I went to a foster home until my family could be located. I was there for two months. Six months in the one after that. And so on. Bouncing around until I ended up here."

"Bouncing around? You mean, between foster homes?" Babcock seemed only slightly surprised, but someone with his experiences would understand the issues inherent in the system. "What happened?"

"Let's just say I wasn't a normal child."

Thinking back to the events of the previous night, Babcock replied, "I hate to break it to you, but you aren't exactly a normal adult."

Alex sighed. "I'm aware. Back then, when I was in foster care, nothing like what happened last night ever happened to me. The nightmares were the biggest problem. In the middle of the night, I would just wake up screaming. And those nightmares would draw me in and hold tight. It was almost like they were alive. Like they didn't want to let me go. Pulling me out of something like that was rough. Not the kind of thing you'd want to deal with in your own kid, never mind one you don't have any real connection to. And then there was the sleepwalking."

"You walked in your sleep?" Babcock asked, his breakfast completely forgotten.

"Yeah. Usually, someone would stop me before I left the house or sometimes on the front lawn, but occasionally I would make it to a neighbor's. Made it to downtown twice in two places I lived. It was upsetting enough for my foster parents, but imagine finding a kid wandering around your house in a daze at three in the morning. Or waking up to a blood-curdling scream as that sleepwalking kid woke up on your lawn. Didn't exactly enhance my reputation in the neighborhood."

"I can imagine," Babcock replied, suddenly remembering his almost full coffee cup and taking a sip.

"So I'd get shuffled off to another foster home. And another. And another. For two years. In all that time, no one came forward with any information as to who I was and where I was from. The authorities were absolutely clueless. I had no identity at all aside from the name the state gave me: John Doe."

Babcock chuffed. "How original."

"Yeah," Alex chuckled slightly. "You can see why I changed it."

Babcock set his coffee cup down, refocusing his attention on Alex. "So you had no family and no legal guardian. Bounced around the system for a while. What happened then?"

Alex shrugged. "The state decided, with advice from Dr. Carlton and a physician whose name I can't remember, that I was at least eighteen and therefore the state was no longer responsible for my well-being. Basically, they cut me loose.

"And...?" Babcock prompted.

"I got a job, hated it and quit. Got another job, hated it and quit. And so on and so on. Then I went to work for the DiArona's over at Antonio's. Things were different there. Antonio and Isabella, they really cared about me. They knew I was in a bad way and they gave me so much more than a job. They gave me a sense of self-worth. I had no idea what that felt like until them. I realized then that if I was going to have a future, I was going to have to make it happen myself. So I scraped and saved and worked to pay for college, going to school during the day and working in the restaurant at night. I busted my ass for four years between work and school, but it paid off. Graduated at the top of my class. Met Rachel my sophomore year, and the rest is history." Alex stated, sipping his orange juice and sitting back on the couch.

"Whoa there, lover boy! It wasn't that easy," Rachel interjected. She turned to Babcock, a sly grin on her face. "What he's not telling you is that he had to chase me for six months before I'd even talk to him. He followed me around like a lost puppy everywhere I went. Kind of pathetic, really. But he was cute, so I thought I'd take pity on him and give him a chance."

"Looks like you lost that one," Babcock said, returning to his coffee.

Rachel nodded, smiling. "Big time."

"Excuse me," Alex interrupted, a faux pained expression on his face. "Who's telling this story?"

"Oh, you are dear," Rachel replied. "I just thought the detective should have *all* the facts."

Alex gave her a sideways glance and a half smile. "As I was saying, after an interminably long time of wearing her down with my persistence...."

"*Now* the truth comes out!" Rachel exclaimed, disappearing into the kitchen with a pile of dirty dishes.

"Anyway, after graduation, Henreson and Foright offered me a job. They're the biggest architectural firm in New England, so I snatched it up. A month later, Rachel and I were married and living in Boston. We spent two and a half years there hating every minute. We realized that city life didn't suit us, so we came back to Pine Haven and set up shop here. My best friend and I opened our business, and the rest is a rather pleasant piece of history."

"Until now," Babcock said. "When these dreams started again."

"Right. Except now they're more than just dreams. They seem to be...." Alex paused, searching for the right way to describe the dreams to Babcock without sounding like he was completely over the edge. "They seem to connect me with something from my past."

"You mean dredging memories out of your subconscious?" Babcock leaned forward, his gaze fixed on Alex, his hands tightly wrapped together in front of him. His curiosity had moved past professional consideration.

"No," Alex replied, uncertain about how the conversation was going to play out. "I mean, they're *actually* connecting me to something. Or someone."

"Like what happened between you and me last night?" Babcock talked so casually about it, as if discussing something as mundane as the weather. Either he was just naturally less skeptical than most people or his firsthand experiences had given him more pliable beliefs.

Alex nodded. "Something like that. But this connection is stronger. There's more than simple emotion involved. There are thoughts and experiences and desires as well, all jumbled together. And it's not just that I feel it, like what happened last night with us, I live it. I remember it like I experienced it myself. I feel this person's pain and pleasure, happiness and anger. It's almost as if we're..."

"Twins," Babcock muttered.

Alex stopped, stunned. "What?"

"As if you were twins," Babcock stated more firmly. "It's a documented phenomenon with identical twins that they will sometimes be identical in more than just appearance. Sometimes it goes as far as their fingerprints and even DNA are completely indistinguishable. And it can go deeper than that." The big man set his coffee cup down and rubbed his hand across the stubble on his chin, his eyes staring into a void as he thought out his next words. "I see it in my girls. They'll finish each other's sentences. They have a sense of where the other one is and what she's doing even if they haven't talked to each other all day. Sometimes they claim they can feel what the other is feeling."

A chill crept up Alex's spine and gripped him firmly. "That sounds a little freaky."

"You don't know the half of it," Babcock replied. "The other day I walked into the living room and Tina was there, just watching TV. Suddenly, completely out of the blue, she turns to me and says, 'I think Lucie and Jack broke up.' Now, it's not like this wouldn't be welcome news to me, Jack's a real jerk-off, but I ask her where she heard that from. These kids and their cell phones, they get news before it happens these days. Thing is, Tina had her phone taken from her that morning for talking back to her mother. She hadn't had it since breakfast. So I ask her why she thinks that. She says she just feels it. Next thing I know, Lucie comes bursting into the house and runs upstairs to her room, crying the whole way. When my wife finally gets her calmed down and talking, she tells us all about the breakup. The breakup Tina knew about before her sister even came home because she 'felt it'. Maybe that's what this thing is with you and this other guy. Maybe he's a twin brother you never knew you had."

Alex shuddered, thinking about the dark stranger from his dreams. "No offense to your theory, but I sure as hell hope not."

It was Babcock's turn to look confused. Alex explained to him in detail about his dreams and the part the mysterious stranger played and how, so far, it seemed to fit in with Dr. Carlton's warning about protecting Rachel and the baby. The pieces of the puzzle were coming together little by little, and Alex had to admit he didn't care much for the complete picture.

Before they could delve any deeper into the conversation, the computer chimed, indicating the completion of the data download. The two men stared at the machine as a thick silence descended on the room. Rachel wandered in from the kitchen, following the same chime they had just heard. None of them immediately moved to the computer.

Taking a deep breath, Alex lifted himself off the hearth, brushing away a few remaining crumbs of breakfast. He looked to Rachel, then to Babcock, then said, "I suppose if we're going to get answers, this is as good a place as any to start."

Rachel smiled a weak smile. Babcock nodded, simply said, "Then let's get to it."

Alex sat in front of the laptop. On the screen sat a small box with two other boxes inside reading 'Run' and 'Cancel'. His hand shaking slightly, Alex grabbed the mouse and moved the cursor to 'Run', clicking the button. The computer hummed lightly again. In a moment a single word, 'Password?', came up on the screen, a blinking cursor next to it.

Alex paused, frozen. Rachel's hand gently landed on his shoulder and she squeezed slightly, as if trying to transfer some of her strength to him. After all the searching and agonizing over his life and history, he was finally about to get some answers. To fill in the void that was his life. All it would take is typing one word. One short word. He inhaled sharply and reached for the keyboard, his hands quivering visibly.

"You don't have to do this, Alex," Rachel whispered, giving his shoulder another gentle squeeze. "It's all right. We understand."

Alex laid his hand over hers, squeezing gently, as if to affirm her presence there with him. To make certain he wasn't alone. Her touch calmed him, as it always had, but it also emboldened him. She was his strength, and he felt certain he could accomplish anything with her beside him.

"Yes. Yes, I have to do this." He reached for the keyboard again. His hands still trembled, but not quite as much as before. Slowly and deliberately, he typed Z-E-U-S.

Again, the computer hummed and his screen was suddenly filled with the face of Dr. Simone Carlton. The image stared at him, motionless, as the drive hummed again. Alex locked eyes with the eerily still image, pangs of regret and guilt stabbing at him. Without warning, the image of the doctor came to life, the abruptness of it startling him as he sharply exhaled a breath he hadn't been aware he was holding.

Dr. Carlton's words didn't immediately register with him; he was simply lost in her voice. A voice as crisp and powerful as Alex remembered it, from before her health had failed her. For a moment, he almost forgot that she had died the previous night, but then the reality of it set in. She was gone, this recording nothing but a faint echo of her life and spirit.

Realizing he hadn't heard a word she had said, he clicked the start of the progress bar at the bottom of the screen to replay the first few seconds of the video. Again, her voice sprang confidently from the laptop, a testament to her inner strength.

"Hello, Alex. I hope this message finds you well, but if you're viewing it, I can only assume that things are not well at all. I know these are confusing times for you, but if you bear with me, I will try to add some clarity for you.

"Before I proceed, there's something I need to tell you. A confession, if you will, of the most regretful thing I have ever done in my life. A betrayal of my professional oath and dedication to protecting and aiding my charges. All the years I was helping you get past your memory block, to help you regain your life, they were all a lie. Every step I took, every action, wasn't meant to help you. Just the opposite, in fact."

In the video, Alex could see tears welling up in the doctor's eyes as she spoke. Whatever it was she was claiming to have done had taken a heavy toll on her. Given the type of person she was, the kind not known to dwell on weighty emotional subjects and allow them to drag on her, Alex felt a deep sense of concern settle in. If she was that visibly shaken by what she claims she had done, it was extremely serious. Once again, he reached for Rachel's hand, still perched on his shoulder. He needed her strength right now, possibly more than ever before.

On the screen, Dr. Carlton wiped away tears and replaced her glasses on the bridge of her nose. "You're probably very confused right now, and that is perfectly understandable after everything you have no doubt been through. But please, be secure knowing that there *are* answers for you, Alex. Your life is not an enigma. You have a history, and I'm going to get you started on discovering it with the information in these files. I have to warn you, you will not like everything you discover here. Point of fact, you will not like most of it. But this is who you are, do with it what you will and make the most of it. But be extremely careful. The intention was never for this information to be public. Many people have died keeping it a secret, and the people who want it kept quiet have no qualms about killing anyone who threatens their agenda. Life has no meaning for them, they only crave power. They will do whatever it takes to attain that power and to keep it."

Suddenly, the fixed camera angle moved back, exposing Dr. Carlton's wheelchair. "Look at what they did to me. It wasn't a genetic nerve disorder that put me in this chair. It was my punishment. Punishment for when I first tried to tell you the truth years ago. A sharp reminder that they will not tolerate disobedience."

She shook herself out of her reverie and refocused the camera to frame her face again. "Enough about that. Review the documentation here and you will have a beginning to understanding it all. However, you will never have all the answers until you talk to two men. To complete the picture, you will need to speak to Dr. Elliot Forrester and Robert Penders of PenTech."

There was a pause as she absently pushed her glasses up the bridge of her nose, turning her eyes away from the camera for a moment. She shifted in her seat, composing herself, as her drawn and tired face softened. Finally, she lifted her eyes back to the camera and continued.

"Before I go, I have to tell you how sorry I am. Just saying it doesn't make it better, doesn't fix the problem, but it is all I can do now. If I'd acted before, done this years ago, maybe I could have saved you all those painful years of agonizing soul-searching. That pains me the most, that I was capable of bringing your pain to an end and I chose not to act. Worse, I chose not to act out of fear. I was a coward. Afraid. Well, I am not afraid any longer. Use this information well and bring an end to this. Make those responsible pay. Then make the best possible life for you and your family. You deserve that happiness, as do they. I can't change what I did, although I wish with all of my heart that I could. All I can do is give you this gift and hope that someday, somehow, you can find it in your heart to forgive me. You are a good person, Alex Carter. Never forget that. No matter what you discover moving forward from this point, never forget that."

The image on the screen froze as the progress bar at the bottom of the screen reached its end. It was done. Over. Just like the life of the woman in the video, her light snuffed out like a candle. No one moved or spoke. Alex, Rachel, Babcock, all were still and silent, either out of respect for the dead or shock at what her voice had said from beyond the grave. Alex simply froze, his eyes fixated on the unmoving face of Dr. Carlton as his mind raced to process what he had just seen. His face felt flush as a range of emotions ran through him, from anger to fear to shame. He didn't know what to focus on, what he should be feeling right now. It was simply too much.

Three short beeps burst from Babcock's cell phone, breaking the silence. He quickly pulled the phone from his pocket and looked at the message, his face contorting in confusion.

"It's Dr. Tanner, the pathologist," he stated. "Is there somewhere I can go to give her a quick call back?"

Rachel faced him, seemingly grateful for the distraction. "The kitchen. Let me show you."

Babcock put out his palm. "No need. I can find it."

Babcock went into the kitchen and Rachel shifted her attention back to Alex, who remained seated motionlessly at the computer, with his eyes fixed on the unmoving image of

Dr. Carlton. As far as she knew, he hadn't moved, hadn't even blinked, since the video ended. She could only imagine what was going through his mind. One of the few people he felt he could trust had betrayed him. Trust didn't come easily to Alex. He struggled to overcome the fact that people who were supposed to be taking care of him had repeatedly let him down throughout his life. But as time went by, he had learned to trust, to give certain people the benefit of the doubt and let them into his life. To expose his fears and insecurities. And one of those people had now not only betrayed him but endangered his family through their actions. She wanted to say something to lessen the hurt he was feeling, but she knew there was nothing she could say that would ease the pain he was in. The most she could do at the moment was to let him know she was there for him. That she was always there for him.

She wrapped her arms around his shoulders and kissed him gently on the neck. His shoulders were like granite, tensed and coiled. He didn't move when she touched him, just stared ahead at the laptop screen. A vista of dazzlingly colorful tropical fish had replaced the image of Dr. Carlton. Alex seemed oblivious to the change.

"Are you all right?" Rachel whispered lightly into his ear.

Tears rimmed his eyes as he continued to stare at the screen in front of him. "She betrayed me, Rachel. You heard her. I trusted her. I mean, I truly trusted her. Trusted her with my darkest secrets. And she still betrayed me. How could she do that? Why would she just let all of this happen to me?" His eyes finally drifted away from the computer screen and came around to hers. "How could she do this to *us*?"

Rachel gently touched her husband's face, his cheeks dampened by tears. Taking his chin in her hand, she gently turned his face toward hers. "You heard her. She didn't want to do what she did. She regretted it. All of it. And don't forget, in the end she died helping you. That has to count for something."

He sighed a heavy sigh and threw his arms around her waist, resting his head on her belly. She was warm, her midsection rising and falling in a gentle rhythm with her breath. "Thank you," he said, his voice choked with tears. "I love you."

She lightly stroked the back of his head, flattening his hair. "I love you, too. More than you could ever imagine. And we will get through this. Whatever it is, we'll get through it just fine. You'll see."

Babcock entered the room, clearing his throat loudly and deliberately from the kitchen doorway, pretending not to have noticed their tender moment. Alex and Rachel relaxed their embrace slowly, reluctant to let go of that one moment of normalcy that had crept into their frenzied lives.

"Dr. Tanner has almost completed the autopsy on Dr. Carlton." He paused, his expression completely neutral. "So far it looks as if she died from the natural progression of a degenerative condition."

Alex snapped to his feet; his fists clenched at his sides. "So that's it? Case closed?"

"Hold up a second," Babcock continued, extending his palm to Alex. "I said 'so far'. She isn't finished yet. But she said she found something unusual. Wouldn't say what it was over the phone, just that she wants me to come down there right away to take a look at it. Said it was strange."

"Strange? In what way?" Rachel interjected.

"Again, she wouldn't say. I'm going to head over there now, see what she's got." He paused, his eyes coming up to meet Alex. "I'd like you to come along, too."

"Why me? I'm no forensic expert, what good would I be?"

Babcock shrugged indifferently. "Maybe none. But I have a feeling you're the key to busting this whole can of sardines wide open and I want you someplace I can keep an eye on you when the shit inevitably hits the fan."

Alex couldn't argue with that. Everything that had happened seemed to revolve around him, even though he had no idea why. Maybe Babcock had something. Maybe he could help to put all the pieces together. Perhaps whatever the coroner found would help jog his memory, get back a few more pieces of his lost past. Either way, he had nothing to lose by trying.

He took a deep breath and slowly exhaled, allowing his hands to release the tension they held and unclench. "OK, we'll go."

Rachel turned to him, taking his hands in hers. "No. I can't. Not right now. I need some rest and I need it badly. I understand that you have to do this, but I just can't. I have more than just my health to think about right now, too." She glanced down, her eyes falling to her belly. "You go. Do this. I'll be fine. I just need some sleep."

Alex's hands tightened around hers, like he was afraid to let go. "I can't just leave you here alone. Not after everything that's happened. Not after Dr. Carlton specifically told me to *not* leave you alone."

Babcock stepped forward, closing the distance between them. "She makes a good point. She hasn't slept in well over a day by now. Rest is important. I'll post a couple of uniforms outside to monitor the house. She'll be safe."

"No offense, Lieutenant, but if this thing goes as far up as it seems to, I don't feel all that keen to place my trust in anyone." He knew what he had said may hit Babcock on a personal level, but he didn't really care. All that mattered was the safety of Rachel and the baby.

Rachel stepped toward him, taking his hand and squeezing gently. "Alex, go. You need to find out if this discovery is significant, and you may be the only one who can tell if it is. I'll be fine. If it's my safety you're worried about, I can't do much better than having a police presence on our front lawn. Not gonna lie, it's going to create some scuttlebutt around the neighborhood, but I'll be perfectly safe."

Her deep emerald eyes met his and his resolve to argue the point melted. "Okay," he relented, "I'll go. I don't like it, but I'll go. Just promise me you'll be all right."

"I promise," she replied, smiled slightly back at him.

Babcock interrupted their moment. "I guarantee she'll be safe. I've got a couple of guys in mind for this detail and they're the best. Don't worry, she'll be in excellent hands. Worry about getting to the bottom of this instead."

Alex shifted his gaze from his wife to the detective, Dr. Carlton's warning ringing through his head. *Don't leave her alone.* He couldn't exorcise that nagging concern in the back of his brain, the feeling that doom was closing in on them. But in his rational mind, he knew that solving this mystery was the best way to keep his family safe.

"Okay," he said, reluctantly releasing Rachel's hand.

"Everything'll be fine," Babcock said, offering no other encouragement.

Babcock's men arrived in ten minutes. Both were intimidating in height and physique, made even more impressive by their uniforms and stern faces. Their plan had been to watch the house from the outside, but Alex insisted they stay inside and close to Rachel. She wanted to argue that it wasn't necessary, but realized that would be Alex's breaking point and thought better of it.

Alex climbed into Babcock's car and looked back at his house as they headed away. Rachel stood on the front porch, waving. Rachel's form dwindled and then vanished altogether as they rounded the corner, and he was struck with the horrible feeling that nothing would ever be the same for them again.

20

The town of Pine Haven was everything he expected it to be. A picturesque little hamlet on the shores of Lake Winnipesaukee comprising hotels, resorts, seasonal residences and businesses designed to cater to the needs of upscale out-of-town visitors. At the moment the only people out and about were town residents going about their daily business, closing up shop for the summer and preparing for the coming onslaught of skiers, snowmobilers and other winter sport enthusiasts that would descend on the tiny town with the first snowfall.

Adam had stopped at a small restaurant called The Bagel Stable, which had a sign in the window with the food pyramid and a tagline stating, 'We've got it all in here!' Proper nutrition wasn't foremost on his mind at the moment, all he wanted was to fill the gnawing emptiness in his stomach. He had driven all night, non-stop, eager to reach Pine Haven. Eager to reach the town that Rachel Carter called home. In his obsession to get there, he had neglected to have so much as a snack during the drive, and now he was absolutely famished. The Bagel Stable's promise would serve his needs nicely.

The place was small, but cozy. It had what some might describe as small-town charm, adorned with the kitsch that urban visitors from out-of-town might find 'quaint' and 'charming'. A viewpoint The Bagel Stable no doubt used to charge them four times what they should reasonably pay for eggs and toast.

A counter ran along the left side of the restaurant, behind which was a pass-through window leading to the kitchen. The right side was adorned with a series of booths. The air was heavy with grease, carrying the smells of breakfasts in the process of preparation from the kitchen. A few customers spread out among the booths and the counter, engaging in what was no doubt local gossip, while others simply sat, perusing the morning news over their coffee and eggs. Most people were scrolling through smartphones, but Adam was surprised to see a few reading actual print newspapers. He didn't know what was more surprising, that they chose to get their news that way or that this town still printed newspapers.

He opted for a seat at the counter. A look at the menu was promising, and he decided on a sausage and cheese omelet with onions and tomatoes and a side of blueberry pancakes purported to be made with fresh Maine blueberries. That, along with some toast, should fulfill all his food groups, especially if grease could be considered a dietary supplement.

"Good morning! Coffee for you today?" The voice was bright and cheerful and attached to an attractive young woman on the opposite side of the counter. She was slender and tall with a toothy smile and glowing blond hair pulled tightly into a ponytail. Her eyes were a deep sea-blue that stood out curiously from the light tone of her face. She was not excessively beautiful, but he found her appearance appealing enough.

"Sure, that'd be great," he replied, gently nudging the overturned cup on the counter toward her. She grabbed it, flipped it over and filled it in what was almost a single motion, setting the steaming cup back in front of him. Despite the temperature, he gulped down a good half the cup. Even the burning sensation as it raced down his throat was invigorating.

"There's cream and sugar on the counter there, sweetheart. Help yourself."

"Thanks," he replied, taking up the cup and inhaling the bitter aroma of the black coffee. The smell alone was enough to give him a quick shot of energy.

"So," she said, taking a small order pad and pen from her apron pocket, "what can we get for you today?"

Adam recited his order, and she wrote it down meticulously, passing the order sheet to the cook through the window. Turning back to him, she grabbed the coffeepot and refilled his cup.

"So where you from?"

Adam paused, the question taking him by surprise. It seemed like a simple enough question, something most people could easily respond to without a second thought. For him, it wasn't so easy.

"Pardon me?" It was the only reply he could think of in the moment.

"Leaf peepers are gone. Winter folks won't be here for another few weeks. You aren't one of our regulars, so that means you aren't from around here. If you lived around here, I'd know it."

Adam sipped at the coffee more lightly now. "What if I said I just moved here?"

"You married?"

"No."

"Then you'd be lying," she said, a wide grin spreading across her face. "A new single guy moves into this town, which is almost never, and the grapevine goes wild. I would have had everyone from Alicia's salon in here yapping about it. So again, where you from?"

Despite himself and his usual desire to remain anonymous and disconnected, he couldn't repress a smile. "Connecticut."

"Nice place. Whereabouts?"

"Just a stopover in Waterford," he answered. "I never stay in one place very long."

She planted her elbows on the counter and cupped her chin with her hands. "Ooh, a nomad. So what brings you to Pine Haven?"

"You this chatty with everyone, or is this inquisition a special?" Adam asked.

She threw up her hands in a mock gesture of self-defense. "Hey, just trying to be friendly. Usually means better tips if I'm friendly." She lowered her hands again, setting them lightly on the counter as she leaned into Adam. "So, what brings you to Pine Haven?"

Adam sighed. There would be no putting her off, apparently. She seemed to know a lot about the town and its citizens, however, so she may have some use if he played the situation right.

He waved his hands in a gesture of surrender. "I'm sorry. I don't do well with strangers sometimes. I'm a bit of an introvert, casual conversation can be an issue for me. Especially with an attractive woman." He smiled an awkward smile to put her at ease. "As for what brings me here, I'm visiting relatives. The Carters. You know them?"

Her face lit us and her smile broadened. "The Carters! Of course I know them. They come in here all the time, at least when they aren't at Antonio's down the street. Now that you say it, I can see the resemblance. You and Alex could be brothers." Her face darkened a bit, the smile fading. "Except Alex doesn't have any family. So who are you?"

Adam chuckled. "Yeah, we get that a lot. It's weird because I'm Rachel's cousin. I was hoping to stay with them for a bit while I plan out my next steps. I don't seem to have a lot of luck finding them. These streets make absolutely no sense to me."

The smile returned to the woman's face, her eyes lighting up once again. "Welcome to New England. The streets around here have never made much sense. Most started out as horse paths a few hundred years ago and gradually turned into streets. Makes for a confusing set up. There's been talk of making changes, but it would take so much time and money it just isn't worth it, I guess. Plus, people around here are a bit resistant to change. Another New England trait."

"Well," Adam exclaimed, "looks like I'll stay lost."

The cook interrupted them, handing Adam's breakfast to the server, who laid it out on the counter in front of him. A tempting mixture of sweet and spicy wafted up to him and his stomach responded with a low groan. Hunger got the best of him as he hastily shoved a healthy bite of the omelet into his mouth. Melted cheese oozed out from the egg and slid onto his tongue, burning it at the touch. It was painful, but offset by the pleasure of the spicy flavor of the sausage exploding on the burned areas of his tongue.

"The roads around here can be confusing," the server continued, absently wiping down the counter for lack of anything better to do. "You need a guide."

Adam looked up and smiled. "Would you know a good one?"

She abandoned the pretext of cleaning and leaned across the counter, bringing her face unprofessionally close to his. "Only the best guide in town there is."

"And that would be...?" he teased.

"You're looking at her. I've lived here all my life. Grew up here. I know this town inside and out. No one can show you the local flavor like I can! What do you say?"

She kept the close distance between them as she waited for him to answer. The smell of her perfume hit him, overtaking the scents of coffee and sausage. It was a very floral scent, light and summery, no doubt meant to evoke an emotional fondness for the warmer seasons. He had to admit she was attractive, and it had been a while since he'd been with a woman. The urge didn't strike him often, but when it did, it could be powerful. While he was certain he could find the Carters' place on his own, her help would certainly speed up the process. Aside from that, she might make for an interesting way to pass the time until the evening.

"I don't know," Adam said, invoking as sincere a voice as he could. Normally, he was very convincing and very capable of getting what he wanted from people, either directly or indirectly. This was going to require a more indirect approach. "Are you sure you don't mind? I don't want to impose."

She waved her hand dismissively. "It's not a problem at all. I'd love to do it. Things have been pretty boring around here since summer ended. I'm dying for a way to liven things up. Besides," she continued as a playful smile overtook her lips, "I think an afternoon with you could be... interesting."

Adam returned her smile with one of his own carefully rehearsed expressions. It was a pleasant, yet mischievous, boyish smile. "I think you are absolutely right."

It was going to be a very interesting day, after all.

21

Like most small towns, Pine Haven had no morgue of its own. Most of the deaths in town could be attributed to old age, reckless living or a simple stab of fate and required little or no investigation. Corpses were sent to their respective funeral homes in accordance with their final wishes, or to cold storage in the county hospital to await the next phase of their final rest. But when the occasional mysterious death popped up, the town turned to the William Harris Funeral Home. In case of need, the funeral home could transform one of the three embalming labs into a forensic laboratory that was just as good, if not superior to, the State Police forensic lab in Concord. Dr. Carlton had been taken to the William Harris Funeral Home the night before and Dr. Tanner had worked through the night sifting through whatever clues she could find that might make the death stand out as suspicious. Apparently, at some point, she had found something because Alex and Babcock now found themselves at the funeral home's front door at her request.

"Lieutenant Babcock, a pleasure to see you. I wish it were under more pleasant circumstances." The man greeting them was short, roundish and balding, with enormous ruddy cheeks and a bulbous nose to match. He wore a dark gray three-piece suit tailored to his unusual build. Despite his awkwardness, he moved with a surprising grace, which was unexpected for a man with such a full body type. Stanley Harris was the son of the late William Harris and had inherited the family business, showing as much, if not more, talent for it than his father had ever displayed. In the twelve years since his father's death, Stanley had built the funeral home into four times the operation it had been in his father's hands. His client base had quadrupled as he had driven three other funeral homes in the surrounding area out of business, leaving the William Harris Funeral Home as the only viable option for funeral services of all denominations in the county. It might not be pleasant work, and maybe that was what drove Stanley to the bottle and his wife to divorce court years ago, but it was extremely lucrative and that seemed to be enough to keep Stanley happy and in business.

"Alex, I'm so sorry," Stanley continued, his voice taking on the tone of the consoled funeral director. "I know you were close with Dr. Carlton. If there's anything I can help you with, please don't hesitate to ask."

"Thank you, I appreciate that," Alex replied, repressing a shudder. Alex knew Stanley Harris as a happy, friendly, easygoing type of guy from the few times he had interacted with him around town. This was the first time he had ever spoken to him in a professional capacity, and his voice seemed cold. Distant. Detached. There seemed to be a façade of caring wrapped around the man. Stanley no doubt had genuine feelings for the pain of his customers, but he had become so desensitized to it over the years that he reverted to the character he had created in order to distance himself from their pain on a personal level. In a way, it was sad, but also rather ironic that the man who had made mourning his life's work had lost the ability to truly mourn. Conversely, much like Babcock's insatiable curiosity, Alex supposed it could be considered a professional asset as well. Still, he wondered if Stanley Harris felt as if his soul were still intact.

"Is Dr. Tanner in her usual spot?" Babcock asked, gently trying to hurry the pleasantries along.

"Of course. In the basement, room number three. That's the biggest room we have, and she usually needs the extra space with all the equipment she brings along with her." Stanley paused, an almost inaudible sigh escaping him. "Good thing business is slow right now. Normally we can prepare two at once in that room, but with all of her things, we can't get any customers in there."

"The department appreciates your sacrifice, Stanley," Babcock replied, the slightest hint of sarcasm in his voice.

"Yes, I understand, and I'm not complaining. I'm always willing to do my civic duty. I'm just glad these types of things don't happen too often. You do not know what a backlog of work can be like in my business." Stanley chuckled at his own joke, his cheeks quivering like mating jellyfish. "Sorry, just a little joke. I get so little opportunity to exercise my sense of humor here at work. You understand, I'm sure."

"I get it. But if you'll excuse us, we really need to see Dr. Tanner." Babcock sounded hurried, a slight quiver of anxiousness in his voice, as if he were eager to get away from the cherubic funeral home director.

"Of course, of course. I'm so sorry to hold you up. I have a few things I need to attend to myself, now that you mention it. There are some people that are just dying to see me." Stanley laughed out loud at his joke and the jellyfish reached climax, shaking and quivering in the throes of their ecstasy. "Two jokes in one day, now there's a workday to remember. You two really should stop by more often."

"You'll have to forgive me if I decline the invitation," Alex replied, smiling slightly and feeling awkward for having done it.

"Oh my goodness, Alex! I am so sorry! Here you are hurting and I'm making jokes. I am truly so terribly sorry. All I ever see day in and day out around here is grief and death. It can get overwhelming, so I try to lighten things up from time to time. The more we laugh while we're alone here, the easier it becomes to deal with mourners when they arrive for services. I did get carried away in this instance, though, and I am so very sorry."

Stanley was apologizing hard, his demeanor somehow trapped and looping between his civilian happy-go-lucky self and the desensitized professional veneer his career demanded. It looked to Alex as if he might split either way at any second. Left with no more words of apology, the plump little man moved in and placed a hand on Alex's shoulder in a gesture of comfort, then gently squeezed to add a sense of friendly familiarity. At that moment, Alex may have been comforted by the man's practiced gesture if it had not been for the stale reek of alcohol on him. He wasn't drunk, but he wasn't a long way from it either. It was barely past breakfast now; Stanley had gotten an early start. Subtly, Alex pushed away from the man and his hundred and twenty proof breath.

"It's all right. Really, I understand. Pressures of business and everything. No worries. But Lieutenant Babcock is right, we need to see Dr. Tanner. Right now. Excuse me." Alex shouldered his way past Stanley to the hallway that led to the basement stairs, not bothering to check if Babcock was following. He stopped at the end of the hall just before a small brass sign engraved with 'Employees Only'. Babcock was still at the opposite end of the hall engaged in conversation with a very nervous-looking Stanley Harris, who occasionally shot a glance in his direction. Alex had shoved past Stanley as if he were being threatened, pushing him aside and rushing away from him in what would seem to be a blind panic. It made little sense. Stanley wasn't intimidating. Quite the opposite, in fact. Every time Alex had encountered the man in the past, he had been nothing but friendly and pleasant. Something had triggered him to run, though. Something he saw, or heard.

Or felt.

It was something he had felt. Just like with Babcock the night before. Without knowing he was doing it, some odd sense of his had reached out to the little mortician. But unlike the night before, he had somehow sensed the connection taking place and was able to pull away before being drawn in by it. Like a psychic early warning system.

Suddenly he felt dizzy, the surrounding hallway refusing to stand still. Closing his eyes, he leaned against the nearest wall for support. The wall felt warm on his back, which he thought was unusual. He thought everything in this place should have the same coldness as death. Bright bursts of color bounced around the inky blackness of the world behind his eyelids as he let the feeling of disorientation pass. Too much was happening at once. It was too much for one person to be expected to absorb and cope with without a few momentary lapses in judgement, reason, or sanity. He needed a few moments of quiet and solitude to take a few breaths and sort things out. Since yesterday, the world thrust him at breakneck speed into a situation he couldn't possibly comprehend. It had been continuous, one hit after another without a break, and he was exhausted.

Breath. In. Out. He felt the air filling and leaving his lungs. The bursts of color in the darkness of his closed eyes slowed and faded. He would be fine in a moment. Just needed a little rest. A brief break. That was a much tidier explanation than a psychic knee-jerk reaction. He breathed deeply a few more times and felt the knots in his stomach loosen. It was still a tangled mass of nerves in there, but at least he didn't feel like he was going to pass out now.

"You okay?"

Alex's eyes shot open, and he bolted upright, startled by the sudden intrusion of another voice in his internal dialogue. Babcock stood facing him, framed by sunlight streaming in from the window. If Alex hadn't gotten to know the burly cop over the last day, he would swear in that moment he looked positively angelic.

Alex waved one hand while rubbing the bridge of his nose with the other. "Yeah, I'm fine. Thanks. Just needed to rest for a sec, that's all. Catch my breath. Center myself a bit."

"And get away from Stanley," Babcock stated.

Alex sighed, looking back at where the little man had been before. "Yeah, that too, I suppose."

"He might seem a little strange to the untrained eye, but don't let that fool you. He *is* strange. His old man was as solid as they come. He had no problem letting the department use the facilities, even had a background in forensic medicine himself. Stanley just sees us as an inconvenient thorn in his business. But a thorn he has to put up with in accordance with his father's wishes, who had the foresight to add a right of usage for the department to his will as long as the business remained in his family. Like I said, solid as they come. Stanley tries to be polite and accommodating, but you can see the resentment in his eyes." Babcock gave a heavy sigh. He looked tired as well, having suffered the same sleep deprivation as Alex had, but the cop was no doubt more accustomed to it.

"Sometimes I miss his old man," he continued, blinking fatigue from his eyes. "At least he knew when to just shut up and get out of the way. And he knew when to lay off the joy juice."

"You noticed that too, huh?" Alex asked, feeling stupid about it. There was no way to not notice it.

"Yeah, I've gotten pretty good at it over the years. Occupational hazard. Stanley's drinking was never a problem in the past, but you never know about the future. One of these days, he's going to take it too far at the wrong time and either get killed, kill someone else, or get sued out of business. So much for the old man's legacy." Babcock rubbed the bridge of his nose, mimicking Alex from just a moment ago. "But enough about the Harris family history. You ready?" He motioned to the door with the engraved brass plate.

"Yeah, just one more second," Alex replied, his stomach again constricting into a tangle of knots.

Babcock moved to him, placing a hand on his arm. "Maybe this wasn't such a good idea. Look, Alex, you don't have to do this. I can go down there myself and get the information from Dr. Tanner. We can get out of here and compare notes someplace else."

Alex closed his eyes and shook his head, bursts of color brightening again for the briefest of moments like fireworks against the sky of a summer night. "No, I need to see this though. It's not the body down there that's bothering me. Or finding out what Dr. Tanner has to say. It's something else. I haven't figured out what that is yet, but I can do this." He straightened up, running his fingers through his thick black hair, immediately taking in and letting out a deep breath.

Babcock's intense stare cut into him. "If you're sure. But if you need to leave for any reason, do it. There's no shame in it."

Alex nodded. Babcock pushed open the thick wooden door, which didn't creak menacingly as Alex thought it might, and descended the stairs. Taking one more sharp, deep breath, Alex followed.

The stairwell was surprisingly well lit and painted the same neutral beige as the rooms upstairs. It was cheerier than Alex thought it had any right to be. As they approached the bottom step, the sting of chemicals assaulted Alex's nose, causing his face to twitch. He pushed the air from his lungs to exorcise the odors assailing him, but they returned with each intake of breath. He coughed lightly, placing his hand over his nose and mouth to ward off the smells.

Babcock chuckled slightly. "You'll get used to it. And this smell is nothing compared to what you get when you cut into somebody. Trust me. We've lost more cadets in the academy to that than anything else. One whiff and they're flat on the floor, stiffer than the corpse."

"If I remember correctly, Ernie, weren't you one of those guys?"

Alex came around the corner to see a woman emerging from a pair of stainless-steel doors. She was small, no taller than five feet, wearing surgical scrubs and stripping off a latex glove as she approached. She had a nearly flawless olive complexion with only a few visible wrinkles and eyes so dark it was hard to discern the pupil from the iris. A few tufts of salt and pepper hair, the only outward sign that she may be a few years Babcock's senior, poked out from beneath the surgical cap stretched over her head.

"That's what I like about you, Celeste; you keep me honest." Babcock grinned widely and wrapped his thick arms around the tiny woman, completely engulfing her in his embrace. The entire upper half of her body disappeared into the hug.

"Well, somebody needs," Dr. Tanner replied, returning his hug. Her arms were like two thin vines encircling a redwood.

Babcock released her and turned, indicating Alex. "Celeste, this is Alex Carter. The one I told you about."

"Of course. A pleasure to meet you. Circumstances aside." Dr. Tanner extended her hand.

Alex grasped her hand, impressed by the grip she had in relation to her size. "It's a pleasure to meet you as well, doctor. Circumstances notwithstanding."

"I was hoping you might give us some answers. We've stumbled on something pretty mysterious here," she said, turning back toward the stainless-steel doors.

"Seems to be the buzzword of the day," Alex muttered as he fell into step behind her.

Dr. Tanner turned back to him. "Excuse me?" She appeared genuinely confused.

Babcock intervened, shooting Alex a wary glance. "It's complicated, Celeste. I'll lay it all out for you later. In the meantime, tell us what you found."

"Of course. After all, if there's one thing I've learned in my years in this business, it's that when cops don't want to talk about something, you can't force the issue." Her voice was thick with sarcasm and tinged with a bit of resentment. She was all business again when turning back to Alex. "Do you have a weak stomach, Mr. Carter?"

Alex shrugged. "Not particularly. Why?"

"I want you to be prepared for what you're going to see in there. It's not pleasant, as Ernie has pointed out. What he didn't get into were the details." She turned to face him fully, subtly closing the gap between them. "I think you need to know precisely what condition your friend is in before we proceed."

Alex met her gaze, her dark eyes drilling into his. "She wasn't my friend. She was my psychologist."

"Still, you knew her, and that makes a difference. You knew what she was like before she died. " She hesitated and averted her eyes, her stance softening. "Listen, I'm not trying to frighten you, but these are the facts. When performing an autopsy, the doctor, in this case, me, needs to have everything accessible. That means opening the body up to expose as much of the interior as possible. To do that, we make a y-shaped incision ranging from the shoulders to the sternum to the pubis. From there, we can pull the flesh back, remove the ribcage and proceed. That's the condition of the woman in there right now. She is lying naked on a cold metal slab with her insides exposed to the world. She has been poked and prodded, and I'm not finished." Allowing that to sink in for a moment, she continued. "Do you think you can handle that?"

Alex wasn't certain he could. Not after watching her die in his arms last night. Not after seeing her face again this morning and listening to her voice as she talked about her part in the series of betrayals that had been his life. For so many reasons, he had no desire to see what was beyond the double stainless doors looming behind the doctor. But he didn't really have much of a choice. There were so many questions still unanswered, and he needed every shred of information he could get to protect his family.

"If not, you and the good Lieutenant will be the first to know," he said lightly, trying to hide the trepidation he was feeling.

Dr. Tanner held his gaze firmly for a moment, her dark eyes boring into him, before shrugging and saying, "Suit yourself. I just wanted you to know what you were getting into."

A supply tray sat by the door. Dr. Tanner removed two filtration masks and handed one each to Alex and Babcock. "Take these and put them on. They're lined with a potent scent, like mild ammonia. It's powerful, but you'll appreciate it once we get inside. Trust me. Humans don't smell so good on the inside."

"A lot of 'em don't smell so great on the outside," Babcock muttered, putting on the mask.

Alex slid the paper mask over his mouth and nose as Babcock had. Instantly, he was hit by the strong ammonia smell Dr. Tanner had warned them about. It burned the back of his nose and throat and he felt as if he might gag, but a hearty cough suppressed that. After another hard cough, he lifted the mask away from his face and breathed in the stinging chemical air again, which he found oddly refreshing compared to the smell in the mask. Subconsciously, he wondered if the burning in his throat would ever go away.

A sly smile crossed Dr. Tanner's face. She didn't mention his reaction, instead politely sliding a mask on to her own face. She pushed open one of the steel doors and gestured inside, saying, "This way, gentlemen."

Upon entering the room, the first thing that struck Alex wasn't the smell, it was the intense brightness of the space. Two surgical lamps burned like twin suns over the steel embalming table that doubled as an autopsy table. The white walls reflected that glare like a blanket of fresh snow on a sunny day, effectively blinding him momentarily. He closed his eyes, blunting the impact of the glare and allowing them a moment to adjust.

When he opened his eyes, the scene was exactly as Dr. Tanner described it. He saw Dr. Carlton, naked and laid out directly beneath the surgical lamps. Her eyes were closed and there was a look of peace on her face that Alex might have found comforting had his eyes not wandered away from it and to her body. The incisions started at either shoulder, met in the middle of her chest and proceeded along her body before finally terminating just above her crotch. It was held open by clamps that Alex was certain had a technical name but didn't really care much about at that moment. The examiner had removed several organs and placed them on a tray next to the autopsy table.

He turned away, bile rising in the back of his throat as his stomach rebelled at the sight. He felt dizzy; the room wobbling uncontrollably around him. Or maybe it was his legs that were wobbling, he couldn't tell. A utility cart stood nearby, and he grasped at it for support, edging a tray of surgical instruments from it and sending them skittering across the floor in a whirling, glinting rush that only added to his nausea. His eyes clouded, and the room closed in on itself as he felt his shaky knees finally give way beneath him, sending him to the floor. Closing his traitorous eyes, he sat where he was for a moment, still grasping the leg of the utility cart to ground himself. Shielded by his closed eyes, he was at least unaware of the spinning world around him, but the comforting darkness soon gave way to new terrors.

Despite having his eyes firmly squeezed shut, an image formed in front of him. Three men, doctors, standing over the bloodied corpse of a young woman. Her face was beaten brutally. Blood and fluids leaked from her eyes, nose, mouth, and ears, leaving her midnight black hair matted and streaked with blood. Alex winced in pain at the sight of her right arm, twisted at a grotesque angle, undoubtedly broken in at least six places to bend in such a way. There was nothing remaining but a ragged stump where her left leg had been, as if someone had viciously torn it off. Her torso displayed a mass of purple and black bruises, horribly swollen, suggesting internal bleeding and the accumulation of fluids within her distended flesh. Alex tried to scream at the horror he was witnessing, a horror that had once been a beautiful young woman, but found he couldn't. Rooted to the spot, unable to speak or move, he was helpless to do anything except watch as the doctors casually poked at her, their faces completely devoid of expression at the loss of the vital young life in front of them. They circled her remains, pointing and poking and scribbling notes in a notebook, completely oblivious to the brutality of what had happened to her.

"Alex!"

His name. Someone was calling his name. Except that wasn't his name. Was it? Not then. His name now, but not then. If not then, what was his then-name? Why was someone calling his now-name if this was then? Why didn't they use his then-name?

Suddenly there was a loud crack and a sharp pain exploded in his face, dispelling the scene before him. The doctors and the corpse of the young woman exploded into the ether as Alex was shocked back into the present. Babcock was leaning over him, shaking him and shouting his name. Alex. That was his name. It wasn't always his name, but that was what he answered to now. It would do.

Seeing awareness returning to Alex's eyes, Babcock grabbed him under the armpits to help him to his feet. "Sorry about the slap, kid. You okay?"

Alex paused, the fog in his brain dissipating as reality reasserted itself. "Yeah, I think so. What just happened here?"

"Why don't you tell us?" Dr. Tanner replied, her voice pitched high. "One minute we're talking and the next you're mumbling about doctors and blood before passing out! What's going on?" She spun to face Babcock. "I think I need an explanation."

Alex stood on wavering legs, Babcock standing by in case they gave out completely. He thought about what he had just seen, trying to focus on details that would help answer Dr. Tanner's questions, but his memories of what he had seen were already fading like a bad dream. It was as if his mind was purging them to maintain his sanity. All he could remember was the image of the battered and brutalized young woman on the table and the expressionless faces of the surrounding doctors. He struggled to maintain the image in his head, focusing on the woman's face. And then it hit him. The black hair. The brown eyes. High cheekbones on a slender face. It was uncanny, her resemblance to him. Like she could be his sister.

A shudder grasped him as the thought raced through his mind. Was that the reason for his amnesia? Was his mind trying to protect him from some traumatic family event, like the horrible death of a sister? Or mother? Was that why he had no memory of his family? Had it all been taken from him as a defense against some dark past?

"I need some air," he announced, pulling away from Babcock and pushing past Dr. Tanner. Slamming through the steel double doors, he felt relief leaving the glaring lights of the embalming room, with its smell of chemical death, behind him. Once out in the hall and away from the corpse of Dr. Carlton, he doubled over and braced his hands against his knees. He could feel his stomach rebelling and breathed deeply to thwart it, but the breath filled his lungs with the dry sweetness of baby powder, causing him to gag again. Tearing the mask from his face, he threw it to the floor and took another deep breath, but this was almost worse as the air still reeked of harsh chemicals. His lungs burned, but that seemed to have taken the attention from his rebellious stomach, so that was a plus. At the far end of the hall was a door with an exit sign glowing above it. He didn't know where it would lead him, but he was certain it had to be better than where he was at the moment.

As he opened the door, a blast of frigid air greeted him, hitting him in the face, slapping him awake far more effectively than Babcock's physical blow had done. He breathed deeply, saturating his beleaguered lungs with cold air. He would have thought of it as intoxicating, except it had the opposite in that it cleared his head instead of clouding it. The fog was lifting and clear thought was returning, but it was taking the memories he had just experienced with it as well. By the time Babcock emerged from the exit door, the memories had almost completely faded from his mind.

"Are you gonna be okay?" the detective asked, sidling up to Alex as he removed the filtration mask from his face. He breathed deeply, relishing the cold, fresh air as much as Alex had a moment ago.

Alex nodded slightly. "I think so. As okay as I can be, I suppose."

Babcock pulled a small cigar from his inside coat pocket. "You mind?"

"Kinda, yeah," Alex replied, added, "But after today I'm not going to deny you small pleasures. After all, they're your lungs."

Babcock bit the tip off the cigar and spat it out in the nearby grass. "You sound like my kids."

"Then you must have extraordinarily brilliant children," Alex retorted, sliding away slightly from the detective as he searched for a light.

From his jacket pocket, Babcock produced an old-school book of matches. "I do," he said, lighting the match and holding it to the tip of the cigar. The end flamed up and then died down to a dull orange glow, a wisp of bluish-gray smoke emitting from the tip. "Although you look like you could benefit from one of these yourself at the moment."

Alex followed Babcock's eyes to his own hands, which were shaking vigorously. He quickly thrust the unruly appendages into his jacket pockets.

"Must be the cold."

Babcock smiled. "Must be." He sucked on the cigar, the end going from a dull orange to a blaze of the color. From his nose came two plumes of gray smoke, staining the pure white of his crystallized breath. "You want to tell me what happened in there?"

Alex stared down at his feet, which were shuffling nervously. "I wish I knew."

"Can you tell me what you saw, at least?" Babcock said, placing the cigar between his lips and again inhaling hard, lighting up the tip.

"Not much. It's pretty well faded already." He paused, wanting to say more as much as the detective wanted to hear it. "It was... gruesome."

"How's that?" Babcock asked, his voice unwavering.

"There was a young woman, not much more than a girl, really. It's fuzzy, but she... She had been completely torn apart. Literally. It was horrifying. And the worst part was her face. She looked like she could be related to me. A sister, or a cousin, or something. But that wasn't the worst of it."

Babcock blew out more plumes of gray and white. "What was?"

Alex shuddered uncontrollably, wrapping his arms around himself. "I felt somehow as if I was responsible for it."

Babcock stopped, the cigar bouncing limply from between his lips. "What do you mean? That you killed her?"

Was that what he had felt? That he had killed her? The memory was almost completely reabsorbed into the murky darkness of his subconscious. He was hesitant to go chasing after it, even to be certain of such a vital piece of information. For now, it was another mystery that would have to remain a mystery.

His eyes fell to his feet once more, and he shrugged. "I'm not sure what I mean."

The reply hung between them for a moment, neither of them sure what to say next. It ceased to be a problem as the door behind them swung open and Dr. Tanner emerged into the chilly morning air.

"How are you holding up, Mr. Carter?"

"I'll be okay. Just a passing thing, I suppose." He took his gaze from the ground to meet the doctor's. "And please, call me Alex."

"Very well, Alex it is." Dr. Tanner cleared her throat before continuing, and when she did, her voice was softer. "I owe you an apology. I shouldn't have been so graphic with you before you went in. While I wanted to prepare you for what you were going to see, I'm sorry for setting you up for such a reaction."

"No need to apologize. Really, Doctor, it wasn't anything you said or did. It was...." Alex trailed off, looking to Babcock for support. The big cop shrugged. "It was something else entirely."

"Something you're not going to tell me about," she replied, the harder edge coming back into her voice.

Alex shook his head. "At the moment, I think that's for the best."

Dr. Tanner breathed a heavy sigh, her breath billowing in a great white cloud that quickly dissolved into the early morning air. "I suppose I'll have to live with that. For now. But I have to tell you, I am really looking forward to an explanation for all of this."

"Celeste, have I ever let you down before?" Babcock asked, dropping the remaining stub of his cigar to the ground and stomping it out.

She gave him a sideways glance. "Don't even tempt me into answering that, Ernie."

Babcock placed a hand over his heart, a mock look of indignation crossing his face. "Celeste, I'm hurt."

"Good, you deserve it," she replied, turning her attention away from Babcock and back to Alex. "There was a reason I called the two of you here and it wasn't to act as your support group. Alex, do you think you're up to going back in there?"

"I should be okay now, knowing what I'm walking into." There was confidence in his voice, but it didn't translate to how he was feeling. He had no idea if the same thing would happen. Or worse. But he kept those thoughts to himself.

"Well then, shall we try this again then, gentlemen? Either way, I am freezing my ass off out here, so I am going back inside." Before either of them could comment, the doctor disappeared through the entrance.

"Lovely woman," Alex said, watching the door close behind her.

"Hey, at least you caught her on a good day," Babcock said, pulling the door open and slipping his huge frame inside.

Once again, Alex found himself alone in the cold with his thoughts. He sighed a heavy sigh, his crystalized breath vanishing in the morning air.

"What have you gotten yourself into?"

Fearing a reply to his question, he quickly ducked back into the warm, odoriferous air inside.

****

"As you can see, it isn't organic."

Alex barely heard Dr. Tanner as he turned the small glass tube over and over in his hands, watching the tiny piece of metal within spiral around with each turn. The object was about half the size of a grain of rice and was shiny and smooth, with no visible markings. He had no idea what he was looking at or what it might have been doing inside Dr. Carlton.

"And where did you find it again, Celeste?" Babcock asked, leaning close over Alex's shoulder to get a look at the object.

"At the base of her spine. Here." She tapped Alex's back, just above his buttocks, at the spot where his spine ended. "How it got there is anyone's guess. It could have been from an accident. My guess is it was placed there intentionally. Most likely injected or implanted surgically."

"Could you find any evidence of that?" Babcock inquired, turning his full attention to the Medical Examiner.

"I doubt it," she replied. "Injections rarely leave any noticeable scars, and the surgical implantation would have been done laparoscopically, leaving very little traceable scarring. I'll check, of course, but I wouldn't count on finding anything conclusive. Someone purposefully made it difficult to detect."

Babcock scratched his face, his fingers rasping against the three-day stubble. "Any idea what it was used for?"

Alex spoke up first, almost hypnotized by the glint and motion of the small metallic object encased in the glass he was holding. "I think it was used to introduce something into her system. Some foreign agent. A virus, or something like that." Setting the glass tube on the tray next to the embalming table, he turned to face the others. "Dr. Tanner, you said your autopsy found that she died as the natural progression of her disease?"

Dr. Tanner nodded. "Yes, that's correct."

"Are you absolutely certain of that?" Alex asked.

The question elicited a confused look from the doctor. "I sent various tissue samples to the state lab for confirmation. They're supposed to check for signs of nerve and muscular degeneration, which would confirm my diagnosis. I'll know more when I get that report." She paused, her eyes falling to the glass tube containing the mystery object. "But that was before I stumbled on this. And whatever secret the two of you are keeping. My diagnosis certainly fits with her medical history, but now I just don't know anymore."

"I'm sorry to keep you in the dark like this, Dr. Tanner. I have a theory." He paused, glancing between the detective and the doctor. "It's pretty wild, though."

"Wild or not, I'm sure it's better than anything we've got so far," Dr. Tanner replied, indicating herself and Babcock.

"Don't be so sure until you hear it," Alex replied, his stomach once more dancing wildly in his gut as he thought about what he was about to say. It was outlandish and insane, but given the events of the last few days, it was also the only thing that made any sense to him. "I don't believe Dr. Carlton's disease was actually genetic. At least not in the sense that she inherited it at birth. I think someone introduced it into her system from an external source." He stopped and looked down at the small metal object beside him. "Possibly by injection."

Dr. Tanner stood motionless for a moment, as if she were still absorbing his statement. After a few seconds, she shot a look at Babcock before turning back to Alex. "That does kind of qualify you for the Tin Foil Hat Society." She paused, taking a moment to look over the body of Dr. Carlton and the glass-encased metal object that had been removed from her body. "But, given the evidence we have, it does kind of fit. But I can't think of a single virus or nerve agent that would do this to a person as slowly as this one has."

"And why would it conveniently kill her now when she was so coincidentally about to help you out?" Babcock interjected. "That's an awfully intelligent virus."

"I think that's where this came into play," Alex stated, grabbing up the glass vial containing the metallic grain of rice. "I think this disease or condition or whatever it is was a warning to her. A warning that she needed to fall in line with whatever her benefactors were telling her to do. I think her condition was a punishment for trying to help me years ago. I think at the same time they gave her the condition, however they did it, they also introduced this capsule into her body as insurance. A second dose of the virus, lying dormant, waiting for someone to push the right button to release it." Alex paused, his eyes moving to Dr. Carlton's body. "Which is what they did yesterday. They found out she was trying to help me again and they killed her. She was trying to get information to me and they killed her for it. She said it was something important, something about my past. Something that was worth destroying a life to keep secret." He turned to Babcock and Dr. Tanner, who had been silent throughout his explanation. "Well?"

Dr. Tanner shrugged. "I don't know what to say. As far-fetched as it sounds, and it sounds way far-fetched, with the evidence we have so far, it's a credible theory. But intentionally injecting a communicable virus into someone? People will notice an outbreak, it's not exactly easy to keep a low profile."

Alex pondered that for a moment. "What if there was no chance of anyone else catching this disease? What if Dr. Carlton was the only person susceptible to it?"

The edge of Dr. Tanner's filtration mask moved slightly, and Alex imagined the look of concern on her face beneath it. "A target-specific virus? That's science fiction. Coding for a single specific target would require extensive gene mapping and then you would have to re-engineer a virus to suit that person's individual genetic code. If the first is improbable, then the second is impossible. Sure, we've developed gene therapies for cancer treatments and the like, but even those are targeting generic DNA of diseased cells. There is enough commonality to make the treatments more generic. And the results are still far from perfect. What you're suggesting would go so far beyond that. It would take massive amounts of time, experimentation and, of course, money, that the effort would far outweigh any potential gains. After all the investment, what are they going to get? The ability to kill a single person? Maybe a family, depending on how they engineer the thing? It's just not worth the effort."

"What it would give them," Alex countered, "is the ability to kill any person they want at any time without arousing suspicion. Think about it, a genetic time bomb attached to the right senator or congressman or even the President. The simple push of a button or flick of a switch, your troubles with that person are over. And it's absolutely untraceable." He held out the glass vial with the metal capsule. "Unless you know what you're looking for."

"What you're suggesting would require a lot of capital to finance," Dr. Tanner stated. "I mean, we're talking about hundreds of millions of dollars just to develop the thing. Not to mention the fact that there are about six people on the surface of the planet that could pull it off." She sighed and rubbed the back of her neck, throwing her head back to stretch the tensed muscles there. "It's just not feasible. But it makes for a fun theory."

"But is it possible?" Alex pressed.

"I just told you..."

Alex cut her off. "Okay, but let's say some mysterious assailant has infinite resources. They have the money, the materials and have managed to find one of those rare people with the know-how. Could it be done?"

Dr. Tanner glared at him. "First off, don't cut me off." Her face softened as she paused, letting the idea bounce around her head. "Theoretically?"

Alex nodded, a bit sheepishly. "Yes. Theoretically."

She sighed. "Yes, it's possible. But it stretches that theory beyond all scientific creditability to the breaking point and beyond."

A name suddenly jumped to the forefront of Alex's memory. "Does the name Elliot Forrester mean anything to you?"

"Dr. Elliot Forrester?" Dr. Tanner's face shrank around the corners of her surgical mask, noting a hidden expression of surprise. "He's a scientist. A...." She paused as the impact of what she was about to say sank in. "A geneticist, actually. He had some crazy idea about how to manipulate the human genome. For the betterment of humanity, he claimed. Even talked about being able to create life, intelligent human life, from nothing more than an aberrant collection of DNA. They laughed him out of all credible scientific circles."

Alex glanced at Babcock, a scowl spreading beneath his own mask. Dr. Elliot Forrester was a name given to him in Dr. Carlton's last message. One of the names of people who might be able to help him uncover his past. The confirmation that he was a geneticist gave greater credibility to his theory of genetic homicide.

Babcock broke his silence. "You wouldn't have any idea where he is now, would you, Celeste?"

Dr. Tanner shook her head. "No. I haven't heard anything about him since his theories were... harshly debunked. He probably took some private sector job. Some companies will fund anyone if they think there's some profit in their research."

"That's okay, Celeste," Babcock said, gently squeezing her shoulder with a meaty hand. "Thanks. We owe you."

"Anything for you, Ernie. You know that." She patted his hand gently. "I don't suppose I get to know what's going on at this point?"

"Not just yet, Doctor," Alex said, extending his hand to her. "But thank you for all of your help. You've given us a place to start, at least."

She grasped his outstretched hand and shook with a hard, firm grip. "My pleasure. Just do me a favor and don't forget about me when you can finally talk about this thing, okay?"

Alex smiled. "It's a deal." He glanced back at the body of Dr. Carlton on the table. "And thank you for taking care of her."

"Of course," she replied quietly. "If what you think is true, I hope you can bring these bastards to justice."

Babcock's grin was so obvious on his wide face that the mask almost slipped off when he smiled. "That's my job. And if I'm going to do it, we need to get out of here."

"Right," Alex replied. "Thanks again, Doctor."

"Just one more thing," Dr. Tanner stated. "How the hell am I supposed to put all this in my report?"

22

"That's Dr. Hendrie's office. He's the best dentist in town."

The server from The Bagel Stable, whom Adam had learned was named Jackie, pointed to a house across the street. "He used to be the only dentist in town until last year, when Dr. Robbs and Dr. Hodkins opened up. They're nice enough and all, but they're so young. I swear Dr. Robbs isn't much older than me, hardly old enough to be out of dentist school. And Dr. Hodkins, well, something about the way he looks at me gives me the creeps. You know how some people do that to you for no good reason? They've never done anything to offend you or anything, but you just don't ever want to be left alone in a room with them. Especially under anesthetic."

Adam smiled and nodded in agreement as she spoke, pretending to be attentive but not really caring at all about what she was saying. It wasn't going to be any different from anything she had blathered on about for the last three hours, anyway. Since they had left The Bagel Stable together, she had gone on about the town and her life in it, none of which had any interest to him. He was thinking her company wasn't worth the trouble.

"And this is Lake View Drive," she announced, coming to a stop. Adam continued walking past her, nodding his head, not realizing initially that she had stopped. He halted and looked up at her, feigning a look of embarrassment.

"Sorry about that," he lied. "Guess my mind was elsewhere at the moment. Did you say this was Lake View Drive?"

She pointed to the sign above his head and he craned his neck around to get a look at it. It did indeed say Lake View Drive. He was here. He was so close now. She was nearby, he could almost feel it. Rachel. Surveying the homes that lined the street, he wondered which one she lived in. Which one had been her prison. He would find it, and tonight he would take her away from her life of misery. And if the pretender was there, he would kill him. Without hesitation and without mercy, but not without some level of satisfaction.

"Hey, Earth to Adam! Can you hear me?"

Jackie again. Her voice was seemingly shriller than it had been even a moment ago. She had been useful to him in finding Rachel, but no more so than a GPS. Her usefulness had come to an end. Almost. There was still one more thing she could do for him. If she would do it willingly, all the better. If not, well, the Project had seen to it that he could be very persuasive when required.

"I guess I'll be going now. It was fun showing you around. I hope you enjoy your visit." Her face had taken on a pouty look as she said goodbye, yet still managed a smile. She was flirting with him, trying to tempt him. He smiled back. This was going to be even easier than he'd hoped.

"You aren't going yet, are you? It's still early and they aren't expecting me until later. I thought we could....." He paused, creating a space for her to fill, confident that she would respond in his favor.

"You thought maybe we could what?" she replied, her gaze softening, her voice turning low and breathy.

He responded in kind. "Oh, I don't know. It's just that I've really enjoyed your company. I'd hate for you to leave now. I feel like we've only just scratched the surface of each other."

Her eyes were alight with potential now. "I suppose there's something we could do. Listen, I've got a bottle of wine in the fridge at my place. I live right next to Holmand Park. You'll love it. It's beautiful. We'll sit under the trees and drink wine and you can tell me all about yourself, okay? And then....." She took a step towards him, her finger lightly brushing against his chest. "Well, who knows what happens then. I guess we'll just have to wait and see."

She winked then, and an odd shudder of excitement ran through him. She was turning out to be very interesting, after all. Passionate, exciting, full of life. She would be able to supply him with everything he needed. Then he would be ready for what he needed to do tonight.

Tonight, he took back his life.

23

Alex nibbled slightly on half of a turkey sandwich; his appetite was practically non-existent after his experience at the morgue. It wasn't the morgue itself or even seeing Dr. Carlton splayed out the way she was. It was the visions. The terrible visions that plagued him. The thought that maybe he had actually done those horrible things. But Babcock had treated him to lunch, even over his strenuous objections, so he attempted to eat in an effort not to offend the detective.

"Okay," Babcock said through a mouthful of pastrami as he flipped through the pages of his small, worn notebook, "let's see where we stand. We have one dead psychiatrist, who we suspect was murdered with a smart virus. Before she died, she left a video message and files of information, along with a few key names. Since then, one of those names, a geneticist, has come up in conversation about the aforementioned smart virus." He flipped back to a previous page. "And let's not forget about these funky dreams and waking visions of yours with the murderous yuppie. And our little shared 'experience' at the dead psychiatrist's house." He paused, taking an audible gulp from the mammoth cup of coffee next to him. "Have I missed anything?"

"That's my life, welcome to it," Alex replied, taking a sip from his Diet Pepsi. The drink was larger than Babcock's coffee by far, which is to say that the U.S. Navy could conduct training exercises in it and still leave room for the U.S. Olympic synchronized swim team to practice. Glancing down at his sandwich, he noticed he had absently eaten almost a third of it, yet it looked as if there were still a sandwich and a half remaining. Babcock had suggested that place for lunch because it was a favorite hang-out of cops for years now, and because the food was apparently great. Alex had to concede to that last point, the food was great, but he couldn't imagine anyone being able to eat that much in one sitting. He wondered if having a voracious appetite was a prerequisite for becoming a cop.

"Thanks, but no thanks. From what I've seen so far, your life isn't the most pleasant place to visit right now. I certainly wouldn't want to live there." The detective pushed back from the table, the thin legs of the plastic chair screeching loudly against the tile floor. "I'm going to get a cookie. They have the best chocolate chip cookies here. Six inches across if they're an inch and baked right here twice a day. You want one?"

"No thanks, I'm having enough trouble with my sandwich." Alex put down the half of he had been nibbling on. "I seem to have lost my appetite. Besides, I thought you guys were all about the doughnuts."

"Usually, yeah, but I've always been a somewhat unorthodox cop." He stood, hauling his massive frame out of the almost comically small chair. "Don't worry about the appetite. It'll come back. Trust me."

Alex looked away from the food. The very thought of it made his stomach churn. "What do you mean?"

"I mean, you'll get over it. A little loss of appetite is expected after the first trip to the morgue. Celeste wasn't kidding about recruits losing their lunch the first time. Happened to me. Right after lunch that day. Lost it all over the floor. I'm sad to say it, but you get used to it after a while. I wish we didn't have to, but it becomes routine." He slapped Alex on the back. "What I'm saying is, you'll forget about it. And even if you don't forget it, after a while it'll fade."

"That's the thing, though," Alex said, his mind once again tiptoeing through the fields of memory. "I don't feel like this was my first trip to a morgue. Almost like it was a place I was familiar with. Intimately."

Babcock sat back down, his cookie craving momentarily forgotten. "What do you mean, 'familiar with'?"

"Like I've spent a lot of time there. Not there, as in the funeral home basement, but someplace like it. Someplace cold. Sterile. Reeking of sanitizing chemicals and decay. And blood. I can't imagine ever being in a place like that but, I don't know, there was just something so damned familiar about it." Alex's mouth was suddenly dry, and he reached for the Diet Pepsi, gulping down just short of half the enormous cup without a breath. Placing the cup back on the table, he noticed a slight tremble in his hand. His vision went blurry at the edges and he felt foggy, but at the same time sharper and more aware than he had ever been before. The world spun around him, moving at a breakneck pace. Yet he could discern certain things, certain people. Babcock. The clerk behind the counter cutting a sandwich. The other patrons were caught up in the world's blur, as if they weren't important enough to take notice of. His muscles tensed as sounds, smells, and feelings assailed him. It was a cacophony of sensory information, setting his nerves on fire.

Babcock's voice cut through to him. "You okay, kid? You look pale. Do you feel like you could use some air?"

It was then that Alex felt someone touch his shoulder and his world exploded.

He bolted up from his seat, sending the plastic chair careening across the tile floor with a loud clatter. In one fluid movement he turned, grabbed Babcock's wrist and twisted it savagely until the angle forced the cop to turn with the momentum or have his hand snapped clean off. The cop's face became a mask of pain as he fell to his knees, Alex's grip like a vise.

"Alex, what the fuck are you....." The sentence was cut short by a scream as Alex jerked the Lieutenant's arm back further, sending jagged waves of pain shooting through his shoulder and down his back. He didn't know what Alex was doing to him, but he knew it shouldn't hurt this much. It felt as if he knew exactly which nerve to squeeze to cause the most pain in the most efficient way.

A low growl escaped Alex's lips and Babcock pushed through the haze of pain to see the look on his face. A mask of naked aggression stared back at him, a twisted vision of anger, hatred and fear. Three things that, when mixed, could create an explosive combination.

Alex leaned into him while keeping the pressure on his arm even. When he spoke, his words were half growls and Babcock felt like someone was running a cheese grater down his spine. The voice was gravelly, deep and rough, and was unlike anything he had heard from Alex in the brief time he had known him.

"I told you never to touch me again."

"Alex," Babcock choked out through the pain, "please, you have to let me go. This has to end before someone gets hurt. Or worse."

"Shut up!" Alex yelled, his voice raising an octave like a child having a tantrum. His eyes shot wildly around the room, landing on the other patrons as they cowered in fear. "You're all against me! Right from the beginning! You wanted me dead! You never wanted any of us to live!" His attention shifted back to Babcock, the wild look in his eyes narrowing into one of pure, blind rage. The icy ball of fear that had been gathering in the detective's stomach exploded, sending chilling shards throughout his body. Less from the pain and more from the realization that he was going to have to stop Alex.

Alex spoke again, his tone calmer but still keeping the same dangerous edge as before. Like the fires of hell were crackling just inside him, trying to leap out from their confines and consume the world.

"I won't end up like the others. I won't let you do to me what you did to them. They never saw it coming, just followed like blind lambs to the slaughter. I won't go to slaughter! Do you hear me? You'll have to hunt me down to get rid of me. I want a life. I want to live! You owe me that, damn you! You owe that to me! And no matter what I have to do, who I have to go through, I'll see that I get it." His grip tightened on Babcock's wrist, sending new shockwaves of pain cascading through the detective's body.

A dark shadow encroached on the edge of the detective's vision. To get rid of it, he shook his head sharply. He couldn't pass out now, there was no telling what Alex would do to the other patrons if he were unconscious. He had to stop the kid, but first he had to escape the iron grip Alex had on him. There was no hope of physically breaking free. Alex's grip was unbelievably strong, and he had Babcock's arm torqued in such a way that any attempt to escape would cause a dislocated shoulder. At the very least. His only hope was in talking to Alex, getting him to see reason.

"Alex? Alex, it's me. It's Ernie. Listen, I don't know what's going on, but I know you need help. And I'm going to help you. I swear I am, but I can't do that like this. Please let me go so we can discuss this and get you the help you need." Babcock's voice had the commanding tone of an experienced police officer, but it was decidedly tinged with pain and a touch of fear.

In response, Alex gave the detective's wrist a slight yet sharp twist, and Babcock's world threatened to go black again. He grimaced, unable to suppress a slight grunt of pain as he twisted his body slightly to compensate for the pressure on him. It helped to clear the haze of pain from his vision, but not by much.

"You're lying!" Alex shouted; his face contorted into a mask of rage. "We're nothing to you! The rats in your lab are more important to you than we are!"

Babcock was getting desperate. By now, someone must have called 911. If the police arrived at this scene, it was going to escalate beyond control and end badly. Very badly.

Suddenly it hit him, through the pain and the noise. A way to strike a nerve with Alex. To make a connection. A verbal slap in the face to bring him back to reality.

"Alex, think about Rachel."

Alex's face went slack at the mention of his wife's name, slowly transforming from a crunched bundle of rage back into the calm, innocent face Babcock had met a few days ago. His grip, however, remained painfully firm.

"Rachel?" Alex stated, his face trance-like.

Babcock shook his head to push back the darkening gray at the edges of his vision. It was a battle he was losing. "Yes, Rachel. Your wife. The mother of your baby. Think about them. You need to be there for them. You can't bail now. Come back to them." The gray darkened a shade more. "They need you. Please."

Just as the black cloud swirling at the edge of his vision threatened to consume Babcock, Alex released his grip on the cop's arm. The detective crumpled to the floor, cradling his wounded arm and catching his breath.

Awareness returned fully to Alex as shock and disbelief overtook his face. "Oh, God! Oh Jesus, I am so sorry! Oh my God, oh my God..."

Alex reached out to help Babcock up, but the detective instinctively shrank away from him and took on a defensive posture. Hurt and confused, Alex pulled back his hand as the detective got himself up from the floor.

"Oh man. Oh shit. I could have hurt you. But how? How could I have hurt you? How did I do that?" Alex's words were all over the place as his conscious mind tried to comprehend what his unconscious had just done. Thoughts of rage and anger still clung to him, mixing with the anxiety and uncertainty over what had just occurred. He felt as if the final shreds of his sanity were falling away.

Turning away from Babcock's hard gaze didn't help him, either, as he met the eyes of the other patrons of the restaurant that had just been witness to his outburst of violence. Their looks of sheer terror made him want to run, to escape his insanity, but he couldn't move. Their fearful yet accusatory eyes froze him in place. Of all the things that had happened to him in the last few days, he hadn't really been a threat to anyone but himself. But now he had hurt another person. Worse, it was one of the few people in the world willing to help him right now.

"Dear God," he muttered to no one in particular, "what is happening to me?"

The question hung in the air, greeted by silence.

24

Adam breathed deeply of the sweet, fresh air, stirred gently by a light breeze that ruffled the leaves overhead. The air caressed his naked body as he lay on a blanket under the canopy of trees, basking in the glow of the immense pleasure he had just received.

He had been right about the woman, Jackie Phillips. She had given him everything he needed, and she had given most of it up on her own. And she had been magnificent. While it had been a while since he'd had a woman, she had certainly been one of the better ones he could remember. Having had to listen to her prattle all day about the town of Pine Haven had been worth the time spent, after all.

They had come to the park, to this place Jackie claimed she knew well. He had no doubt she did and no doubt he wasn't the first person to share this space under the looming trees with her. She had brought a bottle of wine and the heavy camping blanket with her; her claim being the blanket was protection from the cold, wet ground. They sat and drank and talked. To his surprise, the wine had been quite good. It was an inexpensive brand, easily found at any convenience store, but his newly acquired taste for cheap wines made it seem appropriate.

The conversation with Jackie had been almost painfully dull as she rambled on about all the hopes and dreams that life in Pine Haven had quashed, lamenting the life choices she had made since graduating high school and how they had resulted in her being a 'lifer' in town. "The one thing we have here is lots of peace and quiet," she spat after the fourth glass of cheap wine, "along with more than our fair share of boredom." It seemed as if her love affair with Pine Haven only went so far.

She had asked about him and he told her a few lies drawn from the various cover identities he had used when with the Project. About his stint in Afghanistan, where he had lost his best friend to a disease caused by a chemical agent used by either our side or theirs. In actuality, neither side had used it. It had been a third party with a dark agenda. And the man in question hadn't been his friend but a stranger he had watched with fascination slowly die from the strange chemical infection. He recalled for her the sad tale of his mother's passing from lung cancer and his subsequent bid to quit smoking. Of how his brother's alcoholism tore his family apart and how that brother was now serving a life sentence in prison for murdering his wife and her new lover. He told her tales of missed opportunities and romances lost. By the end of his speech, he had woven a sorrowful story that was certain to tug at her heartstrings and bring her closer to him.

Everything he had told her was a lie, of course. But a well-placed lie always got him everything he wanted from people, this case being no exception. Before he could even finish his string of made-up stories about his life, she had leaned in and kissed him. A long, sensual kiss. A lover's kiss. A kiss of deep desire that had led to their making love under the watchful eyes of the birch and oak trees above.

They had finished a short while ago and Jackie had fallen into a peaceful sleep beside him, her blond hair stirring lightly in the cool autumn breeze and catching the few rays of sun that penetrated the thick tangle of branches above in a sparkle of gold. He had thought her attractive when they met that morning, but now she was absolutely radiant. The near flawlessness of her naked form pressed against him, protected from the chilly evening air by the camping blanket and his body heat. She had been remarkable in satisfying him sexually, her skills were well-honed and her technique beyond reproach, but now another need was stirring within him. A need that was as important to him as food or sex was to any average man. Jackie had exceeded his expectations on the sexual front, he had high hopes for her here as well.

Leaning against the trunk of the tree, he closed his eyes. Darkness enveloped him, and he let his other senses take over. A light, cool breeze touched his exposed chest. Birds sang nearby. He could hear small animals scurrying through the brush nearby, most likely squirrels or chipmunks. Most importantly, he felt the warmth of Jackie as she lay pressed against him, her chest rising and falling rhythmically as she slept. He focused on her warmth and her breathing, bringing his body into synch with hers. More than feeling her, he could sense her now. Her mind. Her consciousness. Slowly, he penetrated the veil of her mind as he had penetrated her body earlier. Far more gently this time, however, so as not to disturb the delicate veil of her sleep. If he could take what he needed from her without waking her, it would make things much easier and more comfortable for them both. He owed her that much for all she had done for him.

With slow and methodical precision, he penetrated the misty gloom surrounding her sleep-clouded mind and was promptly met with the tumultuous duality of her personality. It wasn't unexpected, as most people's minds radically divided into passionate and logical sides, each showing the other a different perspective of the world and helping to make sense of it as a whole. However, as victims of their own nature, these two halves were also in direct contrast to one another. This extreme difference created a powerful storm, an undercurrent of thoughts that threatened to drag an untrained or unsuspecting visitor to destruction.

Adam was anything but unskilled. In fact, it had been his talents in this area that had made him such a valuable asset to the Project. With no hesitation or doubt, he submerged himself in the storm of radical indifference, searching for his objective.

It wasn't hard to find. In fact, it was the most prevalent corner of Jackie's mind. Her fear center. It rose before him like a dark spire, multi-colored tendrils of thought emanating from it and worming their way into other areas of her consciousness. Her fear was a powerful side of her; it had already taken over most of her emotional centers and was still leaking into other aspects of her persona. There wasn't an area of her mind that was untouched by fear. It motivated everything she did, every event of her day, sowing doubt, chaos and discord throughout her psyche.

Adam reached out to that dark spire, dabbing it with his mind. The darkness there enveloped him completely, taking him into it psychically, just as Jackie had taken him into herself physically. A rush of panic, of pure unadulterated terror, rushed through him. He quivered in delight at the feeling. Her fear was exquisite as it caressed him, washing over him in wave after wave. Despite himself, a small gasp of pleasure escaped his physical body.

He probed deeper into the spire of fear, searching for the most terrifying horrors that lurked in its heart. As he passed, tremors of nightmares and phobias shook him and elicited more expressions of pleasure from his physical body. But it wasn't enough. There was more here, so much more. And he needed it. Like a junkie needing a fix, he needed the fear in her. The fear was pleasure. Sustenance. Life itself.

As his psychic self moved toward the heart of the dark spire, his physical ears detected a sound as recognizable to him as his own breathing. Still lying next to him, caught in the night dark strands of sleep's web, Jackie whimpered softly. As expected, his foray into her fear had elicited a nightmare unlike any she had experienced before. His trip into her consciousness was releasing all of her latent fears; every shiver, scream or phobia she had ever experienced, all at once. Together, it formed a miasma of terror that was slowly poisoning her, attacking every other aspect of her being.

The terror flowed around him and he drank it in, intoxicating him like wine. For a moment he wondered if it were possible for Jackie to generate more fear than he could handle, that he might overdose on her terror like an addict would with cocaine, destroyed by his inability to control his desire for the drug that fed his addiction. Consumed by need, drowning in pleasure.

The physical world intruded again as Jackie made a series of choking, gurgling sounds. She couldn't tear herself out of sleep, out of the nightmare, and was choking on her own terror.

Adam barely took notice. All that mattered to him at this point was the sheer, stark terror that surrounded him. He drank every bit he could, savoring the sweet taste as it exploded around and through him.

His physical body shook with delight, an expression of pure and complete ecstasy on his face. Conversely, Jackie's face had contorted into a twist of absolute terror. Her eyes sprang open and stared upward, rapidly tracking ghouls that existed not in front of her, but in her mind. Freeing the totality of her terrors had given them life and substance, and they were now as real to her as the branches swaying overhead. She shuddered and thrashed violently to escape, but it was hopeless. She had created and carefully nurtured the demons chasing her for her entire life, feeding and growing them. There was no escaping them now. The rational mind that had kept them in check for so many years had fallen like the walls of Jericho under the weight of their singular assault.

In the real world, under the canopy of trees brought to frenzied life by the breeze, Jackie tried to scream. Only a scratchy whimper escaped her throat. Her eyes were wide and wild, as if they were trying to escape the confines of her skull. Her heart was pounding wildly inside her chest, trying to escape the terror on its own. Again she tried to scream...

Then she was silent, falling back into the warm folds of the camping blanket, her eyes locked in a stare at the thick tangle of branches overhead. Slowly, consciousness faded from her eyes as her mind shut down to escape the terrors it had unleashed upon itself. Her body was quickly following. After twitching twice more and expelling a rattling breath, she lay silent and unmoving.

Next to her, Adam also shuddered violently as a final look of sheer pleasure and excitement crossed his face. His eyes fluttered open, dark and unfocused, like those of a heroin addict who had just injected himself with his favorite poison and was now experiencing a remarkable high. The comparison was close to the truth. As Jackie had died, he had soaked up the last remaining vestiges of her persona. He absorbed everything that remained of her, everything she had been and experienced. Like all the others, it had been a bittersweet connection, and she had been the most interesting at the moment of her death. Death had always seemed to enhance the experience, and the last bit of mingled emotions left behind as life exited the vessel were the nectar of the gods. The essence of life, to be thoroughly savored.

As the high passed and the world reasserted itself, it seemed to take on a new radiance. A new life. The rays of sunshine that broke through the dense canopy above carried a far deeper golden hue, sparkling with energy as the light danced and played with the shadows. With its intense purity, the green of the grass surrounding him was nearly blinding, making him hesitant to gaze upon the brilliant bursts of color displayed by the autumn leaves above. The entire world glowed with a newfound energy and exuberance, igniting a sense of wonder within him he had never experienced before, as he had never been a child. All the terrible fears Jackie held had provided him with a wondrous outlook on the world.

"Thank you for this wonderful gift," he said to her, receiving only a blank stare in reply. Reaching over, he gently pulled her eyelids down over her wide eyes, giving her the eternal rest of the ages she so richly deserved. She was now free of the fears and worries that had plagued her in life and was no doubt thanking him as vehemently from the other side as he was thanking her lifeless form here. As always, releasing a soul in torment was so very gratifying, and he felt a renewed sense of accomplishment.

As he dressed, he realized this was the first time he had ever killed anyone without being ordered to do so or out of necessity. He had killed simply to fill the need within him. The longing. Yes, Jackie had obviously suffered in life and was as burdened as every other soul he had freed, but beyond that, her death had served no purpose. He didn't know why that would make a difference in the experience, but it did. The very nature of her fear had been so rich, so abundant, so overpowering. It had completely intoxicated him. But he had no idea why. Perhaps it was because, for the first time in his life, he had selected the donor. He had found a suitable candidate that met his needs, not the needs of the Project. Because he had done it of his own volition.

That was all something to be pondered later. His time with Jackie had provided him with immense pleasure and a deep sense of personal satisfaction, but it was time to move on to other matters. The sky was being consumed by the gray of dusk, made even darker by thick rain clouds that threatened to open up at any moment and drop cold fall rains. Time was running short.

Rachel was waiting.

25

Alex sat with his face buried in his hands as he had for the last hour and a half, afraid to so much as look up for fear of losing control and hurting someone again. It had gone too far this time. The thought of hurting someone else, especially someone he cared about, was more than he could bear. It was better at this point to withdraw from the world and remove the risk he posed.

The door opened across the room, and he heard someone shuffling in. His stomach seized and his heart raced as the heavy footfalls approached him. He knew it was Babcock simply from the sound of his footsteps. A shroud of shame engulfed him and he pushed the palms of his hands harder against the closed eyes, sealing them from all light and sending a fierce pain through his skull.

"Well," came Babcock's deep voice as he moved closer to Alex, "that's taken care of. I told Angela we were going to be busy in here for a while and didn't want to be disturbed. The kids are all out of the house, so there shouldn't be any issues." Something clinked on the bench next to Alex, a rattling noise. "I thought you might be hungry, so I threw together a sandwich. It's not all that impressive, but it's edible. You, ah, didn't get a chance to eat much lunch."

Alex's stomach tightened again at the reminder of what had happened a few hours ago at the sandwich shop. Tears struggled through his tightly shut eyes and dampened the palms of his hands, still pressed firmly against them.

"There's some soup there, too. Some of Angela's best homemade minestrone. She makes a killer soup. Really, a great cook all around." Alex didn't move. Didn't budge. Didn't even so much as acknowledge the detective's presence. "You going to eat?"

"I'm not hungry." He hadn't been hungry all afternoon. He hadn't been much of anything for the last few hours except ashamed and worried. Contemplating his mind, wondering if he had stepped off the path into full-blown insanity. Was his insanity creeping beyond the confines of his mind and leaking into the world, affecting anyone unfortunate enough to be around him? He couldn't allow that to happen. Next time he lashed out, he could hurt Rachel. Or Rick. Or someone else close to him. To keep them safe, he needed to get away from them. For that, he needed Babcock's help. To get it, he would have to convince him it was the right thing to do.

But Alex may have underestimated the hulking detective. The man didn't seem quite ready to give up on him just yet. After the incident at the sandwich shop, Alex had thought that was it, that the cop would arrest him on the spot. Or, at the very least, remand him to a psychiatric facility. That hadn't been the case. Instead, they retreated to Babcock's home. His home, where his family lived. Not into the house but to the small workshop behind, where Alex had spent the last twenty minutes contemplating the events of the last few days. In that time, he concluded that dwelling on it wouldn't be helpful. He had to face the consequences and move into the future, whatever that was going to be.

"Look, I told you we'd sort this out and we will, okay? But I can't have you passing out from hunger, so will you please just eat something?" Babcock said, pushing the plate closer to Alex.

Alex lifted his face from his hands and looked up at the lieutenant. Dark shadows rimmed his eyes, and they no longer held the sparkle they once had, now resembling murky pools where monsters of incalculable fury lurked. That pent up fury startled Babcock, who hadn't been prepared to see Alex like that. Granted, they had only known each other for just over a day now, but the intensity in the other man's eyes, the look of anger and despair there, was a surprise. Babcock was accustomed to seeing that look, but normally on people who had no one to fall back on, who were at the end of all hope, and who had nothing to look forward to. It was the look of a frightened, lonely person who felt backed into a corner with no escape. It didn't belong on Alex's face.

Alex turned away and picked up the sandwich, taking a small bite. Another quickly followed and in just a few quick seconds, half the sandwich was gone. The other half disappeared just as quickly, with the soup soon to follow. Alex marveled at the sudden reappearance of his appetite. A few moments ago, the mere thought of food would have made him sick, and now he was suddenly ravenous. It was as if his mind and body were completely out of synch.

Babcock had remained silent in the short time it had taken Alex to devour his dinner, amazed by the immediate turnaround from even just a few moments ago. "I thought you weren't hungry," he finally said, stacking the empty plates and setting them aside on the workbench.

Alex wiped his mouth with his sleeve. "Neither did I. Guess I found my appetite."

Babcock chuckled. "Yours and about two other people, I'd say. Thirsty?"

He hadn't thought about it until Babcock mentioned it, but he was absolutely parched. "Yeah, I could stand something to drink. Thanks."

"I've got just the thing you need." Babcock made his way to the workbench and the micro fridge set underneath. From it, he produced two bottles of Sam Adams, popped off the caps, and handed one to Alex.

The beer swirled around the dark glass, giving it a murky appearance. As dry as he was, Alex couldn't seem to lift the bottle for a sip. "You sure this is a good idea? With everything else that's happened today? When I was stone cold sober?"

Babcock waved him off. "Don't worry about it. You need to relax, and this will help do the trick. Besides, I think this afternoon was an isolated incident not related to your unstable psyche, so a beer won't hurt." The bearish cop grinned and took a healthy swig from his bottle, wiping away the foam that had caught in the stubble of his chin.

Alex regarded the bottle like it was a grenade in his hand. "And if you're wrong?"

"Simple," Babcock deadpanned, "I shoot you."

Alex couldn't keep a grin from his face. "Fair enough," he replied, taking a substantial pull from the bottle. The beer filled his mouth with a slightly bitter taste before running down his throat in a cold rush. He'd never been much of a beer drinker, but at that moment he couldn't think of anything that might have tasted better to him. He felt a warmth in his stomach as it overtook the cold in his throat, the familiar warm feeling that always came after his first sip of any alcohol. It radiated out, gradually enveloping him in a comfortable glow.

Babcock took another sip from his own bottle, which was now half empty. "Feel better?"

"Much," Alex replied as he leaned back, setting himself against the wall of the workshop and closed his eyes. There, in the purple shadow world, he felt himself relax ever so slightly. Felt the tiniest release of tension in his muscles. It wasn't much, but it was there, this almost imperceptible sense of relaxation. For the moment, it was enough.

Until Babcock shattered it. "Look, I know this is probably the last thing you want to think about right now, but we have to talk about it."

Alex opened his eyes and leaned forward, leaving the comfort and warmth of the shadows behind and falling once again face first into harsh reality. "Talk about what?" he asked, knowing full well what Babcock was referring to.

Babcock leveled his eyes with Alex, who unconsciously slid back an inch on his seat. "About this afternoon."

Alex took another sip from his bottle. Even though the beer was still as cold as it had been a few moments ago, the feeling inside him wasn't nearly as warm as it had been.

"What about it?"

"How does it fit in with what we know? What do you remember about it? There must be some connection to your recent... issues. People don't just go off like unless they're drugged or psychotic." Babcock felt regret hit him in the chest the instant the words left his mouth, but it was too late. Even though Alex hadn't mentioned the possibility, he knew it must have been on the kid's mind. There was no way someone could go through what he had who wouldn't question their sanity.

Despite that, he still felt bad about the slip. "Alex, I'm sorry. Sometimes I just don't think before the words come out of my mouth. It's a major fault of mine. My worst, if you listen to Angela. I know you're having a tough time with all of this; I don't want to make it worse."

Alex shrugged off the detective's apology. "No offense taken. I can tell you, it's a thought that's crossed my mind a time or two in the last few days. And that was back before I became a bona fide menace to society." He sipped at his beer, a bit more conservatively this time. If he still had some rampaging left in him, he didn't want alcohol to cloud whatever judgment he may have left.

Pulling the bottle from his lips, he said, "So, how long have you been a psychiatrist?"

A confused look crossed Babcock's face. "What do you mean?"

"What makes you think I won't have another episode like this afternoon? Why do you think it's safe for me to have a beer and relax? You barely know me. Why do you have all this confidence in me when...." He paused, a cold rush of shame and fear pushing the comfortable warmth from his stomach. "When I don't have any?"

Babcock sighed, placing his empty bottle on the table next to him and popping the top off another beer. "This job, dealing with people day in and day out, seeing the absolute worst the world has to offer. It gets hard sometimes. Really hard. Wife beaters. Drug dealers. Rapists. Child abusers. Worse, child molesters. You see the horrible things they've done to other people. It affects you. It chips away at your own humanity, tearing you down to the bone. The only way to stay sane? To keep from becoming the people you're putting away? You look for the good in the world. It's hard to find sometimes, but it's out there. You look for it everywhere you go. As a result, you get to know people. To recognize the good when you find it. Those little beacons of light that keep you from completely giving in to the darkness you see in the world every god-damned day. You get to know people, what's in their hearts. You get to tell the good from the bad. And you? You are definitely one of the good people. At your heart. At your core. You're good. What happened to you this afternoon? That's not you. At least not you now. Granted, you seemed pretty fucking pissed at me, but I'm not so sure it's actually me you were mad at."

"What do you mean?" Alex leaned forward again, the cold rush of shame giving way to morbid curiosity.

Babcock swallowed half of his second beer in a few loud gulps. He gestured to the small fridge beside him. "You want another one?"

Alex's was still half full. "No thanks. Never been much of a drinker." He sipped lightly again as if to make the point. "What did I say? I honestly can't remember a thing."

"Yelled at me to take my hands off you. That you weren't going to take it anymore. But it wasn't so much what you said." Babcock paused; his lips stopped just over the top of his beer bottle as his mind drifted back to that afternoon. "It was the look in your eyes. They were cold, but filled with rage. Emptied of everything that's you and replaced with something else. Something dark. Angry. Primal." His eyes were unfocused as he relived the events, absently taking the delayed drink from his bottle. "You were talking about 'the others', how you weren't going to end up like them. That mean anything to you?"

A chill that had become far too familiar to him in the last few days crept once again up Alex's spine. He shook his head in response, but his mind drifted back to the dark stranger from his dreams. And to the dark-haired girl lying dead on a slab, her body looking like wild animals had torn her apart. Was it possible these were 'the others' he had apparently talked about?

"Was there anything else?"

Babcock nodded slightly. "Yeah. It was garbled, but you kept mentioning 'experiments' and 'lab rats'. I couldn't make out the context, between your growly voice and the pain of my arm being torn out of its socket. But it didn't make you happy, I can tell you that much."

Alex froze, his face ashen. His vision from yesterday. The man in the white coat. The dark stranger. Piles of gore and viscera around them. The man in the white coat taking notes and conferring with others like him. Studying them. Analyzing them. As if they were part of an experiment.

As if they were lab rats.

Lab rats that had just murdered scores of people.

Bile rose in the back of his throat, carrying with it the pungent taste of beer mixing with stomach juices. Jumping up, he raced to the door of the workshop and dashed out into the night, promptly vomiting the dinner Mrs. Babcock had been so kind to make for him all over the manicured lawn. Even with his stomach empty, he felt sick. Sick in a way that he wasn't sure he would ever feel right again.

Babcock burst out of the shed behind him, taking a few steps before realizing what Alex was doing and stopping abruptly. His years as a patrol cop picking up drunks had taught him that when they were throwing up the previous night's binges, most wanted to be left alone to do it. And unless he wanted to spend the rest of the evening cleaning his shoes, it was best for him to just stand back and wait until Alex finished.

His stomach had finally stopped reeling and twisting enough to allow Alex to sit back on his heels, tilting his head to the night sky as the cool, fall air caressed his face. Physically, the nausea was passing. Inside his head, he was still in turmoil.

He was a murderer. Worse, an emotionless and dispassionate killer.

"How could I have done that? Why did I let them to do that to me?" he sobbed at an unaffected moon. "How?"

"Do what?" Babcock asked, slowly approaching. While he wanted to help the kid, the events of the afternoon were still fresh in his mind. The persistent throbbing in his shoulder was a fairly consistent reminder, urging caution with each step forward. "I don't understand. What did you do?"

Alex's voice was ephemeral, barely audible. "I killed people. A lot of people."

Babcock stopped at those words, his advance frozen. "What does that mean?"

"The experiment, I think that was part of it." Alex's voice was quiet but calm, his breath becoming an eerie white wisp with each word. "A lab rat, surrounded by piles of meat that used to be living human beings. Covered in blood, surrounded by carnage, and I didn't care about any of it. I can almost feel the heat of their blood on my hands. Taste it in the air. But I can't feel any pain. Any remorse. Any..... anything."

"And *he* was there."

"He?" Babcock stammered. "He who?"

"Him. The dark stranger. The one from my dreams. He was there." Alex had almost moved into a trance as he recounted the experiences, the images, that were flooding back to him. Jumbled and disjointed flashes, as much emotion as memories.

The men and women in white coats. The torn piles of bodies. The dark stranger. The jigsaw puzzle pieces of images whirled around him like a hurricane, stubbornly refusing to come together in a coherent picture.

One image came into focus. An image that chilled him to the core of his soul.

There, amidst the broken bodies, the dark stranger smiled. He smiled a smile of deep satisfaction at what he had done. At the carnage he was responsible for.

Alex shivered hard. Involuntarily. He wanted to scream but couldn't get the sound to come from his throat. The memories swirled again like leaves on the fall wind and his stomach sank. Then he noticed something else. One particular, tiny image among all the others. One little fragment of memory that struck him.

The image was of him. His face. And glistening in his right eye was the barest hint of a tear. A sign of regret. Of silent anguish at the death and destruction around him. The familiar chill faded from his gut, leaving behind a feeling that had been entirely alien to him the last few days.

Hope.

"I'm not a killer." Alex's voice was distant, quiet. The images in his mind didn't fade this time, but instead stood still and coalesced, giving him a more complete image of his past. He still didn't understand the circumstances that had brought a young him to this point, but he knew one thing for certain: He may have killed, but he wasn't a killer.

Alex looked Babcock directly in the eyes for the first time since that afternoon. There was something different in that look. Something lighter. "I killed people, but I'm not a killer. It wasn't me doing the killing. It was.... something else."

Babcock's face tightened in confusion. "What the hell is that supposed to mean?"

"It means someone used me," Alex replied, pulling himself up off the lawn. "I was the instrument of their deaths, but I wasn't in control. I was a tool. A gun, but someone else aimed me and pulled the trigger."

Babcock's face seemed to cinch up even further the more Alex spoke. "That's great to hear. Really. It is. Still leaves a few very important questions without answers, though. Like, if you were the gun, who pulled the trigger? And what happened to the other gun?"

Babcock's words hit like a hammer, smashing Alex out of his trance-like reverie. His eyes filling with panic, he yelled in a shrill voice, "I have to get home! Now!"

Startled at Alex's entirely unexpected outburst, Babcock dropped his nearly full bottle of Sam Adams onto the lawn, white foam spraying across the grass. "What? Why?"

"He's coming after her!" Fear and urgency filled Alex's voice as his body tensed. "That's why Dr. Carlton told me not to leave her alone! He's coming for Rachel!"

Babcock put out his hands, palms up, and stepped in front of Alex. "Whoa! Slow down! What are you talking about? Who's coming after Rachel?"

The cold in Alex's gut returned hard and suddenly, like a physical punch.

"The other gun."

26

Night came fast, dropping from the sky like a cloak. A few streetlights valiantly tried to dispel the onslaught of darkness, but they were rewarded meagerly for their efforts. Across the street, avoiding the spotty light from the streetlamps and hidden under the cover of shadows, was Adam. After leaving Jackie to her final rest, he wandered slowly through the town of Pine Haven, making his way to his final destination. To his destiny. He had been there for an hour now, watching the house across the street for signs of her. Of Rachel. Whenever she walked past the front window, he felt a renewed sense of purpose, and his mission became clearer with each passing. Soon he would go to her. They could be together and start the life they were destined to live. The life that had been denied to them for so long. He would take her from this place of lies, of her imprisonment, to some place safe. Someplace they could be together.

She passed by the bay window in the living room again, looking out into the night. Her fiery red hair hung loosely, gently caressing her shoulders as she turned her head, framing her perfect face. A face that seemed to have been meticulously crafted from the finest porcelain. His heart raced at the sight of her, her perfect hourglass form, the graceful fluidity of her movements. The perfection of her being.

She pivoted her head suddenly in response to something out of his view and disappeared. A dark empty feeling welled up in his chest at her absence, as if her simply being out of sight created an incompleteness in him. As if he had discovered a missing piece of himself, only to have it ripped away again. No more. Tonight was the night their destiny begun and he would let nothing stand in the way of that. Not the Project. Not Robert Penders. Not Elliot Forrester. Not Burke Darnell.

Not Alex Carter.

Especially not Alex Carter. He wasn't like the others. They were obstacles to be overcome. Hurdles to jump. Alex Carter was more than that. His was a case of malicious theft. He had stolen a life that wasn't his and then had conspired to keep it for himself. All the happiness he had experienced in the last fourteen years was nothing more than the spoils of war; his memories a treasure vault of plundered goods. Now the intended owner was back to reclaim that life, and he wasn't about to let anything stand between him and his redemption.

****

Something was wrong.

As she stared out into the street, watching the coming night slowly devour the remaining daylight, Rachel couldn't shake an ominous feeling. It had settled over her that afternoon as she had stood on the front steps and watched Alex ride off with Lieutenant Babcock. As she waved and the car vanished around the corner, it had hit her like a fist; the feeling that things would never be quite the same with them again. At first she thought it was just a nervous reaction to the recent upheaval in their lives, but in the time since it first hit her, the feeling had refused to recede even the slightest. It had lodged its icy claws into her gut and refused to budge. Now, looking out into the shadow-stained street, the claws dug even deeper, spreading frozen venom.

Something was out there, waiting in the night. Watching. Even though the street looked the same as it had every night, she could feel some malevolent force out in the dark. It tried to be invisible; it wanted to remain undetected, but like oil trying to mix with water, its very nature prevented that. And like oil, the thing outside skimmed along the surface with hardly a ripple marking its passage. An unseen danger. But it was there. She knew it was there. And it scared her like nothing else ever had.

"Mrs. Carter?"

She startled slightly at the voice behind her, so caught up in her inner thoughts she had forgotten he was even there. The voice belonged to Officer Dave Timmins, one of the police officers assigned by Lieutenant Babcock to watch over her. Timmins looked far too young to be a police officer, much less one with as distinguished a career as Babcock had described. His curly blond hair twisted uncontrollably in every direction despite his best efforts to rein it in. As she turned to him, he was pushing a lock away from his eyes, which were as startling a blue as she had ever seen. Framing those beautiful blue eyes were two clusters of freckles that screamed little boy to her, and it was those freckles more than anything else that contributed to Officer Timmins' youthful appearance. She had to fight the urge to reach over and muss his hair before sending him out to play with his little friends. The only thing intruding on the illusion that this was simply a game of cops and robbers was the gun that protruded from the young officer's hip, providing a constant reminder of genuine danger.

"Mrs. Carter, it's probably not a good idea for you to stand in front of the window like that, ma'am."

She smiled and moved away from the window; a bit taken aback by being called ma'am so seriously by this young cop.

"Sorry, Officer Timmins. I'm just worried about my husband and this is what I do when that happens. I stand by the window and wait for him to come home. You're right though, now probably isn't the right time for that." She moved further from the window and found her way to the couch. "Besides, I wouldn't want to get your guys in trouble with Babcock. That guy's a bear."

From the crook of the L-shaped couch, Officer John LeFranc looked up from the television to the other two people in the room. He and Timmins may serve on the same force and act as partners more often than not, but they were as different in appearance as night and day. LeFranc's eyes were midnight black, standing in stark contrast to his younger counterpart. His close-cropped dark hair sat atop a face that looked as if someone had chiseled it from granite. Rachel had wondered throughout the evening if his face hadn't actually been granite, seeing as he had barely changed his expression the entire evening. His affect was one of stern seriousness and complete dedication to his role as protector. Every move he made appeared to be a calculated use of personal energy, as if he were storing up his reserves for the need to spring into action at a moment's notice. The same someone who chiseled his face must have sculpted his body as he filled out his uniform in a way Timmins did not. The light-haired officer had a slight build that contributed to his youthful appearance. LeFranc was solid, like a bodybuilder.

Or a bulldozer, Rachel mused as a grin slid across her face.

"Actually," Timmins said, sliding his thumbs into his equipment belt like he was in an old Western, "the Lieutenant is more of a teddy bear. Just don't tell him I said that. He doesn't like that to get out. Wants everyone to think he's hard as nails when really he's like a marshmallow. That right, John?"

From the couch, LeFranc grunted a reply, his eyes once more affixed to the television.

Timmins smiled a warm smile. "You'll have to excuse John; he can be anti-social. Not exactly our best public relations officer, right, John?"

Another grunt. If he hadn't greeted her earlier, Rachel would have to wonder if the man was even capable of speech or if his vocabulary consisted entirely of a series of slightly different grunts. These two were such polar opposites of one another, she couldn't imagine how they got along as partners. It was like a sitcom in her living room.

"That's all right. I'm feeling a little anti-social myself right now, anyway. If you gentlemen will excuse me, I think I'll just putter around with a few things. No offense." Rachel moved to excuse herself from the room.

"None taken, ma'am," Timmins replied, his tone only enhancing the old-timey deputy vibe he gave off.

Rachel winced a bit at the use of 'ma'am' again and slipped out of the living room, leaving Timmins and LeFranc to amuse each other. Try as she might, she still couldn't shake the feeling that something was about to happen. That there was someone or something out in the deepening shadows, waiting. She was feeling like a paranoid psychotic, pacing the house, expecting to be attacked at every turn. She needed a distraction. Something to take her mind off of the events of the last few days and the sense of dread building inside her. Something that would make her feel useful, like she was contributing more than just wearing a hole in the rug from pacing.

She sat at the computer, left dormant since Alex's hasty departure that morning, and called up the message Dr. Carlton had left for Alex. The thumb drive contained much more information than just that message, but he and Babcock had rushed off before having the opportunity to look any deeper into it. There wasn't much else she could do to help them at the moment, but she could at least examine what else the message contained and if it provided any new insights into their situation.

She set her earbuds in so as not to clue in either Timmins or LeFranc as to the contents of the data drive and played Dr. Carlton's spiel again. Retrieving a pad of paper and a pencil from the desk, she jotted down the names of Robert Penders and Elliot Forrester, the only names mentioned in the message. She wasn't familiar with Forrester at all, but Penders struck her. She couldn't recall how she knew the name, only that she had heard it before.

Dr. Carlton finished her speech, her face once again frozen on the screen. Rachel sighed, dropping her head back and closing her eyes for a moment. She searched her memory, running the message through and looking for anything that may have been missed during the first two play throughs. Other than the odd and foreboding nature of it, she was drawing a blank. Lifting her head again, she looked into the eyes of the dead woman on the screen. There had been fear in her voice, to be sure. More than that, though, a sense of strength. Of resignation. She had been drawing a line. There was more to the message. More than she wanted to tell Alex about. To warn them about. So where would she have kept that information?

As if on cue, Rachel noticed something at the bottom right of the screen. It was practically invisible, but it was certainly there. A small arrow, blending in almost perfectly with the background. Hovering the mouse over it made the icon become slightly more visible, and she let it rest there. Her finger floated over the left mouse button. She wanted to click the arrow, but a sense of dread and uncertainty filled her. With everything that had happened to them so far, she wasn't sure if what was on the other side of that click would bring them answers or more questions. Or worse, more pain and trouble.

She sighed again, steeling herself. It didn't matter at this point. They needed answers. There were most likely some on that drive. They had to know. She took a sharp breath and held it, then gently pressed the mouse button.

There was a light click and the image of Dr. Carlton slid off the left edge of the screen as a new screen came in from the right. It was a simple screen, a gray box containing a list menu detailing the options available to the user. The options available were:

Eden Project

PenTech Research and Development

Adam Subjects

Eve Subjects

Project: Sleeper

Fallen Angel

Project: Gabriel

The list presented itself innocuously enough, but with the events of the last few days, she wasn't sure what she should click on, if anything. The options looked equally mysterious to her, and equally frightening as well.

Oh well, she thought as she moved the mouse over each choice in succession, watching as it lit up with the passing of the cursor as if begging to be chosen*, might as well start at the top and see what happens.* Taking in a sharp breath and holding it, she clicked on the button marked Eden Project.

A middle-aged man appeared on the screen, seated behind a large and expensive looking desk with a breathtaking city skyline framed in the floor-to-ceiling window behind him. His salt and pepper hair was carefully pushed back to create a casual look, but Rachel could tell it was meticulously coiffed to achieve that appearance. He wore a deep blue pinstripe suit that was painstakingly tailored to fit his every angle. Wrinkles lightly seamed the corners of his eyes and mouth, the rest of his face so far remaining untouched by the unforgiving ravages of time. His nose resembled the beak of a bird of prey, but not unpleasantly, rather in that his features were sharp and angular. A disarming and contagious smile spread out beneath his nose to dispel predatory comparisons. But the feature that drew Rachel in more than any other was his eyes. They were a deep blue and calm, like the sea. But, also like the sea, there was something lurking beneath them. Something dangerous.

Once the video loaded, it played, his voice sounding light and syrupy. Like a politician. Or a car salesperson. "Welcome to the Eden Project," the syrupy voice dripped in her ears, "the pride and joy of PenTech. I am Robert Penders, CEO and, to date, the sole financier of this project."

This was Penders. Having a face to put to the name didn't help her remember where she had heard it before, so she simply made a note next to his name as 'CEO–PenTech' for later reference.

He continued, a welcoming smile on his face. "Many of you, the most wealthy and influential people in your respective circles, have expressed an interest in joining me on this venture. I have prepared this presentation to address questions you may have. You can find everything you may want to know about the project here, except for a firsthand look at the amazing results we have yielded so far. There have been some rather interesting developments since this project's inception, and we are very excited to share these developments with you. We sincerely hope we can count on your support in what we feel will be the largest wholesale commodity of the twenty-first century."

So far, he had failed to inspire her with his speech. If he were looking for her to invest, he would have already lost her. But she most likely wasn't his target audience. Presumably, the intended audience for this presentation had a bit more advanced knowledge of whatever the project was. That's why Penders could be as vague as he had been and still entice his prospective investors without overly admitting to any illegal activities. He could cover his own hind end while still trawling for investors. Tricky.

Penders continued. "After this introduction, we will bring you back to the main screen so you can browse the options there. Each one will provide further insight into the massive scope of this undertaking. I hope you enjoy and appreciate it, but more than that, I hope you pursue it. Thank you all for your time and attention."

He turned away from the camera, only to turn back a moment later. His face, with that politician's smile, had changed noticeably. Gone was the pleasant demeanor of a salesperson, instead he had the leer of a reptile. "Ladies and gentlemen, this information is extremely sensitive. Please do not share this with anyone. Be assured that to do so would incur the full wrath of PenTech and its subsidiaries." Like the passing of a storm cloud, the cold leer vanished, replaced once again by the sunny smile. "Thank you, and have a pleasant day."

What was that all about? Rachel wondered as the screen transitioned back to the main menu. In appearance, it seemed innocent enough. A business type in an expensive suit, trawling for investors for a new project. But her mind kept drifting back to what the exquisitely dressed older man in the video had actually said. He had referenced the Eden Project, but hadn't elaborated. Her mind was throwing around thoughts of secret cabals and government conspiracies. Things that had once been the province of tabloids and dark web conspiracists but had leached into the mainstream. Tales of dark money and black sites. Of the powerful elite that lived just outside the light of day, riding the shadows at the fringes of society and acting as the puppet masters of humanity. She usually dismissed these things as the paranoid ramblings of weak minds, susceptible to whatever ridiculous pop culture fantasy they were ready to buy into to escape their mundane lives, but the events of the last few days clung in her mind as well. The lines between reality and fantasy were starting to blur a bit recently. With everything that had happened, everything they had been through, what if it was all connected? And what if it were connected to some greater conspiracy? Alex's lifetime of persistent amnesia. The insane nightmares he suffered from. His odd appearance on the beach all those years ago, with no family stepping up to claim him. More recently, there was Dr. Carlton's mysterious death and the weird interactions he'd had with Lieutenant Babcock. All far too weird to be coincidental. If that were the case, then who were these people? What could they possibly want with Alex? More importantly, what could an architect and a pregnant woman possibly be able to do to stop them?

She didn't know, but she did know that information was always valuable. Turning her attention back to the menu screen in front of her, she selected the next item; PenTech Research and Development. As she clicked on it, the screen resolved into another face. An older man with a far kinder and less intense demeanor than the last. His thick glasses accentuated his deep brown eyes, making them jump off of his face. Peppered throughout with equal parts silver and brown, his hair was rather unkempt, waving like seagrass in the wind whenever he moved his head in the slightest. Accenting all of that was his face, lined with wrinkles that gave him an image of sage wisdom with a pleasant smile and a gleam in his eye that displayed a genuine passion for his work.

Looking up as if surprised, the older gentleman spoke. "Good day to you. I am Dr. Elliot Forrester, a specialist in genetics. Specifically, the human genome." His speech was careful and measured, as if he were reading from a script. It was apparent that Dr. Elliot Forrester had not spent a lot of time in front of a camera.

He continued. "Some of you may have heard of me. No doubt in less than kind terms. I can assure you that whatever you may have heard is true. I have conducted what some would say are dangerous, foolhardy or even outrageous experiments in the name of human evolution. Yes, I have done all of those things. But science never progresses by being meek, and I believe that my quest to advance the human genome is about to bear significant fruit."

The doctor waved his hand awkwardly, indicating the laboratory in the background. Technicians in lab coats and surgical masks bustled around the room, checking charts and readouts and adjusting various settings on various technological devices. Lined up on the far wall directly behind the doctor was a row of glass containers, each about seven feet long and looking roughly coffin shaped with various tubes and wires leading to and away from each one. Rachel didn't know the purpose of those tubes and wires, and based on their appearance, she wasn't sure if she wanted to find out.

The doctor spoke again, his voice pulling her attention from the mysterious machinery. "I am certain you are all familiar in some respect with the field of genetics. Since the dawn of humanity, genetics have been used to produce fruit and vegetable crops that are adaptable to difficult growing conditions or that can better repel diseases or damaging pests. We have bred better dairy and meat animals who can produce more food with fewer or more scarce resources. Since time immemorial, humanity has used genetic modifications to not only survive, but to thrive. To master their surroundings and reach past their humble origins, taking control of nature to best meet their needs. Even with all that we have accomplished and discovered; we have not even begun to uncover what this science can do for us."

He staggered back a few clumsy steps, looking like a high schooler in his first play as he tried to move naturally and failed miserably. With a measure of strained reluctance on his face, he took his eyes from the camera and looked down to find the location of a small tomato plant, its almost unnaturally green stalk holding excessively bright red and flawless fruit. It almost didn't look real, more like some bit of Hollywood magic designed to make the plant as appealing as possible to the viewer.

Dr. Forrester moved his eyes awkwardly back up to peer directly into the camera once more, his eyes magnified almost comically by the thick lenses of his glasses. Between that and the near perfection of the tomato plant next to him, Rachel felt as if she were watching a Saturday Night Live sketch instead of a promotional video for potential investors. He directed the viewer to the too-perfect tomato plant again, once more with all the grace of a high school drama production. "Consider this tomato plant. At one time, it and its kind would have been at the mercy of insect plagues, or drought or disease, or an intense and unexpected frost. Ancient humans recognized these failings of nature, however, and found similar fruits that were hardier. Some varieties were naturally resistant to pests. Others could thrive with less water. Still others grew well in lower temperature environments. Ancient humans recognized these attributes in the different varieties of the same fruit and started intentionally cross-pollinating these plants. The result was a stronger and more resilient food product that could survive harsh conditions and feed them in less ideal growing environments. Move forward to today and we now have tomato plants that produce natural pesticides and can survive in temperatures below freezing."

His face morphed in that moment, the awkward high school theater kid disappearing as the face of the passionate scientist came to prominence with a gleam in his eye. "That, my friends, is the true miracle of genetics."

"The miracle doesn't have to stop with plants, however," he continued. "Continuing with the same ingenuity that ancient humans used on the food plants they depended on, imagine what we could achieve with a better understanding of human DNA and how it influences us as a species. With the proper tools and knowledge, we could conquer disease, master the elements, perhaps even stop death itself. The possibilities are truly without limit."

Excitement caught up with him, his complexion turning a few shades darker as blood rushed through him. He paused again, gathering himself up to his full height and once again gazing into the camera. "This is what we are striving to accomplish here at PenTech, to advance humanity to new heights using the miracles already locked within our bodies."

His comically oversized eyes lit up once again with the passion of scientific discovery. "Inside every one of us, there is the possibility of life everlasting. The opportunity to be free of disease. Or frailty. Or mortality. Free of the trials of the world that have plagued humanity since we first stepped beyond the Neanderthal on the evolutionary ladder. We have the keys, all we need do now is find out which locks they open and what treasures await within. That is why we are here today. Robert Penders is here as an entrepreneur, asking for you to lend financial support in the expectation that you will be the first to profit from these remarkable advances. I am here as a scientist, begging you to allow me to continue the work I believe will lead humanity on the path to immortality. Perhaps more. Possibly into godhood. We are the god makers, ladies and gentlemen. It is within our reach. With your support."

He inclined his head ever-so-slightly, diverting his eyes from the camera intentionally for the first time since the video began, as a sign of thankful deference to the audience. "Thank you," he finished, and the video ended abruptly.

Rachel was dumbstruck, staring blankly at the still video on the screen before her. He couldn't possibly be serious. Couldn't have meant what he had just said. It was a hoax. It had to be. The god makers? It was pure insanity.

Back at the main menu, she passed by Adam Subjects, Eve Subjects and Project: Sleeper, settling on Fallen Angel. With a quick double-click, the main menu dissolved once more, transforming into another image. She expected another face, another video guide to take her deeper into the insane fantasy world that seemed to be unfolding around her. This time, there was no face. There was a single image, one picture that filled the screen before her. A picture she told herself she couldn't possibly be seeing, even though it was right before her eyes in full color and sharp resolution. An image of the impossible.

"Oh my God, that can't be real," she muttered to herself, taking in the details of the picture before her. She blinked twice, thinking maybe she wasn't actually seeing what was in front of her. The picture remained. Unchanged. Unwavering. Unbelievable.

And then the screen went blank, along with all the lights in the house, plunging her into total darkness. Leaving the impossible image burned into her memory.

It couldn't be true.

27

Burke turned the cell phone over and over in his hands, a habit he had developed when there was a call he dreaded making. For years, Burke had struggled with the ritual, viewing it as an open display of nervousness that people around him might interpret as a sign of weakness, but he had had little success. Instead, he reassured himself by considering the fact that such calls were rare and only ever made to a specific individual. And any reasonable person should be afraid to deliver this individual bad news.

He couldn't put the call off any longer. It was bad enough he had failed to either capture or destroy Adam Nine, further delays in communicating that fact would only make things much worse. He stilled the phone tumbling between his fingers and quickly hit the name of Robert Penders in his Contacts list. The phone trilled in his ear a few times, each tone adding to the icy ball of anxiety gathering in the pit of his stomach. On the fourth ring, someone answered.

The voice was thick and deep. It rumbled through the phone like not-too-distant thunder. "Yes, Mr. Darnell? You have some news for me?"

"Yes, sir," Burke replied, feeling the tremor in his own voice. Compared to Penders', Burke felt his voice was high-pitched and creaky, like a scolded child. He took a deep breath and tried to push that down before continuing. "We lost Adam Nine at the rest area, sir. He grabbed Forrester and impersonated him to get close to us before we could open fire. He commandeered a helicopter and executed an escape. We lost him after that."

"And his subdermal tracker?" Penders asked. His voice, while still a low rumble of power, showed no trace of ire. It didn't make Burke feel any better.

"He used that as a decoy in his escape. He removed it and placed it in a vehicle near where he landed in Massachusetts. A truck headed to Providence, Rhode Island. I had a team intercept the truck. We located the tracker, but there was no sign of the subject." Burke paused, waiting for a reply. An ominous silence greeted him. The iceberg in his gut was expanding, and his throat tightened a bit. He continued. "I have a theory where he went. We are currently en route to intercept."

"And your hypothesis would be....?" Penders asked calmly.

"Pine Haven, sir."

Once again, a deafening silence hung over the call. Burke chose not to break the silence this time, wanting to give Robert Penders all the time he needed to process the bombshell that had just been dropped.

When Penders spoke, his tone was as flat and calm as ever. "You believe him to be aware of the other?"

"Yes," Burke replied, his mind racing as he carefully worded his reply. "I believe he may have gotten the information from the files he stole when he escaped the safe house."

"And you believe him to be headed there now?" Penders' voice was still level and evenly paced, without the slightest concern about what this information could do to him and his considerable empire if it ever got out.

"Yes, sir," Burke answered simply.

"Why?"

Now it was Burke's turn to supply the dead air in the conversation. The question had taken him completely off guard. He had carefully planned responses to every conceivable question he could prior to making the call to Penders, but this simple one word question was one he had never considered. There was no good reason for Adam Nine to go to Pine Haven. He was certain the other subject was completely unaware of Adam's existence; he certainly wasn't going to offer help. Why would Adam risk his newfound freedom by going to one of the first places the enemy is bound to look for him? Penders, in his simplistic response, was absolutely correct. It made little sense. And yet, logical or not, Burke felt certain that Adam was headed there.

"I can't say, sir," Burke finally answered.

"Neither do I, but I would love to find out." Penders' response was distant, introspective. Hearing it wasn't something Burke was accustomed to. It didn't last long as he shifted to the usual even and commanding cadence. "We believe the other may be in possession of sensitive material about the Project. A copy of the investor pitch. You know what that contains."

A nervous bolt of electricity shot through Burke at that news. Yes, he was aware of what that bit of information contained. And he knew it could be damning for many powerful people if it ever got out.

"Yes, sir."

Penders continued. "If he delves too deeply into that, if he becomes too much of a liability to our efforts, we may have to clean house and start again from scratch. I don't want to do that. We've come too far to have to go back to the beginning. But if there's no other alternative, eliminate them both if necessary. Recovery is still our primary aim, but extreme measures are acceptable if warranted. Are we clear on this?"

"Crystal, sir." There's nothing Burke would have liked better than to put a bullet right between the eyes of that smug shit, Adam. But, as a professional, he was aware of how much it would cost PenTech to go back to the beginning. He would have to move forward with the plan according to Penders' instructions and secretly continue to hope for an excuse to eliminate Adam.

"One more thing, Mr. Darnell," Penders continued. "The woman. Rachel Carter. She is not to be harmed under any circumstances. If we do have to start over, she could be extremely helpful to us. Cut down on some costs of research and development involved. Do you understand?"

"Yes, sir. The woman is not to be harmed." Burke shifted a bit in his seat to ease some of the discomfort of the conversation, but it didn't do him much good. His gut was still a roiling pit of rage and anger at losing Adam the way he had, topped off by a genuine sense of fear at disappointing the man on the other end of the phone. He wanted to be done with the conversation and moving forward to correct his mistakes, but there was one thing that nagged at him.

"Sir, if I may ask. The pitch data. How did the other come to be in possession of that?"

Again, silence on the other end of the line. Penders finally spoke again, and his voice carried a hint of something Burke had never heard before: regret.

"It was a... questionable act of judgement on my part. It seems as if our initial warning to Dr. Carlton wasn't effective enough and she had another attack of conscience. I overestimated her loyalty to the Project and to me." He paused again, and when he spoke next, there was no trace of regret in his tone. "But we have sorted that out. She won't cause us any further problems. I'm afraid, however, the problems she's already caused are enough. What is your ETA to Pine Haven?"

"Twenty minutes, sir. Once we're on the ground, we'll be proceeding directly to the Carter's home. That's where we expect to find Adam. We hope to intercept him there."

"And what about Dr. Forrester? Has there been any fallout or further issues from his recent interaction with Adam Nine?"

Burke glanced across the helicopter cabin to where the odd little scientist was seated. He was looking wistfully out the window at the dark terrain passing below them and didn't seem to notice Burke's stare. "Nothing yet, sir. I'm keeping a close watch on him."

"You have full authority to act, Mr. Darnell. I don't want a repeat of the Dr. Carlton situation. Preserve the Project at any cost. Is that understood?"

"Yes, sir," Burke answered, bitter venom in his voice as he watched the old man across from him continue to take in the darkened countryside, completely unaware of the murderous intent being shot his way. "At any cost."

"Good," Penders stated, his tone implying that the conversation was ending. "Keep me apprised of any new developments and let me know the instant you have either reacquired or eliminated Adam Nine. And Mr. Darnell?"

"Yes, sir?"

Penders' voice, while still deep and resonating, took on a frosty edge. "Don't disappoint me."

Before Burke could reply, there was a sharp tone in his ear that indicated the call had disconnected. Normally Burke would be seething at being dismissed so casually, but he expected it from Penders. The man wasn't the type for casual conversation or lingering small talk. The quick disconnect was his way of punctuating the conversation. And it had been very effective on Burke as Penders' final words rolled around in his head. He had seen what disappointing Robert Penders looked like, and it wasn't pleasant.

Seated across from him, Harriman was just finishing a phone conversation of his own. The Colonel only contributed occasional affirmative or negative grunts. The call ended with a curt, "Harriman out."

"News, Colonel?" Burke inquired, still perseverating on Penders' last line. With his reputation and position in the company at stake, Burke was going to be sure he was one hundred percent informed of every aspect of this operation.

"I just heard from some of my people on the ground in Pine Haven," the Colonel replied, slipping his phone into one of the many pockets his jacket afforded him. "The word is that Alex Carter has been in the company of a detective all day. Detective Ernest Babcock of the Pine Haven police. Seems it's been an interesting day for the two of them."

Harriman paused there to check some new piece of information on the tablet in front of him. Burke's impatience swelled as he waited for the Colonel to check his data and continue. He had been ignored, dismissed, and disregarded all day today. It was getting to be intolerable, and when all of this was over, every person who had slighted him that day was going to pay dearly. But for now, he needed them all in top form and focused on the task at hand. He would just have to weather his impatience and wait for Harriman to continue.

What seemed to Burke like an excruciating amount of time passed before Harriman continued. "They visited what passes for a morgue in that backwater town at the request of a Dr. Celeste Tanner, state pathologist, to attend the autopsy of Dr. Simone Carlton." Harriman looked up from his tablet. "Isn't she one of ours, sir?"

"Not anymore," Burke replied without embellishment. That was sufficient information for Harriman at this point.

Unaffected by the brush-off, Harriman continued. "From there, they went to lunch at a local sandwich shop."

"Followed up an autopsy with lunch? Wonderful." Burke chuffed at his own joke. Harriman simply stared humorlessly at him, waiting to continue his debrief. Burke nodded assent for him to continue.

"It seems there was an altercation at lunch. Witness accounts say Carter attacked the cop. It was sudden and there was no provocation they could discern. They left before more officers could arrive." Harriman's attention was once again pulled to the tablet.

That last bit of news took Burke aback. There was nothing in Alex Carter's files to indicate that sort of violent response. Not since leaving the Project, anyway. What was going on? Could he be regressing? Regaining some memory of his past life and the behaviors that came with it? That wasn't supposed to be possible. Dr. Carlton had been thorough in her erasure of his past. But then again, she had turned out to be less than loyal to the Project, who knows if this had been part of her agenda from the start?

"Anything about Adam?" Burke asked, knowing full well what the answer would be. The Colonel's people were elite soldiers, the best in their field, but they were only human. Adam was so much more than that.

"No sir," Harriman answered, confirming what Burke had thought. "They've been with Carter and Babcock all day, but there's been so sight of the target."

"And the wife? Rachel? Where is she?"

Harriman glanced back at the tablet again. "At home, sir. There are two Pine Haven police officers with her."

"So she's essentially unguarded," Burke said, almost to himself, an almost imperceptible smile sliding across his face.

"That seems to be the case, sir," Harriman replied.

"Do you think Adam knows about her?" Burke mused distractedly.

"If he accessed the files he took from the safe house, then yes, sir. There is no doubt he knows about her."

Now it was Burke's turn to stare out the window at the darkness beyond. "But does he know everything?"

The question wasn't meant for Harriman, but rather served as a rhetorical question to help Burke gather his thoughts. However, the Colonel took it upon himself to answer. "I've been reviewing the files that were taken from the safe house. There is nothing there beyond the fact that she is Alex Carter's wife and that there is active surveillance on her. I can't see how he could infer anything further from that. And even if he could, what would it matter? What could she possibly mean to him?"

Burke took his eyes from the nothingness outside the helicopter and turned back to the Colonel, his face stoic. "I don't know any more than you do, Colonel, but you have to remember what we're dealing with here. He doesn't think like you or me. Maybe he sees the woman as a convenient way to get at Carter. Maybe he thinks she'd make a great trophy that would display his dominance. Who knows? I certainly don't. Also, I don't care. I want to find him and retrieve him. Or eliminate him, whichever is more convenient. Dealing with this whole thing has been nothing but a pain in the ass, and I'll be happier once this fiasco is cleaned up."

Harriman was about to reply when the pilot announced they were approaching the landing site. After buckling his restraint, Burke took his Glock from its holster, ejected the magazine, confirmed it was fully loaded and slammed it back into the butt of the weapon before returning it to the holster again. He made sure to confirm that the spare magazines he carried were also fully loaded and easily accessible if they were needed. This time, he would be prepared. Adam wouldn't get away from him again. He wouldn't disappoint Penders again.

They touched down on a grassy field a few miles outside of town. A few small raindrops fell against the window of the helicopter and Burke wondered if the storm they had left in Connecticut had caught up with them or if he just had extraordinarily bad luck. He decided on the latter and recovered the poncho Harriman had given him earlier from beneath his seat and slid into it. As he did, the few smattering drops of rain intensified and larger drops smashed against the glass. The wind was picking up as well, brewing up one hell of a storm. A storm he had to go out into. Again. And he had just dried off. If there had been any chance of a reprieve for Adam, it had just been rescinded. Burke was going to burn the man to the ground, along with every other hateful thing associated with this complete disaster of a situation.

Except the woman. No, she was the only person who was completely safe in this whole scenario. She unknowingly played the most important role in this unfolding drama, and the ironic thing was that she had no idea of the part she had been assigned to play.

28

"Mrs. Carter, are you all right?"

Officer Dave Timmins whispered into the freshly darkened Carter house. His gun was in his hands, having cleared his holster nearly the moment the lights had gone out. He listened intently for any unusual sounds, any thumps or scrapes that could show someone was trying to make their way through the blackness of the Carter's living room. The only sound he could hear was the fast and steady pounding of his own heart.

He felt the weight of the gun in his hands and was surprised at how quickly he had drawn the weapon. His training had stressed assessment of a situation before reacting aggressively, but tonight he had ignored that piece. Everything about this had felt wrong to him from the start of the night, from the moment Lieutenant Babcock had tapped him and LeFranc for this special duty assignment and then swore them to secrecy about it, he had felt that something was off. That they didn't know the entire story. And now the lights suddenly going out, it had created a heightened sense of preservation that had caused him to react the way he had. But even now, thinking it all over rationally, his gut still told him not to holster his weapon and to keep it ready. And he had always been inclined to trust his gut.

His heart was still pounding in his chest, distracting him from hearing much else in the nearly silent house. Pushing that aside, he listened intently to the darkness and could make out a slight, raspy breathing a few feet to his right. That was where his partner, John LeFranc, had been sitting all evening. No doubt that was John he could hear, and based on the pace of his breathing, he was in the same elevated state of awareness and anxiety Timmins was.

"Mrs. Carter, where are you?" Timmins' eyes were adjusting, and he could discern the outline of LeFranc's enormous frame, standing right where Timmins had thought he would be. "Mrs. Carter, can you hear me?"

"I can hear you. We're in the same room. I'm pregnant, not deaf. I'm by the computer." Rachel stood up and edged her way through the darkness, then thought better of it and stopped to let her eyes adjust. She was completely blind at the moment, the sudden darkness so complete and consuming.

A beam of white light unexpectedly cleaved the darkness as suddenly as the lights had gone out. Her eyes, just now adjusting to the blackness, snapped shut for a moment at the appearance of the beam. She eased them open as a second beam followed the first, both scanning the room until one came to rest on her.

"Mrs. Carter, you shouldn't be moving around the house like that in the dark. It could be dangerous, especially for someone in your condition." It was Dave Timmins' youthful voice behind the point of light that shone in her eyes.

"Condition? If you're referring to my pregnancy, don't worry about it. I think the baby can survive a bump to the shin from a coffee table." She immediately felt bad about the sarcastic comeback. Timmins was only worried about her welfare. She imagined his baby blue eyes were alight with concern at the moment. Sarcasm was a stress reaction for her, and the events of the last few days were more than enough to justify it. But she shouldn't take it out on the person charged with protecting her.

She sighed deeply. "Sorry, Officer Timmins. Just a little on edge here. Any idea what happened?"

As if in reply to her question, the wind outside suddenly picked up with a howl. In the dim glow of the streetlights, leaves whipped wildly through the air as the wind intensified, creating a frenzied swirl.

"Guess it was the storm," Timmins said, moving his flashlight beam off Rachel and scanning the room. "The wind must have knocked down some power lines. Nothing to worry about."

It was a logical and reasonable explanation, but it didn't make the nagging little feeling in the back of Rachel's head go away. The sensation that something was out there in the darkness watching them was still with her, still gnawing at her. Except now the darkness outside had moved inside. Maybe whatever was outside watching them had moved inside, too.

"Except for one thing." The deep, gravelly voice of Officer LeFranc came from the kitchen doorway.

"What's that, John?" Timmins replied.

"How come this house seems to be the only one that's lost power?"

A hard lump formed in Rachel's throat as she looked out the front window and into the street. The streetlights just outside cast a creeping glow, and Rachel noticed lights in the windows of the Barton's house across the street.

She ran to the window, heedless of Timmins' earlier warning about making herself visible, and looked up and down the street. Every other house on the street had lights shining brightly through their windows, not to mention the streetlights still dropping amber light all over the street. It couldn't be the storm. Someone had targeted her house. Someone was out there in the night, watching. Watching and waiting for them to make their next move.

"You're right, it couldn't have been the storm. Someone killed the power to this house. They needed it to be dark, and they wanted to catch us off guard." Her mind was racing with possibilities, kicked into overdrive by an excess of adrenaline rushing through her system. She wanted to know who was out there, who was doing this to her family and why they were doing it, but those questions would have to wait. Whoever this person was, their plan was working.

They were vulnerable, trapped in the dark of her living room. They needed to get out of the house and get some place safe.

Her cell phone! In all the excitement of the last few minutes, she hadn't even thought about calling for help. She reached into her pocket for the safe, familiar feel of that small plastic box, and her heart sank when she found it empty and realized she must have left it by the computer.

"Can one of you call for help?" she whispered to the two officers. "Walkie talkie? Cell phone? Anything?"

She heard a rustling and watched the flashlight beams bounce as both men rummaged for a device of some sort to call for help. "I've got my phone," came Timmins' soft voice. She waited a beat until the telltale dull light of a phone screen came to life, illuminating the young cop's baby face in an eerie glow.

"I don't have any signal," he said, his voice tinged with surprise. "That's impossible. I always have a signal in town. Everyone does. We have three towers in the area, and the mountains surrounding us bounce the signals around. There's always coverage. This can't be right."

"Right or not, I don't have a signal either." LeFranc confirmed.

"What about a walkie talkie? Do you have one of those?" Rachel asked, the desperation showing as her voice went up an octave.

"You mean a radio?" LeFranc replied, as Rachel fought the urge to scream at him about the uselessness of semantics. "No, we didn't bring one. When Ernie asked us to do this, he said it was an off the books assignment and to use our cells instead of a radio. There's one in the cruiser, outside."

"Come on," she said, moving toward the front door. Timmins shouted after her, his flashlight beam moving in her direction and illuminating the floor in front of her, allowing her to miss tripping over Alex's boot.

Why doesn't he ever put these things away? The errant thought darted through her mind as her subconscious made a desperate grasp at normalcy. She turned from the front door and faced Timmins and LeFranc, who almost disappeared in the inky blackness surrounding the house. "We need to get outside. In here, we're sitting ducks. We can't see our hands in front of our faces without the flashlights, and those are like lighthouse beacons for him. Outside, we at least have the same advantages he has. We can see him coming. It's not much of an advantage, but it's a lot more than we have right now."

"In here, he has the same disadvantages we do, if we kill the flashlights," Timmins argued from the shadows. "We can use that against him. Whoever 'him' is."

"He cut the power. Somehow he's jamming the cell phones. He planned all of that out. You don't think he has a plan to deal with the dark?" Rachel snapped.

She hadn't meant to sound so harsh, but she was scared. So very scared. She squinted into the shadows of the living room, searching for any signs of movement. Everywhere she looked, she saw shadows in the darkness, and her heart stammered each time. They needed to move. He was coming. The dark stranger wasn't a concept any longer. He was here. If he wasn't actually in her house, he would be soon, and she very much did not want to be here with him.

The cone of light that had been hovering by the kitchen doorway suddenly snuffed out, leaving a single beam illuminating the space. "She's right, Dave," came LeFranc's gravelly voice from the newly darkened doorway. "At least out there we stand a chance. The cruiser is parked right outside, at the curb. We get to it; we can get Mrs. Carter out of here safely. And that's the main reason we're here."

"Okay, okay," Timmins relented. "But we stay away from the cruiser, too. Like Mrs. Carter said, this guy has planned for everything. He might have rigged the cruiser somehow, too. We get outside and hoof it to a neighbor's house where we can wait for back-up. Okay?"

A moment of silence. "Okay," LeFranc grunted. "The nearest neighbor."

"That's Walt and Betty Barton, straight across the street." Rachel's voice was a whispered shout as she rallied herself to leave the house. She had always felt safe there, in her house, in the community she and Alex had chosen to live in. Tonight, everything that made her feel safe had been ripped away. As she thought about the loss of safety and security in her life and everything they had endured the last few days, rage and determination slowly supplanted panic, and she steeled herself for what was about to happen.

LeFranc joined her and Timmins at the front door as Timmins clicked off his flashlight. Only the dirty amber wash of the streetlights seeped into the house, elongating shadows and deepening pockets of darkness. She reached for the doorknob, willing the fits of panic in her stomach to subside long enough for them to get across the street to the Bartons' house.

Those fits of panic exploded, jolting through her entire body as she felt a hand grasp hers and pull it away from the doorknob. She started to let out a cry, but stifled it when she realized whose hand was on hers.

"I think I should go first, Mrs. Carter. We don't know where this guy is." The deep blue eyes of Dave Timmins, muted only slightly by the glow of the streetlights, stared back at her. The breath that had caught in her throat, the scream she had held a moment ago, exploded from her in a sigh of relief.

She stepped back from the door, allowing Timmins space to position himself directly behind it. Her eyes were adjusting to the lack of light and she saw Timmins slide his pistol from its holster as he rested the other hand on the doorknob. He glanced back at LeFranc and the two men locked eyes until LeFranc nodded acknowledgement to the younger man. He raised his pistol halfway into a firing position as he faced the door, readying himself for whatever was on the other side.

"Mrs. Carter, please move over here?" Timmins whispered, nodding to the left of the door. Rachel positioned herself where he had directed, and she realized what he was doing. When the door opened, she would be hidden from the view of anyone on the other side. She would be the last of the three of them to be spotted, and it would give her the element of surprise and the greatest chance of escape. Timmins and LeFranc were intentionally placing themselves between her and danger. New pangs of fear cropped up at that as she looked into the faces of the two men. They had never met her before tonight, but were now readying themselves to compromise their own personal safety for hers. Fear, guilt and gratitude all fought for dominance inside her at the thought.

With one more glance back to his partner, Timmins turned his attention to the door again. He twisted the doorknob slowly until there was an audible click and carefully pulled the door open, blocking Rachel's view of what might be on the other side. For a moment, Timmins and LeFranc remained motionless, suspended like insects in dark amber. After what seemed like an agonizing eternity, during which her heart tried to pound its way out of her chest, Timmins whispered, "It looks clear. Mrs. Carter, you follow me and John will cover us from the rear."

Rachel nodded, the gesture imperceptible in the cloying darkness. Moving from her position of safety behind the door, she stepped in behind Timmins and moved as close to him as she could. Earlier, in the light, he hadn't seemed very big. But standing behind him now, as he acted as a human shield, she was surprised at how the young officer made her feel tiny in comparison. Timmins glanced back at her to be sure she was in position before moving through the doorway and onto the porch.

He had barely cleared the door frame when the stranger appeared. Rachel couldn't see where he had come from, he seemed to have just slithered out of the surrounding shadows to appear in front of them. When he raised his hand, the meager glow from the streetlights glinted off of an object he held. Rachel gasped as she saw the gun, but that was all she could do at the moment. She was stuck between Timmins and LeFranc, unable to surge forward into the open night or back into the house. All she could do was wait for the loud crack that would issue from the weapon. The stranger had timed his appearance perfectly, trapping them all together, bottlenecked at the door.

The explosion she was expecting from the weapon didn't happen. Instead, what came from the gun was a light whisper and a wisp of smoke that was torn viciously from the barrel and carried off into the night by the fierce winds. Timmins fell back against her, his limp form pushing her back as she stumbled through the doorway with his full weight on her. LeFranc tried to work around them and out the door, shouting at her to move out of the way, but she was stuck where she was as the dead weight of Timmins' body carried her to the floor.

She hit the floor with a jarring impact that sent jagged waves of pain up her back, forcing the air from her lungs in a single whoosh. LeFranc had worked his way to her but not around her and now stood directly over her, his weapon thrust out from his body, ready to fire as he scanned the doorway for signs of the stranger. Rachel gasped, refilling her lungs with air, and struggled to get out from under Timmins' unmoving form. As she pushed against him, her mind once again marveled at how much bigger and more solid the young cop was than she had thought when she first met him. Two more whispers sounded from the porch and with a familiar yet pained grunt, LeFranc fell away from her into the shadows of the living room. Desperation gave her newfound strength, and she pushed as hard as she could against Timmins' body, rolling him a few inches to the side. It wasn't much, but it was enough to allow her to disentangle herself from him. Once free, she dashed back into the darkness of the living room. Her leg hit the coffee table, webs of pain shooting through her as she fell to the floor with a grunt.

"Ouch. That sounded painful." A voice in the dark. The stranger's voice, cold and devoid of feeling.

On the floor between the couch and the coffee table, Rachel froze. She was certain the stranger couldn't see her, between the darkness and her makeshift hiding place, but there was still an icy tingle on her back as if his eyes were boring into her at that moment. Between being slammed to the floor a moment ago and then just now tripping over the coffee table, her body was throbbing with pain. She fought the urge to stretch, to dispel some of the discomfort. She didn't dare to even breathe at the moment, much less move. So she sat in the dark, listening intently for signs of the stranger, trying to ignore the pain.

Her mind tried to push it away, but she couldn't help thinking about Timmins and LeFranc. They had only been trying to help her. To protect her. And now they were both dead. The image of the blue-eyed young cop, with his boyishly captivating smile, wouldn't leave her mind. She could feel a white-hot ball of anger building in her as a tear ran down her cheek. She fought back a sniffle, again trying to remain completely silent. The longer she sat there, silent in the dark, the more the fiery anger was overtaking the chill of fear. She would not let their sacrifice be for nothing. She would escape and she would survive.

The only sound in the room was the howling of the wind outside the open front door. She hadn't heard the stranger move into the house to look for her, but she also hadn't heard him retreat to the porch. She couldn't tell where he was at the moment. He had moved so stealthily before, just before shooting Timmins, that it was possible he was moving around the living room now, searching for her, and she didn't know it.

She needed to get away. Even if it meant exposing her position, she couldn't delay any longer. Every second she lay still was another second she gave the stranger to find her. As quietly as she could manage, she pulled herself forward, each movement generating what she perceived as thunderous noise as she scraped across the carpet. Thankful for the roar of the wind and the pattering of the rain that had fallen against the windows, she moved forward in the hopes it would mask some of the noise she made.

She reached the end of the couch, peering carefully around the corner of the coffee table and into the living room. Dim amber light fell into the room from the open door, illuminating the motionless form of Officer Timmins just inside.

A fresh burst of icy panic washed over her with the renewed realization that Timmins and LeFranc were dead. This man, this stranger, had callously and efficiently murdered two trained and decorated police officers in less than half a minute. What hope did she have of escaping him? Of surviving him? Practically none, she decided, but she wasn't about to let that stop her. There was too much at stake, too much depending on her and her survival. With everything she had learned from the files Dr. Carlton had given them, Alex needed her now more than ever. For the sake of both him and her, she had to escape. He needed to know what she had found. And then there was the baby. The little life hadn't even had a chance to start. She was not about to let this psychopath take that away from him. Or her.

Once again, white-hot determination pushed back the chill of fear and panic. Her mind sharpened, enabling her to better consider her options. The light spilling in from the front door wasn't a lot, but it was enough to prevent her from escaping that way without being seen. She didn't know where the stranger was, but she didn't feel certain she could make it out the front door without being shot. She considered a break for the kitchen, but that was the same situation. The shaft of light that bled in through the front door cut a path across the entire length of the living room and ended right at the foot of the kitchen entrance. It essentially split the house in two between the living room and the kitchen. She would most likely be seen if she tried to make a break for the front door. The same if she tried to escape through the kitchen and out the back door. The river of dim light also flowed across her path to the spiral staircase leading upstairs, cutting off that potential escape route. She considered the windows behind her, still masked in shadow, and trying to open one of those and slip out. Too much motion and noise in that scenario, she was sure to be seen and most likely shot.

She was trapped.

An icy hand gasped at her heart and lungs as a shadow rippled through the band of amber light. Her eyes darted to the front door, fully expecting to see the stranger moving into the house to search for her. What she saw instead filled her with a new sense of hope.

Officer Timmins was pulling himself upright, with an assist from the front door to prop him up. With each movement, his face twisted in agony, revealing the intensity of his pain. He didn't look good, but at least he wasn't dead.

She had to get to him. He was still at the front door, across the darkened living room and all the tripping hazards that contained. She couldn't risk a mad dash for the front door. Even though she felt confident she knew the layout of the room, even in the dark, she had already had one panicked collision with an unyielding piece of furniture. Another simple fall like that would slow her down and, worse, would attract the attention of the stranger.

She decided the best way to reach Timmins was to stay low and quiet. She would crawl across the living room on all fours, staying in the shadows as much as possible until she could reach the front door and get herself and Timmins out onto the lawn. From there, they could get to a neighbor, or at the very least attract some attention and call for help. There was still the stream of light from the front door bisecting the room, but she'd have to cross that as best she could when she got there.

Moving slowly, she slipped past the end of the coffee table and into the living room. Her eyes had adjusted somewhat to the dark and, aside from the light streaming in from the front door, she couldn't make out any significant obstacles between her and Officer Timmins. Still, she swept one hand slowly in front of her from side to side as she moved forward to check for anything that might be in her path. Her heart jumped every time her knee scraped the carpet, the tiny noise thunderous to her ears. She was sure it would give away her position and intentions and the dark stranger would be on her in a moment, raining a hail of quiet bullets on her from his silenced weapon. Her breathing was shallow, almost to the point of being non-existent, as she carefully dragged herself across the room. A shock of electricity jolted through her as her sweeping hand came into contact with something unexpected, and she once again cursed Alex and his lazy housekeeping skills when she felt the spine of the book he had dropped on the floor next to the chair.

She reached the edge of the river of light washing in from the front door and froze, listening for any movement or activity in the house. All she could hear was the driving rain against the windows and the wind rustling the bare trees outside. She swiveled her head to either side, scanning the room for any sign of the stranger. She saw no movement. No flittering in the darkness. No shadows moving against the black of the room. She couldn't be sure he wasn't there watching and waiting for her to expose herself, but she had run out of choices. It was now or never, and never wasn't an option.

Quietly pulling herself to a kneeling position, she scoped out the last few feet between her and Timmins. It was bathed in that ugly, amber glow from the streetlights, spilling onto everything in her path. That glow offered nowhere to hide, leaving her completely exposed as she ran the last few feet to Timmins and helped him get up and out the front door. The cold gnawing of fear overtook the fire of determination in her, and she felt her hands shake. Her mind flashed through all the things that could go wrong. All the things that would slow her down. Expose her. Make her an easy target. She felt dizzy as what felt like hundreds of potential ways to die spun through her head.

No. Mentally, she put her foot down. She had to do this. No matter the risk, it had to be done. It was a few more feet to Timmins. No more. She could cover it in seconds. Besides, it wasn't like she had any other options at this point.

Edging herself as close to the front door as she could while remaining under the cover of dark, she pulled herself up, standing in a crouch. Each movement was a new note in the symphony of pain her body was playing. Despite the chill in the air, her palms were slick with sweat as she inched closer to the river of light and got ready to dash to Timmins. Her heart was racing, sending blood pounding through her ears, blocking out even the incessant rain. She closed her eyes and once again quieted the little voice in her head that insisted on listing all the ways she could die in the next few minutes and readied herself to move.

She hesitated, listening intently once more, directing her auditory senses into the house. Despite her best efforts to block out the howl of the wind and the crash of rain from just outside the door, all she could hear were the sounds of the storm and the anguished gasps from Timmins. She had no idea where the stranger was, but she had no choice now except to move.

Releasing all the gathered energy in her tensed leg muscles, she ran forward into the light of the doorway. She reached Timmins' side in no less than a half-dozen steps, even though every second exposed to the stranger felt like an eternity. She dipped into a crouch next to him, still propped against the front door. His hands clutched his chest, bunching up his otherwise immaculately kept uniform, and every breath he took was sheer agony. His eyes were glassy and unfocused, his complexion pale, taking on an eerie and almost supernatural luminescence in the dim light. To Rachel it almost appeared as if he were glowing, like a host of angels sat nearby waiting to take him on the ultimate trip into the afterlife. Suddenly, he blinked and took in a loud, shuddering breath that shattered the illusion.

She stooped down low enough to throw his arm over her shoulder, wrap her arm around him, and try to pull him to his feet. He winced at the effort, breath escaping him in a sharp huff, his eyes snapping open wide as if they were attempting to leap from their sockets. But he was able to muster enough strength to help her help him up.

"Mrs. Carter, I...." he started.

"No time," Rachel snapped, cutting him off, as she glanced back into the darkness of the house. She fully expected to see the stranger burst from the shadows in pursuit of them, but the house was completely still inside.

"We need to get out of here," she said, her voice edging into panic. "I need you to move with me!"

"Leave me..." Timmins' voice was barely a whisper. She couldn't stop to see how badly he was hurt and, for all she knew, she was helping to kill him by moving him. She knew for certain that if she left him behind, he would be dead at the hands of the maniac stalking them, and she wasn't about to let that happen if she could help it.

The intensity of the storm had reached a fevered pitch. The Barton's house was so close. They had to hurry.

"No can do," she said in response to his request to leave him behind. She nodded her head toward the street and the house just beyond it. "Look, the Barton's house is just a few hundred feet away. We can make it. But you have to help me. I can't carry us both. Just move as fast as you can and I'll take up the slack." She took a step forward, only a few inches, and pulled him along with her. Her injured leg and back burned with the effort, but the sounds coming from Timmins indicated that her pain was nothing compared to his.

As they moved forward, Timmins suddenly jerked his head around frantically, back to the front door of the Carter house. Rachel's heart froze in her chest as she imagined what he had seen or heard. She could almost feel the stranger's gun on her back as she imagined the bullets tearing through her. She turned to look, but stopped at Timmins' face. His eyes were darting around the area of the porch where he had just been, searching desperately. Panic filled his clear blue eyes.

"What is it? What's wrong?" Rachel asked, her anxiety reaching a crescendo in her stomach. The stranger would have heard them by now, even over the noise of the storm. He would know where they were, and he'd be coming soon. They couldn't afford any delays.

"My gun...." Timmins stammered, trying to pull himself away from Rachel.

"Forget it!" she yelled, pulling him back against her and nudging him toward the Barton's house again. "We need to get out of here!"

"But Babcock'll.... have my hide.... finds out.... I left my gun..." he replied, his words staggered through labored breaths.

Rachel reached up and cupped his chin in her hand, swinging his face to meet hers. "Don't take this the wrong way, but right now, I don't care what Babcock will say about your missing gun. Now move!" She pulled him forward, the two of them falling into lurching steps as she dragged the young cop along with her. She fought the nagging urge to look back at the door, certain that if she did, she would see the stranger there. Pushing the image to the back of her mind, she continued forward.

The storm was in its full fury, with grape-sized raindrops driven into them by raging winds. With her free hand Rachel brushed her rain-soaked hair from her eyes to clear her vision, but without the barrier her hair provided the rain pounded directly into her face, momentarily blinding her and forcing her to slow down every few steps to clear it again. The added effort of lugging Timmins along didn't help.

For as long as she could, she fought the urge to look back, to see if the stranger was behind them. She couldn't stand not knowing any longer and risked a glance back toward the house, wiping away at the rainwater covering her eyes. She couldn't see any sign of him. On the surface she felt relieved, but that was immediately washed away by the fear of not knowing where he was. Fresh waves of anxiety washed over her as she scanned the pockets of darkness around the house, looking for movement. She cursed the storm as rain fell and trees shook in the wind, each bit of motion catching her eye. Her mind created threats at each tiny movement, and dread once again overcame her. Turning away from the house, she redoubled her efforts to get her and Timmins to the Barton's house. They were vulnerable in the street and all she could feel were his eyes on her, waiting to put a bullet in her back.

Glancing left and right revealed no traffic out on the street. A passing motorist would have been too much to hope for, she supposed. Once again sloughing the rain from her eyes, she focused on the Barton's. As it was on most nights, the front window was lit with a soft, warm glow. Betty and Walt were creatures of routine. By now they would have finished dinner and sat down in front of the television to watch *Jeopardy!*. They were a kindly couple who had lived in the same home for as long as anyone in town could remember. Never having had children of their own, they had a habit of taking care of anyone who needed help, becoming de facto parents and grandparents for the entire community. If she could reach them, they would help. All they had to do was make it to the front door.

"C'mon, we're almost there," she gasped as she shifted her weight under Timmins' arm. He let out a sharp gasp of pain in response, but he was putting less of his weight on her. She hoped that was a good sign.

She risked another look back at her house. The front door still stood wide open, inside a mass of darkness. Through the wind-buffeted rain and dim glow of the streetlights, the house looked terrifying to her just then, a funhouse mirror of the place she knew and loved. That house had been her sanctuary. Her comfort. She and Alex had built a life there. Yet in one night the stranger, whoever he was, had taken all the happy memories and hopes for the future her home represented and turned it into a nightmare. A flash of anger flushed through her, driving back the fear. She had never been one for hate. In her mind, hate accomplished nothing except creating more hate, and that was a cycle she didn't want in her life. But tonight she knew what hate was. How complete, total and all-consuming it could be, because she hated the stranger that had come into their lives. No matter what he had endured, no matter what his past, he had chosen hatred and vengeance himself. He had decided to destroy her family. And she hated him like she had never hated in her life.

That hatred was guiding her now, pushing her forward as she led Timmins off the pavement and onto the Burton's lawn, the sopping wet ground sucking at their shoes as they did. Teeth gritted, she continued on, the front door only a dozen feet away now. She fought the urge to shout for help, to draw Walt and Betty away from *Jeopardy!* and to the front door to help them. If the stranger didn't know where they were, she didn't want to give that away needlessly. Instead, she slogged forward, dragging along the increasingly less dependent Timmins with her.

When they reached the bottom step of the porch, Rachel gently sat Timmins down and raced to the front door, frantically ringing the doorbell and knocking at the same time. When there was no reply, she let out a whispered cry for Walt and Betty, begging them to hurry and come to the door. There was still no reply. It must be the storm. The older couple were both hard of hearing already, the storm was most likely making it impossible for them to hear Rachel at the door. She tried the doorknob, and it turned in her hand. It didn't really surprise her. Pine Haven was a small, safe little town. Crime typically comprised the occasional drunk and disorderly charge or breaking up teen parties. No one felt compelled to lock their doors. She had always felt safe in the community. Until tonight, when her entire world had been shattered.

Swinging the door open, the house greeted her with a flood of light that momentarily blinded her. She had been moving through the dark for so long now her eyes were no longer adjusted to light and the bright lights of the Barton's living room and the flickering light of the television assaulted her vision. Squinting, she made her way towards the twin easy chairs the older couple frequented during most evenings. Racing from the entryway into the living room, she moved past the chairs and positioned herself in front of the television to get their attention.

And froze at what she saw. Walt and Betty, seated where they would normally be on any given night, in their easy chairs watching *Jeopardy!* and enjoying an after-dinner drink. They sat there now, as they had every night before for as long as Rachel had known them, their wide eyes staring at the television in front of them. Except tonight, each had a neat hole in the center of their foreheads.

Rachel's heart sank and adrenaline surged. "Oh no. Oh God, please, no." Tears were welling up in the corners of her eyes, mixing with the rain from the storm. Anger and grief filled her with a burning core of emotion. Walt and Betty Barton were good people. Happy people. They were people who had brought nothing but happiness and joy to their friends, neighbors, and community. And now they sat in the living room of the home they shared for so long, their lives ended simply because of who they were close to.

"It's not fair," Rachel muttered, reaching out and gently touching Walt's hand. "I'm so sorry." The hand was warm, but there was no spark of life in the man's eyes. None of the warmth and joy that had always been in his eyes. Everything he was, everything he had been until that moment, was simply gone.

The tears came hard now. These two people had cared for her, treated her as if she had been their own daughter, and now they were dead because of her. Her throat tightened and the tears, mingled with the rain, fell down her cheeks. They were dead, and it was her fault. Her fault because she had come to them for help. Somehow, the stranger knew she would come to them. He knew it. And he killed them for no other reason than they were in his way.

"Don't feel sorry for them, Rachel. They're in a much better place now, no doubt grateful to me for freeing them from the burdens of this life."

The voice came from behind, startling her. The voice was deep, even-toned, possibly even melodic. All the tension, fear, and anxiety she had been pushing down exploded within her, mixing with the rage, grief and despair that had consumed her at the sight of Walt and Betty dead in their chairs. Her mind was screaming warnings of danger to her, but she no longer cared. She knew she was going to die soon. But she wasn't going to do it while whimpering on the floor. He was going to kill her; she might as well die facing him with the full fury she was carrying.

"Who are you? Why are you doing this?" she asked, trying to muster as much bravado as she could. It was much easier with the cooling corpses of two people she cared for next to her.

"He really has confused you, hasn't he? He'll pay for that." There was an edge to that last statement that made her blood run cold.

"Who are you?" she repeated, taking a few slow, almost imperceptible steps backward. Her eyes darted around the room in search of anything she might use to defend herself. There wasn't much to choose from. To her left was a magazine rack with a stack of old copies of People and Yankee Magazine, to her right nothing but the couch. The entrance to the kitchen was further to her right, but the couch partially blocked her way. With the throbbing pain in her leg and back, she wasn't sure if she would clear the couch before the stranger was on her, let alone be able to quickly find a decent weapon.

She was trapped. Again.

As if sensing her thoughts, the stranger shifted from the inky shadows and stepped into the living room where he could be seen in full light. Seeing him clearly for the first time, Rachel noted he didn't look like a murderer, as if there were a physical prerequisite for being a psychopath. It was more than his appearance that thrust the thought into her head, his demeanor was one of complete harmlessness. He was average looking. About her age, average build, dark hair and a soft face that held a beautiful pair of haunting blue eyes. Eyes that, despite their icy color, looked warm. Possibly even inviting, under different circumstances.

Beyond his appearance, he carried himself with a sort of quiet calm. An inner sense of confidence that comes from a sense of surety in oneself. It wasn't swagger; he didn't feel the need to advertise his belief in himself, it was just there. In his stance. In his eyes. When he spoke. In another time and place, she might have considered him attractive.

But not here and now. In the now, all she could think about was how she could get away from him alive and get to Alex. He strode two more steps into the Barton's living room, moving closer to her but still keeping a distance. Rachel had the thought that she was being baited. That he was slowly and methodically closing the distance between them in a way that was almost imperceptible, letting him get closer without her panicking. It might have worked if she hadn't known that he had murdered at least three people that night. In response, almost with a visible sense of defiance, she backed away an equal number of steps. It was a limited strategy. He had the entire living room to cross; she was running out of places she could easily move into. If he continued to advance, she would have no choice but to make a break for the kitchen or risk being caught where she was.

"You're confused," he said, taking another small step forward. His voice was smooth and gentle, warm and inviting. The tone was neither forceful nor passive but completely neutral, like he was ceding half of the conversation in an effort to hear and understand you. To build trust. Underneath that, she could detect the slightest sense of bitterness in him. Bitterness that became stronger and more acidic as he continued speaking. "The lies you've been told have taken a firm hold. I'm sorry about that. We'll get through them together and show you the truth soon enough. And then you'll understand why all of this was necessary."

Anger coursed through her at that last sentence and she was ready to rage against him, but he moved forward again slightly at that moment, his right arm swinging out from behind his back. Her breath caught in her throat at the sight of the gun in his hand. The gun that had killed Want and Betty and Officer LeFranc and no doubt countless others before that. He carried it nonchalantly at his side, as if it were nothing more than a tool to him, like how a carpenter carries a hammer or a plumber carries a wrench. He wielded the weapon with the same casual confidence he carried himself with, and that frightened her even more than the fact he had a gun. That level of confidence meant he had experience, that he knew how to use the gun and wasn't afraid to.

It was then that she noticed the extension attached to the barrel and her heart sank. She knew little about guns, but she knew that piece of equipment wasn't something the average gun owner would carry around with them. It was then that she knew, for certain, she wasn't dealing with a garden variety psychopath. The man standing before her, slowing moving toward her, was a professional killer. He had murdered three people without hesitation or remorse just to get to her. Why he had done that was still a mystery, a mystery she hoped to have time to ponder. That possibility was looking less and less likely with each advancing step the stranger took.

He paused, holding out his empty hand to her. His clear blue eyes locked on her and what she thought was a look of concern crossed his face. Slowly and deliberately, he slipped the hand with the gun behind his back again and took a half step away from her. He held her gaze the entire time and his eyes, while still cold, seemed to soften a bit with some odd realization.

"Don't be afraid, Rachel." The voice was like warm ice as it slid across her ears, both soothing and frigid at the same time. "I'm not here to hurt you. I'm here to rescue you. To free you. To put things right."

"Who are you?" What do you want from me? Why did you kill all these people?" The questions tumbled from her in rapid-fire succession, not giving her sudden burst of courage and resolve time to fade. But as soon as she finished, a smile spread across the stranger's face that again turned her insides into icy jelly.

"Killing these people was unfortunate, but it was necessary. They were standing in the way of my mission. My destiny. They were standing between me and you." He paused for a moment, his smile unchanged. Some of the warmth it previously held dissipated, exposing more of the cold darkness that lay underneath. Rachel shivered.

"As for what I want from you," he continued, "I only want to give you the best possible life I can. To shield you from all the lies. The deceptions. The pain. I want to allow you to live the life you were truly meant to live; with the man you were meant to live it with."

Her mouth was dry, her knees suddenly buckling a bit as his true intentions sank in. He wasn't here to kill her. It was so much worse than that.

"And that man would be...?" she asked, trailing off at the end, her bravado failing her.

The stranger's head shook slowly, as if a great weight had suddenly been placed on him. "They really have brainwashed you, haven't they?"

It seemed to Rachel at that moment that he actually seemed despondent about the level of her apparent brainwashing. She wasn't sure whether to hate him or feel sorry for him.

"I am that man," he stated.

"No...." Rachel whispered, her chest tightening. She glanced at the lifeless forms of Walt and Betty, thought about Officer LeFranc. He had killed them all over some strange obsession with her. They were dead because of her. She could feel the dead eyes of Walt and Betty on her, their usually kind faces twisted into masks of pain and accusation, and squeezed her own eyes shut. Hot tears streamed down her cheeks; her fists balled up beside her. This was insane.

She opened her eyes again and wiped at the tears. The stranger remained where he had been, not making any further advancement toward her. As he looked at her, his face twisted into an odd mix of compassion, concern, confusion, and pain. His icy cold eyes bore straight into her as if he were laying bare her soul. She shivered again, harder, drawing an arm across her chest and shrank back from him as much as she was able.

The stranger saw this and his face went slack. "I'm sorry. I didn't mean to frighten you. It's just that, seeing you now, being here with you, I..." He paused, searching for the next words. In that instant, Rachel saw the tiniest glimmer of vulnerability in him, a shy little boy completely out of his element.

"Please," he continued, his voice almost pleading, "trust me. I can help you navigate through this web of lies you've been living in, and together, we can live the life we were destined for."

Pushing his gun hand further behind his back, the stranger held out his other arm, palm resting up and fingers slightly splayed open in an invitation to her to take his hand. His voice had changed once more. It was warm and soothing without the malice that had permeated it earlier. He was like a teenage boy making an overture to his first girlfriend, convincing her of his undying love and devotion. Except his obsession wasn't a harmless teenage fling, he was a killer who had callously murdered people in his pursuit of her.

Rachel's mind spun as she grasped at her next move. She was about to respond to his outstretched hand, to tell him what he could do with his offer, when she noticed a shadow slide across the darkness of the hallway behind the stranger. She couldn't make out who it was, whether it was a friend or an enemy, but at this point she didn't care. Any distraction that might allow her to slip into the kitchen and out the back door would be a welcome one.

She would have to keep him occupied, keep him from noticing whoever was behind him. Keep his attention on her. The best way to do that was simply to talk to him.

"I'm married, you know," she stated flatly. It was a risky thing to lead with, but the goal was to keep the stranger focused on her. She didn't want to shatter his delusions entirely, as that might send him over the edge and into a killing rage. But she needed his attention focused solely on her at the moment, and that seemed to be the best way to do it.

The stranger took it better than she imagined he would. "We can take care of that," he replied, dropping his outstretched hand. "We'll need new identities. That will effectively dissolve your marriage. It was a sham from the beginning, anyway."

The figure crept closer. Rachel was making out an outline in the darkness, the shadow slightly deeper than the surrounding dark. A slight build, moving at a slow but steady pace, holding some sort of blunt object in their hands. So far, the stranger hadn't noticed this new player, but Rachel had to keep the blue-eyed psycho talking to keep it that way.

"What was a sham?" she asked the stranger, building on his delusion. Keeping his focus on her.

"Your marriage," the stranger spat, venom returning to his voice as it lost the soft edge it had a moment ago. "It was meant to be us from the beginning. Until someone stole it from us."

"Who stole it?" Rachel blurted, watching as the figure in the darkened hallway came into the light of the living room. It was Officer Timmins, moving slowly and meticulously closer to the stranger, armed with one of Walt's golf clubs. He must have slipped in through the garage after Rachel left him on the front steps. The young cop moved well, despite being shot twice only fifteen minutes ago. As he moved further into her field of vision, she saw the two bullet holes in his shirt, right above his heart. There was no blood in sight. She silently said a thank you for the miracle of Kevlar.

"It's best you don't worry about that and leave it to me," the stranger stated, his voice again cold and dead.

Timmins was directly behind the stranger now, almost close enough to hit him with the golf club that was now held high above his head. Timmins' stance was shaky and his eyes were glassy and wild, once again skating the edge of consciousness. Rachel's heart raced; her gut knotted in anticipation as Timmins edged closer. The cop drew back his arms, positioning himself to strike.

Suddenly and without warning, the stranger turned, raising his gun toward the advancing cop. Timmins' eyes went wide with surprise for a fraction of a second before the gun coughed once, this time blowing a neat hole through Timmins' forehead where Kevlar offered him no protection. For what seemed like an eternity, Timmins stood there with a look of shock etched on his face before sliding to the floor with a thud that resounded like thunder through the room.

Shock and horror seized Rachel as Timmins fell to the floor and lay there, a deepening crimson pool spreading out beneath him. She couldn't move, couldn't breathe. He had survived before. He had been shot and survived. They had dragged themselves away from this madman and survived. And now he was dead on the floor. Dead because he came back for her.

Disbelief paralyzed her as she stared at Timmins' unmoving form, until she realized the stranger was also firmly fixated on the young cop's body. In that moment, she simply reacted, her body moving without thought. She darted past the edge of the couch, out of the dim light of the living room and into darkness once more. But this time was different. This time, the darkness was her ally, not her enemy. She knew the Barton's kitchen well, almost as well as her own, with the time she had spent there during the many neighborhood barbeques and holiday parties Walt and Betty hosted over the years. With only a few seconds advantage over the stranger, she raced past the refrigerator and stove to the far end of the small kitchen, falling hard against the counter there, her hands smacking down with a loud slap. Fumbling in the darkness, she found a drawer next to the sink and yanked it open, pulling it right out of its niche in the wall. Silverware clattered to the floor, noisily sliding across the linoleum. She fell to her knees and grasped the first item her hands fell on. In the dark, she couldn't tell exactly what it was, just that it was heavy and sported a wooden handle. She hoped it had a sharp edge, but whatever it was would have to do. She didn't have time to search for anything else.

As soon as that thought crossed her mind, there was a flutter of motion in the kitchen entry. The stranger stood there, silhouetted by the dim yellow light spilling in from the living room. Her hand tightened around the wooden handle and her body tensed, ready to move.

"Please don't make this difficult, Rachel." His warm, almost welcoming voice was back, the malice once again buried. "You'll be happy in our new life, I promise. Just come with me now." Something jingled in his hand. "I have the keys to the Barton's car. It's right out in the garage. We can get in and drive far away from here. We can be together, as we were meant to be. You just have to come out."

The slightest touch of darkness reappeared with his next words. "Don't make me have to come looking for you."

"You can go rot in hell," she muttered, wrapping her hand tightly around the wooden handle of her mystery weapon, and chided herself for swearing. When she got out of this, she'd have to remember to feed the swear jar.

The stranger took a step into the kitchen and away from the entry, slipping into the darkness. Rachel pulled herself to a low squat, her sore body protesting every movement, as she duck walked around the island that took up the center of Walt and Betty's kitchen. If she survived this, she would treat herself to a long, hot bath. With bubbles. Definitely with bubbles. And wine.

A clattering noise erupted to her right, too close for comfort. He had wandered into the scattering of silverware left behind by her search for a weapon. He was so close to her now, just around the corner of the island. She resisted the urge to strike out blindly in that direction. She couldn't depend on dumb luck to hit him, she had to let him get close before she struck. And she had to strike hard to be sure she would hurt him enough to keep him from chasing her. Possibly hard enough to kill him.

A chill ran through her at that thought. Even after everything she had been through tonight, she still mentally recoiled at the thought of taking another person's life.

Another loud clank of silverware being scattered across the floor. He was getting closer. Her grip on the wooden handled whatever-it-was tightened further, to where she doubted even death could break it.

Another clatter of metal, this one almost right next to her. The sensation of his breath on her neck was almost tangible. She couldn't allow herself to strike impulsively. She had to wait for contact. Had to be absolutely certain where he was before she could make her move. Her heart raced, knowing he was so dangerously close.

Something brushed against her lightly and pulled away, then doubled back and grabbed at her. She felt his hands scrambling to grasp and she let out a cry before swinging her weapon toward the searching, grasping hands. There was a soft *thunk* as the weapon hit something, followed immediately but a shriek of pain and something warm and wet spraying over her. The hands that held her suddenly let go and without hesitation she raced for the living room, wrenching free the weapon with a wet sucking noise that elicited another cry of pain from the stranger. She hadn't been able to move more than a step before she felt his hand close around her ankle and pull hard on her injured leg, tripping her and sending her crashing to the cold linoleum in a timpani of spilled silverware. Again she flailed blindly with the weapon and again she found her mark as the stranger cried out in pain and released her again.

He was still screaming as she reached the living room, running past the cooling corpses Walt, Betty, and now Timmins, before bursting out of the front door. She ran blindly into the storm, racing to the street where she hoped she could attract the attention of a neighbor or a passing car. A sinking feeling hit her as she thought that maybe the stranger had anticipated this and had already killed all her neighbors, leaving them dead during their nightly routines as he had Walt and Betty. Pushing that thought down, she moved forward, hoping desperately that someone would hear her cries for help or see her frantically waving. This was a small town; someone would recognize her and stop to help her. They had to.

Just as the thought of help ran through her mind, the glow of headlights appeared around the corner, growing brighter until two glowing orbs split the night with yellow beams. She couldn't make out the type of car it was, but it was moving at a dangerous speed and in her direction. As she wondered who could be out driving like that on a night like this, her heart dropped. The stranger. Maybe he wasn't acting alone. Maybe he had back-up. A partner. A protégé. It wasn't uncommon for killers to work together in pairs.

She ducked down behind the big oak tree in the Barton's front yard, shrinking as close to the trunk as she could to hide herself in the shadows. The car slowed as it approached her house, coming to a full stop at the curb just outside. She tensed, tightly gripping the weapon in her hands. The weapon that she now realized had been a large kitchen knife, the one Betty had often used to cut meat. Blood sluiced off the blade as the rain diluted it, and she felt a sudden sense of satisfaction in the fact that she had hurt her attacker.

No one had yet gotten out of the car across the street. She couldn't make out any distinct features through the rain dappled windows of the vehicle, but she could see there was more than one passenger inside. Her heart pounded, blood rushing noisily through her ears, knife gripped firmly in her hand as she waited. The car doors opened and her breath stopped in anticipation as two figures stepped into the storm. Between the darkness and the rain, Rachel couldn't determine who the driver was, but the identity of the passenger was unmistakable to her.

It was Alex. His build, his walk, it was definitely him. He had jumped from the passenger's seat and quickly joined the driver, who could only be Babcock, who handed something to Alex as they raced to the house and the still-open front door. As they paused there, she moved out from behind the tree, calling out and waving her arms frantically.

Unaware of her shouting, the two men split up, with Babcock moving toward the back of the house and Alex disappearing into the darkness of the front door. They were out of her view, her warnings drowned out by the howling winds of the storm.

Her heart jumped into her throat as Alex disappeared into the house. She had to warn them; they had no idea of the danger they were in. The stranger may have seen them coming, might have circled around her and was already in the house waiting for them. They would be completely unprepared. She had to get to them first.

Her injured leg protesting, she started across the Barton's lawn toward her house. She made it only a few steps before she felt a heavy hand on her shoulder grip her from behind and hold her fast, the grip like a vise. She struggled against that grip and in response her assailant twisted her arm around her back, her shoulder and elbow exploding in pain. The more she moved, the more she struggled, the more intense the pain became. The knife was knocked from her hand and she watched it tumble away onto the lawn, desperation and hopelessness quickly mingling with the pain. Someone kicked her feet out from under her, causing her to land hard in the cold, wet grass. Mud and rainwater invaded her already soaked clothes, and her injured body cried out in protest. She tried to scream but was stifled by a hand suddenly and brutally thrust against her face. She fought as best she could against the weight pressing down on her back, but between her earlier injuries and the fresh pain shooting through her arm, escape was looking impossible. Off to the side, the blade of the knife glinted, reflecting the streetlights. It was out of her reach and completely useless to her now.

At least the stranger was focused on her. Alex was safe.

As if he could hear her thoughts, the stranger leaned in close and whispered, "Don't worry, I won't let him come between us ever again. I'm here to save you, Rachel. I wish you could see that." He pulled her to her feet, her clothes wet with cold autumn rain. "Come on, it's time to break ties with this sham of a life."

He pushed her toward the darkened house, keeping her arm firmly pushed against her back, the constant throbbing in her arm and shoulder leaving her immobilized and with no choice but to go where he led her. She again caught the glint of the knife blade where she had dropped it in the grass. It gleamed like it was taunting her, calling her to come and pick it up. She kept her eyes on the knife until it was out of sight, hoping against hope she could somehow reach it, that she could stop the stranger herself before he could hurt anyone else. She just needed an opportunity, but that was quickly fading behind them in the grass.

Ahead of her loomed her home, dark and foreboding. In all the years she had shared the house with Alex, she had never thought of it in that way, and it made her sick to think of it that way now. She had always considered it her sanctuary, but now dread filled her as they came closer. Not because of the house itself, because of the man leading her and what he intended to do there. He was going to kill the two men inside, one of whom she loved with all her heart.

And there was nothing she could do about it.

29

After Alex suddenly recalled the Shadowy Stranger, he tried to call Rachel. There had been no answer on the first try, and that was concerning. The second try with no answer became frantic. Panic had set in by the third try. She didn't answer her phone. She didn't respond to texts. Babcock had tried to contact LeFranc and Timmins as well, with no luck. Alex, beyond himself with panic, insisted they get to the house immediately. Babcock agreed. Given the lack of contact with the two officers he had stationed with Rachel, he had called for back-up at the Carter house.

Unfortunately, back-up wouldn't be coming anytime soon. The storm was playing havoc with power lines, and most of Pine Haven's small police force was out on clean-up duties, watching over downed lines until repair crews could arrive. They would be on their own.

The tail end of Babcock's car skidded on a patch of wet leaves and he eased off the accelerator a bit. As the rain pounded against it, propelled by the wind and the car's velocity, the windshield became pure chaos. The wipers, set on high, flew frantically across their forward view in a desperate battle with the elements. A battle they were losing.

"What are you doing? Why are you slowing down?" Alex's voice was filled with palpable anxiety, just short of explosive panic. "The house is still a block away!"

"I'm aware," Babcock replied calmly. "That's why I'm slowing down. If we approach at this speed, two things could happen. First, with this weather, we go off the road and get killed before we even get there. That doesn't help anyone. Second. If we approach the house at this speed, this frantically, that 'stranger' you keep talking about is going to know something is wrong. And I can tell you from years of experience, the last thing we want to do right now is make this guy nervous. Trust me. I know it seems counterintuitive, but barreling in there will only get people hurt. Understand?"

Alex nodded. He didn't like the idea, but Babcock had the edge in experience. He would have to defer to the other man's judgement. It didn't help the fact that he was nothing but nerves at the moment. His hands were shaking, caught between the need to act and the inability to. His stomach roiled, and he was sure that if he hadn't already emptied it out on Babcock's lawn he'd be vomiting right now.

As Babcock slowed to a normal driving speed, he glanced over at his passenger. "Try not to worry, kid. She'll be okay."

"How can you be sure?"

Babcock shrugged his massive shoulders. "I've done this a few times. You get a feel for it after a while."

Alex didn't reply, instead sinking back into the well-worn seat of the police cruiser, turning his face to the storm-tossed night. He hoped Babcock was right. He desperately wanted the cop to be right, but a nagging feeling prodded at him, telling him that this was only the beginning. That after all this was over, their lives would never be the same.

"Here we are," Babcock announced, bringing the car to a stop at the curb.

Alex's chest tightened at the sight of his house. It was dark and still in a way that didn't seem natural to him. "There are no lights on."

Babcock looked the house over, peering into the driving rain that once again obscured the windshield. "Must have lost power because of the storm."

Alex looked up and down the street. "No, the Bartons and the Petersons still have lights. Usually the entire street goes out in a storm." He pushed down the gathering lump in his throat. "It must be something else."

"Maybe it's just the lines to your house," Babcock suggested. "This wind is pretty fierce."

Alex squinted out the window, peering past the rivulets of rain. "I don't see any loose cables. Any more suggestions?"

Babcock sighed slightly. "None that you'd like."

"So now what do we..... Hold on!" Alex shot up straight in his seat like a jolt of electricity hit him and pasted his face against the window to see through the storm.

Babcock tensed at Alex's sudden outburst. "What? What is it?"

"The front door." Alex's voice was low, tinged with anxiety.

"What about it?" Babcock asked.

"It's wide open."

Babcock looked warily at the house as he gently applied the brake, bringing the car from a slow crawl to a complete stop. "So it is," he answered distractedly, his eyes scanning the front of the house for activity.

"No, you don't understand. Rachel would never leave the front door open like that. She was born and raised in the city; you just don't do that. It's a habit she's never been able to get over. Every night before bed, she locks all the doors securely. If that door is open, she's in trouble! I need to get in there!" Alex grasped the door handle and pulled open the door, stopping when he felt Babcock's heavy hand on his arm.

Babcock held fast to Alex's shoulder. "I get how you feel, kid. But you have to let cooler heads prevail here. If she is in there and in danger, we could make it worse by busting in there and surprising this guy. We need to know what's going on in there. Let me go ahead and assess the situation. I'll let you know when it's clear to come in. Until then, I think it's best if you wait out here."

Alex pulled away from Babcock and pushed open the steel reinforced door of the cruiser, allowing the wind and rain to come pouring into the vehicle. "I'm sorry, I can't do that. If Rachel's in danger, I need to get in there! I can't just sit here and wait. I'm going in there, with or without you."

Babcock sat silently for a second, considering his options. He didn't want Alex to get hurt, or worse. Under normal circumstances he would order Alex to stay put and, if he still resisted, arrest him for his own good. But what he had experienced in the last day was anything but normal, and the response would have to go outside normal procedures as well.

"Okay," Babcock relented, "you win. We'll both go in. But remember, I'm in charge. What I say goes. You listen and do what I say without question. Understand?"

Alex nodded vigorously, his eyes never wavering from the yawning blackness of the open front door.

They got out of the car and were immediately assaulted by the pelting rain driven by the punishing wind. "One more thing," Babcock said, his voice practically a shout over the wind. He opened the back door on the driver's side and removed a long object that was unmistakable to Alex, even in the dark and rain. "Do you know how to use this?"

Alex reached out and took the weapon, a shotgun, and felt its weight. It was heavy, but strangely comfortable in his hands, as if he was intimately familiar with it. The feeling made him as uneasy as the gun itself.

"It's weird, but I think I do," he replied.

Babcock continued. "That's a Beretta 1200 auto shotgun. There's no need to pump it to chamber another round, just point and shoot. You don't need a lot of precision or experience to use it. Just make sure you know who and what you're pointing and shooting at, understand? I don't need any dead civilians here."

"Then why give me the gun?" Alex asked, absently looking over the gun and still amazed at how completely familiar it felt to him.

"Because I can't keep you from going in there. And if this guy is as dangerous as you think he is, I don't want you running in there without a way to defend yourself. Just be careful! If you get killed in there, I'll have mountains of paperwork to fill out, and I hate paperwork. So do me a favor and don't get killed, okay?" Babcock nodded at him slightly, asserting the seriousness of the matter behind his glib tone.

Alex nodded.

“Good. Remember what I said, follow my lead. Do whatever I tell you whenever I tell you to do it. No questions asked.” Babcock reached under his coat and produced a revolver. He popped open the cylinder, checked that it was fully loaded, flipped it closed again, and then he turned back to Alex. “Last chance, kid. Are you sure you want to do this?”

“Whatever it takes to keep Rachel safe,” Alex replied.

Babcock’s sigh was imperceptible in the wind. “Just wanted to make sure. Stay behind me and keep your eyes open.”

Alex fell in behind the detective, matching him step for step as they climbed to the front door. In all the time they had lived here, Alex had never thought of their house, their home, as anything less than a happy place. Tonight, their home looked foreboding. Uninviting.

It was true; after that night, none of their lives would ever be the same again.

30

"What's their status?" Burke asked as ducked into the back seat of the car that had arrived to pick them up at the makeshift airfield.

Burke sat next to Sergeant Todd Rutters, a stocky, ruddy-faced man in his early thirties. He was Harriman's man in the field, the head agent for this region. Until Burke had arrived, that is. Rutters wore his resentment at having his position taken over by some suit and tie wearing desk jockey on his face like a badge. That was fine with Burke. Rutters didn't have to like him, all he had to do was what he was told. If he could do that, they would get along fine. Anything other than that would be completely unacceptable and dealt with harshly. This whole situation had gone on far too long and Burke was through screwing around. It had to end tonight.

Rutters took his eyes of fire off Burke to check his tablet. "As near as we can tell, sir, they've all gathered in one place."

Burke noted how Rutters had spit out the word 'sir' like it was poison. "And that place would be....?" Burke asked, his tone dripping with sarcasm.

Rutters' reply came through nearly clenched teeth. "The Carter house, sir."

Burke ignored Rutters and turned to Harriman, seated on the other side of him. "What did I tell you? I knew the whole Providence thing was a trick. He found the bug we planted on him and he used it against us. Why the hell Forrester couldn't work out the kink that makes them vibrate when they get close to the tracer is beyond me. The man's incompetence is staggering."

Harriman inclined his chin slightly, as close to a nod as he ever got. "Yes, sir."

Burke turned and focused his gaze on Rutters, but directed his next question to Harriman. "You don't tolerate that sort of incompetence in your ranks, do you, colonel?"

"No sir," Harriman replied, never taking his eyes from the flow of data on the tablet he held. "All of my people are hand-picked and trained by me personally. There is no room for that level of performance from them."

While the Colonel spoke, Burke and Rutters locked eyes. If hate were a visible thing, it would have been thick between them. They were like wolves determining who was the alpha of the pack, a question Burke could answer easily. If push came to shove, he would eat the young sergeant alive and enjoy every minute. Rutters probably realized that as well, based on Burke's reputation alone, but he wouldn't admit it. Their eyes remained locked, each one trying to stare down the other, neither willing to look away or even blink. After a few moments of tense silence, Rutters finally looked away, conveying the position of top dog to Burke. For now, at least.

Burke allowed himself a smug smile of satisfaction. He was feeling as if he were in control of his environment again, and he liked the feeling. Now, all that was left for Burke to do was clean up this mess, the one blemish on his otherwise spotless record.

"What is our plan of action on arrival, sir?" Harriman asked, glancing up from his tablet.

"Do whatever it takes to get Adam off the board. Capture him if you can, kill him if you have to. I don't really give a shit which. Just get it done and ensure the Project isn't compromised." At this point Burke actually preferred Adam dead, but as a businessman he understood the necessity of not wasting resources.

Harriman continued. "Under whose authority will we be operating?"

Burke considered the question for a moment. "Adam is a fugitive we are attempting to apprehend. I'd say U.S. Marshals would be appropriate? Do you agree?"

Harriman gave another nearly imperceptible nod. "Yes, sir. And what about the Carters?"

"The preferred course of action is to get in and get to Adam without disrupting their lives. There's still a lot of valuable control data they can provide. If that's not possible, and by now I would say there's a good chance it isn't, then we are to deal with Mr. Carter as needed. As long as the Project is not compromised, we are open to taking any measures." Burke heavily emphasized the last statement.

Harriman continued. "And the woman?"

Burke leaned in. "No harm of any kind is to come to her. Under no circumstances. She is to be taken alive and unharmed, regardless of any mission challenges. Are we clear on that?"

"Absolutely, sir," Harriman replied, this time without a nod.

Burke turned to Rutters again. "And you, Sergeant? Are you clear on my orders?" He emphasized the words 'my orders' in an obvious show of authority.

"Yes, sir. Clear as crystal, sir," answered Rutters, spitting out 'sir' each time.

Burke smiled a humorless smile. "Good. I think we're ready. Remember, take him alive if you can. If you can't, make certain you kill him. This son of a bitch has eluded and tricked us before. I either want a living, breathing body to transport home or I want his head on a pike. We need to ensure with absolute certainty that we have neutralized him. If anyone screws this up, you will answer to me personally."

Neither of the soldiers said a word for the rest of the ride. That was fine with Burke, he had said what needed to be said. Harriman was clear on his instructions and Rutters had been put firmly in his place. He leaned back in the soft seat and closed his eyes, thinking about the look that would be on Adam's face when he realized his little trick had backfired. It would be almost as satisfying as the look on his face when Burke killed him. And he would kill him, despite Penders' instructions. Adam had made this personal. There was no way Burke could let such a blatant challenge to his authority go unanswered.

Burke let out a contented sigh. Sometimes his job was immensely satisfying.

31

Dr. Elliot Forrester rode in the second car, cruising through the stormy night behind the car carrying Burke, Harriman, and the stocky young field commander who had met them when they landed. Nervously, he wrung his hands together and fidgeted in his seat. He felt like a child awaiting punishment, knowing it was coming, but left with his imagination what and how bad it would be. Burke would soon find Adam Nine and Alex Carter, the last two of Forrester's children, and there was no doubt in the doctor's mind what would happen then. Burke had been on an enraged tear to find Adam ever since the humiliation he suffered at the rest area, where Adam had so skillfully eluded him. The only thing that might abate that anger would be for Burke to see Adam dead. Odds are he would want to see Alex dead as well, just for good measure. And at the root of it all was Forrester himself, who was the progenitor of it all and whom Burke would want punished as well. Harshly.

Forrester stopped wringing his hands and sat up straighter between the two soldiers seated on either side of him. He was not about to let Burke Darnell destroy him or his life's work. This project had consumed him, absorbed his entire life. His fellow scientists had made him an outcast in the scientific community, stripping him of all legitimacy and leaving him to ponder the path of a career that had come at the cost of absolute alienation. He had suffered so much personal and professional loss already, losing his last two children would simply be too much.

But how could he prevent it? He couldn't make an outright stand against Burke; the man was untouchable. Not only did he have Harriman and his mercenaries at his disposal, he also had the entirety of resources offered by the Eden Project. That web of spies and information easily covered the entire globe, insinuating themselves into even the tiniest nooks and crannies of power. Whatever he was going to do, Forrester realized he would be doing it alone.

Or maybe not. Maybe there was still one ally he could trust. One person he could still depend on. If he could only reach this person before Burke did, convince him of the validity of his work and the founding principles of the Eden Project, he might sway them to his side. The timing would be difficult to get to this person first, but there was a way. There had to be. Maybe he could show Burke and Penders that he was more than just a withering old scientist.

Content with the framework of a plan, Dr. Elliot Forrester allowed himself an exceedingly rare indulgence in these days. He smiled. Maybe just this once Burke Darnell would get his comeuppance.

32

Alex silently cursed the pre-winter storm as he swiped rainwater from his eyes. It didn't help him much as another river flowed from the sodden mass atop his head, keeping his vision obscured. He pushed his fingers through the mass of wet hair, slicking it straight back against his skull, hoping he could keep it out of his eyes for a few minutes.

Babcock stood on the opposite side of the open front door, struggling with the same ritual of pushing back his own soaked hair. He had an easier time than Alex did, but then again, he had considerably less hair to worry about. Now under cover of the porch, the detective rubbed water from his eyes and blinked furiously to clear his vision. Slowly he leaned around the edge of the door and into the house to get a look at the interior, but beyond the doorway all he could see was a mass of darkness split by a meager streak of light from the roadside streetlights. In that thin band of light the only detail of the room he could make out was what he remembered to be the Carters' coffee table, other than that the house was as dark and still as a crypt.

"I can't see a thing in there," Babcock said, pulling his head back around the corner and into the wind again. Almost instantly, his face glistened with rain propelled by the unrelenting winds of the storm. Swiping at his face again, he tore what he could from his eyes. "This goddam storm isn't helping, either!"

"Do you think he's in there?" Alex asked, gripping the shotgun close to him.

"I have no idea," Babcock answered, eyes darting back into the darkness to scan for movement.

Alex swallowed hard and gripped the shotgun tighter. "There's only one way to find out," he said, pushing himself away from the wall. Before Babcock could register an objection, he dashed through the open door and into his darkened house. Once inside, he darted to the right and into the smothering darkness that enveloped most of the interior, doubling over at the waist to make himself as small a target as he could. He had no idea why he did it, just that it somehow felt like the natural thing to do in this situation, to make himself small and a tough target. If anyone had seen him burst through the front door as he had, they would hopefully assume he was still standing up straight and aim high while firing blindly, buying him a few precious seconds to track his opponent and return fire.

His head spun from the sudden burst of strategic thinking. He had no idea how he knew that, just that it was the logical tactic to employ in this situation, given the darkness and the enemy's unknown position. It gave him the best chance of evading enemy fire. Once again, his head reeled at the thought. How did he know this? Where did it come from? Why was he aware of it in the first place, much less that this situation was perfect for that attack plan? It disturbed him in the same way that the shotgun Babcock had given him felt so comfortable in his hands. It just...fit.

He was ripped from his reverie by the sound of Babcock, cursing in a low tone at Alex's impetuousness. The detective was right; it had been impulsive and irresponsible. It had also felt right, as if he had been training for it all his life. All that aside, Rachel needed him right now. Until she was safe, he would use any advantage he could get, whether he understood it or not.

Being inside the darkness didn't make it any easier to navigate the living room. If he were going to find his way around, he would have to do it by memory. Judging by where the edge of the coffee table was, he estimated it was only a dozen steps straight ahead to the kitchen. The couch was slightly ahead of him to his left, a wall to his right, but nothing ahead in his way.

Except the shaft of light from the front door. To get to the kitchen, he would have to cut straight through it. And then.....

And then what? It hit him at that moment; he had no plan. Despite his apparently newfound tactical knowledge, he had rushed into the situation with no sort of plan. He stopped, freezing in his tracks. Why was he heading for the kitchen to begin with? What was he hoping to accomplish there? What was he accomplishing now, standing around in the dark?

Mentally, he reigned in his wayward thoughts. Doubting himself now wouldn't help, he needed to organize. To plan. He had gone off half-cocked, and that was a mistake. That was something he couldn't change. He needed to plan his next steps more carefully.

He glanced behind him to the illuminated rectangle that was his front door. Since he had entered the house, he hadn't seen or heard anything from Babcock. He felt sure the detective hadn't entered the house; it was pitch black and he would have had to traverse the stream of light just as Alex had. In the pitch-black darkness, that wouldn't have gone unnoticed. So where was he? Waiting outside for Alex to realize he had made a mistake? Or was he still wisely waiting for back-up?

Standing here now in the darkness between his living room and kitchen, feeling exposed, Alex had to admit that any of those choices were better than the one he had impulsively made. His own burning need for action had tripped him up and now he was stuck here, alone in the darkness.

At least he hoped he was alone.

As that last thought burrowed its way into his subconscious, biting fear supplanting impetuous bravado, the lights in the house suddenly snapped on. The sudden eruption of illumination blinded him and he squinted, trying to filter through it. A loud sound to his right startled him and he turned, swinging the shotgun to bear in that direction. His eyes quickly adapted to the light, and he could see his attacker.

He had nearly killed his television. The television must have been on when the power went out and came back to life when it was restored. Breathing out a heavy sigh, he reached out to shut it off, but pulled his hand back as a sudden realization hit him. Why did the power suddenly come back? How did it get restored? Who had done it? And, most importantly, where were they now?

There were only two ways he could think of to cut the power to his house. The first was to damage the power lines, but they had been intact when he and Babcock had arrived. The second was to flip the master switch in the circuit box. That action would result in cutting off the power to just his house, and flipping the switch back on would restore the power just as effectively as it had been disconnected. But it would have to be done at the circuit box, and since the power had just come back, whoever had opened the circuit to restore it was still in the house. At the circuit box. Which was in a closet next to the washer and dryer.

In the kitchen.

Sudden panic exploded in his gut, and he flattened himself against the wall, bringing the shotgun to bear on the kitchen entrance. He took a few small, cautious steps forward, his wet sneakers squishing against the carpet with each step. He winced at each wet, sucking sound, hoping the newly revived television was loud enough to cover the noise. Staying as flat against the wall as possible, he took more loud steps and stopped a few feet from the entryway to the kitchen and listened, trying to discern any noises from the other room. All he could make out were the muted sounds of the storm still raging outside. Beyond that, the house was still and quiet.

His stomach tightened. It was too quiet for Rachel to be in there. There were no sounds of struggle and there was no way she would keep quiet on her own. If she were in there, he'd have been able to hear something, but no noise issued from the kitchen.

There was only one way to figure out what was going on in there and no more time to wait. Checking the shotgun one more time, he stepped to the kitchen entrance, his sneakers seeming to squish even more loudly with each step. He cursed the rain, but hoped the sound wasn't as loud as he imagined it was. Two feet from the kitchen entrance, he gripped the shotgun tightly. Holding it ready, he was sure to keep his finger off the trigger. The weapon was very effective at close range for obliterating everything in front of it; he didn't want one of those things to be Rachel.

Letting go of the barrel, he wiped more moisture from his face. A cold, nervous sweat had formed on his brow and was slowly trailing into his eyes. Relaxing his neck, he let his head drop slightly to quell the discomfort there. The last thing he needed at that moment was pain clouding his reflexes. Even though he had never been even a remotely religious person, a prayer found its way up from the recesses of his mind.

Steeling his resolve, he slipped through the entryway and into the kitchen, gun raised. His heart hammered in anticipation as he burst into the room, ready for a fight. None came. Scanning the kitchen, listening intently to hear past the sounds of the storm and his pounding heart, Alex realized he was alone in the room.

Something caught his eye that caused his heart to seize in his chest. The sliding door stood ajar in the closet where the washer and dryer were kept, where the breaker box for the house was. He swallowed hard, turning the barrel of the gun toward the closet, and slowly made his way across the room. Thoughts and scenarios ran through his mind like a sieve, terrible images he didn't want to consider but couldn't stop them coming. He saw the stranger in there, gun in hand and waiting for Alex to get closer. He saw himself pulling open the door to find Rachel's lifeless body stuffed inside. Each variation hit him like a fist.

He reached the closet, flattening himself against the wall. Again, he couldn't hear or see anything out of the ordinary. His mind was still showing him horror after horror as he reached for the handle, gripping it in his sweaty, shaking hand. Slowly, heart in his throat, he pulled the door open, shotgun ready.

There was a sudden flurry of movement and Alex jumped back from the closet, bringing the shotgun stock to rest on his shoulder and taking aim at his attacker. His finger slid onto the trigger, his heart and breath freezing in the moment...

...as his laundry, which had been unceremoniously dumped on the washer, fell to the floor. Exhaling the breath he didn't realize he had been holding in, he silently cursed himself for this habit of his, piling dirty laundry on top of the washer instead of putting it in the hamper. Rachel had fought with him about this for their entire relationship, and in that second he finally saw the logic in it and silently swore to mend his ways.

The circuit box was to his left, hidden in a recessed box. The door stood open at the moment, which struck Alex as unusual since Rachel was obsessive about keeping everything in the house orderly. Even something as minor and inconspicuous as the circuit box had an order in her mind. She would have been sure to close it the last time she was in that closet.

And then he saw it, the reason someone left the door to the breaker box uncharacteristically open. At first glance everything seemed normal, but as he looked closer he noticed the gleam of moisture on the main switch. A matching trail of rainwater ran across the surface of the dryer as well and out onto the kitchen floor. The trail led to the back door. Alex moved to the door and quietly pulled it open, the wind and rain of the storm pelting him immediately.

The door had been left unlocked. A familiar feeling of dread crept back up his spine as he thought back to earlier that night when he and Babcock had left Rachel in the care of the two officers Babcock had brought in. He had locked this door himself. Had checked it twice to be sure. Now it stood open and vulnerable, with obvious signs that someone had come in this way while the storm was raging. That was how he had done it. He had snuck in under cover of the dark, aided by the wind, rain and confusion of the storm. He must have picked the lock to get inside and shut down the main breaker to kill power to the house.

The feeling of dread that had been gathering along his spine suddenly exploded into his chest. The lights were back on. That meant he had come back into the house again and switched the power back on. Recently. The power had only been back for moments.

Which meant he was in the house right now.

Senses suddenly on high alert, he searched for anything out of the ordinary. He strained to filter out the raindrops pattering against the windows and the sounds of the wind tearing through the trees. The smells of the last meal cooked in the kitchen lingered. The presence of the gun in his hands. He crept back to the entryway to the living room, alert for movement or noise. The light made him feel exposed. Vulnerable.

A sudden burst of wind caught the still-open front door and slammed it into the wall, startling him. He turned to the noise and froze, his breath caught in his throat. He had missed it previously in the dark, but there it was now. Laid out before him like an omen.

It was one of Babcock's men, LeFranc, he thought he had heard Babcock call him. He was lying spread-eagled on his back on the living room floor, shock and surprise permanently etched on his face. Blood had pooled around his shoulder and under his head, and in his forehead was a ragged hole. Given the amount of blood gathered on the rug, Alex had no desire to see what the back of his head looked like. Still firmly gripped in his hand was his pistol, which had been drawn and ready when he encountered the stranger.

Despite that, he had died.

A trained and, according to Babcock, decorated police offer who had his gun at the ready had encountered this dark stranger and couldn't save himself. Suddenly, Alex felt the weight of the shotgun in his hands more than he had since he first took it.

Thump!

The noise came from the second floor; a soft, muffled sound that couldn't have been made by the storm. Alex's eyes followed the twisting curves of the spiral staircase to the landing above, but couldn't see anything from his vantage point. The lights had come back on downstairs, but up there he could see nothing but darkness. He would have to climb the stairs to investigate. Climbing the stairs would be a slow process, and he would be exposed the entire way. If he encountered the stranger at the top of the stairs, he'd be trapped.

But that maniac could have Rachel up there.

Thump... thump... thump.

Three more quick pounding noises, like a struggle going on upstairs. His mind suddenly flashed horrible images at him again, terrible things that psychopath could be doing to Rachel, and all thoughts of caution retreated from his mind. He raced for the stairs, taking them two at a time, spinning faster and faster upwards as if caught in a wrought iron tornado before being deposited at the top. He stopped for a moment, listening. There were no more noises, but there were only a few places they could have come from: a bedroom or the bathroom, all at the far end of the hall. The hall that just two nights ago had been filled with alien queens and other vicious monsters waiting to rip out and feast on his steaming entrails. But the danger then, as real as it may have seemed, was born of his overactive imagination. Now an actual monster was lurking in the eerie green glow of the nightlight. A monster that looked human but was more dangerous than any creature spawned by imagination.

It was that same reality that also made this monster vulnerable. He was human, or close to it at least. A well-placed shot from the gun Alex carried would kill him just like it would any other human being. Alex could end this nightmare. All he had to do was walk down the hall and find the monster. Just three choices at the end of a brief walk; make the right one and it would be all over with.

Thump!

The sound was louder this time and accompanied by a small, almost imperceptible whimper. It had to have been Rachel. Anger welled up inside him, a rage that built to a crescendo as he charged headlong down the hallway towards the doors at either end of the hall. The first door was the extra bedroom, the room that would soon be a nursery. Right now it was nearly empty, with nothing but a crib still in the box and a few cans of paint in the room. He wouldn't have her in there. He moved on to the next door down, the bedroom he shared with Rachel, and readied the shotgun. His subconscious flashed the image of Officer LeFranc on the floor with a bullet hole in his forehead, his dead hand still clutching the gun he hadn't had the chance to use.

Alex exploded into the room, motion to the right catching his eye. Turning, he saw Rachel lying on the bed, gagged and bound with electrical tape. Her eyes were wide, filled with panic and desperation, as a figure stood over her.

A figure with a knife.

He raised the shotgun, bracing the stock against his shoulder, and pointed the weapon at the armed intruder standing over Rachel. Rachel locked eyes with him and the look was wild and pleading as she shook her head and grunted in warning at him.

"Get the hell away from my wife," Alex growled, fury building in his belly, "or I swear I will fucking kill you right now."

Rachel struggled against her bonds, grunting and looking from Alex to the stranger, while the stranger slowly rose from the edge of the bed and dropped his knife. Alex, heart hammering in his chest, kept the gun trained on him and tracked his movement. Despite the power being restored, shadow still shrouded the bedroom and Alex couldn't discern the man's features. All he could tell was that the man was big. Imposing.

"Step away from the bed!" Alex commanded, trying to put as much bravado into his voice as he could. If he could even keep his voice from quivering, he would consider that a win at the moment.

The stranger looked up at him, dark eyes glinting in the dim light, before he spoke in a gruff tone. "Put that damned thing away! We need to get out of here!"

Alex's blind fury subsided as recognition set in. "Babcock? How the hell did you get in here?"

The detective turned to Alex, a hard look on his face. "After that incredibly stupid fucking stunt you pulled, rushing in here alone, I looked around the perimeter for another way in. That great big maple tree you have out back got me up to your bathroom window, and I got in that way. I figured I could meet you in the middle, or we might box this guy in somehow. Trying to take advantage of your incredible fucking stupidity, especially after I warned to you to not do that exact thing! The lights came on a few seconds after I got in the house and I found your wife here, trussed up like a pig." He turned to Rachel, who was still bound and gagged on the bed. "No offense, Mrs. Cater." Babcock picked up the knife again and started hacking through the tape on her ankles. In a second, her legs were free, and he started on her wrists.

Alex rushed forward, dropping the shotgun to the floor and hugging his wife, kissing her hard on her forehead. Clumsily, he tore the tape from her mouth and she gasped in pain, but ignored it and kissed him back. He savored the sweet taste of the kiss, grateful that she was alive and seemingly unharmed. Babcock sliced through the tape binding her wrists and she threw her arms around Alex, pulling him in tight. Alex could feel her hot tears on his cheek as she held him, feeling her shake in his arms.

"Are you alright? Did he hurt you?" he asked, gently pushing her away and looking her over. Aside from being wet from the storm, he didn't see any obvious injuries.

"I'm fine," she said, then patted her stomach and amended with, "We're fine. But Alex, whoever this guy is, it's so much worse than we imagined."

Alex was about to reply when Babcock broke in. "And that's why we need to get out of here before that asshat comes back."

Alex nodded at him and then turned back to Rachel. "We'll talk about it as soon as we can. But we need to get moving. Are you okay to get out of here?"

She nodded. "More than ready. But Alex, I have so much to tell you. To show you. You won't believe it. You just won't believe what I found."

A wave of concern ran through Alex at that. Genuine fear resonated in Rachel's voice, which was not something he was accustomed to hearing from her. Whatever she had found out had shaken her badly, and coupled with the events of the last few days and the complete upending of their lives, he was worried about how that had affected her. She had always been strong, one of the most resilient people he had ever met, but no one could experience what she had and walk away from it with no repercussions. After this was over and they had the chance, there was a lot they were going to have to unpack together.

He reached up and gently touched her cheek. "Whatever it is, we'll figure it out together."

"It changes everything," she whispered back to him, a slight tremor in her voice.

"Looks clear." Babcock was at the bedroom door, peering into the hallway. "We need to go."

They shuffled over to join him, Alex pausing just long enough to retrieve the shotgun. Babcock took another glance down the hall, then turned back to them. "I can't see anyone, but that doesn't mean he isn't there. Before we go out there where we'll have almost no cover, I have to ask; is there any other way out of this room besides going down that hall?"

"There's the emergency fire ladders," Alex volunteered. "They're rolled up in a little box under each window in case of a fire. All we have to do is open the box and unroll it down the side of the building."

Rachel shook her head and pointed to the window where the ladder was kept. The box was open; the ladder ripped from its mooring in the wall. "It was the first thing he did after he got me up here and tied me up. Said he didn't want me thinking about leaving him so soon after we were reunited."

Alex turned to her, a quizzical look tinged with anger on his face. "What the hell does that mean?"

"I have no idea. Nothing he does makes any sense." Rachel shivered, thinking about Timmins and LeFranc and Walt and Betty. "He's a psychopath," she added, her voice barely audible.

Alex put his free arm around her, feeling her shiver. She was soaked through and probably freezing, but that wasn't the reason for her shaking. "We'll be okay," he said, hoping he could back up the statement.

"The fire ladders are out. Any other suggestions?" Babcock asked, seemingly oblivious to the exchange between husband and wife.

"What about the way you came in? Through the bathroom window?" Rachel blurted. There was still a trace of fear in her tone, but more of her natural bravado had seeped back in.

Babcock shook his head. "Won't work. It was hell to get in and that was with my weight bending the branch toward the window. I don't think we could reach it from inside the house." He glanced back down the hazy green hallway once more. "Looks like this is it."

Babcock heaved a heavy sigh, half of it stifled in his throat as he tried to keep quiet. The situation wasn't ideal, to say the least, and he felt a nagging sensation of doubt, regret and a lot of fear settling in on him. Whoever this guy was, he had already killed two cops tonight and at least two civilians that he knew of, according to Rachel. Two good cops. Good men who were also good friends. And now he was the sole remaining officer with no backup and a psychopath on the loose. Well, no back up except for the kid, who had already proven himself to be an unreliable hothead in the thick of a situation. And Rachel, who was in no shape to take on a killer currently. So yes, he was scared. Scared as hell. Scared he wouldn't make it home tonight. Scared that Angela would get the phone call every cop's spouse dreads. Scared that his kids would have to finish growing up without him.

As he had done so often during his career, he pushed down his fear and focused on the situation at hand. He had sworn to do a job, and tonight that job was to protect the Carters. A job he had never shirked or abandoned, and he wasn't about to start now.

Checking his revolver again, he turned to face Alex and Rachel. "Okay, I don't like it, but I guess this is our only option. Stay close to me and stay quiet." He shifted his gaze directly to Alex, eyes boring into the younger man. "And this time, do exactly what I tell you to do and nothing else. Is that crystal clear?"

Alex nodded, as did Rachel. Babcock grunted and turned back to the hallway. "I'm going out. I'll go to the end of the hall and wait by the stairs. Once I determine it's clear, you two join me. Once at the stairs, I'll scout out the lower level and if everything's okay we can waltz right out the front door."

Alex and Rachel remained silent as Babcock slipped into the green glow of the hallway, pushing as far up to the wall as he could to stay hidden in the shadows. There wasn't much shadow to be had as the nightlight permeated every corner of the hall, making him a target no matter where he stood in the short, boxed-in shooting gallery. With his revolver held at the ready, he sharply focused his eyes on the wrought-iron railing at the end of the hall. It looked so close, but seemed so distant. Still, he wasn't comfortable speeding up his progress. Haste makes waste, his wife is fond of saying. It also makes you careless, and in this situation, that could be lethal.

Nothing moved ahead of him and a quick glance behind showed him only the nervous faces of Alex and Rachel in the bedroom doorway. He slid as quickly and quietly as he could along the wall, trying to hover just over it so as not to make a noise by scraping along. After what seemed like an eternity, he finally arrived at the end of the hall. He peered around the corner, to either side of the expanded landing that overlooked the Carter's living room. Nothing. Glancing behind again, he waved the Carters forward, watching as they emerged from the bedroom and started down the hall.

As he turned back, Babcock heard a scuffling sound and saw a dark shape leap at him from around the first bend of the spiral staircase. It moved like some predatory beast, black raincoat flapping behind him like a dark nightmare creature. Babcock brought the revolver around quickly, but the stranger was too close now as he reached out and grabbed the cop's gun hand, forcing his arm straight up. Babcock's finger jerked on the trigger and the gun boomed once, sending a round straight up into the ceiling and sending bits of plaster and sheetrock falling around them. The stranger glared at the detective; his cool eyes filled with an unnerving apathy for the man he held.

The stranger smiled then, an evil, predatory smile that chilled Babcock to the core, and said, "That wasn't nice at all. I think you need to be taught some manners. Discipline is important."

The voice was warm, almost comforting, like speaking on the phone to a friend you haven't seen in years. But his eyes, despite the light shade, were dark. Evil. Dangerous. There was more to this than pleasure for him, although he certainly seemed to enjoy it. This was a crusade. A religion. A righteousness of his actions. It was a look, a demeanor Babcock had encountered before in his career, but never with the intensity he saw in this man's icy blue eyes. Even just that second of looking into his eyes told Babcock that he was a fanatic, a committed zealot, which made him more dangerous than a hundred garden variety killers.

Suddenly Ernest Babcock, veteran police officer, was very afraid.

A smile crossed the stranger's face as he tightened his grip on Babcock's gun hand while simultaneously driving his free hand into the cop's abdomen, just under his ribcage, and forced his hand up. Babcock's world erupted in pain as his breath exploded from him.

The stranger's smile widened. "You're afraid, aren't you? I can tell, you know. I can sense the fear. The panic. The desperation. It's the gift given to me when they brought me into this world. I wish you could experience it like I do. Your fear has an especially sweet flavor, like an aged wine. You don't let it out to breathe much, do you?" A flutter of movement at the far end of the hall caught his eye. Alex and Rachel were there, frozen at the sight.

The stranger's smile dimmed slightly as he turned back to Babcock. "It seems we've run out of quality time. It's been a pleasure making your acquaintance, sir. I wish it could have lasted longer."

Babcock stared into the man's eyes, sensing what was about to come. A sudden rush of adrenaline quelled the pain in his arm and abdomen and he kicked savagely at the man holding him, putting all the strength he could muster into it. The stranger, seeming to sense the attack, reacted at the last second to block the kick, but was a bit too slow. Babcock's kick connected solidly, and the stranger lost his grip on the detective and fell back against the railing, panting and grabbing his side. He struggled up to his knees, his once cool eyes now filled with a furious hatred. Babcock, still trying to recover his breath, could only watch. His mind seemed only dimly aware of the danger he was in, the lack of oxygen muting the sense of fear that had been so prevalent moments ago. He heard muted sounds to his left and turned to see Alex and Rachel racing up the hall toward him, seemingly in slow motion. They were screaming something at him and pointing in his direction, but his mind was still hazy as pain and fear ran their course. He was only vaguely aware of the figure before him rising to his feet. As his breath returned and the haze cleared, he remembered the gun still in his hand.

It was too late. Babcock watched dully as the stranger reached under his coat and produced a silencer-equipped handgun and was bringing it to bear. Babcock's mind suddenly exploded in a flash, clarity coming back to him in a flood. As the fuzziness in his head cleared, he realized it felt familiar to him. More than just the effects of pain, fear and confusion; it was something more. It was the same sort of confusion he felt after his experience with Alex at Dr. Carlson's house the night she died. Somehow, this guy had done the same thing to him. But it was different. Targeted. He knew what he was doing and how to do it.

As the realization hit him, the barrel of the stranger's gun came level with Babcock's chest, finger tightening on the trigger. Babcock stopped breathing, anticipating the discharge of the weapon and the feeling of the bullet ripping through him. He had been shot before; he knew what it felt like, but never from this close. He wondered if he would feel the pain or if he would be dead before it hit him.

The question became moot as Alex ran headlong into the stranger, slamming him against the waist high iron railing that separated them from an eighteen-foot drop to the living room floor below. Upon impact, the finger of the stranger tightened on the trigger of his gun, and the weapon discharged a round with a whisper. From behind them came a grunt and a scream Alex recognized as Rachel's, fear gripping his heart. He wanted to look back, to be sure she was all right, but to take his eyes off of the man pinned beneath him would be suicide. Rage filled him at the thought of his wife lying on the floor of their home with a bullet from this man's gun in her and he tightened his grip on the stranger's throat, pushing him further over the railing. The stranger grasped at Alex, trying to free himself from Alex's hands around his throat. His gun hand flailed wildly, unable to draw a bead.

"I'll kill you, you son of a bitch!" The words came as a growl deep in Alex's throat with savage ferocity. He tightened his grip on the other man's throat, feeling the soft cartilage start to give way beneath his fingers. Deep inside, he knew this should sicken him, but it only encouraged him to squeeze harder as a red haze of rage filled the periphery of his vision. After everything they had been through, everything they had suffered because of this monster, Alex wanted to keep tightening his grip until the other man's windpipe collapsed from the pressure.

Until he could watch the man's life drain from his body as he should have done all those years ago, the first time they fought to the death.

The thought, that suppressed memory, exploded inside Alex's head like a bomb. Images flooded back as if a mental dam had broken. The blood-soaked arena. The broken bodies. Panic from the researchers and guards as their experiments went completely out of their control. Screaming and wailing in the chaos of the carnage. With him in the middle of it all. Him, and one other. Someone Alex was in a struggle to the death with, their hands locked around each other's throats. Someone with unmistakable blue eyes.

The stranger. Those blue eyes stood out in his memory as much as they did in the current moment. Deep, cold and haunting. Unfeeling. Alex felt the same rage now as he did then, but it triggered something in him now that he didn't have the capacity for earlier.

Compassion. Even as filled with rage as he was at this man for what he had brought into their lives, a spark of compassion burned inside the man Alex was now. It flooded over him, that feeling of empathy for the stranger, and his grip loosened slightly on the other man's throat.

Pain erupted in Alex's side as the stranger took advantage of the momentary distraction. Gaining enough leverage, he brought his knee up to connect with Alex's mid-section, forcing the air from Alex's lungs and causing him to lose his grip entirely. Feeling the pressure on his throat give way, the stranger pressed his attack, pushing Alex hard off of him and driving him into the wall. The pictures that hung there rattled and fell, grass cracking and falling from frames as Alex slid down amongst the shards. Breath came to him in quick gasps, his chest an explosion of pain with each one. His ribs throbbed, and he thought he could feel one of them moving, twisting itself into a strange angle. Most likely broken. He tried to stand but was met with a kick to the jaw that sent him sprawling onto the carpet. His mouth welled up with blood, the taste of it warm and coppery.

"I had hoped to make this last longer, but you had to spoil all my fun." The stranger's voice was both warm and chilling, but the tone was unmistakably one of menace, the duality of it betraying the façade of the man it belonged to. It chilled Alex as much here and now as it had in his nightmares, only this time it was much worse. This time, the nightmare was real.

"Who are you? Why are you doing this?" Alex asked, his jaw exploding with each word. Something there must be broken as well.

His only answer was another savage kick to his med-section. This time he could hear and feel ribs break with the impact, a sickening, wet crunching noise like stomping on seashells wrapped in a blanket. He wanted to scream, but his lungs couldn't take in enough air. Blood continued to well up in his mouth, running onto the carpet and forming a pool. For there to be that much blood, he must have a punctured lung, which would also explain why he found it so difficult to breathe.

Alex's vision was becoming a red haze of pain. Through it, he saw Babcock moving toward the stranger. The detective had a clear shot now, and was going to take it. A flash of hope filled him, only to be dashed a second later. As fast as Babcock was, the stranger was faster. He whirled to face the cop, his coat billowing around him like a flock of angry black birds, and fired his gun twice in quick succession. Babcock fell back against the iron railing, clutching his chest, revolver still firmly in hand. He wasn't ready to give in yet as he steadied himself against the railing and tried to bring the revolver around for another shot. But his hand was unsteady, and the stranger had already closed the distance between them, looming over the detective.

"Ah, ah, ah! Can't have you shooting holes in me, now can I?" The stranger reached out and casually took the wounded detective's revolver from his hand. As weak as he was, Babcock was in no condition to resist. With the gun gone, his arm flopped against his side like a puppet with cut strings.

"You see, I just recovered from some very severe injuries, and I really have no desire to go through the recuperative process again. I'm sure you understand, a man in your line of work. You must have suffered a good number of injuries over the course of your career. I'd be willing to bet even that gunshot wound is nothing new to you, now is it? Painful, but nothing you haven't been through before, I'm sure." Babcock said nothing in response to the stranger, merely slid to the floor as the patch of crimson on his shirt spread like a blooming flower. His white dress shirt quickly became stained with a glistening red. His eyes stared ahead, glassy and unfocused. Alex could hardly make them out, but he could see they had the look of death in them. If Babcock wasn't dead already, he would be soon.

The stranger squatted next to the wounded police officer. "I know this may seem cruel and unjust, but you really have to see my side of things. I mean, all my life, people have lied to me. They mislead me. They use me. For the first time in my existence, I'm getting my life in order and I simply can't let anyone impede that. Unfortunately, you are in my way. So, you have to be eliminated. But trust me, once all of this unpleasantness is over and you are finally at peace, you'll thank me for it. I won't be able to hear your thanks, which is also cruel and unjust, but at least I'll have the satisfaction of knowing that you are free of all your worries and are finally truly happy."

Standing again, he examined the gun in his hand. "Now, just close your eyes and this will all be over in a moment. I promise."

Babcock's eyes remained open, and he offered no response.

The stranger stood and leveled his pistol at Babcock's temple, only three inches from his head. There was no way he could miss, and no way Babcock would survive it. Alex wanted to cry out, to stop or delay the killer, to distract him from killing the officer he had come to know as a friend, but there was nothing he could do. His own injuries prevented him from moving without tearing up his insides with the jagged remains of his shattered ribs, and he had dropped the shotgun somewhere when he charged at the stranger. He could do nothing now except watch as the stranger from his nightmares murdered his friend.

Alex braced himself for the inevitable whisper of the silenced handgun and the wet splatter of gray matter against the wall. The whisper didn't come; instead, a sound he hadn't expected nearly deafened him.

There was a tremendous explosion as the stranger's shoulder burst into a red mist. Screaming in pain, the impact of the shot jarred the gun loose from his hand as it threw him against the iron railing. He somehow managed to grasp the rail with his other hand to keep from going over and pull himself up straight as he turned to face the source of the attack. His face was a deep red of rage. A killing rage that quickly melted into surprise and shock when he saw who had shot him.

Rachel stood in the center of the hallway, still reeling from the massive recoil of the shotgun, but again bracing the stock against her shoulder and raising the gun for another shot. She grimaced as the rifle set on her shoulder, the first shot no doubt bruising her. But she was undeterred and ready to take another. Despite the pain in his jaw, Alex smiled.

The stranger gingerly touched the pulpy mass that had been his shoulder just a moment ago, wincing in pain at the contact. He stared at the blood on his fingers, his blood, which was even now flowing down his back in a river.

"How could you do this to me?" he rasped; his voice drained of the chilling fear it contained previously. He sounded more like a jilted teenager than a cold-hearted killer.

"After everything you've done tonight, you have to ask? Why don't you ask Walt and Betty Barton? Or Officer LeBlanc? Or poor Officer Timmins? Or how about Lieutenant Babcock?" Her voice quavered in anger as she spoke their names, remembering how she had seen each of them murdered or ravaged at the hands of this killer. The quavering vanished, and her voice took on a hard edge with her next sentence. "What about my *husband*?"

The stranger's face contorted in a mix of pain, anger, sadness, and desperation. "They were trying to keep us apart; don't you see that? Why can't you see that?"

For the first time since encountering him, Alex heard a loss of control in the other man's tone. A sense of desperation and anguish at his situation. Not fear. Confusion and disappointment. He could feel it coming from the stranger in waves. He genuinely couldn't understand Rachel's apparent betrayal.

In an instant, Alex felt the stranger's feelings shift. Where there was doubt, confusion, pain and betrayal, suddenly it coalesced once again into anger. A burning rage consumed him as he turned to Alex, realization crossing his face just as anger filled his heart. The frosty edge returned to his eyes as he spoke in a low growl, spitting hatred at Alex with each word. "You did this to her. The lies went deeper than I thought. You kept her from me! She and I were meant to be together, but you kept her from me!"

Alex could feel the rage still emanating from him, but his voice softened and regained some of the control he exhibited before. "Well, we can't have that anymore. I need to make sure you can't ever come between us again. Then we can finally be together, as was intended."

Those last words hung in the air, carried by the howl of wind and the patter of rain. He eyed Rachel, who kept the shotgun steadily trained on him, before redirecting his gaze to his gun on the floor. Rachel saw his body tense, and she knew what he was about to do a moment before he did it, but didn't have time to shout a warning to the stranger before he made a move for the gun. He dove to the floor and came up with the weapon in his hand. Instead of going for the obvious threat, he ignored Rachel and instead turned the gun on Alex. Alex squeezed his eyes shut and waited for oblivion.

There was another ear-splitting boom and just above the knee, the stranger's leg became shredded meat. While still reeling from that wound, another explosion shattered the night and the right side of his chest blew apart. The momentum of the impact threw him against the railing, his bottom half hitting hard while his top half found nothing but open space. He tried to grab hold of the railing and steady himself, but his hands were slick with blood and he couldn't find a grip. He toppled over, disappearing as he fell to the living room floor below and landing with a sickening thud.

There was no movement or sound in the hall, save the muted sounds of the storm outside. Rachel stood with the shotgun still perched on her shoulder, wisps of white smoke lazily drifting from the barrel. Her eyes were wide, transfixed on the spot where the stranger had stood just a moment ago.

"Rach? Rachel, honey?" Alex forced out the words through the pain in his chest, but she ignored him and continued to stare.

Alex gently pushed himself up on his elbow, his tortured body protesting each movement. His mind screamed at the thought of trying to stand, but there wasn't much choice. With generous help from the wall, he pulled himself up to his feet. While his body screamed with the effort, everything that had previously felt mangled inside him seemed to hurt less than he might have imagined. Maybe the simple act of getting up off the floor and changing position had relieved some odd pressure, but at least he didn't feel as if he were ready to pass out.

He limped over to his wife, searing jolts of pain coursing through him. With each step, he felt the pain lessen and was amazed at how well he was moving after the beating he had suffered. He was certain his ribs had shattered and punctured a lung, but he couldn't feel the bones grinding and noticed his breathing had eased considerably. Even his jaw felt better. By the time he reached Rachel, he was moving easily and there were almost no outward signs of injury; no limp, no stagger, nothing except a slight hunch in his posture. Except for the blood staining his shirt, it would have been nearly impossible to tell he had been injured at all.

Slowly and gingerly, he reached out and took the shotgun from Rachel, who still stood with it firmly braced against her shoulder and aimed steadily at where the stranger had stood only a minute ago. It was as if she was waiting for him to spring back up over the railing and come after them again. As the gun was pulled from her grasp, her expression suddenly changed from firm determination to fear and anguish. Her arms dropped to her side, most likely exhausted from the strain of holding the shotgun up as long as she had, and her shoulders slumped as all the adrenaline and anger fueling her strength left her body. Tears flowed freely down her cheeks and her body rocked with sobs as the events of the night finally caught up with her. Alex put his arms around her and pulled her in tight to him, feeling her shake with each sob. He didn't have any words to offer her and settled for kissing her forehead and stroking her back as she cried.

After a moment, she spoke, her voice quiet and desperate. "Oh God, Alex! What did I just do?"

He pulled away from her slightly, taking her face in his hands and pulling her gaze up to his face. "What you had to do. Rachel, honey, you had no choice. If you hadn't done what you did, he would have killed me. Me and..." He trailed off as a thought burst into his brain. "Babcock! Oh, my God!"

The detective still sat propped up against the wall, his shirt front almost entirely a mass of wet crimson. Two jagged holes gaped back at them, one at his shoulder and the other just above his belt. It was at that wound the red stains were darkest. His breath came in sharp gasps, and his eyes were wide and glassy.

"Lieutenant!" Alex shouted at him, breaking into the cop's field of vision. His eyes remained unfocused and unchanging.

"I'll call 911," Rachel said, Babcock's plight momentarily supplanting her conflicting feelings over having to shoot the stranger.

"Lieutenant! Babc... Ernie, can you hear me? Please, hear me." Alex pleaded as he hastily tore off his own bloodstained shirt and tore it in half. He pressed one half against the wound in the cop's belly and Babcock winced in pain, his already shallow breathing stopping all together. Alex froze. He hoped he hadn't aggravated the man's injuries. Almost before he could finish the thought, a series of hacking coughs wracked Babcock, spraying specks of spittle and blood across the carpet. Alex realized he must be bleeding internally and wished he knew more than the basics of emergency medicine. He had no idea how severe Babcock's injuries were. For all Alex knew, he might be okay for hours, or he could be dead in minutes.

Rachel came running back a few moments later as Alex was applying the second makeshift bandage to the detective's shoulder. By the time he finished, the first bandage was already soaked through with blood.

"An ambulance will be here in a few minutes." She looked over the wounds Alex had just hastily dressed, a grim look on her face. "He's already lost so much blood, and he's still bleeding pretty heavily. The bandages should help to slow things down."

"But will it help him?" Alex asked, almost pleadingly.

Rachel shook her head. "I just don't know. I know what to do for bee stings and skinned knees. I don't know anything about gunshot wounds. We can try to slow down the bleeding as best we can, wait for the emergency crew to arrive and hope for the best. Pray for the best."

"You...need to...get out of...here. Can't be here... when they show up."

Alex and Rachel both jumped in surprise when Babcock muttered the words. So much so that it took a few seconds for the meaning of his words to sink in.

"Just take it easy," Rachel said, taking his hand in hers. It was already cold. "Stay with us. Help is on the way."

"Heard," he said in a light rasp that was barely audible over the pattering of the rain. "Can't...be here when it comes. Can't trust... them. None... of... them."

"What do you mean? Who can't we trust?" Rachel asked, not sure if she should press him for answers.

Alex understood Babcock's warning. He gently touched Rachel's arm, urging her away from Babcock. "Rachel, we need to go. Now."

"What do you mean, we have to go?" She pulled Babcock's hand in closer, tears once again welling in her eyes. "Alex, we can't just leave him here. Not like this. Not after... everything."

Alex placed his hand on hers, the hand that rested on Babcock's. "We have to. We don't have a choice. There are still people out there looking for us. Dangerous people. They could be on their way here right now. For all we know, it could be the cops or the ambulance crew. We can't afford to stay here and find out."

Tears streamed freely down her face. "Alex, look at him! He saved our lives! We can't just leave him to die alone like this! I can't abandon him! I won't!"

"Yes, you will," came Babcock's painful, whispered voice. He gently squeezed Rachel's hand while attempting to force a grin on his face. "Don't you dare... let those... bastards win because of... of me. Get out of here. Now. Protect yourself and... protect your baby. Find help. Find someone...you can trust."

"Who can we trust?" The slight shake returned to Rachel's voice. She bit her bottom lip to stop crying. The tears still gathered in her eyes.

Again, the detective gave her hand a reassuring squeeze, albeit weaker this time. "Alex knows who...to trust. Follow... him." With those words, he closed his eyes. Although his chest continued to rise and fall sporadically, the detective was done speaking.

Over the noise of the rain came the sounds of a siren a few streets over, coming closer. There wasn't much time. Alex stood, his hand still on Rachel's arm, and gently nudged her to her feet.

"They'll be here soon," he said, a sense of urgency creeping into his voice. "We have to go."

Rachel looked at him as if she were about to protest, but said nothing. Turning back to the unconscious form of the police officer who had risked so much to save them, she whispered, "Thank you," and followed Alex to the top of the spiral staircase.

Alex kneeled and picked up the shotgun, his ribs offering a minor protest. The pain from the beating he took had almost faded completely. It was strange. Right after it happened, he was sure that his ribs were shattered, his lung was punctured and his jaw was broken. Now that he was up and moving around, it didn't seem nearly as bad. He had a few aches and no doubt some hidden bruises, but he could move without a lot of pain.

Except for the pain in his belly. Ever since he started moving around, he noticed a gnawing feeling in his stomach; a deep, incessant hunger in the pit of his belly. He needed something to eat badly. He had thrown up the contents of his stomach earlier at Babcock's house, but he had never felt a hunger like this before. Not even the other night, when the nightmare woke him up at the start of all this weirdness. Even stranger was his sudden need for orange juice. It wasn't more than a simple craving; it was a deep need. As odd as it was to be fixating on in this moment, he couldn't get the thought out of his head. He was ravenous, and it was getting worse.

He snapped out of his reverie when Rachel, standing at the top of the staircase, gasped sharply in surprise. She was staring down into the living room where the stranger would be after his fall from the loft. After she had shot him. Her face was ashen, a shocked expression etched on her.

Alex moved to her, placing a reassuring hand on her back. "Rachel, honey, don't look. You did what you had to do..."

She cut him off sharply, her voice thin and shaky. "He's gone."

Alex felt her body shudder involuntarily. He moved up closer to the rail and looked over into the living room, expecting to see the bent and broken body of the stranger below. A sudden jolt of electric terror ran through him at what he saw.

The body wasn't there. There were spatters and smears of blood as evidence it had been there, but the body was gone. That was impossible. Rachel had hit him three times with the shotgun, he had seen it himself. The shotgun that was loaded with scattershot. Even if she had only clipped him with each shot, it would have been enough to incapacitate him. Add the fall over the railing to that, there was no way he could have survived.

Yet the body was gone.

His mind was reeling, the icy hand of terror momentarily displacing the hunger in his belly. It just wasn't possible. With his leg torn apart like it was, there was no way he could just get up and walk away. There had to be another explanation. There had to be.

The sirens were getting closer, easily audible over the wind and rain. If they were going to leave ahead of the emergency personnel, they would have to go now. The mystery would have to wait.

"Alex, where is he?" Rachel's voice was filled with a quiet desperation as she gripped the iron railing, her knuckles as white as paper.

"I don't know. I don't know," was all he could offer. He had no rational explanation, only a bad feeling settling in among the hunger pangs in his stomach.

Alex pushed down the growing bad feelings. "We need to go. Now. Take this." He held the shotgun out to Rachel, who pulled away from it. Alex understood her reluctance. "I know how you feel about this right now. About this gun. About what happened just now. But we need to get moving and get out of here. And we have no idea where that guy went, what shape he's in or what he might be planning. We have to be ready for him if he comes at us again. I need you to take this. And I need you to be ready to use it if you have to. I can't do it without you. Can you do that?"

She stared silently at the gun for a moment, hesitation visible on her face, then nodded and took the weapon from him.

"Good," he said as he reached down and retrieved the stranger's dropped handgun. He released the clip into his hand and checked to be sure there were still rounds in it before replacing it with a hard slam and chambering a round. He completed the process in a swift series of movements, confidently, as if it were part of his daily routine. Like it was second nature to him. Which surprised him, since he couldn't remember even holding a gun, much less being proficient with one. And yet, the gun in his hand felt like a natural extension of his arm.

Once again, he pushed those thoughts to the back of his head. Those were mysteries for later, right now they had to move. "Okay, we'll do this one step at a time. I'll go first, you follow close behind me. When we get to the bottom of the stairs, head straight for the front door. Don't stop and look around, just go. Once we get outside, head for the garage. The Pathfinder is there, we'll take that."

Rachel shook her head. "No. You and Babcock believe these people are well connected, so they likely know what car we drive. They'll spot us before we can even get out of the neighborhood."

"Damn, I hadn't thought of that," Alex admitted. "But what choice do we have? We can't take Babcock's car for the same reason."

"Yes, we do. When we get out the front door, head across the street to the Barton's." A lump formed in her throat and her stomach churned at the thought of going back there, but it was the only option she could think of.

The sirens wailed through the night, closer now. Possibly even turning onto their street. "Let's get moving," she urged Alex, nudging him slightly with her elbow.

Alex heard the wailing of the emergency vehicles and understood her urgency. Time was running out fast, there wasn't any time for debate. Besides, he'd never had cause to question her judgement in all the time they'd been together, he wasn't about to start now.

He nodded at her and started down the stairs, pausing at each turn in the wrought iron spiral to check for movement. At the bottom step he stopped, Rachel directly behind him, and scanned the room once again. Nothing stirred. He couldn't hear anything but the storm outside. Going against what he had warned Rachel not to do, he glanced over to where the stranger had landed after going over the railing. There was a good amount of blood spattered on the floor, with smears that showed whoever left it there had pulled themselves up. A crimson trail led off to the left, through the kitchen. He must have somehow, miraculously, gotten up and slipped out through the kitchen door into the storm. The garage was on that side of the house, more reason to not head out that way.

Moving off the bottom step, Alex refocused on the front door, which still stood open. Stepping carefully over the blood trail, he headed for the exit, pausing only long enough to be sure Rachel was still behind him. He moved swiftly through the small living moving until he came to LeFranc's body. There he stopped cold, his heart seizing at what he saw.

"Alex, what is it? What's wrong?" Rachel's suddenly panicked voice came up from behind him.

"His gun."

"What about it?" There was a tangible tension in Rachel's voice, so thick he could almost feel it creeping up his back as she spoke.

"He was still gripping his gun when Babcock and I came in." He nodded toward the officer's body on the floor. "Look."

Rachel's eyes dropped to where he indicated, and her heart sank. LeFranc's fingers splayed apart as if someone had forcibly pried the pistol from them.

Not only was that maniac still alive, but he had also armed himself again.

"Come on, let's get the hell out of here." Alex bolted for the front door and into the storm, which had abated since he and Babcock had first arrived at the house. He scanned the surrounding night, zeroing in on the pools of light provided by the streetlamps and neighboring homes. A flicker of motion to his left caught his eye, startling him. He turned, the pistol ready. A flash of blue cut through the storm, followed almost immediately by another and another in quick succession. Flashes of red blended in a second after, coloring the trees and the rain. Emergency vehicle lights, police and rescue. They were just around the corner and would be in view in seconds.

"Run!" Alex yelled, grabbing Rachel's arm and breaking into a sprint toward the Barton's house, pulling her behind him. The rain-soaked ground of their front lawn sucked and pulled at their shoes, slowing their pace. The red and blue emergency beacons became brighter as a police cruiser, followed closely by an ambulance, rounded the corner a few houses down. In seconds, they would be dead on in the headlights of the lead vehicle.

Alex hit the pavement, instantly gaining traction. Still gripping Rachel's arm, he flung her ahead of him, across the last stretch of street and into the small stand of shadowed birch trees that marked the Barton's property line. He dove in next to her, landing with a wet smack on the lawn, conveniently out of reach of the streetlights. The beams of the police cruiser's headlights panned the road where they had been standing a second ago.

Rachel moved for the house, but Alex put a hand on her shoulder and kept her down behind the tangled trunks of the birches. "Not yet. They might see us. Give them a second to get inside."

She kneeled back down in the sodden grass beside him, and the rainwater that had not yet been absorbed into the ground soaked into her jeans. A chill ran through her as a trickle of water penetrated entirely through her sweatshirt and cascaded down her back, coming to rest at the uppermost curve of her buttocks. She was wet and freezing and had been for so long she wasn't sure she'd ever feel warm again.

Across the street, the police cruiser and the ambulance came to a stop in front of their house. A single police officer exited the cruiser while the ambulance disgorged one man from the driver's side of the cab and a woman emerged from the back, carrying two large black bags. She handed one to her partner before the three of them headed for the still open front door of the house. The police officer led the way into the house, weapon drawn.

Alex and Rachel sat still for a moment, expecting to hear gunshots from inside. When none came, Alex stated, "It looks okay. I think we can go."

Rachel stood up next to him, the tiny pool of water tumbling further into her pants. It felt like a chilled insect crawling down her leg. She shivered again and turned to head for the Barton's house. At the porch she paused, glancing across the street to the house she had lived in happily with her husband. The place they had started their lives together, made plans for their future, started a family. Just this morning it had been home, but now it seemed so alien to her. It was just a house now; she couldn't bring herself to think of it as home any longer.

"Rachel? What's the matter?" Alex asked.

She replied, her voice a flat monotone. "We can never go back there again."

He stepped down from the front door and put his arm around her, turning her to face him. Her eyes, normally alight with life, were faded and dimmed. There was no fire there, no fight. Just pain, exhaustion and hopelessness.

"Don't talk like that," he said. "When this is over, when everything is sorted out, we'll go home again."

Rachel lowered her eyes, unable to keep looking into his. She couldn't, not after everything she had seen on that thumb drive. Not after everything she knew. After everything that had happened because of it. From now on, their lives would never be the same.

"We can't ever go home again," she whispered.

Alex wanted to argue the point, to tell her she was wrong, but he couldn't. Deep down, he could feel that change was stirring. He loved his wife with all his heart, and it pained him he couldn't offer her any comfort right now. Because she was right.

"Come on," he said, vainly trying to ward off a chill that wasn't the result of the damp night. "Let's get inside."

They turned, his arm still tightly wrapped around her, both of their thoughts weighed down by the dark cloud over their future. Neither one of them saw the line of black town cars that rounded the corner and pulled up across the street in front of their house.

33

The emergency beacons from the ambulance washed over the town car as it pulled up at the Carter's house, staining the interior a bright red. Burke watched as two paramedics leaped from the rear of the emergency vehicle and raced for the open front door of the house, burdened by heavy bags, no doubt containing medical supplies. He sighed a deep sigh and pinched the bridge of his nose between his thumb and forefinger, rubbing slowly yet with a substantial amount of pressure. He closed his eyes to the swirling red flashes that raced around the back seat of the car, the commotion of the lights being more of a strain on him than the cacophony of sounds assaulting him. The wind, rain, sirens and Rutters' incessant chatter were wearing on him.

"Sir, are you all right? Can I get you anything?" It was Harriman, seated across from him. Burke found the man's voice slightly unnerving in their current surroundings. Since they had disembarked from the helicopter, the Colonel hadn't said more than a few scant words, simply sitting and staring at the screen of his tablet and occasionally typing now and then. Now that the tablet was put away and the Colonel rejoined them, Burke felt uneasy by the man's sudden attention.

Waving him off, Burke replied, "I'm fine, Colonel. Just thinking about things have gotten more complicated." He turned his attention to Rutters, meeting the man's eyes with a hard, unflinching stare. Indicating the ambulance and police cruiser parked at the curb, he growled, "We should have arrived ahead of them. Now we have to do things the hard way."

Rutters broke Burke's gaze and hung his head like a scolded dog. "I apologize, sir, but the medical aid call was unexpected..."

Burke held up his hand, cutting him off. "Enough. I don't need excuses right now. We'll handle your numerous fuck ups in the debriefing. For right now, we'll just have to deal with the shit pile you allowed to happen. Fortunately, I'm prepared for situations like this."

He removed a thin wallet from the inner pocket of his suit coat; the kind used by law enforcement to house badges and identification. From his pants pocket, he produced another small case, this one designed to carry business cards. Burke's carried something far more useful. He removed a single laminated document from the small pouch and placed it behind the plastic window in the wallet. Harriman reached across and handed him a small item taken from a case the Colonel carried, a badge that Burke then pinned on the wallet opposite the laminated card. He then placed the small wallet with the badge and ID card back into his suit pocket, completing the transformation. In that moment, he was no longer Burke Darnell, personal attaché to Robert Penders.

"Who are you, sir? In case I need to address you?" Harriman casually inquired.

Lowering his voice an octave, Burke replied, "Special Agent Lance Barrymore, F.B.I."

Harriman nodded before reaching beneath his seat to produce a small briefcase. He popped it open to reveal the tools of the trade for any F.B.I forensic technician; fingerprint powder and applicator brush, small glass evidence vials, a Xacto knife, tweezers, a magnifying glass, latex gloves, a spray bottle of phosphorescent fluid, and paper bags. While the Colonel was trained in forensic collection techniques, he primarily used the case for show to reinforce Burke's current identity.

"All right, gentlemen," Burke stated, "let's go. Remember, don't speak to anyone if you can avoid it. If you can't avoid it, remember that everything is classified and you cannot talk about it. Understand?" There were two affirmative responses. "Good. And Colonel?"

"Sir?" Harriman replied.

"I want to keep Forrester out of there. We're going to have to dance around this situation and I don't want him in there screwing up the tempo. Have your people keep him in the car and out of trouble," Burke ordered.

"Understood," Harriman replied. He turned to Rutters and grabbed the younger man's cell phone. "I'm commandeering this, son."

Rutters' face flashed with a hint of rage, but he reined it in quickly. "Yes, sir," he replied curtly before opening the car door and stepping into the storm. Burke smiled at Rutters' response. To Harriman, it was simply efficiency; he was the ranking officer there and didn't have a cell phone to direct operations. Rutters had a phone he would not need; it made perfect sense for the Colonel to take it. But Rutters saw it as another challenge to his authority and it ate at him. A fact that sat warmly in Burke's belly.

Harriman finished a call on his newly gained phone and Burke stated, "I don't think he likes either of us, Colonel. What do you think?"

"I don't think it matters, sir," Harriman replied flatly.

Burke's smile became a sarcastic grin. "It matters, Colonel. Believe me, it matters. If that man gets it in his head that neither one of us should be running this show, we could be headed for trouble.

"I'm certain it's nothing we can't handle." The Colonel's reply was even and emotionless. Burke wondered if the man was even capable of inflection.

"And if he gets out of hand?" Burke continued. "You have no problem 'handling' one of your own people?"

Harriman leveled his eyes at Burke. The Colonel's face remained as steady as ever, but something in his eyes shifted ever so slightly in a way that made Burke's stomach twist. "If he ever needs to be 'handled', he's no longer one of my people."

"I see," Burke replied, unable to shake the chill that came over him from locking eyes with Harriman. "And if you were called upon to 'handle' one of your superiors?"

With no noticeable shift in tone, Harriman stated, "If I were called upon, they would no longer be my superior. Sir."

Burke's smile faded from his face completely. "I will keep that in mind."

Harriman sat in silence.

Burke broke the tension he was feeling. "Well, now that we've settled that, we should get to work." He opened the car door, wind sweeping in and driving rain into his unprotected face. Flinching, he leaned back into the protection of the vehicle.

"You may need this, sir." Harriman handed Burke a raincoat. Not a poncho, like last time, a black dress raincoat. London Fog.

Burke took the coat. "Thank you, Colonel. Prepared once more, I see."

"Always prepared for anything, sir."

Burke nodded knowingly, slipping into the raincoat and back out into the storm. It was cold and wet, but he was better off out in the cold rain than back in the car with the deep chill that had come over the Colonel.

****

Dr. Forrester looked out on the scene as the paramedics raced from the ambulance to the front door of the Carter house. A parade of horrible thoughts marched through his head as he wondered who had been hurt and how serious it was. As much as he hoped it wasn't either Adam or Alex, he was especially concerned for the woman. Rachel. Losing one of the men would be a setback, but it would be recoverable. Losing the woman would be tragic to his research.

Opening the car door, he stepped out into the wet night and made his way to the house and the commotion there. He needed to ascertain what was happening inside, who had been injured, and to what extent. Aside from that, while his chosen area of expertise had been genetics, he was a doctor. He may be able to render more assistance than the paramedics that had preceded him into the house.

He didn't make it more than a few steps before one of Harriman's mercenaries, a large no-nonsense sort with more muscle than mind and absolutely no neck to speak of, stopped him.

"I'm afraid I can't let you go any further, sir," the human gorilla stated, placing a surprisingly gentle hand on Forrester's shoulder.

Forrester looked up at the brutish man who had just laid a massive hand on him. Rain was cascading down his thick glasses, obscuring his vision, but he could see the serious expression on the man's face. "Why not?"

"I have my orders," was the reply, the man's voice low and thick. There was a slowness to the response, confirming Forrester's earlier suspicion that the man hadn't been hired for his intellect.

"And who gave these orders?" Forrester asked, puffing himself up and lowering the tone of his voice as much as he could. It made little difference; he was still small and squeaky-voiced compared to the man-mountain before him. No one could accuse Elliot Forrester of being intimidating.

"Colonel Harriman, relaying orders from Mr. Darnell," the mercenary stated flatly. His hand remained firmly on Forrester's shoulder. "We're to keep you away from the scene until further instructions are issued."

Forrester deflated at that. "No. He can't shut me out. Not now, when we're so close."

"I believe he just did, sir."

"Damn him! I need to get in there to assess the damage! I need to know what's going on!" Forrester tried to move toward the house again, but the other man firmly held him in place with a hand on his shoulder.

"I can't allow that, sir," the man stated, his voice devoid of any notion of feeling. "I have my orders."

"But," Forrester protested, "I need to..."

"I think what you need to do, sir," the man interjected, the slightest bit of irritation creeping into his voice, "is step back into the car and cool off for a bit. I'm certain if Mr. Darnell needs you, he'll call for you."

Dr. Forrester found himself being forcibly turned around and moved back into the car, the door closing behind him with an angry sounding thump. He wanted to protest further, to argue his case, but he knew it would be futile. He would have to wait while Burke Darnell grandstanded and manipulated the events. All Forrester could do at the moment was sit and stew about how Burke and Robert Penders had taken over the Project, and had co-opted his life's work. He found a silver lining in the dark cloud, however, and soon he would get some satisfaction. Soon Burke Darnell would learn that life wasn't always what it seemed to be. That sometimes even your own life wasn't what you thought it was. But he would, and with the pace of recent events, it would be soon.

Very, very soon.

****

"Who's in charge here?" Burke bellowed as he erupted through the Carter's front door, phony badge and ID held high. The paramedic to his left made no motion to answer, his attention firmly on the second-story landing. Burke followed his gaze to see the other two paramedics, the ones he assumed had jumped from the back of the ambulance when he arrived, working feverishly just on the other side of the wrought iron rail that ran the length of the landing. Next to them was the officer who had arrived first at the scene with the ambulance. No one acknowledged him.

"I said, 'Who's in charge here?'!" he yelled, heading for the lone paramedic, his attention still riveted to the activities of the others above. Burke shoved his fake ID into the man's line of vision, stepping between him and the action. "Special Agent Lance Barrymore of the F.B.I. and I need some questions answered. Who can do that for me?"

"I can, if you keep your God-damned shirt on for a minute!" The response came from the top of the spiral staircase, a cop glaring at him from above.

In a few moments, the three paramedics worked to lower their patient securely over the rail in a back brace and transfer him to a stretcher for transport. Burke was surprised when he didn't see either Adam or Alex on the stretcher and was relieved it wasn't the woman. Judging by the description Rutters had given, it must have been Detective Lieutenant Ernest Babcock, the cop who had been seen with Alex Carter since the investigation into the death of Dr. Simone Carlton. It appeared he had been shot twice, with wounds to his shoulder and stomach.

The three paramedics, having secured the detective to the stretcher, hurried out the door to the ambulance in an impressive amount of time. Seconds later, Burke could hear the vehicle's siren fading into the distance.

"Now, what can I do for you?" The cop who had rebuffed him a few minutes earlier was descending the spiral staircase. He was fairly young looking, Burke estimated his mid-thirties, but with a worn look on his face and just a touch of gray peppering his hair.

Burke flashed his phony credentials. "Special Agent Lance Barrymore, Federal Bureau of Investigation. Were you the first one on the scene?"

"I was." The cop's reply was cold, distant. Distracted. Burke surmised it was most likely because he had just seen a fellow cop taken out on a stretcher and he was trying to piece things together. Whatever, it didn't matter to Burke. He needed information, no matter what this hick town Barney Fife was dealing with.

"Was there anyone here when you arrived?" Burke continued. "The owners of the house? A neighbor?"

"No one," the cop answered. He seemed to stare off into space while answering, deep in thought, as if he was still processing the events of the night. In a moment, he continued. "That was the strange thing. There had obviously been a pretty massive incident that occurred, but Ernie was the only one here. It was as if he had just been..." He paused again, searching for the right word. "Abandoned. That's the only way I can think of to say it. Someone was definitely up there with him just after he was shot. Just before I arrived on the scene. But he was alone when we found him. Someone called 911, and there was definitely someone else here, but they had just abandoned him alone up there, bleeding, until we arrived."

"What do you mean, there was someone up there with him just before you arrived?" Burke asked.

The cop turned back to Burke, his eyes still distant. Burke could almost see him reliving the events of the last hour, sorting through the details. Burke needed to push him faster. The more time he had to think about the details, the more it would fill in blanks by itself, covering up actual events and important facts. A situation made even worse if there's an emotional response to the event. It's why witness testimony is the most unreliable evidence in any investigation, but if it was necessary, it was best to get to it quickly while the memories were still raw and undamaged.

"How would you know that there was someone with him right before you got here?" Burke asked. He hastened the pace of dialogue, lowered his voice an octave and raised his tone to create a sense of urgency to force the cop to answer more quickly.

The cop's expression changed as Burke's tone did, seeming to snap him back to attention. "Someone tore off a piece of their shirt and used it as a bandage to slow Ernie's bleeding. They didn't do that long before we go here, though."

"And you know this how, Officer?"

"Sergeant," the cop replied. "Sergeant Tim O'Neill." Sergeant Tim held out his hand to Burke, who grasped it and gave a vigorous shake.

"Pleasure to meet you," Burke lied. "Again, how did you know this bandage was applied just before you arrived?"

"When we got to Ernie, there was hardly any blood soaking through the bandage. He was bleeding pretty damned heavy, let me tell you. But there was hardly any blood soaked into that piece of shirt. Someone would have had to apply the bandage to Ernie's wounds no more than five minutes prior." A bit of anger seeped into the Sergeant's voice as he recounted finding Lieutenant Babcock.

Burke was losing him. He had to wrap it up. "Do you have any idea who it might have been that shot the Lieutenant?" He had a pretty good idea who it was, but he wanted to see how far off the mark the local police were.

The answer was exactly what Burke expected. "I have no clue. And now that you're here, I guess it's not really my place to figure it out, is it? So, if you'll excuse me...." Sergeant Tim stepped around Burke and headed for the door, pulling a pack of Marlboros and a lighter from his jacket pocket. As he tapped a cigarette from the pack, he turned back to Burke, a thoughtful expression on his face. "I'm sure you'll find this out when you get all your forensic reports back, but I can tell you right now, Ernie wasn't the only person injured here tonight."

That piqued Burke's interest. "Why do you say that"?

"This may be a small town, Agent Barrymore, but we see our fair share of gunshot wounds. Mostly hunting accidents, idiots who drink too much and go out shooting at anything that moves, but we have a few of the deliberate kind, too. I've been doing this job for ten years now and I've seen people bleed from almost every kind of wound there is, and while Ernie was bleeding pretty severely, there's no way he left all that blood up there by himself. Look at this." Sergeant Tim led Burke to a spot beneath the loft overhang. Using his unlit cigarette as a pointer, he indicated several spatter patterns of blood on the floor. Patterns that seemed to erupt from a central point. "Ernie sure as hell didn't leave that."

Burke bent down to examine the red spatters. Whoever left this blood, a gunshot wound was only one of their problems. The spattering showed they had fallen from the loft after being shot. Yet somehow the blood trailed away. That meant this person had been shot more than once, had fallen from a height of at least fifteen feet, and then somehow dragged themselves up and out of the house.

It had to be Adam. No one else could have taken punishment like that and just walked away. It wasn't humanly possible. Whatever else Burke thought of Eliot Forrester, he certainly had to admire the man's craftsmanship. He built them to last.

But this time, there was a trail. A fresh blood trail leading outside. "Harriman!" Burke bellowed.

"Yes, sir?" came the Colonel's voice from above them as he leaned out over the edge of the loft.

Burke craned his neck upward. "I need you. Now. We may have a lead."

Harriman didn't respond, but raced down the spiral staircase at a pace that made Burke nauseous just watching him. At the bottom of the staircase, he bounded over to Burke and Sergeant Tim.

"Yes, sir."

Burke pointed to the blood staining the hardwood floor. "I think this might belong to our man. It's still fresh and there's a trail leading outside. Get your people on it!"

Harriman nodded, producing a radio and barking instructions to his people outside. When he finished he turned again to Burke. "They're on it, sir. But I have to remind you of the weather. Odds are slim there's much of a trail to follow out there."

Burke waved him off. "A slim chance is better than no chance. Get moving."

Harriman nodded in response and raced out the front door, vanishing into the storm swept night.

Sergeant Tim let out a long whistle. "Man, you guys don't waste any time, do you? Which brings me to my next question; this barely happened, why is the F.B.I. here before any local police? Don't you have to be called in on cases like this?"

Burke noted the suspicion in the cop's voice. Fortunately, he had prepared for that question. "There are no cases like this, Officer," he stated. "I also can't discuss the details. Matters of national security. You understand."

Sergeant Tim looked Burke up and down. There was a bit more hesitation in his reply as the adrenaline of the evening faded and his cop instincts kicked in. "Honestly, I can't say I do understand, Agent Barrymore."

Burke tensed a bit. He was losing the shock element as more time went by. Sergeant Tim was turning out to be more perceptive than he expected. "Well, I don't have the time or inclination to explain it to you. This is a federal matter, and we are in charge from here on. Oh, and there's one other thing." He locked eyes with the Sergeant and paused to let the effect sink in. "I need you and everyone else involved here tonight to keep this quiet. Including the Lieutenant's condition."

Sergeant Tim's eyes widened at that, but he kept his composure. "Why?"

"We have our reasons. Just do as I ask." Burke fell back into his official, menacing tone once more.

Sergeant Tim held Burke's gaze for a second, and Burke could almost see him turning the situation over in his yokel cop brain. He braced for a confrontation with the cop.

Sergeant Tim broke his gaze. "Okay. I don't understand it, and I certainly don't like it, but okay."

Burke relaxed a bit on the inside but kept up the hard-edged attitude. "Good. Make sure not a word of this leaks. If it does, there could be... consequences."

"Is that a threat, Agent Barrymore?" Sergeant Tim pulled himself up to his full height, which was considerable compared to Burke's, and took a half step forward.

Burke didn't back down. "Take it any way you like, just be sure to take it back to whoever was here with you tonight." He locked eyes solidly with the bigger man, a test of dominance.

It was a test he passed as Sergeant Tim turned away, breaking eye contact. "Have it your way," he replied, retreating a step. "I don't give a shit. I have work to do. Are we through here?"

Burke nodded. "For now. But stay available for further questioning."

Sergeant Tim turned and practically stomped out of the room like a scolded child, practically running over Harriman who was on his way back in.

"As I thought, sir, practically nothing remains of the blood trail," the Colonel reported. "The rain has been very effective in washing away any evidence that may have been left outside."

"No worry," Burke said, his attention fixed on the blood pattern on the floor.

"Excuse me, sir?" There was an unmistakably perplexed tone in Harriman's voice.

Burke flashed Harriman a cryptic smile. "Let's just say I think the fly will come to the spider soon."

34

Alex entered the Barton's house and his stomach almost revolted. Not that the scene was particularly gruesome or gory, it was the fact that the victims had been people he knew. People he cared about. It was like passing the scene of a fatal accident and discovering the third victim is your neighbor, or teacher, or boss; it takes on a new meaning. No matter how well you knew them or in what capacity, the simple fact that they were a part of your life adds a personal connection to death. The people splayed out before him had recently been living, breathing people who laughed and loved. He had seen them alive, seen them *living*, and now they were gone. Except these deaths weren't random acts of fate. These were once vital lives that had been consciously and intentionally cut short. Cut short by someone with no aversion to killing whoever stood between him and his goals. Ruthlessly. Without conscience.

The same person who was hunting them right now.

Rachel moved past him toward the kitchen, feeling along the wall for the light switch. Clicking on the light, she grabbed him by the hand and pulled him along past the bodies. "Come on, we don't have a lot of time. He could still be waiting for us nearby. We need to get away from here."

Alex squinted in the bright light of the Barton's kitchen, easily three times as bright as the living room. The kitchen was half wrecked, a result of Rachel's earlier encounter with the stranger. Silverware of every description littered the floor, pouring from an overturned drawer that sat just beneath the empty socket it had been pulled from. More startling were the streaks of deep crimson that stained the linoleum.

"What the hell happened here?" Alex asked as he took in the scene.

"I did," Rachel replied, stepping around the silverware and making her way to the pegboard on the far wall, decoratively painted with the word 'keys' on it. "Me and our friend, that is."

A startled look settled on Alex's face, his eyes wide. "You did this? What happened? Are you all right? Why didn't you tell me about this?"

"We've been a bit busy," she replied, grabbing a set of keys from the pegboard. "I'll tell you all about it when we get out of here."

"I don't understand," Alex stammered. "What happened? Why were you here? What happ..." He stopped mid-sentence as Rachel put her forefinger to her lips to silence him.

"We don't have time for that right now." She tossed the keys to him across the cluttered floor. He snapped back to attention and snapped them out of the air as she moved back through the clutter on the floor. "We need to get moving. Now."

She headed back to the living room. As she moved past, Alex reached out and touched her arm, stopping her cold.

"You know, eventually you're going to have to talk about this," he said, nodding slightly toward the Barton's living room and the bodies of their friends.

"I'm fine," she replied, but her voice wavered slightly, and she didn't bring her eyes up to meet his. She could feel the tears gathering. It was all coming back to her in a rush. Walt and Betty were dead, and she was responsible for it. Timmins was dead, and it was her fault. She wasn't directly responsible, she knew that, but what if she hadn't come running to them for help? What if she hadn't dragged Timmins over with her? What if she had stood her ground in her own home, by herself, and hadn't dragged innocent people into it? She knew she would most likely be dead right now, but she wondered if that wasn't preferable to the crushing guilt she was feeling right now.

"You're not fine. But you're also right, we don't have time right now." Alex placed his free hand on her other shoulder and gently nudged her around to face him. She refused to lift her head and meet his eyes. "This wasn't your fault, Rachel." He leaned forward and kissed her gently on her forehead. "Believe me, this wasn't your fault."

"I know that. In my mind, I know that no matter what else I might have done tonight, I couldn't have stopped this. I mean, Walt and Betty were dead before I got here! But Alex, in my heart, looking at them, all I feel is responsible. He was after me! Me! Timmins was trying to save me. Walt and Betty didn't do anything, he killed them just in case I came to them for help! They were between me and that... that psycho, and they died! If not for me...". She trailed off, leaning her head into his chest. She couldn't hold back the flow of hot tears any longer and her body shook as she sobbed uncontrollably, unable to contain all the emotions that flowed through her in a rush. He slipped his arms around her and pulled her in tight as the events of the night took their toll.

She pushed herself away from Alex, sniffling back emerging tears and wiping at her eyes to clear the existing ones. The danger of their situation came flooding back to her, shocking her back into action mode. Soon their house would be crawling with legitimate police asking questions they had no answers for. Before long, they would spread their investigation throughout the neighborhood and would discover the brutal scene at the Barton home. They needed to get away from there. She had plenty of questions of her own she needed answers to, being detained by the police would delay them and the few sparse clues they had would go cold. Better to get out now and explain everything to the authorities when they had actual answers.

Without warning, the image she had seen earlier that evening on the thumb drive burst into her mind. "I can't believe I almost forgot this!" Reaching into her pocket, she retrieved the USB drive. "These are the files Dr. Carlton left for you at her house. We have to get to a computer! Alex, you need to see this!"

"What are you talking about?" he asked, surprised by her sudden outburst.

"I think this can answer a lot of our questions," she replied, dropping the USB drive back into her pocket. "It also brings up a whole lot more. Come on, let's get going before the police go door to door."

She moved toward the living room again but stopped cold just before the arch that separated the rooms. "I don't think I can go in there again."

Alex thought about the bodies of friends littering the room. About Walt and Betty, who had been more like family to them than neighbors. He wasn't sure he wanted to go through there again himself. "We'll go out the laundry room door."

"There's a direct view of that door from our house," she said, still staring into the misty amber light of the living room. "We might not make it to the car before we're spotted."

Alex sighed heavily, grief settling in his heart. "That's a risk, yes. But it's that, or we go back through there."

Rachel didn't move, transfixed at the border between rooms. She turned back to the kitchen again. "The laundry room door."

"In just a sec," Alex said, turning and making bis way across the scattered junk to the Barton's refrigerator. He pulled open the door and took stock of the contents.

Rachel stared at him, slack jawed. "What are you doing? You want a snack now? Do I have to remind you of the crazed psychopath who tried to kill us a few minutes ago? The psychopath who could still be around?"

"I know," he replied, shoving the silenced pistol into his belt and rummaging through the refrigerator. "I don't get it, I just know that if I don't get something to eat right away, I'm not going to make it even as far as the car." He emerged with his arms loaded with food; a deli bag of sliced ham, cheese, milk, two apples and a pizza box with half a leftover pizza inside. Stacking the other items atop the pizza box, he closed the refrigerator door but stopped when something caught his eye. A half-gallon of orange juice. Dropping the rest of his haul on the counter, he grabbed the juice and snapped the bottle open, immediately downing half the contents. As the cold juice flowed down his throat, he felt the same sense of satisfaction he had experienced the other night in his own kitchen when he had gone on an unexplained snack frenzy. The juice seemed to ease some of the intense food cravings that were consuming him. He stopped drinking and exhaled loudly, recapping the bottle and placing it on top of the pizza box with the rest of the food. "There, that should do it for now. Grab the shotgun and let's get out of here."

Rachel picked up the weapon and followed him to the adjoining laundry room. It was exactly what the name implied, a small space containing a washer, dryer and a rack of various detergents and laundry aids. A door on the other side of the room led to the yard, where a clothesline stood. Betty had always preferred to hang their clothes outside to dry; claimed it gave them a cleaner, more natural scent and feel. Rachel remembered how Betty would often leave the clothes on the line during a brief summer rain and let them dry again because the scent of them reminded her of her childhood. Rachel's stomach clenched again at the thought of her neighbor, her friend, and how she would never enjoy that simple pleasure again.

Alex had placed his pile of snacks on the dryer and opened the door a crack. The rain was as intense as it had been all night, coming down in a fury. Alex peeked out, squinting his eyes against the backsplash of rain on his face, and craned to see across the street. He made out a line of four large black cars parked directly in front of the house, along with the police cruiser that arrived with the now departed ambulance. A few people in dark rain ponchos were moving about around the yard, but he couldn't determine exactly what they were doing. Some rushed through the storm, stopping periodically like they were searching for something. Others merely stood and stared into the night. Regardless of what they were doing, they all moved with a sense of purpose and a militaristic rigidity.

A glint of light from one of the poncho wearing figure's flashlight briefly illuminated the trunk of one of the black cars and Alex could make out the Lincoln emblem. The cars were certainly not the property of the Pine Haven Police Department. Pine Haven had a fairly affluent tax base, but Lincoln Town Cars were too expensive and impractical for a little town. No, these were something else. Something that meant trouble for them.

"See anything?" Rachel asked, trying to peer over his head with little success.

"A line of black town cars parked outside the house and a bunch of people in equally dark clothes along with them. I have to say that I don't much like the looks of it." Turning his head slightly, he looked across the small driveway that held Walt and Betty's Grand Am. It was roughly a fifteen-foot dash to the car, but it seemed like a mile. All it would take was for one of the black-clad figures across the street to look over at the wrong moment and catch them cold. Even if they could reach the car unnoticed, they would lose the element of surprise once they started the engine. It was definitely a risky operation.

"What are we waiting for?" Rachel asked. "Grab your snacks and let's get out of here!"

"I hope it's that easy," Alex replied, pulling back into the tiny room and closing the door behind him. Moving to the dryer, he gathered up the pizza box with the contents on top of it. It was clumsy in his hands, tilting from side to side as the uneven weight on top shifted with even the slightest movement. He wouldn't be able to move four steps like that, never mind fifteen feet. And certainly not as quickly and quietly as they needed to be. He thought about abandoning the food here, but he needed it. Hunger was tearing at him like he'd never felt before and, as ridiculous as it seemed, he felt as if his pants were about to fall off. As if he'd suddenly lost a tremendous amount of weight. He could almost feel his waist shrinking away from his pants.

On the shelf above the washer, he found the answer to his problem. He reached up and grabbed the mesh bag, normally for carrying laundry, and stuffed all the food that would fit inside. Cinching up the bag, he threw the strap over his shoulder, testing the distribution of weight and deciding whether it would hinder him as they escaped. The bag wasn't designed for that purpose, and the strings dug uncomfortably into his shoulder, but he found the load balanced and could easily carry it the short distance to the car.

"That should do it," he pronounced.

Rachel looked at him, dumbfounded. "Can't you just leave all that? We can get you a snack along the way!"

"Honey, I wish I could explain it to you, but I can't. Just please trust me when I say I need this now." His stomach roiled, cramps of hunger rippling through him as if to enforce what he said. "I already feel sick. I don't know why, but I know this will help. And it has to be soon."

His eyes were pleading for her understanding. She could see the pain in them, hear the desperation in his voice. She had to admit to herself that he looked thinner, even more so than he had been a few minutes earlier. Gaunt, approaching emaciated.

"Okay, okay," she relented. "Can we just go now?"

Alex smiled at her, and even that was weak. She was amazed at how well he held up despite the severe beating he endured earlier at the hands of the stranger. It looked now like it was catching up with him.

"Give me the keys." She held out her hand. He opened his mouth to argue, but she cut him off. "I'll drive. Don't argue. You need to eat that badly, this will give you the chance to do that. And you don't exactly look like you're fit to operate a vehicle right now."

Although he hated to admit it, she was right. He wasn't in any shape to drive or to argue with her. He reached into his pocket and retrieved the car keys, handing them over to her.

"Fine," he said. "You were always a better driver, anyway."

"You know it," she replied, snatching the keys from his hand.

He turned to the dryer where the pizza box and the shotgun sat. Running the choice around his brain for a second, opted for the shotgun, grabbing it up and moving to the door. Opening the door just a crack, he peered out across the street. The cars were all still there, but the number of figures moving around through the stormy night seemed to have decreased. Now was as good a time as any to head for the Grand Am in the driveway.

Without looking back at Rachel, he asked, "Ready?"

"As I'm ever going to be," she replied, a noticeable tinge of anxiety in her tone.

"Okay, when I go, head out right behind me. Don't stop for anything, just head straight for the car. If Walt didn't change his habits, the car should be unlocked, so we'll have that in our favor. You just get in and get the car going. Don't look back, don't look around. Leave that to me. I'll be right behind you, so be ready to get us out of here." He checked the crowd across the street again. He could make out four dark forms, none of which seemed to pay any attention to the Barton's house at the moment. Between that and the rain, the coast was about as clear as it was going to get.

He swung the door wide open and said, "Now!" Rachel slipped under his arm and bolted straight for the car, her attention focused solely on getting the vehicle fired up for their escape.

Alex followed directly behind her, scanning the surrounding yard as they moved. He couldn't see anything he took to be a threat, but he felt something that wasn't right. It was as if they were being watched. Scrutinized. He paused, trying to peer through the rain and darkness, but saw nothing. The same feeling of dread came over him again, the same feeling he'd been having for the last two days, but stronger this time. So much stronger. He was being watched right now. He could feel the cold, hateful stare on him. And it wasn't hard to guess who was behind that stare.

You tried once and failed, you bastard, he thought, projecting it as loudly as he could into the night. *I know you're out there. I can feel it. You won't get another chance.*

Just then, an intense wave of hatred hit him, so strong it turned to nausea as it struck his already roiling stomach. Then a thought, a thought he didn't originate, wormed into his head; *We'll have to wait and see*.

His head spun as the alien thought bounced around his skull. It was more than the thought; it was the driving emotion behind it that screamed inside his head. Anger, hatred, loathing; they all tore at him at once. It was like a physical thing, each new emotion slashing through his psyche. He felt his knees buckle beneath him at the onslaught and he wanted to cry out, but he held back. If he were to scream now, it would alert the authorities across the street, and that would put a quick end to their escape.

"What are you waiting for?" Rachel's urgent whisper-yell cut off the internal barrage of emotions. "Come on!"

Alex shook his head, a physical effort to clear the mental attack. Pulling open the passenger door, he dropped the shotgun on the floor in the back and flopped into the seat, closing the door behind him as gently and quietly as he could. Laying his head back against the headrest, he let out the breath he hadn't realized he'd been holding.

That couldn't have been real, he told himself. The voice in his head, it must have been his imagination. A stress reaction to the events of the last few days. A part of his subconscious, conjured up by anxiety, adrenaline, and intense hunger. It was the only explanation he could accept. Other than that, it meant he was losing his mind or, worse; he had actually heard someone else's voice in his head. Neither one of those options was terribly appealing.

"What was that about?" Rachel asked, hastily inserting the key into the ignition and starting the car. In practically the same motion, she threw the car into reverse and hit the gas, the car careening toward the end of the driveway and into the street.

"Trust me," he replied, "you don't want to know."

Across the street, the commotion sent black-clad figures scrambling. Rachel slammed the gearshift into drive and stomped on the gas pedal, the tires squealing on the wet pavement as the car lurched forward.

Ahead, as they sped past one of the town cars, a gnomish man was stepping out to see what the commotion was. Rachel pulled the steering wheel hard to the right to avoid him, nearly sending the Grand Am off the road and into a tree. As she regained control of the car, the headlights illuminated the man, revealing his features. In that moment, her brain registered recognition. She had seen him before, but she couldn't remember where. She pushed the image of the little man to the back of her brain and refocused her efforts on escape.

As she burst onto the Main Street extension and headed for the center of town, she glanced in the rearview mirror for signs of pursuit. There didn't seem to be anyone following them, so she slowed to the speed limit to avoid any undue attention.

"Where are we headed?" she asked Alex, who had already broken into the bag of goodies from the Bartons.

"My office first," he answered between bites of sliced ham, "then the Willian Harris Funeral Home."

"The funeral home?" she parroted. "Why the funeral home?"

"There's someone there who might be able to help us," he replied, shoving the last bite of ham into an already full mouth.

"And then...?" Rachel asked, trepidation in her tone.

Alex didn't answer right away, instead looking out the window at the storefronts as they raced past, thinking about the life they had lived in this town. A pang of remorse struck him. It had been a good life, and now it was over.

"And then," he answered absently, "I just don't know."

35

Dr. Elliot Forrester threw up his hands as the car careened toward him, as if he could magically prevent it from turning him into roadkill. It was a futile effort, he knew, and braced for the immediate impact that would shatter bones and crush organs. At the last moment, the car jerked to the right, pulling back onto the road and regaining control. He let out a tremendous sigh of relief as the car set itself right and raced past him for the end of the street. In that moment he caught of flash of the driver.

It was her. The woman. Rachel Carter. For a fleeting second, as she pulled the car back onto the road and resumed her breakneck pace toward Main Street, their eyes locked through the rain-streaked window. A second later the car jerked forward, tires squealing, and disappeared into the storm.

"Was it them?"

Forrester turned to see Sergeant Rutters, the young man that had met them on their arrival in Pine Haven, running up behind him. He was a hulk of a young man, standing as wide as he was tall yet lean at the same time. He was physically imposing, but more than that, the look in his eye stated without a doubt he was not a man to be trifled with.

"I, uh, I'm uncertain," Forrester lied. It wasn't something he was good at, lying. "I wasn't able to get a good look at them." He tried to contain his stammer as best he could to give the appearance of honesty and cover his subterfuge.

Rutters didn't seem to have picked up on Forrester's deception as he turned to the soldiers who had gathered. "Find that vehicle!" he shouted. "I don't care if you have to block off every road from here to the Massachusetts border, find them! Move!"

The soldiers scrambled to follow the vague order when another voice, much more familiar to Forrester, rose above the din. "Hold that order!"

All activity set off by Rutters' command came to a sudden halt. A sense of confusion filled the night as the soldiers looked from Rutters, whom they had accepted as their commander, to Burke. Burke was a new variable for them, a new level of authority they didn't know how to react to, so they stopped to wait and see who would prevail. Burke stared through them, each one in their turn, with eyes as cold and empty and Forrester had ever seen. No emotion, no compassion, no life; just a deep stare that cut right to the bone and chilled straight to the marrow. The already damp and chilly night suddenly felt much colder.

"Is there a problem?" Burke asked no one in particular. A moment of confusion passed between the soldiers as they looked at each other and tried to decide if they should respond. Burke eased their confusion by going directly to the source. "Sergeant Rutters, is there a problem with belaying that order?"

Even in the rain-obscured darkness, Forrester could see Rutters' face go bright red, his brow dropping and lips pursing. This was a man unaccustomed to having his orders questioned, never mind reversed. And never in front of people under his command.

"Sir," replied the younger man, the word carrying the strain of his attempt to control his temper. "The longer we delay in going after them, the further away they get. If that was them, we could acquire the targets now and move back to a safe position. If we move now, we can still catch them."

Burke shook his head, a droplet of rain spattering from the hood of his drenched raincoat. "Why expend all that energy, especially if we can get them to come to us?"

Confusion momentarily replaced the anger on Rutters' face. "I don't understand, sir."

Burke let out a chuckle. "That doesn't surprise me. And you don't need to understand, just follow my orders. Is that understood?"

The anger came back to Rutters' expression again; the rage peaking at Burke's dismissive tone. Forrester braced for a physical altercation, feeling nearly certain the Sergeant had reached his breaking point. A part of him was hoping for it, actually. Rutters was much larger and trained in physical combat. He could easily destroy Burke without so much as breaking a sweat. But a moment later, Rutters backed down, flashing a look of disdain at Burke before turning back to his troops. He ordered them to stand down, per Burke's order, but the malice in his voice was unmistakable. Rutters kept himself in check this time, but Forrester firmly believed that it was only a matter of time before Burke pushed him too far. He just hoped he was there to see it.

Burke watched with satisfaction as Rutters re-tasked his people, satisfied once again in his dominance over another. He basked in his authority for a few moments before finally turning back to Forrester, who was still transfixed by the near altercation between the two men.

"Dr. Forrester, we need you inside to confirm something," he said, turning back and heading toward the house without waiting for a response. Forrester followed.

The house was much the way Forrester imagined it would be; the perfect small town country home. At least it would have been, if not for the pools and smears of blood. It was one pool of blood that Burke directed him to.

"We think this might belong to Adam," Burke stated, indicating the excessively large patch of blood that streaked off toward the kitchen. "Can you find out for us?"

Burke had phrased his request as a question, but Forrester knew it was anything but. "I can," he replied, removing his glasses and wiping the remnants of rain from the lenses. "There are certain properties inherent to the blood of our subjects that make them unique. Identifying their blood won't be an issue. I will, however, need access to a laboratory."

Burke glanced at Harriman, who simply nodded. "Done. Anything else?"

"Yes," the doctor started, pausing briefly to gather his courage before continuing. "I need to know what you plan to do with the Carters when you apprehend them."

Burke turned and, for the first time that night, fully regarded the scientist. "I have my instructions. Alex Carter and Adam are to be retrieved and returned. If possible."

"And if that's not possible?" Forrester asked, a lump forming in his throat.

"Both are deemed expendable," Burke answered.

The tone of Burke's voice had a note of finality to it, but Forrester pressed his luck with another question. "What about the woman? Rachel?"

Burke's expression didn't change, his face a portrait of determination. "You are aware, I'm sure, that she has value to us. She is not to be harmed under any circumstances. She is to be retrieved and sent to Gabriel's Nest. Any more questions?"

Forrester froze at the mention of Gabriel's Nest. It was the code name for the laboratory he had spent years toiling in to perfect the subjects of the Eden Project. He had been party to unspeakable horrors there, horrors that had been committed in the name of his beloved science. Horrors he could not condone even as a serious researcher and originator of the Project. Now the same people who had taken and perverted his work for all these years wanted to return his last surviving children to those horrors, as well as giving over two more innocent lives to it. It had gone too far. The desecration of his work had to be stopped.

"Doctor?" It was Burke speaking to him again. Forrester snapped himself out of his memory induced trance and faced the young executive. "Are there any more questions?"

Forrester put his glasses back on and shook his head. "No, thank you. I'll get to work now. If you'll excuse me."

He shuffled off to collect some samples of the blood, leaving Burke alone with Harriman. Burke watched him go, waiting until the doctor was out of earshot to speak to the Colonel.

"I want him watched." Burke's voice was a low growl. "I don't want to give him the chance to fuck things up any more than he already has. Make sure your people know that."

"Yes, sir," Harriman replied with his customary nod.

"Keep an eye on Rutter, too," Burke added. "I have a feeling he's going to get sick of my shit soon and I want back-up if things get ugly."

Harriman nodded again and added another curt, "Yes, sir."

The sound of sirens broke through the storm. "Sounds like the locals finally got off their asses. I suppose even this storm couldn't keep them off our back forever." Burke sighed, rubbing the bridge of his nose with his thumb and forefinger as he so often did when stressed. "When you find out who the head hillbilly in charge is, send them my way. I don't, under any circumstances, want them talking to Rutters' people. We can't risk any dents in our cover here. Make sure everyone sticks to the F.B.I. standard backstory. The last thing we need right now is to have to clean up a blown cover."

"I'll take care of it," Harriman answered, turning and vanishing into the stormy darkness.

The sirens drew closer, the wail of them giving Burke a headache. Each rise and fall of their shrill tones was a spike being driven into his brain. He rubbed at his temples, trying to soothe the building agony. It didn't help. As they got closer, they didn't even sound like sirens anymore.

They sounded like screams.

A shiver ran up his spine that had nothing to do with the rain and chill. He repressed a shudder, stretched to his full height, and shook his head to clear the noise. The pain seemed to subside a bit as he moved and shifted his concentration. Headaches were unusual for him, but it had been an unusual couple of days. There was something in the air, an intangible feeling of change. A feeling that when all of this was over, his life would be radically different. It was an odd sensation for him. He normally wasn't one for introspection like that, but it nagged at him and he couldn't seem to ignore it. It was something he was unfamiliar with.

Dread.

As the sirens and flashing blue lights of the police vehicles pulled up out front, he forcibly stuffed the thoughts of gloom down, once again retreating into the comfort and safety Special Agent Lance Barrymore offered. He'd have to deal with whatever that was later, right now he had work to do.

36

Rachel woke to a bright orange glow filling her world. She opened her eyes, blinded momentarily by the sunlight that permeated the room. Sitting up, she stretched her arms to work out the kinks from last night's slumber. As she stretched, she winced at the multiple bruises and scrapes on her body, each one a painful reminder of the previous night. As she looked around, her heart sank, overwhelmed by the full gravity of their situation once again. She found herself on the couch in Alex's office, with him stretched out on the floor next to her. He was still asleep, mumbling something incomprehensible to her she supposed she should be listening to. It was his dreams that had started all their recent troubles, whatever he was muttering could be another clue to figuring out their situation. She was just too tired to care right now. Tired and depressed that the events of the previous night hadn't turned out to be a nightmare of her own.

Gently stepping over the sleeping form of her husband, she found a way to the bathroom, complete with a shower. Alex and Rick had installed that amenity when they first opened their office because of the number of times they would work straight through the night and needed to be ready for a presentation in the morning. As their business grew and they brought on more staff, their schedules became more manageable and they could go home at a reasonable time each night, so they hadn't used the shower for some time. She was eager to rectify that situation.

Being as quiet as possible so as not to disturb Alex's rest, she slowly closed the bathroom door. She approached the mirror with trepidation. She knew she looked terrible, but how bad was a question she wasn't sure she wanted an answer to. Risking a glance reaffirmed her fears. Her hair was a mess of wild red curls from the rain it absorbed the night before, her face smeared with dirt and blood. Her clothes were destroyed; soaked through last night, and then slept in for the last few hours. She couldn't remember a time when she thought she looked worse. A shower was most definitely in order.

Breathing a deep sigh, she unbuttoned and unzipped her jeans, pushing them down past her waist. Hidden bruises came alive as the denim rubbed against them and she winced at each eruption of pain, but got her pants down to her ankles where she could step out of them. Removing her top had the same effect, and she paused before she moved on to her underwear and socks, taking another look in the mirror. She barely recognized the face looking back at her. The red hair and green eyes were hers, but between the dirt and blood and the fatigue that dragged on her, she felt like she was looking at a haggard stranger.

She finished undressing and stepped into the shower, twisting the knob to start the water flowing. At first, a blast of numbing cold hit her, causing her to gasp in surprise, but before long, waves of warmth caressed her. She emptied her mind of any thoughts except for the pleasure of the shower, focusing on the warm water as it cascaded over her body.

Breathing deeply, she took in a lungful of cleansing steam that spread throughout her core and warmed her from the inside as much as the shower warmed her outside. She felt mildly more human, slightly renewed and refreshed. She looked around briefly for something to wash with, the only product being some men's shampoo that the bottle said smelled like leather and spice. Figuring it was better than nothing, she squeezed a generous portion into her hand and cleaned the filth of the last day from her body.

As her hand passed over her belly, she thought about the baby growing inside her. She and Alex had been ecstatic to discover they were going to be parents. They had been trying for so long and had been thinking that having children wasn't going to happen for them. After two years of trying without success, they resigned themselves to the fact they would not be parents, at least not in the traditional way. They explored adoption that same day. Sometimes fate has a way of throwing curveballs, though, and two weeks later Rachel discovered she was pregnant.

That was three months ago, which felt like a lifetime to her now. They had been so happy in that moment, having defied the odds and received this remarkable gift. They knew there was still a long road ahead of them with a lot of potential pitfalls, but at that point their greatest hurdle was behind them.

How wrong they had been.

Now, after everything they had been through, she had to wonder if this baby wouldn't have been better off never having been conceived. At least then they wouldn't have been caught up in all of this, whatever this was. She caught herself with that thought and pushed it aside. No, this was their child. The product of the love she and Alex shared. There was no way she was going to give up now and wish the baby away. They would get through this, and their baby would have an amazing life.

Without warning, the image she had seen on the thumb drive from Dr. Carlton flashed through her head. Her stomach tightened as she connected that with her baby, a connection she hadn't made before. If what she had seen was real, what did that mean to their baby?

She had done the best she could to clean the blood and grime from her, and the warm cascade of water had lost the soothing qualities it had possessed. She shut off the shower and grabbed a towel, giving herself a cursory drying off before wrapping it around her and heading back into Alex's office.

Alex was no longer asleep on the floor, having moved to his desk. She found him staring blankly, mouth agape, at his laptop screen. Dr. Carlton's thumb drive protruded from the side of the computer. Alex stood transfixed, witnessing the same thing she had witnessed the previous night just before the lights went out. And being hit with the same disbelief and shock she'd had.

"Alex?"

He didn't answer. He hadn't so much as blinked since she entered the room.

"Alex," she repeated, stepping around the desk, "are you all right?" Grabbing Alex by the shoulder, she spun him around to face her. Even though he was looking straight at her, his eyes didn't immediately register recognition, his attention still on what he had been looking at a moment ago.

Silence hung between them. She wanted to speak, to talk about what he had just seen, but he wasn't ready yet. He was still trying to wrap his head around the true gravity of the situation. Not that she had any words for him just then, she still hadn't fully absorbed it herself.

After a few seconds of deep silence, he finally spoke, his voice low and distant. "Is that what you saw yesterday? What was so important?"

She nodded. "Yeah. That was it. I still don't get it. Don't know what it means, or if it's even real. But I know Dr. Carlton wanted you to see it. She was killed while trying to get this information to you, so it must be serious."

He twisted around in his office chair to face the computer. She placed a hand on his shoulder again and gave it a light squeeze of encouragement, leaning in to get a better look at the image. Even though she had only caught a brief glimpse of it the previous night, she remembered every detail. It was exactly as it had been then. Although after what happened last night, the picture took on a far more sinister appearance.

The image was slightly grainy and fuzzy; the color muted. A group of people stood around what appeared to be a mound of earth that had been driven up by a great impact of some sort. All were busying themselves; analyzing the dirt and the surrounding trees or having what appeared to be intense conversations. It was just a picture, a moment frozen in time, but there was a sense of frenetic energy in it. Rachel felt a physical vibration as she took it in, like a buzzing beehive.

At the center of the picture, half buried by the mound of earth its impact had pushed up, sat the reason for the storm of activity. An oblong silver object jutted from the ground, gleaming in the sunlight. The reflective surface, surprisingly clean after being half buried in dirt and debris, created a mirror-image of the scene. It appeared to be about the size of a school bus compared to the trees, vehicles, and people alongside it. A caption at the bottom read, 'Fallen Angel: Recovered April 23, 1979'.

"Yeah," Rachel muttered, "that's what I saw."

Disbelief filled Alex's face and his jaw went slack. "Why didn't you tell me about this?"

"I was a little preoccupied last night. You know, staying alive," she answered, sarcasm and bitterness mingling in her tone.

He turned back to her, his face drawn. "I'm sorry, honey," he said, repentantly. "You're right. I get it. I'm just in a bit of shock right now."

She sighed and leaned forward again, her hands on his shoulders. She touched her forehead to his and rocked them both slightly. "I get it, believe me. I just can't believe what we're seeing here. How do we know this isn't a hoax?"

"We don't," he replied, pushing back from her gently and turning his chair to the laptop again, leaning into the screen to inspect it. "That's why I'm going to talk to someone who might be able to help us. Maybe even authenticate this picture, if that's even possible."

Rachel noticed him squinting at the screen. "What are you looking at?"

"I'm not sure. I wish I could enlarge this section of the picture," he replied, pointing to a gathering of people standing near the silver object.

"I might be able to. Might take me a few minutes to clean it up, given that the image isn't great to begin with. Let me see what I can do." She patted his shoulders. "Get up and let me in there."

He stood, and she moved into the seat he had just vacated. "Since this'll be a few minutes, I think I'll jump in the shower myself and clean up a bit. I have a feeling this is going to be an interesting day."

"Good idea," she answered. "While you're at it, see if you can dredge us up some clothes. Mine are completely unwearable."

"You got it, chief!" He gave her an informal salute and vanished into the bathroom.

Rachel sat back, smiling at Alex's affable demeanor. Even now, with trouble at every turn and the unknown staring them in the face, he wasn't about to give up. He was determined to protect her, the way he always had since the moment they met. She had found it irritating through the years, but mostly, it was just sweet. A warm feeling settled over her with the thought that maybe, by working together, they could get through this.

With that thought in mind, she returned to her work on the picture.

37

In about twenty minutes, Alex showered and dressed himself in a fresh pair of jeans and a long-sleeved black t-shirt. He had kept the clothes at the office for the occasional all-night-and-into-the-morning work sessions he and Rick had endured early in their practice and was glad now he had the foresight to keep them on hand.

Along with his clothes, he was fortunate enough to discover a pair of Rachel's jeans that had been mixed up with his. Along with that, he brought her one of his work shirts, a red and black flannel, that hung to her knees. By rolling up the sleeves and tying the shirt at her waist, she could achieve a passable sense of normalcy.

After getting dressed, Alex made a pot of coffee and served it with a half-empty box of stale powdered donuts for breakfast. The donuts had the consistency of old drywall paste, with the taste to match, but they were passable if left to soak in the coffee long enough. As they ate, they reviewed the contents of the thumb drive.

"Look at what I found when I enhanced that segment of the picture," Rachel said, pointing to the small group of people gathered at the base of the object. The faces became much clearer, reaching the maximum clarity given the original resolution of the picture, and now it was possible to discern individual features. "I have no clue who most of these people are, but I came across a few interesting finds." She manipulated the mouse, enlarging the image even further to focus on two men in particular.

Alex leaned in to examine the image, squinting at the highly pixelated square. He leaned back again and shrugged. "The one on the left looks a little familiar."

"He should," Rachel replied, pointing to the younger of the two men. "This is Robert Penders."

Alex gave another passive shrug. "So?"

Rachel sighed. "You know, there are other uses for the internet besides funny animal videos. Robert Penders is the president and founder of one of the largest scientific research firms in the world. Also, one of the richest. Last year, he made Forbes' list as the ninth richest person on the planet. Rumor has it he may move up a few slots this year."

Alex's expression remained unchanged. "I reiterate; so?"

"So," she responded, "what is one of the world's richest men doing at a UFO crash site?"

"UFO crash site?" Alex asked, incredulous. "What makes you think this is a UFO crash site?"

"Let's see," Rachel replied, sarcasm dripping in her voice like honey. "A big silver cigar falls out of the sky, shearing off treetops and plowing up a half-mile of ground. After it crashes, it's surrounded by very serious sciency types with very serious sciency equipment, examining it in a very serious sciency way." She gave an exaggerated shrug, a smug grin spreading across her face. "Yep, you're right. Sounds like the county fair to me. What was I thinking?"

Despite his best efforts, Alex returned her smile. "Okay, fine. We'll go with UFO crash site. But if that's the case, what was he doing there? And what does any of this have to do with us?"

"You've heard the name recently," she replied. "It's one of two names Dr. Carlton mentioned in her video message. One of the two she said was crucial in helping you solve this mystery."

It came to him suddenly. "That's right! Penders, and..." He paused, searching his memories for the other name. "Forrester. Dr. Elliot Forrester!"

"Speaking of which..." She pointed to the man standing to the right of Penders.

"He's there, too?" Alex stared intently at the two faces. "How are you for coincidence?"

"I'm not," she replied. "There's a connection here, Alex. And once we figure it out, I think it'll blow this whole thing wide open."

Alex took a deep breath and closed his eyes. His stomach rumbled. The stale donuts had done little to ease his hunger, he needed something more substantial. There was nothing left to eat in the office, so for the moment he pushed the feeling down and did his best to ignore it while they puzzled out their next move.

"Okay, we have a picture of a crashed UFO. In that same picture are two men who are supposed to know something important about me." He shuddered slightly at what he said. It sounded ridiculous to him; insane that he was saying it, never mind giving it credibility. But after what they'd experienced recently, he was learning to embrace the impossible more and more. "What about the other files? What did they say?"

Rachel clicked the 'Main Menu' button and the UFO, Penders, and Forrester vanished, replaced by a list of options. "Project Eden is Penders' pitch to prospective investors. He never comes right out and says what it is exactly, no doubt covering his ass by distancing himself from the details, but it sounds like a massive and expensive proposition. PenTech Research and Development was Forrester's spiel...." She froze in mid-sentence, her eyes wide.

Alex's stomach tightened at her expression. "What is it?"

"Last night," she replied, "the man that was getting out of the car as we were leaving Walt and Betty's, the guy I almost ran over! I thought he looked familiar. It was Forrester!"

"Are you sure?" he asked. "He was here? In Pine Haven? At our house?"

"As sure as I'm looking at you right now, I know it was Forrester I saw last night." Without warning, the speech she had heard him giving on the modern miracle of genetics popped into her head, accompanied by a sour feeling in her stomach. She didn't yet know how it figured into their current situation, but she knew she wasn't going to like the answer when they found out.

Without warning, a realization hit her and she leaped from her chair, turning to Alex and grabbing him by his shoulders. "We need to get out of here. Now. They were at our house last night! How long do you think it'll take them to figure out they should look for us here? They might be watching this place right now!" She dashed to the window and, after a furtive glance outside, drew the blinds shut. "Alex, what if they know we're here? What if they're watching us right now, waiting for us to leave? How could we have been so stupid, coming here?"

Alex took it all in, his mind trying to sort it all out. She was right, coming here was the last thing they should have done. Of course, the logical place to look for them, aside from their house, would be his office. So far, they hadn't seen any unusual signs of activity; no strangers loitering where they shouldn't be, or unfamiliar vehicles driving up and down the block. Then again, neither of them had thought to keep an eye out for things like that. After getting away last night, they had been completely exhausted, so rational and secure thinking wasn't their top priority. Besides, they weren't spies or agents; they were ordinary people. Except now, some very extraordinary circumstances had caught up with them, requiring them to be more aware of their surroundings. Their lives depended on it.

"You're right, we need to go." He checked his watch, it was nearly 7:30. If everything stayed true to form, Rick would come into the office in about twenty minutes to get his customary early start on the day. A half hour after that, Stevie and Jackie, the two junior members of the firm, would be along. They didn't have much time.

"Can you make a copy of that USB drive?" he asked Rachel as he gathered up their belongings, stuffing the pistol into his jeans at the small of his back. It was uncomfortable, but not so much so that he was willing to risk not having it.

"Yeah, sure," she replied. "Why?"

"I don't think you and I should be the only people in possession of that information. We may need some leverage at some point, and that data seems to be something someone wants very much to keep secret." He peered out the window toward the street, checking for anything out of the ordinary. Pine Haven was a small town. In the off-season, resident's routines changed little, so finding something out of the ordinary wouldn't be that difficult. Nothing appeared off to him. Then again, the people after them were professionals. If they didn't want to be seen, odds are they wouldn't be.

"While you're at it, make two copies."

"Okay," Rachel replied, retrieving two new thumb drives from Alex's desk. "But who can we give them to? Who can we trust?"

As if on cue, they heard the front door of the office open. Alex glanced at his watch; 7:42. If that was Rick, he was earlier than usual. Turning to Rachel, he placed his index finger against his lips, gesturing to her to keep quiet. Slipping the pistol from his waistband, he grasped the doorknob and turned it slowly. It clicked, the sound like a gunshot in the silence, and Alex swung the door wide open and rushed into the reception area, sweeping the room with the pistol.

At the front door, his friend and partner cowered at the sight of the gun, eyes wild and fearful. The paper bag with the logo for The Bagel Stable he had been holding dropped to the floor, and he clutched his backpack against his chest like a shield and froze, the moment suspended in time. It took him a second to look past the barrel of the gun to the person wielding it, his guard dropping as recognition set in. He lowered the briefcase and moved away from the front door, into the office, his body visibly relaxing. His eyes didn't leave his friend and partner, who still had a pistol pointed steadily at him.

"Alex, what the actual fuck are you doing?" Rick yelled, his breath ragged as adrenaline still coursed through him. "You scared the shit out of me! Probably literally!"

Alex lowered the gun but didn't return it to its makeshift holster. "Sorry, I overreacted. You wouldn't believe what's been going on the last few days. Hell, we don't even believe it."

"I'd really like to know," Rick replied, fixated on the weapon at Alex's side. His eyes were wide, unblinking, like a deer unexpectedly caught in the headlights of an oncoming car, unable to move or flee. It took a few moments for him to tear his gaze from the gun.

"I've been trying to reach you since last night," Rick continued, setting down his backpack. "I heard the cops were at your house last night and that it looked like something major was going on. When I stopped at the Bagel Stable this morning, Lou mentioned that a cop got shot. At your house! I thought he was full of shit, but now..." His eyes moved back to the gun at Alex's side.

The implication wasn't lost on Alex. Rick had spent the morning hearing what he no doubt considered to be crazy accusations about his business partner and best friend, only to come to work and find that best friend in their office waving a gun around. Slowly and purposefully, Alex slid the gun back into his waistband and pulled his shirt over it. Hopefully, having the gun out of sight would make the conversation with Rick go a little easier.

Not that the story he and Rachel had to tell would make them seem any saner and more stable than they had a moment ago. "Believe me," Alex replied, consciously spreading his open palms out in front of him to reduce the tension that hung in the air, "there's a lot more going on here than you think. I can't explain all of it. Hell, I don't understand most of it myself, but there are things you need to know. Come into my office and I'll tell you what I can."

Alex turned back to head to his office. Behind him, Rick didn't move. He remained rooted to the spot, unmoving. His eyes were wide and unblinking. Even though he had relaxed his arms and lowered his makeshift backpack shield, his hands still had a vise-like grip on it in case he needed to use it again quickly. Alex's heart dropped at the sight of his best friend, obviously confused and frightened.

"Look, I know this is absolutely batshit crazy," he said, intentionally keeping distance between him and Rick. "I can only guess how all this looks to you, and what's going through your mind right now. I get it. I want to set your mind at ease, to explain it all, but we don't have a lot of time. There are some people after us, really bad people, and we need to get out of here. But I need a favor from you first."

Rick remained still and silent, offering no response. Alex looked at him pleadingly, putting out a hand. "Please," he continued, "I need your help. We need your help. We can't do this alone."

Rick finally broke his silence. "We who?"

"Me," Rachel announced, coming out of Alex's office. "Us." She put her hand on her stomach.

Rick breathed a deep sigh, his clutch on the backpack relaxing as it dropped to his side. "That's not fair, you know," he said, pointing an accusatory finger at Rachel. "You know I could never say no to you. Or my godchild."

She smiled at him; the first real, warm smile Alex had seen from her in days. He had forgotten how much he loved her smile.

"I know," Rachel replied to Rick. "Why do you think he makes me ask you for all the important stuff?"

"Then he's brighter than he looks," Rick replied, returned Rachels's smile with a very slight one of his own.

Alex eased a bit with Rick's grin and light-hearted jab at him. Life may have gone completely off the rails recently, but one thing remained constant; the three of them were family and always would be, no matter how fate conspired against them.

Rick dropped his backpack on a nearby desk. "Okay, what's next?"

"I'll show you," Alex said, gesturing to Rick to have him come to the office. "And hey, thanks. It's good to know we have someone watching our backs right now. It means a lot."

Rick nodded his head slightly, an odd half smile on his face. His eyes dropped to the floor and his feet shifted slightly. "No problem, man. Don't mention it. Really."

A sudden feeling of uneasiness washed over Alex. Rick's discomfort with Alex's words of appreciation struck him as odd. Rick was usually the first person to bask in the glow of recognition. In fact, his lack of humility was one of his few character flaws.

"Hey, you okay?" Alex asked, tensing. "I know things are weird right now."

"Yeah, I'm fine." Rick's eyes wandered to Alex's back, where he had tucked in the pistol. "Just a little shaken, is all. It's a lot to take in."

Alex's trickle of uneasiness became a flood. "Look, if this is too much for you, we can find someone else. I understand that this might be overwhelming for you. I'm there myself. If you want to just step away, we'll understand."

"No," Rick replied, waving off Alex's concern. "I'm good." His awkward half grin became a full smile.

"Yeah," Alex replied. "Okay. Come on."

He gestured for Rick to follow him and went into his office. As they moved, Alex noticed Rick quickly wipe his palms on his pant legs. It was a nervous habit he'd had since they first met, most evident on first dates and final exams. Alex pushed the thought aside. This was as stressful a situation as they had ever been in, but it nagged at him.

Rachel was at the laptop removing a thumb drive. "Finished," she said, handing the drive to Alex.

Rick's eyes followed the hand off, his gaze never wavering from it. The look on his face struck Alex as odd; not concern or curiosity, instead it was more like anticipation. The unease swirling inside him swelled.

"This is it," Alex said, holding up the small thumb drive.

Rick moved toward the device, his eyes never wavering from it. His hand quivered slightly as he took it from Alex. A sheen of sweat formed on his forehead as he turned the drive over in his hands a few times. When he spoke, his voice was oddly disjointed. Distant.

"What's on it?"

"You wouldn't believe us if we told you," Rachel said easily, oblivious to Rick's odd reaction. "UFOs, genetic engineering, big business cabals and cover-ups. It's all there."

Rick's head snapped up suddenly, his face taking on a new expression. His eyes were wide, his jaw set. There was a slight tremble in a corner of his upper lip. Suddenly, he looked far more serious and perhaps even a bit frightened.

"So you've seen it?" he asked, a new sense of urgency in his tone.

Alex didn't like how this was going, the feeling of uneasiness in his stomach growing to vast new proportions. Rick's reactions were completely uncharacteristic of him. He was trying to lead the conversation, to extract information instead of just asking for it. Rick had always been the most honest and straightforward person Alex had ever known. If he wanted to know something, he had no problem just asking. Subterfuge wasn't his thing. It was a trait that had cost them in business meetings, but Alex considered it an invaluable asset for a friend.

"Of course we've seen it," Rachel answered, unaware of Alex's concerns. "We've searched for years for answers about Alex and where he came from. This information promised some of those answers. How could we not look at it?"

"Did you find anything interesting?" Rick asked. He didn't turn to Rachel with the question, keeping his attention firmly locked on Alex.

Rachel started to reply, but Alex cut her off. "Not really. A few pictures and some names to check up on. We haven't had much of a chance to follow up on anything yet. Been a little busy, you know?"

"Alex, we've..." Rachel started, but Alex shot her a quick look and placed his hand on hers, giving it a quick and gentle squeeze.

"What did you say?" Rick asked, the cloud of suspicion around him darkening.

"Nothing," Alex answered quickly. "Nothing at all."

Rick's feet shuffled lightly again, and he brushed his palms against his pants. As he held the thumb drive aloft with his left hand, his right hand slipped into his pocket. "Okay. Tell me what is it you want me to do with this?"

Alex paused, again squeezing Rachel's hand in the hope she'd give him the opportunity to answer. As he contemplated how, scenarios flew through his head about how this situation could end. None of them were positive. In the end, he chose the only option he felt gave them the best chance to come out ahead.

The truth.

"We want you to safeguard that for us," he answered. "Keep it where no one will find it. If you don't hear from us in a few days, I want you to leak it to the public. Everywhere. News outlets. Social media. Get it out to the public any way you can, to anyone who will listen. Make sure the entire world knows what's on that drive."

Alex finished speaking and silence hung between them. No one moved. No one spoke. Alex could feel the pounding of his heart, his muscles tensing and gathering energy for action. Rick simply stared at the small device in his hand. His face shifted slightly, almost imperceptibly, from suspicion to deep remorse.

"I really wish you hadn't said that."

"What do you mean?" Rachel asked, her confusion evident in her voice. "What's going on?"

Rachel was piecing together what Alex had understood almost since the conversation started. Rick had dropped all pretenses. He wasn't even pretending to be the man they knew. The revelation was shattering.

"Rick," Rachel pleaded, "what are you doing?"

In a quick motion, Rick's right hand reemerged from his coat pocket, carrying a small pistol. "I'm so sorry for this. Please trust me when I say I'm doing this for you." He looked directly at Rachel, then at her belly. "For all of you."

Despite the appearance of the gun, when Rachel spoke again the pleading was gone from her voice. In its place was a hard, angry edge that surprised both Rick and Alex alike. "You're supposed to be our friend. Our family. Why are you doing this to us?"

Rick's eyes dropped, unable to stand her angry glare. "I'm not who you thought I was," he said, a quavering in his voice. "I never have been."

"You've been lying to us the whole time you've known us?" Alex's voice was a cold monotone, devoid of the emotional upheaval happening just beneath the surface. "Twelve years. You've been like a brother to me for twelve years. Aside from Rachel, you're the only family I've had. We trusted you." He lowered his head, hot tears gathering in the corners of his eyes. "We loved you."

"Please, Alex, it's not like that. What I'm doing, what I've done, it's only ever been for your own good. For the good of your family." Rick looked at him pleadingly. "Please understand, this is so much bigger than just us. There's so much at stake here."

"Enough to make my best friend become my Judas?" Alex's voice was still low and steady, but there was obvious venom in his words.

Rick didn't answer, instead pulling a small flip-phone from his left pocket and dialing a number. Silence was thick in the room for the few seconds it took for someone to answer.

"I have him here, at the office. He came here, just as you suspected he would," Rick stated, pausing as the person on the other end of the call spoke. "Yes, they're both here. No apparent life-threatening injuries. A few bruises." Pause. "No, I don't expect any problems." Pause. "Burke's luck has been running cold lately, anyway. See you soon." He clapped the phone shut, turning his full attention back to Alex and Rachel. "It won't be long. I promise you'll understand everything soon."

"Will I understand why you're such an enormous fucking asshole?" Alex asked, a dark sarcasm in the question.

Rick ignored him and motioned to the couch. "Just sit over there until my associate arrives."

Rachel looked to Alex, who simply nodded as he proceeded to the couch she had slept on the night before. Rick reached out and stopped Alex after a few steps.

"I'll take that," he stated, reaching behind Alex and taking the pistol from his belt. "Things are tense enough around here right now. I don't want any accidental gunfire if we can avoid it."

Alex glared at him. "You'd really shoot me?"

Rick avoided the question. "Just sit down, please."

When Alex and Rachel were on the couch, Rick took up a position behind Alex's desk. Closing the laptop, he dropped the thumb drive on top of it. "Is this the only copy?"

Rachel nodded. "Yes. I only made one to give to you. Guess I'm a lousy judge of character."

"The original?" Rick asked, avoiding her question.

She sighed. "In the middle drawer of the desk."

Rick reached in and retrieved the original drive, the one Dr. Carlton had given them. Placing it next to the copy Rachel provided, he leaned back in the chair. There was nothing comfortable about his posture, and he didn't lower the pistol.

Suddenly, there was nothing but silence between them. Each one was waging a private battle with their inner demons, contemplating betrayal and its cost weighed against the greater good, each searching for an answer that would ease their souls. None would be forthcoming. In the end, they would have to reconcile their roles in their own ways and live with the consequences they created.

If any of them lived at all.

38

Burke woke early the next morning, his stomach turning to discover he was still in Pine Haven. He found it difficult to fall asleep after the events at the Carter house, but as he did, he held a slight hope that when he woke up, all of this would be a dream and he wouldn't be trapped in this backwater shithole. Why anyone would want to waste their vacation here or, even worse, live here was beyond comprehension. The town, the whole damned state, was nothing but a haven for retired fossils who had nothing better to do with their time than gawk at a bunch of dying leaves. If he ever reached that stage in his life, where looking at leaves was considered a thrilling pastime, he hoped someone would show mercy and end his misery.

He dragged himself out of bed and into the shower, trying to ignore the supposedly charming kitsch that decorated the room. It just oozed country charm, with images of farm animals stenciled or stitched onto everything. If it wasn't animals, it was some ridiculous saying like, 'There's No Life Like Lake Life!' or 'A Bad Day Fishing Beats the Best Day of Work!'. It was physically nauseating to him. He fought through it long enough to finish his shower, shave and dress before heading for the restaurant that serviced the motel, another horrible mecca of quaint, homey trash. God, he hated it here.

Sitting around a table, he found Harriman, Rutters, Forrester, and the local police representative, a rather unpleasant woman by the name of Maggie McCall. Without a word, he slid into an empty chair at the end of the table next to Harriman.

"Good morning, Agent Barrymore. I trust you slept well?"

The question had come from Detective McCall, who could no doubt damned well tell just by looking at him he hadn't slept well at all. After all, she had kept him up well past midnight and into the early hours of the next day with a constant stream of questions about his investigation and several accusations of trying to shut out local law enforcement. That been only the beginning, though. Burke had got her to back off by promising he would keep her informed of any future developments and would involve local police in the investigation. While not satisfied with his concession, it had been enough to get her to leave him alone for a while. It was at that point the real nightmare started.

After leaving the scene at the Carter's house, he made his way to the motel Rutters had set up for them, a little waking nightmare of country hell called the Dew Drop Inn. The décor was as dated and unimaginative as the name of the place, looking as if a country craft fair had vomited all over it. With deep brown paneling on the walls and a fiery orange carpet of deep shag that made it feel like the foliage outside was creeping in, the rooms appeared untouched since the sixties. The final touch in the dizzying array of color was the lime green bedspread that assaulted his eyes when he opened the door. Normally, he would have turned around and left, but he had been exhausted. He forced himself to use the ancient bathroom to brush his teeth before climbing under the lime monstrosity that was his bed. He had thought the color of the bedspread would be the worst thing about it. He was wrong. He felt as if he were sleeping on a slab of granite. An uneven, jagged slab of granite.

He had managed a few hours of uncomfortable, off-and-on-again sleep. His reflection in the mirror the next morning confirmed his lack or rest with the appearance of large, dark circles under bloodshot eyes. The two days' worth of stubble on his face didn't help matters. A quick shave offered him a moderate improvement on his appearance, and he figured a cup of coffee would take care of the rest. If the savages in this backwater burg knew what coffee was.

To his surprise, they did. A steaming cup waited for him at his place at the table and he took an exploratory sip. There wasn't a trace of bitterness, and he swore he could detect some minor hints of cinnamon as it washed over his tongue. Surprised, he took three long swigs from the cup before sitting down. The warmth swirled around his gut for a moment, and he reveled in the feeling of it, the best thing he'd experienced in days.

"No stomach for late nights, Agent Barrymore?" It was McCall again, a broad grin on her face. She locked eyes with him as her grin became a smirk before she raised a cup of coffee to her lips.

The pleasant warmth in Burke's stomach turned sour. Maggie McCall was a reasonably attractive woman, sporting short dark hair and a stern but not displeasing face. Her body was perfectly honed, a testament to her commitment to her work. She wore a dark gray suit precisely fitted to her, accentuating her feminine form while conveying a seriousness that befitted her profession. Burke appreciated that, the outward display of her no-nonsense approach. It was something he had always striven to exude for himself, to be taken seriously. Even so, he didn't like this woman. Her need to assert dominance was going to clash with his expectation of it, and that was something he simply couldn't allow. But for the moment, he needed her help. And butting heads with her wouldn't be productive.

"It's been a while," he conceded, choking down the urge to argue with her in defense of his constitution.

The server, an excessively perky woman with gray curls and more lines in her face than a topographical map, appeared at the table to take their orders. McCall kept her order to coffee and a blueberry muffin, as did Forrester, while Harriman and Rutters ordered something the menu referred to as the Logger's Supreme Breakfast which consisted of two eggs, bacon, pancakes, toast, home fries, juice and coffee. To his surprise, Burke found himself ordering the same thing, with extra home fries and bacon and a large orange juice. He had never been much of a breakfast person, usually sticking to coffee and a Danish or croissant. Today he was famished, a fact he hadn't really noticed until just now. Out of nowhere, his stomach rumbled like a wild bear, anticipating the obscene amount of food he had just ordered. It had been a long day yesterday, and his main meal had comprised a granola bar and water, so he pushed aside concerns and focused on the conversation at hand.

"How is Lieutenant Babcock doing?" Burke asked. Not that he really cared, but he had a cover to maintain and needed to keep up appearances. Special Agent Barrymore would be concerned about the welfare of a law enforcement brother-in-arms.

"Not good," McCall replied, her voice heavy. "Whoever shot him did a real number on him. The doctors say he'll recover, but they had to practically rebuild a good part of his guts. Won't be back at work for a long time. If ever."

"I'm not surprised," Burke said, falling into character. "That's how this guy operates. Maximum damage. Babcock was lucky there was someone else there to drive him off, otherwise there'd be someone digging a hole for him right now."

McCall bristled visibly at that comment. "Who is this asshole, anyway? What's his story?" She sipped from her coffee, a slight tremble in her hand as she lifted the cup to her mouth.

Detective McCall was shaken. Not only by what had happened to Lieutenant Ernest Babcock last night, but because the shooter was still out there. And he was dangerous. And she was now in charge of bringing him in, at least as far as she knew. All of that frayed her nerves, which is exactly what Burke needed.

"We're not entirely sure," Burke lied. He had gone through this story last night while stretched out on the torture mattress. As with every cover story, it was easier to pass off if there were a basis of truth at its core. He had concocted a lie that would satisfy the local authorities, weaving in enough truth to make that lie simple to sell.

"We think he's a headcase from the Midwest. Maybe Colorado," Burke continued with his narrative. That much was true. Adam was a headcase, and he had been 'born' in Colorado. He had simply omitted a few choice details. "Beyond that, the only thing we know is that he kills using a variety of methods and weapons in no discernible pattern and we have absolutely no clue what drives him."

"Basically, you're clueless," McCall replied, setting down her coffee mug and locking eyes with Burke.

Burke felt his fists clench involuntarily. "Not entirely," he said, forcing himself to relax. "True, we don't have many leads, but we're far from clueless."

McCall pressed the issue. "Then where are you?"

Burke tensed again at her question. This was going on far longer than it should have. "We're here. Where he is."

"That's it?" McCall replied, her voice jumping to double the casual volume she'd had a moment ago. "You have no clue when he might strike again? Or where? He could be hundreds of miles away by now!" She realized she had raised her voice and glanced around to see if she had drawn the attention of the other patrons. Once she was sure everyone's attention was firmly on their eggs and individual conversations, she continued. "Just two hours south of here, there are a million potential victims for him to choose from. Victims of all shapes, sizes, ethnicities, religions, genders or any other damned things he wants. It's a fucking customizable gourmet buffet of murder for any serial killer! What makes you think he's going to stay here?"

"He won't stray far from here. Not yet," Burke answered, his tone thick with confidence.

McCall chuffed. "What makes you think that?"

He leaned across the table to her, his voice low. Not so much to keep quiet, more for a dramatic spin on his next words.

"Because Lieutenant Babcock isn't dead yet."

McCall drew back, her face indignant. "What the fuck does that have to do with anything?"

Burke noticed they were drawing some attention from the other diners. "Please keep your voice down," he requested, as pleasantly as he could muster. "The last thing we need is for the local citizenry to find out there might be a killer on the loose in town."

"Hell with that," she spat back. "Tell me why you think this killer is staying in town because of Ernie."

Burke sighed heavily and again rubbed hard at the bridge of his nose. This was exasperating. Once Burke took care of Adam and brought the woman and baby to Gabriel's Nest, he planned to request a vacation. A month-long vacation. No, two months. He deserved at least that much.

"This man has never failed killing anyone he's set out to, intentionally or by coincidence," Burke said, squeezing thoughts of warm tropical islands with no dead leaves blowing around out of his mind for now. "He's not about to start now. Your Lieutenant, Ernie, wasn't his intended target, but getting in the way like he did made him one. Once he finds out Babcock is still alive, he'll be back to finish the job. And when he does..."

"We nail him," Rutters interjected, slapping his palm with a fist.

McCall jumped almost imperceptibly at the noise, startled. Although whether it was the sharp noise or the fact that someone besides her or Burke had joined in the conversation, Burke couldn't be sure. What he could be sure of was that Rutters made McCall nervous. He watched as she looked him up and down, stopping finally at his steely eyes. Burke chuckled slightly to himself. Maybe the muscle-headed idiot would have his uses after all.

Reluctantly, McCall pulled her eyes from Rutters and came back to Burke. "You're suggesting a trap?"

Burke nodded. "With the help of your department, yes."

She sat quietly, thoughtfully, for a moment before speaking. "Agent Barrymore, Ernie is more than a co-worker. More than a boss. When I first made detective here, no one in town would accept a woman, especially one as young as I was, in that position. Pine Haven may look like a perfect little town, and in a lot of ways there have been some huge strides made in acceptance overall, but there are still some big prejudices here. No one wanted to give me a chance. No one except Ernie. When I asked him why he was willing to go against the system that way, he told me he saw potential in me. Raw talent, is what he said. He took me under his wing, trained me, even protected me at first. Everything I am, everything I have, I owe to him. I want whoever did this to him. I want him to pay."

Burke leaned forward again, bridging the gap between them. "With your help, he will. I promise."

"When do we start and what do you need from me?" she replied, a renewed sense of action in her voice. Revenge could be a remarkable motivator.

"I need the hospital locked down," Burke replied. "Quietly, though. We need for him to get in, then we can tighten the net once we have him inside."

"Done," she answered, the sharpness of her reply like a gunshot. "Then what?"

Burke risked a slight smile. "Then we wait. Shouldn't be long. I have a feeling that by this time tomorrow he'll be in our custody."

The server appeared with their breakfast just as Forrester's cell rang and he politely excused himself from the table. After a brief conversation, he returned and announced he would have to skip breakfast, that something had come up that required his attention. Before Burke could inquire what was taking him away, Forrester abruptly excused himself and left.

Burke shot Harriman a glance. The Colonel stood and also excused himself, exiting after the scientist.

Burke was left to finish his breakfast in the company of two people he couldn't stand. As if the food wasn't already enough to give him indigestion. But soon, none of that would matter. Possibly as early as tonight, this assignment would be over, and he could finally get his life and career back on track.

Yet somehow, something in the back of his head nagged at him. He couldn't shake the feeling that the worst was still yet to come.

39

As soon as the call came in, Forrester excused himself, exiting the meeting and the breakfast table as quickly as he could while trying not to arouse Burke's suspicions. He was certain he wouldn't succeed on that front, but this development was worth the risk.

Once clear of the restaurant, he searched the parking lot for the most convenient vehicle belonging to the Project. Two black Lincoln Town Cars sat at the far end of the lot along with a similarly black Lincoln Navigator, all with tinted windows that practically matched the bodies of the cars. Milling around the vehicles were several men and women in either dark suits or black fatigues, the hired muscle of the Eden Project. That presented a problem. The guards would certainly not be willing to step aside and allow him to take a car. Not without direct orders from Burke, Harriman, or Rutters first. They were trained soldiers; orders were their lifeblood, and they lived and died by them. He couldn't expect any favors, either. None of the security team cared for him much, he could see it in their eyes. He was an intellectual; they were accustomed to action. They regarded him as weak, nothing more than dead weight on an operation like this. All of that, along with the soldiers' deep-rooted fear of Burke and Harriman, meant that he would have to find another method of conveyance to his destination.

"Can I help you get somewhere, Doctor?"

Forrester jerked visibly, surprised by the voice that came up from behind him. The two guards by the car laughed lightly at him, no doubt mocking the doddering scientist. Ignoring them, he turned toward the voice and found Harriman standing there. While it had startled him when the Colonel spoke, it wasn't particularly surprising that he was there. He must have followed from the restaurant under Burke's orders, Forrester supposed. Forrester knew Burke didn't trust him in the slightest, but he didn't think he would assign his top watchdog to keep him in line. This could complicate matters more than he had expected.

"Colonel Harriman, you startled me," Forrester stated, trying unsuccessfully to conceal the slight quavering in his voice. "I thought you were still inside having breakfast."

"Seems I'm not as hungry as I thought," Harriman answered. "Can I offer you any assistance, Doctor?"

Forrester's mind seized momentarily as he processed Harriman's offer and struggled to formulate an appropriate response. He was a brilliant scientist, but in this arena of deception and subterfuge he was decidedly out of his depth. A wrong answer to even this simple question could mean the difference between success and failure in his mission. Failure would carry far more severe tertiary consequences as well, so this was indeed a life-or-death decision. It was critical he formulate the correct response.

He swallowed hard, looking up into the stoic face of the Colonel. "I would appreciate if you could arrange a vehicle for me."

There wasn't more than a heartbeat between the question and Harriman's answer, but to Forrester it was as if time had stopped. Stopped in order for him to be judged.

Harriman nodded in response. "Will you be needing a driver?"

The question seemed ubiquitous, but Forrester knew better. Harriman no doubt knew what was going on, that Forrester was trying to sneak away from Burke and his entourage for some subversive reason. The offer of a driver was a trick question. If he said yes to a driver, it would show he wasn't averse to being tracked and was working in the interests of the Project. If he refused, Harriman, and by extension Burke, would consider that confirmation of their suspicions regarding Forrester's loyalties. At that point, his mission would be over. Forrester steadied his nerves as best he could. He had come this far; he would stay the course and see it through.

"No, I don't think that will be necessary. I hold a valid driver's license and should be able to operate one of these vehicles without too much difficulty. Just the car. The car will be fine, thank you. Thank you, Colonel." He was rambling, but he couldn't stop himself. It had always been a nervous habit of his, a way for his subconscious mind to make sense of situations his conscious mind had no way of dealing with, and he couldn't think of a time he had ever been as ill-equipped to deal with a situation as he did right now.

Harriman looked him up and down, his face betraying nothing but the grim look he always wore. Forrester, like many of the Colonel's own soldiers, wondered if his face wasn't actually made from stone. His expressions were consistent. It was impossible to read anything in the man's face.

In the next moment, the last thing Forrester would have ever expected to happen, happened. He was convinced that if he lived an eternity and was granted an audience to all the miracles that occurred throughout time, he would never have expected this to be one of them.

Colonel Harriman smiled.

It wasn't much of a smile. More of a half grin, half amused leer. While it faded almost instantly, Forrester knew he hadn't imagined it. He had seen it, and he would never forget the sight of it.

Without another word to the scientist, Harriman shouted past him to the soldiers by one of the town cars. "Give Dr. Forrester the keys to that vehicle for use at his discretion. Provide him with whatever he asks for. Understood?"

The two young men exchanged quizzical glances. One of them spoke up, hesitancy thick in his voice. "On whose authority, sir?"

Harriman's chin dropped slightly as he locked on the soldier who voiced the question. "Mine," he answered, his tone low and firm.

The guard shifted his feet slightly. "But sir, we have orders from Mr. Darnell not to let Dr. Forrester out of our sight," he said sheepishly, glancing at Forrester. He swayed a bit on uncertain feet, unsure if he should have revealed that information in Forrester's presence. Not that it mattered to the doctor, he suspected as much already.

"And who did those orders come though?" Harriman sounded like a teacher asking a student if they understood the rule they had just broken. A very stern teacher.

"Y-you, sir," the young guard stammered.

Harriman pressed him. "And who is issuing new orders?"

"You are, sir." The guard could sense where the conversation was headed. His shoulders relaxed visibly as his stance firmed.

"Doesn't it make sense that these new orders would also come from Mr. Darnell through me?" There was no inflection in Harriman's voice, making it seem less like a question and more like a reinforcement of his authority.

The young soldier nodded. "Yes, sir. Will there be anything else, sir?"

"Just whatever Dr. Forrester may need," Harriman replied. He turned away from his soldiers and back to Forrester. "These men will see to your needs. Is there anything else I can get for you, Doctor?"

Once again, Forrester's mind froze at the sudden influx of impossible information. He simply stared at Harriman, incredulous at what had just occurred. Not only had Harriman smiled, which was enough of a miracle, but now he had lied to his own people on Forrester's behalf. It had to be a lie; Burke would never allow Forrester free rein. He had no idea what Harriman's motivations might be. More importantly, he wondered what the cost would be should the Colonel ever call in the favor.

"Doctor?" Harriman repeated.

Forrester shook himself out of his contemplative trance. "Uh, no, thank you, Colonel. I think that is more than sufficient."

"Well then, I have other duties to attend to," Harriman stated, turning back to the restaurant. Before leaving, he leaned in close to Forrester, his voice practically a whisper. "You have my cell number if you need anything else, correct?"

Forrester nodded weakly.

"Good. Be careful. I'm not sure I'll be able to do anything like this for you again, so whatever you're doing, you had best get it right the first time." He stepped back, resuming his usual rigid stance. "Good day, Doctor," he stated. Without waiting for a reply, he disappeared back into the restaurant, leaving Forrester and the two soldiers standing outside in the bitter fall cold, very bewildered.

****

Harriman returned to the table where Burke, McCall, and Rutters were silently engaged in eating their breakfasts. Rutters and McCall had eaten, leaving a few crumbs of their food behind as they sipped their coffee. But Burke surprised him. He had ordered more food than Harriman had seen him consume in the entire time he had known the man, and his plate sat before him completely clean. Not only that, but he was also currently in the process of eating Forrester's abandoned muffin. It was certainly unusual for the man. Normally he ate enough to sustain maybe the average bird. Today, he had apparently found his appetite.

Burke chewed up the last of Forrester's muffin and dabbed at his mouth with his napkin. After quickly sipping coffee to wash it down, he turned to Harriman. "Did you tend to the matter?" Burke was careful to be vague in the presence of Detective McCall.

Harriman nodded slightly, saying nothing. As he sat down to breakfast once again, he realized he had lied to Forrester earlier.

He was hungry, after all.

40

Rachel's leg had fallen asleep. When Rick had herded her and Alex to the couch at gunpoint, she sat with such haste that her leg ended up beneath her. She realized now that this was a mistake, that she should have adjusted, but given how jumpy Rick had been she was hesitant to shift position and get shot accidentally because of it. Worse, the pain in her hip had returned from her collision with the coffee table the night before, so her hip was a burning mess of pain just out of reach of the tingling of her sleeping leg. Still, he sat quietly and tried to ignore the discomfort. It was more comfortable than a bullet wound, at least.

Alex sat next to her; fists clenched tightly at his sides. Rick sat behind Alex's desk, propping his elbows up to avoid fatigue from keeping his gun trained on them. There had been a brief yet decidedly awkward period of silence and staring between the two, but they had started talking again. It was a tense exchange, filled with accusations from Alex and defenses and reassurances from Rick. The tension in the room had grown into a palpable thing, so thick it was like a gray shroud smothering them.

"When is your friend supposed to get here?" Rachel asked, cutting into their circle of blame with one another. It was as much to get them to stop sniping as it was to take her mind off the growing numbness in her leg.

Rick's head snapped to her, his eyes hard and glossy from the constant stream of bickering between him and Alex. The office was cool, but an almost imperceptible sheen of sweat clung to his forehead. No doubt a nervous sweat, not a good sign from a man holding a gun.

"He'll be here when he gets here," Rick replied, his expression softening as he spoke with Rachel. "And he's not a friend."

"Seems you don't have a lot of friends these days," Alex murmured, his gaze boring into his former best friend. From the beginning of their whole accuse and defend session, he kept his eyes solidly locked on Rick. Even now, Rachel could almost feel the seething hatred in her husband as he glared at Rick. She understood the feeling, the deep betrayal they had experienced, but she didn't like the depths to which Alex's hatred was consuming him.

Suddenly, without warning, she felt a surge of overwhelming warmth wash over her. A wave of love, comfort and happiness so intense it brought a tear to her eye. Instinctively, she moved her hand to her abdomen, where she felt the wave had originated. At that moment, another wave of warm feelings passed over her, like she had just received a reassuring hug. As impossible as it seemed, she felt as if the child within her was comforting her, letting her know everything would be alright. It was impossible, her rational mind knew that, but her heart grabbed on to those feelings and she dared herself the luxury of imagining it to be true.

Rick moved his gaze back to Alex, his face hardening again. "You think I wanted it to go like this? Do you really think this is what I wanted? Sure, in the beginning you were just another assignment. Another job. But it became so much more as I got to know you. I've wanted to tell you for years. About me. About you. About who, and what, you really are. Because, whether you believe it or not, I am your friend. It's because of that friendship I'm doing this now. Alex, I know it doesn't seem that way, but I'm trying to save you!"

"You talk a good game, I'll give you that," Alex replied, his voice low and even, his eyes unwavering, "but in the end, all I see is a man with a gun, keeping us hostage."

"I know how it looks, but you are not a hostage. I just need you to wait until my associate arrives and hear him out." Rick's voice went from demanding to almost pleading. "How do I make you realize I'm still your friend?"

"For starters, you could put down the gun. Then you could let Rachel up to use the bathroom. We've been sitting here for a while and she is pregnant, you know." Out of the corner of his eye, Alex saw Rachel swing her head around, her face curious. She knew his concern for her bladder wasn't foremost on his mind. Before she was pregnant, she had been a camel when it came to the need to relieve herself. On road trips, they would stop at least twice for Alex to every one stop she needed. So far, pregnancy hadn't affected that much. The need to empty her bladder struck only slightly more frequently than it had before. There was another reason for his request. Did he expect her to run? To escape? Even if she could get away, where would she go? There was no one left for them to turn to. No, there was something else he needed.

A diversion.

He wanted her to distract Rick away from him. Whatever he had planned after that, she had no idea, and a part of her felt she might be better off not knowing. But as nervous as Rick had been, there was no way he was going to just let her waltz out of that office on her own and out of his sight.

Or was he?

"Okay," Rick conceded, much to Rachel's surprise. "Rachel can use the bathroom. She has two minutes. As for the gun..." He placed his weapon on the desk in front of him, next to the one Alex had been carrying. "I'm afraid this is as far as it goes." He glanced at Rachel. "Go."

She pulled her numb leg out from under her, pain cascading through her injured hip. Slowly, she stood, steadying herself. She hoped she wouldn't have to run anytime soon, it would take a while for her leg to come back. She grinned slightly at Rick. "Sorry, my leg fell asleep."

Rick ignored her, checking his watch. "Two minutes. If you aren't back here, I'm going to come after you."

Rachel nodded as she limped to the bathroom, the pins and needles shooting through her leg as it came back to life. She glanced back at the two men, both watching her, both with decidedly different motives. Closing the door behind her, she searched frantically around the small bathroom for anything that would provide enough of a distraction for Alex. She saw little. A small holder bolted to the wall by the sink held three toothbrushes. A bar of soap lay in a soap dish next to that. An empty plastic cup completed the contents by the sink. The shower didn't offer any better options with only the shampoo and another, slightly more worn, bar of soap. Nothing there she could use.

A minute and a half left. She was running out of time.

Under the sink, she found nothing but a few extra rolls of toilet paper and a plunger. She considered the plunger for a moment, but thought better of it. She needed to distract Rick, not confront him. Besides, the plunger wouldn't be much use to her against his gun. She kept looking, moving on to the medicine cabinet. There she found a razor, shaving cream, and a bottle of mouthwash. Those had potential, but she had the same dilemma as she did with the plunger; how could she effectively use them and not get shot? Aside from that, she didn't want to hurt Rick. Until an hour ago he had been their closest friend, a member of their family. No, no matter what he had done, she couldn't bring herself to harm him.

"Ouch!" She snagged her shirt on a ragged edge of the paper towel holder that was screwed into the wall, tearing the denim and digging into the flesh of her arm. "Shoot!" she spat, dabbing at the thin line of blood welling up in the slight cut, staining the edge of the shirt. "Stupid thing," she said, hitting the paper towel rack with an open hand. As she did, she knocked over the cup. It clattered into the sink and slowly spun to a halt there. As it did, an idea popped into her head. An idea she could live with. An idea they could hopefully all live with.

Thirty seconds left.

****

"Thirty seconds left, Rachel!" Rick shouted, checking his watch. "Please come out. I'd hate to go in there after you."

"Would you, really?" Alex asked, his voice taunting. "Or is that something you'd secretly enjoy, going in there and catching her with her pants down, so to speak?"

"What? Why would you say that?" There was a hint of hurt in his tone. "I love Rachel, but not like that. She's more like...like a sister-in-law to me."

Feeling an opening, Alex pressed forward. "Sure. But just think, once this plan of yours plays out, I'll be out of the way and she'll be available again. You'll have a shot at her."

"I don't want a shot at her," Rick replied. "What do you mean, you'll be out of the way? Do you think I'm going to kill you? I've told you; I'm trying to save your life!"

Alex cut him off sharply. "Then show it! You say you're still my friend, prove it! Let us go! We still have a chance to get out of here, to get away from these people! You asked me what you needed to do to prove to me you're still my friend? That's the thing! Let us go!"

Rick looked away, unable to keep Alex's gaze. "I can't," he whispered, the hurt in his voice replaced by regret.

"Then I guess our friendship is over, if it ever existed at all," Alex replied flatly.

Rick bristled slightly at that. "I guess so. I only hope that when this plays out, you can see I was doing it all to protect you. And as for Rachel, I had no true intentions with her of any kind. Ever. But now that you say it, sometimes I thought she might be better off with someone else. Someone less dangerous. Someone more..." He stopped as he searched for the right word. Unable to find anything less hurtful, he went on.

"Human."

The word cut through Alex. His stomach fluttered. He didn't want to ask the next question, but it couldn't remain unasked. "What do you mean, more human?"

Rick opened his mouth to reply, but was cut off as Rachel emerged from the bathroom. She held the small plastic cup and rubbed her forehead lightly.

Cautiously, Alex stood up from his position on the couch and took a step toward her. He stopped halfway across the office, an equal distance between her and Rick.

"Rach? What's wrong?" Rick asked, turning his attention to her.

She shook her head lightly. "I'm not sure. I feel kind of... of... of..." Before she could finish, she crumpled to the floor. Rick raced forward to catch her, his gun forgotten on Alex's desk. In two strides, he was next to her and reached for her arm to steady her. Before he could, she lurched back up and stepped away from him. He tumbled forward slightly, losing balance from his forward momentum, stumbling past her as she tossed the contents of the cup at his face, green liquid splashing across Rick's eyes.

His eyes exploded in pain as the mouthwash burned savagely in them. Howling in pain, he instinctively jumped back away from Rachel, his right buttock slamming hard into the edge of the desk. Crying out again at the fresh pain, he lurched forward again, rubbing intensely at his eyes to ease the burning and clear the fluid.

Alex wasn't going to give him the opportunity. Closing the distance between them, he grabbed Rick by the wrist and savagely twisted his arm behind his back. Blinded by the mouthwash in his eyes, Rick didn't see it coming and a sharp cry of surprise and pain erupted from him, his face contorting into a horrific mask of agony.

Seeing the pain his former friend was in, Alex instinctively eased up on his hold. It was a mistake Rick took full advantage of. Bracing himself, Rick kicked hard at Alex, catching his knee. Alex's leg wobbled at the impact and he stumbled, but kept his grip on Rick's wrist as he tried to right himself. Rick found Alex's knee joint with his foot and pressed hard against it, stopping just short of dislocating the joint. Alex's leg flared with pain as his knee extended and he finally released his grip on Rick and pulled away to avoid having his leg snapped in half. Once separated, the two men, as if thinking with one mind, dashed for the desk where the two handguns sat. Rick was a few inches closer and snatched up his pistol, turning to bring it to bear on Alex. But Alex was too close and moving too fast. Before Rick could fully turn and put Alex in his sights, he dove over the desk and threw himself into Rick, both of them going down in a mass of flailing arms and legs.

Rachel moved toward them to help Alex as they thrashed and grunted, each trying to gain the upper hand. She hadn't gone more than a step when a thunderous crack stopped her cold. Silence immediately pervaded the room and she froze, her chest seizing. It only lasted a second, but it was the worst second she had ever endured.

After a heartbeat there was motion from behind the desk. She couldn't see what was happening, who was shifting around, and she was afraid to move any closer. Instead, she waited, unable to move or breathe.

Another heartbeat and a hand reached up and slapped the surface of the desk. The owner of the hand slowly pushed himself up, trying to steady himself on wobbly legs.

It was Rick, gun still in hand.

"Oh, my God!" Rachel screamed, time suddenly moving again. Her eyes went to Rick's chest.

Rick looked down to see what had brought about her scream. A circle of blood covered the front of his sweatshirt, trailing into his jeans. His face went ashen, his jaw slack. The gun slid from his hand and hit the floor with a resounding thud. Absently, in a state of shock, he padded at his chest to find a wound. When he found nothing, he turned his gaze to the floor.

Alex hadn't moved.

Rachel raced to him, shoving Rick away. A deep crimson stain had already formed beneath him, spreading out into an ever-widening arc on the carpet. "Oh, God," she breathed, kneeling beside him. He was on his side, she couldn't see where the blood was coming from. Gently grasping his shoulder, she moved him on to his back, revealing a horrific hole in his chest just beneath his sternum. She gasped as more blood, an impossible amount of blood, flowed from the wound.

"Help him!" she screamed at Rick, who stood paralyzed, watching his friend bleed. "We have to help him!"

Just then, the door to the office was pushed open and in came the gnomic man Rachel had seen the previous night in the street outside their house. His eyes widened beneath his thick eyeglasses, distorting them into a cartoon parody of shock.

He looked at Rick. "Good Lord, what have you done?"

On the floor, Alex gasped and closed his eyes.

Then he was still.

41

As soon as breakfast was finished, Harriman quickly and quietly separated himself from Burke under the pretense of planning their upcoming operation. In truth, he had already effectively planned out a simple 'snag-and-run' operation, but he needed an excuse to get away from the young executive's prying ears.

He found a quiet spot across the street from the hotel, a beautiful grassy area normally shaded by maple trees. Late fall had robbed the trees of nearly all their leaves, but the weather was cool enough that a lack of shade wasn't much of a concern. A cool breeze punctuated that thought and he pulled the collar of his jacket tighter around his neck. A few dozen feet ahead, ducks were cavorting wildly in a pond, splashing and chasing each other around the small confines of their watery playground. Even though he was alone in the park, it was easy to imagine lovers picnicking and children laughing as they played games with their families.

With a heavy sigh, he pushed away thoughts of happy families. There was no use thinking about that. He had made his choices in his life and there was no turning back now. His military career had consumed his youth, and PenTech had taken the balance of his vital years. He had never married, never had a family of his own. Worse than that, his work had alienated him from the family he had, leaving him effectively alone. As the years progressed, he could feel his usefulness ending as his youthful strength slowly retreated from him. He had considered retirement, but what would that be for him? He had nowhere to go, no one to spend that time with. What would he do, sit in a park like this and feed ducks while brooding about the wrong turns he made in life? No, he wouldn't spend his last days withering away like one of the many leaves that fell to the ground around him. He had lived as a soldier; he would die the same way.

Cementing that thought in his mind, he turned his attention from the playful ducks and took his cellphone from his pocket. Briefly, he checked the area to be sure he was alone and not within earshot of anyone before punching in the special number and waiting for an answer. He didn't have to wait long. After half a ring, a cold, electronic voice asked him to say his name. He did as requested and waited as Genie verified his voiceprint. In the span of another heartbeat, Genie's soulless voice announced that the line was secure and the call was being forwarded.

"You have news for me?" The voice on the other end of the line was deep and authoritative, the question sounding less like an inquiry and more like an expectation. He spoke faster than usual, though, showing a bit of anxiety as well.

The thought of this man ever being anxious amused Harriman. A perverse feeling of satisfaction ran through him like a shiver as he relished the minute bit of power his unspoken knowledge gave him. It wasn't much, but a man in his position needed to savor and cultivate all the power he could. Sometimes it was all a person had.

"Yes, I have news," Harriman replied, feeling his power slip away with each word.

There was silence on the other end. He wouldn't be asked to continue; it was simply expected of him. Whatever power he had coveted momentarily was completely gone now.

"The operation is a success to date," he continued, "but there have been some complications. Adam has eluded us still, and he left a mess that Mr. Darnell is cleaning up. The Carters are in the wind and they may know more about the Eden Project than we would like. This is also being dealt with." He gave his report without embellishment. If the voice on the other end of the phone wanted details, he would ask for them.

"And what of Mr. Darnell?" the gruff voice asked.

A bit of the feeling of power slipped back into Harriman as he answered, this time directed at Burke Darnell and not the voice on the other end of the phone. "Everything seems to be proceeding as expected."

A heavy breath that carried a minute sense of relief came down the line. "Good. Keep me apprised of any further developments. Find Adam. He may have outlived his usefulness to us, but we still can't have a loose cannon running around unchecked. And keep a very close eye on Mr. Darnell. Understood?"

"Understood," Harriman repeated.

"Report back to me when the situation is under control, or with any further developments." The call ended with a sharp beep.

Harriman leaned back against the edge of the picnic table, spreading his arms and letting the warmth of the sun soak into him as he watched the ducks at play. He thought about all the years he had answered to Burke Darnell. All the assignments. Everything he had done to elevate the man's status at PenTech. He wondered what Burke would have to say when it was finally revealed it had all been a sham? When all the players laid out their cards for the final hand?

If nothing else, it would be interesting to see what happened.

42

"Help him!" Rachel cried, cradling Alex's motionless form.

Rick didn't move, frozen from shock. The other man, the man Rachel recognized as Dr. Elliot Forrester, quickly made his way to them and kneeled by Alex's side. He examined the wound and gingerly touched Alex's throat to check for a pulse.

"This is not good," he stated. "Not good at all." He refocused his attention on Rick, who hadn't moved since Alex got shot, except for blinking furiously at the mouthwash that still stung his eyes.

"What did you do?" Forrester asked, concern and accusation mingling in the question. "You were supposed to watch them, keep them from leaving until I could arrive! They were not supposed to be harmed!"

"Things escalated," Rick replied flatly. "They knew about Fallen Angel. They were piecing together what the Eden Project is all about. As soon as I got here, they were scared and ready to bolt. I couldn't talk them down. I had to detain them with force. It was unavoidable." He looked down at Alex and a slight quiver appeared in his voice. "This wasn't what I intended."

"We will address this later. For now, help me get him onto the couch!" Forrester barked the order more like a trauma doctor than an aging scientist, snapping Rick out of his state of shock and moving to assist Alex. Rick slipped his arms under Alex's shoulders while Forrester grabbed his legs. After a brief count of three from the scientist, they lifted him from the floor. As they did, blood flowed more heavily from the wound, falling to the carpet in bright scarlet drops. Forrester grunted and wheezed, the strain apparent on him, as they carefully moved to the couch and placed Alex there as gently as they could.

Rachel couldn't believe the amount of blood that had already spilled from her husband. She didn't know how much more he could stand to lose and still live. A sudden panic gripped her at the thought of losing him, her chest tightening and new tears coming to her eyes. That couldn't happen. It just couldn't. She wouldn't allow it. Pushing the thought of Alex's death and the anxiety that came with it aside as best she could, she refocused herself on the task at hand, saving his life.

Rick's cell phone sat on Alex's desk. "I'll call 911," she stated, reaching for the phone.

Forrester stopped her before she could grab it. "It's too late for that," he said, turning back to the still form on the couch.

All the feelings she had been trying to control suddenly burst inside Rachel. Her insides churned as her legs turned to jelly and she grabbed onto the desk to keep from falling to the floor in a heap. New tears filled her eyes and her throat tightened as grief and panic filled her to overflowing.

"What are you saying?" she managed. "He can't be dead. He just can't. Not now. Not after everything we've been through."

"He's not dead," replied Forrester, "but no hospital can help him now. No, he needs a different help, my dear. The kind of help only you can give him."

Rachel blinked back the tears in her eyes. "Me? What can I do for him?"

"You can provide something for him no one else can," Forrester replied. "The will to live."

"That's insane! He needs a doctor! A hospital! I'm calling 911!" She broke away from Forrester and snatched Rick's cellphone up again, bringing up the phone app and dialing. She had dialed nine and one, and stopped. A small spark of doubt burned at the back of her mind as her finger hovered over the dial pad. What Forrester was saying seemed impossible. Ridiculous, even. But was it any more insane than what had happened to them already? It sounded impossible to her she could save Alex from a gunshot wound to the chest simply because she wanted him to live, but she had already experienced so much impossibility. What made that any more far-fetched? She had already learned there was so much more to Alex than she could have ever imagined, why should she draw the line now?

Dropping the phone on the desk again, she turned back to Forrester. "What do I have to do?"

The little scientist moved closer to her, placing his hand lightly on her arm. "Talk to him. Convince him to come back to you. As you've already discovered, there is much more to your husband than meets the eye. He has gifts that have yet to be tapped, abilities that are beyond imagination. You need to persuade him to dig deep inside himself, deep in places even he isn't consciously aware of, to discover those abilities. To use them to heal himself. The power is there, inside him. He simply hasn't discovered it yet. Help him do that."

Rachel looked down at Alex. His face was ashen, his features slack. Blood was gathering again beneath him in an ever-widening pool. Glassy eyes stared into the void. Her heart sank in her chest at the sight of him. It was like he was dead already.

Kneeling beside him, she took his hand. It was cold to the touch, clammy and slippery with blood that had already cooled. A shallow rasp of breath escaped him and she saw the almost imperceptible rise and fall of his chest. It wasn't much, but it was enough to let her know he was still alive, that there was still hope.

She softly spoke, as if gently trying to wake him from a nap. "Alex, I don't know if you can hear me, honey. It's Rachel." His hand twitched slightly at the mention of her name. Her heart swelled slightly with hope, and she squeezed his hand a bit harder. "I know you're hurting, baby. I know you may feel like the easiest thing to do right now is to just give up. To just let go and leave the insanity behind. Please don't. Alex, I'm so scared right now. So confused. I don't know what will happen to me, to our baby, without you here with us. We need you so much. So much..." She trailed off as a soft sob escaped her. With desperation in her breast, she checked for a reaction from Alex. Anything that would show he was hearing her, that he was fighting to stay with her. She expected little, but when she looked at him he appeared different. There appeared to be some color returning to his face. She thought his hand felt warmer. It might be her imagination, but even the flow of blood from his wound seemed to have slowed.

A tiny bloom of hope rose in her and she continued. "We need you, this baby and me. Please don't give up on us. Please. We're a family, and we haven't even had a chance to start. Your baby needs to know their father. Needs to have you in their life."

The same remarkably warm feeling she had before once again welled up in her belly. Happiness and compassion. Unadulterated joy. It was as if their unborn child was adding its own strength to Rachel's, helping its father. Spurred on by this, Rachel continued. "I just don't know how we can go on without you." She held his hand up to her tear-streaked face. "You can't leave us. We love you."

"I love you," she choked out before again being silenced by an uncontrollable sobbing.

She simply held his hand against her face, feeling the warmth from her belly flow through her. Her own hand warmed with it and she consciously tried to will that energy into Alex, to infuse him with the light and hope she felt at that moment.

"It's working!"

Dr. Forrester's exclamation startled her from her trance, her eyes springing open at his voice. He stood above her, above Alex, a smile across his face and his eyes alight with excitement. Rachel risked a look at Alex to see what Forrester was so excited about, and went slack at what she saw.

The gunshot wound in his chest, the ugly hole there, was closing as if it were occurring in a time-lapse video. It closed in on itself; the flesh knitting together until nothing remained but a slight red mark. A small welt. His breathing became stronger and steadier, his chest rising and falling with increasing regularity. She no longer had to strain to hear him draw breath.

Rick, eyes wide with wonder, muttered, "It's a miracle."

"A miracle of science, perhaps," replied Forrester. He placed his hand on Rachel's shoulder, giving it a reassuring squeeze. "And perhaps a miracle of the heart, as well."

Rachel wiped tears from her eyes and smiled at him. "Thank you."

"Don't thank me, my dear. It was you who did the work. You and your husband, that is. I just started the ball rolling, so to speak." A wide grin of self-satisfaction crept across the doctor's face. "It is rather wonderful to see one's life work come to fruition, don't you think?"

Rachel lowered her gaze from the doctor and back to Alex, the tears on her face replaced by a chill in her heart. She had a suspicion she knew what Forrester was referring to as his life's work and, even though she was ecstatic Alex was alive and recovering, the facts of his lineage were still going to haunt them. Silently, she held on to her momentary happiness. She was certain it wouldn't last.

A sudden gasp of shock from Rick pulled her from her reverie. His face was pale and distended, his eyes wide. Rachel followed his gaze to Alex, still lying prone on the couch, and understood why. She hadn't expected it to happen so soon, but she felt her last bit of happiness drop away.

Alex looked again like he was at the edge of death. Not from the gunshot wound, this was different. His face and features were gaunt. Emaciated. His skin hung from his bones as if there were no muscle to support it. It looked as if he was being eaten away from the inside.

"What's happening to him?" Rachel asked, trying her best to suppress the rising panic in her chest and keep her head clear.

Dr. Forrester, still beaming like a proud father, explained. "He will be fine, child. The process he underwent to save his life is very taxing and requires a large amount of energy to fuel it. Fuel the body can only supply as calories. He just needs to get some food into him, that's all. Quite a bit of food, actually."

"Well then," he continued, loudly clapping his hands together and startling Rachel, "we had best get him out of here and get him something to eat." He absently waved Rick to him. "Help me get him to his feet again, would you, my boy?"

They pulled Alex to his feet, supporting him between them. When standing, he looked even worse, his clothes hanging off of him like they were for a man three times his size. Despite Dr. Forrester's assurances that Alex would be all right, at that moment she didn't feel reassured.

"Rachel?" It was Alex, his voice barely more than a raspy whisper.

"I'm here," she replied, taking his hand. It was a frail, bony thing in hers, like an old man's. Despite herself, she winced at the touch.

"We have to get out of here," he croaked.

There was an urgent quality in his voice that pierced her soul like an icy dagger. "We are," she replied, trying to keep her tone encouraged and confident. "We're going right now. We'll get you some food, get you well again."

Alex took in a deep, shaky breath before he continued. "No time for that," he said in a desperate whisper. "We have to leave right now. Get as far from here as we can."

Panic rose in Rachel's chest. "Why? Why do we need to leave now?"

"Because he knows where we are. He's coming for us, and this time he won't be stopped until we're all dead." His voice cracked and faded on the last few words. He was weakening with every second.

Still, Rachel pushed him with one more question. "Who, Alex? Who's coming after us?"

With the last of his strength, Alex replied, "The stranger."

43

Adam stretched, shaking out the stiffness of a night's sleep. Not that he slept much, with the healing dreams tearing at his mind all night, but his body was stiff.

He glimpsed his arms as he stretched. They were almost skeletal, his skin clinging directly to the bones. The healing had ravaged his body, eating away muscle and fat to sustain and repair him. But all the physical and psychological torture had paid off. There was no evidence of the gunshot wounds he had sustained to his shoulder and leg. Once he ate and built his body back up to peak strength, he would once again be in perfect physical condition.

The perfect condition for hunting.

Of all the wounds he had received the past night, there was one that had stung him the most: Rachel's betrayal. He understood why Alex Carter had attacked him; he was about to expose the man's lies and put an end to the sham of a life he had been leading. The life he had so maliciously stolen. He could even understand the cop getting involved, having fallen under Alex Carter's web of deceit and manipulation. But Rachel, poor darling Rachel, was just an unfortunate pawn in an ugly game. A game that was growing uglier and more dangerous every minute. He knew he should feel loathing for her, a need for revenge, but he couldn't. It was obvious to him that her will was no longer her own, that she was an innocent thrall of the man she called her husband. He couldn't bring himself to hate an innocent flower whose only crime had been falling under a deceiver's spell.

No, he couldn't hate her. She had to be freed, released from his influence so they could finally be together and build the life that had always been intended for them. A life that corruption had tainted. That was his course. He had to kill the deceiver to free her.

He had to kill Alex Carter.

But what if that didn't free her? There was no telling how deep his influence was, how much damage he had done. He had thought that just by seeing him, the man she was intended to be with, Rachel's mind would be cleared. That assumption has proven to be in error, and it had nearly cost him his life. But what if she was too far gone? If there was no way to break the hold of the deceiver?

He squared his shoulders in resolve. He knew what he would have to do. There was no other option. He cared too much for her to allow her to live under his control, even after Alex Carter was dead. He wouldn't allow her to suffer misguided conceptions for the rest of her life. In the absence of freeing her mind from the deceiver's influence, there would be only one option for her.

He would have to kill Rachel Carter.

It would tear his heart in two to do it, but she would be better off for it. Better to die than live mourning the man who had brought so much deceit and pain to her. Because Alex Carter would be dead, there was no question of that. His last, fleeting hope was that seeing Alex Carter die would dispel the brainwashing she had been suffering under all these years, but if that didn't work, he would have no choice but to kill her. To let her continue to live under his thrall was simply unthinkable. As much as it would destroy him to do it.

First, he had to find her. After last night, they would no doubt have gone into hiding, which would normally make them marginally more difficult to locate. Not impossible, not with his skills and resources, but it would be more time-consuming. Last night, while in his healing trance, in the midst of the dreaming terrors that always plague him, he received a great gift. A revelation..

A sign.

Somewhere off in the distance, his quarry was preparing to run again. He knew this. He had been shown this. Even now, he could sense it. Like magnetic North drawing the point of a compass, he could feel the presence of the deceiver. Emotions not his own swirled over him; confusion, betrayal, fear, anger. Like a predator catching the scent of prey, they swirled around him, fueling his determination. His conviction. Despite his starved and weakened body, he felt rejuvenated.

Once again, he had purpose.

He knew where his prey was. He knew where they were going. Soon he would find them, and then he would experience the greatest satisfaction he could imagine.

He would kill Alex Carter.

44

"He knows where we are. He'll be coming after us soon," Alex repeated between bites of a bacon, egg, and cheese sandwich. It was the fifth sandwich he had eaten since they stopped for food, not to mention the four one-quart containers of orange juice. Stuffing the last bit of sandwich into his mouth, he reached for the fifth orange juice.

They had driven to the edge of town to avoid drawing the attention of Pine Haven's locals, who may recognize them. When they felt they were far enough out, they had stopped at a roadside gas station and deli that made their own homemade breakfast sandwiches, which had both looked and smelled amazing. There were some tables hidden in the back of the place behind the stacks of potato chips, beef jerky, and sweet snacks, and they were fortunate enough to grab a spot that wasn't easily seen from the parking lot. Feeling as secure as they could, they ordered breakfast, no doubt giving the little spot its best day of sales in a while.

"How do you know?" asked Forrester, lightly sipping at his coffee. Steam wafted up from the cup and frosted his thick glasses. Annoyedly, he wiped at them with a napkin, then absently took another sip and was forced to repeat the process. Frustrated, he put the drink down and faced Alex. "How can you be sure?"

"I don't know how I know, I just do. I feel... connected, somehow. It was vague at first, just an odd little feeling at the back of my skull. But the stronger I get, the stronger it gets. It feels like we can tune into each other, like a radio." He paused and drained the last of the orange juice. "Or a homing beacon."

"Fascinating," Forrester muttered inwardly. His eyes went wide, creating a cartoonish appearance behind the thick lenses of his glasses. "It worked."

"What worked?" asked Rachel as she collected the empty wrappers from the table and dropped them in a nearby trash can.

A cloud passed over Forrester's face, changing his expression from one of pleasant surprise to guarded secrecy. "It's, umm, nothing, dear. Just something I suddenly remembered, that's all."

"I see," she replied. She didn't believe him, but they had more pressing issues right now. Still, she packed the information away for later.

"Where is he now?" Rick asked through a mouthful of his own sandwich. He had been quiet for most of the drive and all of breakfast, only piping up when necessary. The shooting of Alex was still fresh in everyone's mind and a thick cloud of tension still hung between them. So far, Rick's silence had been enough to placate Alex, but everyone at the table cringed when he spoke.

Alex answered in a calm and even tone, surprising Rachel. She was sure he hadn't forgotten what had happened, but he seemed to focus on more critical problems right now. "I haven't been able to pin him down yet. I only know that he's not far away. And he's getting closer."

"You think he's homing in on you? Can't you do the same thing to him?" Every word Rick spoke grated on Rachel.

"Not yet," Alex answered, reaching for another breakfast sandwich. "Like I said, this is new to me. As I get stronger, it gets stronger." He took a healthy bite from the sandwich. "So shut up and let me get stronger."

"So, what do we do next?" Rick pressed. "If this guy can find anywhere we run to, where do we go? And what do we do when he catches up with us? Because I feel fairly secure that he will catch up to us, eventually."

"Alex?" Rachel asked, turning to her husband. The uncertainty in her voice made him uncomfortable, mostly because this wasn't a problem that could be fixed with a kiss and a smile. "What do we do?"

"You mean what do I do," Alex replied flatly.

Forrester piped up in a voice loud enough to draw the attention of the two employees of the gas station. "My boy, you can't seriously be thinking about going off on your own to face that madman, can you?"

"It's me he can sense. He can find me anytime he likes. That makes me a danger to all of you just by being around you. It only makes sense that I break off from the rest of you and draw him out. Face him and end this thing, once and for all." Alex never took his eyes from his breakfast during his spiel, not daring to look at any of them. He knew what their reactions would be.

Rick spoke up first. "That's stupid. You've seen what this guy is capable of. You need help. I'll go with you to back you up. Dr. Forrester can get Rachel someplace safe in the meantime. Besides, I owe you this much, at least."

"And that brings to a close this installment of Macho Bullcrap Theater," came Rachel's response. It amazed Alex how, though everything that had happened to them over the last few days, she maintained her commitment to not swearing. No one could blame her if she dropped a few curse words right now.

Rachel reached across the small table and took Alex's hand in hers. "I have way too much time and energy invested in you to just let you go and waste it like that. I love you, and we're in this together. 'For better or worse', remember that?"

"Besides," chimed in Dr. Forrester, "defeating or escaping Adam only represents half the problem."

"What do you mean?" asked Alex, uncertain he wanted the answer.

The doctor continued. "The people I work for, or used to work for, I suppose, have a vested interest in both you and Adam. An interest they will not readily give up. So not only do you face escaping Adam, but the Eden Project as well. Even if you survive Adam, the Project will be almost impossible to elude. You see, you've given them something far more valuable that either of you represent. A new commodity for them to exploit."

"And that would be?" Rachel asked, a slight crack in her voice.

"Your child, my dear."

"They want our baby?" Alex replied, anger and fear tinging his voice. "What does our baby have to do with all of this?"

"It's simple," Forrester replied, his voice infuriatingly calm. "Because the child is yours. And it shouldn't exist."

Rachel's hand moved unconsciously to cover her belly. "What do you mean, shouldn't exist?"

Dr. Forrester pointed to Alex. "Because *you* are supposed to be sterile."

"What?" Alex asked, through surprise and confusion. "How would you know that?"

Dr. Forrester smiled. It was a warm, friendly smile. Perhaps even a fatherly smile. "I know because I created you. You and Adam."

Silence fell like a cloak around them.

45

Stunned silence hung uncomfortably in the air. Alex and Rachel, still reeling from Forrester's bizarre revelation, could only stare numbly at the round-faced geneticist. Rick shifted in his chair, his face conveying his concern about the impact from the worst of all betrayals. Dr. Forrester fidgeted with his coffee cup. They were at an impasse; none of them certain what should, or could, be said next.

Rick broke the silence as he leaned in and whispered, "Maybe this isn't the best place to be talking about this?"

Dr. Forrester surveyed the room, noting they had drawn the attention of the facility's staff and the customers that had since come in. "An excellent idea. Let's adjourn to the car and take to the open road. Aside from avoiding prying eyes, we also won't be a stationary target for one of our many pursuers."

"I'm not sure I want to go anywhere with you people," Rachel stated, crossing her arms tightly across her chest. "How can you ask us to trust you? We're putting our lives into your hands. How can we be sure we'll be safe? I mean, I've never met you before," she indicated Dr. Forrester with a nod. As she turned to Rick, her eyes turned misty and forlorn. "And I'm certain I don't know you."

A shadow of pain crossed Rick's face. "You can't imagine how sorry I am for all the hurt I've caused you. I can't change that, or make up for it. And I know you don't have any reason to trust me, but I'm hoping you can get past that for now, because what I'm telling you is the truth. We are all in very grave and very immediate danger right now. You, Alex, the doc. Even me. Yeah, that's right, even me. When the Eden Project finds out I've turned and I'm helping you now, they will issue a termination order on me without hesitation. This thing has become so big that killing to keep it quiet is just the cost of doing business. And with the personal knowledge I have, there's no way they can let me walk away. I am taking a bigger risk than any of you by helping you, because of all of us, I am the only one who is one hundred percent expendable. So do what you want, trust who you want. I just hope you can find enough trust in me to at least hear Dr. Forrester out. What he has to say could save your lives. At the very least, you'll know what you're up against and why."

Rick leaned in across the small café table, his face coming withing a few inches of Alex's. "Ever since I've known you, you've wondered where you came from. This is your chance to find out. The man with all the answers is literally standing right in front of you. You're so close, don't walk away now."

Alex slowly pulled back, keeping his eyes locked with Rick's. "We'll go with you. For now. But I'll be watching you, both of you. If there is even the slightest hint of danger to

Rachel or the baby, we're gone. No matter what we need to do or who we have to go through to do it. Do I make myself absolutely clear?"

"Clear as crystal," Rick answered, his gaze never wavering.

Forrester cleared his throat and stood up. "Well then, gentlemen, if you are done with your macho posturing for now, we really should be going." He gathered up the various wrappers and cups on the table and dropped them in the nearest trash can. "If Adam is indeed as close as Alex seems to think he is, we can't risk him finding us. At least not yet." He rummaged around in the pockets of his tweed coat for a moment before stumbling on the car keys. "Ah! There they are. Shall we?" He pointed out the exit with a sweep of his arm.

"After you," Alex said to Rick, stepping back to clear a path to the front door.

"If you insist," Rick replied, his voice thick with an angry sarcasm, and headed for the exit after Dr. Forrester.

Gathering up the last two containers of orange juice, Alex followed him out, with Rachel close behind. When they reached the car, Forrester had already slid into the driver's side while Rachel opened the back door on the passenger's side and dropped into that seat.

Rick looked at Alex. "Front or back?"

"I think I'll take the back with Rachel for now," Alex replied. He didn't move for a moment, waiting for the other man to get into the car.

Rick took the hint. "Suit yourself," he replied, slipping into the passenger's seat next to Dr. Forrester.

Alex made himself comfortable next to Rachel as Dr. Forrester left the gas station and pulled back onto Main Street, heading south. That way would take them away from Pine Haven and toward Concord, about a half hour away. Although Alex knew they wouldn't be going quite that far. Not yet. Everything they needed to accomplish was in Pine Haven. They weren't ready to leave just yet.

Alex was struggling to find a reason to stay. There was nothing left to keep them in that tiny town. Nothing but memories. They couldn't go back to their home, that much was certain. Even if they could clear everything with the police and go back to their lives again, he was certain he could never sleep in that house again. And then there was his business. He couldn't see a way through this that allowed him to forgive Rick and pick up where they left off, as if none of this had happened. That chapter of his life was definitively closed. Forever. The business would have to be dissolved and he would have to start all over again on his own. Something he could just as easily do somewhere else, where there weren't so many ghosts chasing them. Every time he thought of a reason to stay in Pine Haven, he countered with another not to. It seemed as if that part of their life was dead forever, no matter what happened in the coming days.

But he would hold on tightly to his family. Rachel and the baby. If he came out of this with nothing else of his old life intact, he was determined to hang on to what he and Rachel shared. His family would be safe, no matter the cost or who had to pay for it. They would remain together, and somehow, somewhere, raise their child together peacefully.

First, they had to survive the next few days. And for that to happen, he needed information.

"Dr. Forrester, when you said you created me, what did you mean by that?" Alex asked. "Are we... related?"

Forrester chuckled slightly. "You could say that, my boy. You could say that."

Anger rose in Alex's chest at the old scientist's answer. Just once, he wanted to get some answers without more riddles. But losing his temper now would be counterproductive to what he needed to accomplish. Pushing down his anger, he addressed Forrester again. "Could you elaborate on that for me, please?"

"I'm sorry to be vague," Forrester responded, the smile on his face undiminished. "It's far more complicated than you might imagine. Putting everything into simple terms is difficult at best, especially with you and your siblings."

Alex jumped at the word siblings. Rachel reached out and took his hand, squeezing it gently. He glanced at her and gave her a slight smile to demonstrate he was okay, but a familiar look in her eyes caught his attention. A look he had seen far too frequently over the years, but especially in the last few days. A look that warned him not to get his hopes up too high. Pushing down his feelings of hope and anticipation, he turned back to Forrester to continue questioning the diminutive doctor.

"Siblings?" he asked. He tried to hide his anxiousness, but there was no mistaking it as his voice rose an octave and cracked a bit at the end of the word. "Are you saying I have brothers and sisters somewhere that I know nothing about?"

The smile on Dr. Forrester's face faded as a dark cloud crossed his face. For a moment, Alex was sorry he had pressed the issue. A glance from Rachel convinced him otherwise.

"Doctor," he pressed, a pang of guilt settling into the pit of his stomach. "My siblings. How many are there? Brothers? Sisters? Both? Where are they now? Please, I need to know. I've been searching for this my whole life, it's important to me."

Dr. Forrester's face fell at Alex's words. The smile he had worn just moments ago was completely gone now, buried under a mountain of grief and pain. For a moment, Alex felt a pang of guilt at his incessant questioning of the man, but a glance at Rachel reminded him of what was at stake.

"Doctor?" he pressed, despite the pang of guilt that settled into his stomach. "My siblings, what can you tell me about them? Where are they? Please, Doctor. Anything would help."

Without warning, Forrester pulled off the road and into the breakdown lane, put the car in park and shut off the engine. There was silence for a few moments as he simply stared ahead at the open road. A car raced past them, shaking their car slightly in its wake. After a few more moments of quiet reflection, Dr. Forrester twisted in his seat to face Alex as best he could. He looked like a shadow of the man they had known, his face drawn and pale, his eyes dull and lifeless behind his glasses. The jovial bug-eyed look was gone, replaced by the face of an anguished old man who had been witness to far too much pain and suffering in his time. The pang of guilt in Alex's stomach surged at the sight of the man, but he had been telling the truth when he told Forrester the information was important to him. It was more than important; it was crucial.

But that didn't make the guilt any easier to live with.

Forrester removed his glasses, his eyes appearing unnaturally tiny. Rubbing the bridge of his nose hard, he exhaled and asked, "It's imperative to you that you know?"

Alex nodded.

"Now?"

Another nod.

Forrester sighed a deep sigh and replaced his glasses on the bridge of his nose. "Very well then. To answer your earlier question; yes, we are related. But not in the sense you may think."

A puzzled look fell on Alex's and Rachel's faces. Dr. Forrester continued. "Are you aware of what genetic engineering is?"

"You mean cloning?" Rachel asked.

"Not exactly," Forrester replied. "Cloning creates an exact duplicate of a living organism. Like what those Scottish scientists did with a sheep all those years ago. And what some less than reputable companies are claiming they can do with deceased pets now. What I'm talking about is a far more complex procedure."

"Like genetically modified crops," Alex chimed in. "Crossbreeding different strains to make them able to grow in harsh conditions. To grow with less water. To create natural pest control measures. Things like that."

Forrester took another deep breath and pursed his lips, which had suddenly gone dry. "That's much closer, but not precisely correct." He paused for a deep breath and a moment to gather his thoughts. "Please bear with me. I am going to attempt to explain this in the simplest way possible. I mean no offense to any of you, but the science involved here is complex even to those who have spent their lives immersed in it. But I will do my best."

He paused again, clearing his throat before continuing. "The goal was the creation of the ultimate expression of a human being. To accomplish that, we selected the best genetic traits from the most perfect human specimens we could find. Elite athletes. Preeminent scientists. The greatest military and strategic minds. People at the peak of physical, mental, and intellectual capability. Once we assembled that genetic material, we could create a complete genetic map of the most perfect human being. We recreated a gestational experience by placing those traits in a simulated egg and stimulating growth through the use of applied electric shock and regular chemical immersion. We carefully balance all nutrients to maximize the embryo's growth and development, conducting the process outside of any woman's body. When the embryo reaches the proper state of development, the subject is removed from the artificial womb, a blank slate in the world. From there, the child is placed in an accelerated growth chamber, where they are fed educational, instructional and training information while they grow. Within a few short months, they emerge from the growth chamber, accelerated to an effective age and carrying the knowledge they will need to achieve their life's mission." The doctor finished his rhetoric, like a college professor delivering a lecture. "Questions?"

Alex and Rachel both sat in stunned silence. Questions raced through both of their heads, but they couldn't pin down just one to ask. Finally, Alex stumbled a few words out. "So, I was created? In a lab? I'm... not real?"

"You are as real as the rest of us, my boy," Forrester replied, leaning back into the soft leather of the driver's seat and closing his eyes. "Perhaps more so than those of us who came into the world in the natural way."

"But," Alex stammered, "how? You can't just create a person out of nothing!"

"I can," Forrester replied calmly, "and I did."

"Why?" Rachel asked, her voice somber.

Forrester's eyes popped open, and he sat upright, turning to face her again. "Excuse me?"

"Why did you do it?" Rachel repeated.

Forrester sat in silence for a moment, stunned by the question Rachel had just posed to him. When he finally spoke, he turned away from her to face Alex. "Have you ever been sick? Have you ever missed school or taken time off from work because you had the flu, or even just a bad cold?"

Alex shook his head. "No, I've always been really resistant to things like that."

Dr. Forrester continued. "Have you sustained any injuries you had difficulty recovering from? Do you have any scars from past injuries?"

"No," Alex replied warily. "I've always been a fast healer."

Dr. Forrester nodded slightly in assent. "Of course you are. Now tell me, son; you're in excellent physical condition, correct?"

This time Alex's voice was shaky, uncertain. "Yes. I've been in great shape for as long as I can remember."

"And do you ever exercise?" Forrester asked.

Alex shook his head slowly, absently. "No. No, I never do. Just a gift of genetics, I suppose."

"More than you can imagine," Forrester stated, turning back to Rachel. "That is why I did what I did. Genetic engineering has been used to create everything from the perfect dairy cow to the perfect potato. I simply went one step further and created the perfect human being."

"Perfect?" Rachel shot back. "After the last few days we've endured, I certainly wouldn't use the word 'perfect' to describe his life!"

"Think of it," Dr. Forrester continued, the light returning to his eyes as he talked about his work. "Your husband will never get sick. As demonstrated earlier, he can recover from even the most egregious injuries. He never has to work at maintaining the physique of a premier athlete. He is one of the most perfect human specimens on the planet. And then there are his special abilities..." The scientist trailed off, either retreating deeper into thought or stopping himself before he revealed too much.

Alex was about to press him for more information, but another voice distracted him. The last voice he expected to hear.

Lieutenant Ernie Babcock's voice.

It was more than simply hearing Babcock's voice, there was more to it. Not only could he hear him, but Alex could also feel his presence. It was like a distant memory that lingered in the back of his mind, something he tried to forget but that refused to be forgotten.

"Help me," the voice of Ernie Babcock said. It was a weak sound, almost lost to the static in Alex's mind. Like a radio signal that was right on the edge of transmitter range. But the pain, the desperation, behind it was very real. Alex could feel the anguish in his plea, as faint as it was.

And then it was gone. Just as quickly as it had come, Babcock's presence faded from Alex's mind.

"Alex?" It was Rachel's voice this time, but in his ears instead of his head. "What is it? What's wrong?"

"I just heard Ernie," he replied, his voice quiet and distant as he processed this new experience. "More than heard him, though. He was in my head, Rachel. Calling out to me for help."

Rachel continued, surprised that this new revelation did not put her off. "What did he say?"

Alex seemed to snap back to the real world with that question. "He asked for help. But he was so weak. I could feel him in my head, all the pain he was experiencing. He's scared, Rachel. I don't know how much longer he can hold on."

"His injuries must have been worse than we thought," she replied, gently putting her arm around her husband's shoulders and pulling him in close.

"Poor bastard," Rick whispered. "Never had a clue about what he was getting into."

"And that," Alex announced somberly, "is why I have to help him."

Rachel pulled back a bit. "Help him? How can you help him?"

"Just like I did this morning for myself. Don't ask me how I know, but I know I can help him, Rach." Alex took her hand in his, returned the gesture of reassurance she had given him earlier that day. Looking into his eyes, Rachel saw a fire burning there that she had never seen before. Despite the cool blue color of them, they were alight with new purpose. As frightened as Alex was about their future, all the recent discoveries they made were invigorating him as well. Changing him.

She couldn't help but smile. "I believe you can. And I'll be there to help you do it."

"Thank you," he replied quietly, leaning forward and kissing her lightly. "I love you."

"I know," she replied, her smile widening.

"That's fine," Rick interrupted from the front seat, "but how do you plan to get to him? A cop was shot, the hospital will be crawling with police. Furthermore, since the cop was shot at your house, I have a feeling the police will want to question you. Not to mention that fact that Burke has probably set a trap for you already."

"Yes," interjected Dr. Forrester. "I had completely forgotten about our young Mr. Darnell."

Alex had never heard the name before, but from the way Forrester and Rick were talking about him, it sounded like he was someone to get to know. "Who is this Burke Darnell guy?"

"He's Penders' right-hand man," Rick explained, "and about as sleazy as they come. He's been on a fast-track to the top and he never lets anything get in his way. And if something does get in his way, he removes it efficiently and with extreme prejudice. The man is cold. Calculating. Ruthless. And he hates Adam. I have no idea why, but if Burke hadn't been ordered to bring him in alive, I'm sure we'd be seeing a far more aggressive manhunt than the one we have now. It's almost like him hating Adam is, I don't know, instinctive."

"There will be a trap for you, Alex," Forrester cut in, his tone becoming dark, "but it isn't the local authorities you need to be wary of. The Eden Project considers you and the child Rachel is carrying to be their personal property, and they are extremely obsessive about their possessions. They will be looking for you, and they are tenacious and resourceful. So be aware and be cautious."

"This Darnell, is he dangerous?" Alex asked.

"He has been given explicit instructions to deliver Rachel and her unborn child to the Eden Project," Forrester stated. "I believe she is in no immediate danger from him, or the Project. They would prefer to bring you back to the Project alive and intact as well, Alex. Provided you don't become too much of an impediment to their objectives, I believe you are reasonably safe. For the moment."

"Mr. Darnell's intentions toward Adam are not as generous," the scientist continued, "and I can't say that's such a bad thing anymore."

Picking up on the trepidation in the older man's voice, Alex pressed him. "What do you mean?"

Forrester became sullen again, his eyes adopting the gray pallor they held previously. "There was a time I regarded all of you as my children. True, I wasn't your father in the biological sense, at least not entirely, but it was I who took the raw genetic material gathered and created you all. I saw you incubated and educated in vitro. As you reached maturity, I saw each of you birthed. I managed your transition into the world, helping you go from blank slates to fully realized human beings in a matter of days. Yes, I may not have been your father in the traditional sense, but I was prouder of you and your siblings than any father had ever been in his progeny. But I failed you all after your births. I lost control."

"How did you fail?" Alex asked. "How did you lose control?"

"After your incubation and in vitro training were complete, when it was time for you to be 'born', Penders took control of your development. He had a plan for you and your siblings, and even though it was a plan I vehemently opposed, I had no choice but to follow him. It was the only way I could stay close to all of you. To stay involved and try to keep you from harm." Tears formed in the scientist's eyes and his voice cracked slightly as he spoke. He looked as if he had suddenly aged a lifetime in the last few minutes, years of regret and pervasive sadness bubbling up from his soul and showing on his face. He removed his glasses again and swiped at the new tears.

A question caught in Alex's throat as he was about to voice it, not sure he wanted to know the answer. But he'd come this far. There was no turning back now. "What happened then?"

I failed," the old man said simply, a missed tear running down his cheek.

"Failed what?" Rachel interjected. Her voice was soft, like the eye of a storm. Calm in passing but heralding greater destruction in its wake.

"I failed to keep my children safe," the doctor said, deep sobs suddenly bursting from him. He buried his face in his hands as his body heaved heavily with each sob.

Rachel leaned forward and gently placed her hand on the doctor's arm, giving a slight but reassuring squeeze. "How did you fail them?"

Forrester didn't speak right away, waiting until the sobs wracking his body subsided enough for him to regain some of his composure. After a few moments, he was able to take his face from his hands and replace his glasses, smoothing the front of his coat. He had recovered the appearance of the staid scientist. When he spoke, even his tone had regained its analytical aspect, the emotional response of a moment ago completely buried. "Penders plan was to turn you into the most viable commodity of the twenty-first century: Designer human beings. You would be trained as soldiers, spies and assassins, then sold off to the highest bidder. I disagreed with him. I thought you were better suited to use your gifts for the greater good of humanity. You could go where normal humans can't, surviving conditions that would be lethal for even the hardiest of humans. Think of the advances in viral research from a researcher who could work unprotected and unhindered around even the deadliest virus! Or someone able to withstand high levels of radiation for prolonged periods! Rescue workers who could survive for days on end in the most inhospitable of climates! The potential benefits to society were endless! Penders, however, was interested only in his profit margin. I couldn't dissuade him. He threatened to terminate me from the Project if I didn't go along with his plans. He was going to cut me off from my children! I couldn't allow that to happen. So I stood by and observed as Penders and Harriman worked to turn you into engines of destruction. Weapons training. Espionage techniques. Unarmed combat. Every destructive thing you learned tore another piece from my heart. I wanted to stop it, to put an end to the madness, but I was powerless. I clung to the idea that I was your only hope for a productive life. Then that hope died, too."

Forrester stopped again, reining in the thoughts and memories that careened around his head. He was determined to finish his story, to get the whole truth out, to clear his conscience. But there were so many memories bubbling up to the surface, each one carrying with it a heavy load of emotion. Sorting through it all, detaching the emotion from the facts, was taking a toll on him. He was tired, but the truth had to come out. Alex had a right to know, as did Rachel, about the reality of his existence.

After a few moments, he let out a deep and loud sigh before continuing. "It was the eighteenth month of your training. You had all advanced to the physical maturity of the average sixteen-year-old, but mentally several of you were showing signs of fatigue. Instability. Training was intense, and you were all absorbing a lot of data entirely too fast. You were absorbing and grasping concepts in days what normally would take months or even years to learn. But your minds, as exceptional as they are, have limits. As we found out."

Another pause, but whether it was to gather thoughts or just stall the inevitable, even the doctor himself couldn't say. Regardless, he forged ahead. "Eve Seventeen was the first to break. It was dinnertime, and you were all gathered in the cafeteria for your evening meal. Baked chicken, I believe. Everything was proceeding normally until it happened. Until Eve Seventeen grabbed her knife and thrust it into the throat of the boy seated next to her, Adam Twenty-Three. It was more than just a simple stabbing. She was vicious in her attack, yet also remarkably precise in efficiency. By the time security could restrain her, she had nearly decapitated the boy. He died right there and then, with no opportunity to heal himself."

Forrester turned back again to face Alex. "Remember that, my boy. You *can* die. It might be more difficult to accomplish, but it can be done. There are some injuries you simply cannot come back from."

Alex swallowed hard and sat back in his seat. He had questions he wanted to ask, but somehow he just couldn't get them out. Forrester's tone had been steady and informative, but the message it carried was anything but. Alex could feel his mortality closing in around him, suddenly becoming less of a concept and more of an inevitability. The realization sat on his chest like a stone.

Rachel was both repulsed and captivated by the story all at the same time. She wasn't sure she wanted to hear more, but she knew she needed to. This was something that would affect the course of her life from here on, not to mention Alex's life, and the life of their unborn child. Holding onto that thought, she pushed her revulsion aside and embraced her morbid curiosity.

"What happened next?"

"Chaos. Mayhem. Seeing such a blatant act of violence play out incited others to action. Some followed Eve Seventeen's lead, grabbing weapons and attacking anything nearby. Others moved to stop them, doing what they could to subdue their siblings. By the end, we lost three more of you, not to mention six support staff. It was..." Another pause from the doctor. The proper words were proving hard to find.

"... horrific," was what he finally settled on, even though it didn't seem sufficient to describe the situation.

Forrester went on. "I went to Penders immediately to convince him to suspend the Project. He wouldn't hear of it. Said it was a minor setback, and he had every confidence that I could fix this little 'bug'. Ten people were dead, and he called it a 'bug! The tenacity of the man. The unmatched ego of him. I wanted to leave right then. But I couldn't. Despite what had happened, I felt a sense of responsibility. I had to do whatever I could for you."

"Oh my God," Rachel breathed. It was all she could get out. She felt numb, hearing what she was hearing. A few days ago, if she heard that, she would have laughed it off, knowing the person her husband is. But in the last few days, she had seen and done things she never imagined she could, and made discoveries about their lives that would have been inconceivable before. Now, she wasn't sure what to believe.

She turned toward Alex to offer him what comfort she could, but stopped cold at the sight of him. His face was white as a cloud, his eyes wide and glassy and simply staring into the void. He lost himself in his own mind, his own thoughts, possibly his own horrific recollections. She wanted to reach out and take his hand, but at that moment, she didn't dare. As much as she felt for the man she loved, as much as she wanted to offer him comfort, she also realized she was in the grips of a new feeling. A feeling she never had before with Alex.

Fear. For the first time, she was afraid of her husband.

A few seconds of nerve-shattering silence went by before Alex finally spoke. "Did I kill anyone that day?"

The question hung in the stale air of the car. Forrester averted his eyes from Rachel's before finally answering. "Not that day, no."

Alex's mind wandered back to the flash of memory he'd had at Babcock's, the image of him and the man he now knew as Adam standing amidst a pile of gore and broken bodies. He shuddered slightly at the memory, then went on.

"Did I kill anyone, Dr. Forrester?"

Forrester hung his head, his gaze falling to the floor. Tears were now streaming down both cheeks, gathering at his chin before dropping off in tiny crystalline forms that shattered on the edge of the steering wheel. He remained silent.

Alex did not. "Dr. Forrester, did I kill anyone?"

"Alex," the scientist muttered, "you must understand the circumstances. It wasn't you there that day. Not the man you are now. That was someone else. Someone who had never learned compassion. Caring. Friendship. Love. Things were..."

"Answer the damned question!" Alex suddenly exploded, any remaining sense of composure a casualty of his outburst.

Rachel and Rick both jumped in surprise at Alex's sudden explosive anger. Rachel shrank back into the seat as far as she could, the fear she had acknowledged for her husband just a moment ago suddenly bursting inside her. Rick's hand went to the gun in his belt, not knowing if he could actually shoot Alex if it came down to that. But he wanted to be prepared, regardless.

Dr. Forrester finally, with great effort, lifted his head to meet the eyes of the man who was, in some twisted way, his son. His eyes were red and rimmed with tears, some of which tumbled down his cheeks. When he spoke, it wasn't in the confident voice of the man of science but the soft whimper of a defeated man who had seen all his dreams crumble to dust before him.

"Yes, you did. You killed more than I care to count. With your bare hands, you tore into them savagely, ripping them and pummeling mercilessly until they were no longer recognizable as human beings. You did it with the intensity of an animal on a kill, but with the zeal only humans take in killing. Some might say you were simply defending yourself, that they were trying to do the same to you, but the look in your eye was unmistakable: you enjoyed it. The blood. The shattered bones. And you loathed me for putting an end to it. If you could continue, you would have gleefully murdered everyone in that room; Penders, Harriman, me, all of us. You would have continued killing until someone found a way to stop you. You had become a horrible machine, an engine of destruction the likes of which I hope to never see again as long as I live. And, God help me, I created you."

Forrester stopped and went silent, an oppressive quiet once again falling over them. Alex stared forward, his eyes were vacant and unfocused. Rachel reached out and gently touched his hand.

Alex's movement was quick and definitive as he snatched her wrist and snapped his head around toward her. His eyes were no longer vacant, but filled with anger and fear as he squeezed her wrist. Without warning, he pushed her hard away from him, into the soft leather seat behind her. Unconsciously, she shrank back from him, grabbing her wrist where he had just held her.

The fear on his wife's face softened Alex's expression, anger giving way to fear. "Don't touch me! If you know what's good for you, you'll get as far away from me as you can!"

He pushed the door open, stumbling out of the car and onto the road. Picking himself up and, without so much as a glance behind him, he ran across the road and disappeared into the woods on the other side. As Rachel started after him, someone gently but firmly placed a hand on her arm to stop her.

"Let him go," Rick said.

"Are you crazy? I can't let him run around like that! Did you see the look in his eyes? He might hurt himself! Or, worse, someone else!" She pushed Rick's hand free, got out of the car, and began crossing the street but was stopped by a sudden line of traffic. She heard Rick's door as he got out of the car.

"Rachel," he said, his voice soft and pleading, "he needs to think this through by himself for a while. To process everything. It's a lot to absorb. He needs some time."

She turned to him, her eyes alight with green fire. "What do you know about him? After all those years of pretending to be his friend, don't you dare tell me what he needs!"

"I understand what you're worried about," Rick continued, heedless of her angry condemnation of him. "You don't need to be. Dr. Forrester is right, he isn't the same person now that he was then. That person died years ago. The Alex you know, the Alex you love, is the only Alex there is. I know it. Deep down, you know it too. Now he needs to figure it out for himself, and he needs some time to do that."

"How do you know?" Rachel snapped, her tone filled with equal amounts of anger, sarcasm, and venom.

"Because," Rick replied calmly, "whether or not you want to admit it, I helped create that Alex. Just like you did."

She whipped around to face him. "Excuse me?"

"When they found Alex, his mind was almost a blank slate. That was Dr. Forrester's doing, an attempt to reset him and forget all the horrible things he was a part of. That was the day *that* Alex, the one Dr. Forrester just described, died. His memories of all those horrors, the dark impulses that went with them, were wiped away. He was given a clean slate. Everything he is today, the Alex we know, started that day. He was reborn, given an opportunity most people never get; the chance to literally forget your past sins and become someone new. All the experiences he's had, the people who have influenced him, have made him a new man. And that new man is all that exists today. He'll figure that out soon enough. He just needs time. But he'll remember the people who loved him, and he'll be back." Rick finished with a weak smile. It seemed awkward, but elicited the same from Rachel.

"Are you sure about this?" she asked, staring into the dark woods on the other side of the road.

"I am," Rick replied.

"You really do care about him, don't you?" she said, her voice softening.

He nodded. "It started out as a job, but he has a way of growing on you."

"Yeah," she replied, "he does." She turned to face him, the smile melting from her face. "I'm sorry about before. About doubting your motives."

"Well, I *did* hold you hostage at gunpoint," Rick replied. "That sours most relationships."

Rachel turned back and looked out across the road once again, to the spot where Alex had disappeared into the woods. "Do you think we'll make it through this?"

"I have no idea," Rick answered honestly. "But I do know we're going to give it our damnedest try."

She reached out and squeezed his hand. "Thank you."

"For what?"

"For being here. After listening to Dr. Forrester talk about those horrible things and the people like Penders, I think I understand the risk you're taking for us. The danger you're in. I just want you to know that I appreciate it. So will Alex, in time."

"I hope so. I really do," Rick replied, turning his gaze to the woods.

Together, they stood in silence, waiting for Alex to come back to them.

46

Alex ran as fast as he could, crashing through branches, ignoring the slashing cuts they inflicted on him. He had to run, to get as far away as he could. Faster and faster, running from the demons that snapped at his heels as he went. The demons from his past that were coming back to devour him. He ran faster with every step, but in his heart knew there was no way to escape these demons. No matter how fast or far he ran, they would always be with him. They were a part of him now and there was no escaping them.

He burst into a small clearing, his foot catching on a root as he did. He tumbled to the ground hard, dead leaves and dirt kicking up around him as he fell. An intense pain exploded in his shoulder and ran through him like lightning, setting nerves on fire through his arm and along his spine. He stopped rolling and came to a rest in the middle of the clearing, face down in a patch of dew-soaked moss. He rolled over slowly, trying not to aggravate his injured shoulder, but the worst of it had passed already. Only a dull ache persisted, throbbing in his shoulder and neck. He relished the pain like it was a penance for his sins, even though he couldn't begin to make up for the atrocities he committed. He simply laid there on the ground while staring up at the deep blue fall sky that shone through a thick canopy of brightly colored leaves, and let the pain run its course.

The throbbing pain faded to nothing more than a dull ache, not nearly enough to be any sort of atonement any longer. Still, he didn't move. He remained where he was, staring up at the small patch of blue sky overhead, shrouded by a burst of red, gold, yellow, and orange. It was truly beautiful and for a moment he felt guilty appreciating it. The faces of those who died at the Eden Project, particularly those who died at his hands, flashed through his mind. Guilt gripped his chest with a cold iron fist. They would never be able to appreciate beauty like he was seeing now. The frigid grip on his heart suddenly became a jolt of energy that ran through his nervous system before coming to rest as a sharp pain at the base of his skull. He winced at the pain, but again did nothing to ease it. It was his punishment, divine retribution. If God even recognized him. After all, it wasn't like he was one of His creations. He was nothing more than an aberration, a sty in the eye of God.

There was a sudden rustling in the brush just ahead of where he lay, in the opposite direction from where he had run from Rachel and the others. Startled, he sat up quickly and scanned the woods, pain erupting once again in his skull. His fight-or-flight instincts kicked in and he once again ignored the pain, scanning the woods for the source of the rustling.

In a last burst of dry, rustling leaves, a fox jumped into the clearing. The animal stopped suddenly, its dash through the woods interrupted by the sudden appearance of a human in its habitat. It simply stood and stared at Alex with large brown eyes. Unblinking, unmoving, unwavering.

It took a moment of staring down the fox before Alex noticed something dangling from its jaws. A chipmunk hung limp and unmoving, its eyes dark and vacant. The fox's breakfast, no doubt. That was the harsh reality of the food chain, Alex mused to himself. The fight for life. Struggling for survival, the chipmunk fights for its life. To survive, the fox fights to kill and eat the chipmunk. Two opposing needs, and only one would come out on top. Today it had been the fox. The larger animal gets to live another day, thanks to the sacrifice of the chipmunk. Tomorrow, the fox may fail in catching his prey. It wasn't fair, it's just the way things are in the animal kingdom. Your survival so often depends on the demise of something else. Not just with animals, either. Eventually, life devours us all, consuming us with no regard for any accomplishments or station a person may have attained in their life. Fate is cruel and life is fleeting, gone in the blink of an eye. Except with humans, fate can exercise a special brand of cruelty. Fate can rob us of everything we hold dear, making us suffer before finally delivering death to us.

That was the worst of it, Alex thought. Having the life he loved ripped away from him. Much like the chipmunk had its life torn from it, Alex's life was being ripped apart by the wolves that surrounded him. Adam. Robert Penders. Burke Darnell. All the wolves that conspired to break him. They devoured him while also leaving him whole, aware of what they had done to him. Leaving him broken and helpless, yet alive and aware. Across the animal kingdom, it was a practice engaged in by only one animal, only perpetrated by the vilest creatures on the food chain. The practice is intentional cruelty, and only humans engage in it. Humans are the only animals who want their prey to suffer. Who *crave* their suffering. Much like the fox would feed on the flesh of the chipmunk to sustain itself, humans feed off the suffering of their prey to sustain and nourish them.

Alex stared into the eyes of the fox, thinking about everything that had happened to him and the people he cared about over the last few days. Rachel's life had been completely demolished, forced to flee her home after being brutalized by an unknown assailant with then-unknown motivations. Chased and hunted simply because she had fallen in love with the wrong man. Babcock had intervened and tried to help them, when he had no reason to, and now was lying in a hospital bed with death looming over him. Whether he was a police officer or not, he had gone above and beyond for Alex and Rachel and definitely deserved a much better fate than what he had suffered. Dr. Carlton had done much the same, going against the people she worked for to give Rachel and him the opportunity to get some answers they had been looking for and to prepare them for the fight ahead. She died trying to help them, giving up her life so they might salvage theirs. Muck like Dr. Carlton, Rick and Dr. Forrester were not without blame in this whole thing, but they were still here and risking their own lives for Rachel and him.

Slowly, a sense of understanding filled him. He wasn't the monster Forrester had painted him to be. Whoever that person had been, he died when Alex Carter was born. And in that moment, Alex would lay any memory of him, any regrets or insecurities, to rest once and for all. All that remained now, all that mattered now, was the man he was today.

The fox locked eyes with Alex for another moment, its rich brown eyes penetrating deep into his as if it were trying to see his soul to gain some insight into the odd creature it had encountered. Alex smiled at that. If the fox could see into his soul, it would be witness to a remarkable transformation as light overtook darkness and hope displaced despair. A new animal being born of the old one. Suddenly, as if baffled by this strange and soundless transformation in Alex, the fox bolted off in search of a better place to enjoy its breakfast.

Alex sat still for a moment after the fox vanished. The sun was finding its way through the canopy of branches above and was slowly beginning to drive out the chill in him. The chill that had held him since the first dream took hold and shook his life. As the sunlight touched him, it expelled all darkness from within him. Driving out despair and hopelessness. For the first time in days, he felt as if he could go on. As if he had purpose. As if there were actually hope.

Closing his eyes, he smiled and sat for a while longer in the morning sun's warmth.

Rachel shifted uncomfortably on the hood of the car, unable to find a comfortable position. She couldn't find any genuine comfort since she and Alex were attacked in their home the previous night. Between the bruises and scrapes of her run-in with Adam, sleeping on that awful couch in Alex's office and then being forced to sit unmoving at gunpoint, all coupled with the normal discomfort that comes with pregnancy, she was starting to think she would never be comfortable again.

Adam. Something about the name had set off an alarm in her head after Dr. Forrester had attached it to the stranger who attacked them. She had heard it or seen it recently, but with everything that had gone on, she hadn't had the opportunity to process where. All she knew was it made her skin crawl and her belly cold whenever she heard it.

Suddenly, it hit her. The thumb drive Dr. Carlton had left for Alex. That was where she had seen it. Last night, just before Adam attacked. There was a file titled 'Adam 1-50'. At the time she hadn't given it much thought, but as she sifted through what Dr. Forrester had told them, things clicked into place. But there were still some gaps, she needed more information. She still had the thumb drive on her, but without a computer, she was dead in the water. Unless there was another source of information close at hand, a source even more reliable than the data on that drive.

Dr. Forrester sat still in the driver's seat of the car. He had barely moved since Alex had run off into the woods, simply staring vacantly into the distance with empty eyes. She could almost see him reliving his past failures, lost in a sea of reverie. She hesitated for a moment to disturb him, especially to dig deeper into a past he seemed so desperate to escape, but she had to know what was happening with her husband. What was happening with her family.

Pulling open the passenger's side door, she sat down next to him. She left the door open to allow in the cool fall breeze and breathed deeply of the sweet, moist air that followed the storm of the previous night. Dr. Forrester remained silent and still.

"Dr. Forrester?" she said, low and gently, easing into the conversation. She didn't want him to think he was being attacked or interrogated, but she also hoped he wouldn't ignore her entirely. "Is it okay if I ask you a few questions?"

"About your husband?" he replied, his eyes never moving from the road ahead.

"Among other things," she answered.

He signed a deeply pained sigh, as if his soul itself hurt, and turned to her. "Very well. You should know the whole truth, anyway. Ask."

"The story you told before, about the genetic engineering, is that true?"

"If you knew anything about me, you wouldn't be asking that question. Yes, it's true. I created life through science. A modern-day Dr. Frankenstein, as Adam once called me. I suppose the reference isn't entirely without merit. My creations have certainly come back to haunt me."

Rachel continued quickly to keep him from slipping back into his memories. "What's the connection between Alex and Adam?"

Forrester sighed again as another piece of his soul died. He removed his glasses and rubbed the bridge of his nose in that way that had become so familiar. Each question was obviously a source of immense anguish for him, the corresponding memories painful and tragic. But he continued.

"A side effect of the experiment, one that Robert Penders thought he could exploit. When the Adams and Eves were brought to physical maturity..."

"Adams and Eves?" Rachel interrupted. "There was a file on Dr. Carlton's thumb drive. Two, in fact. One titled Adam 1-50 and another Eve 1-50."

"That would be accurate," Forrester replied. "Those were my creations, my children, named after the biblical first man and woman. They were named such because they were to be the first of a new age of civilization, a new era for humanity. The future of this world." He paused then, his expression darkening. "Unfortunately, nature has a way of protecting its patents."

"I'm sorry," Rachel replied quizzically. "I don't understand. What happened?"

"Everything you heard in the story I told earlier. After being released from gestation, the Alpha group, the test subjects, underwent a rigorous training program under the guidance of Penders. I tried to warn him they weren't ready for anything that intensive yet, but he pushed forward. He had investors to worry about and a timetable to follow, he said. I believe it was that program, the violence of it being pushed on minds that unprepared, that made them all snap." Forrester paused, once again staring down the empty road in front of him. His eyes were unfocused, his mind once more lost to memory.

"Snap?" Rachel repeated, the word sounding no less ominous coming from her.

A weighty sigh escaped the scientist. "A few weeks into the program, some of them started showing signs of stress from the intensity of their training. Remember, physically they had the bodies of post-pubescent teens, but inside they were still little more than children. Children who had been force-fed information while in the 'womb' and were now being indoctrinated to become the ultimate soldiers and killers. It was bound to have a detrimental effect on them."

Rachel interrupted again before he could continue. "Hold on, wait a minute. Still children? Force-fed information in the womb? Released from gestation? I'm afraid I don't understand, Doctor."

"No, of course you don't. I never did adequately explain that amidst the emotional upheaval of earlier, did I?" He stopped to clear his throat and gather his thoughts, his demeanor suddenly shifting from grieving 'father' back to scientist. "Adam, and your husband, are human engineered genetic constructs of my design. They were not born and bred in the natural way, but rather by science. I carefully designed and developed each strand of DNA, cultivated and examined each cell at every step of the process. In the beginning, their development was the stuff of miracles that all scientists hope for. To see your hypothesis and research coming to fruition. I'm convinced that if I had been able to observe my timeline, things would have been markedly different. But Penders wanted viable subjects in a much shorter time. I had no option but to accelerate their development."

An increasingly familiar icy fist grabbed Rachel's stomach and squeezed. "Accelerate their development?"

"Their aging, yes. As well as the information being delivered to them in vitro. Although each one of them was no more than a month old when they were released from their gestation, they had the physical characteristics and mental acumen of an above average fourteen- to sixteen-year-old." He paused, again rubbing the bridge of his nose. "Children in adult bodies."

"You mean that Alex and Adam and all the others were..." She choked on the last word, unable to complete the thought.

Dr. Forrester picked it up for her. "I mean, they were all children. Artificially conceived, gestated, and educated. And all no more than a month old, pushed into adulthood before their time."

Rachel was frozen. Speechless. There was so much she wanted to say, so many questions she wanted to ask, but the words were lost in the storm in her brain. After a minute of recuperating, she was able to choke out a few words.

"But Alex just turned thirty. We just celebrated his birthday. There was a party and everything. A cake...." She trailed off, slumping back into the soft leather of the passenger's seat.

"What you celebrated," Dr. Forrester replied flatly, "was Alex's fourteenth birthday. Give or take."

"Fourteen?" She wanted to say more, but this new information paralyzed her brain once again, locking it up with an overload of emotion that she couldn't process.

"I don't know what effect this will have on your child," Dr. Forrester stated.

Rachel looked down to where she was absently rubbing her stomach. She tried to envision the tiny life she was carrying inside her, but suddenly found she couldn't. It was the first time she could remember since discovering she was pregnant that she hadn't been able to envision the baby. As if in response to her fear and doubt, a familiar warm, soft feeling cascaded over her again. It was slight, but it was there. It brought with it a very slight feeling of hope, and right now that just might be enough.

Feeling calmer, she looked over at Forrester to continue the conversation, but caught sight of Rick approaching the car. With a quick nod to the woods on the other side of the road, he said, "The prodigal son is returning."

They all turned to see a figure emerging from the woods. A man, walking tall and proud and practically glowing in the emerging morning sunlight. This figure was nothing like the person who had run off into the woods earlier. The warmth in Rachel's belly intensified, reaffirming what she was thinking. Gently, she rubbed her belly where the warmth originated. The glow inside her intensified as Alex approached.

Early morning commuter traffic had picked up, and Alex had to weave his way through a few cars that sped past them. Rachel noticed a difference in how he moved, a renewed sense of energy in him. A new drive and purpose.

"You look better," Rick stated as Alex rejoined them on the side of the road. "Not a tremendous feat, though. You looked like shit before."

"I feel better," Alex replied, ignoring the jab. "You have no idea how much better I feel."

Turning to Rachel, his chin dropping a bit to meet her eyes, Alex simply stated, "I'm sorry."

Rachel stood for a moment, taking in the man before her. She was right; he was different. She wasn't certain exactly what it was. His posture was upright and confident, not slouched as if carrying some heavy existential burden. His eyes seemed to shine a brighter blue. But what she noticed most of all was the almost imperceptibly serene smile he wore. The smile that, until a few days ago, had been a permanent fixture on his beautiful face. The smile that drew people to him, had drawn her to him. It was that smile that settled her and made her feel like everything could be alright again.

She threw her arms around him and hugged him to her tightly, tears gathering in her eyes. "Don't be sorry. Never be sorry for being who you are. I love you, no matter where you came from or what kind of past you've had. All that matters is the Alex Carter standing here with me right now. You are the man I love, and nothing will ever change that."

He pulled her in closer to him, feeling her comforting warmth. "I love you, too. It took a weird encounter with a fox in the woods to realize it, but I know now anything that happened in the past is just that, the past. It doesn't change who I am now. The person Dr. Forrester talked about is long gone. All that matters now is the life we've built together, and preserving that." He cupped her chin in his hand and raised her face to his. "And we will preserve that, no matter what it takes." Leaning forward, he kissed her lightly, lingering for a moment.

"I hate to be a bother here," Dr. Forrester interrupted, "but now that Alex is in a better place and we've put some of the drama behind us, I think we should move along. The world seems to be waking up. It's only a matter of time before one of Penders' people or a member of the local constabulary drives by. We really should be gone before that happens."

"A very good point," Rick agreed, "but to where?"

"To the one person who may be able to help us," Alex replied. Then, with a bit of trepidation in his voice, said, "If I can convince her to trust us."

"Where are we going?" Forrester asked, sliding back into the driver's seat.

"The William Harris Funeral Home," Alex answered as he opened the back door. "There's someone there who may be the only friend we have left."

They piled into the car once again and Dr. Forrester pulled back onto the road, making a U-turn and heading back into Pine Haven. "Who is there at a funeral home who could be helpful to us?" he asked.

"Dr. Celeste Tanner. She's a forensic specialist with the police," Alex replied. Then added tentatively, "And she's a friend of Ernie Babcock."

"The cop?"" Rick exclaimed, his voice uncharacteristically high pitched. "She's a friend of the cop you're suspected of shooting. Why would she help us?"

"I don't know that she will," Alex replied. "This may be a huge mistake. But I don't see a lot of other options for us. Plus, she could be a big help when I go to the hospital for Ernie."

As impossible as it seemed, Rick's voice jumped up another octave. "You're still going to try to get to him in the hospital? That's insane. Absolutely insane."

"If I don't, he'll die. I can't let that happen, not after everything he did for us. He believed me when any other cop would have taken the easy way out and thrown me in jail after Dr. Carlton's death. I'm the reason he's in the hospital in the first place. I have to do this."

Rachel reached over and took Alex's hand, smiling a slight smile. "I understand."

Rick let out an exasperated sigh and slammed his head hard against his seat like a toddler having a tantrum. "I don't! We're going to have enough trouble getting away from the Eden Project as it is, now you want us to walk right into the lion's den? We're serving ourselves up for them! And for what? How do we know you can actually do anything for this guy?"

"He can," Dr. Forrester interjected.

"How do you know that?" Rick yelled, trying desperately to find an outlet for his frustration. "What if all we accomplish when we walk in there is we get ourselves captured by the Project? Or worse? There are a lot of cops out there right now who would love a shot at the guy who put their lieutenant in the hospital. I mean that *literally*. And as far as they're concerned, Alex is that guy! We should get as far away from here as fast as we can!"

"We will," Alex replied. "But not until Babcock is out of danger."

"Alex, look..."

Alex cut Rick off with a wave of his hand. "I'm sorry, but that's just the way it is. You have a choice; you can leave now and maybe salvage something of a life for yourself, or you can stay and we can face this together like we always have. The choice is yours."

A deep scowl fell over Rick's face. "Damn it, you know what I'm going to say. Why even give me the choice?"

"Torture," Alex replied, his voice thick with sarcasm.

Rick's scowl became an uneasy grin. "Twisting the knife?"

"Hard and fast," Alex replied, returning the smile.

Rachel couldn't help but grin herself at the back and forth between her husband and the man who had been, until just yesterday, his best friend. It was good to see them bantering again. Maybe they could salvage this relationship, after all.

If they survived, that is.

47

Dr. Celeste Tanner wasn't sure what was becoming of the small town she had chosen to live in. When she left Atlanta fifteen years ago, she thought she was escaping what she thought of as 'big city problems'; crime, poverty, homelessness, a basic lack of civility and empathy toward others. That was why she had come to Pine Haven. A small, quiet town in a small, quiet state.

All that had changed. In the last few days, she had seen more death and violence than in the entire twelve years she had been the state's Chief Medical Examiner, and now it had hit close to home for her. Ernie Babcock, her long-time contact with the Pine Haven Police Department, as well as her close friend, was lying close to death in the hospital. She had spent most of the night at the hospital with his wife and children, offering what advice she could as a doctor and whatever comfort as a friend. There had been no change in Ernie's condition throughout the night, so when the sun started coming up that morning, she decided she was better off in her office distracted by work than sitting helplessly in his room.

When she arrived at her makeshift office in the basement of the Willam Harris Funeral Home, she found a fresh case on her desk. Like all the others this past week, this one was personal, a long-time resident of Pine Haven. Jackie Phillips, who had graduated Pine Haven High School just a few years earlier and had taken a job at the Bagel Stable, a job she insisted was temporary until she could get herself to New York or Los Angeles and carve out her niche as an actress. She certainly had the looks for it; blond, tall, excessively skinny and with a little wiggle in her walk that could turn any man's head. Jackie Phillips was only missing one thing in her quest for fame: Talent. Since leaving high school she had gone to New York once and Los Angeles twice in bids to break into the business, each time returning to Pine Haven and resuming her job at the Bagel Stable, waiting for her next big chance.

Now that chance would never come. Instead of the glamourous life she was looking for, Jackie had earned distinction another way; she had become a statistic. Just another number added to hundreds of thousands of others that make up the annual statistics on violent crime. No past, no history, no story; just a name and a number. A momentary blip on some number crunchers computer screen and then Jackie Phillips, aspiring actress and superstar server, would vanish forever. That seemed tragic and woefully inadequate to Celeste, but she had learned in her years as a medical examiner that was the way of things. Her job was to finish Jackie's case file quickly and efficiently and make room for the next statistic. The next Jackie Phillips. That was the part of the job she struggled with the most. She had tried to change the status quo when she arrived in Pine Haven, given the overall lack of violent crime cases crossing her desk, but the bureaucracy remained the same. Do your job, make your reports, and step aside. She had discovered it had nothing to do with the number of cases; it had more to do with how quickly those cases were closed. As disheartened as she was by that, she had had no luck in changing it. For her part tonight, she would shed a tear for Jackie Phillips and her lost future, as she did for all the poor souls unfortunate enough to end up on her table. It wasn't much, but it was something she could do to bring some meaning to their deaths.

With a heavy sigh, she collected her coffee mug and Jackie's file and left her small makeshift office for the embalming room that doubled as an autopsy room when needed. The room had been used entirely too much lately, both for its intended purpose and for hers. Death was becoming too friendly with Pine Haven.

And now, Ernie became entangled in it, whatever 'it' was. Why couldn't he have just told her what this was all about before going and getting himself shot? Maybe if she'd had more information she might have been able to help more, to better prepare him for what was coming. Maybe he wouldn't be lying in a hospital bed right now, waiting to die.

A noise down the hall, a sound like footsteps, broke her train of thought. It couldn't be, this early in the day she was the only one in the building. Stanley's staff wouldn't be in for another hour yet, and Stanley himself wouldn't be sufficiently pickled enough to face the day at least until noon. Still, she stopped and listened intently in the direction she thought the noise had come. Standing perfectly still, unmoving, she strained to hear another noise.

Nothing. She must have been imagining it, thinking about the death and oddness she'd encountered in the last few days. Her mind playing tricks on her. She cursed herself for being ridiculous and entered the embalming room.

Then she heard it again. Footsteps, but with a muffled scraping sound, as if someone were stepping lightly in an effort not to be heard. Not only was she not alone, whoever was in the building with her was trying very hard not to let her know they were there. Her stomach tightened and her heart raced as she placed her coffee mug and Jackie's file on the autopsy table and exchanged them for a scalpel. It wasn't a big blade, but it was extremely sharp and it might be enough to turn the tide on an attacker. Unless he was significantly bigger than her. Or better armed. Her mind raced with those possibilities as she heard the muffled footsteps again, closer this time. It didn't matter if she was at a disadvantage now, whoever was out there was getting closer. Steeling her entire five-foot tall frame, she gripped the scalpel tightly in her hand and peered out into the hallway.

A current of cool air wafted past her and she shivered slightly. Feeling a draft down here was unusual since the basement was sealed practically airtight to prevent unsavory odors from wafting upward into the funeral parlor or out onto the grounds. Celeste couldn't remember a time when she felt a draft in the basement that wasn't because of a door opening and disrupting the air seal, despite the building's age and imperfect sealing. Someone had opened one of the two doors that accessed the basement rooms. Either the door at the far end of the hall that opened to the parking lot or the door at the top of the stairs entering the public area of the funeral parlor. She had a line of sight to the bottom of the stairs that descended from the first floor and couldn't see any movement in that direction. It must have been the outside door. But that door was locked, she was certain of it. She had locked it herself before leaving last night, and she had been the last person to leave the building. The only other person with a key to that door would be Stanley, and even when he could shake off a drunk, he never entered through that door. The basement both frightened and depressed him, and he always entered through the lavish front door of the building when he came to work.

Another option popped into her head and chilled her spine; what if her mysterious company didn't require a key? She could be caught in the middle of a break-in, maybe body snatchers coming in search of fresh corpses for black market organ trade. It was unlikely, things like that didn't happen in Pine Haven. But then again, a lot of what didn't happen in Pine Haven had happened in the last few days and she wasn't about to discount any possibilities, no matter how ridiculous they might seem.

She was about to call out, thinking that if it were thieves they may be driven out by the fact that there was someone else in the building, but paused as a new scenario flashed into her mind. The tiny cylinder she had removed from Dr. Carlton's arm was still in her office, encased in a glass evidence vial. While she hadn't yet figured out what it was, it was possible someone else knew all about it. Someone who wanted it back and was desperate enough to break into a morgue in the early dawn to retrieve it.

She heard the light, scraping footfalls again and reached for her phone in her pocket. All she found was an empty pocket as she realized she had left her phone on her desk in her office. She thought about turning back and trying to reach it, but the echo of the empty halls made it nearly impossible to pin down where the footsteps were coming from. Whoever was down there with her could be between her and her office, she couldn't take the chance. Odds were against her making it up the stairs to the funeral parlor without being seen, either.

As slowly and quietly as she could, she slipped back into the embalming room through the double stainless-steel doors. Outside in the hallway, the footsteps grew louder with each step. Celeste thought the steps sounded bolder, more confident, as they moved in her direction. Whoever was out there knew she was here, possibly knew where she was, and was coming for her. Courage and resolve were quickly dissolving, replaced by fear. She scanned the room for some place, anyplace, she could hide. Or for a better weapon she could use. There were the two small equipment carts that had the tools she would need for Jackie Phillips' autopsy. A small desk in the corner with a laptop and a few file folders. Jackie's body, covered with a sheet and lying on one of the embalming tables. She had no place to hide and no route for escape, and the most lethal weapon in the room was the scalpel in her hand. She was out of options, and now she was out of time.

Just outside the stainless-steel double doors, the footsteps came to a halt. She gripped the scalpel tightly in her fist and strained to hear any noise on the other side of the door. There was nothing but an all-encompassing silence. Her heart pounded incessantly in her chest, beats coming so hard and fast they were nearly indistinguishable from one another, each pounding through her head like the frantic beating of a bass drum. Her body went numb as adrenaline flooded her system, preparing her to fight whatever was coming after her.

Suddenly, as the left door swung open, her heart froze completely. Fear kept her firmly in place, freezing her to the spot as her body struggled between wanting to rush forward and slash wildly with the scalpel in a desperate attempt to save herself and being transfixed by the door swinging open suddenly before her. It seemed to open in slow motion, each inch feeling like a mile and each second feeling like an eternity, before someone opened it wide.

A figure stood in the doorway, looming over her. The bright light of the hallway assailed her eyes, the person in front of her nothing more than a shadow. It was a man, that much she could tell from his poise and stature, but nothing else. Gripping the scalpel even tighter, she took a step backward into the room. As she bumped against it, the cold metal of the embalming table melted into her, blocking her retreat. Stepping into the room, the figure closed the door behind him. The light from the hallway withered away and the shadow before her coalesced into a recognizable human form. The form of someone she knew.

Alex Carter stepped completely into the room as the door finished closing behind him. "Dr. Tanner, are you all right? I've been looking all over for you!"

Celeste was still in shock, still in the grip of fear, as her mind processed and reacted to Alex's presence. The adrenaline high dropped, feeling returning to her extremities, and her heart rate dropped with the presence of a familiar face. The arm holding the scalpel fell to her side, until a new fear burst from the back of her mind. Ernie, lying near death in the hospital. Shot by an unknown assailant. At Alex Carter's house. And Alex had fled the scene, leaving nothing but questions and uncertainties behind. And now he was here, where he had been earlier with Ernie. Where he had learned about the small device that had been removed from Dr. Simone Carlton's body.

Her mind flashed again to the small vial in the desk behind her. Was that why he was here? Why Ernie had been shot? Was Alex here now to cover up that dangling end? The scalpel raised again to a defensive position as her hand closed around it tightly once more. Slowly, she took a small step toward the desk, closing the gap between it and her.

She thrust the scalpel in his direction, backing up toward the desk again as she did. "What are you doing here? What do you want?"

Alex stopped, his face a mask of shock and confusion. Putting up his hands in a defensive gesture, he replied, "Dr. Tanner, I get why you might not trust me right now. Please believe me, I had nothing to do with what happened to Lieutenant Babcock. In fact. I'm here because I'm trying to help him."

"How can you help him?" she asked, the scalpel still held in her outstretched arm between them. "What did you have to do with all of this?"

Alex kept his hands firmly in front of him, palms facing her. "I know how this looks. I was at the center of two crime scenes in the last few days. Babcock was shot in my house. He ended up there because he was helping me, and he got caught up in something so much bigger than he ever could have expected. But I didn't hurt him. He was hurt by... someone else."

"Who?" Dr. Tanner shot back.

"That's a bit more complicated. I'm happy to discuss it at length with you, but right now, we don't have time." Keeping his hands in front of him, he took a tentative step in her direction. "I think I can help Lieutenant Babcock. Ernie. I can help Ernie. But I need your help to do that."

Celeste's mind was racing. There was no reason to trust the man standing in front of her. In fact, there was every reason not to trust him. But somehow, even with every bit of evidence screaming to the contrary, her gut was telling her Alex was telling the truth. She wasn't sure why she felt that was; it was almost like the man projected an aura of trustworthiness, a genuine air of goodness and righteousness. For whatever reason, she instinctively felt she could trust him.

She dropped her arm, placing the scalpel on the desk behind her. "Alex, what are you doing here? You know the police are looking for you? And they're not exactly thrilled with you. Hell, I'm an officer of the law myself. I should take you into custody right now."

"I understand that. But if you do that, I won't be able to help Ernie." He lowered his hands, but still kept them firmly by his side and visible to Dr. Tanner. "We need your help."

She eyes him suspiciously. "Who's 'we'?"

"Rachel," he answered, his eyes scanning the walls and ceiling of the room. "Dr. Tanner, can we speak here? Safely?"

"As far as I know," she answered, a bit unnerved by his suspicions.

"Good," he replied, retreating through the steel door. "Wait here for a minute. I'll be right back." He turned to leave, but hesitated. Glancing back over his shoulder, he added, "And Dr. Tanner? Thank you for believing me."

With that, he disappeared back into the hall and Celeste collapsed into the chair behind the desk with a heavy sigh. "I hope you know what you're doing, Celeste," she said out loud to herself. She was usually driven by facts and evidence. Things she could examine and verify. Irrefutable. Undoubtable. Science had ruled her worldview for as long as she could remember. As had common sense. Right now, it felt to her as if common sense had abandoned her. Given the facts of recent events, she had no reason to trust Alex Carter. Everything she had seen, heard and examined since hearing his name led her rational mind to believe that, even if he wasn't directly responsible for the death of Dr. Simone Carlton and the near fatal shooting of Lieutenant Ernest Babcock, he was certainly involved. She should call the

Pine Haven Police Department right now and have him arrested. But she wasn't. Something inside her, some instinct, was telling her she was right about Alex. That he was trustworthy. She had never been one to trust her instincts, her gut, over scientifically verifiable data, but in this instance it just felt right to do so.

There was also her scientific curiosity to consider. Ever since performing the autopsy of Dr. Carlton, she had been consumed with questions. Question that Alex could answer, or at least provide a path to answers for her. She would help him help Ernie, but in exchange she wanted to know everything he knew about the mysteries she had recently discovered. Starting with the tiny metal piece removed from Dr. Carlton.

She closed her eyes and relaxed the muscles in her neck and shoulders, letting her head flop over the back of the chair. "What have you gotten yourself into this time, Celeste?"

Her only response was a silence as quiet as death.

Alex returned a few minutes later, accompanied by a red-headed woman who could only be Rachel, and two other men.

Ushering them inside, he made quick introductions. "Dr. Celeste Tanner, this is my wife, Rachel," he said, indicating the woman standing next to him.

"A pleasure to meet you, Dr. Tanner," Rachel said, holding out her hand to Celeste.

She took the woman's hand firmly. "Please, call me Celeste." Rachel nodded slightly, a kind but weary smile on her face.

Alex introduced the younger of the two men. "This is Rick Banning. He's... complicated."

Rick didn't offer a hand, instead simply smiled and nodded at her.

"And this," Alex said, gesturing to the distinguished-looking gentleman, "is Dr. Elliot Forrester."

"Not the Elliot Forrester?" Celeste sputtered. "The world-renowned geneticist?"

The gnomic white-haired man with the abnormally thick glasses smiled and nodded gingerly. "Yes, that is me."

Celeste stood, stunned into silence for a moment. When she continued, her voice had gone up a full octave, like a teen girl meeting her boy band crush. "I'm a follower of your work, Doctor. I was in a lecture of yours when I was in medical school. It must have been thirty years ago now. You were speaking about the possibility of cloning human organs for transplant patients that would have a zero chance of rejection, and cultivating human skin for burn victims without the risk of harvesting skin from another part of the body. It was a very controversial lecture for the time, as I recall. People did not treat you kindly."

The Doctor's smile faded slightly at that, but Celeste continued. "However, we now routinely cultivate human tissue for skin grafts. And the science around the cloning of organ tissue has advanced tremendously, almost to the point of human trials." She paused for a moment, taking a breath and getting back her composure. "You predicted that, and more. Despite the pushback from your peers, there were several of us who were certain you would be at the forefront of a revolution in genetic engineering. What happened to you?"

Dr. Forrester glanced sideways at Alex before pulling his gaze back to Celeste. "I pursued my work in the private sector."

Celeste noticed the quick glance at Alex and her eyes narrowed in suspicion. "Does your work have anything to do with what's been happening recently?"

"I think now would be a good time for that explanation I promised," Alex cut in. "Although I have to warn you, a lot of it is pretty unbelievable."

"Seeing who you're with," Celeste replied, nodding toward Dr. Forrester, "I think I'm ready to believe anything."

"Don't count on it," Rick muttered sarcastically.

"What does that mean?" she replied, turning to him.

Alex stepped in again. "Please, bear with us. It's a long and complicated story. To be honest with you, I'm not sure I believe all of it myself."

Dr. Tanner sat still and allowed Alex to speak uninterrupted as he told the story of everything that had happened to them in the last few days, sparing no details. The thumb drive Dr. Carlton had left for them, the Eden Project, Adam, Dr. Forrester and his research and experiments, and the involvement of Robert Penders and PenTech. He selectively omitted the image of the alien spaceship they found on the thumb drive, figuring that may be a bit too much for her to absorb.

"And that's how we ended up here tonight," Alex finished.

An eerie silence hung in the stale air of the morgue, the tension gathering like a thick fog. When Dr. Tanner finally spoke, her voice was only a whisper, her eyes wide and glassy.

"That's... amazing." She turned her wide-eyed gaze on Dr. Forrester. "This is all true? You did all of this?"

Forrester nodded, his eyes falling away from her as he fixated on the tile floor. "Not some of my finer moments," he mumbled.

"Ridiculous!" Dr. Tanner announced, her voice taking on a stern tone. "Yes, some of what happened was tragic. But Dr. Forrester, that wasn't your fault. You are a scientist and you had a theory to prove." She turned to Alex, taking him in at his full measure as she looked him over. "And prove it, you did. Quite successfully."

Dr. Forrester dropped his head like a man in search of penance. "But all those deaths, aren't I responsible for those? Doesn't the blood of those innocents rest with me? If I had waited longer, I was certain I could have isolated the aggressive traits in them and curb their violent tendencies, but Penders was insistent he have them right away..."

Dr. Tanner cut him off sharply. "See? Right there! 'Penders was insistent.' You said it yourself. Given more time, you could have curbed or even eliminated their aggressive tendencies. But Penders kept pushing you. And, based on everything else Alex has told me tonight, those aggressive traits were important to Penders and the Eden Project. There was no way he was going to allow you to complete your research and alter their code for the better. What happened is not your fault, Dr. Forrester. The blame lies with Penders and his greed."

Forrester lifted his chin slightly, his eyes coming up to meet those of the diminutive Medical Examiner. "Thank you," he whispered to her.

"Look," Rick broke in, "I hate to interrupt this therapy session, but that Project we've been talking about? The evil group that we all agree did all those terrible things? They're still out there looking for us, and they are some mean sons of bitches. Would it be possible to put all this new age feelings stuff behind us and focus on a way out of this mess? Please? I promise, you can go back to getting in touch with your inner feelings later."

"And just who the hell are you?" Dr. Tanner snapped, turning sharply to Rick. Her stance changed considerably as her fists planted firmly on her hips and she leaned toward him, her face a scowl.

"Rick Banning," he replied, holding out his hand toward her for a handshake. "Former best friend of our resident genetic construct, former employee slash spy for the Eden Project, and current fugitive from my former employers with no real expectation of living past tomorrow. And you are...?"

Dr. Tanner ignored his outstretched hand. "Are you always this rude?"

"Only when people are trying to kill me," he replied, a sly grin sliding across his face.

"Hmph, with that attitude, I'd think that would be more often than not," Dr. Tanner responded before turning curtly away from Rick and back to Alex and Dr. Forrester. "But I suppose he's right. A rude twit, but right. You said you came here because you needed something from me. What is it?"

"A couple of things, actually," Alex said, refocusing on the task at hand. "First off, do you still have that tiny piece of metal that was removed from Dr. Carlton's body?"

"Right here," Dr. Tanner answered, reaching into the top drawer of the desk and producing the small glass vial that contained the metal cylinder she had taken from Dr. Calton during her autopsy. She handed it to Alex, who gave it to Dr. Forrester.

The moment Dr. Forrester saw the object in the glass tube, his face drained of all color. His eyes went wide, and his breathing slowed to a near halt.

"Do you recognize it?" Alex asked, fear rising as he saw the look of familiarity cross the doctor's face.

Dr. Forrester slowly, almost absently, nodded. "Yes," he gasped, "I recognize this piece."

"What is it?" Rachel chimed in, moving closer to better see what had so completely captivated their attention.

"It's a transport module," Dr. Forrester explained, slipping back into scientist mode, his voice the even monotone of a college lecturer. "It's used to introduce new genetic material into an existing form via a viral medium. The intention behind it was to use it in gene therapy, to introduce a specific DNA requirement, like flu or measles resistance, or to treat a genetic predisposition towards cancer or diabetes. In this case, it appears as if it were used to introduce a degenerative nerve disorder into Dr. Carlton's genetic code, and then again to advance the disorder."

"I recall when she told me about the onset of her disease," Alex said. "But she told me it had manifested in her years ago. Are you saying they gave her the disease and advanced it with that same gadget? How could they manifest the disease initially and then kill her with it years later?"

"The tube," replied Dr. Forrester, "is only meant to be injected once. While inside the host, it can perform a variety of tasks, including secondary releases of any genetic material it may be carrying. It could have easily been injected into her years ago, infected her nervous system, and then remained dormant before being reactivated to perform its secondary function of introducing the second genetic agent. The one that ultimately killed her." He paused, holding the tiny glass cylinder up against the light to examine it. "Quite ingenious, actually."

"To a psychopath," Rick muttered. "How do you know so much about that thing, anyway?"

"Simple," Forrester replied, "I invented it."

"You invented this?" Alex said, bolting upright and leaning in toward the doctor. "You created that? The thing that killed a woman who was only trying to help me recover my life? And you're okay with that?"

"Alex, please calm down." Forrester was still in lecture mode, his tone cold and indifferent. Alex bristled visibly at his neutral tone, but backed away from him. "The uses I envisioned for this device were remarkably different from what the Project had in mind. But the device is only a tool, subject to the whims of the user. Neither it nor its creator are inherently evil."

"Tell that to Dr. Carlton," Rachel said, the quietness of her words a sting to the heart of the scientist.

Rick stepped forward, slapping his hand down hard on the autopsy table. "We're running low on time here, people. We can put the doctor on trial later, but can we please get on with what we came here for?"

"Good point," said Dr. Tanner, happy to move the conversation away from Dr. Forrester and the discussion of the moral implications of his scientific discoveries. "You said there were two reasons you came here, what's the other one?"

"The tough one," Alex replied. "We need your help to get into the hospital. We need to get to Lieutenant Babcock. To Ernie."

Silence filled the stale, odoriferous air of the morgue. Rachel shifted slightly, the scraping of her jeans almost thunderous in the moment. Dr. Tanner lowered her glasses and peered over the top of them at Alex, sitting unmoving.

"You're an idiot," she stated flatly. "You are currently the number one most wanted individual in the state. Right on the heels of a young local woman being murdered, someone shot a decorated and respected police officer in your home. And now you want to just waltz into the hospital, where nearly every cop in town has taken up residence, and head straight for the room of the man they're protecting? Not to mention the other, more shady characters I've seen lurking around the hospital that the police seem to give a very wide berth to. I imagine they're connected to this 'Eden Project' you've talked about. Those do not sound like good people." She paused, placing her glasses on the desk in front of her and rubbing her eyes vigorously. "Alex, this is a bad idea. A very bad idea."

"I know," Alex answered, "and I can't explain to you why I feel so compelled to get to Ernie. I just know that I do. That I can help him."

A look of suspicion darkened Dr. Tanner's already gray eyes. "Even if you could get near him, what can you do for him that his doctors can't? Aside from getting arrested, that is. Or worse."

"I'm not sure," Alex answered honestly. "It's just a feeling. Almost a compulsion. If I can get to him, I know I can help him." He shrugged lightly. "That's all I know. That, and I owe him. He saved my family. We're the reason he's in there. I need to do this for him."

Dr. Tanner held his gaze for a moment before turning to Dr. Forrester. "Why do I feel you have more to do with this than I'm being led to believe?"

"For now," Forrester replied, "let's just say I have some theories and leave it at that." He offered her a friendly half-smile, but no further enlightenment.

Dr. Tanner sat quietly, contemplating Alex's request. It seemed impossible that he could help Ernie, but she had experienced so much impossible recently she wasn't sure where to draw the line between the real and the fantastic anymore. She looked from Alex to Dr. Forrester and back again, going over in her mind everything she had learned and experienced between the two. Forrester's work most certainly had the potential to create what he claims it had. And Alex had proven himself to be a resilient and determined young man. As she considered all the variables and outcomes, one more image popped into her head. One that had no business among the weighing of scientific data. An image of Angela Babcock and her children mourning the loss of their husband and father. It was then she settled on her choice.

With a heavy sigh, she placed her weighted gaze squarely on Alex. "Okay, I'll help you. But know this; if anything bad happens to Ernie while you're there, if you harm him, I will turn you over to the police so fast you won't know what hit you. Understood?"

Alex nodded. "Thank you, Dr. Tanner. Have faith, everything will be all right."

Dr. Tanner chuffed at the suggestion. "Faith is something I left behind a long time ago. This career will do that to you. I'm not yet certain I trust you, so don't ask me to believe in an idea that vanished from my life years ago. If you can do what you say you can do, that will be more than enough for me."

Alex was about to reply when a sudden twinge of pain erupted in his skull. Going back to the healing technique he worked out earlier in the day, he focused on it, trying to drive it away, but the pain refused to subside. In fact, it got worse with each second. In less than half a minute, the pain was so intense he felt his legs give out, his knees buckling beneath him. He fell to the cold, hard floor and lay there, still trying to push the pain from his head. It wasn't like any headache he'd had before, this pain felt like it was targeting him, hammering away until he would finally crumble under the incessant pounding. He tried to push past it, to focus on the cold of the tile floor on his cheek, but it continued to hit him in wave after wave of unrelenting agony.

Until it suddenly stopped. The undulating waves of pain disappeared almost as quickly as they had hit him, becoming nothing more than a dull throbbing to remind him it had been there. A dull throb in his skull and the deep ringing in his ears. Ringing that slowly changed in tone and modulation, slowly becoming a voice in his head. Quiet as a whisper, slithering through his head like a venomous snake readying to strike. The voice called to him, and in that moment he knew it wasn't a dream or a hallucination. The voice he was hearing now had chased him through his nightmares for as long as he could remember and had now become the darkness that invaded his waking hours. The dark stranger.

Adam.

"I know where you are," Adam's voice sounded in his head. "I'm coming for what's mine. Don't run. I'll find you no matter where you go. And when I do, you'll pay. She's suffered enough at your lying hands, it's time for her to come back to where she belongs. Back to me."

"Don't count on it, you son of a bitch," Alex said aloud, focusing his anger on the message. There was a sudden snapping sound in his head and the pain that had overtaken him disappeared completely. Even the dull throbbing that had been there while Adam 'spoke' was gone. It was as if it had never happened.

Except that it had. Adam had contacted him. Reached out to him through the ether and touched his mind. He had found the link they shared and exploited it, and now he might know how to find them.

A reassuring hand touched his shoulder while a powerful arm grabbed him and picked him up off the cold floor of the morgue. Rick helped him to his feet and steadied him, holding his weight. Rachel's hand went from his shoulder to his cheek as she stared into his eyes, her face a mess of worry.

"Alex, honey, are you okay? What happened?"

"It was him," Alex replied, pulling himself up to his full height and taking his weight on his own feet. Rick felt the shift in Alex's balance and let go of his arm, allowing Alex to stand and fully regain his balance on his own.

Dr. Tanner piped up from behind Rick. "Him who?" she demanded, a look of understandable confusion on her face. "Who are we talking about?"

"Adam," Alex stated, the name sending a shiver up his spine as he spoke it out loud. "He dropped in to remind me he's still here. That he can find me whenever he wants and not to forget that he's coming for me. As if that's possible."

"Does he know where we are?" Rick asked, urgency and panic mixing in his tone as his façade of bravado dissipated.

"I don't think he does," Alex replied. "At least not yet. I think that may be why he made contact just now. It wasn't to taunt me, that was just a surprise bonus for him. No, I think he was trawling for me. Like me, he's felt the connection between us and knows it exists. He's decided to use it to his advantage. He cast a psychic line, hoping to snag me, which he did. But it was weak, he couldn't sustain it for long. I could feel his struggling to keep the link. He couldn't maintain it, but now he might have an easier time finding and locking on to me. For right now, though, I don't think he's been able to establish a clear link."

"How do you know?" Rachel asked, her tone mirroring the urgency and panic in Rick's. "How can you be sure?"

"I don't know how I can be sure," Alex answered. "I'm still new to this telepathy thing. But there's no background noise. No psychic static. No mental feedback. Nothing. The pain that hit me, it must have been him forcing his way into my mind when he found me. Everything I experienced then just disappeared when he lost contact. So yeah, I think I'll know when he's in contact with me."

Dr. Tanner's face went slack. "Telepathy?"

"It was an unexpected side effect of the genetic engineering," chimed in Dr. Forrester.

She turned to him, her face a mask of confusion. "You have got to tell me about that sometime."

"I'd be delighted," replied Forrester, a wry smile on his face. "It's been so long since I've been able to truly share my work with anyone. At least with anyone who might sincerely appreciate it."

"That's fine," Rachel cut in, "but we still have work to do. And we need to get away from here before Adam can get an actual lock on Alex. I don't know about the rest of you, but I never want to see him again. Once we take care of Lieutenant Babcock, Alex and I are going to get as far away from here as we can."

"It won't be far enough," came Alex's solemn answer.

Rachel's face dropped as she turned to her husband. "What do you mean?"

Alex shook his head slowly. "Anywhere we go, he can find us. It might take him some time, but there's no place we can go to outrun the connection between us. Eventually, I'll have no choice but to face him."

The already frigid air in the room seemed to grow colder as Alex spoke. His words chilled them all, but Rachel in particular. She had feared for Alex's safety, and that fear came back to her like a tsunami as the reality of what Alex was saying sank in. He was right, there was no escaping. No running. They were trapped, and Rachel could see the few options they had slowly diminishing before her eyes.

As if sensing her fear, Alex reached out and took her hand in his with a gentle squeeze. "I know how you feel, Rach," he said softly, "but this is the only way."

"How could you know how I feel?" she muttered, tears filling her eyes. With her free hand she swiped them away, keeping her head low so that maybe Alex wouldn't see the desperation in her eyes.

"Because I can feel it, too," he replied, patting his chest over his heart. "These abilities I have, they let me feel what you're feeling. They create an empathic connection, and it's getting stronger all the time. I can sense what everyone in this room is feeling. I have no idea what this will become as it grows, but it really is remarkable, and I want to share it with you. But we won't get that chance if we live our life on the run, constantly looking over our shoulders, waiting for the inevitable day when Adam finally catches up to us. This has to end, once and for all."

"And how do you intend to do that?" she asked, a tremor of expectation in her voice.

"The only thing I can do," Alex replied, his voice becoming hard and cold. "I'm going to kill him."

48

"Are you sure this place is secure?" Burke asked, surveying the hallway of the hospital. Three uniformed police officers were positioned just outside Babcock's room, with two undercover officers at the nurses' station posing as nurses. Harriman had positioned his people around the building's perimeter and on the roof, and had placed a few people a little further down either end of the hall from the local police presence. Harriman himself was staying close to Babcock, taking up a position just around the corner in a waiting room turned command center with Burke and Detective McCall.

McCall sighed and rolled her eyes, not even trying to hide the disdain she had for Burke. Or Agent Barrymore, as she knew him. "A mouse couldn't fart in here without us knowing it," she replied.

Burke shot her a look of daggers. "That's hilarious. Very creative. I hope you keep that sense of humor after your people fuck this up."

"My people won't be the ones to fuck this up, Agent. Their job is to protect Lieutenant Babcock, and they will do that or die trying. Catching your guy? That's on you. Now, I have some work to do," she replied coldly, turning back to the patrol officer she had been previously briefing.

"You better hope they don't," Burke continued, speaking to the back of her head. "We need Babcock protected for our operation, too. We both have a dog in this fight. Remember that."

McCall finished up with the officer and dismissed her, sending her hurrying away to return to her assignment. "I've been meaning to ask you about that, Agent Barrymore. In all the meetings and briefings around this operation, you never once mentioned what the connection is between the Carters and your guy. I mean, I don't even know what to tell my people. Half of them know the Carters personally and don't believe there's any way they could be involved in this... whatever this is. They seem to think this is some type of federal witch hunt, a coverup of some sort. Apparently we're talking about people who have always been honest and law-abiding to a fault. I don't know them personally, and even I'm developing suspicions about your motives."

Burke stepped close to her, his face mere inches from hers. When he spoke it was quiet and low, with all the authority expected of a federal agent. "First, I don't give a rat's ass if you question my motives. I don't give a sweet homemade shit what you think of me or my intentions. Just know that everything we're doing here is for a reason. Second, did you ever consider, in all your great Barney Fife wisdom, that I might know information about Carter that I haven't disclosed to you? That maybe, just maybe, in my capacity as a federal law enforcement agent, I haven't seen fit to share all my resources with a Podunk dep-u-tee from East Fistfuck?"

McCall's hard eyes tore right back into his. "I have to admit," she answered, her voice heavy with sarcasm, "I never imagined you would know something I don't. About anything. Now, if you'll excuse me, I need to report back to Sherrif Andy. Want me to have Aunt Bea save you a slice of her famous apple pie?"

Burke's hands balled into tight fists at his sides. "Don't fuck with me, McCall. I promise you'll regret it."

She smiled a sickeningly sweet smile at him. "We'll just have to see about that." Without another word, Detective Maggie McCall marched out of the waiting room turned command center, and headed for the nurses' station to check on the progress of her end of the operation, leaving Burke and Harriman alone.

"Y'know," Burke said, watching as she marched away from him, "I hate to admit it, but something about that woman really turns me on. It's strange. On the one hand, I want to strangle her to death with my bare hands just for the sheer satisfaction of watching her choke to death, but on the other hand I'd really like to see what she's packing under that badge, if you get my meaning."

"Unfortunately I do," answered Harriman as he checked the reception of the hospital security cameras on his laptop screen. Immediately after they had arrived he had patched into the system, covertly co-opting the entire network of security cameras and alarms. He was in total control of anything seen or heard throughout the building, as well as any responses to incidents. A calm settled over him as he watched the mundane daily activities play out on the screen in front of him. He enjoyed having control, being able to manipulate situations in order to achieve a desired result. He'd heard it said that control was an illusion, but in his experience it had been very real and had served him very well. Tonight, he would ensure that there were no exceptions.

Burke sensed the disdain in Harriman's answer and changed the subject. "Heard anything from Forrester yet?"

Harriman twinged slightly. He knew exactly what had happened to the Doctor. In fact, in another exercise of situational control, he had orchestrated it. It just wasn't information he could share with Burke.

"Not since this morning," he lied comfortably, his attention never wavering from the images of the hospital security cameras. He was good at lying, it had been a staple of his career and he had mastered it over the years. Another useful tool in controlling and directing a scenario. His voice remained the usual calm monotone he presented to the world, with no trace of nervousness or deceit. There had been many aspects of his military training he had been thankful for over the years, but above all else he was grateful to the United States government for teaching him how to lie effectively. It was a handy skill that, over his career as both a military officer and a corporate security operative, had proven to be useful.

"Damn him!" Burke exclaimed, turning to the picture window at the far end of the room and the majestic view of the mountains it presented. The spectacular view did nothing to calm him down. "What is he up to? I swear, if he blows this for me I'll kill him myself, no matter what Penders wants!"

Harriman said nothing, keeping his attention firmly on the happenings in and around the hospital. He knew where Forrester was and had a good idea what his intentions were, but could only imagine what would happen when Burke discovered them.

"I need a cup of coffee or something," Burke said, turning away from the view outside the window. He pinched the bridge of his nose between his thumb and forefinger and rubbed hard. It hurt, but it was a good pain. Just enough to keep him alert and focused. "Keep an eye on things and call me immediately if anything happens."

"Yes sir," Harriman replied simply. As Burke left the room, he made a mental note of how he had just rubbed the bridge of his nose in a moment of stress. Much like Dr. Forrester did when deep in thought or deeply troubled. It was quite a coincidence that two men who couldn't stand the very sight of each other possessed an almost identical nervous habit. He would have to ask Dr. Forrester about that the next time he saw him.

That is, if Burke didn't kill the man first.

"There's more security there than the White House," Rachel remarked, surveying the police presence at the front entrance of the county hospital.

"Close, but not quite," Alex remarked. Although he had to admit that her assessment may be closer to the truth than he cared to admit. In the last half hour since they had been watching the hospital, they had seen a dozen uniformed police officers, possibly the entire contingent of Pine Haven's uniformed division, patrolling the grounds. Besides that, there had been several individuals in dark suits prowling around, people that were certainly not part of the regular hospital staff. "Do you recognize any of the cops, Dr. Tanner?"

"Celeste," she corrected him. "If I'm going to lose my job and possibly go to prison for someone, I want to be on a first name basis with them." She scanned the crowd of officers, looking for familiar faces. "A few, but I can't say I know any of them. I don't know too many of the patrol officers. My business is usually with the detectives."

"That could work to our advantage," Alex said, watching as two uniformed officers snuck a cigarette under cover of some shrubbery.

"Speaking of which," Rachel said as she stretched herself out across the back seat of Celeste's Volkswagen Jetta, "how do you plan to go about doing that?"

"I have a plan," Alex replied, watching the two officers stub out their cigarettes and resume their patrol of the grounds.

"And that plan would be...?" Rachel pressed.

"So complex in its simplicity my brilliance will simply astound you," Alex answered, evading her questioned.

"I doubt that," she replied, a slight edge of anger in her voice. He had been sarcastic and evasive ever since she had refused to stay behind at Celeste's house with Rick and Dr. Forrester as he had asked. It would have been safer for her, as he had insisted, but she couldn't let him do this insane quest on his own. She had to be here, to be sure he was safe.

"Do you really want to know?" he asked, squinting to make out some movement in the shadows at the far corner of the building. A second later, another of the unknown, dark-suited people emerged into the light of the hospital entrance.

Rachel let out an exasperated sigh. "I wouldn't have asked if I didn't."

"It's simple," Alex answered, a wry smile on his face. "There's only one way for me to get into that hospital."

"And that is?"

"If I'm dead."

As the night wore on, boredom consumed both the police officers and Burke's people. Their attention was not as focused as it had been earlier in the evening, affecting their focus on their primary task; watching for Adam or Alex. The police were making work for themselves, checking food carts as they passed, as well as randomly interrogating visitors as to their business in the hospital. For all the boredom tinged with nervous anxiety in the hospital, the wait went on.

The passing of so many uneventful hours didn't affect Colonel Harriman. Burke was a different story, leaving the makeshift command center and walking the grounds to be certain their people were still on task. The longer the night went on, the more restless people were becoming. Minor conflicts with the Pine Haven officers were becoming more frequent, and Burke made it a point to solve these problems himself. Every time he returned, he found Harriman in the same spot, riveted to the security monitors and occasionally issuing new orders to his troops via cell phone or radio. Most of the orders were nothing but useless shuffling of their forces, but it kept their people busy and refocused them on the job at hand. Another trick he had picked up during his military service, idle hands lead to idle minds. Burke had to admire that about the man, Harriman knew how to keep his people in line and on task.

Unlike Burke himself. He had lost count of the number of times he had cursed Forrester since his earlier discussion with Harriman and McCall. Or how often he had fantasized about taking the little man's neck in his hands and choking the life out of him. Or shooting him in the knees, working his way up and saving the crucial head shot for last. Or any other of a dozen tortures he imagined visiting on the diminutive scientist.

He turned his attention away from the violence in his imagination and clicked on the small television mounted in the corner, immersing himself in the world of television violence for about an hour before boredom overcame him again. "I'm going to take another walk around the perimeter," he announced, pulling himself off the couch and sliding into his coat. "Call me immediately if you see anything."

"Yes sir," Harriman replied, as he had the last dozen or so times Burke had made the same announcement as he left the room. He was feeling certain nothing important would come up while Burke was gone. Until his cell phone rang.

"Harriman," he stated, expecting to hear Rutters' or Burke's voice on the other end of the line. The voice he heard instead was a surprise.

"Colonel," the voice on the other end of the line said with a barely noticeable quiver. They were silent after that one word.

"Doctor," Harriman replied in his deep and steady tone.

A pause. "You told me to call if I needed anything else from you," Dr. Forrester said. He hesitated, drawing out his words as if testing the waters before continuing.

"I did," Harriman replied, his voice entirely neutral.

There was silence on the other end of the call. No doubt the doctor was trying to decide whether he could trust the Colonel. His breathing came through the phone, hard and labored. Harriman remained quiet and waited. A moment later Forrester went on, committing himself.

"I need something."

Harriman glanced up from the security feed and checked the hallway to ensure it was empty. "What can I do for you, doctor?"

"I... ah... I assume you're monitoring all the hospital security cameras?" Forrester asked, trying and failing to hide the nervousness behind his voice.

"Correct."

"I also assume you've taken full control of those systems as well?"

"Correct."

The doctor hesitated again and a loud gulping sound like a hard swallow emanated from the other end of the line. "At ten thirty this evening, there will be a body moved into cold storage in the basement. I would like to make certain that no one aside from you sees that happen."

"Done," Harriman replied curtly.

"After that," Forrester continued, "Someone will make their way to Lieutenant Babcock's room. It would be appreciated if you could do everything in your power to ensure that he arrives there."

"Who would this person be?"

"Someone you know," Forrester replied. "Or at least know of."

It was Harriman's turn to pause this time as likely scenarios played out in his head. He needed to be certain this incursion wouldn't become a liability to him and his assignment if things went bad. "I see. What are this person's intentions?"

There was no hesitation from Forrester at all this time. "Entirely beneficial to the Lieutenant and his well-being, I can assure you."

"I'll do what I can," Harriman replied, his concerns placated somewhat by the confidence in Forrester's answer. "Is there anything else?"

"I think that will be enough for now, Colonel," Forrester stated, sounding relieved the conversation was ending. "Thank you for your assistance."

"May I offer you some advice?" Harriman asked, his tone lighter than normal.

"By all means."

"Stay away from Burke Darnell," the Colonel stated flatly. "Far away."

"If I'm able, Colonel, I fully intend to. Trust me."

"No offense, doctor, but I don't trust anyone," Harriman stated. "But I will try to help you."

"That's all I can ask," the doctor replied. "Thank you. I trust we'll speak again."

"I'm certain we will. Good luck, doctor."

Before Forrester could say anything further, Harriman hit 'end' on his phone, finishing the conversation. Something was going to happen tonight after all, something that would not sit well with Burke Darnell. An almost imperceptible and uncharacteristic smile struggled onto Harriman's face. It looked like it was going to be an interesting night, after all.

The back door leading downstairs to the hospital's cold storage was unguarded, just as Dr. Forrester had promised it would be. Alex had no idea how the doctor had accomplished that, but it was done and the way was clear. It was probably better he wasn't aware of the details, anyway.

As he and Celeste made their way briskly through the small employee parking lot to the back door, he stole a quick glance back at Celeste's Jetta parked in the shadows and out of the way of surveillance cameras. Even though he couldn't make her out in the darkness, Alex was sure Rachel was still fuming. Alex knew he'd pay for his decision to have her wait in the car, even though Rachel had begrudgingly agreed with his logic that it would be best if she were to act as a lookout and potential get-away driver if they came out 'hot'. She had agreed, but he knew she saw right through him to his true intent, keeping her and their baby away from danger. She'd be plenty angry, but at least they were relatively safe at the moment, and that was all that mattered to him. He could weather the rest later.

Provided there was a later.

They reached the back door and Celeste rooted through her bag for the electronic card that would grant them entry. Her hands dug into her satchel, pushing through the contents and squinting into the open bag in search of the small card. The longer she searched, the more frantic she became. Her eyes grew wider and her breath shorter as she rifled through the bag's contents, desperate to find that one item.

"God damn it! I should have grabbed this before we left the car! I swear it was right on top!"

Alex put a reassuring hand on her shoulder to calm her. "It's okay. I didn't think of it, either. Just relax and take another look. You know it was in there, right?"

"Yes," she answered frantically, thrashing around the contents of the bag.

Alex watched her as she searched in a near panic. He glanced away, looking up at the cold, dark concrete building, and felt as if a fist were tightening around him, crushing him.

"Got it!" Celeste exclaimed in an excited whisper as she tore the credit card-like key from her satchel.

"I didn't doubt you for a second," Alex replied as she swiped the card through the reader.

"Sorry," she said, stuffing the card into her front pocket, "it's been a while since I've had to use it. I don't come here very often. The bodies are usually delivered to me."

"How convenient for you," Alex replied absently, scanning the parking lot for any movement. The ethereal fist around him tightened further as he felt sure they'd be caught and he'd end up back at the Eden Project, the last place he wanted to be if his slowly returning memory was to be believed.

The indistinct murmur of voices from around the corner caught his ear and the fist slowly squeezing him suddenly grabbed his heart and tightened around it. Every muscle in his body tensed as his breathing stopped completely as he listened to the approaching voices. Low tones, definitely two men. A crackle of radio static burst into the night and Alex grabbed Celeste's arm, ready to make a dash for the Jetta, as the LED indicator on the electronic door lock changed from red to green. Before he could react, Celeste pushed the door open and dragged him in behind her, silently closing the door behind him.

Inside, with the door closed and secured behind him, the fist around his heart loosened and he started breathing again. "That was about as close as I'd like to cut it."

"Me too," Celeste replied, "but I have a feeling things are only going to get worse from here." She scanned the dim hallway, squinting into the shadows that gathered at either end of the hall. "Come on. What we want is this way, if I remember correctly."

She led him down the hallway; the light becoming increasingly dim the further they got from the door. Small piles of abandoned and obsolete electronics dotted the hallway, along with a few wheelchairs that looked as if they hadn't seen use in quite some time. This area of the hospital was like a graveyard for unwanted and broken things, and he realized as both sad and ironic that this is where the dead waited before being moved to their final destination. It was a disturbing statement about the finality of life, ending up with the rest of the discarded and unwanted things.

Celeste stopped at a set of double doors with a sign that read 'Morgue', drawing the access key from her pocket and sliding it into the card reader mounted next to the door. The light went from red to green and a lock audibly disengaged as she pushed the doors open. Stepping inside the dark room, she felt along the wall until she stumbled on a light switch and flipped it up to turn on the lights.

The cold storage room was nothing at all like Alex assumed it would be. Considering the hallway they had traversed to get there, he had expected a dark, damp, dingy place where the dead waited before being taken to their final resting place. The room he had just stepped into was anything but that. Overhead lights cast a bright yet soft glow throughout the space, creating a sense of warmth and comfort. The stark white walls were broken up by a well-placed plant or subtle painting. Oddly, he felt at ease in the space. The hospital had made every effort to create a serene and comforting space for individuals who may need to identify a loved one's body or bid farewell to a recently deceased family member or friend. No doubt, the serenity of the room provided a soothing environment for the employees who were constantly surrounded by death, keeping them in a positive state of mental health.

"Nice cold storage area," he commented.

Celeste chuffed as she made her way to one of two doors on the opposite end of the room. "This isn't the cold storage room," she stated, swiping her ID card once more through another electronic lock. With a soft click, the LED once again went from red to green and she pushed the door open, holding it for him as she moved into the next room.

A sudden drop in temperature hit Alex as he followed her through the door, chilling him instantly. Celeste felt around the wall behind her before stumbling on a switch and flipping it up, flooding the room with a harshly bright light as the overhead fluorescent snapped on with a low hum. The small room had sparse furnishings, including a desk in one corner and a tall steel cabinet secured by a simple padlock in another. The far wall displayed four small steel doors, each adorned with a handle. Television and movies had taught him that if he were to open one of those doors, there would be a slide out rectangular tray inside, perhaps with a corpse on it. He decided against opening any of the doors.

"This is the cold storage room," Celeste stated, scanning the room. "The other room is the public face of the hospital morgue. A place to make death seem a bit more cheerful. This room is the stark reality of the cold, hard finality of it."

"Very cheerful," Alex replied, a shudder running through him. Whether it was from the cold or the bleakness of Celeste's words, he couldn't be sure.

"What we need should be this way," Celeste said, moving toward the desk. Behind it was a small door marked with a sign that simply said, 'Equipment'. She pushed the door open and ducked inside the small room. Alex heard her rummaging around as she swore under her breath, digging through the contents of the large storage closet. A moment later, she emerged pushing a gurney with a large blanket and three white lab coats. Snatching up one of the coats, she pushed her arms through the sleeves as the coat fell around her slight frame. It was about three sizes too large and hung just a few inches from the floor, but it was the smallest of the three, so it would have to do. Still, Alex couldn't help but think that she looked more like a child playing doctor than the actual doctor she was.

After settling the coat over her as best she could, Celeste moved the gurney away from the wall and pushed it toward Alex. "Take off your clothes and lie down. I need to find a toe tag." She moved to the small desk and rummaged through it, coming up with a small white card.

Alex did as she told him to and undressed down to his underwear. He stopped there as an odd sense of modesty came over him. Celeste was a doctor, he had nothing on his anatomy that she hadn't seen countless times before, but a brief twinge of shame and anxiety refused to allow him to go any further. Based on everything he had seen and experienced recently, maybe deep in the recesses of his brain he was afraid that maybe he *had* something she hadn't seen before. Something different. Something no other man on Earth possessed, simply because there weren't a lot of men on Earth like him. He knew it was an irrational thought, but his underwear remained on.

He stretched out on the gurney, the cold metal burning like icy flames on his naked back. It was a morgue gurney, designed to carry the deceased, and was without the comfort of any sort of padding between its passenger and the hard metal surface. No doubt no one gave a second thought about the comfort of the gurney since the patients never complained, but as icy knives cut up and down his back, Alex could attest with certainty they were not comfortable in the least. Between the coldness of the metal gurney and the ambient chill of the storage area, he shivered involuntarily.

"Quite moving, you're supposed to be dead," Celeste admonished him. She grasped his foot hard and held it still while she tied the tag around his big toe.

"I'm going to actually die of hypothermia if we don't get out of this icebox," he responded, his voice quivering as another series of chills shot through him.

"Just one more minute," Celeste replied as she moved back to the desk. She returned with a clipboard and a large white sheet that she draped over him, stopping just short of covering his face. "We lucked out. I found a patient chart that fits our needs perfectly. Says no autopsy is needed, but the doctor wanted some x-rays of the body. Congratulations, you are now Mr. John Alarton, the proud papa of one massive coronary."

"Great," Alex replied. "My clothes?"

"Grabbing them now," Celeste answered as she shoved his street clothes into a plastic bag labeled 'Patient Belongings'.

"Good thing," Alex replied. "I'd hate to make an emergency get away in my Fruit of the Looms."

"That would make an interesting target for a trigger-happy cop," she replied, smiling. "Now be still and be quiet. People have to believe you're dead."

"Give me a minute," he replied, settling onto the cold slab of steel and letting the chill of it flow into him. Thinking back to what Dr. Forrester had taught him earlier that day, he closed his eyes and pictured his body, prone on the gurney. In his mind, he slowly removed his surroundings. The padlocked cabinet. The cluttered desk. The cold storage drawers. The storage room entrance. Even the walls surrounding him. All that remained in his mind was him resting on the gurney in a stark white space. The last thing to go was the gurney, slowly fading into nothingness and leaving him suspended in a space of complete emptiness. As the gurney disappeared in his mind, so did the deep chill of the metal at his back, leaving only a comfortable feeling of floating freely in the endless empty around him. As he focused on his body, he turned his attention to his lungs, observing his chest rise and fall with each breath. He slowed those breaths by half, and then by half again, until they were imperceptible. He shifted his attention to his heart and did the same, increasing the time and intensity of each beat until they were nearly nonexistent. Envisioning the cold surrounding him like a cloud, he pulled that cloud around him and allowed it to permeate his body, dropping his skin temperature to a point where he would be cold to the touch.

To all outward appearances, he would be just another corpse on a slab.

"Will that do?" he asked Celeste, his words quiet and slurred as he concentrated on maintaining the illusion of death.

There was no reply at first. When Celeste finally answered, there was an uneasiness in her voice, a flinching of discomfort at his transformation. "Better than I could have hoped," was all she said.

She offered no other comments as she pulled the sheet over his face, completing his transition from living to dead.

The elevator doors slid open onto a bustle of activity as hospital staff navigated around the police officers that packed the floor where Ernie Babcock was currently fighting for his life. Celeste maneuvered the gurney into the corridor as two individuals dressed in vivid blue hospital scrubs hurriedly passed her and her 'patient,' completely ignoring her. Death was just part of the daily routine to them.

Not so with the patrolman standing just to the right of the door, checking the credentials of every person as they exited the elevator. She hadn't even cleared the door before he approached her.

"Pardon me, ma'am," he said, holding a hand up to her, palm out. "I need to see your authorization paperwork."

"Of course," she replied, retrieving the clipboard she had taken from cold storage and handing it to the officer. She didn't recognize his face or the name on his uniform, Samson. With his baby-like features, she estimated him to be in his mid-twenties. He couldn't have been with the police department for very long.

"Thank you," he replied, intentionally lowering his voice to sound more authoritative and compensate for his youthful appearance. He reviewed the paperwork she gave him, glancing up occasionally at her and the covered body on the gurney.

"This the stiff?" he asked, his voice slightly gruffer than before.

She nodded.

"I'll need to take a look," he said, reaching for the sheet covering Alex.

Celeste's heart jumped into her throat. Alex's simulated death was astonishingly authentic, and she was convinced that this inexperienced, youthful police officer had never encountered a dead body before and would never suspect the ruse. Still, she fought to maintain a neutral expression as the officer took hold of the cover's upper edge.

He pulled back the sheet to reveal Alex's face. His skin had an unnatural paleness, and a chilling shade of blue tinged his lips. No breath moved his chest. Not a flicker could be seen beneath his closed eyelids, his eyes completely motionless. She felt sure that if the cop braved touching him, he would find Alex's skin cold and clammy to the touch. Even to her trained eye, he appeared dead.

He must have appeared that way to Officer Samson, too, because he immediately pulled the sheet back over Alex's face and took two involuntary steps back. His face was slack, his skin ashen, his eyes wider than they had been a moment ago. She was right; he had no experience with death. Not even a clean death like this one was pretending to be. She could only imagine how he would react at the scene of a car accident or a shotgun suicide where the victims would be far less presentable. If this was how he reacted today, she thought, he really should think about another line of work. Death and law enforcement often travel hand-in-hand. It's not a career for the squeamish.

"You, ah, you can go," he stammered, stepping clear of her path. His eyes remained fixated on the face beneath the sheet, filled with a mix of fear and anticipation, as if expecting the body to spring to life like the zombies in movies.

She nodded in response and quickly pushed the gurney down the hall toward the imaging lab and away from the young police officer. She didn't want him to find his courage and decide to take another look. A quick glance back took away that concern as the young officer sat by the elevator door, face in hands, no doubt pondering his choice of career. He wouldn't be detaining them any longer. Which was a good thing, she wasn't sure how long Alex could maintain the illusion of death.

Upon reaching the medical imaging lab, she scanned her badge for entry and maneuvered the gurney inside, quickly securing the door behind her. No staff technicians were on duty this late at night, and there was no guard stationed here since the rooms containing valuable supplies or equipment were securely locked. This room was the end of the line for them, though. The other labs required a combination of an electronic keycard and a passcode to enter, which she didn't have. But this room gave them access to everything they needed for the next phase of their incursion into the hospital.

She yanked the sheet off Alex, revealing his eerily still and pale body. Even with all her years as a medical examiner, she would not have been able to tell he wasn't dead just by looking at him. It was unsettling to see him like that, and she silently hoped it wasn't a portent of things to come.

"Wakey, wakey," she said, rubbing his sternum lightly. There was no response. "Come on," she said, pushing harder on his chest. Still no response. A cold tide of fear washed over her as she pushed as hard as her tiny hands allowed into his chest. "Wake up, damn it!"

With no warning, his eyes popped open as he exhaled loudly, followed by a desperate sucking in of fresh oxygen. A healthier pallor returned to his complexion as he pulled himself into a sitting position, pulling his feet over the edge of the metal gurney and letting them dangle there.

"That was close," he said between harsh gasps. "I wasn't sure how much longer I was going to make it without more oxygen. That's something I never want to try again."

In response, she slapped him hard on the shoulder. "Don't you ever! You scared the living shit out of me!"

"Sorry," he replied, rubbing the spot where she hit him. "Believe me, it was no great walk in the park for me, either. You have my clothes?"

She opened one of the instrument drawers on the morgue gurney and produced his clothes, which he gratefully accepted. As he came back into full awareness again, he was realizing how cold he still was, not only from the environment but also from his simulated brush with death. Eager to get into some warm clothes, he jumped from the gurney, his legs buckling under him. Just before he crumpled to the floor, Celeste caught his arm and saved him from falling.

"Take it easy. Your body went with very little oxygen for much longer than it should have. You're bound to be disoriented. You need to ease back into it." She pulled him up until he was standing up straight, positioning her compact frame under his arm for support. Slowly, she moved away from him, letting him stand on his own. He teetered for a moment and she moved back in to catch him, but he waved her off.

"I'm good, thanks," he said, standing up straight again without so much as a wobble. The color had completely returned to his face, and he no longer struggled to breathe. It was hard to believe that just a few minutes earlier, he had been all but dead. There were no outward signs of his recent ordeal.

"Amazing," Celeste whispered, astonished. "Your metabolic rate and regenerative abilities are astounding."

"Thanks, comes from good genes," Alex quipped, uneasy with the analytical way she was regarding him.

"I'm sure it does," she replied. "The question is, whose genes?"

Alex had no retort, so he let the rhetorical question hang between them for a moment before he shifted to the subject at hand. "Where do we go from here?"

Celeste visibly pulled herself out of conjecture and back into the moment, indicating a grate in the wall just above their heads. "That leads to the intensive care unit where Ernie is. After that, I'm afraid you're on your own."

"No problem," Alex replied as he pulled his shirt on. "You've done more than enough for us already. I don't know how to even begin to thank you."

"Help Ernie," she stated, "and we'll call it even."

"He means that much to you, huh?"

"To me and pretty much everyone else who's ever met him. He's truly one of the good guys."

Alex couldn't deny that. He and Rachel had met Ernie Babcock on what had been the worst night of their lives. He came across as gruff and even rude, but they had put their trust in him almost immediately. And they had been right. He had gone far above and beyond his duty in helping them and, because of that involvement, had ended up in the hospital near the brink of death. He was certainly one of the best of the good guys, and Alex was determined to do whatever was in his power to help him.

Before beginning his ascent to the ventilation grate, he took a moment to carefully position the gurney against the wall, ensuring that the wheels were locked in place. The grate was secured by clips at each corner and not screwed in place, and he breathed a sigh of relief. That would make this a lot easier on both ends. He popped the grate off and handed it to Celeste, who propped the metal square against the wall.

Inside the duct itself it was dark, dusty and tiny and he was suddenly grateful that claustrophobia wasn't a fear of his. The trip wouldn't be comfortable, but he was certain he could squeeze through.

"You'll be ready at the other end?" he asked, turning back to Celeste.

She nodded. "As soon as you're in the duct, I'll head for the Ernie's room in the ICU and wait for you there."

"What if they won't let you through to see him?" Alex asked.

Celeste chuffed and grinned. "I may pass my time as a mild-mannered coroner slash forensic specialist, but underneath all that, I'm still a cop. Also, as senior forensic tech, I technically outrank any officer in this building right now. Add to that the fact that Ernie and I are close friends, and top it off with knowing that I can be the worst bitch you've ever encountered if I need to be. Given all that, I think they'll let me through."

Alex gave a wry smile. Celeste was a tiny woman, but there was no way he would ever argue with her. He felt secure in the fact that she would be waiting for him when he arrived in Babcock's room.

"All right then, I'll see you soon."

He raised himself into the tight shaft, maneuvering through the space by tugging and propelling his body until he finally squeezed in completely. There was considerably less space than he thought there would be, and dust and cobwebs caked the interior. As he shimmied forward on his belly, he noticed he could feel the top of the shaft scraping his back as he moved. He had to keep his hands extended out in front of him to pull himself along, with no space between the walls and his body. The tight grip of the metal walls made him feel trapped, like Thanksgiving leftovers tightly wrapped in aluminum foil. A mild pang of fear gripped his stomach as he pulled himself deeper into the narrow labyrinth, but he pushed it down and focused on the goal ahead.

"Alex," Celeste called from behind him, "be careful. I don't want to have to explain to Rachel why you didn't come back."

With that she replaced the grate, and Alex felt at once like she was nailing closed the lid of his coffin.

Harriman was still reviewing video surveillance throughout the hospital, but after his conversation with Dr. Forrester, his search had become much more intense. He wasn't sure precisely what he was looking for, just that he would know what it was when he found it. With the goal in mind, he scrutinized every image, hoping to discover an anomaly that would give him the information he needed.

And then suddenly, there it was. It had gone unnoticed all evening, but now it stood out like a lighthouse, demanding attention amidst the chaos. Except this lighthouse was not to be avoided, it was to be embraced. Events were finally falling into place.

He needed to get away to take advantage of the gift fate had provided him. Some diversion that would occupy the attention of the police, as well as his own people, long enough for him to grasp this opportunity.

He barely had time to wish for a distraction before one materialized before him. A red light flashed violently on the screen in front of him, an alarm indicator showing a disturbance of some sort in the ventilation system. The alarm was near the imaging laboratories and the intensive care unit. Harriman was certain this was the intrusion Forrester had asked him to ignore, that he had promised he would allow to go unimpeded. However, Harriman had made that promise before fate handed him this opportunity, and sadly, his interests in this case would have to come before the promise he had made to the doctor. It was a pity; he had always prided himself on his honesty and dependability and the strength of his word, but when that conflicted with his pride and integrity in his work, there was no question what would come first.

Retrieving his cell phone from his pocket, he began dialing Rutters, but abruptly halted. While it was true he would have to break his promise to the doctor, he could at least give whoever was creeping through the ventilation duct a fighting chance. Moreover, if he waited a few more minutes before sounding the alarm, it would probably trigger a more aggressive reaction, causing a widespread commotion that could serve as a smokescreen for his endeavors.

Setting the phone back on the table, he leaned back and stretched his muscles. It was the first time all night he had stretched his back, and after leaning over the computer watching video surveillance for hours, it felt good. He checked the time on his watch and started a countdown. The intruder had five minutes before he made the call and sicced Rutters on him. No more, no less. It was the least he could do in keeping his promise to the doctor. Then, in the confusion, he would slip out and complete his new mission.

As he completed the stretch, Harriman allowed himself an indulgence. He smiled. It was going to be a very productive night, after all.

As Celeste entered the ICU reception area, she remarked to herself how smooth it had been getting to this point. The two officers posted at the main ICU entrance had let her pass with barely a second glance, sufficiently impressed by her official credentials. From here on, things were certain to be more complicated, regardless of what she had told Alex earlier.

In less than a minute, her instincts were proven right. As she reached the nurse's station, two large and rather imposing men, both with close-cropped haircuts and wearing identical black suits, stopped her. They were certainly not part of the Pine Haven police force. Between their build, stance, and no-nonsense approach, she marked them as military. Taking a deep breath, she continued forward, flashing her police identification. Neither budged.

"I'm sorry, ma'am," the one on the left, who had no neck she could discern, said, "we need to verify all incoming persons regardless of identification. I'll just be a moment."

She nodded her understanding as he turned away and headed down the hall, trying at the same time not to appear on edge to the other black-suited guard that remained. Official or not, she had a valid purpose for being here that would stand up to even the most rigorous examination. There was no logical reason she could think of that would deny her entry to the ICU. Still, she couldn't dispel the cold, prickly feeling on the back of her neck, the feeling that usually warned her of trouble.

No-Neck came back from wherever it was he had disappeared to and handed her identification back. "Someone will be with you in a moment, ma'am," he stated, taking up his position next to his partner and resuming his stance.

Celeste didn't like the sound of that. "Is there a problem?"

Neither of the men had a chance to reply before a tall, slender woman in a business suit appeared. Despite her fresh and young appearance, her face was clouded with consternation.

"I'm Detective Maggie McCall," she stated in a deep and authoritative tone. "I don't know if you remember me, it's been some time since we've spoken."

"I remember you, Detective," Celeste answered, a flicker of recognition appearing in her eyes as the face fell into place in her memory. "You're the young officer Ernie Babcock always spoke so highly about. I'm glad to see the Pine Haven Police Department has been good for you."

"Thank you," Detective McCall answered. "I was very lucky to have him as a mentor. Which brings me to my question. What are you doing here? I'm not aware of anyone putting in a call to the coroner's office."

"Oh, I'm not here as coroner," Celeste replied, looking the young detective up and down, taking her measure. Maggie McCall stood tall and straight in an effort to add height to her slight frame. She cocked her left hip outward slightly, where her detective shield was clipped to her belt. Celeste found it interesting that she stressed the badge on her left instead of the gun on her right. Her posture and demeanor exuded authority in every way.

"Would you join me down the hall, please?" the detective asked, although her tone left no doubt that it was less of a question and more of an expectation.

Celeste nodded slightly and followed as Detective McCall led her around the corner at the far end of the hall and into an empty patient room that had been transformed into a command center for the police. They removed the bed, making room for a makeshift desk that housed an array of computer monitors displaying images of various angles of locations inside and outside of the hospital. A woman in a black suit, similar to the two giants at the ICU entrance, was seated in the center of the monitors. Completely engrossed in the images before her, she didn't bother to look at the new person in the room.

Once inside, Maggie McCall turned back to her and asked, in her authoritative fashion, "If you aren't here as coroner, Dr. Tanner, why are you here?"

“Besides being coroner, I’m also the chief forensic technician for the department,” Celeste shot back, her voice carrying the same authority as her younger counterpart.” As such, it’s my job to collect any evidence relevant to the case. The case here being the shooting of a police lieutenant.” She paused for a moment, softening a bit before continuing. “That, and Ernie is my friend. Has been for a long time. I need to know how he’s doing.”

Detective McCall’s face softened noticeably at the mention of Ernie Babcock. “I get that. It’s been driving me crazy seeing him laid up like that. Ernie has been more than a mentor to me. He’s been like a father. And there’s absolutely nothing I can do to help him. Nothing except maybe catch the bastard that did this to him.”

“I take it that’s why you’re here?” Celeste asked with feigned innocence, even though she already knew the answer.

“Yeah,” Maggie answered, shifting her stance as she ran a hand through her short, dark hair. “The F.B.I. guys seem to think the scumbag who shot him will show up here tonight to finish the job. It’s supposed to be his MO.” Her face hardened again, her eyes shifting between Celeste and the dark-suited woman in the corner. “I don’t know, though. I can’t seem to get any direct intel from these guys. I’ve never met feds so tight-lipped before.”

Celeste was on the verge of interrogating Maggie for more details when a mysterious man in a black suit entered the room. A young man with a ruddy complexion and intense eyes that sharpened the chill on the back of Celeste’s neck and sent it running down the length of her spine. With a glance, she could tell that this man was dangerous. He was someone to tread carefully around.

“Who is this, and why is she here?” he asked, suspicion evident in the question.

“Sergeant Rutters, this is our Chief Forensic Specialist, Dr. Celeste Tanner,” answered McCall, her lips tight and tone low. It was impossible to ignore the palpable tension between the two of them.

"She isn't supposed to be here," he answered, his voice filled with authority, as he turned away from the detective and directed his gaze towards Celeste. “You’ll have to leave. Now.”

McCall positioned herself between Rutters and Celeste. “She’s in charge of the investigation into the shooting of Lieutenant Ernest Babcock and is here on official department business.”

Rutters glared at her, his face contracting in on itself as pure fury at having his authority questioned overtook him. “This is an F.B.I. matter now,” he said through clenched teeth. “She has no jurisdiction here.”

“You listen to me, you crater-faced son of a bitch,” McCall shot back, her voice equally thick with anger, “that man lying in there is the best police officer I have ever know, not to mention one hell of a good human being, which is far more than I can say for you. Your people have said they know who shot him, but so far I have seen absolutely fuck-all when it comes to finding him! So I am going to carry out my own investigation, and Dr. Tanner is a crucial part of that. She stays. You don't like it? Too fucking bad. This is my town. Get the fuck out, asshole." She slammed her fist on the technician's makeshift desk with enough force to rattle the computer equipment there, causing the woman behind the desk to jump up and ensure nothing was damaged. McCall never took her eyes from Rutters.

The man's complexion turned redder by the second as the barely contained rage kept in check beneath a very thin surface of self-control threatened to explode from him in a violent eruption. His ragged breath caught in his throat as he struggled to reply to McCall's challenge, so angry the words wouldn't come to him. His hands clenched tightly at his sides into fists the size of softballs, his arms shaking uncontrollably. When he could finally gather himself enough to speak, the stiff muscles of his jaw muted his words.

"You skank whore bitch. I've been dying to throw you out of here since you first walked through the door, and now you're handing me the excuse I need. Go ahead. Do something really stupid. Just give me a reason to..."

"I think I can clear this up with no further hostilities," Celeste said, squeezing her tiny frame between the two of them. With her back to McCall, she faced the young sergeant, having to crane her neck at an intensely odd angle to look him in the eye. She took a deep breath and kept her voice calm in contrast to his.

He glared down at her, a foot and a half taller than she was and outweighing her by at least a hundred and twenty-five pounds. The chill of fear in her spine was becoming a numbness in her back and stomach, which she was actually grateful for at the moment. It dulled the nausea that was aggravated by her fear, at least.

"The sting operation to capture the shooter is an F.B.I. matter," Celeste continued, swallowing her fear and speaking with the calm authority she was known for, "but the investigation into the shooting of Lieutenant Babcock is still under the jurisdiction of the Pine Haven Police Department. I am a representative of that police department and, as such, am authorized to be here. In fact, with all matters around the case involving Lieutenant Babcock, my authorization here supersedes yours. Given that, I would suggest you stay out of our way and not impede this investigation in any manner."

The red of anger on Rutters' face became a bright crimson as his face contracted into itself, compressing his features. For a moment Celeste was afraid the man's head might implode, creating a tiny black hole of rage, but almost immediately his features relaxed and his face returned to its usual red hue. The fists at his side released slowly, and his chest fell a bit as he breathed out a heavy sigh. His eyes, still pinpoints of his monstrous anger, held Celeste firmly in their gaze.

"Fine," he lamented. "Have it your way. I've got too much to worry about right now. But don't get in my way. I don't care who you are, it won't end well for you."

She nodded and smiled. "Thank you for your understanding," she said, putting as much condescension into her tone as she could.

Before Rutters could say anything that might reignite tensions, McCall grabbed Celeste by the sleeve of her lab coat and pulled her away from him. "Come on, Dr. Tanner. I'll show you to Ernie's room," she said through gritted teeth, pushing back her own seething anger. As the door closed behind them, the detective let out the breath she had been holding in a sharp, angry exhalation that rushed through her clenched teeth with a slight whistle. "I can't believe this fucking assignment."

"What's his story, anyway?" Celeste asked, humoring McCall's tantrum. She didn't want to raise her suspicions by running off to Ernie's room, but she needed to be sure the room was clear before Alex arrived. She thought about him, creeping through the ventilation system, wondering how long she had. If he exited the vent and any of the mysterious federal agents were lurking nearby, it would bring their plan to an abrupt and ugly end.

"I have no clue, but I bet it's a lonely one," McCall replied, the flush of anger fading slightly from her face. "A person can't be that much of an asshole and have a lot of friends." Her expression shifted again, the anger supplanted by concern and suspicion. "I have to tell you, Dr. Tanner, I don't trust any of them. Not Rutters, not Harriman, but especially the guy in charge. Special Agent Lance Barrymore. Nothing sets off my cop alarms like that guy. It's always half-truths and need-to-know with him. I can never get a straight answer. I don't know, I..." She stopped, cut off by the shocked expression on Celeste's face. "Dr. Tanner, are you all right?"

Celeste's voice was a shocked whisper. "Did you say Lance Barrymore?"

McCall nodded. "Yes, Special Agent Lance Barrymore, F.B.I.. Why?"

The name exploded like an alarm in Celeste's head. If this so-called 'Agent Barrymore' was here, that meant Alex was in grave danger. And he was heading right into a trap set for him, with poor Ernie as bait. She had to get to Ernie's room now and warn Alex.

"Dr. Tanner, are you okay?" McCall asked again.

"No," Celeste answered, "everything is not okay." On hearing the name Special Agent Lance Barrymore, her mind raced. His involvement in this was a threat to all of them, and she quickly reviewed the options available to her. Alex was in the ventilation system, nearing Ernie's room and about to arrive at any moment. She needed to warn him, but she couldn't risk catching the attention of the supposed federal agents lurking in the building. They had to speed up whatever plan Alex had to help Ernie, but any action she took would bring attention and suspicion on her. There was no way she would succeed on her own. She needed an ally. The only available option she had was Detective Maggie McCall.

Swallowing hard, she turned to the detective. She was out of time. She was out of options. She would have to put her trust in Maggie McCall and cling to the hope that her suspicions about Lance Barrymore were correct, and that her determination to help Ernie would prevail.

"Listen to me, this is very important," Celeste blurted, needing to get the information out fast before she lost her resolve in trusting McCall. "Your suspicions about Agent Barrymore are correct. He isn't what he says he is, and neither are his people. I don't have time to get into it right now, but I can tell you they are at least indirectly responsible for Ernie's condition. And my reason for being here."

McCall blinked, taken aback by the sudden deluge of information. "Dr. Tanner, you're not making sense."

"I know, but you get used to things not making sense pretty quickly," Celeste answered. "Trust me, I know. And I will try to make everything clear for you when I can, but right now, I need your help."

McCall stared at the smaller woman as she processed what she had said. As Dr. Tanner spoke, Maggie noticed a slight shaking in her arms and how she shifted her feet restlessly, moving unconsciously toward Ernie Babcock's room. While she had questions about what was going on, her training also enabled her to recognize someone who was scared and in need of help. And from everything she could see, Dr. Celeste Tanner needed help.

"What do you need?" she asked.

Celeste paused for a precious second. McCall seemed sincere, and that she wasn't already in handcuffs was a good sign, so she continued. "I need a few minutes with Ernie, alone. I need you to make sure we get that. After that, I need your help to get us out of here."

"Us? What do you mean us? And why do you need help getting out of the hospital?" The suspicion in the young detective's voice was evident again as she barraged Celeste with questions.

Celeste was losing her. She had to reign in McCall's natural sense of curiosity and refocus her on the task at hand. "I don't have time to explain it all right now. Let me just say that we're here to help Ernie, and then we need a discreet escape route after that." There was desperation in her voice and she didn't know if that would help or hinder her efforts with McCall, but she didn't have time to care right now. Everything was coming to a head, and she needed to move fast. "Maggie, you have no clue who these people really are or how dangerous they can be. I need to know if you'll trust me, and I need to know now."

McCall was silent, her face a neutral slate. Her mind, however, was moving at breakneck speed as she ran through her interactions and experiences over the last few days. Even with the crucial details Celeste hadn't shared, the story was incredible. With little to work with, McCall had to rely solely on trust, going against everything she had been taught as a police officer.

The one thing Ernie Babcock had impressed on Maggie when she first joined the force was to trust her instincts above all else. And at this moment, her instincts were telling her to trust in what Dr. Tanner was saying.

"Damn it!" McCall exclaimed, slamming her fist into her thigh. "I knew there was something off about those guys! Even after we verified their credentials, it just didn't feel right. What an idiot I am!"

Celeste reached out and placed a gentle hand on her arm. "No, you're not an idiot. These people are dangerous, but they're also very persuasive. And they have resources you can't imagine. This is not your fault." She glanced back to the makeshift command center, fully expecting to see Rutters burst through the door with his gun drawn. Momentary relief flooded her when she didn't see him there, but they were running out of time. "Can I count on your help?"

"Absolutely," McCall answered. "What do you need me to do?"

Celeste explained the plan in brief, carefully omitting Alex's name. McCall agreed to help make a way into Ernie's room and grant them the necessary time for their plans. The lack of details made her uncomfortable, but she was stuck choosing between the devil she knew and the one she didn't, and the devil she knew in Special Agent Lance Barrymore was more than enough to convince her to side with the unknown.

"You'll only have a few minutes," McCall explained. "That's all I can spare you."

"It'll be enough," Celeste assured her, her voice filled with uncertainty about whether there would be sufficient time for Alex to complete his task. If that was all they had, it would have to do.

McCall turned away and began walking down the hall, but then paused and turned back to face Celeste. "When this is over, I want an explanation. A fully, painstakingly detailed explanation. No more secrets."

Celeste grinned awkwardly at her. "Detective, if we survive this, it will be my pleasure. I'll even buy the drinks. You're going to need a lot of them."

As the women parted ways, Celeste's own words rang through her head: If we survive this...

Alex inched his way along in the darkness, crawling toward his destination. The ventilation system was a maze, but he moved forward confidently, sure in the direction he was going. It was as if he were being guided, like a compass needle pulled toward magnetic north. Whatever it was, he chose to trust the feeling.

Moving through the ductwork wasn't the easiest thing he had ever done. Moving through the ductwork was challenging because of the cramped space, which was designed for moving air and not a person. He had to pull himself along on his stomach, extending his arms in front of him out of necessity. Pulling himself forward, he focused on the beacon in his head as he wiggled through, grabbing at any edge he could.

His arms were screaming at him as he pulled himself along another few inches and he stopped for a moment to rest. The echo of his breathing swirled around him in the chamber, like the breath of Death himself on his neck. His breathing was truncated already as the duct constricted his chest's ability to expand and take in air, which was contributing to the fatigue in his arms and legs. He needed to reach an exit soon or risk passing out from lack of oxygen.

Steeling himself again, he wriggled forward another two feet before the unseen force he'd been following told him to stop. To his left was another ventilation grate like the one he had entered, bars of dirty white light streaming into the darkness. With great effort, he turned his head slightly, peering through the slats of the grate into the room below.

Despite being considered a fairly large room by hospital standards, the amount of machinery surrounding the bed created a cramped atmosphere. Apart from the machinery encircling the bedridden patient, there were two cozy chairs thoughtfully positioned to accommodate family members spending extended periods with their critically ill or injured relatives. Even though they were just chairs, the implications of them struck Alex with a deep sense of morbidity at the thought of keeping a deathwatch over a loved one.

That was exactly what was happening in the room. The deathwatch chair was occupied by a woman in her mid-forties, still radiantly attractive despite her current circumstances. Clad in black leggings and a vibrant blue sweatshirt, both slightly baggy on her slender frame, she seemed to have effortlessly thrown together an outfit in response to the sudden hospital summons. Her raven black hair was pulled back into a hastily assembled bun that somehow sat neatly atop her head. A tiny, pert nose and rosebud lips complimented a perfectly formed face. Deep hazel eyes, no doubt stunning under normal circumstances, now were red and puffy from crying. Alex figured this must be Angela Babcock, Ernie's wife, and he could see why the man loved her as he did. It was obvious she loved him back just as fiercely.

But now he was dying. Alex didn't know how he knew that, he could just sense it. Just like the beacon in his head, guiding him through the labyrinth of ductwork, he could sense the lieutenant's life force gradually fading away. He was running out of time.

The ventilation duct was so cramped that he couldn't see his watch, yet he was confident that he had been in there for at least twenty minutes. Celeste should have been here. It had been a twenty-minute crawl to him, but for her it was less than a five-minute stroll from the imaging labs to the ICU. She must have run into a problem and been delayed or detained. He was on his own, and time was running out for Ernie Babcock. It was time to move forward with the plan without Celeste.

He wriggled forward again, to position himself to allow him to kick the grate free, when the door opened and Celeste walked in. She quickly greeted Mrs. Babcock with a consoling look and a brief hug, but didn't linger. As she spoke softly, Alex couldn't hear her words, but he could sense the gravity of the situation as she hurriedly explained everything to Ernie's grieving wife. To her credit, Angela Babcock listened intently and nodded several times before sitting back down with her husband. Alex felt a sense of relief. Unnecessarily alarming Mrs. Babcock was the last thing they wanted to do.

Celeste brought a stool to the wall and climbed up, removing the clasps on the grate before setting it aside and stepping back down. Alex wriggled his legs out through the space, sliding slowly backward out of the hole before dropping the last few feet to the floor. He extended his arm past Celeste to retrieve the discarded grate and carefully placed it back where it belonged, erasing any signs of his entry into the room.

"Glad to see you made it," he said to Celeste as he took a second to shake out his cramped legs.

She chuffed. "I wouldn't miss this for anything. Although I had a few snags along the way."

"I don't want to interrupt," came a voice from the corner, raspy from hours of crying, "but who are you? And what do you want with my husband?"

"Mrs. Babcock," Alex started, moving around the myriad of equipment to speak directly to her, "my name is Alex Carter. My intention is to help your husband in any way I can, just as he helped me. I owe him that much. I owe him a lot more than that, actually. He's a remarkable man."

Angela Babcock stared intently at the man before her, uncertain how to respond. A moment later, recognition dawned on her. "It's you. You're the young man Ernie brought over to the house last night, just before... before..." She trailed off as tears began flooding her eyes, her voice choked off as grief took hold once more.

"Before he was hurt," Alex finished for her. "Yes, that was me."

"Celeste said you can help Ernie?"

Alex noted the cautious skepticism in her tone, but he could feel the hope that flowed from her. "I certainly intend to try."

Her voice was suddenly tiny, like a child. "How?"

He smiled, a warm and comforting gesture. "Honestly, I don't know. I'm afraid we're all going to have to have some faith and learn together."

The emotions emanating from her were intense and mixed. Grief. Despair. Sadness. Uncertainty. Anger. Alex moved past those, focusing on the small but growing point of light in her that represented love and hope. At the moment they were small, frail things, vulnerable to the swirl of negative feelings within her. Concentrating on the positive feelings in her, the light, he grasped those emotions and pulled them out of the darkness, bringing them to the forefront of the raging storm within her. As he did so, Angela's face changed from one hardened with grief and pain to one that suddenly saw hope.

"You just need to have faith," Alex stated again, stepping back from her.

Angela Babcock looked up at him, the tears in her eyes gone. She was still concerned for her husband, but she felt confident that the young man before her could bring him back.

"Thank you," she breathed, taking his hand in hers. Locking eyes with him, she asked, "Do you know who did this to him?"

The question triggered a rush of memories from the previous night. Babcock throwing himself into the fight to protect him and Rachel from Adam, nearly at the cost of his own life. The look of grim satisfaction on Adam's face as he pumped bullets into the defenseless cop. Yes, he knew he was responsible. It was something he could never forget.

"Yes," he replied as the horrors continued to play in his mind. "I do."

"What about him?" Angela pressed, her hand tightening on his as a bit of the dark storm of anger pushed through the light of hope inside her.

Alex took a deep breath and forced his memories back, at the same time reaching into Angela Babcock's mind and rekindling her light of hope once more. Her grip on him relaxed slightly and she melted back into her chair, still concerned for her husband, but not consumed by her darker emotions.

"Not to worry, Mrs. Babcock. The man who did this to your husband, he'll pay for it. For everything he's done and everyone he's hurt." He squeezed her hand reassuringly. "I promise you that."

"I don't mean to be rude," Celeste interrupted, "but we are on an extremely tight schedule."

"Of course," Alex replied, shaking his head and breaking the bond he had created with Angela. She shivered at that but remained calm and comfortable where she was, her positive emotions at the surface of her psyche. Without Alex's reinforcement, it would change soon. He needed to hurry to help Ernie before that happened, it was impossible to predict what her reaction would be when her darker impulses took hold again.

Releasing her hand, he moved to the opposite side of the bed where Ernie Babcock lay. He was eerily still and quiet, so unlike the man Alex had gotten to know, as the machines surrounding him displayed a weakened heartbeat and low oxygen levels. His chest struggled to rise with each breath despite the machine that was forcing air into his lungs. His midsection bore tightly wrapped thick bandages, which had turned into a deep crimson from the wounds below. Again, Alex felt the strange sensation that he could feel the detective's life as it left him, like heat radiating from a rock cooling into the night after sunset. Alex knew what he needed to do. He needed to keep that escaping life inside. Needed to contain it and amplify it.

As if acting on their own, Alex's hands found their way to the chest and forehead of the dying man, gently laying on him. On contact with Babcock, a sharp tingle, like a burst of electricity, ran up his arms and through his chest. Startled by it, his instinct was to pull away, but Alex soon realized there was no pain in the sensation. It was quite the opposite. The feeling of warmth washed over him. Warmed him in a way he had never known before. Warmed him to the core of his very soul. Deep inside him the warmth, the energy, pooled and grew before spreading out through him again like wildfire. It touched every part of him, physically and psychically, charging him up and filling him with its power. His entire being was overtaken by the warmth, as if every cell in his body was basking in its comforting embrace. He basked in it, letting the energy in, letting it draw on his own reserves of life energy until it became an inferno he couldn't contain any longer. Reflexively, he focused on the injured form of Ernie Babcock and gathered the power inside himself, pushing it into Ernie's near lifeless body. Alex could feel the warmth leaving his body and seeping into the detective, leaving him suddenly chilled, his own life force teetering on the edge of depletion. Still, he moved the life-giving energy into Babcock, forcing the last of it into him. In an instant, it left him, accompanied by a sudden surge of electricity, a sharp snap that reverberated in his ears, causing him to stumble away from Babcock and collapse in a heap on the floor.

This time, there was pain. A lot of pain. His arms screamed from the final jolt of energy that cut the circuit between him and Ernie, the nerves alight with fire. In contrast, his chest felt devoid of warmth, as if a chilling emptiness had settled within, leaving behind a cold and hollow sensation. The cold emptiness inside him burned as well, but it burned with all the emotions he had been suppressing for so long. Anger, fear, and resentment mingled with love, compassion, and happiness as they coalesced into an uncontrollable storm in his core. He felt a tear roll down his cheek and heard a sob, a sob he knew was his. Someone was beside him. He could feel them, but he had no idea who it was. They were speaking to him, almost yelling at him, but the burning rage of the icy fire within him drowned out their words. He barely felt it as this person touched him, numb from cold and pain.

He was going to die. As sure as he had felt Ernie Babcock's imminent death, Alex knew with certainty he was going to die. Darkness closed in around him, consuming him. He tried to push it back, to keep a grip on the world, to anchor himself to life, but he was too weak. As the last vestiges of life faded around him, he uttered one word.

"Rachel."

Harriman picked up his cellular phone and punched in Rutters' number. As he hit the final digit, he offered a silent apology to Dr. Forrester for betraying his trust. After four rings, Rutters answered.

"What?" he yelled; his voice thick with anger.

Under normal circumstances, Harriman would not have tolerated behavior like that from someone under his command and Rutters would have been the subject of a severe reprimand. But he was on a schedule and time was of the essence. Besides, having Rutters in an agitated state only made him more useful to achieving his endgame.

"You have an alarm in the ICU ventilation corridor, Sergeant," Harriman stated evenly. "I would suggest you investigate immediately."

"Shit! God-damned bitch! I knew she was up to something!" Rutters yelled. Before he could reply, Harriman heard the phone crash onto the floor as Rutters hastily dropped it and sprinted out of the room, abruptly abandoning the call.

Harriman punched the 'end' button on his phone and set it down again, a deep sense of satisfaction welling up inside him. Rutters was an incompetent who had to be terminated anyway, this failure would only accelerate the process. It would also serve as the perfect diversion Harriman needed to accomplish his own goals.

Burke Darnell would be next. For a moment, Harriman thought about calling Burke and letting him know the intruder was here, but that would be too quick. Better that Burke find out later, after it was too late for him to do anything about it, that his life was falling apart right under his nose.

Checking the surveillance video one more time to make sure his objective was still in sight, he rose and collected the few items he would need. Then, with a few keystrokes, he locked down the security system completely, including all cameras. Burke was now completely blind. In time the technicians could restore the system, but by then Harriman would be long gone with his prize.

Satisfied he would have time to carry out his objective, Colonel William Harriman disobeyed orders for the first time in his career and abandoned his post. It was a feeling he didn't relish, but one he could cope with. The ends would justify the means, after all.

With that thought, he left, taking with him a deeply satisfied feeling. He wasn't a big believer in fate, but this night had handed him a remarkable opportunity. The kind that he simply could not ignore.

Things were going remarkably well.

McCall waited nervously at the nurses' station; eyes riveted to the door of Rutters' makeshift command center. Despite her earlier bravado with him, she had no desire to face off with him again, especially now that she knew he wasn't what he claimed to be. He had been dangerous before, but now there was nothing holding him back. Facing him down could cost her more than just her career now; it could cost her life.

"I hope you appreciate this, you ox," she muttered, thinking about Ernie lying in his bed a few yards behind her. The immediate threat to him was the only reason she was ready to stand her ground against a maniac like Rutters. The only reason she hadn't sought reinforcements. The danger to Ernie was imminent, but she didn't dare use her radio to bring in reinforcements. The fake F.B.I. had been monitoring Pine Haven police frequencies all day, making her hesitant to call for reinforcements and risk drawing attention. She was afraid to use her cell for the same reason. She was on her own. Alone and facing a man half again her size and weight, with a temper that could swallow a city and still be hungry enough for dessert.

Almost as soon as she had the thought, that anger exploded onto the scene as Rutters burst out of the command center and stomped toward Ernie's room, with her standing between them. His face was a much deeper shade of red, his eyes mere slits as his face contorted in rage. He approached, his fists tightly clenched and swinging wildly at his sides, each the size of a softball. Without a moment to consider her options, she stepped in front of the charging man-mountain.

"What seems to be the problem?" she asked, trying to keep the quaver of fear in her stomach from leaching into her voice.

"Get out of my way," he snarled in a low growl. "You do not want to piss me off right now."

McCall took a sharp breath to calm the knot in her guts. "Look, I have a right to know..."

In a seamless motion, Rutters pulled out a handgun from beneath his coat and aimed it at McCall's face, the barrel positioned just half an inch away from the bridge of her nose. "The only thing you have a right to is a bullet in the fucking brain if you don't fucking move the fuck out of my way!"

"Whoa!" yelled McCall, feeling her insides melt as she stared into the barrel of the gun. "What the hell is this? We're on the same side here!"

Fear gripped Maggie tightly, as it never had before. In all her time with the police department, she had never once had to draw her sidearm, much less face down an armed opponent. It was something she had trained for, and given how she excelled in her academy training, she thought she would be prepared for it should it ever happen to her. But staring down the barrel of an actual weapon, especially one wielded by a psychopath of the character she was facing now, was decidedly different than it was in a training scenario. What made it worse was the fact that the masks were off now, there was no more pretending. Rutters didn't care anymore if she knew who he really was, the anger that blazed behind his eyes and the snarl on his lips was evidence of that. Something had set him off, and he was beyond seething with anger. He was pure rage, ready to explode. He just needed a reason to go off, and she was giving him one right now.

"You have until the count of three to step aside, bitch. After that I will blow your whore head off," Rutters snarled between clenched teeth.

Maggie's instincts kicked in, calling on her training in hostage negotiation. It was another skill she had never used before, but if ever a situation needed de-escalation, it was now. "I get that you're upset and I want to help you. If you'll lower your weapon, we can figure out how we can both get what we need out of this situation."

Rutters' teeth were grinding audibly, the hand holding the gun shaking slightly with barely contained rage. "One."

"You don't have to do this. We can find a solution." Her stomach balled up on itself and threatened to rebel against her.

"Two," Rutters said as his other hand gathered into a tight fist.

Maggie looked into his eyes, the eyes of unstoppable violence. Nothing she could say would change what he was about to do. His countdown was merely his way of playing with his prey before going in for the kill. There was no doubt in Maggie's mind that he had always intended to kill her, and now in his deranged mind he had the justification for it.

"It doesn't have to be this way," she stated, her voice eerily calm in the moment.

"Yes, it does," he growled. "You had your chance to walk away. You didn't take it. That was stupid."

She watched his finger tighten on the trigger and snapped her eyes shut, waiting for the shot that would end her life. For a fleeting second, she wondered if there would be pain or if there would be a loud bang and that would be it. At the same time, she berated herself for working into a corner like this, with no escape and no opportunity to reach for her own weapon. Rutters had been right about one thing; she had been stupid. But it wouldn't matter in a second. Nothing would matter.

The sound of the gunshot came, possibly the loudest sound she had ever heard. Her eardrums exploded with pain as the noise echoed down the narrow corridor, reducing her hearing to a mere ringing as it faded. A hot wetness slapped her face, and she heard a low grunting noise. Her eyes opened just in time to see Rutters crumble to the floor, blood flowing from a quarter-sized hole in his forehead. His gun fell from his hand and clattered across the floor; the sound strangely muted to her noise-damaged ears. He fell to his knees and slid backward, his body coming to rest face up. His eyes, the eyes that had held so much rage just seconds before, now stared vacantly at the ceiling.

A voice came from behind her, one that was unmistakable even through the ringing in her ears. The last voice she expected to hear.

"Three."

She turned and there he stood, blood-soaked bandages still tightly wrapped around his midsection and wearing only his boxer shorts. He leaned against the wall to support himself and looked as if he had just walked through Hell, his eyes sunken and unfocused, his body shaking from the effort of keeping him standing. Despite all that, at that moment, Ernie Babcock was the most beautiful sight in the world.

"Ernie!" she exclaimed as she ran to him, throwing her arms around him, heedless of his recent injuries. If her embrace was uncomfortable, he didn't show it, although he leaned into her for support.

"You all right?" he asked, his voice like sandpaper.

"I'm fine," she replied, shifting her weight slightly to add more support underneath his considerably larger frame. "How are *you* feeling?"

Grunting, he pulled himself up to his full height. He didn't take all his weight off Maggie's shoulders, but he was at least able to stand up straight. "Better than expected."

"Ernie, I...." Maggie's voice caught in her throat as she choked back tears. "Thank you."

"No problem," Babcock replied through a strained grimace. "Do me a favor?"

"Anything," she replied.

"Get me back into my room so I can sit down. I'm dead on my feet."

She smiled at his joke, the morbidity of it not lost on her. "Can do, partner."

Matching his pace and keeping as much of his weight on her as he needed, she led him back to his bed, a bed that was going to be his deathbed until a few minutes ago. While helping lower Ernie into a sitting position, she caught sight of Dr. Tanner kneeling over someone on the other side of the room. She couldn't make out who it was, only that they appeared male and were shaking uncontrollably, as if caught in a winter storm. Once Ernie was safely on the bed with Angela by his side, she turned her attention to the fresh problem in the room.

As she approached, she could finally get a look at the face of the young man writhing on the floor, curled into the fetal position with his arms wrapped tightly around himself. His face had completely lost color, his lips had turned an unhealthy shade of blue, and his cheeks and eyes were sunken into his skull. An occasional spasm would wrack his body and he would whimper with each one, marking the fact that there was pain to accompany the chill he was feeling. Despite all that, Maggie recognized him as Alex Carter, the man who was a current subject of interest in the shooting of the police officer whose hospital room he was currently on the floor of.

"What's wrong with him?" she asked as she approached, her hand moving to the weapon at her hip. He didn't seem dangerous, but she had been caught off guard once tonight, she wasn't going to let it happen again.

"I don't know," Celeste answered, a mild panic in her tone. "One minute he's standing over Ernie, the next minute he's crumpled up on the floor like this!" She turned her attention to Angela Babcock, the doctor in her taking over and subjugating the panic. "Angela, will you please hand me those blankets?"

Angela Babcock was still in shock, reeling from the bizarre events unfolding in front of her. Despite feeling shocked and confused, her maternal instincts kicked in and she immediately helped the man who had miraculously saved her husband. Grabbing the neatly folded set of blankets from the foot of Ernie's bed, she brought them to the young man quivering on the floor, promptly unfolding them and laying them carefully over him. His shivering continued, accompanied by the occasional whimper.

"Is he going to be all right?" she asked, kneeling beside Celeste and moving to take the man's hand into hers. As their hands made contact, she recoiled abruptly, as though stung by an unseen electric current.

Ernie Babcock was instantly at his wife's side. "Ang, are you all right?" he asked, taking her hand to check for any physical damage. "What happened?"

Angela Babcock's eyes went wide. Her face went stiff, but her eyes and her tone contained the warmth of caring and concern. "His hand, it's as cold as ice. As cold as death."

"Rachel! No! Rachel!"

Without warning, Alex shot straight up into a prone position as he shouted his wife's name, his eyes wide open and his face a picture of panic, as everyone in the room started at his sudden awakening. To her credit, the already unnerved Angela didn't move from his side.

"Rachel," he repeated, more sedate this time.

Ernie stepped forward, squeezing his huge frame between Angela and Celeste. "What is it? What about Rachel?"

Alex's face was still a mask of panic, his eyes unfocused and staring ahead as if watching something only he could see. After a moment, he went slack and fell back toward the hard floor. Angela reached out and caught him, guiding his head gently to rest on the tile. Tears formed in his eyes, running down his cheeks in silver rivers.

"They've got her."

Rachel was tired of waiting. Tired of worrying. She wanted to get out of the car, walk right into the hospital lobby, and find her husband. No more sneaking around. No more hiding. Whether or not they were looking for her, the hospital was a busy public place. There were always plenty of people around, even at this hour of the day. These people, this 'Eden Project', wouldn't dare try anything with that many witnesses around. She could walk right through the front door and be perfectly safe. Alex was worrying for no reason.

No matter how many times she told herself that she still hadn't dared to leave the car. Despite the front entrance of the hospital being only fifty feet away from where she was parked, she hadn't dared to leave the car. She didn't want to admit it to herself, and she would certainly never admit it to Alex, but she was afraid. She had good reason to be, given the events of the last few days, but she had always thought of giving in to fear as a weakness. Something to be ashamed of. Then again, until recently, she had never known what actual fear looked like and she was rethinking that stance. The fear and the shame of it weren't going away soon, so she sat in the darkness of Celeste's Volkswagen and waited for them to return.

She had been afraid to leave the car, but as the shadows of late afternoon grew into the all-encompassing darkness of night, she had grown afraid of staying. That uncertainty had been at the back of her mind when Alex and Celeste had left the car, but it had grown as the gray of twilight become the black of night. She attempted to brush it off as childish and silly, this sudden fear of the dark, but it held her in an icy grip.

She checked her watch. Alex and Celeste had been gone for just over a half an hour. Closing her eyes, she let her head fall against the headrest as the vinyl seat creaked beneath her. She wondered in silent frustration what was taking them so long. Each second they spent there increased their risk of getting caught. Alex should have known better. It's true they owed Lieutenant Babcock an impossible debt, and maybe Alex could help him somehow, but she was certain the police detective would not want them to be captured. Especially by the people who put him in the hospital in the first place. Despite that, she knew this was the only way this was going to happen. Alex's deep sense of conscience and loyalty guided him in everything he did, and he was loyal to a fault. This was one of the reasons she had decided to marry him and create a life with him. She couldn't demean those same values now that it wasn't easy or convenient.

She opened her eyes and glanced at her watch again. Five more minutes had ticked by. Her sense of anxiety and frustration was becoming difficult to keep in check. What was taking them so long? She sat up and scanned the front of the building, looking for any sign of them. The building looked the same as it had the last dozen times she had checked, but there was something different about it now. Something important.

The guards were gone. The people in black suits that had been patrolling the grounds were nowhere to be seen. A few uniformed police officers remained, stomping their feet and trying to keep warm in the chilly night air, but the mysterious black suits were gone.

Her stomach shrank into a tight knot. Alex had been gone too long. Something had gone terribly wrong with the plan. She regretted listening to Alex and not trusting her own instincts to go with him, cursing herself for it. She should have known better. Alex always led with his heart before his head. Normally, she found it sweet and endearing, but now it terrified her. She had to help but had no idea what that something might be.

Before she realized it, she was out of the car and halfway across the parking lot, heading for the front entrance of the hospital. After silently admonishing Alex for his terrible plan, she was now rushing headlong into the lion's den with absolutely no plan of her own. All she had going for her was a loud voice and lots of bluster. She had spent all that time in the car just waiting and worrying when what she should have been doing was coming up with some contingencies in case the original plan went south, because it was looking like it did. Now she had no other options but to burst into the hospital and hope she could make enough of a scene to give Alex and Celeste a chance to escape.

"Mrs. Carter?"

The sudden voice from behind startled her, causing her to jump. A sharp gasp escaped her as she turned, wild-eyed, to face whoever had just spoken her name. Standing next to a black SUV, the kind she had seen surrounding her house the previous night, was a man clad in one of the ubiquitous black suits. He was shorter than most of the others she had seen, with a slight shock of gray running through his close-cut hair, but his build was broad and strong. Despite his height, he carried himself in a way that commanded respect, even from strangers. The confidence of his stance and deep, resounding voice reinforced the fact that this man was a leader. The knot in her stomach tightened further.

"Are you Mrs. Rachel Carter?" the man asked again in a polite yet demanding tone.

Rachel involuntarily took a few steps back away from him. "Please, whoever you are, just stay away from me and my family. Please."

"I'm sorry to have to do this," the man said as he quickly closed the distance between them, "but I have my instructions. I have to bring you in. You've been the subject of this mission from the beginning, you see."

Rachel froze as the words hit her. "What do you mean?" she asked, her voice only a whisper. "Alex is the one you've been after."

"I'm afraid not," the man continued, his deep voice calm and even. "The moment your child was conceived, your husband became expendable."

The knot of fear in her stomach suddenly released as a rush of anger hit her. Planting her feet firmly on the pavement, she stood straight against the man in the black suit. "I hope you rot in hell."

His lip curled up slightly at one end in a sad smirk. "I'm certain I will, Mrs. Carter. Someday. But for now, I have a job to do."

Before she could so much as make a sound, the man's hand flashed out from behind his back and darted towards her like a striking cobra. She felt a sharp but brief pain, like the bite of a snake, in her neck. Almost immediately, the world around her blurred and her legs crumpled beneath her. She never hit the ground, but she didn't feel anyone stopping her fall as all feeling left her and the world became a void around her. The already dim light of the parking lot quickly faded to black, the sounds of the night becoming ever more distant. Just before she left the word entirely and fell into a warm, comfortable blackness, she heard the man in black whisper softly to her.

"Sleep tight," he said, and she slid into oblivion.

"We need to get the hell out of here," Babcock said as he pulled himself out of bed and crossed to the small closet that held his belongings. He rummaged through, pulling out the clothes that Angela had optimistically brought for him earlier in hopes he would recover. Ernie was grateful for his wife's hopefulness as he slipped into a pair of jeans and a button-down shirt. "Those goons'll be on us any minute."

His recovery had been nothing short of miraculous since Alex's laying on of hands as he was nearly back to being his old self again, with only a diminishing limp as evidence of injuries that were fatal an hour ago. Already he was on the move, gathering his clothes while strategizing his next move. He moved like a man possessed and singularly focused on his mission, which tonight was ensuring the safety of the people in his care.

"Let me see what I can do about that," McCall said, reaching for her radio. "I may not be able to stop them, but I'm sure I can slow them down a bit."

Babcock nodded at her as he shrugged into his shoulder holster before turning his attention to Alex. "You gonna be okay, kid?"

"Yeah, I think so," Alex answered, although he wasn't sure how close to the truth that was. Healing Babcock had taken a lot out of him, and he wasn't going to get much time to rest and recoup his energy and strength. It would come back, he was sure of that, he just didn't know if it would happen quickly enough. And time was something they didn't have a lot of.

"We have to get to Rachel. They've got her," he announced, heading for the door. The first few steps caused his head to swim, and he thought for a moment he might black out, but the feeling passed quickly and he was able to keep his footing.

"So you've said," Babcock chided as he slipped into his shoes. "Where is she?"

"Still by the front entrance," Alex replied. He had no idea how he knew that, he just did. It was like he could feel her there. Like he could sense her presence.

"Then that's where we're going," Babcock stated, slamming the cylinder of his revolver back into place and slipping the gun into its holster. "Celeste, will you make sure Angela gets home okay?"

Celeste nodded in reply. "Be careful, you dumb ox," she said with a smile, gently punching his arm.

He returned her smile with a smirk of his own. "Nothing but."

"Ernest Jonathan Babcock, if you think I'm going to let you just walk out of here after everything that's happened, after almost losing you, you're insane!" Angela Babcock stepped up to her husband, shaking an index finger at him. She was a good two heads shorter than him and at least a hundred pounds lighter, but she made no concessions about letting him know exactly what was on her mind.

Babcock looked down at her, his face softening. "Ang, please. The kid's in trouble. His wife is in trouble. You know I have to do this."

"I just got you back," Angela replied, unsuccessfully choking back tears. "I don't understand the connection between this man, his wife, and everything that's happening. All I know is that I can't bear the thought of losing you."

"I love you too," he replied, his own voice little more than a whisper, "but I have to go. Please understand."

She lifted her head to meet his eyes and smiled a weak smile. "I understand. I understood that when I married you. This is who you are." She rested her head against the middle of his chest as tears dropped from her eyes. "Please, just come back in one piece."

He bent his massive frame down and gently kissed the top of her head. "You know I always do my best. I'll be back, Ang. I'll always come back."

"You better," she choked out, glistening tears on her cheeks. Stepping back from her husband, she turned to Alex. "I'll be honest, I have no idea what just happened here. I also don't care. Whatever you did, thank you for saving my husband's life."

"My pleasure," Alex replied, an awkward smile on his face. He was unsure how to handle her appreciation for something he didn't understand how he accomplished.

"Make sure I get him back," Angela continued.

Alex nodded. "I will. You have my word on that."

She nodded back in reply and left the room with only one more lingering glance at Ernie before going. Celeste started after her, then turned back to the two of them.

"I'll stay with her until you get back," she said directly to Ernie.

His voice soft, Babcock replied, "Thank you."

"Please be careful," Celeste continued, her eyes darting between the two of them. "Both of you." Without another word, she slipped out of the room to catch up with Angela.

Babcock turned his attention to Alex, his demeanor all business again. "Do you know where Rachel is now?"

Alex felt through the night, through the distance between them, to find her. When he did, it was faint. Almost nonexistent. His stomach coiled around itself as he realized he was losing track of her.

Babcock had gotten to know the look that crossed Alex's face. "What's wrong?"

"She's gone," Alex replied, his heart falling to his feet inside him. "We're too late. They've got her."

Babcock came forward and planted a massive hand on Alex's shoulder, squeezing gently. "It's not too late. We're going to find her, and we're going to get her back."

Alex didn't answer, instead holding tight to the dwindling psychic impression of his wife as she was being taken from him. Ernie was right, they would find her. They would get her back. And once she was safe, he would burn the entire Eden Project to the ground.

Closing his eyes, he whispered into the ether. "Be safe, Rachel. We're coming."

49

Alex gripped the steering wheel of Celeste's Jetta and yanked hard, forcing the car around the corner in a protest of squealing tires. He and Babcock were harshly thrown to the right as the car made the left turn, just barely still on two wheels, before evening out again as Alex shot down the narrow road.

"For the love of Christ, will you take it easy!" Babcock yelled as he pulled himself upright in the passenger's seat. "We can't help anyone if you wrap us around a tree, damn it!"

"Sorry," Alex answered. His voice was distant and vacant, responding more out of habit than being part of the conversation. His attention was on the road ahead.

He had been in a mad rush since the police had started sorting through the mess back at the hospital. McCall's people had rounded up a few of the faux federal agents that had lagged behind, but they remained as stone-faced and intractable as ever. Not one had said so much as a single word since their arrest. Not to the police, not even to each other. No pleas for lawyers, no threats, nothing at all. Just silence. Alex found that silence to be more frightening than any threat they could have voiced, as it meant they were loyal to whomever they worked for. Loyal to where they would risk prison, or worse, before they divulged any information that might compromise their operation.

Even the mousy technician McCall had thought might be easy to break had kept up the same icy façade as the others, although she was prone to breaking out in a sweat whenever Babcock or McCall were around. She was frightened, that much was certain. She just wasn't frightened of them. It was something else that was spooking her, or more likely someone else. The someone that was the key to finding Rachel.

Babcock's cell phone suddenly rang. "What the hell!" the cop exclaimed, the noise startling his already jangled nerves. He fumbled through his jacket pocket before finally grasping it in his sausage fingers and answering the call. "What is it?"

He listened to the caller on the other end of the phone intently, remaining so silent and still that Alex wasn't even sure if he was breathing. After listening intently for another minute, he breathed out a heavy, exasperated breath. "Holy shit. What the fuck are we into here?" A few more seconds of silence. "We'll keep you posted. Let me know if anything else comes up. And bring Celeste in on this. We're gonna need her." With that, he disconnected the call and sat staring at the phone.

"Who was that?" Alex asked, navigating around an enormous puddle left by last night's storm.

"McCall," Babcock answered. As he spoke, Alex felt something radiating from him he had never felt from the man before. A powerful emotion, intense like the heat from a winter bonfire.

It was fear.

"The phony feds she had in custody are dead."

"What?" Alex exclaimed, pulling the car back onto the road after veering to avoid another huge puddle. "They're dead? All of them?"

"Yeah," Babcock replied, "Looks that way." He rubbed his chin absently, the three days of stubble there rough on his hands. "Suicide, apparently. All except for one."

"There's still one alive?"

The fear Alex was sensing from Babcock took a sudden turn, becoming a nauseating feeling as terror and uncertainty settled in. "No, she's dead," the detective answered. He paused again, clearing his throat before he continued. "Wasn't suicide, though. She was murdered by the others."

"Oh my God," was all Alex could manage.

"It was a technician, apparently. McCall said she had seen her with someone named Rutters, one of the higher ups. He's the guy I shot, the one who was about to kill Maggie."

"Yeah," Alex answered, letting Babcock sort through everything in his own time. For good people, killing didn't come easy. Even for someone as hardened as Ernie Babcock appeared to be, taking someone else's life left deep psychological scars. It would take some time to reconcile that. Time they didn't have now, unfortunately. For now, they simply had to allow each other whatever moments they could take to keep themselves moving forward. Especially knowing the violence and death weren't over yet. Not by a long shot.

"She was the one who was murdered," Babcock continued, his voice regaining some of its usual rough edge. "McCall seems to think she was ready to spill some information, and that's why the others killed her. Just before killing themselves."

"How did they do it?" Alex asked, somewhat surprised, and a bit frightened, by his sudden morbid curiosity.

Babcock looked up from his lap and met the younger man's eyes. "The murder or the suicides?"

"Both," Alex stated flatly.

Babcock took a deep breath and exhaled loudly. "The killing was pretty basic. Snapped her neck. Clean and easy and relatively painless."

Alex shuddered. It wasn't the worst way to go he could imagine, but it certainly wasn't a great way. "The suicides?"

Babcock paused again before continuing. When he did, Alex could hear a deep sense of desperation, almost defeat, in his voice. "McCall was pretty sure it was poison, but she couldn't figure out how it might have happened. She called Celeste who, on a long shot, had Maggie check inside their mouths. Specifically, their dental work."

"What did she find?" Alex asked.

"Three of them had false molars that were cracked in half." She stopped there, assuming they'd all be the same."

Even though it was the answer he'd been expecting, it still hit Alex like a punch to the gut. "Holy shit. Phony teeth filled with poison, inserted into phony federal agents. That's some James Bond level shit right there! Who are these guys, and what the hell were they doing with suicidal dental work?"

"Suddenly I feel like we're in way over our heads," Babcock replied, almost under his breath.

A fresh wave of fear and doubt radiated from the man. It was intense, an almost physical feeling of hopelessness. Intermingled with that was a sharp sense of responsibility, duty and resolve as the two fought against one another. Babcock's dedication to protect the innocent, clashing with his sense of self-preservation and duty to his loved ones. Knowing the man, Alex had a feeling which one would win out, the only decision Babcock would make. Alex felt a twinge of quiet guilt.

"Ernie, I...."

"There!" Babcock interrupted suddenly, thrusting a thick finger forward and pointing into the darkness ahead. The headlights of the car cut through the country night and a sign appeared ahead, reading 'Drake Farm' with the names Burt and Edna Drake beneath it.

"That's the place," Alex replied, slowing the car as they passed an old farmhouse sitting atop a slight rise near the road. "This is where Forrester said to meet them."

"There's the stone wall," Babcock announced. In the night's gloom, they could barely make out the ancient-looking stone wall that lined the property. "The turn should be just ahead."

Suddenly, out of the night ahead of them, two points of red light sprang up, peering back at them like the eyes of a demon in the darkness. Alex recognized what they were, but he couldn't help feeling his stomach jump and clench, as the effect wasn't lost on him. A few more yards forward and two granite posts with red reflectors marked an opening in the stone wall that led onto a dirt road that was barely a road in the middle of a field. As he turned the car and navigated the narrow opening between the posts, Alex noticed an odd set of lights in the field about two hundred yards ahead. Small red, white, and yellow lights flashing intermittently in the total darkness.

"What's that?" Babcock asked, leaning forward and squinting into the night.

Alex shrugged. "Only one way to find out, I guess."

He drove on along the rough road, the car violently jumping and jolting over unseen potholes and crevices carved into the dirt from the previous night's rain. The second time the car loudly scraped its bottom on a hidden rock, Alex stopped, afraid to keep moving forward. If they had to escape quickly, Celeste's Jetta was their only option for that. Stranding it on the exposed edge of a buried boulder wouldn't be prudent to their safety.

He put the car in park and turned off the engine. "Looks like this is as far as we go by car."

"Just as well," Babcock replied. "We can be a lot sneakier on foot if need be."

Alex nodded agreement, then opened the car door and stepped out into the night. He carefully adjusted the pistol he had taken from Rutters, ensuring it was snug against the small of his back for quick access, and then slipped into his coat. As he emerged from behind the car door, a burst of cool air hit him like a slap, causing his eyes to sting and his hair to dance in the breeze. This initial blast was quickly followed by a succession of identical gusts, creating a wavelike sensation that washed over him. It wasn't a natural wind, certainly not like any storm he had ever experienced. In the distance, in the open field where he and Babcock had seen the blinking lights, he could make out an odd whooshing noise that seemed to be the center of the unusual windstorm.

Babcock came up next to him, annoyedly slapping at the collar of his coat as it repeatedly blew against his face. "Sounds like your friends came through."

"C'mon, let's go," Alex replied, cautiously making their way along the dirt road towards the flickering lights and the gentle rustling of the wind.

The terrain was difficult to traverse in the dark, but they eventually came close enough to the field of blinking lights and whooshing sounds they could perceive a shape in the darkness. A massive outline, black against black, like a sleeping dragon waiting to devour any travelers unlucky enough to wander too close to its maw.

A cone of blinding white light, like the fiery breath of the dragon, cut through the darkness and fell on them. Alex froze, half expecting to burn at its touch. His hand snapped to his waistband and retrieved the pistol there. Babcock already had his revolver in hand. Their eyes fought against the intense light, still adjusting from the darkness they had just left behind. As they strained their eyes against the glaring light, the relentless wind whipped against their faces, making it impossible to make out anything in the field of pure white. Unable to see behind the light, both men raised their weapons and took aim at what they thought was the center of the field.

"Whoa! Hold up!" came a voice from behind the light. "Didn't mean to scare you, just wanted to make sure you were friendlies."

Alex stepped forward past the cone of blinding light that had trapped him and Babcock like mesmerized deer. As the light receded, he could distinguish Rick sitting near the passenger door of an enormous helicopter, a type that seemed straight out of a war movie. The war movie analogy was further driven home by the fact that Rick had an assault rifle cradled in his arms.

Slinging the rifle over his shoulder, Rick jumped from the helicopter's side platform and stepped forward to greet Alex. "Like it?" he asked, sweeping his arm toward the helicopter with all the enthusiasm of a child with a new toy.

Alex took in the full scope of the machine. He had seen helicopters in his life, but never a military gunship like this one. And never one painted completely black.

"It's incredible," he replied, running a hand over the smooth metal of the exterior. "How did you pull it off?"

Rick shrugged. "The pilot owed me a few favors, so I called 'em all in."

"Pretty big payback," Alex replied.

"Not as big as you might think," Rick said, turning back to the gunship's platform to click the searchlight off. "Like Dr. Forrester and me, the pilot is a rather disgruntled employee of PenTech and the Eden Project. When I called him and explained the situation, particularly the part about bringing down the Project, he was all in."

Alex's mind flashed back to the murdered technician in the Pine Haven police department's holding cells. The Eden Project, or Robert Penders for that matter, did not take kindly to disgruntled or disloyal employees.

As if on cue, a man emerged from the cockpit, a man Alex didn't recognize. Carefully, Alex reached his hand behind him, his fingers wrapping around the cold metal of the pistol. He still wasn't sure he could trust the man who had been his lifelong best friend, he wasn't about to put his faith in strangers right now.

Rick's eyes flashed to Alex as he reached for his gun. Stepping between Alex and the pilot, he waved a hand up toward him. "Alex, meet Lars Cameon. Our pilot. Lars, Alex Carter."

As his name implied, Lars was a large, Icelandic looking man with long blond hair pulled back sharply to reveal a weathered face that framed ice-blue eyes. The man's face was completely neutral, betraying no emotional state whatsoever. As Alex was rapidly learning, he no longer had to depend on external signals. Focusing on the large Slavic man, Alex sensed the enthusiasm of an adventurer inside him. An almost child-like need to wander and discover which he kept concealed behind a wall of anger, mistrust, and fear of betrayal. It was his fear of being betrayed that had prompted him to help when Rick had contacted him, with Lars seeing it as an opportunity to strike back against his employer. Alex relaxed a bit on learning that. Lars' intentions were more revenge driven than altruistic, but they aligned with Alex's intentions and right now that was all he needed.

Alex offered his free hand to Lars. "Pleasure to meet you."

Lars regarded Alex's outstretched hand for a moment before brusquely turning away. "We should get moving," he said, his baritone voice bearing no hint of the accent Alex would have expected. Without another word, he disappeared back into the cockpit.

"Friendly guy," Alex remarked.

"He may seem gruff and unfriendly, but don't let that fool you. Underneath that grumpy exterior lies an even grumpier heart," Rick replied.

Alex smiled, but something looming over Rick's shoulder swiftly refocused his attention. "Won't our take-off wake the neighbors?" Alex asked, indicating the farmhouse about a quarter mile behind them.

"I doubt it," Rick replied. "That house and the four sub-basements beneath it are an Eden Project safe house. They established it here shortly after you arrived. According to Lars, Harriman has mobilized all the security personnel, leaving the safe house nearly empty. Might be a few techs still inside, wrapping things up and sanitizing evidence. Burt and Edna will still be there, but they won't bat an eye at another helicopter taking off from their field. They'll think we're just stragglers, the last of the group to bug out. Besides, the whole farmhouse won't exist after tomorrow."

"What do you mean, it won't exist?" Alex asked. "What will happen to it?"

Rick shrugged. "Same thing that always happens in these situations. At some point tonight, the Pine Haven Fire Department will get a call about a gas line explosion. When they arrive, they'll find the house destroyed, the explosion having conveniently filled in the sub-basements as well. Two bodies will be discovered, eventually identified as Burt and Edna." Rick looked up at the house. Alex felt a twinge of regret in him as he did, not for the house or its occupants, but about how its destruction represented his own life at that moment. "The Eden Project is very good at covering their tracks."

Alex took a step toward him and placed a hand on his shoulder. "You worried about them coming after you?"

"I'd be an idiot if I wasn't," Rick answered, the usual bravado in his voice giving way to a slight quavering. "They're powerful, Alex. More powerful than you can imagine. What you've seen, everything you've been through, that's the tip of the iceberg. Penders is powerful, but he's only one arm of the monster. I don't know how many others there are or how far their reach is, but I know they control powerful people and their resources are practically endless. It's possible there's no escape from them. I don't know about you, but I find that possibility scary. Damned scary."

The same thought had run through Alex's mind more than he cared to admit. And now the same shadow organization that instilled crippling fear in the hearts of every life they touched had just kidnapped the most important person in his world. It didn't matter how powerful they were, he would get her back. No matter what it took.

"It is damned scary," Alex replied, "but right now, I don't really care. I want Rachel back and I don't care who I have to go through to get her. Once that's done, I'll worry about the future."

Rick turned to him, a lost look in his eyes. "After today, we may not have a future." He turned away again and, without another word, slung the rifle over his shoulder and climbed on board the helicopter.

"Cheery thought," Babcock said, coming up behind Alex.

Alex turned around to face the detective, raising his voice to be heard over the sound of the rotors. "He makes a good point. I met your wife tonight. Amazing woman. Incredible cook. Braver than she looks. Strong, too. And those pictures you showed me of your kids, they're beautiful."

"Alex, I...."

Alex raised a hand to cut him off. "Go home. Be safe. Be with your family. This thing is so big, so dangerous. You've already given more than your fair share to it. And to me. I can't ask you to give up anything more. I don't want to see you get killed over this. That's something I couldn't live with."

"What about Rachel?"

"Don't worry about Rachel, she's more than capable of taking care of herself. We'll get her back." Alex reached out, offering his hand to Babcock. "Have some faith."

Babcock took Alex's hand, the cop's gigantic hand devouring Alex's. "Good luck."

"Thank you," Alex replied. "For everything you've done for us. For believing in me. For everything."

"Sounds final," Babcock said, a sly smile crossing his face. "I hope you plan on coming back. I want to see that baby."

Alex didn't reply, instead simply nodding.

Babcock released Alex's hand and smiled awkwardly. "Don't worry about what happened at your house. I'll smooth that over."

Alex returned the smile. "Thanks," he murmured, his voice trailing off as he turned to climb into the helicopter. But then, with one foot on the landing, he reconsidered and turned back to face Babcock. "There is one more thing you can do for me."

"Name it."

"That farmhouse." Alex nodded towards Burt and Edna Drake's house on the hill. "At some point tonight there's going to be a massive gas line explosion there that will completely level the house and kill the owners."

"Jesus," Babcock breathed. "What can I do?"

"Don't let it happen. Get McCall and every other cop, firefighter and EMS personnel you can up here and stop that explosion from happening. Keep the evidence from going up in flames and get whatever you can that might expose PenTech, Robert Pender, and this Eden Project, whoever they might be. Don't let them disappear without a trace again."

Babcock's smile widened. "It'll be my pleasure."

Alex acknowledged him with a nod before swiftly entering the helicopter, not saying anything more. For now, they had said all that needed to be said. Strangely, Alex hoped this wouldn't be the last time he saw Babcock. When they first met, Babcock had been ready to run him in for the murder of Dr. Carlton. A few days later here he was, ready to rush headlong into who knows what kind of danger to save the life of a woman he barely knew. Men like that were rare, and Alex felt lucky to have met one of the best.

"Everyone strapped in?" Lars called from the cockpit.

Rick and Dr. Forrester already sat securely fastened in their seatbelts. Alex sat across from them and buckled his, giving Lars the thumbs up signal.

The door of the helicopter's passenger compartment remained open and the wind outside picked up suddenly as the rotors spun faster to gain enough lift for take-off. Alex watched the field below as Babcock's silhouette faded, eventually being swallowed up by the all-encompassing darkness. As the detective's silhouette vanished into the darkness, Alex redirected his focus to the interior of the helicopter. Rick, Dr. Forrester and Lars. Two people he barely knew and one whose betrayal was so recent and complete it left a bitter sting in the open wound that was their friendship. Aside from Rachel, the only person he felt he could trust was dwindling away with each foot the helicopter climbed, consumed by the night. Everything had happened so fast. Without any time to think or plan, he found himself thrust into this situation, and the weight of reality was settling in. He had to get Rachel back, no matter what it took. He was willing to go to any lengths, even making a pact with the devil, to ensure that it happened.

As he looked around him at his companions in the deep black interior of the helicopter, illuminated by a slight red glow from the interior light, he wondered if that wasn't exactly what he had done.

50

Adam watched the helicopter lift off from the field, the running lights eventually becoming nothing more than moving stars against a larger field of glittering gems. Carter was on the move again, off to find his lost bride. Love had made Alex Carter rash. Stupid, even. He was running headlong into the mouth of the beast with no idea of what waited for him.

The players were coming together. The end of the game was near, and Adam could already feel victory swelling in his chest. Soon, Adam would finally claim what should have been his, and he would see the pretenders and persecutors all dead or broken, thrown from their ivory towers. Everything was falling into place.

Almost everything.

Retrieving his cell phone from his jacket pocket, he dialed the familiar number with a methodical slowness, savoring each digit his finger landed on. A giddy feeling seized him as the phone rang. Once. Twice. Thrice. Four times. It didn't matter; he was patient. Besides, the person on the receiving end of the call was sure to be quite busy right now. He could wait.

The fifth ring was interrupted halfway through. "Darnell here! What the hell do you want?"

Adam smiled. Burke Darnell sounded haggard. It must have been quite a night for him. "Having a rough night, Burke?"

Dead air followed for a moment as Burke realized who he was talking to. "Adam," he said, drawing the name out in an exasperated breath.

"Correct," Adam replied, reveling in the shock value of his voice.

Burke wasted no time on pleasantries. "Where are you?"

Adam chuffed. "You really don't believe I'm going to tell you that, do you?"

"One can hope," Burke replied. "Why are you calling me?"

"I was there tonight," Adam said. "At the hospital. I saw it all. A shame what happened. Really. I almost feel bad about it."

"You were here?" Burke stated, his voice strained.

"Yes, I was," Adam confirmed. The warm, giddy feeling in his stomach grew, expanding toward his groin. It excited him. "Such a shame for you, losing so many people who, at one time, you believed were loyal. First me, then Dr. Forrester, and now Colonel Harriman. I must admit, that one shocked me a little. He was always such a good little toy soldier."

Anger crept into Burke's tone. "What do you know about Harriman?"

Adam didn't answer right away, savoring the silence that Burke no doubt found infuriating. "I know he disobeyed your orders. And in doing so, got in my way."

Adam could almost hear Burke pinching the bridge of his nose in frustration. "Look, Adam, I'm completely out of patience here. If you have something to tell me, say it. If not, leave me alone so I can concentrate on finding you so I can kill you."

"Harriman absconded with Mrs. Carter," Adam answered, brushing off Burke's threat. "Took her right out from under my nose, so to speak. He left the Drake Farm a short while ago in one of those black helicopters you're so fond of."

"Fuck!" Burke exclaimed, this time not even trying to conceal his anger.

"I'm sure you know where he's going," Adam teased.

"Yeah," Burke replied through clenched teeth. "I know."

"Then you should get yourself there," Adam suggested. "Things are bound to be getting interesting by the time you arrive. Oh, and as for looking for me, you might as well quit right now."

"Why would I do that?" Burke asked with both anger and curiosity.

"Because I'll see you at Gabriel's Nest." Adam reached for the 'end' button, but stopped himself suddenly.

"Before I go, I want to leave you with a final thought."

Burke let out an exasperated sigh. "And what would that be?"

"Harriman has never disobeyed an order in his life. Until today, I wouldn't have thought him capable of it. Yet he disobeyed yours."

"Yeah, so?"

"So, it makes you wonder. He must have had an order from someone else that contradicted yours."

"Your point being...?"

Adam closed his eyes, savoring his final comment. "There's only one person in the Eden Project whose authority supersedes yours. If he gave the order, one has to wonder why you were left out of the loop?"

Before Burke could reply, Adam ended the conversation and tossed the phone out the car window, then leaned back in the driver's seat with a satisfied smile. *Now* everything was falling into place.

51

Alex stared out the cabin window, absently watching the dark landscape as it roiled and tumbled beneath him. The way the terrain seemed to heave and shift in the darkness as the helicopter sped past, lacking shape or substance and instead appearing like some bizarre surrealist painting in motion, reminded him of his life right now. One long stretch of constant turmoil.

It didn't appear as if the tumult would abate soon, either. In fact, if the last few days were any sign, it was about to get worse. Much worse.

As evidence of that, Rick was seated directly across from him, meticulously inspecting weapons that Alex had only seen in action movies. Rick had produced the arsenal from the storage compartments under the seats just after they had taken off from the Drake Farm.

"Just a few things I'm sure we'll need when we get there," he had said, setting the weapons down one at a time on a toolbox that was doubling as a workbench.

It had been a surprise when Rick had produced the weapons, but what shocked Alex more was the fact that he seemed to have a working knowledge of each gun Rick laid out. As he eyed each gun, different tactical scenarios ran through his mind that would maximize the efficiency of the weapon. Ways to modify them as needed for any situation. These images ran roughshod through his head, even though he had no memory of ever seeing or touching guns like those laid out in front of Rick.

Turning his attention away from Rick and his work, he focused on the handgun on the seat next to him. It was the gun he had taken from the late Sergeant Rutters, whom he had since learned from Rick was yet another member of Penders' elite security force. It hadn't thought about it at the time, but when he first picked it up it had felt so natural to him. The weight was comfortable in his hand, like it was a natural extension of him. With no conscious effort, he had engaged the safety and slid the weapon under his belt at the small of his back, where it would be least conspicuous. The action had been a natural one for him, as if he had been born to it.

"Are you all right?"

Startled, Alex looked in the direction the voice had come from. Dr. Forrester had moved from his seat at the opposite window to sit next to Alex. His face was a mask of concern, but whether it was concern for Alex as a person or an experiment he couldn't be sure.

"I'm fine, thanks," Alex replied, turning his attention back out the window and onto the churning darkness again.

"I understand these are difficult circumstances you find yourself in," Forrester said, his tone almost parental. "But I have confidence you will get through them, my boy. You must. If not for your sake, then for that of your wife and unborn child."

"Doctor," Alex began, turning slowly from the darkness out the window and focusing his attention on the scientist, "I could pick up any of those guns right there and know exactly where to aim to do exactly the amount of damage I want to inflict. I could kill you instantly, before you could even so much as blink. Or I could draw it out and make you suffer for hours. Or I could kill or maim you a dozen different ways with my bare hands. I'm discovering information hidden in my own mind that I never would have imagined was there, and that isn't even what scares me the most. Do you know what scares me more than that?"

"What?" Forrester asked, trying not to register on his face the fear Alex could feel radiating from him.

"The fact that, as recently as three days ago, I had never even seen guns like those. And as for unarmed combat skills, let's just say that before all of this happened, Rachel could have knocked me on my ass easily if she wanted to."

"That's true," Rick interjected without looking up from his work.

"What I'm saying here, Doctor," Alex continued, "is that before you came into my life, I had a happy, normal existence. I lived in a quiet little town where my best friend and I owned a prosperous business. I was married to a beautiful woman, the love of my life, and we were expecting our first child. I was planning to paint the baby's nursery next week. I had a happy, normal, boring life, and I loved it. What I didn't know was my happy life was as fragile as a soap bubble that would burst at the slightest touch. Then you and the Eden Project came along with the harshest touch imaginable and completely obliterated my life."

Alex paused, letting the anger settle inside him before continuing. "Granted, it's a life I owe to you. Without you, I never would have existed. But in all honesty, given the choice, I would have chosen nonexistence."

"I know," Dr. Forrester replied, his voice heavy, "and it fills me with regret. Still, despite everything you've endured, think of the benefits you have to offer the world."

"Benefits?" Alex answered, eyebrow raised. "What benefits?"

"My boy," Forrester continued, a renewed sense of hope in his tone, "think of the remarkable abilities you've displayed! Think about what happened at the hospital! I knew you had an ability to heal yourself, I never imagined you might heal another person! Who knows what else you are capable of?"

"That," Alex interrupted, "is what scares me most. If even you, the person who created me, aren't certain what I'm capable of, then how could I possibly know? Worse, what about my baby?"

"What about the baby?" Dr. Forrester asked.

"The baby has half of my genetics. Genes that aren't... normal. What will he or she inherit from me? What will they be capable of? Worst of all..." Alex paused, not sure he wanted to voice his next thought as he may manifest it into reality. "Worst of all, what will they choose to do with their abilities? Will they be like me, or end up like... him? How can you be certain about the baby when you don't even fully know what I'm capable of? Who knows what the genetic soup you concocted might do when passed on?"

Forrester turned away, afraid to look the younger man in the eye. "That," he stammered, "isn't entirely true."

The heavy, cold feeling in Alex's stomach, the one that had been with him since the first nightmare invaded his sleep, took hold again. Pushing it down, he faced the doctor. "What's not entirely true?"

The doctor was quiet, staring straight ahead and not returning Alex's gaze. Alex could sense the fear and uncertainty in him as he considered how to answer the question he had just been asked. It wasn't something he wanted to address right now, that much was certain, but there was also a sense of determination in him to be straightforward.

His honest side won out. "Where your gifts came from," he stammered, "I have an idea."

The chill in Alex's stomach became a raging blizzard. "Go on."

The doctor continued, a slight quiver in his voice. "The data you recovered from Simone's office, there was a file titled 'Fallen Angel'."

"Yes," Alex replied, even though the doctor hadn't phrased it as a question. Alex felt certain Forrester knew exactly what they found on that thumb drive. He wouldn't be surprised if Forrester had arranged for them to discover it in the first place. "Along with other things."

"The other files aren't a concern right now," Dr. Forrester continued. "Just Fallen Angel. Did you see it?"

The picture they had found in that file suddenly sprang to life in his head, the crashed flying saucer surrounded by men and women in military fatigues and hazmat suits. He hoped that wasn't what Forrester was referring to, but the ice storm in his stomach was telling him differently. Nodding, he said, "Yes, I've seen it."

Forrester took off his glasses and wiped his forehead with his coat sleeve. "Then you know I was there."

"I saw you in the picture," Alex answered.

"And you know what was in the picture?"

"I know what I think was in the picture," Alex replied, hoping with all his heart he was wrong.

"When I was building the DNA structure for all of you, I found I couldn't complete key segments of it. Segments that were crucial to the viability of your genetic make-up. There were bridges that had to be built to close those gaps, to create an ideal human being. You can't imagine how frustrating it was to be so close to achieving my dream, only to come up a few components short. I was so eager to finish my work..." Dr. Forrester trailed off, pausing for a moment. Closing his eyes, he rubbed hard against the eyelids with the palms of his hands, as if he were trying to crush the images behind them only he could see. After a few more seconds of silence, he put his glasses back on, leaned back, and sighed. "I suppose I was a bit too eager."

Alex felt a slight trickle of frigid sweat on his back. "What do you mean?"

"At first, I was skeptical," Forrester said, slipping once again into his scientist persona. "I'm a man of science, after all. Statistics certainly support the existence of extraterrestrial life, but to face the reality of it was daunting. Almost impossible to believe. Imagine my surprise when I arrived at the crash site and found myself in charge of the salvaging of a genuine otherworldly craft. The excitement was almost too much to contain."

"Hold on," Alex said, holding out a palm to the Doctor. "Are you saying that picture was real?"

A slight grin crossed Dr. Forrester's face, and he nodded. "Yes. Yes, it was."

"The Eden Project salvaged the wreckage of the ship?" Alex asked, incredulously.

"I didn't say that."

"Yes, you did. Just a minute ago, you said you had been in charge of the salvage operation."

Forrester nodded. "My apologies, I misspoke. Yes, I was in charge of the scientific end of the operation. What I meant was, there was no wreck. The ship was undamaged by the crash."

Alex's world suddenly dropped out from under him. He felt light-headed, like he might pass out. He dropped his eyes to the floor of the helicopter cabin, finding a rivet there to focus on. One small piece of normalcy he could use to bring himself back to reality. After a moment of staring at that rivet to center himself, he continued.

"You're saying the Eden Project took possession of an alien spacecraft? An intact, undamaged spacecraft?"

"That's correct," Forrester answered.

"And you didn't contact the Air Force about this crashed, yet undamaged, UFO?"

The doctor's grin widened. "Who do you think called us?"

"The U.S. government called a shadow organization to recover and research a downed UFO?"

"I think you underestimate the resources and influence of both PenTech and the Eden Project," Dr. Forrester stated, the grin gracing his face now vanishing altogether. "There isn't anything out of their reach."

The ominous tone of the doctor unnerved Alex. He focused the direction of the conversation away from the Eden Project. "What was inside the spaceship?"

"Very little, yet more than you can imagine," Forrester answered cryptically.

"You'll have to be more specific," Alex answered, not bothering to hide his irritation with Forrester.

"Yes, of course," replied the scientist, bringing his focus back to the conversation. "For the engineers, there has been very little. They've been examining that ship for years and are no closer today to understanding how it works than they were the day it was recovered. In fact, they haven't yet figured out to even open the damnable thing! But for me? For me, it was a veritable treasure trove." He leaned back fully in his seat and closed his eyes, as if savoring some sweet memory he didn't want tainted by the present-day world. "We discovered the body of the creature we assume to be the pilot just outside the craft, dead but otherwise completely undamaged."

Alex's jaw went slack. Dr. Forrester paused again to savor his reaction.

Alex was speechless. Literally. His head was spinning with the revelation Forrester had just made. He pushed down the swirling mess inside his head as best he could and was finally able to find his voice.

"You found an alien? An actual alien? From outer space?"

Dr. Forrester chuffed at him. "When you say it like that, it sounds so pedestrian. Like a bad 1950s science fiction film. But yes, we did find a genuine extraterrestrial being. A lifeform not of this Earth, proof that we are not alone in the universe. Truly, the scientific discovery of the century, if not the millennium. I will admit, I was awed by it. But then again, it would be difficult not to be. That sort of event tends to put a marker on your entire life, as if you're starting life over from that point, counting down the days from that one critical moment in time. An event so monumental you no longer have anything to look forward to because anything that comes after couldn't possibly measure up to it."

Alex's head was still swimming with the ramifications of this new information. He had always had an interest in flying saucers and aliens, speculating about life on other planets, watching the documentaries that talked about aliens and abductions. But that was different.

That was just him and his friends engaging in harmless speculation over a few drinks, where seemingly outlandish theories can be easily explained away by alcohol. But this, this went far beyond speculation.

"I understand how you feel," he finally replied. "I think, for me, that day is today."

"That day for me wasn't the day we recovered the craft and its pilot. No, for me, that day came later. For me, it was the day I made a discovery far more staggering than the mere existence of the creature." Dr. Forrester paused as if once again savoring the memory. "You recall I mentioned the missing pieces in the DNA sequences that had stymied me for so long?"

Alex nodded.

"Interestingly enough, it seems as if the DNA of the creature, the alien, fit perfectly as a compliment to our own. So perfectly, in fact, that I could use its genetic code to patch and complete the DNA sequencing that became the building blocks for you and your siblings."

Forrester spoke as an interested scientist, savoring the excitement of exploration and discovery. Like a child exploring the world for the first time, filled with wonder. To Alex, the words hit like a hammer.

"I'm not really human?" he said, the question catching in his throat as he asked it. "I'm... whatever that thing was?"

Forrester turned to the younger man, his face dropping. When he spoke, his tone was a mix of remembered excitement and current regret. "I was so excited my work would finally be completed. It was to be the culmination of my entire life's work. Regrettably, because of that, I rushed to complete the project without taking the time to examine the outcomes. My zeal in discovering the missing piece of the puzzle blinded me to the ramifications of utilizing such an unknown variable. The ultimate unknown variable, really. And I ignored all scientific principles and forged ahead like a maverick. I knew there would be some unpredictable results, that's all part of the scientific process of discovery, but I imagined nothing like what has happened recently." He turned back to Alex, the tears welling up in his eyes magnified to almost comic proportions by the man's thick glasses.

"I'm sorry, Alex," he continued. "If I had taken the time to consider the potential consequences and not foolishly rushed headlong into feeding my ego, then none of this would have happened."

"I'm part alien," was all Alex could say in response. The doctor's words left him stunned, his mind racing to make sense of the shocking news. Among all the betrayals and secrets that had been revealed to him in the last few days, this was the most difficult for his mind to process. As monumental as each event had been previously, they paled compared to this revelation. Not only had he learned that advanced extraterrestrials actually existed, but he had also found out that he carried genetic material from those same extraterrestrials. Despite the abilities he had already displayed, how would that affect him? How much of his DNA was human and how much of it was not of this Earth?

Suddenly it hit him, squeezing his heart like a vise. It wasn't just him he had to worry about. "If I have alien DNA in me, that means the baby..." He couldn't bring himself to finish the sentence as the invisible hand grasping his heart worked its way to his throat.

Forrester nodded. "Yes, your child will most likely inherit some of your genetic traits. I'm afraid I can't offer even a hypothesis on how or which aspects of your DNA might manifest in your offspring. Admittedly, I didn't consider it as a factor, given that you were engineered to be sterile. In fact, it was most likely the unpredictability of the extraterrestrial DNA that allowed you to conceive in the first place."

Alex, still stunned, sat silent.

"Yes, well," Dr. Forrester continued, not comfortable with the conversation, but even less so with the silence that hung between them. "You also weren't supposed to have any sex drive to speak of, either. Too distracting." He huffed. "Look how that turned out."

"How can you do that?" Alex asked, his gaze held by the tumbling landscape below, afraid to take his eyes from it for fear of what they would find elsewhere.

"Pardon me?" Forrester responded.

"How can you do that to people? How can you screw with their lives, their very existence, and claim it's all in the name of science? What gives you the right to play God?" Alex turned away from the window to face the doctor, the man who was his maker, his creator. "You aren't a god maker, doctor. You're a megalomaniac, wrecking people's lives in the interest of your own curiosity with no regard for the effect it has on anyone else! You're a child with a new toy, a very dangerous toy. A selfish child, at that. You had no right to play with life itself to satisfy your own needs. You've most likely condemned an innocent child to never live a normal life! And what about Rachel?"

"I... I don't understand," Forrester stammered, taken aback by Alex's outburst.

"When it comes time to deliver the baby, will it be a normal delivery? Will Rachel be in danger? Will she survive the birth? And what about the baby? Will they be normal? Just how much of the baby's genetic make-up is human and how much is... not? What kind of life can we expect for him or her? A life like this, on the run? Is that how my family will spend their lives? Running? Is this what you had in mind when you started all this? Is this what you wanted, doctor?"

"No! No. I only wanted to...to..." Forrester hung his head. "I only wanted to help people."

"The first rule of medicine," Alex replied, "is to do no harm. You really shattered that one, Doc."

Dr. Forrester sat silently, still not comfortable with the silence between them but afraid to say anything further. He had done enough harm already.

Alex leveled his gaze at the scientist. "I have to ask; how did I end up on that beach? Why don't I remember anything that happened before that?"

Dr. Forrester shifted uncomfortably in his seat and once again wiped away beads of sweat from his forehead, despite the chilly temperature in the helicopter cabin. "That was another act of rebellion on my part. An act of rebellion meant to save you. Penders declared the experiment a failure and demanded the destruction of all test subjects. He wanted to start over. I couldn't bear to see that happen to you. You had such potential. So at that moment, I decided to get you away from the Eden Project. To set you free. To see how you would adapt and survive in the greater world. It wasn't easy to get you away from the Eden Project, and for a while I thought perhaps you hadn't survived, but then there was the news..."

"The news about the emaciated, amnesiac boy who had washed ashore," Alex broke in.

Forrester nodded. "That was it, yes. I was so relieved when I saw that, you can't imagine. I thought for sure after the gunshot and the fall that you would most certainly have died."

"Hold on a second," Alex interrupted. "Gunshot and fall? What are you talking about? I don't remember any of that, and it seems like the kind of thing someone wouldn't easily forget."

"I'm not surprised you don't remember," Forrester said, closing his eyes and sliding into his own memories. "You see, I had wiped all your memories. At least, I thought I had."

Alex shook his head. "Wiped my memories? You can do that?"

"Oh yes," Forrester answered, the excited scientist creeping back into his voice. "It was a standard procedure during the Eden Project. The purpose of it was to create a more stable, controllable environment with the subjects. It was... often less than successful. But in this case, it was meant to give you a new start, a chance at life. With no memory of your past in the Eden Project, what would your life become? My plan was to wipe your memory, take you a few towns over and set you free. The idea was for you to be found by the citizens there, dazed and confused, but otherwise unharmed. After a while, you could establish a new life for yourself. Become your own person. I hypothesized that, with no memories of your past and without the Eden Project's influence, you would imprint on the people and circumstances around you and develop your own ethics and morality. That was the plan, until Colonel Harriman showed up."

Alex started at the name. "Harriman? The guy who took Rachel? How does he fit into that day?"

"Colonel Harriman has been in charge of Robert Penders' security and enforcement needs almost from the beginning. Whenever Robert wants something..." Forrester paused, searching for the right word, "... unsavory, done, he would rely on Harriman to take care of it. Here Harriman's job was to be sure all the subjects, every remaining Adam and Eve, were destroyed. Which he had done, with two exceptions; you, and Adam Nine. When he discovered I was missing, he surmised I must have been with at least one of you and tracked me down. I yelled at you to run, but you were still stunned from the memory erasure. You didn't know how to react to his sudden appearance until he drew his gun. Seeing that weapon activated something in your brain, some base instinct, and you ran from him into the nearby woods. He took chase, and you both disappeared. I tried to keep up, but even back then this old body didn't have the strength to be taxed that way. I ran as fast as I could until I heard the shots. By the time I caught up to Harriman, it was too late."

Forrester paused again, collecting his thoughts. Alex sat silently through the pause, fearful of what the man had to say next.

"He stood near a sharp cliff overlooking a river about thirty-five feet down. Near the edge of the drop there was blood spattered on the ground. Harriman's weapon was still in hand. Between gunshot injuries, the fall, and the current of the waters below, I was certain you hadn't survived."

"By the time the story came up about an amnesiac boy washing up on a nearby beach, you had become a media curiosity. If you had disappeared, then it would have been too suspect and invited more attention than Robert wanted, so he decided to leave you alone. He told me he was going to back my 'experiment' with you, but that you were to be closely monitored. Several inside agents were placed in key positions in your life, such as Dr. Carlson and Rick, and you were left to live your life." The doctor sighed a heavy sigh. "The rest, you know."

Alex was silent as he let that all sink in. As far as secrets and revelations about his life were concerned, that one was mild, but it still impacted him. To know what he had overcome to become who he was now, it was staggering.

He was about to question Forrester further when Rick chimed in. "We're almost there. Lars says we'll be landing in a few minutes."

A lump formed in Alex's throat. He'd been so focused on what Forrester had to tell him he hadn't prepared for what was coming. He quickly snatched up the SIG Sauer from beside him and once again dropped it into his waistband at the small of his back. At least he had that.

Alex approached Rick, who was gathering up the weapons and equipment he had been working on for the entirety of the flight. "Where are we landing?"

"About a mile out from the Nest," Rick replied. "That's about the only decent landing site nearby. We'll have to walk the rest of the way."

"Won't they know we're coming?"

Rick shrugged. "Probably, but we don't have any other options I can think of. Besides, I have a way inside the compound. Just follow my lead."

Alex wasn't comfortable with that idea, but he didn't have another choice. He still wasn't sure he could trust Rick. He couldn't be sure that he wasn't being delivered to the Project by his old friend, that his whole repentance thing hadn't just been a set-up to trick Alex into willingly walking into the lion's den. Even if it was, it didn't matter. Rick was his only way into Gabriel's Nest. Without him, Alex wouldn't have been able to find the compound, much less get inside. Trust or not, he needed Rick.

"Is it just the four of us?" Alex asked.

"Three," Rick replied, placing the last few items into a backpack. "Lars only flies the chopper. He won't get involved beyond that. He also won't wait for us once we're gone, so we'll have to find our own transportation out once we get inside and find Rachel."

"What?" Alex asked, his voice jumping an octave. "How are we supposed to do that?"

"Relax," Rick answered, shouldering the backpack and picking up a long hardshell case Alex knew carried a rifle. "I have a plan."

Alex sighed heavily. "Great. Can't wait to see how it goes. So, there are three of us. A supposed 'advanced human soldier' with no active memory of his training, an ex-operative of the Eden Project, and a geriatric scientist with no combat training and vision so bad he needs half-inch thick glasses. How are our odds?"

Rick smiled a humorless smile. "Don't ask."

Alex let the conversation drop with that. Despite Rick's declaration of having a plan, Alex decided he'd have to come up with a counter-initiative on their hike to the Nest. He still didn't trust Rick or Forrester completely, and the stakes were too high to not have a plan of his own. Rachel's life was at stake, not to mention the baby. Their safety was the only thing that mattered.

As the helicopter settled onto the ground amidst the shadowy woods, he felt his bravado fade. Looking into the impenetrable darkness, he felt as if there were a thousand eyes watching him, just waiting for the right moment to strike. Waiting for his moment of weakness.

As much as he wished it to be all part of his imagination, he knew the predators were out there somewhere, waiting for him in the dark. He could almost feel their eyes on him, see their fangs gleaming in the moonlight. And yet, he had no choice but to walk straight into those waiting jaws.

52

Awareness was returning to Rachel Carter. Slowly, she lifted from the comfortable haze of unconsciousness as reality coalesced around her. Her memory was returning as well, as she slowly pieced together what had happened to her. She had been at the hospital with Alex, having gone there to help Ernie Babcock, who had been near-fatally wounded helping them escape from Adam. There was something else, too. A memory right at the fringe of consciousness. Something about a gray-haired man in a black suit.

The man in the parking lot. On her way into the hospital to help Alex and Celeste, he had approached her. He called her, knew her name. She couldn't recall ever having seen him before. Should have known better, girl. Don't talk to strangers. But at that moment she didn't know better, and now here she was. Absently, she rubbed the spot on her neck where the needle he had stuck her with had penetrated. There was no pain, but the motion was comforting, so she continued.

She was forgetting something, but her head was still so hazy from whatever the man in the black suit had injected her with, she couldn't seem to form a truly coherent thought. Everything was still just scattered images in her mind, like a jigsaw puzzle waiting to be assembled.

She opened her eyes, thrust from a comfortable darkness into the harsh light of her surroundings. The brightness from the lights above stabbed into her eyes and she reactively shut them again to protect herself. Turning her head to one side, away from the lights above her prone form, she slowly opened her eyes again. It still hurt, but it was tolerable this time, and she was able to give herself a few minutes to adjust.

Sitting up slowly, she winced as bolts of pain sliced through her head, intensifying with even the slightest motion. Whatever the black-suited man had given her had left her a pretty decent hangover. She hadn't felt this way since the night she graduated from college, but she was grateful the fog was clearing from her brain.

At least when she had woken up hung over in college she had been some place familiar. Now she was completely lost, with no clue about her whereabouts. Not that it wasn't nice; in fact, it was very comfortable. Under different conditions, she might even consider the space cozy. She was sitting in the middle of a black leather sofa, facing into what appeared to be someone's office. An office unlike anything she had ever seen outside of television or movies. The office of someone with a very large bank account and a great deal of both power and ego, by the looks of it. In the far-right corner of the room, there stood an enormous mahogany desk, its polished surface reflecting the soft glow of the room's warm lighting. A matching bar stood nearby, stocked with bottles that appeared both old and expensive. The coffee table, bookcases, and curio shelves that made up the rest of the room were all the same rich wood as the desk and bar. The desk chair and bar stools were all covered in the same supple, buttery leather as the couch she was seated on, leaving her to ponder the number of cows and trees that were sacrificed to furnish this room.

A flickering light drew her attention to the fireplace that took up most of the opposite wall. Made from polished black marble, the fire burning inside created a mesmerizing play of light and shadows on its surface. It was hypnotic to watch the dancing flames as the light echoed their rhythm, flickering and fluttering throughout the room. Her eyelids felt heavy as she watched the dance, and she wanted nothing more at that moment than to sink back into the soft leather of the sofa and let the dance of flames lull her back into a peaceful sleep.

Reluctantly, she fought against the comfortable drowsiness and pulled herself off the couch, only to land hard on the floor as her legs gave out beneath her. She was grateful for the deep, comfortable carpet that cushioned her and kept her from taking the full brunt of the fall to the floor. Her head was suddenly spinning, a feeling of nausea gripping her stomach. To ease the pain and nausea, she leaned forward and tucked her head between her knees. Neither was being terribly cooperative at the moment. Whatever the man in the parking lot had given her must have been potent. She'd have to wait it out for a while longer.

Just then, she heard a door open, most likely the ornately carved door she had seen earlier opposite the immense fireplace. Reactively, she pulled her head up sharply to see who had entered the room, and immediately regretted it. A barrage of pain, nausea and dizziness hit her again, and she felt as if she were either going to vomit all over the plush gray carpet beneath her or simply pass out. Closing her eyes again, she took a deep breath and leaned back against the sofa, waiting for the feeling to pass.

"You really should relax for a bit, Mrs. Carter. The after-effects of the sedative will wear off much more quickly if you don't exert yourself."

The sound of a man's voice, resonant and powerful, filled the room. A voice she recognized, although right now she couldn't remember from where. She listened to his footsteps as he crossed the room, passing the enormous desk and heading for the equally large bar. A moment later she heard a glass clink and water running, the sound deepening as the glass filled. The water stopped running, and she heard him moving again, his footfalls muffled by the thick carpet. She listened intently and, even with the soft noise of his footfalls, could tell he had moved to her and was now standing over her.

"Here," she said, gently taking her hand and wrapping her fingers around a cold glass. "Drink this. Slowly. It'll help."

At first, she wanted to snatch her hand away from him, but she thought better of it. Right now, she was being treated as a guest, whether willing or not. It might benefit her to play the part for the time being, to see what she could learn by playing the gracious hostage instead of being belligerent.

"Thank you," she replied, taking the glass. The nausea was subsiding and she slowly opened her eyes, revealing a world that was still a painfully bright jumble of light, even more so after her ill-fated attempt at standing. Each flicker of the fire, the same dance of light she had found so comforting a few moments ago, was now a painful jab in her skull. She fought the urge to shut her eyes and block out the light and pain, making a conscious effort to keep them wide open.

She gripped the glass between two hands, neither one steady enough on their own. Gingerly, she lifted the glass to her lips. Stopping just short of taking a sip, she sniffed slightly.

"It's only water, I assure you," her host said. "Please, drink. It will help to dispel the effects of the drug you were given."

She had figured as much, considering she was still incapacitated from whatever the black-suited man had injected her with. There was no need to drug her again. But if the last few days had taught her anything, it was caution.

Her host was still standing over her, nothing more than a silhouette against the bright overhead lights. She squinted, trying to make out some of the man's features. She could distinguish the faint outline of a nose, the curve of a mouth, and a tousle of hair brushing against his forehead. Not enough to identify who he was.

She sipped lightly from the glass he had given her, the water cold and comfortable as it trickled down her throat. In that moment she realized just how thirsty she really was and sipped a few more times, taking larger and deeper gulps each time. Before she knew it, she had drained the entire glass.

"Feeling better?" asked her host, relieving her of the empty glass and retreating once more to the bar.

"Somewhat," she answered. "No thanks to you."

"I am sorry we had to take such drastic measures, but you are very important to us, Mrs. Carter. And I feel certain you wouldn't have come if we'd asked."

"I'm pregnant, you know," she replied, her voice tinged with anger she couldn't hide. "That drug could have harmed my baby."

"We are well aware of your condition. Rest assured that the drug you were given won't cause any harm to your child. You and your baby are both quite safe with us."

"You'll forgive me if I withhold my opinion at the moment," she quipped, then silently chided herself about her attitude. She was supposed to be cooperative and submissive, not antagonistic.

"I wouldn't have expected anything else," her host answered, a slight tone of amusement in his voice.

The fire was slowly dying, the dance of flames coming to a conclusion. The stabbing pain in her head was also subsiding, the room coming into focus. Slowly, she turned her head towards her host, who was still standing at the bar, hoping to catch a glimpse of his face. Although she could see him more distinctly, he continued to have his back towards her. All she could make out was the dark suit he was wearing and the full head of gray hear he sported.

"I'll take my leave now, give you some time to rest and recuperate. Gather your strength. If you need anything, simply push the intercom button on the desk and someone will be in right away to assist you."

He turned from the bar and headed for the door, never turning his face to her. His back still to her, he placed his hand on the door handle and pushed it open.

She needed to see his face.

"Wait!" she shouted, startling herself with the outburst. It was an instinctive thing, a last desperate effort to get him to turn around. She had no idea how to proceed from there.

Her host stopped at the door. "Yes?" he said, and turned toward her.

She *had* seen his face before. Not in person, but in a context that would make him forever unforgettable to her.

"I just wanted to know who my host was," she said. "Thank you, Mr. Penders."

Robert Penders smiled a slight smile. "You know me?"

"I've seen you before," she replied, thinking back to the speech she had discovered on the thumb drive Dr. Carlton died bringing to Alex. "I'm familiar with a few aspects of your work."

"That's good," Penders replied as he opened the door. "That should make all of this that much simpler."

He slipped out the door and it closed behind him with a resounding click, no doubt the lock engaging. Rachel was alone once more.

She braced her arms against the soft leather of the sofa and pushed herself up from the floor, slowly this time to avoid the dizziness and nausea that had hit her before. As she stood her legs still felt a bit weak, wobbling slightly beneath her, but that passed in a few seconds. There was no nausea this time. No dizziness. No disorientation. Her vision was clear, and she felt steady on her feet. The drug must have passed through her system completely, clearing up the side-effects from before. Except it had happened way too fast. Based on how she had felt just moments ago, with her head pressed against her knees and fighting the urge to be sick, whatever they had given her should have kept her incapacitated for another half-hour, at least. Now here she was, minutes later, with all the adverse side-effects gone. It felt like she had never been drugged in the first place.

Gently, she laid her hand on her stomach. "That was you, wasn't it? You were protecting your mom, weren't you?"

In response, Rachel felt a warm, comforting feeling in her stomach that soon spread throughout her body. The baby had answered her. Either that or she was hallucinating, either of which was entirely possible at the moment.

She decided to err on the side of hope. "Don't worry, baby. Mommy will get us out of here. Have faith."

The warm feeling rippled through her body, a wave of complete and absolute happiness and trust. Despite her situation, Rachel smiled.

"I love you, too, baby."

53

Alex stared intently out the cabin window and into the darkness, trying to glimpse something that would justify what he was sensing. It had happened just after they landed, the overwhelming feeling they weren't alone. That there was something out there in the night waiting for them, ready to pounce. He sensed tension, fear, and anxiety on a level far beyond what he might expect from Rick, Dr. Forrester, and Lars. But the darkness was so intense he couldn't make out anything past the small pool of light from the helicopter's exterior floodlights. He couldn't see any mysterious figures lurking in the shadows. He couldn't see anything at all. But he could feel them out there, waiting and watching. Tensed and ready to attack.

A loud rumbling noise startled him out of his search and he snatched up his pistol, leveling it at the source of the noise. At the other end of the weapon was Rick, his face a mix of shock and surprise as he stared into the barrel of the gun, his hand still on the handle of the cargo door.

"Are you insane?" Rick yelled as the deafening noise of the helicopter's engine, accompanied by the rushing wind of the spinning rotors, filled the cabin.

Alex lowered the pistol, but slowly. He was still under assault by a cacophony of emotions emanating from all around him, uncertain of what was coming from where. Or who. He was still uncertain who he could trust, and the waves of intensely fearful emotions cascading over him weren't helping him figure it out.

"We can't go out there," Alex stated, placing a hand on Rick's shoulder and nudging him gently back into the cabin.

"Well, we can't get any closer with the chopper," Rick answered, slinging a rifle over his shoulder. "If we wait any longer we'll miss our window of opportunity. It's now or never."

"Hold on for a moment," Dr. Forrester interrupted, shifting his focus to Alex. "Why can't we leave the helicopter?"

"I'm not sure, to be honest. It's just a feeling." Alex paused, searching for the words to explain what he was sensing. "I can... feel people out there. Waiting. Watching. It's just a jumble of emotions; anger, fear, anxiety. There's also a sense of determination, a very strong sense. That's it. I can't get anything else."

Dr. Forrester frowned, his already enormous eyes widening further. "That's good enough for me. Rick, inform your pilot friend we need to take off again. Now."

"I'm afraid I can't do that," Rick answered, his voice low and suddenly thick with regret.

Dr. Forrester seemed oblivious to the change. "And why would that be?"

Forrester may not have noticed it, but Alex picked up on it right away, his heart sinking. "Because this is where he promised he'd deliver us."

"What are you talking about?" Dr. Forrester asked, still unaware of what was happening.

Alex clarified it for him. "What I'm talking about," he answered, his eyes narrowing on Rick, "is betrayal. Again. Rick is here to turn us over to the Project, isn't that right?"

"That can't be," Forrester stammered as the reality of the situation sank in. "Please, Rick, tell him he's wrong."

Without warning, Rick produced a pistol and leveled it at Alex, shattering any remaining illusions of his loyalty. "I'm afraid he's right, doctor. The Project expects the two of you to be delivered to them immediately." He reached out and gently removed the gun from Alex's hand. "I'll take that if you don't mind. I don't want you to get any ideas that could be potentially dangerous for either of us."

"How can this be true?" Dr. Forrester said, a genuine sense of shock and hurt in his voice. "We've planned for months now how we could liberate Alex and Rachel from the Project. I trusted you. Your experience. Your expertise. Most of this was..." He trailed off, the reality of the situation coalescing in his mind. "Most of this was your idea."

Rick nodded. "Your passion and commitment to your work made you easy to manipulate, doctor. And I'm sorry for what I did, but you understand I had no choice. The Eden Project, PenTech, Robert Penders, they control everything about my life. Everything. If I betrayed them... Well, let's just say it wouldn't be conducive to me leading a long life."

Alex stepped forward, closing the distance between them until the barrel of Rick's gun poked firmly into his chest. "All I know is, if I get the chance, I won't give you the opportunity to betray me or my family again."

"I suppose I'll just have to make sure you don't get that chance," Rick answered defiantly.

"What are you going to do, shoot me?" Alex pushed forward again, feeling the barrel of Rick's gun dig into his chest. "I can heal, remember? Take your shot, I'll still take you down."

"You might take him down," came a voice from behind them, "but can you take us both out?"

Even though he had heard little of it, Alex recognized the deep, gruff voice even before turning to see the tall blond man with the pistol leaning out from the cockpit. It seemed Lars wasn't the disgruntled Eden Project turncoat Rick had made him out to be. Big surprise.

"Besides," Lars continued, a shark's grin spreading across his face, "who did you think was going to fly this bird for you?"

"I guess I hoped you were the upstanding moral citizen Rick had made you out to be," Alex quipped back. "But then again, consider the source."

Lars laughed a hearty laugh that would have been jovial in some backwater hole in the wall bar, but in their current situation only made Alex more tense. He was trapped between the two of them, Lars and Rick, with no quick escape. Even if he could somehow get past the two of them uninjured, he would still have the soldiers outside to deal with. And he had Dr. Forrester to consider as well. With the scientist between him and Lars, any gunfire would put the doctor in the middle of the line of fire.

"That's enough," Rick shouted, the grimace on his face tightening. "I may have to do this, but I sure as shit don't have to like it. Now get over here so we can get this over with."

Lars lifted his massive frame out of his seat and navigated his shoulders between the pilot and co-pilot's chairs. He had to turn his shoulders to get through, but still kept his pistol trained on Alex. Coming up behind Dr. Forrester, he pulled back his gun hand and slammed the weapon hard into the spine of the geneticist, eliciting a sharp cry of pain. Forrester stumbled forward a step before catching himself, but before he could so much as stand up straight Lars struck him again.

"Stop! Can't you see he's hurt?" Alex yelled, taking a step toward Forrester. The barrel of Rick's gun stopped him.

"Enough," Rick said, taking Alex's arm and pulling him back toward the open cargo door. "Step out."

Alex stepped back, his heels on the edge of the door. "If anything happens to him, you'll regret it." That said, he turned and stepped out into the maelstrom of wind created by the rotors.

"Time to get moving, Doc," Lars said, drawing back his gun hand and preparing to hit Forrester again.

Rick took a step forward. "That's enough of that. We got them here, our job is done. You don't have to hurt him."

"Sure, I don't have to, but it was because of this piece of shit and his boy Adam that my brother got killed in the Pennsylvania safe house. I want payback. So, get out of my way." Lars put his massive hand on Rick's chest and pushed him back. "Let's go," Lars growled at Forrester, once more slamming the gun into the doctor's back.

Forrester cried out again and fell to his knees, gasping for breath as tears welled up in his eyes and ran down his cheeks. "Please," he wheezed, "don't hit me again. I beg you. Please."

"Shut the fuck up, asshole," Lars yelled, raising his gun hand high above his head as he wound up to deliver a finishing strike to the cowed doctor.

Taking advantage of the momentary opening, Rick shoved the barrel of his gun hard into Lars' chin. "I said that's enough. Now drop your gun, get back in the cockpit, and wait for us to leave. Once we're gone, you can fly this bird to wherever the fuck you want to. I really couldn't give a shit about what happens to you. But if you don't do what I say, I am going to splatter the wad of shit you call a brain all over this cabin. Understand?"

Lars nodded, the action driving his chin further into Rick's gun. Not taking his attention from the massive pilot, Rick helped Forrester to his feet. "Dr. Forrester, please join Alex outside."

The aging scientist moved toward the open cargo door, carefully nursing his back where Lars had beaten him. As he disappeared from view, Rick slowly pulled his gun away from Lars' chin. The big man took a step back, rubbing the spot where the gun had been, his face an angry scowl.

"I don't know why you did that, and I don't really care. But if I ever get the chance, I'm going to kill you. Believe it."

"I believe it," Rick said, breathing a heavy sigh. "So many people out there, wanting to kill me. Burke. Adam. Alex. Now you. That's too many. I guess I'll have to make sure you never get the chance."

Before Lars could so much as move, Rick pulled the trigger. There was a deafening boom, amplified by the confined space of the cabin. It was immediately followed by a wet slapping noise as blood and viscera splattered the ceiling. Lars' head snapped back violently and his legs buckled, but he didn't immediately fall. Instead, his body struggled to stand as his life left him, as if it were trying to deny its inevitable death. A second later, it was forced to acknowledge the inevitable, and Lars crumpled to the floor.

"I appreciate your help," Rick said, nudging the unmoving body with his foot, "but I'm afraid that everything you may have heard on this trip has to be kept confidential. Sorry. Besides, you were always kind of an asshole."

Tucking his gun back into its holster, he turned and followed Alex and Dr. Forrester into the night.

■■

Alex's fears became a reality the moment he hit the ground. A tight half circle of at least a dozen soldiers faced the helicopter, their weapons trained on him. The sense of tension in the air was so palpable he didn't need his special abilities to detect it. These people were on edge. They had taken up a standard defensive position to contain him, but each was uneasy about what to do if this living weapon were to get out of control. Alex could feel their fear of him as it rushed at him like the breeze from the rotors. Every soldier there was afraid of him.

No, not every soldier. One man stepped forward, gracefully slipping between the others. The soldiers parted for him in a way that seemed almost instinctive or somehow rehearsed. More likely, it was due to the potent combination of respect and fear they had for this man. This man who, unlike the people under his command, felt no fear. Not just of Alex, but of anything. Despite his average height and build, everything about this man exuded confidence. Both his body language and empathic resonance were those of a man who hadn't experienced fear in a very long time, if ever.

"Alex Carter?" the fearless man asked when he had moved close enough to be heard over the whirring blades of the helicopter. The voice of the man was as soft as a breeze, yet deep and commanding. A stern paternal voice, the voice of someone people would be eager to please. No wonder his soldiers regarded him as they did; he was someone to be respected, but also someone to be feared.

"I am," Alex replied, trying to match the tone and pace of the man's voice.

"I am Colonel William Harriman," the smallish, gray-haired man stated, his expression unchanging. "It is my duty and privilege to escort you to Gabriel's Nest."

Before Alex could reply, Rick came up alongside them and greeted the Colonel with a sloppy salute.

"I heard a shot," Harriman said, his voice unwavering. "Is there a problem?"

"Not anymore," Rick replied. "Everything's been taken care of."

Harriman nodded almost imperceptibly. "Good. Mr. Penders is expecting you. Report to him as soon as you reach the Nest."

"Got it," Rick replied, trading nervous glances between Alex and Harriman.

Harriman picked up on it right away. "Are there going to be any issues here?"

Rick swallowed hard, keeping his eyes firmly on Harriman but fully aware of Alex staring him down. "No sir," he answered.

Harriman let his own gaze bore into Rick for another few seconds before continuing. "You have fifteen minutes to meet with Mr. Penders. Don't be late. And get someone to stow that helicopter before you head for the Nest."

Rick nodded, casting wary eyes on Alex. "I'll get right on it." Without another word, he was gone, fading into the surrounding night.

Harriman turned his full attention back to Alex. "This way, please," he said, gesturing to a nearby Hummer.

Alex stood firm for a beat, his mind racing to find an escape route. There was none he could find. Harriman had completely closed any avenue of escape. Alex had no choice but to follow Harriman's instructions and continue searching for an alternative.

As they approached the vehicle, Harriman opened the rear passenger door for Alex, who stepped past him and ducked into the vehicle without a word. He had lost track of where Dr. Forrester had been taken, but he assumed he was in another vehicle, keeping them separated for better control measures. He hoped the scientist would be all right on his own.

Harriman gently closed the door behind him, only to reappear a second later and seat himself in the front passenger's seat directly in front of Alex. The Colonel nodded to the driver, who immediately put the vehicle in gear and pulled away from the landing site and onto a darkened mountain road. Judging from the way they were being jostled around inside the Hummer, Alex assumed it was more of a trail than a road.

Neither the driver nor the Colonel had said a word since the trip began. Alex chose not to start a conversation and remained silent. He felt certain he wouldn't be able to get any important information out of the Colonel, anyway. And the driver would never speak without the explicit permission of the Colonel, so that would be a dead end. For now, he found himself at a stalemate.

He watched the dark terrain go by, shapeless forms undulating in the night. Somewhere in that shapeless darkness was Rachel. He could only assume she had been taken to the Nest as well. That part of the plan had worked, at least. Maybe not how he imagined it, but he was on his way to Gabriel's Nest right now. And he would get inside without an issue.

The only question he had was what he would do after that. The darkness offered him no answers as they sped to their destination.

To his birthplace.

He was on his way home.

54

They traveled in the dark along the winding mountain road for what seemed like an eternity. In the distance, Alex could see a slight glow of light, most likely from a town half-asleep at this hour. Other than that, and the illumination from the headlights of the Hummer, everything else was an all-consuming darkness. Inside the Hummer it was the silence that was oppressive. No one had spoken so much as a word since they left the landing site, the only sounds being the rhythmic thrumming of the engine and the pinging of road debris kicked up into the vehicle's undercarriage.

Alex risked breaking the silence. "How much longer until we get there? These seats are murder on my ass."

The driver glanced at the Colonel, who returned a curt nod. "ETA is another five minutes, sir," the driver stated.

"And what happens when we get there?" Alex asked.

Again, the driver glanced at Harriman. This time the older man shook his head slightly, then continued to stare ahead at the path the headlights blazed through the night. The driver returned his concentration to the road ahead as well, not offering even a courtesy answer to Alex's question.

He turned back out into the darkness, a different feeling settling in on him. He felt something strange, something he couldn't quite put his finger on. It was as if the darkness was staring back, watching him as much as he was watching it. Watching and waiting. Waiting for what, Alex could only imagine.

Leaning back in the seat, he drew his field of vision and imagination back into the cabin of the Hummer. He joined the Colonel and the young soldier in staring out the windshield at the road ahead, lit up by the Hummer's powerful headlights. He couldn't shake the feeling of being watched, but at least he felt some security in being able to see what was ahead of them.

Until the headlights washed over a chain-link fence and gate. The fence before him was in good condition, maintaining most of its original silver hue, but to Alex it was something else entirely. His heart hammered in his chest as his eyes took in a rusty, twisted, time-worn fence, as foreboding as it was familiar. At the center of the gate was a sign, a sign that sent chills running the course of his spine, his blood frozen where he sat.

UNITES STATES GOVERNMENT FACILITY.

TRESPASSERS ENTER UNDER RISK OF BEING SHOT.

"We're here," the Colonel stated as he rolled down his window to speak with the gate guard.

Alex didn't hear him. He wasn't hearing anything right now. Nothing except the echo of long-faded screams. He could still feel the darkness watching him, but now the darkness was a pair of icy blue eyes that pierced his soul and injected him with fear.

Somewhere in the night, a shadowy figure laughed.

55

The gate swung open, granting them entry, but for Alex, it was like entering the depths of hell. Stepping aside, the guard waved them forward, snapping off a sharp salute as they passed. Harriman sharply returned the salute.

As they entered the facility, Alex assessed his surroundings. As he navigated the dark streets, the sodium vapor streetlamps bathed the makeshift buildings in an eerie, pale light, amplifying his sense of fear.

It was exactly as he had dreamed it. To either side of him were identical, squat, nondescript gray buildings, completely devoid of any character. The only thing that differentiated them were the large white numbers stenciled on the front of each one, no doubt denoting what that hut was for. The roadway they were on was simple concrete, making for a much smoother ride than the dirt road they had gotten them here. Except for the occasional guard wandering the night, the place looked utterly deserted. It was as lonely and desolate a place as he could have ever imagined.

The driver parked in front of one of the dull gray buildings. He remained seated, anxiously watching as the Colonel stepped out of the vehicle. Then he quickly scrambled to the back passenger door, nearly stumbling in his haste. He rested his hand on the door handle and stood completely motionless, waiting for his next instructions. Alex thought about surprising the young soldier by opening the door himself, but he noticed at that moment there were no handles on the inside of the Hummer's back doors. He realized he had been trapped inside all along.

Seconds after they parked, three soldiers exited the building, each armed with what Alex recognized as semi-automatic tactical shotguns. Each weapon could fire multiple rounds of scattershot in seconds, creating a veritable wall of moving lead that would completely shred anything in its path. The soldiers walked in step toward the rear door of the Hummer, taking up a three-point position outside of the door he would be exiting. Whatever his hosts were expecting of him, they certainly weren't taking any chances.

The young driver pulled open the door as Colonel Harriman stepped into view behind the armed soldiers. "Mr. Carter, please follow me."

"I'm not sure I should move," Alex replied, indicating the heavily armed men surrounding him.

"I assure you; they are just a precaution. If you continue to cooperate with us, I guarantee no harm will come to you." The Colonel took a step back, creating space for Alex to exit the Hummer. "Now, if you will, please follow me."

Alex hesitated. It was easy for Harriman to say these soldiers were only a precaution; he wasn't the one staring down the barrels of three semi-automatic shotguns. One twitch interpreted the wrong way and he would end up as nothing more than a splatter on the concrete road.

He braced himself, lifting both hands to ear level with his palms facing out as he slowly turned in the seat. Pausing there, he smiled an awkward smile at each of the three guards and the young driver. Only the driver smiled back. He let his feet fall to the concrete and stood, moving as slowly as he could, always keeping his hands in plain sight. As he moved to follow the Colonel, the three guards took up new positions to flank him, with one on each side and the other directly behind him. They moved in unison with him, their weapons always trained on him.

Colonel Harriman stopped at a plain-looking door, as featureless as the rest of the buildings in the compound. Turning to Alex, he said, "You may lower your hands, Mr. Carter. As I stated previously, you are safe here as long as you continue to cooperate. So please, relax and be comfortable."

Alex glanced at the two guards on either side of him, their shotguns still diligently tracking his every move. "Do these guys know that?"

"They are under my command, and were trained by me," Harriman replied, his expression still unchanging. "They are fully aware of their duties and how to execute on them, I assure you."

Alex bristled at the word 'execute' but lowered his hands anyway. He didn't have any other option right now, aside from trusting Harriman's word. To his pleasant surprise, neither of the guards he could see moved or reacted as his arms dropped to his side. "Thank you," he said to Harriman.

The Colonel turned back to the door without a response, and it was then Alex noticed the small digital security keypad mounted just to the right of the doorframe. Alex watched as Harriman tapped out a five-digit code, not bothering to block Alex's line of sight with his body. Alex carefully noted each number Harriman entered, putting them in the back of his mind for later. He let them go a second later as Harriman placed his thumb on a small black square just above the keypad. To enter, both a code and a verified thumbprint were required. Alex sighed quietly. He had the code, but he was fairly certain he was lacking the viable thumbprint.

A chime sounded, and the door slid open. Flanked by the three guards, Alex followed Harriman into the next room, a dimly lit and deserted office. Gray metal desks with matching chairs lined the walls on either side of the room, the only splashes of color being an institutional printer in the corner and a water bubbler against the far wall. The room was clean and, judging from the personal items on some desks, functional during the day.

Another door and another keypad were at the far end of the room. Harriman repeated the procedure from the first door, albeit with a different code this time. A moment later, the door slid open, revealing an elevator. Stepping to the left of the door, Harriman motioned for the guard behind Alex to move into the elevator. The man moved quickly from behind Alex and took up position at the back of the elevator, his weapon now pointed directly at Alex's chest.

"Now you, please, Mr. Carter," Harriman stated, gesturing for Alex to enter the elevator. Still flanked on either side by the other two guards, he stepped inside and turned his back to the third. Harriman followed, pushing an unmarked button on the elevator's control panel. As the doors closed, Alex couldn't help but notice how cramped it was with all five of them squeezed inside, and how unnervingly close the guard's weapons were. As he was about to make a remark, the car came to a halt. The doors slid open, revealing something that again took his breath away and made his blood run cold.

Just outside the door hung a sign with black lettering on a yellow background that read:

BIOLOGICAL AND GENETIC RESEARCH – WARNING!

POTENTIAL BIOHAZARD AREA!

Just beneath that was a second sign:

XENOBIOLOGY DIVISION

An arrow beneath that sign pointed right.

Without a word, the Colonel stepped from the elevator and turned right, moving at a brisk pace down the brightly lit hallway. Alex was momentarily too stunned to move until the guard directly behind him prodded him in the back with the muzzle of his weapon.

"Please follow Colonel Harriman, sir," he said, again giving a gentle nudge.

Alex pulled himself back into the present, pushing away the memories of his nightmares the signs triggered in him. As he stepped out of the elevator he had to squint his eyes against the sudden brightness of the overhead fluorescent lighting, which was a sharp contrast to dim and moody lighting of the sodium vapor lights used on the levels above. He pivoted to the right, the direction Harriman had moved in, and picked up his pace. Upon catching up with him, he found Harriman stopped before yet another locked door, going through the same process he had already done twice, once again with a different numerical code. Alex wondered how the man could remember so many codes, not to mention which code went with which door. Colonel William Harriman was likely an extremely meticulous and obsessive-compulsive individual who spent his nights perfecting every aspect of his life.

The door opened and Alex followed Harriman through. What lay beyond this door was not anything he expected or was prepared for, and he stopped dead in his tracks, completely mesmerized by what he saw.

He was standing on a catwalk above what appeared to be a huge cavern carved out of rock. Interconnected catwalks crisscrossed the cave, spanning its entire length and width, and hundreds of halogen lights adorned the ceiling, illuminating the entire space in an almost angelic blue-white light. The place was enormous, a true feat of engineering big enough to house a professional football stadium, but it wasn't the size of the cavern that amazed Alex.

It was what it held that took his breath away.

Stepping to the edge of the catwalk, he pressed his stomach against the guardrail and leaned over as far as safety would allow to get a look at what lay beneath him. He couldn't believe what he was seeing. It was impossible.

On the floor of the cavern sat the same silver disk-shaped object he had seen in the picture from Dr. Carlton's thumb drive. The ship that Dr. Elliot Forrester had overseen the recovery of after its apparent crash. The ship that had traveled who knows how far, to end up on this one insignificant planet. The ship that had no doubt been witness to countless wonders in its travels through the universe. It was here, now, right in front of him. In that moment, he was so shocked that he completely forgot about the Eden Project, Robert Penders, and the danger he faced. He forgot all about Adam and his ice-cold killer's eyes. Time stood still as he gazed at the silver spaceship, and in that instant, his worries lost their weight, overshadowed by the sheer magnificence that lay before him.

But only in that moment.

"It's beautiful, isn't it?"

Alex turned, startled at the appearance of a new person. The mesmerizing presence of the extraterrestrial spaceship had completely distracted him, making him oblivious to the silver-haired man in the flawlessly tailored suit who had silently approached him.

"Absolutely awe-inspiring," the man continued. "Makes you realize just how insignificant we really are in the grand scheme of the universe."

"That's just what I was thinking," Alex replied.

"I've been here thousands of times, but it never ceases to amaze me." The silver-haired man turned to the guards that surrounded Alex, their weapons dutifully trained on him. "I think that's enough of that," he said, waving them off. "I don't think Mr. Carter means us any harm. Do you, Mr. Carter? Mean us harm?"

"I still haven't decided," Alex answered flatly.

"Regardless, I think we can do without the distraction of guns in our faces while we talk. So, gentlemen, if you please," he said, gesturing to the door and indicating that they were dismissed.

Alex turned his head slightly to look at the guards, and what he saw in that moment solidified the structure of power within the organization. After being dismissed by Silver Hair, the three guards glanced at Harriman. With a slight nod from the Colonel as affirmation of the order, they lowered their weapons and exited the way they came without a word. Silver Hair might give the orders, but Colonel Harriman was the one calling the shots. At least as far as the military personnel went.

"Thank you, Colonel," the older man acknowledged with a slight smile. Harriman nodded in response but didn't return the smile. Silver Hair turned his attention to Alex once more.

"Would you like a closer look at it?" he asked, indicating the giant silver ship below.

"I believe I would," Alex answered simply, suppressing the urge to run down the stairs like a kid on Christmas morning.

His silver-haired host turned and gestured to the stairs. "This way, then."

"Of course, Mr....?" Alex said, trailing off in the upward inflection of a question.

His host turned back to him, a shadow of surprise on his face. It was gone in the blink of an eye, but Alex was sure he had seen it. And he was positive he could feel it coming off the man like bad cologne.

"You don't know who I am?" Silver Hair asked.

Alex shook his head. "Sorry, I'm afraid not. There is something familiar about you, but I just can't seem to place it."

The older man smiled a wide smile, a feeling of confidence and superiority supplanting the previous surprise he had felt. "My name is Robert Penders," he stated boldly, as if announcing himself into a room, "and I am the man who created you."

"Penders," Alex said, his voice nothing more than a whisper. This was the great Robert Penders, the man who deemed to make the world a better place by creating more durable inhabitants for it. Or, conversely, the man who intended to make a tidy profit from selling his new-age marvels into modern day slavery. The man who had Dr. Carlton murdered because she dared to disagree with him.

The man who had kidnapped Alex's wife.

"I see you recognize me by name, at least," Penders said.

"Yes," Alex replied, trying not to let his voice quiver with the rage building within him. "I recognize who you are. Robert Penders, visionary business mogul and murderer."

Alex had emphasized 'murderer' for effect, but Penders' didn't show any sign that it had affected him. Alex couldn't sense anything from him he might have expected; no anger, no anxiety, no fear. The only thing he could feel from the man was his smug sense of self-assurance, which only served to further fuel the anger in Alex.

"You're half right, at least," Penders replied evenly, unshaken. "I am an entrepreneur, that much is true, and quite an intuitive one at that. But a murderer? I think that's a bit harsh, wouldn't you say?"

"I don't know," Alex spat back, "why don't you ask Simone Carlton?"

"Yes, Simone. She wasn't entirely on board, Alex. For the sake of this project and everyone involved, you and your lovely wife included, she had to be brought back in line. Unfortunately, we couldn't ignore her resistance to what we are trying to accomplish here any longer, as it became an obstacle. I feel terrible about the outcome and wish it could have been different, but what's done is done. It can't be changed, there's no sense in dwelling on it. If we intend to change the world, we have to look forward." Once again, Penders swept his arm to show the stairs leading to the floor of the cavern. "Are you prepared to step into the future with me, or will you stay mired in the past and dwell uselessly on things you can't change?"

Outwardly, Alex glared at the man, but his other senses bored into him to see his real self. The emotions he found there were anything but the remorse he claimed. Greed, ambition, and lust for power were all there in abundance, but there was little else. Penders was nothing he claimed to be, but if he wanted to find Rachel, Alex would have to play along with him. For now.

Without another word or even a glance at the older man, Alex stepped past Penders and preceded him down the catwalk, following the winding path until he reached the floor of the great cavern. The shift in perspective, seeing the craft from below rather than above, instantly magnified its size and made it seem enormous. From ground level, Alex could see the cavern dominated by the massive silver ship, with technicians, scientists, and armed guards buzzing around it, creating an atmosphere of intense activity. Like a beehive, the place hummed with constant activity, with the silver ship reigning as the queen of the bustling scene. It was the hub of the universe.

"It's even more magnificent up close, isn't it?"

Alex hadn't heard Penders as he descended the last steps to the cavern floor, being mesmerized as he was by the great ship. As he stared in awe at the spaceship, he was bewildered by the fact that all these workers could go about their mundane tasks while in its presence. No doubt these workers had been around it so often now it was no more out of the ordinary than an office building.

To Alex, it was life changing.

"Come here," Penders said, gently touching Alex's arm and nudging him forward. "I want you to see it up close."

Penders guided Alex through the buzzing throng of workers, none of whom acknowledged either man. They were intent on their tasks and nothing else, the perfect worker bees, furthering Alex's beehive comparison. Very little conversation occurred, and none of the workplace chatter that might be expected in other settings was present. Each person's focus was singular of purpose. Alex found it to be a bit unsettling, like a b-grade horror movie, and wondered what might motivate them. As he glanced back at Robert Penders, he quickly decided it was best to let that thought go.

Penders led him under the curvature of the ship, stopping when the hull of the craft was about six inches above them. Alex looked up into the perfectly smooth silver skin of the ship at his reflection, which was stretched and distorted like a funhouse mirror reflection. The surface of the craft was perfect, without a smudge or speck of dust to be seen.

"What do you think?" Penders asked.

Alex continued staring at his shifting reflection. "It looks smooth. Like polished metal."

"It is," Penders replied, reaching up and running his hand over the surface. His funhouse reflection did the same, neither of their hands leaving even so much a trace or smudge of dirt or oils. "It seems to be completely indestructible as well, at least against everything we've tried. Cutting torches, lasers, corrosives, radiation, explosives. Nothing we've done has made so much as a dent or scratch in its surface. It's entirely sealed, as well. Not a seam or crease anywhere. No sign of a door or hatch. We've been working on it for twenty-five years now and we've never seen the inside. We're no closer to understanding its secrets than we were when we first brought it here. You can imagine the frustration."

"Yeah, I feel for you," Alex replied absently, studying the metal surface for any sign of a flaw. There were none. As far as he could tell, the surface was absolutely perfect. "You've never been inside? Never seen inside?"

"No," Penders answered, his tone darker in response to Alex's flippant remark. "Never."

Alex turned his attention from the ship back to Penders. "What about the pilot? I thought the pilot was recovered?"

A slick smile crossed Penders' face. "It seems you are better informed about the history of our organization than I was led to believe. I'll have to have a conversation with Dr. Forrester about that. But to answer your question, yes, we have the occupant of the ship. Or the occupant's remains, to be more precise. The lifeless body was located just a few yards away from the ship."

"The pilot left the ship?" Alex asked. "Why would they do that?"

Penders shrugged ever so slightly. "That's why we'd like to get inside. To answer some of the many questions we have."

"No doubt, there's more to exploit in there," Alex muttered, shifting his attention back to the ship's belly above. "Wish I could help you," he lied, reaching up to touch the surface of the ship, "but I'm afraid I'm not much use..."

Alex stopped cold as his hand contacted the underside of the ship. At his touch, the surface changed, transforming from cold, unyielding metal into a sparkling, shifting, translucent energy. Wherever he touched the ship, the metal seemed to melt as swirling colors danced around the tips of his fingers and gently caressed his hand. The metal seemed to give way to his touch, his hand sinking into the surface as if he were pushing on sand. He knew it should shock and alarm him, but all he could feel was tranquility. His entire body was warm. There was music, he thought. Nothing he recognized, and he felt it resonate inside him more than hearing it, but it was there and it calmed him in a way he hadn't felt in a very long time.

Suddenly, a voice shattered the warmth and peace the ship had brought him. "Remarkable," breathed Robert Penders, his eyes wide with wonder.

Alex pulled his hand away from the ship. Almost immediately, the calming feeling and soothing vibrations ceased, slamming him headlong into the reality of his situation again. As soon as he broke contact with it, the ship's surface returned to the state it had been in before he touched it; cold and shiny metal.

"What was that?" Alex gasped, examining his hand. It was the same as it had always been, with no evidence of the remarkable scene he had just witnessed. For a moment he thought he had maybe imagined it, but the look of amazement on Penders' face confirmed he hadn't been the only witness.

"A major leap forward," Penders answered, a child-like look of wonder still on his face. "The most we've had so far. Simply amazing."

Alex was still examining his hand when he noticed the silence. The buzzing hive of activity that had surrounded them had suddenly come to an abrupt halt. Apart from humming computers and rasping air circulators, there was not another sound in the cavern. Alex found himself to be the new center of attention.

"Try it again," Penders said.

"And maybe lose my hand this time?" Alex replied. He knew that wouldn't happen, the ship had as much as told him that with the feelings of calm and serenity it projected onto him, but he certainly didn't want to give Penders any more access to it than he'd already had. "Yeah, I don't think so."

A change came over Penders' expression, as if some dark cloud had swept over his face and washed away the look of wonder, leaving behind a scarred landscape of anger. "Mr. Carter, do I need to remind you that you are here at my sufferance? From this moment on, your future, your fate, is solely at my discretion. As is that of your wife and unborn child. A word of advice; do not disappoint me."

Alex suddenly understood how Robert Penders motivated people; fear. It was that fear of the man that had kept Dr. Carlton from betraying his confidence for all those years. Looking around at the faces of the workers who had stopped to witness this fresh development, this 'major leap forward' as Penders had called it, he could see one common factor in all of them.

Fear.

There was no escape for him. Not right now. He was surrounded by people entrapped by their fear of one man. People that would fight for the man, regardless of the danger to themselves. It didn't matter if they might get hurt, whatever Penders would do to them in the wake of their failure would always be significantly worse.

Caught between the Devil and the deep blue sea. The line suddenly sprang into his head, something he had read in college. He couldn't remember where he had seen it, but it summed up his current situation. And if there were ever a devil on Earth, it was Robert Penders.

"Well, Mr. Carter?" Penders asked impatiently.

"All right," Alex replied, his options exhausted. "I'll do it."

"A wise choice," Penders answered snidely.

Just as before, Alex reached up and brushed his fingertips against the smooth metallic surface, and just as before, the metal gave way to a simmering dance of colors at his touch. The warmth filled him again and the calming resonance reverberated through his body, but this time it was slightly different. There was an undertone of something else there. Not quite fear or anxiety, more like caution. Apprehension.

The light expanded further outward from where he contacted the ship, creating a mesmerizing display of shifting colors - from vibrant reds to soothing greens, deep blues to sunny yellows, and countless combinations in between - all moving in a slow, easy pattern. There was nothing frenetic about it, it was pleasing and comforting to watch as the colors mingled and floated like neon clouds. The effect continued to ripple outward, eventually enveloping the entire underside of the craft in its luminous glow.

Out of curiosity, Alex pushed inward slightly. As before, the metal that was previously unyielding allowed his hand to sink slowly into its surface. The lights rippled outward in concentric circles with a greater intensity where his hand passed through, as if he were gently sinking it into a calm pool of water.

Behind him there were whispers and awed utterances, but he ignored them. His attention was absorbed by the mesmerizing flow of lights and the peculiar rippling sensation that his touch created on the ship's surface. It was hypnotic in its effect, drawing him in completely.

"What does it feel like?"

Penders' voice was like a sledgehammer, shattering Alex's concentration. Now that the trance was broken Alex realized his arm had been absorbed up to his elbow and, despite the warm calming feeling and gentle harmonic resonance flowing through him, he panicked and withdrew his arm until only his fingertips remained enveloped in the metal-turned-lights. As he retracted his arm, he noticed the colors shifting around him, changing from mostly blues and yellows to a predominance of reds and greens. Once his arm settled into a more comfortable position, the blues and yellows again became prominent.

"It feels like nothing I've ever felt before," Alex replied. "There's a warmth, a feeling of ease and comfort, that I can't put into words. It's like.." He paused, not entirely sure how to explain what he was feeling. Trying to put it into words felt almost sacrilegious. After a beat, he settled on the only words that seemed right, although they were woefully inadequate.

"It's like coming home."

Penders turned from the glowing ship and nodded to Harriman, who stepped forward without hesitation and reached up to touch the underside of the ship. When he made contact with the vessel, the dancing colors vanished, receding from his touch and leaving behind simple chrome-like metal. He reached out with his other hand and that section also became metal once more. Harriman broke contact completely and the swirling colors again overtook the spots his touch had corrupted.

"Nothing, sir," Harriman said, stepping back away from the ship. "Just metal."

Penders turned to Alex. "Step away from there," he commanded, his voice a low growl.

Alex broke contact with the ship and stepped away. Instantly, the craft reverted to its previous metallic form. Once again, Alex examined his hand and arm, finding nothing wrong. It was exactly as it had been before being drawn into the shifting lights.

Penders came up beside him and placed his own hand on the underside surface of the ship. As it had before, it remained unchanged. Pristine metal. Even the smudges from his fingers vanished, as if they had never existed.

His hand dropped to his side, clenching into a tight fist before relaxing again almost instantly. "How did you get it to do that?" Penders asked. His voice was calm and even, but Alex could sense a definite edge of frustration in him. "What did you do?"

Alex shrugged. "I have no clue. I just touched it and... Well, you saw what happened."

"All right," Penders said. "I think that's enough for now. We need to analyze the data from this and determine next steps. This is only the beginning." He gestured to Harriman, who advanced with two armed guards in tow. "Make him comfortable, but keep him under a close watch. Is that clear?"

"Yes, sir," Harriman replied, giving the two guards a slight nod. At that, they moved forward and flanked Alex, weapons once again at the ready.

"You got what you wanted," Alex addressed Penders. "Now take me to my wife."

"All in good time, Mr. Carter. All in good time." Penders was examining the underside of the ship again, staring intently at it as if he could open it by sheer force of will alone.

"If she's been hurt," Alex snarled, "I swear to you..."

"Please, Mr. Carter," Penders said, absently waving the threat away as if it were a bothersome fly, "don't make threats you are in no position to carry out."

Alex's rage surged once more, and he felt an overwhelming desire to unleash his fury on the smug little man, but the presence of armed guards made him think twice. Even with his remarkable healing abilities, they could cut him down before he moved more than a few steps towards Penders. Taking a breath, he pushed his anger down. As difficult as it was, this was a time to be patient.

"Okay," Alex said, falling into line between the two guards. "I'll follow your lead. For now. But as I was about to say earlier, if Rachel or the baby are hurt in any way, I guarantee I'll kill you."

"I'll keep that in mind," Penders replied, a smirk crossing his face.

"See that you do," Alex answered.

"By the way," Penders called to him as the guards led him away. "Welcome home."

56

Burke stormed out of the helicopter as soon as it touched the tarmac, pushing past the ground crew and security. Several people offered greetings to him as he passed, but he ignored them all as he stomped his way straight to Robert Penders' office.

Reaching the office, he crashed through the oversized and elaborately carved wooden double doors, a great crack resounding through the corridor as the door slammed hard against the walls of the reception area, straining against the confines of their hinges. Marjorie Haskill, Robert Penders' personal assistant, leaped up from her desk in wide-eyed surprise at Burke's explosive entrance.

"Mr. Darnell! What is the meaning of this?" Her voice was the low yet authoritative tone of an elementary school principal, the image completed by the bifocals that swung wildly around her neck on a gold chain, caught up in the ruffles of her white blouse peeking out from beneath her green wool business coat. Her hands had been tightly clenched, and she released one of them to steady her glasses.

"I'm here to see Penders," Burke answered as he rushed past her desk to the second set of heavy wooden doors that led to Penders' office.

Marjorie reached for the intercom on her desk. "One moment while I see if he's in."

"Don't bother, I'll find out for myself," Burke answered without a look back.

Behind him, Marjorie was yelling something about calling security, but she was out of his focus now, lost in the periphery of his tunnel vision. He had a singular focus and was being driven by rage and a sense of betrayal. As with the first set of doors, he hit them hard, his momentum carrying him forward. While these doors were just as thick as the first set, they were also smaller, and they flew open with a noise that resounded through the office like a shotgun blast. The lone occupant didn't so much as flinch at the commotion. Burke wasn't surprised.

"Burke, please come in and sit down. I've been expecting you." Robert Penders sat turned away from Burke in a high-backed leather office chair behind an enormous modern-looking black desk. He faced a wall of monitors that covered the far side of the room, hundreds of screens, each displaying different images. No sounds accompanied the images, which only intensified the eerie feeling the flickering screens gave to the otherwise darkened room.

"Thank you, Marjorie. That will be all." Penders waved a hand dismissively at his secretary. She merely nodded and backed out of the room, pulling the doors closed behind her as she went.

Penders turned away from the wall of monitors to face Burke. "Please, have a seat," he again suggested, gesturing to one of three seats on the opposite side of the desk. The light from the video screens behind him continued to flicker wildly, making the shadows perform a macabre dance around their master. Penders remained silent and motionless as the mesmerizing play of light and shadow unfolded around him.

Burke glanced up at the screens behind Penders. News programs, sitcoms, police procedurals, documentaries, cartoons, movies, internet videos; everything broadcast or internet related was represented on this wall of monitors. Each displayed a different channel or website in a massive conflagration of information. It was too much to take in all at once, and he lowered his head away from it.

"A little distraction?" he asked, indicating the flickering, dancing monitors behind Penders.

"It would seem that way, wouldn't it? But all of this is actually a valuable tool for our organization." Penders stood, his form blotting out a few of the screens. The light that seeped in formed a halo around him, bathing him in a frenetic sort of heavenly light. Burke grinned at the image of Penders as some sort of attention deficit angel as the other man continued to speak.

"I'm certain it seems to you that this is just a random, jumbled display of programs, but every image you see has something in common. Whether it's news or a sitcom, a cheesy movie or a trashy talk show, or a mindless internet stunt. Whatever goes across the many screens we surround ourselves with, each program has one thing in common with all the others: information. A vast, sprawling network of information. Every conceivable fact or misconception humanity has ever held will eventually come across one of those screens. And when it does, the Eden Project will be there to capture it, tag it, analyze it, catalog it, and preserve it for future use." Penders sighed the sigh of someone taking in the beauty of a tropical sunset.

"Media," he continued. "The power of it is staggering. The implications of it are endless if you have the imagination and the foresight to make use of it. Fortunately, the Project has both."

Penders sat again, leaning back in the black leather chair and steepling his fingers in front of him. "So, as you can see, it is far more than a 'little distraction'. But that's not why you're here, is it?"

"No," Burke blurted. "I want to know exactly what the hell has been going on around here. Why haven't you kept me in the loop about all operations? Why are my orders being overridden without my knowledge?" Burke realized he was yelling, ignoring all conventional rules of politeness and business etiquette, but he'd had enough. He had been loyal to this organization and its mission for as long as he could remember, politeness and etiquette were not on the forefront of his agenda at the moment.

Despite Burke's breach of decorum, Penders' face was a study in stone, betraying nothing about what lay just beneath its surface. He sat in silence, his eyes running over the younger man as he took his measure. The video screens behind him continued to flash and flicker, creating a jumble of activity that, despite the silence, seemed deafening.

The older man shifted slightly in his chair and cleared his throat. "I suppose I owe you that much, at least."

"At least," Burke repeated, venom in his voice.

"You know what the Eden Project's ultimate goal is?" Penders continued, ignoring the anger in Burke's tone.

"To control, either overtly or covertly, all aspects of society. To eliminate undesirables and bring about the renaissance of the class system," Burke rattled off. It was the first thing Penders drilled into him when he was brought on the Eden Project.

"Correct," Penders acknowledged. "To that end, we have created, with the research provided by Dr. Forrester, a worker class. A class that will perform the more dangerous or mundane tasks to keep society running, bred and born specifically to that task. At least, that was the intent of the group. Some of us had... other ideas."

Burke startled visibly at Penders' statement. "Are you saying your personal goals are no longer in line with those of the rest of the Eden Project's founders?"

"Not entirely," Penders replied, leather creaking as he leaned forward and placed his elbows on the desk. "I simply believe that the possibility of profit is too prevalent to ignore. We have created a new race of human beings; smarter, stronger, faster, and far more physically resilient than those of us born in the typical fashion could ever hope to be. They are the perfect biological weapon, simple to use and easy to control. A target specific weapon, more focused and less messy than nerve agents or germ weapons. No fear of making a target uninhabitable due to radiation, or subject to an extensive and expensive clean-up. Imagine what people would pay for that. They would be wasted picking up our trash, as the other founders would have them doing. It's too great an opportunity to let slip away."

Burke sat quietly for a moment, wary of where this conversation was heading. Robert Penders was a man of vast, almost limitless power and influence. But so were the other members of the Eden Project, and they would not respond well to one of their ranks deviating from the plan. Burke's mind raced, searching for options. He had been completely loyal to Penders for as long as he could remember. If the Eden Project took action, it would drag him into it as a part of Penders' camp. He needed to rectify the situation, to bring Penders back on track with the Project's goals.

A single idea surfaced amidst the tumultuous thoughts in his head. "Sir, I'm willing to concede that there is a huge financial opportunity here. However, you must see that what we've produced so far consists largely of damaged goods. Look at the results. Most of the subjects went feral and ripped each other apart. As if that weren't bad enough, the remaining two haven't been much better. Adam has run amuck, killing at random while in pursuit of some goal no one can quite pin down. Carter has proven to be completely uncooperative and uncontrollable despite the deep programming we put into him, even developing emotions that are counter to his programming and purpose. Then there's the baby, a child that never should have existed in the first place since the subjects were all supposed to be sterile! Look at the data, this phase of the experiment has been an abject failure. We can't offer the services of our products until we first create better products!"

"We have a better product," Penders stated, leaning back once more into the soft leather of his chair. As he did, shadows rushed in to fill in the details of his face where the light couldn't reach, masking everything but his eyes. His cold blue eyes. "We have the Sleeper."

"The Sleeper?" Burke repeated. He had heard rumors of an experiment with that name, but he had never uncovered any evidence of its existence. As far as he knew, it was just another urban legend among the rank and file.

"I don't know who or what this Sleeper is," he continued. "I can't count on the success of something I know nothing about."

"Oh, you know more about this project than you think, Mr. Darnell," Penders replied cryptically. "Much more than you think."

A smile crossed Penders' face, one that Burke had seen countless times before. Never on that face, though. It had always been staring at him from somewhere else, and seeing it now on Penders chilled him to the marrow. Not because it was a particularly chilling grin, just that Burke knew what sort of dark thoughts lay behind it. He knew this because the smile was usually staring back at him in his own reflection. And the dark ideas behind it were usually his own. Ideas that meant something bad was about to happen to someone.

As usual, he was right. Even though this was the one time he wished he could have been wrong.

57

Although he was locked in a detention cell, Alex drifted off to sleep. He'd had so little rest the last few days and it had all finally caught up with him. Now that he wasn't running or fighting for his life, fatigue overtook him, dragging him under in an unrelenting wave.

But somehow, even in sleep, he couldn't find rest. As he drifted deeper and deeper into the dark areas of his mind, places only his subconscious allowed him to go, he heard a voice calling to him. It was faint, hardly audible at all. In fact, it was less a voice and more a small, tinny sound, like a mixture of musical notes. Whether or not it was spoken, its meaning was unmistakable.

Set me free.

Three simple words that spoke volumes. Someone was calling him for help. A psychic connection, reminiscent of the way Ernie had reached out during his near-death experience in the hospital. But this was different somehow. This was closer. Stronger. Just... different. He couldn't explain how, just that it didn't feel the same. It wasn't a call he heard in the traditional sense, but a call that stirred something within him, like a gentle tug on his soul. And unlike Ernie, it wasn't a desperate plea; it was more of a gentle nudge.

Set me free.

He started to follow the call, to see how he could help whoever was reaching out, but he was stopped suddenly and violently by another voice that screamed from the surrounding void. Unlike the pleasant urging of the first call, this one was dark and intrusive, forcing its way into his head like a runaway train, its message as unmistakable as the force behind it.

I'm coming for you.

Through the gray-black haze of his mindscape, Alex could see a dark shape moving towards him. It moved like oil through water, darting fluidly through the flotsam of his crowded subconscious. It was angry and vengeful, intent on a singular purpose as it moved closer. There was no mistaking who was behind this intrusion into his mind.

It was Adam. And he was close.

Alex slipped to the side, dodging as the dark mass swept past him. It hadn't touched him, but its mere presence in close proximity was enough to send shockwaves of pain through his body as the miasma of anger and revenge that made up its being washed over him in its wake.

I'm coming for you.

The line rang through his head, resounding painfully. A chill of fear gripped Alex as he realized Adam was stronger than the last time they fought. More focused. More powerful. Maybe powerful enough to swallow Alex's psyche whole.

As if in response to his realization, the dark mass turned back toward him, slithering along its former path, seeking its prey once more. Alex turned to escape, to find a way out of his own psychic plane, but panic trapped him like a fly in honey. He felt slow and sluggish, weighted down by fear, helpless to do anything but watch as Adam set upon him like a shark on a seal. His heart felt like it was going to explode as the dark mass sped closer to him. As it was almost on him, he thought he could see its ice-blue eyes and jagged predator teeth.

Suddenly, a brilliant burst of pure white light erupted, flooding his mind with its radiant glow and dispelling every trace of darkness. The dark creature burned and withered at the light's touch, screaming and writhing as the purity of it consumed it. One last time, Alex heard the voice in his head as the creature that was Adam faded from this plane of existence.

I'm coming for you.

Then it was gone, as if it never existed. The creature that sprang from Adam's mind withered away instantly as the blinding white light consumed it. Alex scanned his surroundings, desperately trying to locate the source of the inexplicable presence, but there was no sign of anything. Nothing but the light itself. It was as if it simply was and always had been. Then he heard it again; the light, musical chime of the voice that had drawn him here.

Set me free.

Unlike Adam's psychic voice, this one didn't come from a single source or direction. It surrounded him, enveloping him in warmth and comfort. Not just around him, but through him as well, permeating him with calm and peace. In that instant, although it had spoken nothing to him besides those three words, Alex understood what was being asked of him.

"I will," he responded, and suddenly found himself staring wide-eyed at the ceiling of his cell, the tinny musical voice already fading once more into the misty depths of mind and memory.

But the memory of the shadow creature that had invaded his mind was still fresh, refusing to drift away as the other had. He sat up on the bunk, not wanting to fall back to sleep, afraid that the horror would find its way back to him. His logical mind knew what it was, that it wasn't some nightmare creature. Adam was flesh and blood, just like he was. And maybe that was what scared him most, that they were so similar. Maybe, at the core of his being, he was less afraid of the reality of Adam and more afraid of the possibility he could become like him.

He pushed off the bunk and crossed the small cell, stretching the sleep from his body. Before he lay down to sleep, he had taken off his shoes and now he felt the plush carpet crush beneath his feet with every step. The room, despite being a holding cell, was rather comfortable. The light green paint on the walls created a comfortable and inviting atmosphere. A small refrigerator stocked with food and beverages sat in the far corner, along with a microwave for convenience. He noticed a mounted television on the wall, but he hadn't turned it on to explore its offerings. The atmosphere inside felt more like a college dormitory than a prison.

The locked and guarded door shattered the illusion of safety and comfort. For all the comfort provided, there was no mistaking the fact that this was still a cage.

A loud rumble from his stomach interrupted his thoughts as he realized he had had nothing to eat since the previous morning. As he stared at the fully stocked refrigerator, doubts about Penders' intentions and the safety of the food crept into his mind, causing him to hesitate. Being kidnapped and locked up already, he couldn't shake the fear that the Eden Project might go as far as drugging him, too. Then again, they really didn't need to drug him to get his cooperation. As long as they had Rachel, they had him. Something Penders was fully aware of.

His stomach rumbled again, practically screaming at him. Regardless of trust, he couldn't concentrate on finding Rachel and escaping if his stomach was growling with hunger. Deciding to risk it, he selected a microwave dinner of turkey and mashed potatoes, along with a can of Pepsi. With a clatter, he dropped the plastic tray of frozen food into the microwave and punched in the cooking time. As the microwave hummed, he grabbed a soda and chugged it down, anticipating his meal. Before the microwave alerted him that the food was ready, he was already halfway through another can of Pepsi. The food was pleasantly warm, and he ate rapidly, more to fill the space in his belly than to enjoy the taste of it. He had to eat two more frozen dinners, one lasagna and the other some sort of chicken something, along with another Pepsi and two bottles of water before his stomach finally stopped begging for more. After disposing of the empty plastic and aluminum containers, he sat back on the bunk and leaned his head against the light green wall. Closing his eyes, he waited for any ill effects from drugs that might have been in the food. After what seemed like hours in his own personal darkness, he opened his eyes to the brightness of the cell, feeling nothing but full. Seems he had been right, Penders hadn't felt the need to drug him.

That was one problem taken care of. Unfortunately, it was the easy one. Next, he needed to get out of his cell, then find Rachel and get the two of them as far away as they could get. That, and find the source of the musical voice that had rescued him in the mindscape. And maybe figure out why the mysterious spaceship back in the cavern had reacted to his touch the way it had.

So many questions he wanted answers to, and so many answers he was sure he wouldn't get. First thing first, get out of this cage and find Rachel. That was all that really mattered. Everything else was just a distraction. Unfortunately, he was at a loss as to how he would even begin to tackle that challenge.

As if in response to his thoughts, there was a muffled thump outside his cell door, followed almost immediately by another. A jolt of pure fear and adrenaline shot up his spine and he jumped up from the bunk, turning to the source of the noise. Seconds passed by, stretched out into an eternity, with no further noise. He searched the room for anything he could use as a weapon, but found nothing. Anything that had the potential to cause damage was carefully fastened and secured in place. The only thing available to him were a few cans of soda that remained in the refrigerator. In the absence of any available options, he hastily seized two cans of soda, steadying himself as he confronted the door. At any other time, he would have thought it was absurd, but at that moment, his mind was consumed by the need to survive and get away.

Abruptly, the silence was shattered by a series of sharp beeps coming from the electronic door lock. The lock required a seven-digit code to disengage, and Alex counted the tones, his heart racing faster with each one. As the seventh beep echoed through the room, Alex's heart raced as he quickly pressed himself flat against the wall next to the door. Staying out of sight might gain him the element of surprise and maybe gain an advantage over whoever came through the door.

The door lock clicked loudly, signaling that it was now open. The door pushed inward and Alex pressed himself further into the wall, sliding into the space behind the opening door. A shadow fell across the room. Someone was at the entrance, waiting. Maybe waiting for him to make a move to escape. Or maybe surprised at not finding him sitting placidly on his bunk. Either way, it appeared as if his plan had worked and he had surprise on his side.

The shadow rocked left and right as if searching the room before advancing, growing menacingly larger in the light from the hallway. Slowly, he elevated one of the soda cans, getting ready to strike. The toe of a boot appeared just beyond the edge of the open door. One more step and Alex would have him. His hands tightened around the soda cans, which felt wet and slippery against his palms. Either the cans were sweating, or he was. He loosened his grip slightly, afraid of squeezing them out between slick fingers.

The boot took another tentative step forward, placing the wearer just on the outside edge of the door. Just one more step, and Alex would be fully visible. If he were going to strike first, it would have to be now.

Alex leaped from behind the door, thrusting a fist full of aluminum can and carbonated beverage at the intruder. He felt his fist connect hard, the seal at the top of the can coming apart under the crushing force. A brownish foam followed by a burst of dark bubbly liquid came spurting from the top of the crushed can as the intruder yelped in a mix of pain and surprise and fell backward, toppling over into the hallway. Something fell onto the carpet next to Alex and he glanced down to see a silencer-equipped pistol lying next to his sock-clad foot. He swiftly picked up the gun and directed it towards the fallen intruder, who sat on the floor, his hands pressed against his face as he groaned in pain. Dark brown soda and bright red blood ran between his fingers.

"My nose!" the black-clad man exclaimed in a hushed yet pained tone, desperately trying to avoid attracting any unwanted attention. "I think you broke my damned nose!"

Alex stepped forward, leveling the gun at the man's head. "Shut up, or your nose will be the least of your problems!"

Stepping out of his cell, Alex almost stumbled over the motionless form of the guard who had been responsible for his surveillance. It was one of the three that had greeted him when he arrived at the compound. His semi-automatic shotgun lay on the floor next to him, his hand still tightly wrapped around it. A pool of blood was forming on the floor from a gunshot wound to his chest, his eyes wide open and empty. Against the far wall, a second man, unknown to Alex, remained slumped with a gaping wound in his chest, while blood trailed down the wall. That explained the thumps he heard earlier.

The intruder stopped groaning in pain and struggled to his feet. Alex kept the pistol trained on him, tracking his every move with his finger lightly on the trigger. As he struggled to his feet, he swayed unsteadily and let out grunts of pain from the vicious soda can attack. He lowered his hands and gradually turned to face Alex. Despite the bruises, blood, and soda, the face was unmistakable.

It was Rick.

"You son of a bitch!" Alex shouted, and without thinking, struck Rick with the pistol. Rick crumpled to the floor again, groaning in pain and holding the side of his head where Alex had connected. Alex moved forward and shoved the barrel of the pistol hard against Rick's nose.

"Give me one reason I shouldn't kill you right now," Alex growled through clenched teeth.

"Because I can get you out of here." Rick stated, returning a hard stare. "You and Rachel both."

Rage shot through Alex, his hand tightening on the grip of the gun. "You're lying. You've been lying to me since the day we met. You turned me over to Penders! What makes you think I'm going to believe anything you say now?"

"I got you inside, didn't I?" Rick replied, the slightest hint of snark in his voice.

"You turned me over to them," Alex repeated, his anger at a peak now. "You turned on me *again* and turned me over!"

Rick winced in pain as the gun was inadvertently shoved harder against his face, driven by Alex's anger. Risking Alex's wrath, he reached up and pushed the weapon away from his face. "That was the only way I could get us in here!"

"What are you talking about?" Alex replied. "You said you had a plan to get us inside to rescue Rachel!"

"And I did," Rick said, gesturing to their surroundings. "You're inside, aren't you?"

Alex stood in disbelief, the hand holding the gun falling limply to his side as his rage slowly abated, replaced by confusion and disbelief. "*This* was your plan all along?"

Rick stood again; his legs still unsteady beneath him. Alex reached out to help him, stopping short as Rick righted himself. "I knew there was no way we'd be able to sneak past Harriman's security. He's as good as they get."

Alex scowled. "We've met."

Rick frowned. "Yeah. Anyway, I needed a sure-fire way to get you in here. I knew this place would be locked down airtight, especially after Adam's recent 'resignation', so I figured this would be the best way. They knew I was double dealing with Forrester, so they assumed he'd ask me to try to him get you away. Which I was going to do, by the way. Until they captured Rachel." He paused, wiping soda from his eyes and blood from his chin. "That was when things took a sharp turn. I knew they'd bring her here, and I knew you'd go after her. I also knew that if you came here alone, they'd chew you up and spit you out, right before re-indoctrinating you into the Eden Project. So, I called Harriman before you and that cop got to the rendezvous site and told him we were coming. Before you and that cop got to the rendezvous site, I called Harriman and informed him we were coming. I also made it clear that I would hand you and Forrester over, as long as he assured me that no one would be hurt. From there, I figured I'd be able to get you and Rachel out of here once we were all together inside the Nest. So far, everything has gone exactly as planned." A new trickle of blood ran from his nose, over his lips and down his chin. He swiped at it with the back of his hand. "Well, not everything."

Alex said nothing, simply stared at the man who had betrayed him twice in the last two days. Not to mention the lie that had been their entire friendship. His newfound abilities allowed him to sense nothing duplicitous from him, but he was still conflicted, unsure if he could trust the new Rick. At the moment, he didn't really have much choice. Rick had at least come up with a plan, which was more than Alex had done. He seemed to have some idea how to escape, too, which was certainly more than Alex had. He seemed to know where Rachel was being kept, putting him yet another step ahead of Alex. Whether or not he wanted to admit it, whether or not he wanted to trust him, Alex realized he needed Rick's help.

"Okay," he said at last, "you've got me. But if anything feels even remotely wrong, I'll kill you and take my chances on my own. Understood?"

Rick nodded assent as a sly smile, very much an old-Rick smirk, crossed his face. It was his mischief-making smile, the kind that always preceded them getting into trouble in their younger days. "We have to get out of here. A security detail will arrive here in a few minutes once they realize that someone has tampered with the security cameras in this area. Help me with these guys." He bent down and grabbed the body of one guard, dragging him by the shoulders into the cell. Reluctantly, Alex did the same with the other man. Once they were secured inside, Rick punched some numbers into the keypad and locked the door again with a resounding click. "I've scrambled the codes. It'll take them at least ten minutes to get in there and discover you aren't inside anymore."

"I have a feeling they'll assume the worst," Alex replied, gesturing towards the pools of blood on the floor and the ominous smear on the wall.

"Well then, let's not hang around and see," Rick said as he snatched up one of the abandoned shotguns, handing it to Alex before taking the other one for himself. "Follow me."

Staring at the blood-stained walls and floor, Alex hesitated, a wave of unease washing over him. But then he remembered Rachel, trapped somewhere in this insane asylum, and a fierce determination surged within him. As he fell in behind Rick, he could feel the weight of the shotgun in his hands and the reassuring presence of the handgun against his lower back. He would find Rachel and they would escape to safety, no matter who or what stood in his way.

58

Rachel had relaxed and recuperated for as long as she could stand it. After Penders left her, Rachel dragged herself onto the soft, exceedingly comfortable couch and laid back, waiting for the effects of the drug she had been given to pass. She hadn't felt any further dizziness or photosensitivity since she first laid down, and her fine motor skills seemed to have returned as she flexed her arms and hands over her head. It amazed her she had recovered so quickly; she had expected to be out of it for another few hours at least. She wasn't certain what could have facilitated her speedy recuperation, but she made sure to rub her stomach and say a little thanks to her baby, just in case.

Pulling herself off the couch, she set her sights on escaping Robert Penders and the Eden Project. She scanned the room for anything she might use to get a message out to the police, or something she could use as a distraction to cover her escape.

Or maybe a weapon.

Her heart sank at that thought. She didn't want to hurt anyone else, there had been enough of that. Enough pain and killing. Before this, she would never have believed she was capable of hurting another person, but the last few days showed she wasn't only capable, she was also able. She consoled herself with the fact that she had done those things to protect the people she cared about, but deep inside a dark feeling clawed at her. Gnawed at her conscience and amplified her guilt.

No, she thought, pushing the encroaching darkness back. *Not now.* She would eventually have to address her guilt and reconcile her conflicting emotions around her recent actions, but now wasn't the time. Now she needed to focus on saving herself and her baby.

She ducked behind the bar to search for anything useful to her. Dozens of bottles, filled with undoubtedly pricey liquors, were neatly arranged on the shelf behind her. Below the bar, there was a compact fridge housing a variety of microwave meals, accompanied by a microwave for easy heating, with no other items in sight.

Frustrated, she moved to the enormous desk. A sudden burst of hope erupted in her chest at the sight of a telephone there, and she snatched up the receiver to dial. As she lifted the earpiece to her ear, she heard a soft click and a woman's voice, soulless and mechanical, on the other end of the phone. "Please enter your personal security code to place a call outside of this facility."

The phrase repeated twice before she hung up the phone, the feeling of hope dying inside her. It wasn't surprising that the phone lines would be secured, but she was hoping she could catch a break. She braced herself and carried on, meticulously scouring the left-hand drawer of the desk. The deep drawer had rails on either side, specifically designed to hold file folders. Not surprisingly, in the modern era of electronic data storage, the drawer was empty..

The two drawers on the right were empty as well. A quick look at the small middle drawer revealed what appeared to be just elastic bands and a box of paper clips, with nothing else of note. A closer look revealed a small metallic triangle peeking out from under the box of paper clips. She slid the triangle out of its hiding place to reveal a letter opener. The old-fashioned type shaped like a dagger, not one of the new plastic safety types that hid the blade inside a plastic case.

This was something she could use.

But how? Penders must have left guards posted outside the door. Even if she could somehow lure them into the room, how would she and her letter opener overpower trained and heavily armed soldiers?

She needed a distraction. Something big that would allow her to slip out unnoticed in the chaos and confusion. Something that would keep her from having to use her letter opener in a fight. But what did she have that would create a disturbance big enough for her to escape?

While her thoughts were occupied with finding inspiration, her eyes couldn't help but be mesmerized by the flickering flames in the fireplace. Earlier, before her rest, she had gone to stoke the fire to keep it from dying, only to discover it was a gas fireplace. Simply turning a valve above the hearth could instantly achieve any level of comfort or mood. Convenient, but it took away so much of the reward of building and tending a fire. Her mind flashed back to when she was a kid and went camping with her family, how her father had taught her his special trick for stacking wood just right. How, when her mother wasn't looking, he would douse the wood in lighter fluid to guarantee it would catch fire immediately. She was never fooled, the smell of the lighter fluid was always so thick in the chilly night air, but she never let on and he continued to brag about his fire making skills.

And suddenly, like the flames that erupted from those fuel-soaked pieces of wood all those years ago, an idea exploded inside her head. A bolt of energy shot through her and she dashed back to the bar, fumbling through the bottles, examining each label. Ignoring the cheap stuff, she went straight for the most expensive looking bottles she could find, reading the alcohol content on each, before finally settling on five bottles of brandy. Very expensive looking brandy, at that. It wasn't lighter fluid, but it should suit her needs.

She gathered up the bottles and some bar rags in her arms and made her way back to the fireplace, carefully placing them on the floor in front of the hearth. Taking care not to snuff out the flame entirely, she located the gas valve and reduced the flow to a minimum, anxious about the possibility of not being able to reignite it when needed.

Carefully, she tore the bar rags into strips and soaked them in the brandy, watching as they absorbed the liquid and transformed into makeshift wicks. Once she suffused them with brandy, she positioned the wicks as close as possible to the tiny, flickering blue flames, arranging them in a straight line along the hearth and extending them over the edge until they made contact with the carpet. Next, she poured brandy in different directions on the floor - one towards the bar, the other towards the door. After recapping it, she tightly clutched the remaining half of a bottle to her chest. The bottle was slick with sweat from her hands and slowly slipping from her grip. Worried about dropping it before the right moment, she readjusted her grip and pulled it in closer.

Once again, she reached up and found the valve at the top of the gas hearth. She took a deep breath and muttered, "Here goes nothing," before turning the jets up to their highest setting. As she did, the small blue flames erupted with a massive infusion of gas, spewing orange and yellow tongues of flame outward. She jumped away as the heat seared her side, sliding over the desk and landing with a loud thump on the other side.

The brandy-soaked rag strips ignited instantly, sending bright lines of flame outward like trails from tiny rockets. The wicks burned up quickly, while the fire spread and consumed the brandy-soaked carpet, splitting into two vivid streams. One of the fiery trails slithered towards the door, while the other meandered across the carpet, leaving scorch marks in its wake. It climbed up and over the bar, swiftly maneuvering between bottles on the shelves, consuming everything in its path.

“Fire!” she screamed as loud as she could. “Fire!” Her heart raced as she watched the fire move throughout the office, spreading out from the course she had charted for it with the brandy. As the coffee table caught fire, embers drifted onto the plush couch where she had slept, scorching the leather. “Help, fire!” she screamed again, this time with a touch of genuine panic in her tone. A piercing alarm sounded, its shrillness echoing through the air, signaling a warning.

Suddenly, the sprinklers came to life, showering the flames she had cultivated with a torrent of water.

"No! Not now!" she cried; her words drowned out by the sound of water cascading from above to extinguish the flames.

Across the room, the door opened. Startled, a man dressed in black fatigues exclaimed, "What the hell?" as a wave of flames forcefully pushed him backwards, fueled by a sudden influx of oxygen from the outer office.

Regaining his composure, he shouted, "Mrs. Carter?" The smoke was getting thick as the sprinklers extinguished the smaller fires, and he strained to see across the room. “Where are you?”

“Over here!” Rachel shouted back, staying tucked down. “Behind the desk!”

"Just hang tight, we'll get you out," the soldier replied as he entered the room, his boots thudding against the smoldering rug.

Through the smoke and cascading rain from the sprinklers, Rachel could barely make out another figure standing behind the young soldier, a man of similar build. She had wished for just two guards to be assigned to watch over her, worried that she couldn't handle any more.

As the cold water from the sprinklers drenched her, she kept a low profile, kneeling on the floor by the desk. She hated being wet and cold, but it kept her sharp and focused. She held onto the brandy bottle's slim neck and the letter opener's smooth handle, her hands trembling with anticipation. Peeking over the top of the desk, she saw the two men cautiously maneuvering through the room, sidestepping the crackling fires and spreading puddles. By now, they had covered more than half the distance towards her; a few more steps and she could act.

In that moment, she couldn't help but wonder about the families that these men might have left behind. If they were brothers or husbands or fathers. If they died today, possibly at her hand, she wondered who would mourn them. She vigorously shook her head, trying to rid her mind of the lingering thoughts. It was too late for that now. When they threw in with Penders and the Eden Project, they chose their side. Now they would have to live with the consequences that went with that choice.

Another step. The first one, the young one who had been first in the room, was close now, but the second one was lagging. Her plan hinged on their proximity to each other. She needed them to be closer together. As she looked around, the fires were dwindling, leaving behind a sense of despair.

"Mrs. Carter?" the first man shouted over the din of the fire alarm, rubbing his eyes clear as water and smoke tore at them in equal measure.

Okay, Rachel decided, it was time to shake things up and revise the plan. With each passing moment, her confidence in salvaging anything from it dwindled. Her hands tightened around her makeshift weapons as she stood up from behind the desk, her heart pounding in her chest.

"Here!" she shouted, waving her arms. Her voice caught their attention, causing the men to face her abruptly, their eyes widening in surprise. Without hesitation, she emerged from her hiding spot, effortlessly leaping over a fading trail of fire, and positioned herself confidently between them near the crackling fireplace. The gas jets were still pumping out an inferno, undeterred by the efforts of the sprinklers to douse them. The heat felt good as it lapped at her soaked and chilled body and if she could have, she would have curled up right there and warmed herself. It seemed like it had been forever since she felt warm and safe and comfortable.

"Come on," said the man closest to her, the young one. "Let's get you out of here."

A twinge of guilt struck her at the sound of genuine concern in his voice, and she hesitated. He moved toward her, causing her to freeze in place as indecision grasped her. She shook harder with each step he took, squeezing the weapons in her hands but unable to make her arms work to use them. As he emerged through the smoke, she saw the face of a man only twenty-five years old, wet shocks of blondish hair hanging over his bright ocean blue eyes, light brown freckles dotting his cheeks. Her resolve to fight slowly dissipated as thoughts of families in mourning once again filled her head.

As he approached her, he reached out a hand. His hand abruptly tightened around her arm, his fingers digging into her with a sharp, painful grip. "The bitch is over here!" he yelled to the other soldier. In an instant, his boyish appearance evaporated, melting into a visage of pure rage.

"Did you do this on purpose?" he yelled, shaking her violently. Her fingers tightened around the bottle and letter opener, her knuckles turning white as she desperately held onto her only means of protection.

It wouldn't be easy for her to break free from him, but she knew she had to seize this one opportunity. With a pressing need to free her arms and create space, she realized she had limited options to do so. Without warning, she stepped forward into his grip, pulled back her head, and smashed her forehead hard into his nose. Her head and neck throbbed with intense pain from the impact, but the guard's screams were a satisfying sign that her plan had been successful.

Mostly. Before she could create enough distance between them, he made a desperate grab for her. Despite the pain, blood, smoke, and the constant cascade of falling water, he grasped her arm once again. Awkwardly, he pulled her back and spun her around to face him, causing her heart to race.

"That fucking hurt!" he screamed, shaking her hard. Swiftly and unexpectedly, he pulled his arm back and delivered a forceful strike to her cheek. The impact threw her back, breaking his weak grip on her, and she fell hard to the floor. The young soldier stepped toward her again, his hands balled up tightly at his sides, quivering with rage. Despite Rachel's attempt to retreat, he effortlessly matched her pace. In an instant, he towered above her, his clenched fists poised to strike once more. His blue eyes were no longer those of an innocent young man, but now projected the soul of a remorseless killer. Seized with fear, she could only wait for the blows to start.

Just then, as if on cue, a bottle behind the bar exploded. A spray of half ignited brown liquid shot straight up, spattering the flaming mixture into the ceiling where it continued to burn and spread. Another followed almost immediately as the heat from the fire seared them, causing them to boil and shatter. More bottles followed in rapid succession and the fire leaped back to life, completely engulfing the bar.

The guard standing over her looked away, his arms instinctively moving to shield his face from the chaos of bottles breaking at the bar. Rachel took advantage of the situation and slid out from under the young man, pulling herself up and away from him. In one swift motion, she hurled the bottle of brandy into the roaring fireplace and launched herself towards the nearest guard. The impact was brutal as she landed, putting all her weight on the outside of his right knee joint, causing it to contort at an alarming angle, accompanied by a bone-chilling snapping sound. The young man's face twisted into a mask of agony as he screamed and fell to the floor in a whimpering heap, grasping his wounded leg. At the same moment, the brandy bottle shattered in the gas generated inferno of the fireplace, creating an explosion of liquid fire that splashed across the floor and reignited the dying flames. As she moved away from the screaming heap of what had been a man a moment ago, Rachel saw the second guard advancing toward her, drawn through the haze of smoke and steam by his partner's screams. As he came into view, he was distracted by the writhing form of the other man cradling his wrecked knee, choked sounds between a sob and a scream emanating from him. Remembering her previous mistake, Rachel acted swiftly, throwing herself at him and striking with the letter opener without hesitation. She found her mark, the small blade sinking deep into his thigh, eliciting the same sickening popping-tearing sound she had heard at the Barton's the other night when she stabbed Adam, followed by a similarly piercing scream of pain.

With a stumble, the guard lunged towards her, but she deftly slipped out of his reach and bolted towards the door. She wiped the damp strands of hair away from her face, trying to clear her vision as she squinted through the thick smoke, desperately searching for the door. A feeling of elation washed over her as she caught sight of the dim rectangular outline - she was almost free.

Glancing at the door again, she suddenly came to a halt. Silhouetted against the light leaking through from the outer office was the shape of a man, his identity masked by clinging smoke. Her elation turned to stark, chilling terror as, even through her muddied field of vision, she could make out the gun in his hand. She couldn't launch an attack on him yet; he was still too far away, just beyond her grasp, and she had used up her makeshift weapons. She was defenseless and completely out of ideas, her bid for freedom and, possibly, her life about to end abruptly. Squeezing her eyes shut, she formed a picture of Alex in her mind and waited for the shot to come.

The boom she was expecting didn't happen. Instead, there was a slight chuff, almost inaudible over the din of the screaming fire alarms. Even more surprising to her, she didn't feel any pain or searing heat or ripping impact of a bullet tearing through her body. The cold and wet from the sprinklers told her she was still alive, and a feeling of relief rushed through her.

"Rachel?"

The voice that carried her name was the most wonderful thing she had ever heard in her life. Her eyes snapped open, and she instinctively swiped at the damp red hair that clung to her face. Stepping towards the doorway, she left the swirling cloud of smoke and flickering light behind, finally catching sight of him. It felt like an eternity since she had last seen him, but in this instant, he looked more beautiful than ever before.

"Alex!" she choked out, throwing her arms around him. He returned her embrace with an intense one of his own, refusing to let go as if afraid she might vanish into thin air.

"Are you all right?" he asked, brushing the remaining strands of hair from her face. As he revealed her eyes, his heart practically skipped a beat at the deep green of them.

Another bottle exploded across the room, tearing his attention back to the reality of the situation. "What happened here?"

"I happened," she answered, her voice strong and confident. "Never come between a pregnant redhead and her man."

Despite himself and their situation, Alex smiled. "Noted," he said, and kissed her gently. The kiss was filled with a gentle passion that she returned eagerly, grateful for the first taste of safety in days.

"I hate to interrupt this happy little family reunion," Rick said from the doorway, "but we have got to get out of here. This place is going to be swarming with heavily armed security in a minute and they're going to be none too happy when they see the place. Not to mention their boys."

He nodded at the room behind them, and Rachel turned to take in the damage. Fires still burned, although they were slowly being overtaken by the sprinklers. The smoke was clearing and she could make out the two guards. The first was still lying on the floor, whimpering in pain and grasping his wrecked knee, which stuck out from beneath him at an impossible angle. Positioned about halfway across the room, the second guard remained motionless on the floor, the letter opener still embedded in his thigh. Amid the dissipating smoke, she caught sight of the dark pool of blood spreading beneath him.

"I had to do it, Rach," Alex said, sensing the feelings of guilt and remorse in her. "He was about to shoot you. I had to stop him. There was no other choice."

"I know," she choked out, tears welling up in her eyes before being swallowed up by the rain from the sprinklers. "I'm just tired of all the killing. All the violence. I want it all to stop."

"I know," Alex replied, hugging her close to him again. "So do I."

"Come on!" Rick shouted, waving them on. "If we stay any longer," he cautioned, "you'll just end up right where you began!"

Alex nudged Rachel toward the exit, positioning himself between her, the corpse, and the screaming man. She couldn't see it, but the vivid details of the carnage in that room were etched into her mind, haunting her thoughts. She was responsible for that. It was her doing. She thought back to the person she had been just a few short days ago; happily married, expecting her first child, living an idyllic life in a quiet little town. She missed that person, missed her more than she cared to admit. Mostly because she knew she could never be that person again.

In her mind's eye she took one last look at that happy woman in her happy life, then shut the door on that memory forever. She was a different person now, even though her priorities remained the same; her husband and her child. She had proven that she was willing to do whatever needed to be done to protect them, and apparently she was able as well. She was a new person, and when all this was over, she would make a new life for herself and her family.

59

Harriman wasn't surprised when the alarms sounded. He knew it was inevitable from the moment they brought Alex Carter in. No matter what Penders' opinion of himself was, even he couldn't control something akin to a force of nature. He had gotten himself in way over his head.

And dragged me in with him, Harriman thought as he pulled himself off his bed and stepped into his boots. Now it was his job to pull them both out.

Before he finished lacing up his boots, his phone chirped a high trill, the sound denoting a call coming from inside the Nest. It made sense. When the alarms sounded, all communication to and from the Nest would be cut off, meaning that he could only receive a call from inside the mountain.

He snatched up the phone and answered the call. "Harriman."

"Colonel, we have a situation here." The voice on the other end of the line was young sounding and harried, filled with fear.

"Calm down and explain it to me, son," Harriman replied, taking a fatherly tone to put the young soldier at ease rather than push him over the brink into a blind panic as a bellowing commanding officer.

"We have three dead and one wounded, sir," the young man answered, his voice steadying slightly. "Castillo, Brock, and Williamson are dead. Gunshot wounds. Briar's out of commission with a seriously screwed up leg, sir."

Castillo, Brock, Williamson, and Briar. The four who were assigned to guard Alex and Rachel Carter, respectively. He knew it was only a matter of time before that situation would go critical.

Harriman refocused his attention on the young soldier. "What about the prisoners? Are they secured?"

"No, sir," came the hesitant reply, the anxious edge returned to the young man's voice. "We don't know what happened to them. And there's one more thing, sir."

"What is it?"

"Rick Banning is missing as well," the young soldier replied. "We can't find a sign of him anywhere."

"I figured as much," Harriman muttered.

"Excuse me, sir?"

"Nothing. Who am I speaking to?" Harriman asked, snapping his holster in place and checking his Glock to ensure it was loaded, as well as making sure he had extra magazines in place.

"Wright, sir. Sergeant Lawrence Wright."

"Well, Sergeant Wright, until I can get out there, you are officially in command. Lock the facility down tight, then sweep it again. Search every corner of the Nest. I don't want so much as a microbe getting in or out. Are we clear?"

"Yes, sir," Sergeant Wright replied, a nervous quavering in his voice.

"I want the Carters found and contained. They are not to be harmed. If you can take Banning alive, fine, but you have some discretion on that one. What about Dr. Forrester?"

"Still secured, sir."

"Good. Make sure he stays that way." Harriman was about to end the call as another priority popped into his head. "Wright, ensure that Fallen Angel is secured. No one except security personnel with the highest clearance goes in there."

"Understood, sir," Wright replied.

"That'll be all, Sergeant. Report to me when you have some news." Harriman hit the 'End' button on his phone and leaned heavily against his desk, his body suddenly feeling as if the weight of the world had just landed on him hard.

He sighed and rubbed his temples hard with the tips of his fingers. All the years of work that had gone into the Eden Project were blowing up in their faces and he was low on options to keep it from happening. A part of him wondered if he should even try. He thought about the Carters, about the child Rachel Carter was carrying. He never made time for a family, having dedicated himself to his career, and he never looked back. But now, seeing them, he wondered what he might have given up. What he might have missed out on. And now he was in charge of breaking a family up, a family that had proven repeatedly their determination to stay together. He had a choice in his life and how he lived it; the Carters were victims of other people's schemes and machinations. And he was the cruel hand that had to execute those schemes.

He thought back to that pond in Pine Haven. Enjoying retirement by the pond, feeding waterfowl with breadcrumbs as families picnic by the serene waters. It was a pleasant thought. One he was certain wasn't for him. One that he hadn't earned. He needed to salvage this situation. To balance the scales of his life.

Pushing away from his desk, he felt lighter and stronger than he had in a long time. He had his orders, but he also had his conscience. It was time to put them both together and see which came out on top.

He secured his flak vest, making one last check of weapons, ammunition, and equipment before heading out of his quarters. The moment he entered the hallway, a peculiar sensation tingled at the back of his neck, making him uneasy. A dark feeling, like Death itself was staring him down. Stalking him. An uncharacteristic chill ran through him and he shivered slightly. He attributed it to his newfound mission and shrugged it off, unwavering in his determination to carry on.

Behind him, buried deep in the shadows of the dimly lit corridor, a figure moved to follow.

60

The surrounding sights blurred as Alex ran, trying to keep up with Rachel, who was following Rick. It was then that he felt the call again, pulling at him with an undeniable force.

Set me free.

He slowed, the lyrical voice nagging at him from the back of his mind, pulling him away from thoughts of escape and safety and leading him back into the heart of the Nest. The temptation to turn and run back into the danger they were fleeing from was overwhelming him. The pull grew more intense with every step, almost reaching the point where he would abandon Rachel to answer its irresistible call. He desperately attempted to push the thought aside, his priority being to find a safe place for himself and Rachel, but it stubbornly lingered.

His internal battle became a moot point in the next few steps. Rachel suddenly came to a halt as they turned the corner, causing Alex to collide with her and send her crashing to the ground.

"Oh my God, are you alright?" he exclaimed, reaching out a hand to help her up.

Ignoring his outstretched hand, she sat motionless, her gaze fixed unwaveringly on Alex. Except she wasn't looking at him. It was as if he was invisible to her, as she looked right through him with a vacant stare.

"Rachel?" he said, squatting down next to her.

"Did you hear that?" she asked, her voice quiet and distant.

"Hear what?"

"A voice. No, more like a thousand voices. A chorus of angels in my head. It was so beautiful I can't describe it." She shifted her focus to him, no longer staring into a void. "Did you hear it?"

A jolt ran up Alex's spine. Tentatively, he asked, "Did it say anything to you?"

"It asked to be set free," she answered, taking his hand and allowing him to help her to her feet. "I don't know what it means, but that's what it said. It wants to be set free."

Rachel looked up at Alex, her green eyes wide with wonder and confusion, tinged with a touch of fear. It was understandable, given the circumstances. Alex had been experiencing weird things for days now, which continued to scare and confuse him. It was understandable that Rachel would feel the same way right now. But behind all of that, behind the concern she felt for herself and her family, there was a deep sense of compassion in her amazing green eyes. Feelings of warmth and caring that the strange musical voice had touched. These feelings were so deeply ingrained in her being that she couldn't easily ignore this cry for help.

Alex knew how she felt. They had hooked him too. They were irresistibly drawn back into the heart of the Nest, compelled by the captivating allure of that voice, regardless of whether they liked it or not.

Alex turned to Rick. “You go on. We can’t leave here just yet.”

Rick’s eyes went wide, his body tensing. “Are you out of your mind? You know what kind of people we’re dealing with here! We need to get away now!”

Alex shook his head. “No. Listen, I can’t explain it, but it’s like when Babcock was in the hospital. When I heard him calling me, I don’t know, psychically, I guess. I felt compelled to help him. Well, I’ve been hearing a similar call since we got here. Only this one is a thousand times stronger, and in desperate need of help. I can’t explain it, but I have to go back.”

“I hear it, too,” Rachel interjected. “It’s the strangest thing. Like a thousand voices in my head with a single thought. I don’t understand it, but I have to try to help. I have to get to the source. Which, oddly enough, I know where that is. It’s guiding me, somehow.”

“Besides,” Alex added, “we left Dr. Forrester behind. We need to go back for him, too. We might need him.”

“Why would you need him?” Rick replied, his eyes darting furiously around the corridor for signs of Harriman’s troops. “Isn’t he the cause of this whole mess?”

Alex nodded. “Mostly, yes. But he might also be the only person who can help if Rachel’s pregnancy and delivery aren’t normal. In case you hadn't figured it out, this baby wasn't exactly conceived under normal circumstances. As much as I hate to say it, Dr. Forrester may be the only person who can help them if anything goes wrong.”

“We have to go,” Alex continued, “but if you can escape, do it. We don’t have a choice but to go back, whatever’s back there needs us. But if you can get away from all this insanity, do it. Do it now, while you still have the chance.”

Silence hung in the air between them as Rick mulled over the situation. He was close to getting out of the Nest, to getting away from the Eden Project. To escaping all of this. But, deep inside, he knew he would never be truly free. The Eden Project had a reputation for swiftly dealing with rogue agents, ensuring that no loose ends remained. He might enjoy some peace for a while, but they would eventually catch up to him. The Eden Project's continued existence meant that he would forever be on high alert, constantly watching his back, knowing that one day they would inevitably close in on him.

He sighed a heavy sigh. "Let's go," he said as he brushed past Alex and Rachel, taking point in the opposite direction. “Before I change my mind.”

Alex reached out to him, a hand on his shoulder. “Thanks,” was all he could say. In that moment, there was a sliver of their past that felt right again. That felt like it used to be.

Things had changed, and after the events and revelations of the past few days their friendship would never be like it was, but maybe they could forge something new. Maybe it didn't have to disappear forever.

"You're welcome," Rick replied simply. "Now let's get moving. I think I know where you need to go. What might be calling to you."

"And what's that?" Rachel asked, curiosity creeping past her fear.

"Something I can't adequately explain. You'll have to see it for yourself. But if we don't get moving, Harriman will have the whole place sealed up tight and we'll never get in there, no matter who's calling you." Rick started off down the corridor again, waving at them to follow.

Rachel started after him, but Alex stopped her. "I know this is the last thing you want, but I need you to take this." He held out the shotgun he had taken earlier from the fallen guard. "It's an automatic, like the one you used at the house, so it's just point and shoot."

As she looked down at the weapon, a wave of disgust washed over her. She'd had enough of killing. The thought of being responsible for ending someone's life was something she never wanted to bear. Her stomach roiled at the thought, bile rising in her throat. But she knew that situation might arise again, and it was better to anticipate and be prepared for it.

"Okay," she said finally, taking the gun from him. "Point and shoot. Got it."

"I know how you feel about this," Alex said, as she took the weapon. "I can feel it in you right now. Just promise me that if you have to use it, you won't hesitate."

Her mind wandered back to when she had shot Adam. Thought about how his body had fairly exploded where the shots impacted. Her stomach turned a bit as her head filled with memories of that night, the terror she felt as the gun boomed and tore him to pieces. She never wanted to see anything like that ever again.

But she might not have a choice. That was the reality of it. If it came down to protecting Alex or the baby or herself, there was no doubt in her mind that she was capable of doing it again. Even though it would take another piece of her soul with it, she would do it again to save her family.

"No hesitation," she answered in a strong steady voice, even though her stomach continued to turn.

"Good," Alex answered, confident in the emotions he sensed in her she would protect herself if necessary. It would tear her apart, but she would do it. And her safety and survival were all that mattered to him. They would sort out the rest when they were finally safe.

From behind them came the muffled sounds of footsteps and shouting. A lot of footsteps and shouting.

"Go," Alex whispered, nudging her forward. "Get moving."

She did, heading off in the direction Rick had disappeared in. With a furtive glance over his shoulder, Alex followed closely behind, making sure they hadn't been spotted. They caught up with Rick a short distance up ahead.

"They're coming," Alex said, waving Rick on.

Rick nodded. "This way," he said, taking a sharp left at the next intersection.

The corridor's red emergency lighting abruptly transitioned to a bright, bluish-white light as they rounded the next corner. Rachel gasped and threw her hand up to shade her eyes, squinting into the glare. Rick, knowing what was coming, had shielded his eyes before rounding the corner to make the transition less jarring. Alex's genetically altered eyes adjusted almost immediately, without effect.

As the other two adjusted to the new illumination, Alex took in their surroundings. About ten feet away, the corridor abruptly came to a halt at a glass wall, revealing a massive metal door within its frame. Letters adorned the glass, creating a captivating spectacle as the words seemed to hover effortlessly in the air. The letters at the top, posted in large and blocky font, seemed to shout a warning:

RESEARCH & DEVELOPMENT

Authorized personnel only.

All personnel must clear through clean room protocols prior to entry.

Alex's stomach sank. "Does that mean what I think it means?"

"Yep," Rick answered.

Alex turned to him, his eyes narrowing with renewed anger. The path they had taken led them to yet another dead end, leaving them with no escape as the Eden Project's soldiers closed in. Another betrayal.

"We can't go any further?" he growled.

"I didn't say that," Rick replied, a sly smile on his face. "Over here."

A door, with the word 'Lockers' stenciled in black against its gun metal gray surface, was to their left, which Alex hadn't noticed before. The door was practically invisible, as it was set into a small, naturally occurring niche in the cavern wall.

"How are we supposed to get in there?" Rachel asked, the squint now nearly gone from her eyes.

Rick pushed on the handle and the door clicked and swung inward. "In the simplest way possible," he replied as he slipped inside.

Alex held the door open for Rachel, closing the door behind them with a resounding click. The room was a small space with rows of larger than normal lockers lining the walls. Each locker displayed a hazmat symbol and Alex noticed a shower in the corner marked, 'Emergency Decontamination'.

Before he could comment, Rick moved to a locker and pulled it open. From it, he produced what looked to Alex and Rachel like a sleek, blue space suit and proceeded to effortlessly slip it on over his clothes. Alex recognized it as a hazmat suit, designed to allow people to work around dangerous chemicals, viruses, or bacteria.

"Come on! Don't just stand there, grab a suit and get going," he said, gently gliding his arm into a bulky sleeve.

"Why?" Alex asked, his sense of distrust again getting the better of him.

"First off, it'll be a lot harder for us to be recognized right away in these things," Rick replied, pulling a pair of oversized black rubber boots over his shoes. "Second, if you don't wear one, your skin will melt off in about five seconds once you enter the Decon room."

"Excuse me?"

Rick sighed, pausing his struggles with the rubber boot to address Alex. "In order to get to where I think is the source of this private little psychic distress call the two of you are hearing, we need to go into a clean space. Like, the ultimate clean space. I'll spare you the details, but the process involves spraying a whole lot of nasty chemicals all over you to kill absolutely anything that might be brought in from the outside. So, you need a suit, or you can't go through. At least not without having your body melt."

Alex exchanged a quick glance with Rachel, her hand going instinctively to her belly. Without another word, they each singled out a locker and put on suits of their own. Rick had finished struggling into his boots and continued rummaging through the remaining lockers.

"What now?" Alex asked, zipping up the sole zipper on the outfit. He felt like the Michelin Man.

"The suits will keep us from being recognized," Rick replied as he continued to search lockers, "but we still need identification to get us into the clean room. Aha!" he exclaimed, holding up a small plastic rectangle over his head like a trophy. "Tsk, tsk. Someone is very careless."

"What's that?" Rachel asked as she finished zipping her own suit.

"Identicard. It'll get one of us inside."

"I hate to be the one to point this out," Alex said, "but there are three of us."

"Oh, ye of little faith," Rick answered in a smarmy tone. "To believe that I wouldn't have considered that. Only one person needs keycard access. Once inside, one of us can operate the clean room controls manually, granting access to the other two. One at a time, of course. The room can only process one person in a cycle. Once we get past the clean room, we should have full access to the labs."

"Sounds too easy," Rachel remarked warily.

"It is," Rick replied, his voice still thick with enthusiasm. "In order to get to the labs, you first have to get inside the Nest itself. That's the tough part. It's also the part we already accomplished. Security here isn't as intense as it is a few floors above, because it's nearly impossible to reach this point without authorization."

"So, who goes first to clear the way?" Alex asked.

"I'd be the logical choice," Rick answered. "I know how things work in there; I can get the two of you through the fastest. And in the unlikely event there's a guard on the other side I'm more than capable of handling that, too."

"Sounds reasonable," Rachel replied, a slight quaver of uncertainty in her tone.

Alex nodded in agreement, but a sharp feeling in the back of his skull nagged at him. A feeling he couldn't shake. There was something not quite right. He didn't sense any deception from Rick; it wasn't that. While trust was still an issue between them, Alex felt certain that at the moment he was on their side. There was something else, something he couldn't pin down.

It was also something he didn't have time to dwell on. They were running out of time and their only option was to keep moving forward, no matter the risks. He pushed back on the dark feeling but kept the uneasiness it created close to the surface. A little healthy paranoia could come in handy right now.

"Okay," Alex agreed. "Let's do it."

"Here we go," Rick sighed as he pulled the massive and awkward hood over his head and locked it in place. With a slight hiss, it fell into place, cutting him off from the outside world. The dark Plexiglass face shield made it nearly impossible to see his face. Once the hood was secure, he signaled to Alex and Rachel to do the same. They did, and in a few seconds were both sealed inside a personal microcosm of their own.

Just a second later, Rick's voice broke the silence, startling both of them in their own little worlds. He tapped the side of his hood and explained, "The suits connect automatically through a local radio network to ensure easy communication inside the lab."

"Guess I should watch what I say," Rachel muttered, a light tone in her voice.

"Yes, you should. You know I'm sensitive and if I cry in here I won't be able to wipe the tears," Rick replied in his familiar sarcastic voice, the one Alex knew so well.

"Moving on," Rick said, gesturing towards the left sleeve of his suit. "You'll notice three buttons on your sleeve. The blue one connects to a cellular network that would normally allow you to make calls in and out of the Nest. The eggheads thought it would be useful for conferencing with other Eden Project sites, and I suppose it would, but it's all moot right now because they have completely locked down all external communication. The black button allows you to mute or deactivate the local radio frequency if you need to. Also, radio communication is isolated to each individual room. It was set up that way to avoid interference between labs. So, if one of us is in another room, we can't communicate."

"Does that mean we'll be out of touch when we go through the Decon process?" Alex asked, his voice tinged with concern as he contemplated the possibility of being out of touch with Rachel.

"Yeah," Rick answered, "but only until you get through to the next room. After that, we shouldn't have to separate again."

"And the red button," Rachel interjected, holding up her left arm. "What does that do?"

"Do not, under any circumstances whatsoever, press that button," Rick answered, all humor gone from his tone. "That's the emergency button. The emergency button is used when there's a release of a dangerous contaminant or if there's some other accident. Pressing that button will lock down the entire lab. Entrances, exits, everything. Even the ventilation ducts are sealed. There's no way, and I mean absolutely no way, out if anyone activates the system. Best-case scenario, we're trapped in there until the room is determined to be clean and is unlocked. Of course, by that time, angry and twitchy people with a lot of guns will also surround us, so there's that."

"If that's the best-case scenario, what's the worst case?" Rachel asked.

"Given what they work with in those labs, if the system detects any kind of contaminant, it will start cleansing protocols."

"What are the cleansing protocols?" Alex asked hesitantly, certain he would not like the answer.

"A super-heated plasma will flood the lab, completely sterilizing the environment, including anyone inside."

"So, what you're saying," Alex said, "is don't touch the red button."

"Yes, don't touch the red button."

Rachel nodded, the gesture barely visible under the bulky suit. "Got it. No red button."

"Good. And that goes double for you, butterfingers," Rick replied, smacking Alex on the shoulder with his gloved hand. "I guess we're good to go, then."

"As good as we'll get," Alex replied. "What about these?" he asked, indicating the shotguns and the silencer-equipped pistol that lay on a nearby bench.

"They'll have to go through Decon under the suits," Rick answered. "The chemicals being used would destroy them. Give me the Glock, it's easy to access if I need it when I get to the other side. You'll have to get the shotguns through somehow."

"Right," Alex replied, his own voice echoing ominously back at him through the suit's speakers. The moment he passed the pistol to Rick, a sharp, throbbing ache in the back of his skull heightened, as if a silent alarm was going off inside his head. They hadn't seen or heard any sign of Eden Project security since ducking into the locker room, and the only psychic presences he could feel nearby were the three of them. Granted, he was new to the whole psychic thing, but he couldn't pinpoint any imminent danger to them. Once again, he pushed back on the pain, concentrating on the task at hand.

He unzipped his suit again with a hiss of escaping air and slid the shotgun inside, resting it against his leg. It wasn't ideal, but it was the best option he had. He didn't want to go into the unknown beyond the Decon chamber unarmed.

Rachel lifted the other shotgun, resting the barrel on the floor and positioning the stock under her arm as if the gun were a crutch. Alex couldn't suppress a chuckle, which came through loud and clear through the radios.

"Is there a problem?" Rachel asked as she opened the front of her suit with a hiss of escaping air.

"You need any help there, Tiny Tim?" Alex replied. "There's no way you're going to get that into your suit and still be able to move."

"Are you saying I'm short?" Rachel replied with mock indignation. "I am shocked!"

Alex grinned behind his polarized faceplate, happy she couldn't see it. "Sorry," he answered, "it's the Irish in you."

"True," she replied. "Just remember, there's a lot of that Irish you like, too."

"I'll never deny it," he answered, and gently touched her plastic-covered shoulder with his thick-gloved hands.

"I'll be fine with this," she said as she awkwardly lifted the gun and slid it into her suit, holding it tight against her side as she closed the seal again. "Besides, like you said, I might need it."

"Showtime," Rick announced, closing his suit again. "Wait for me just outside the entrance to the Decon chamber."

Rick slowly cracked open the locker room door, listening for any signs of activity in the corridor. There was no sound, just an eerie silence that filled the air. It was possible the guards had decided the secure laboratories were a dead end and moved on to better options. No matter the reason, it seemed as if the coast was clear.

Slipping out the door, Rick carefully navigated along the wall, his body brushing against it as he advanced towards the glass barrier at the far end of the corridor. Alex and Rachel followed closely, mimicking his movements. Beyond the glass barrier was the clean room antechamber, a small waiting room to process personnel through decontamination. The clean room truly lived up to its name, as the bright white light washed over every surface, leaving no room for shadows and giving the walls a clinically pristine look.

As they rounded the corner, Rick paused. "Hold up," he said. "This could be a problem."

Alex shifted position slightly to see into the antechamber and understood what Rick meant. Inside sat a member of Nest security, a young man most likely in his early twenties. A slight brownish fuzz barely covered his scalp, the skin beneath it glowing as white as the surrounding walls. Obviously, he hadn't spent a lot of time in the sun. As they approached, he shot them a stern look that seemed as out of place on his face as a snowball in the desert.

"This is it," Rick muttered. "Better hope this works."

The security guard stepped up to his side of the glass. "Identification, please."

Without a word of reply, Rick pressed the ID card against the glass as requested. The youngster lowered his face, squinting at the card, and Alex immediately noticed the silence that had fallen over the group. No longer could he hear their breathing through the suit radios, as they all held their breath in anticipation.

Rachel broke the silence. "It's not working," she whispered.

"The whole place is on lockdown," Rick replied, a hard edge to his hushed tone. "He's being extra cautious. Give it a second."

Rachel remained unconvinced. “It’s not going to work,” she repeated. It wasn't just a feeling, there was an unmistakable quality about the guard that made her internal alarms go off. Maybe it was his stance or the look in his eyes. Whatever it was, she was currently fighting the urge to run. The shotgun at her side seemed to suddenly get heavier, more burdensome. It felt hot against her, as if the metal was heating up in response to her anxiety. She wanted to shift position, but she was scared. Scared that whatever she did would be the thing that exposed their ruse. That the guard would sound the alarm and bring all the forces of Nest security down on them, trapping them here. Or worse, in a fit of testosterone laced masculinity, he might try to capture them himself. She was certain how that would end up; with the boy dead and more guilt laid on her soul.

“It’s not going to work,” she said again, repeating it like a mantra of doom.

“Please stop saying that,” Rick uttered, a palpable tension in his voice. Even though he had displayed confidence earlier, a seed of uncertainty grew within him, casting doubt on the feasibility of this endeavor. Having Rachel drive the point home every few seconds wasn’t helping to calm his nerves.

"Both of you, try to relax," Alex said, his voice steady and composed, masking the fear that was consuming him as the young guard meticulously inspected the identicard. It wasn’t easy. In addition to his own mounting fear, he could sense Rachel and Rick's fear emanating from them in waves, reminiscent of the heat radiating off the pavement on a sweltering summer day, amplifying his own fear and uncertainty. He tried to push it away, but it surrounded him like the buzz of hungry insects that threatened to devour him.

Suddenly, the guard stood up straight, moving his gaze from the ID card to the trio of containment suits in front of him. Without a word, he reached for a control panel on the wall next to him, pushing a sequence of buttons. There was a sudden loud buzz, clearly audible even inside the suits, and the fear inside all of them suddenly exploded into panic as their fears of an alarm being sounded suddenly materialized.

The sound came to an abrupt halt after a mere second, leaving behind a lingering stillness. Moments later, the reinforced metal door in the middle of the glass wall clicked open and smoothly slid aside. The guard stepped out and pointed at Rick.

“You,” was all he said, gesturing to the antechamber.

Rick swiveled back toward Alex and Rachel and waved, signaling them to stay where they were, then turned and walked through the door into the outer chamber of the clean room. The baby-faced guard followed and, with the press of another button, the door slid shut with an ominous hiss of hydraulics and a sharp bang. Once inside, the guard turned to Rick. Holding out his hand, he said something they couldn’t hear. His face was stern and commanding, but with a slight edge of anxiousness to it. Alex could make out beads of sweat gathering on his forehead and he shifted his stance slightly, moving away from Rick.

He wasn't the only one sweating. As the guard took the identicard from Rick and examined it as if it were new to him, Alex's tension rose again. Beads of sweat trickled down his face and back, leaving a trail of dampness in their wake. Helplessness washed over him, and his heart raced with the realization that he couldn't do anything for Rick.

This isn't going to work. The thought darted through his mind, unwelcome and intrusive, but he quickly dismissed it before it could slip out and reach Rachel's ears. He could feel her anxiety rising again, the last thing she needed was for him to add to it.

The guard looked from the card to Rick, his face like stone. His eyes widened as if he were trying to peer past the polarized Plexiglass covering Rick's face.

Oh no, Alex thought, his stomach practically collapsing in on itself. *Please don't ask him to take the hood off.*

The thought came too late. Almost simultaneously with Alex's silent begging, the guard motioned to Rick to remove his hood. At the same time, his hand moved to his holstered pistol and rested on the weapon.

"Shit, this is it," Alex muttered, his eyes riveted to the scene playing out on the other side of the glass.

As if in slow motion, Rick reached up to release the catch on his hood. He moved nonchalantly, as if he were complying with the most natural and logical request in the world. Alex's heart jumped into his throat as he fought the urge to grab Rachel and just run.

"What's he doing?" Rachel asked, her voice only a whisper as the question caught in her throat.

"Getting killed," Alex answered. "Getting us killed."

Rick's hands fumbled with the hood's closure, seemingly struggling to release it. Throwing his arms up in frustration, he held up an index finger to signify he needed a moment, his fingers flailing clumsily around his neck. After struggling with the suit for another few seconds, he unzipped the top, just underneath where the body and neck met, and reached inside to fumble around again. The guard watched Rick closely, his hand tight around the butt of his pistol, and slowly released the catch that held the weapon in place. His body was tense, the sweat around his temples intensifying with each passing second, but he kept his gun holstered.

For now.

Rick bent over, still apparently struggling to release the hood of his suit. It was almost comical the way he shuffled and jerked at the loose plastic around him, flailing like a child caught up in their snowsuit after coming inside from playing.

Until it wasn't. Suddenly, with no warning, Rick stood straight up as his hood fell away. Startled, the guard yanked his pistol from its holster, but he was too slow. Before he could get his weapon clear, the front of Rick's suit erupted as two bullets tore through it from the inside. They found their mark as the young guard's chest exploded and he stumbled back, coming to rest against the far wall. For what seemed like an eternity, he stood there, eyes wide with shock, staring at the blue-suited harbinger of death before him. As his arm twitched in a feeble attempt to raise the hand holding the pistol, he collapsed to the floor, motionless, leaving behind a vivid red streak on the pristine white wall.

"Shit!" Alex exclaimed. Next to him, Rachel was too shocked to take a breath.

Rick showed no sign of remorse as he brushed past the lifeless young man to reach the control panel on the wall. He slammed a button, the same one the now dead guard had hit a few minutes earlier, and the door buzzed open again. By the time Alex and Rachel had shaken off their shock and realized the door was open, Rick had already moved the guard's body.

"What did you do?" Alex demanded, as Rick shoved the young man's corpse into the tiny airplane-like bathroom in the antechamber's corner.

"We're in. I did what I had to do," Rick answered, his replied just as indignant as Alex's question had been.

"You didn't have to kill him," Rachel muttered, her voice small and even. "He was just a kid."

"Jesus Christ!" Rick yelled, slamming the bathroom door closed. "That 'kid' would have killed you, me, Alex, or anyone else he was told to without a second thought! Killing him was the only option we had in order to get to where we need to be! I hate to tell you this, but he's probably not the last one! And the next one might be up to you to do! So you," he stabbed a finger at Rachel, "need to put your moralities aside and nut up or there is no way we're getting out of here alive!"

Alex stepped between Rachel and Rick; his face flushed. With his fists clenched into thick, black rubber balls at his sides, he confronted his maybe-friend, their eyes locked in a tense stare. "That's enough. We don't have time to fight each other. But we will talk about this later, believe me."

Rick waved him off. "Fine. There might not even be a later, so whatever." He turned from Alex and slipped the fallen guard's gun into his waistband.

"One more thing," Alex said, his voice low and calm.

"What's that?"

"Never talk to her like that again. Are we clear?"

Rick turned back, his face twisted in a mixture of anger and regret. Slowly, he nodded.

"Good," Alex said. "What's next?"

Rick indicated the Decon room past the glass wall on the opposite end of the antechamber. "We go through there," he said as he zipped his suit back up before reaching out a hand to Alex. "My shotgun?"

"You can take this one," Rachel interjected as she unzipped her own suit and clumsily pulled the weapon out. "I don't think I want it anymore."

Rick's face clouded over and he was about to say something, but thought better of it. "Fine," he lamented, "just stay between us. I don't think we'll run into any trouble in the labs, but you never know."

As Rick moved away toward the Decon chamber, Rachel placed a gentle hand on Alex's arm. "Thank you," she said.

Alex patted her hand. "Always."

She pulled her hand away from his as they moved into the antechamber to the wall on the opposite side of the room. Like the wall behind them, this one was entirely glass, displaying the Decon chamber inside. The door here was glass as well, not metal, and printed on it was a large hazmat symbol. The sight brought to mind movies Rachel had seen, where the tombs of the honored dead were adorned with ancient warnings written in languages long extinct. The sense of dread abated only slightly with the phrase, written in English, just beneath it:

Decontamination Chamber.

Highly dangerous chemicals in use.

Please closely examine suit integrity before entering.

Alex turned to Rick, his eyes fixating on the two holes where the slugs from his Glock had torn through. Rick did the same.

"Shit!" Rick exclaimed, smacking his faceplate with an open palm. "I'll have to go back for another suit!"

"Is there time for that?" Alex asked.

"Doesn't really matter," Rick replied. "Exposure to the chemicals used in the process is lethal. By design. It's meant to obliterate even the most insignificant microbes, and it's damned successful. Sure, if I go back for another suit I might get caught and killed. But if I go through there with these holes in my suit, I will definitely die. And not in a good way."

"Hurry up!" Rachel said as she waved her arms at him to get him moving. "We'll wait for you here."

"No," Rick replied. "You need to go through now. The chamber only allows one person inside at a time, and the process takes a few minutes to complete. At least one of us can get through before I get back."

"One problem," Alex said. "You're the only one who knows how to operate the controls."

Rick chuckled. "Yeah, about that. I may have been keeping the actual complexity of operating the room kind of secret. You know, just in case things got tense between us."

Alex scowled. "Of course you did. How do we do it?"

"Step through the door and hit the big green button on your right. The process starts automatically."

"I think we can handle that," Rachel said, putting a reassured hand on her husband's arm. Now was not the time to confront Rick about his deception.

Rick slipped off his thick black gloves and readied the shotgun. "I should be back in just a few minutes. You need to get going."

"We're good," Alex answered, turning away from the man who had been his most trusted friend. "But hurry up. We might need you on the other side."

For just a moment, Rachel thought she noticed Rick's face drop at the tone in Alex's voice. A touch of guilt, or maybe remorse. It wasn't there for long as he turned and headed back to the locker room, going back into soldier mode as he stopped to scan the corridor for Nest security before proceeding.

For the briefest of moments, her heart longed for their prior simple life.

As Rick disappeared around the corner, Rachel turned back to Alex. "Do you trust him?"

"I don't think he'd intentionally hurt us, if that's what you mean. But he isn't telling us the whole truth, and right now that's dangerous." Alex heaved a heavy sigh. "He had this whole life, Rachel. Before he ever met us, he lived this whole other life. A dangerous one, at that. I suppose secrets are a part of that."

"But can we trust him?"

Alex pondered the question for a moment. "We don't really have a lot of choice right now. But when we get out of here, I don't think we'll be having him over for dinner as much as we used to."

Before she could pursue the subject any further, he nodded at the door to the decontamination chamber. "Would you care to go first?"

"Do I really have a choice?"

Alex shrugged. "It's either wait out here for the troops to arrive or go inside and possibly have to subdue some nerds. Up to you."

"I'll risk the nerds," she replied, pressing a button to the right of the door marked 'Open'. The glass door slid open silently. "After all these years of living with you, I've learned how to handle them."

He stopped her just before she stepped inside. "I know you don't want this, but I'd feel a whole lot better if I knew you had it." He was holding out a pistol to her.

She stared at the gun, thinking about the life it had just taken. Thinking about doing it herself. Again. She had shot Adam, intending to kill him, but he had invaded her home, shot Ernie Babcock, and beaten her husband to within an inch of his life. She felt no remorse in doing what had to be done that night, but the thought of pulling the trigger like Rick had just done made her uneasy.

"I can't," she said, shuddering. "I just can't."

Alex gently placed his gloved hand on her shoulder, the thick material blocking any sensation from passing through. But the gesture was there. "It's okay. I understand. When you get through the chamber, wait just outside there for me. Don't wander off. Okay?"

"Okay," she repeated, and stepped through the chamber door. It was much darker than she had expected, even with the light from the antechamber seeping in, and she squinted to see her surroundings. The room was small, like a shower stall, and sparse. On either side of her, the walls were decorated with six nozzles each, protruding like the spikes of a medieval torture device. The moment she set foot in the room, a wave of unease washed over her, causing her stomach to tighten and her hands to quiver. She paused, standing on the red 'X' marked on the floor. Turning her head to the right as best she could in the bulky suit, she saw two buttons glowing in the dim light, one red and one green.

"Don't touch the red button. Ever," she whispered, repeating it like a mantra.

Between the small space and the bulky suit, she couldn't turn enough to see Alex, but she was certain if she could see his face it would be a mask of concern. It wasn't difficult to figure out why. She was on the verge of being washed with a dangerous chemical mix and then stepping into a potentially hostile setting. She was more than a little concerned for herself at the moment.

"I love you," she muttered into the suit's radio, then pushed the green button.

The door slid shut with a quiet whoosh and almost instantly the jets began spraying a fine mist that covered her completely, obscuring her face shield. She flinched as the mist gathered and clung like a thick fog in front of her.

She jumped as a ping sounded in her ear, letting out a startled cry of surprise. The jets stopped spraying and a robotic voice told her phase one was complete. Exhaling loudly, she relaxed a bit, grateful that Alex hadn't been able to hear her brief outburst. Breathing in a slow, steady rhythm, she watched the liquid coalesce into droplets on her faceplate and slide away, leaving tiny trails of slime as they went.

Another tone announced phase two, and the jets sprang to life again. This time, the force behind them was stronger, and she could feel each spray thumping her. Even through her suit, it was uncomfortable. A sudden blast from an unseen jet above her cleared her faceplate, allowing her to see the small room again.

The jets fired harder at her, stinging where they hit. She adjusted her position to find some relief, but they stopped after a few seconds. Another ping and the announcement of phase three followed. When the jets stopped, a powerful surge of hot air hit her, making her feel as if she could have been knocked off her feet if it hadn't been dispersed. It was like being caught between four hurricanes.

The searing winds stopped, followed by yet another ping. The electronic voice informed her the process was complete and to exit the chamber immediately when the door opened. A second later the door in front of her slid open, and she obliged the robot voice by stepping out into a small waiting area. With a swift scan of her surroundings, she discovered three hallways radiating from the central point, each marked by signs suspended overhead. There was nothing else in sight.

Behind her, the glass door slid shut as the decontamination chamber reset itself for the next user. Pressing her faceplate against the glass, she peered into the chamber, waiting for Alex to enter.

The door didn't move.

A few more seconds passed, and the door remained closed. Her heart hammered in her chest, the blood rushing through her ears, sounding like a tidal wave in the confines of the plastic hood. Where was he? Why hadn't he entered the chamber yet?

The door was still closed. She squinted, hoping to see into the antechamber, but her eyes were met with a blurry darkness that left them strained and aching. A feeling of panic consumed her, causing her heart to race and her head to spin, leaving her lightheaded and overwhelmed. She took a step back and examined the door that had just sealed itself shut, looking for another button that would allow her to backtrack through the chamber. There was no button to be found, but above the door was a sign that made her blood run cold.

No re-entry to Decontamination Chamber.

To exit the labs please use decontamination site 4B.

"No!" she screamed, pounding her fists against the door. "Alex! Alex, what's wrong? Where are you?"

There was no reply save for her own voice, screaming back at her through the speakers in her hood. The door to the clean room remained closed.

Something had gone wrong. She had left Alex there by himself and something had happened to him. Now she was alone.

Alone and afraid.

Alex watched the jets fire as Rachel was absorbed in a fine mist, the spray from the jets gathering in viscous pools that slid slowly down her back, arms, and legs before forming a thick puddle at her feet. He couldn't sense what she was feeling, cut off from her by the walls between them, but he felt sure she was fighting panic as the toxic chemicals flowed over her. He certainly didn't relish the thought of following her. Aside from suffering from a slight case of claustrophobia, the idea of showering in poison didn't sit well with him, even if he was wearing a protective suit. It seemed like a monumentally stupid idea to him, like walking into a den of hungry lions covered in raw meat while eating a roast beef sandwich. It was tempting fate, and he was pretty sure that fate was sick of being teased by him.

The jets stopped their spraying, and Rachel disappeared through the exit on the other side of the chamber. The light next to him switched from red to green, signifying the room was ready for the next user. His stomach tightened. It was his turn. Closing his eyes, he took a deep breath to steady himself. The process wasn't that long. He had just watched Rachel go through it and she walked out of the chamber without an issue. Just step in, close your eyes, and get through it.

No matter how he tried to hype himself up, he hesitated. Even after everything they had been through the last few days, this was what scared him. Standing in a small room. A wave of shame ran through him. He could do it. He had to do it. Not only was it the only option he had, the answer to the mystery behind the voice in his head was on the other side. A mystery that he needed to solve. Bracing himself, he opened his eyes and reached for the button.

As he did, something jumped at his hand.

In a fit of panic and surprise, he jerked it back, his heart racing as he searched frantically for the unseen attacker. There was nothing there. At least nothing solid. Another flicker of motion drew his attention to the glass door, where he saw the reflection of something moving behind him. Something fast. It must be Rick, returning with a new hazmat suit.

He turned to urge Rick on faster and froze at what he saw. The flurry of motion reflected in the glass hadn't been Rick. Beyond the first glass wall that separated the hallway from the antechamber, he spotted eight fully armed Eden Project soldiers. One soldier pointed at Alex and shouted something, the silence eerie as the glass barrier blocked any sound from passing through.

As his breath hitched, he whispered, "Oh, shit," his hand trembling as he swiftly pressed the green button, triggering the Decon chamber. The second that ensued seemed like a lifetime to him as the entry door to the chamber slid open to allow him access. With the door halfway open, he squeezed through sideways, feeling his suit snag on the door latch as he did. With a sense of trepidation, he jabbed the green button on the interior of the chamber, hoping his suit hadn't torn.

The door reversed course and slid closed as Alex watched the soldiers converging on the metal door that opened to the antechamber. As the closest fumbled with an identicard to open the door, Alex searched the advancing wave of black fatigues. Behind them, he caught a fleeting glimpse of bright blue that vanished like a ghost. It had to have been Rick. He hadn't made it back before the soldiers stumbled on them. It was impossible for him to make it back; he was on his own, and there was absolutely nothing Alex could do for him. Grief and guilt hit Alex like dual hammers as the door slid closed, the muffled click of the lock resounding through him like the thud of an executioner's ax.

A ping sounded in his ear, followed by a voice telling him the first phase of the decontamination process was about to begin, and instructed him to face the exit door. As he turned, just before the jets surrounding him began emitting their gooey mist, he glimpsed another dark faceplate peering in at him from the other side.

Rachel. He let out a heavy sigh of relief at the sight of her waiting for him. If she hadn't encountered any security forces on that side of the chamber, there might still be a chance they could somehow make it out.

The start of phase two brought a powerful surge of jets that carved into his side, cleansing away the thick fluid. It passed in a moment, as did phase three, although each one seemed like an eternity to him. With each passing moment, he braced himself for the process to abruptly cease, imagining the jarring sight of armed soldiers forcefully escorting him out of the chamber. He knew that wouldn't happen, the Eden Project soldiers knew how toxic the chemicals used in the chamber were, but he couldn't help silently urging the process on faster. He could almost feel their hands on his back.

Another ping and the electronic voice announced the process was over. As soon as the door was open enough for him to squeeze through, he pushed himself out and fell into Rachel's waiting arms.

"What happened?" she asked frantically.

"They caught up with us," Alex said, desperately feeling around his suit for signs of a tear. The fact that he hadn't died in the Decon chamber led him to assume it was intact, but he still felt the need to double-check.

A loud thump echoed through the room, jolting him from his thoughts. He swiftly turned his head to find a soldier vigorously pounding on the entry door to the chamber. The man waved to someone, and a moment later Alex saw another blue hazmat suit fill the glass door. Panic seized him as he realized they were about to send someone through after them.

Frantically, he grasped at the zipper of his suit and fumbled to open it. The blue suit on the other side disappeared from view as they moved into position to activate the chamber.

Although it went against every instinct he was experiencing, he forced himself to take a deep breath to settle his panic. As he did, he removed the thick black glove from his right hand and grasped the zipper, pulling it open just enough to reach inside and grab the Glock from his waistband.

"What are you doing?" Rachel screamed; her voice so high with panic it was almost a squeak. "Where's Rick?"

"They got him," Alex answered. "I'm going to make sure they can't come after us. Not this way, anyway."

Reaching in through the partially open door, he took aim at the control panel near the chamber's entrance and snapped off two shots. The gunfire boomed in the tiny space as the panel exploded in a shower of sparks and jagged metal, sealing the door. A shrill alarm sounded, warning of a breach and imminent lockdown of the chamber. Alex yanked his arm backed through the door as it slammed shut hard, sealing itself tightly with a hiss of air.

"That should keep them off of us for now," he said as he returned the Glock to its makeshift holster. After the Glock was secure, he pulled the shotgun out of the suit and leaned it against the nearest wall while he zipped himself back up. It was difficult to move with the weapon tucked inside, he'd have to carry it from this point. Which was just as well, considering the Eden Project troops now knew where they were.

"What about the other entrances?" Rachel asked, pointing to the sign above the door referencing Chamber 4B. "What's keeping them from using one of those?"

"Nothing," Alex answered, snatching up the shotgun again. "That's why we need to get moving."

Rachel swept her arm wide, looking like a spokes model for the Federal Nuclear Commission in her hazmat suit, indicating the three hallways. "Which way?"

Alex checked the signs above each exit, but they were useless to them as they had no idea what they were looking for. "I don't know," he answered, exasperated. "Do you feel anything? The pull you felt before?"

Her head shake was barely noticeable under her hood. "No. Sorry, I..."

She trailed off, the rest of her response unspoken. Even though he couldn't see her face behind the polarized faceplate, Alex felt certain she had the same vacant expression as before, staring blankly as if her mind had just shut down.

"Rachel," Alex said, moving toward her. He hadn't gone more than a single step when it hit him again, just as it had before.

Set me free.

The same chorus of angels in his head, pleading for his help. This time, it was stronger. Louder. More insistent. Much more beautiful and compelling.

"There," he said, pointing to the center corridor. "It's that way."

Rachel had already begun moving in that direction, needing no guidance from him. She moved quickly, but her gait seemed odd to him. It reminded him of the way zombies walked in old horror movies, her legs stiff and mildly unsteady. It felt as if someone else was pulling the strings, manipulating her every move. This couldn't be Rachel.

"We have to hurry, there isn't much time left," she said, her voice quiet, her cadence eerily steady. Her voice was the same as her movement, her and yet not her.

"I know," Alex answered, not entirely sure who he was talking to. "I'm not sure how I know, but I know."

Without another word, Rachel shuffled down the bright hallway, passing door after door, somehow just knowing that wasn't where she needed to be. They passed another decontamination chamber and Alex's grip on the shotgun tightened as he envisioned troops clambering through after them like marauding insects. He knew that wasn't possible, they could only come through one at a time, but the thought stuck with him, regardless. It struck him as odd that they hadn't yet encountered any resistance, though.

Rachel suddenly came to an awkward, stumbling stop. "This is the one."

It was a glass door like all the others they had just passed, with one exception. On the door, two simple words were written in thick block letters:

Project Gabriel

"What in the hell is Project Gabriel?" Alex asked. He had a slight recollection of seeing the name on one of the electronic files Dr. Carlton had left for him, but he never had the opportunity to explore it.

"Rach, do you know what that is?" he asked her. "Do you know what's in there?"

She didn't move, simply stared ahead into the lab. "I do," she stated in a robotic Rachel-not-Rachel tone.

Alex reached over to her and touched her arm. "Rach, what is it?"

"The solution," she answered. "We need to get inside. They're waiting for us."

A chill raced up Alex's spine. "Who, Rach? Who's waiting for us?"

"The solution," she repeated.

"God damn it," Alex muttered. The chill in his spine had become firmly entrenched now. He was worried about Rachel, about what was happening to her. He didn't even know if Rachel was still in there or if something else had supplanted her entirely. He wanted to scream, to shake her until he got his wife back, but somehow he knew that wouldn't help. He had no choice but to keep moving forward, to get into that room and hope that whatever was in there truly was the solution.

Next to the door were two lights, much like there had been at the decontamination chamber, one green and one red. The red light was currently lit. Under the lights, there was a slot that seemed to be the exact size to accept an ID card, similar to the one Rick had used previously. The 'Entry' button was lit up, so Alex pressed it, hoping the door was unlocked. As soon as he did, a chime sounded in his ears.

"Please insert the proper identification for entry," said the robotic voice.

"Well, shit," Alex said. No sooner had the words come out of his mouth than another friendly chime rang in his ears. There was a muffled click from the door as the red light went out and the green light lit up.

"Enter when ready," said the electronic voice.

"What the hell...?" he said aloud to himself, reaching down and again pressing the 'Entry' button. This time, the door slid open.

"I'll be damned. How did that happen?"

Rachel didn't answer, but shambled her way past him into the lab. Alex looked back down the hallway once more to ensure no one was following before trailing behind her. Just inside the door there was another set of buttons, one marked 'Lock'. As the door slid shut behind him, he pounded the 'Lock' button. The lock engaged with another audible click. He turned away from the door to follow Rachel...

... and came face to face with a man in a hazmat suit, this one a bright red. Startled, he leveled the shotgun at the stranger's faceplate.

"Don't move!" he yelled, but the stranger didn't react to the threat of the weapon. He seemed entirely indifferent to it, in fact.

"He can't hurt you," Rachel said flatly, slipping past the immobile stranger and moving into the next room.

"How do you know that?" Alex asked, not yet willing to let down his guard or his gun.

"They told me," Rachel responded, continued on into the lab.

Alex moved around the motionless man, never letting the gun waver from him. "I thought I was the one who was hearing voices."

"I don't hear them. Not like you do."

"Who are 'they'?" Alex asked, the chill of concern creeping up his spine again.

"The baby," Rachel replied nonchalantly. "And the other."

The chill of concern suddenly became a blizzard. "The baby? You mean our baby?"

"Yes."

"But..." he stammered, not sure how to continue. "How?"

"They speak to me," Rachel answered.

"Who's the other?"

"The solution," Rachel answered.

"This is insane," he muttered, picking up his pace to catch up with Rachel. Yet, as crazy as it sounded, it also made a certain amount of sense to him. The baby she was carrying was his. She carried his genetics; it wasn't too far-fetched that she would have the same abilities he had. Seemingly much stronger ones, at that. It was mind-bending to consider.

In that instant, it hit him. She. Rachel had referred to the baby as 'she'.

"Rachel," he asked after her, "are you saying our baby is a girl?"

"Yes," was the simple, unenthusiastic reply.

He was about to press the issue when Rachel stopped, pointing to an archway at the end of the room. "In here," she said, dropping her arm and shuffling toward the arch.

"Rachel, be careful," Alex called to her as he dashed around the workstations that dotted the small room. Navigating the space wasn't difficult since, aside from the workstations, the room was entirely vacant. There were no decorations, no papers, no personal items to be seen. It was an orderly, sterile environment.

She vanished through the arch and into the next room as he raced after her, and almost plowed into her as he rounded the corner. She had come to a complete halt just past the entryway and stood completely still, staring vacantly into the dark. As he came up beside her, a motion sensor must have been triggered because the overhead lights instantly flickered to life, gradually illuminating the room row by row in a brilliant white glow, mirroring the brightness of the rest of the lab section.

The room was vastly larger than the one they had just left, and nearly as sparse. In the center of the room there were metal tables containing a variety of medical instruments, laptop computers and other electronic monitoring devices, arranged in a circle like a modern Stonehenge. What stopped him cold was what they were centered on.

A large cylinder, maybe twenty feet tall, stood in the center of the room like a monolith, making the entire scene look like some sort of futuristic ritual site. Upon closer inspection he observed the cylinder contained a brackish fluid, and a body floated within it, swaying slowly, as if in the grip of a mild current.

A body like he had never seen before.

"No way," he whispered, slowly advancing toward the cylinder. "It can't be."

He felt numb as he approached it, the odd body. It appeared basically humanoid; head, torso, two arms and two legs. Towering above the average human, it stood at an estimated height of nine feet and was completely devoid of hair. The creature was naked, but there was no sign of any type of sex organs to be seen. Its skin seemed grayish, but the fluid that suspended it gave it an almost yellowish hue. The texture appeared smooth and rubbery, as if it had the same feel as a dolphin.

The most captivating thing about it was the eyes. Consistent with stories of UFO and alien encounters, the eyes were strangely enlarged and entirely black. But unlike those accounts, these eyes seemed to have life behind them. A cinder left behind by the spark of intelligence that once inhabited them.

Alex suddenly felt very insignificant, staring into the face of a god.

He sensed Rachel moving up behind him. "It's almost like it's still alive," he said with a childlike wonder to his voice. "There's such a... a light in those eyes. Such intelligence. It's...". He paused, not able to find a word to convey the magnitude of what he was feeling. He finally settled on 'incredible', even though that was woefully inadequate.

"It is the solution," Rachel replied.

Something about her voice snapped Alex out of his awe-filled trance. The tone was the same, but the cadence was different. It wasn't as flat, there was a slight hint of anticipation in it. Maybe satisfaction. He turned to her, fear exploding in him as he did.

Rachel stood there, fixated on the creature inside the cylinder, her hazmat suit a bright blue heap on the floor. Before he could react, she casually kicked off her shoes and slipped her shirt off over her head, dropping it with the hazmat suit. In a frenzy, he ran to her, his breath coming in short, sharp gasps, and urgently clasped her arm.

"What are you doing?" he screamed, trying to be heard through the hood of his suit. "There could be all kinds of bacteria or viruses floating around in here! You don't know what you could be exposing yourself or the baby to! Put your suit back on!"

She turned her head to look at him. For the first time since entering the clean room, her face had some expression on it. Her mouth turned up in a slight smile, her eyes alight with joy.

"I'm safe," she stated, her voice still the same mixture of stoic anticipation. "They'll protect me."

It hit him then, like a lightning bolt running through him. Her voice, he'd heard it before. It was the same soulless voice she had in his dreams. The dreams where she was taken from him, just before the dark stranger killed him.

"Rach, I'm not kidding around. Please put your suit back on."

She reached out her hand and lightly touched his cheek. "Don't be concerned. I'm safe. So is the baby. They'll protect me."

"They?" Alex screeched.

"The baby," she answered, dropping her gaze to her stomach. "And him." She lifted her head again, indicating the body floating in the cylinder. "They know. Trust and have faith."

He wasn't sure why, but at that point Alex released her arm. She turned back to him again, still smiling that comforting smile, her eyes still filled with light, and continued to undress until all her clothes lay in a pile on the floor. Now naked, she walked to the base of the cylinder, shifting her attention to the unmoving form inside. Her hands reached out as if they weren't hers and began searching the bank of buttons and switches there, her lithe fingers hovering over the control panel as if she were performing some ancient incantation or mystical prayer of divination. After a moment of searching, her index finger landed on a particular button and pressed.

A loud hiss erupted from the chamber, followed by a gurgle as the yellowish fluid drained from the tank. As Alex observed, the thin, towering shape within the enclosure crumpled against the walls, eventually gathering in a heap at the bottom of the tank, resembling a lifeless puppet discarded by its puppeteer. Even in that awkward position, the creature kept its power to enthrall, and Alex couldn't look away. Something monumental was about to happen, he could feel it. It was like an electric charge in the air itself, running through him and invigorating his every nerve, all centered on the unmoving heap of gray flesh encased in glass before him.

Rachel divined another switch, and the glass separated from the base of the chamber and slid up, disappearing into the ceiling. The alien form dropped from its squatting position and fell along the length of the platform, its limbs splayed out like a cat stretching after a long nap. Its enormous black eyes stared at him, filled with the same spark of life. As much as he might have wanted to look away, Alex found he couldn't. The creature had drawn him in and now held him there. It was almost as if it were trying to say something to him with its gaze, to communicate some urgent message from beyond death.

Rachel moved around the platform, her steps suddenly light and graceful again. More like her. She stopped directly above where the creature's head rested and, with no hesitation, rested her hand on its temple.

Panicked, Alex tore at the hood of his hazmat suit, ripping the plastic and tossing it aside. Suddenly, the risk of exposure to whatever was in the air seemed less significant to him. "Rachel, no!" he yelled. "Don't touch it!"

She looked at him, her face serene. "This is the way it was always meant to be," she stated quietly.

Alex raced around the base of the cylinder to come up alongside his wife. He wanted to grab her, to snatch her hand away from the creature, but the calm quiet of her voice stopped him. Deep down, he sensed he shouldn't meddle with what was unfolding before him, as if destiny were guiding the events.

"What do you mean, it was meant to be this way?"

"I was meant to be here," Rachel replied. "It was me who was supposed to come here all along. Not you. Oh Alex, I wish I could share it all with you. Everything I feel and see and hear. It's so amazing. So beautiful. And the baby..." She trailed off, her eyes going glassy and vacant, as if she were staring at something only she could see.

"What about the baby?" Alex asked frantically.

Rachel didn't answer. Her eyes remained locked in the distance, a contented smile etched on her face, oblivious to her surroundings. Alex caught a glimmer of something in her left eye a second before a tear rolled down her cheek.

"It's so beautiful," she said simply.

Alex reached out to grab her hand but was stopped suddenly. The magical chorus-voice that had been guiding him, and apparently Rachel too, sprang up inside him. There were no words this time, but Alex could sense that whatever the entity was wanted Rachel to be allowed to continue with what she was doing. The song-speak in his head filled him with a sense of serenity, calming his instinct to pull Rachel away from the unknown, assuring him they were all safe. The warmth of the message filled him, giving him the reassurance he needed to release Rachel's arm and move away from her, certain that no harm would come to her.

Until another voice made itself known at the back of his head. A voice in opposition to the musical tones assured him. A voice that told him to fight back and protect his family. To save his wife.

Shaking his head violently, Alex brought himself back into the present moment. The assuring melody in his head dissipated from his mind and he focused on Rachel again, her hand still resting firmly on the alien creature's temple. With no further hesitation, Alex stepped forward again to grab her and pull her away from the alien, but was stopped again. This time there was no pleasant chorus ringing through him with reassurances. This time, there was just pain and immobilization as an unseen hand grasped his mind and pervaded his consciousness. His head was on fire from the assault and he paused as it dug into him, holding him in place. Whether it was the alien in front of him or some unknown force, they didn't want him getting involved with the unfolding events.

He pushed back on the pain, shoving it down as best he could, and continued forward. The second voice pushed him forward, step by step, as he fought through the torrent of pain assaulting him. The entities in his head were at war with one another, each one asserting their power over him. With each step, he felt as if he were trudging through thick mud, his feet sinking deeper into the ground. It was no longer his choice what he did; he was simply a weapon in the battle raging inside his mind.

The new entity was winning, pushing him forward toward Rachel. He was an inch from her, his arm extending toward her. He could almost feel the heat from her body. Then, in one final push, his hand grasped her wrist. As it did, the musical entity struggled forward in his mind and sang out to him.

I'm sorry.

As soon as he heard the words, there was a flash of blue light as a tendril of energy leaped from the creature and stabbed into Alex. As the energy tore through him, his body convulsed uncontrollably, every nerve ablaze with searing pain. He wanted to scream, but the pain was so great he couldn't find his voice, his entire world suddenly consumed by a maelstrom of agony. The second entity within him screamed as well and, just as quickly as it had come, retreated from his mind. As clarity returned to him, Alex glimpsed his wife, her face radiating serenity and tranquility. In that moment, he knew the right side had won, no matter what the consequences to him.

At that same moment, the energy coursing through him exploded in a wave, sending him careening across the room, upending everything that wasn't secured in place as carts full of surgical instruments and electronics flew apart in a spectacular display of metal and sparks. Alex hit the back wall hard, his body wracked with pain from the impact, and he slumped to the floor in a heap. Random convulsions coursed through him as the strange energy discharged itself. Despite the sheer agony he was in, he forced himself to stay conscious. Unable to move, all he could do was lift his eyes to see what had happened to Rachel.

She stood firmly in place, exactly where she had been a moment ago, at the epicenter of the blast that had cleared the room. Rachel was undeniably at the heart of what was unfolding. As he watched her, the smile on her face altered, transforming her into a vision of pure, unadulterated joy. Her green eyes, always alive with a sparkle of life, now practically glowed with a new energy.

No, Alex thought, they *were* glowing. It was faint at the moment, but there was actual light emanating from his wife's eyes. A light that appeared to be getting brighter by the second.

Despite the throbbing pain that continued to surge through his body, Alex fought against it, mustering the strength to rise to his feet. He hurt so much; he wanted to simply lie down and pass out. But he needed to get to Rachel. He didn't know what he had to do, but he needed to be with her.

As he struggled to stand, he couldn't help but notice the ethereal blue glow radiating from the creature, its eyes emitting a faint, mysterious energy. As Alex watched, a tongue of blue light licked up from the creature and ran up Rachel's arm, slithering around her head like a neon snake. While the color of the light was the same as the bolt that had shocked him moments earlier, he didn't feel as if it had the same malevolence. This time, the light moved across her body in a slow caress. In response, Rachel let out a happy, almost giddy, giggle.

The coruscating energy tendrils met at her midsection, just above her belly. As they came together, their energies merged into a radiant sphere of light, bluish hues transforming into a brilliant white that seemed to radiate with intensity. The sphere hovered there for a moment, emitting a faint humming sound as if it was scanning its surroundings. Then, with a sudden burst of blinding light, it disappeared, merging seamlessly into Rachel's midsection. The atmosphere remained still and silent for a few moments, until Rachel's stomach started emitting a gentle blue glow. The glow intensified rapidly, becoming so bright that Alex had to shield his eyes and turn away.

And then the light was gone. Opening his eyes, Alex was met with the sight of Rachel lying motionless on the floor, the alien body looming above her. The creature's large black eyes stared at him, but there was none of the spark of life he had seen in them earlier. They were just simple black orbs now.

The pain that had immobilized him was quickly fading, but every step was still agony as he plodded his way to Rachel. He had barely made it to her when his body gave out and he tumbled to the floor next to her, fighting the urge to close his eyes and just sleep. To forget everything and just fade into a comfortable oblivion.

Rachel stirred beside him, a little groan of fatigue escaping her. It was the same noise she made every morning as she woke, and Alex had always found it adorable. Right now, in this moment, it was so much more than that to him.

Suddenly she bolted upright, her head falling into her hands as if she were warding off a headache. Lifting her head, she looked dazed and confused, like a sleepwalker waking up in strange surroundings.

"Where am I?" she stammered, her eyes darting around the ruined room. "What happened?"

"You don't remember?"

"The last thing I remember is going through the decontamination process and waiting for you to come through. After that, nothing." She took her hands from her temples and rested her head in her hands again, staring toward the floor, when her eyes suddenly went wide with surprise. "Why don't I have any clothes on?"

"You took them off over there somewhere," Alex replied, pointing in the general direction of the pile of abandoned clothes. "I don't know why, but it's been the one good part of this whole adventure."

"You're just a laugh riot," she said, grasping the lip of the cylinder and pulling herself to her feet.

Immediately and without warning, she let out an eardrum splitting shriek. Alex jumped up, and the lingering pain immediately surged back, intensifying. As he stood, he found her staring at the motionless alien corpse, her eyes as big as two full moons.

"What is that?" she gasped, slowly backing away.

"You really don't remember?"

"I think I'd remember *that*," she snapped back at him.

Alex gently took her hand, guiding her to her discarded clothes. While she dressed, he recounted the events with vivid detail, reliving every moment since they left the decontamination chamber. Once dressed, she simply stared at him, dumbstruck, before letting her gaze fall to her midsection where the ball of light had vanished inside her.

"Are you all right?" Alex asked, stroking her arm.

"It's strange," she replied, her eyes riveted to her stomach, "but I feel this warm, comfortable feeling. Like everything is exactly the way it should be."

"Just before I got knocked across the room," he said, "once I was able to push away the other presence in my mind, that's exactly what I felt. That it was meant to be."

She turned her head up to look at him, concern on her face. "Another presence? What was it?"

"I have a feeling," he replied, remembering the force that was pushing him forward, trying desperately to disconnect Rachel from the alien. "If it's what I think it is, it means we're not out of danger yet. In fact, we're in a whole lot more."

She shook her head. "What else is new?"

"True enough," he replied. "But right now, we need to get out of here. The Project's security people have probably bypassed the decontamination chambers and are on their way here right now."

"Correction," came a muffled voice from behind them. "They're here now."

Alex and Rachel turned to see a person, a man judging by his deep voice, in a bright red hazmat suit. He was standing in the archway that led to the outer office, a gun in his hand leveled at them.

"Son of a bitch!" Alex exclaimed. It must be the guard they had encountered when they entered the lab, the very guard who had been paralyzed at the entrance. He must have been released when the alien 'died'.

He also realized in that moment he had lost both the shotgun and his Glock when the energy discharge knocked him across the room.

After everything they had gone through, they were caught again. And this time, there was no escape.

61

The man in the red hazmat suit herded Alex and Rachel back through the arch and into the administrative section of the lab, past the drab workstations to a steel door at the back of the room. The word 'Infirmary' was stenciled in black on the door. With the push of a button, the door slid aside noiselessly, leading into another glass chamber. Unlike the earlier decontamination chamber, this one was larger and could easily fit all three of them together. There were no obvious nozzles in this chamber, nothing that looked like it might dispense any dangerous chemicals, which made Alex relax a bit. Neither he nor Rachel had the opportunity to retrieve their hazmat suits. Not that it mattered, his was torn up beyond repair. If they were about to go through another chemical decontamination, it would certainly kill them both.

Red Suit moved into the room, crowding in with Alex and Rachel, as the door slid shut behind him. Alex could feel the barrel of the man's pistol digging into his back, but it was more than just being in a tight space. Red Suit was aggressively poking him with the weapon, most likely to intimidate him. It was unnecessary, there was nothing Alex could do against the man in the small room, but he apparently felt the need to make sure Alex knew who was in charge.

A sudden blast of air, loud and angry, hit them from above. Alex felt Rachel jump, startled by the noise and assault of it. As surprised and startled as he had been, Alex fought the urge to react as Rachel had. A sudden movement like that would most likely have gotten him a bullet in the back from Red Suit.

The blast of air, which filled the small chamber with the stinging scent of antiseptic, concluded a second later. Alex's eyes stung from the unexpected onslaught and he blinked wildly to clear them, but again didn't raise his hands to rub his eyes for fear of upsetting Red Suit. Rachel wasn't so inclined and rubbed her eyes furiously.

"What was that?" she asked, tears forming on her face.

As the second door opened, Red Suit remained silent, and in front of them appeared something that Alex never could have expected. The room was like every waiting room in every doctor's office he had ever been in, all the way down to the woefully outdated magazines piled on the small coffee table. The walls of the room were a stark white, reminiscent of the laboratory they had just exited, while the floor was adorned with a dull green carpet that perfectly complemented the chairs arranged around the coffee table. A desk sat straight ahead of them, vacant at the moment but with a nameplate that read 'Virginia Hobbs'. Unlike the sterile-looking metal and plastic workstations of the lab, this desk was a dark wood that somehow felt warm and inviting. In contrast to the other workstations, Virginia Hobbs' desk stood out with its personalized decorations. A coffee mug that read, 'This calls for a spreadsheet'. A framed picture of an orange cat curled up near a fireplace. A worn paperback novel with the picture of an impossibly muscled man holding a woman in a Victorian gown on the cover. The entire room seemed designed to instill calm in otherwise nervous patients and seemed entirely out of place.

"Inside," Red Suit ordered, again nudging Alex in the back with his pistol. "Keep going."

"Without an appointment?" Alex quipped, a sly grin on his face.

"I hope you hold on to that sense of humor, asshole," Red Suit replied, again nudging Alex forward with the gun. "You're going to need it."

"Well, you're going to need a good proctologist if you poke me one more time with that gun," Alex said, his smile fading. "He's the only one who'll be able to get it back for you."

Red Suit chuffed at him. "Tough and funny. That'll work out well for you. Especially after what you did back there to Project Gabriel. Now get moving."

The alien was Project Gabriel, Alex thought. It made sense. If the UFO was Fallen Angel, the recovered pilot would have been Gabriel.

"Move," Red Suit said, this time not poking Alex with the pistol.

As they moved forward, they found themselves in an immense room where the stark white walls only amplified the sense of space. A surgical table sat in the center, a mobile instrument table next to it. On the table, a collection of gruesome stainless-steel instruments were laid out, some of which Alex recognized and others that resembled instruments of torture. A bank of screens and other monitoring devices decorated the wall on the far side of the surgical set-up. Directly next to the bed sat a smaller version of the cylinder that had held the body of the alien in the sterile lab.

An uneasy feeling settled over Alex. There was a foreboding presence in this room, suggesting that whatever transpired wouldn't be favorable, especially for him. Or Rachel. As he looked around the room, his mind raced, searching for any clue or object that could aid their escape. The instruments on the table would make for suitable weapons, but they were too far from him. Red Suit would shoot him down long before he could even reach the table, never mind grab a weapon. It was the same with the door at the far end of the room. Even if they could reach it without being shot, they still had no idea where it led to. They could find themselves in an even more dire situation.

Alex's stomach clenched even tighter as the door at the far end of the room opened. Rachel's head snapped to the door, her face frozen in fearful anticipation. They had no plan to escape, and had just run out of time.

Robert Penders strode through the door, his posture tall. Dr. Forrester, sporting a few slight bruises on his face, followed him. Colonel Harriman brought up the rear, keeping Forrester between them. Several men in black fatigues, their assault rifles at the ready, followed closely behind Penders, positioning themselves on either side. Penders' face wore the expression of a disappointed parent, stern and ready to lecture on proper behavior. The look did nothing to calm either Alex's or Rachel's nerves.

"You two have caused me quite a lot of trouble since you arrived," Penders said, slowly pacing the room. His voice was as calm and even as ever, but there was a sense of irritation rippling underneath it. "I let your first bout of spiritedness pass because of what you mean to me and my organization. Unfortunately, I can't be lenient any longer. Losing Project Gabriel is simply too much" Stopping in front of the surgical table, he examined the instruments laid out there. "Is this everything you need to proceed, Elliot?"

Dr. Forrester looked up hesitantly and gave a slight nod before his chin fell once more to his chest. He looked small and frail, like a man completely defeated, a shadow of the person he had been before coming to the Project. The feelings Alex could sense from the man were intense. Fear. Anger. Regret. Sadness. All mingling together in a toxic mental soup. Alex couldn't imagine what they could have done to him that could have broken him so completely. He wasn't sure he wanted to know.

Penders were different. From him, Alex could sense a mix of emotions as well, but they were darker in purpose. He was determined, but that had always been there. A touch of concern tinged the edges of his emotional spectrum, intermingled with regret charged by anger. He appeared to be wavering in his convictions, contemplating his actions and taking measures to rectify his errors. Drastic measures.

He needed to know more than the abstract the man's emotional output provided. "What do you mean? What is he supposed to be doing?" Alex demanded, stepping toward Penders. He was met instantly by the barrel of Red Suit's gun, pressed hard into his face. Instinctively, Alex turned, ready to push the gun away, but stopped. He couldn't see the man's face through the polarized plexiglass of the hood he still wore, but he was certain from the feelings of anxiety and rage flowing from the man that any action like that would get him shot immediately.

"As I said before, my patience is at an end," Penders stated. "These men have orders to shoot if you get out of line. As of this moment, you live at my sufferance, do not wear out your welcome. You are still of some use to me, and that is the sole reason you are alive right now. Test me again and I will have you eliminated."

Penders' tone shifted from threatening to flatly informative. "As for your question; while your usefulness may be coming to an end, there was an unexpected variable in this experiment that cannot be allowed to go to waste. Something that requires more study. I thought we would have to wait months for the chance to examine this remarkable specimen, but your recent actions have made that possibility untenable. Fortunately, the good doctor was able to provide us with an alternative."

The air around Alex suddenly felt thick and oppressive as his entire body went numb with realization. "Side effect. You're talking about the baby."

"If that is how you would like to refer to it, yes," Penders answered.

Rachel crossed her arms over her stomach, instinctively protecting the child nestled within. "No," she said, her voice a hoarse whisper. "No. You can't do this. I won't allow it. This isn't one of your horrible experiments, this is a baby! *My* baby! You monster, you can't possibly be that inhumane!"

Penders took a few steps toward her. Even though he stood a good foot taller than her, Rachel didn't back away. Instead, she planted her feet and stood her ground against him.

"What would be inhumane would be to allow a resource like that child to go untapped," Penders said, his voice a low rumble. "You've seen what your husband is capable of, the sort of abilities he possesses. Dr. Forrester assures me your child will have the same amazing gifts, and so much more. Imagine what that could mean for the future of humanity, Mrs. Carter. I'm not being inhumane; I am trying to bring this child to light for the benefit of our beleaguered world. It's you that are trying to deny humanity the next step in its evolutionary process. Denying it what could very well be its salvation. I ask you, what is more humane? Saving humanity by a small sacrifice, or denying that salvation for your own selfish desires?"

"My baby is not a small sacrifice!" Rachel snapped, standing tall against Penders. "And you will not take her from me!"

Penders motioned to the guards. "That is where you are mistaken."

The guards moved, and so did Alex. Even though it might mean being cut down by gunfire, he was out of options. This was the endgame. Rachel was in danger. Their baby was in danger. Acting out of reflex was the only thing he had left. In two quick steps he positioned himself between Rachel and Penders, sliding her behind him with an outstretched arm. He knew he wouldn't be able to stop the soldiers, but there was no way he was letting them butcher his wife and take their daughter without a fight.

As he steeled himself against the coming onslaught, preparing to make a last stand, he felt a familiar pressure against his neck. The barrel of a Glock handgun, held by Red Suit. Alex cursed silently at himself. He had been so focused on the soldiers at the door he had forgotten about the threat behind him.

"Go ahead," came the challenge. "Move."

And that is exactly what he did. Faster than he ever could have imagined possible. With skill and precision he had never exhibited before. In a swift motion, he ducked under the barrel of the gun and seized the man's arm, gripping it tightly. With a surge of strength he didn't know he had, he lifted Red Suit off the ground and hurled him into the path of the advancing guards. As Red Suit's limp form soared through the air, it collided with the soldiers, sending three of them sprawling to the ground. The two that remained standing jumped aside to avoid being caught in the tangle of bodies on the floor, and Alex took advantage of their distraction. Before they could register what he was doing Alex closed the distance between them and, in one fluid motion too fast to track, landed a solid punch on the windpipe of the first guard while simultaneously knocking down the other with a powerful kick to the sternum. Both men went down hard, joining their compatriots on the floor.

Snatching up a fallen guard's assault rifle, he leveled it at the writhing heap of soldiers. "All of you, stay where you are!" Without taking his eyes off the soldiers, he addressed Harriman. "Colonel, throw your weapon over here."

The Colonel, his expression unchanging, did as he was told, taking his handgun from its holster and sliding it across the floor. Alex stopped it with his foot. "Get it," he said, nodding at Rachel.

She did, lifting the weapon gingerly, her finger resting firmly on the trigger guard and not on the trigger itself. Familiar feelings of guilt and anxiety flooded through her again with the gun in her hand, but she pushed them back as best she could. She didn't want to be holding the gun, didn't want to have to use one again, but right now she didn't really have much choice.

Alex ordered the soldiers to surrender their weapons. After a cursory nod from Colonel Harriman, they complied.

"This is ridiculous," Penders said, stepping around the surgical table and approaching Alex and Rachel. "Drop those weapons right now. You know you can't escape."

Alex aimed his rifle directly at the center of Penders' chest. "Don't test me."

Penders was undeterred by the threat. Shaking his head, he said, "I had hoped it wouldn't come to this."

"What are you tal..."

Without the opportunity to complete his sentence, Alex was struck by a searing pain in his head, causing the world to vanish in a kaleidoscope of bright colors. He felt the floor come up to meet him as he crumpled under the onslaught of unimaginable agony; the gun falling from hands he suddenly had no control over. As he fought to rise to his feet, a sharp pain shot through his head, forcing him to crumble onto the cold tile floor.

And then there was nothing but darkness.

Alex woke to a burst of pain in his skull. Wincing against the assault, he squeezed his eyes shut as the darkness behind his eyelids swirled with bright streaks of light. Streaks of light that flashed by and stabbed into his brain as soon as they were out of sight, each burst of color like being branded with a hot poker.

After a few moments (minutes, seconds, hours – he couldn't tell how much time passed) the pain began to subside, and his mind started to piece together recent events. He recalled the alien in the laboratory, Project Gabriel. Rachel's odd behavior. The internal battle with the forces trying to assert influence over him. The explosion that sent him careening across the room. The ball of light that was absorbed into Rachel's body. He could recall being led to an infirmary and seeing Robert Penders, Dr. Forrester, and Colonel Harriman there. There had been a fight. Rachel and the baby had been threatened. And then...

... nothing. He couldn't remember anything beyond that. He was missing something important, a critical part of the events that transpired in that room, but it eluded him. There was a blank spot, like someone had just erased that part of his memory and left behind nothing but static.

And suddenly, like water over a broken dam, it came flooding back to him. Rachel and the baby. Penders had been planning to take the baby, to transplant her from Rachel's body to an artificial gestation tube, the same kind he had been grown in. Dr. Forrester had been brought there, most likely against his will, to perform the surgery. He was going to take her by force, with no regard for Rachel.

In an instant, his eyes snapped open, and he winced as the harsh lights directly above pierced through his vision. With the massive amount of adrenaline coursing through him, he managed to push aside the pain and clear his mind of the remaining mental static. As he attempted to sit up, he felt an unyielding force holding him down. Panic settled over him as he suddenly remembered hitting the floor, hard, and thought that a head injury might have resulted in some sort of paralysis. But he could feel his arms and legs as they strained to obey the commands his brain was sending them. There was something else preventing them from doing what they were being told.

He could feel pressure across his chest and around his wrists and ankles as he tried to move. Straps. They tied him down, fastening him to a bed like some deranged and dangerous mental patient. But where was he? Other than the sounds of his futile attempts at escape, the room was completely silent. With immense effort, he twisted his head, wincing in pain, and managed to glimpse the room he was in. As he thought, they had strapped him to a hospital gurney. Above him, a large lamp shone bright with white light. There was another table, one designed for surgery, next to his bed. Accompanying that was another metal cart with surgical tools laid out, waiting for a surgeon.

He was in a surgical theater.

As far as he could tell, he was alone in the room. His arms went slack, no longer fighting against the tight bonds, as a wave of terror washed over him. He couldn't shake the nagging fear that Dr. Forrester had already taken the baby from Rachel's lifeless body. But that couldn't be the case. She had to be alive. If she were dead, he would know it. He wasn't sure how, but he was sure he would have sensed it. Felt it, somehow. Empowered by his realization, he mustered all his strength and tugged against his bindings again.

It was no use; they held him no matter how hard he struggled. He could feel them digging into his wrists and ankles with each tug, refusing to give way. With each passing moment, the initial dread gave way to a rising tide of anger and urgency, spreading through him like a slow, steady current. There was a way out, he just needed to slow down and think over his options. Closing his eyes once more, he blocked out the bright light above, allowing himself to analyze his circumstances.

No sooner had his eyes closed than he heard the door slide open, followed by slow but heavy footsteps. Instinctively he wanted to open his eyes, to see who it was, but decided it might be better to play possum. If the straps were removed, it could give him the element of surprise.

The footsteps stopped as the door hissed shut. Again, there was silence in the room. Alex couldn't make out any breathing or even the rustle of clothing. In an instant, the sound of footsteps reverberated again, but this time they were louder and faster, as if the person was in a hurry. A half-dozen steps brought them to his bedside. Alex could feel the stranger's presence standing over him and he fought to keep his eyes closed and maintain the image of unconsciousness. His heart picked up its pace, his skin prickling with nervous energy.

Just then, a hand fell on his chest. A large hand, almost certainly a man's. Somehow Alex managed not to flinch as the hand positioned itself just over his chest and stopped over his heart. Without warning, the hand retreated as quickly as it had come.

Alex winced a bit as it left him. While the stranger was touching him, he at least knew where he was. Now he had no idea what the stranger was doing. There were no more footsteps, so he felt confident they hadn't moved away from his bedside, but that meant they were now standing directly over him, and he had no idea what they might be planning.

With a slight rustle of cloth, the hand grabbed Alex's wrist, turning it over as if it were being examined. He was about to risk a peek, to get a glance at the visitor, when he felt his wrist restraint being unbuckled. He stayed still as the stranger worked, moving from one wrist to the next, then his chest, then his feet.

As soon as he felt the last restraint fall away, Alex lashed out at the stranger with a vicious kick. He felt a solid contact as the man let out a hard grunt and fell to the floor with a hard and painful sounding thud. Leaping from the bed, Alex frantically searched his unfamiliar surroundings for something he could use as a weapon. From the corner of his eye, he saw his opponent unholstering a weapon and kicked at him again, knocking the gun from his hand and sending it skittering across the floor. The gun came to a stop against the far wall and Alex moved for it. A hand grasped his ankle mid-stride. Alex's body hurtled forward uncontrollably, resulting in a painful collision with the unforgiving floor. His injured head bore the brunt of the impact against the chilly tile. Lancets of pain erupted anew, slashing through his skull and shredding his brain. The world threatened to go black. Alex held on to consciousness as the man scrambled to his feet and made a move for the gun. With a swift motion, Alex swung his arm towards the other man's legs, delivering a powerful blow upon impact. With another grunt of pain, the man went down on the floor again, landing face down in a spread-eagle position.

Alex pulled himself up, the throbbing pain in his head now joined by an equally intense pain in his arm, and lunged again at the gun. Simultaneously, the man on the floor smoothly rolled to his side, sitting up effortlessly as he reached for the pistol. Alex, his body crying in pain, was just a second slower. A second that made all the difference. The stranger snatched up the gun as Alex, his equilibrium completely lost, tumbled and fell. Frantically, he pulled himself to his feet, but stopped as he felt something cold and hard pressed against the back of his head.

"Get up slowly and carefully," came a gruff voice. A voice that sounded vaguely familiar.

The pressure on the back of his head released, but Alex was still keenly aware of the presence of the man standing behind him. Slowly, he did as he had been told and stood, standing perfectly still on his feet. He could hear the man's labored breathing as he moved around Alex, coming into his line of sight.

As he came around, Alex was taken aback by the unexpected face that stood before him. "You?"

Colonel William Harriman didn't offer a reply and stood stone-faced before him.

"Where's Rachel?" Alex demanded, oblivious to the fact that he wasn't the one holding the gun.

"She's safe for now," Harriman said. "We'll have to move fast if we're going to help her."

A sense of guarded relief flooded through Alex. His stomach unclenched on hearing that Rachel was safe, but the news had come from a source that was dubious at best. Also adding to his confusion was what Harriman had just said.

"If *we're* going to help her?" he repeated. "Pardon me for not sounding grateful, but don't you work for the other team?"

"Yes. No. Maybe," Harriman said. "It's a long story, one we really don't have time for. Now, we can stand here and discuss my employment history, or we can help your wife. Your call."

Alex found the reticence in the Colonel's voice to be off-putting, but he couldn't sense any malicious intent from the man. A storm of conflicting emotions raged within him, torn between regret and the desire to help. But as Alex sensed the Colonel's emotions, he felt compelled to follow through on his offer.

Alex regarded the other man cautiously. "How do I know you won't just shoot me in the back?"

"Because if I wanted you dead, you'd be dead by now," Harriman replied, his face remaining still and emotionless.

"All right," Alex replied. "It's not like I have a lot of choice. You have the gun, after all. I'll go along with you." Alex narrowed his eyes and stared intently into Harriman's neutral brown eyes, holding his gaze for a hard second before continuing. "But there's no way I'll trust you."

"I wouldn't have it any other way," the Colonel replied, lowering his gun hand but not holstering his weapon. With his free hand, he pointed to the door. "Out that way, down the hall and to the left. The second door down. That's where they're performing the operation."

"Guards?" Alex asked.

"None. I relived them all and ordered a general evacuation. Everyone is to leave, and no one can reenter without my express order. The entire installation should be nearly deserted by now. You shouldn't meet any resistance." The Colonel pointed his finger up at Alex sharply. "But don't get cocky and screw off. I've also initiated the cleansing protocols."

The urgency in the man's voice was unmistakable. "Cleaning protocols?" Alex asked, knowing the answer wouldn't be positive.

It was Harriman's turn to deliver a hard gaze. "In the next thirty minutes, a cascading series of explosions will completely destroy this installation. It will start with the outer ring, the living quarters, and move its way in toward the middle. It will end in the great cavern where Fallen Angel is located. You have exactly that much time to find your wife and get out."

"If you're being honest with me," Alex said sharply, putting a hard emphasis on the word 'if', "it shouldn't be difficult if the only obstacles are Penders and Forrester."

"First, *never* underestimate Robert Penders. He may look like your average stuffed shirt, but he always has a surprise or two up his sleeve. Second, I never said they were the only obstacles." The Colonel paused, seeming to collect himself before continuing, stating, "The Sleeper is awake."

Alex thought he felt a sliver of fear from the man. It was entirely uncharacteristic of him and sent a chill up Alex's spine. In response to the Colonel's statement, a memory flitted through Alex's head. Something he had seen briefly not long ago.

"The Sleeper? Wasn't that one of the files from Dr. Carlton?"

"Probably. It was a project she was heavily involved in." Harriman looked at his watch as digital numbers counted down. "We now have twenty-seven minutes. No more time for chatter."

"One more thing," Alex pressed. "Rick Banning. I saw him outside the clean labs, surrounded by your people. Where is he?"

Harriman sighed. It was a deep, regretful sound, and all at once Alex was sorry for having asked the question.

"He didn't make it," Harriman answered, his voice heavy with genuine regret. "He was cornered, trapped. It was before I arrived. When he fought back, my people reacted, and..." He stopped, his voice choked. "There was nothing I could do. I'm sorry."

Alex wanted to reply, but his head was drowning in a vortex of emotions. Rick was dead. Rick, the man who had been his best friend for as long as he could remember. Who had been his family. Yet Rick was also the man who had been spying on him that entire time, their whole friendship being nothing more than a ruse. A cover. The onslaught of anger, rage, resentment, and loss flooded Alex, leaving him bewildered and unable to process his emotions.

Anger won out in the end. Not at Rick. No, that situation was far too complicated for him to process right now. Eventually, he'd have to unpack all that emotional baggage and reconcile his feelings around Rick's life and death, but today wasn't that day. In this moment, his anger homed in on the person who had orchestrated the elaborate deception that had shaped Rick's false existence. The man who set him up as a spy. The man who, as commander of the Eden Project's security forces, was ultimately responsible for Rick's death.

Colonel William Harriman.

Alex glared at the man, his vision ringed in red. "That almost sounded sincere," Alex spat through gritted teeth, fighting the anger that was trying to claw its way out of him.

Harriman turned sharply to Alex, his face no longer cast in stone. The Colonel's usual stoic visage was now a twisted wreck of anger and resentment. Alex could feel it radiating from him, exploding in waves that cascaded over him and burned deeply as they passed. In the time since Alex had discovered his empathic talent, this was the strongest burst of raw feeling he had ever felt in another person. The sheer power of what Harriman was feeling right now stabbed at Alex, sinking deep into him and mingling with his own complex feelings about Rick. Except Harriman wasn't focusing on Rick, not entirely. His feelings were being fueled by something more. Something with far more power behind it than anything else inside the man.

Guilt.

An immense sense of guilt weighed Harriman down, his mind filled with remorse. It writhed inside him, wriggling through him like a parasite, eating away at any happiness of joy the man may have felt. It was like a wildfire, like an animal in a cage suddenly set free to wreak havoc, tearing down and obliterating everything good around it. Harriman's guilt, long ignored and mistreated, was now unleashed and hungry for revenge.

"Sincere?" the Colonel replied, his voice a low, gravelly growl. His eyes were narrowed and red, his face clenched tight as he spoke. "You want sincere? Do you know how many people I've sent to their deaths over the years? Good people? I hope not, because I couldn't tell you. I've lost count. And what was it all for? Once upon a time, it was in defense of something I believed in. Something they believed in. Something worth dying for. But then..." He stammered, the hard edges of his face softening as the memories poured back into his head. "Then it became something else. It became service to Robert Penders. Sending young people to die in the service of a madman's ideals. And for every one of them I lost, a little piece of my soul died with them." He turned away from Alex, staring down at his open palms. His face bore a haunted, tortured expression as he stared at his hands, as if they were stained with the blood of all those he had lost.

"Maybe that's why I have so little soul left."

Before Alex could react, Harriman turned back to him, his face once more rigid. "But he's dead now. We can't do anything about that except mourn him, which will have to wait. Right now, we need to get you and your wife away from here."

"That's cold," Alex replied, "but you're right. We don't have time for that." He stepped back from the Colonel as muscles he hadn't realized were tensed, suddenly relaxed. "How much time do we have left?"

Harriman looked at his watch. "Twenty-five minutes."

Alex nodded to him, assenting to a temporary alliance. "We better get moving."

As Alex moved for the door, Harriman stopped him. "When we get there, don't be a hero. Grab Rachel and Forrester and run. Forrester knows the way, he can lead you out. Just get out and don't look back. Understand?""

"What about the Sleeper?" Alex asked.

"Not your concern. That's my mess to clean up. I'll handle it."

Alex was about to argue, but saw the haunted look in the other man's eyes. He nodded, and said simply, "I understand."

Harriman returned the nod and slid past Alex, exiting the surgical suite. Alex moved to follow, but stopped as something brushed up against his consciousness. The feeling was almost unnoticeable, like the feeling of dread that comes over someone after shutting off the lights at night as they stumble to their bed in darkness. You know in your logical mind that there are no monsters in that darkness, but your subconscious can't help but conjure them up for you.

He turned back to the small room, seeing nothing there but the bed, surgical table and cart full of medical instruments. Even though he couldn't see anything, the sense of a presence still clung to him. A feeling of déjà vu came over him. This feeling was familiar, somehow. Familiar, and yet not. Like a song heard once long ago suddenly springing into your mind.

With a firm shake of his head, he banished the mental fog that had been clouding his thoughts. He had enough to worry about; he didn't need to create imaginary threats. With one last glance at the surgical suite, he set himself to the task at hand and followed Harriman.

Outside the room, in the shadows of the corridor, something in the darkness moved to follow.

62

Harriman moved quickly and quietly through the complex, taking confident turns down hallways that all looked exactly the same to Alex. After what felt like an eternity of passing by identical doors, the Colonel finally halted outside one labeled Surgical Suite D.

Turning back, Harriman put his index finger to his mouth in the civilian sign for quiet, hoping Alex would get the hint. He did, and hung back, pasting himself against the wall of the corridor as quietly as he could. Harriman silently shuffled up beside him, his Glock firmly clenched in his fist.

"I'll go in first, take them by surprise," Harriman whispered, although his hushed voice felt like it was booming through the quiet, empty corridor. "You follow right after and grab Rachel and the doctor and make a run for it. Understood?"

Alex nodded. It was all he wanted to do, grab Rachel and get out of here.

The Colonel reached for the numerical pad to the surgical suit and tapped out a code, each tone that issued from the device sounding to Alex like a thunderclap. He was sure that Penders and whomever else inside the room could hear it as well and he tried to press harder into the wall, to make himself as flat and inconspicuous as possible. If someone came out shooting, he didn't want to be the first thing they saw.

After what felt like an infinite number of thunderous beeps from the keypad, the indicator light blipped from red to green. Harriman leaped back and fell into a shooting stance, his Glock centered on the thick metal doors. Alex braced for gunfire as his muscles tensed, readying himself to spring into the room and grab Rachel. Adrenaline shot through him as his heart thudded in his chest, his entire body a mass of potential energy yearning to be released. He wished he still had the shotgun. Or the pistol. Or even a slingshot. Anything that would help to tilt the scales in his favor.

The doors slid open with a startling hiss of compressed air and Harriman leaped through, disappearing from view. Alex's coiled leg muscles sprang, launching him after the Colonel. Frantically, he scanned the room, his heart pounding in his chest, desperately looking for Rachel and any potential threat of armed soldiers. Getting her out was the most important thing, but doing it without being shot was certainly preferable.

"No one move!" Harriman shouted, panning the room with his pistol.

Across the room, Alex found Rachel. She lay strapped to a surgical bed, the ominous-looking glass cylinder that Penders had produced positioned next to her. Next to the bed, Dr. Forrester stood frozen, his face half concealed by a surgical mask, his exposed eyes wide with fright as he stared at Harriman and the weapon in the Colonel's hand.

In sharp contrast, Rachel's face was a beacon of happiness and relief at the sight of her husband.

Alex moved from the relative safety of his position behind Harriman and raced to her, pushing the doctor away. Forrester fell against the instrument tray, both going over in a heap with a loud metallic clatter as surgical tools scattered across the floor. Alex was oblivious to it all as he fumbled with the straps holding Rachel, her freedom being his sole focus.

"Are you all right?" he asked, still frantically struggling with her bonds. "Did they hurt you?"

"No, no, I'm fine," she answered as Alex freed an arm. She immediately wrapped it around him and held him tight. "Thank God you're here," she said, her breath catching in her throat. "Alex, what Penders wanted to do. It was... was..."

"I know," he replied, finally freeing her other arm. "But it didn't happen. And now that we're together, we're getting out of here."

Tears streamed down her face as she tightly wrapped her other arm around his neck, desperate to be closer to him. In that moment she was almost afraid to let him go for fear that he would just melt into the ether like the remnants of a dream. Feeling the heat of his body, smelling his sweat, knowing he was real and with her again; for the first time in longer than she could remember, she felt safe. Really, truly safe.

Alex slipped his arms around her waist and hugged her powerfully but briefly, then lifted her from the surgical bed. Her bare feet hit the floor with a shock of cold from the tile floor.

"Where are my clothes?" she asked Dr. Forrester. Still addled with fright by Harriman's sudden armed entrance, he merely nodded toward a locker on the far wall. Without another word, Rachel went to the locker and retrieved her clothes. Hastily, she dressed.

Harriman glanced at his watch again. "Twenty minutes. You need to go."

Alex turned toward him. "Are you sure? You can come with us. We still have time."

Harriman shook his head. "No. You need to go. Get out of here. Live your life. I still have some loose ends that need tending to." He turned to Dr. Forrester, who was just getting to his feet. "Doctor, you need to get them out of here. Penders' secret escape route, you know it?"

Forrester nodded. "Yes, I know of it."

"Good. Take them there. The cleansing protocols have been activated. You have a little less than twenty minutes." Harriman stepped forward to help the doctor up. As he did, the Colonel fixed his gaze on the doctor. "Go with them. Escape. The Project won't end with the destruction of this facility. Bring them down. You have the knowledge, Dr. Forrester. You know, literally, where all the bodies are buried. Find your courage and do the right thing."

Forrester looked at his hand, still entwined with the Colonel's. In that moment, his face hardened, his eyes focused firmly on the other man. "I will, Colonel. I promise."

Harriman nodded, realizing the conviction Forrester had found. "Thank you."

Alex moved to Rachel, who had just finished sliding into her shoes, took her hand, and moved toward the exit, but paused as a realization hit him. "Penders! Where's Penders?"

"That's an excellent question." Harriman said. "Dr. Forrester?"

But Forrester wasn't paying attention to the conversation. Something had distracted him, something that was making him shake uncontrollably. His eyes, already comically large from his thick glasses, loomed even wider. Alex sensed it just then, the stench of fear oozing from the aged scientist, thick and black like oil. More than distracted, he had completely withdrawn from reality out of sheer terror.

Suddenly, without warning, it slammed into Alex as well. A deluge of thick, greasy fear that enveloped him and threatened to drown his psyche. The onslaught came at him from all angles, a relentless force that sought to penetrate his mind. Reflexively he lashed back, pushing the miasma of terror back, feeling out at the same time for its source.

He found it directly above them.

"Look out!" Alex yelled, releasing Rachel's hand and diving for the Colonel and Dr. Forrester just as the glass of the observation window above them shattered, coming down like a tinkling hail as it hit the hard tile floor. Alex plowed into the two men and they went down in a heap of tangled limbs, sliding across the floor before coming to a hard stop against the far wall of the suite.

Behind them, amidst a rain of shimmering glass, a figure fell to the floor, landing with perfect precision. He stood waiting as the last of the falling glass crashed down around him, his eyes riveted on the three men on the floor as they struggled to right themselves.

Alex froze at the sight of him. The man's eyes were an icy blue, like cold death. Devoid of all emotion, driven only by pain. Alex was horribly familiar with the evil of those eyes.

But not on this man.

This wasn't the man Alex knew from his nightmares. This was someone else bearing those nightmare eyes. He was thinner than either Alex or Adam, his frame more slight, but his stature did nothing to diminish the confidence and determination in his stance. His hard, icy gaze remained locked on them as he casually brushed away shards of glass from his shoulders, straightening his tie and suit coat in the same motion before advancing on them.

Forrester's eyes again grew wide with fear, his face draining of blood. His glasses hung loosely from one ear, but even without clear vision he knew what was coming for them and it terrified him beyond reason.

"No," he muttered, trying to back away even further from the slight man in the suit, his back pressing hard into the wall. "Oh please, no."

Harriman pulled away from Alex and Forrester and rolled over to assess the new threat. His face was as unchanging as ever, but Alex noticed a flicker of fear in the man's eyes as he saw their assailant. It was a fear that might have caused others to crumble, as Forrester had done, but Harriman was not like others. He would not go down without a fight.

"Get up and get out of here," Harriman ordered, his eyes darting around for the gun he lost when Alex tackled him. "Grab Rachel and Forrester and get out. I'll keep him busy for as long as I can."

The cold-eyed man took a step closer, the sound of broken glass beneath his feet echoing through the small room like a symphony of shattered bones. Alex shivered at the thought as Forrester whimpered at the man's approach, grasping Alex firmly by the back of his shirt as if pleading for him to hide him. The Colonel simply stared back defiantly, not allowing his face to betray the fear inside him.

"Colonel, Doctor," the man said, his voice a sharp contrast to the murderous look in his eyes. It was an upbeat, confident voice, like a politician. Or a used-car salesman. It certainly wasn't the voice of a stone-cold killer.

Harriman's eyes narrowed into slits. "Darnell."

The name struck a chord with Alex and he struggled to pull it from his memory. Where had he heard it before? And in what context? Forrester. It had been Forrester who had mentioned the name. Burke Darnell. He was Robert Penders' right hand and, according to the doctor, someone to be feared. Someone dangerous.

Alex never imagined he could be dangerous like this.

Darnell's eyes became slivers of ice as his lips curled into a smile that was the stuff nightmares were made of. A handgun materialized from behind him, its barrel trained on the center of Alex's forehead.

"I hope you understand, I have to do this," he stated, his finger slowly tightening on the trigger. "It's not that I want to."

He laughed, a cackling noise that rang through Alex's ears and chilled him to his marrow. "Oh, who am I kidding? Of course I want to do this!" His eyes wandered to Forrester, then to Harriman, the fiendish smile practically engulfing his face in a wicked shroud. "And after him, I'll deal with you two. Trust me, it won't be quick."

Alex's mind raced, trying to conjure up a plan to escape as Burke's gaze locked onto him once again. On one side Forrester still had his shirt in a death grip, on the other was Harriman, who was no doubt doing the same mental gymnastics of plotting an escape that Alex was. Directly in front of him were Burke and his gun. He was socked in with no way to roll or dodge the coming shot. Even if he could, he was sure that would only save him from the first bullet. It wouldn't take long for one of them to find its mark.

This was going to be the end. Burke was about to shoot him through the head, an injury that even he wouldn't be able to come back from. Closing his eyes, he thought of Rachel and silently apologized to her for failing to be there when she needed him. That he wouldn't be able to save her. That they wouldn't have their life together as a family. That he would never meet his daughter.

He heard the deafening explosion of the gunshot and cringed, waiting for the bullet to hit. There was no pain, no slamming impact as he expected. In fact, he felt nothing. Nothing but the insistent tugging at his shirt and the cold of the tile floor beneath him. He heard something hit the floor just a few inches from him, something that let out an almost imperceptible moan.

Cautiously, slowly, he opened his eyes. Next to him, Forrester was still whimpering and clinging to him. Directly in front of him, where Burke had been standing ready to end his life just a moment ago, now lay the man's body, splayed face down as a stream of crimson flowed from beneath his unmoving form. On the opposite side of him, Alex saw Harriman skitter forward and grab the gun from the fallen man's hand and then back away just as quickly.

"Rachel," Alex whispered.

She stood at the far end of the room, her small hands gripping the still-smoking Glock that Harriman had dropped. She was shaking, and her body seemed locked in place, the pistol held out in front of her as if she were afraid Burke would get up again.

Pulling away from Forrester's grip, Alex stood and slowly moved to her. "Rachel? Honey? Are you okay?"

She pulled her gaze from the prone form of the man she had just shot and locked eyes with her husband. A wave of raw emotion washed over Alex, and he felt a mix of things he had never experienced from her. She experienced a mix of emotions - fear, regret, and relief - as she realized that both of them had made it through unharmed. There was a softness to her, deep feelings of guilt from taking a life. But as he looked into her eyes, he could see a hardness in her he had never seen before. She had always been strong, the strongest person he had ever known, but now her strength seemed to have moved to another level in defense of her family.

"Okay?" she answered, her arms finally dropping to her sides. "Not in the least." She turned away from Burke's body and fell into Alex's arms, melting into him, pressing firmly against him to feel that they were both safe and alive. When she raised her head to his, he once again saw a look of steely determination behind her eyes, the cold hardness fading. This was the woman he knew. The woman he loved.

She squeezed him harder. "Can we go home now?"

"Wherever you go," Harriman said as he helped Forrester up off the floor, "it better be as far from here as you can get in..." He checked his watch. "Fifteen minutes."

"Aren't you coming?" Rachel asked.

"There are still a few loose ends I need to take care of. Things I should have tended to a long time ago. Don't worry about me, I still have a few tricks up these old sleeves," the Colonel answered. Just then, the great stone façade of his face cracked, and a smile appeared there. "But in case I don't see you again, ma'am, you take good care of that baby. I have a feeling he's going to be a handful."

Rachel returned his smile. "She. And I will."

Harriman nodded back at her. "I'm sure you will, at that. Now go, you're running out of time."

Dr. Forrester joined Rachel and followed as she left the room. Alex moved to follow, but then turned back to Harriman. "Thank you," he stated with deep sincerity. "I couldn't have done this without your help."

Harriman tipped his head at the younger man. "Take care of yourself. Have a good life. You deserve it. Now get going."

With nothing left to say, Alex followed Rachel and Dr. Forrester, the weight of silence hanging in the air.

From behind came a scuffling of cloth on tile and the crunch of broken glass. Harriman's face once again became stone as he turned, knowing full well what he'd find there.

"Touching," Burke rasped out, his hand pressed against the exit wound in his chest as blood flowed freely from it, falling to the floor in small drops of liquid ruby. In his free hand was a scalpel, plucked from the myriad of surgical tools scattered across the room. "Why did you do it, Colonel?" he asked, circling closer to the two men. "Why did you turn against the Eden Project? How could you sabotage the possibility of a better world?"

Harriman's mind drifted back to the small park he had visited in Pine Haven. Back to the visions of picnicking families and children, laughing as they play. About the realizations he'd had of his life and the contributions he'd made to the world. Of what he would leave behind when he was gone. What his legacy would be.

He shrugged. "Who says I haven't made the world a better place? That's not for me to decide. Or you. All I know is, I no longer have any business in it. And neither do you."

"You're a traitorous bastard," Burke gurgled, blood spilling through gritted teeth.

"And you're an aberration," Harriman answered. "A stye in God's eye. And maybe I'm just now learning what that means."

He raised his gun, aiming squarely at the center of Burke's forehead, as the other man charged him with the scalpel raised high. Harriman squeezed the trigger twice and watched as the bullets tore into Burke's forehead and erupted out the back of his head, his body crumpling to the floor for the last time.

In the quiet, Harriman sighed and again checked his watch. Thirteen minutes. There was nothing to do now but wait.

63

Alex clung to Rachel's hand, their fingers intertwined as they sprinted, the fear of losing her again driving them forward. Behind them, Dr. Forrester panted and wheezed like a punctured bagpipe as he tried to keep up.

"Where are we going?" Rachel asked, her breath ragged. They had been running hard since leaving Harriman and she had no doubt come down from the burst of adrenaline she'd had earlier, and her fatigue was showing.

"There's an escape tunnel up ahead," Forrester rasped out between labored breaths. "Something Penders had installed to escape a lockdown."

Alex, unaffected by the physical demands of their escape because of his genetically engineered physique, hated to slow down, but Rachel and Dr. Forrester didn't share his unique endurance. Particularly the aged scientist who appeared like he might just keel over and die at any moment.

Alex slowed his pace, allowing Rachel to keep up with him and giving Forrester a chance to catch his breath a bit. As they rounded the next turn, Alex suddenly stopped cold. Rachel, unable to curb her forward momentum, crashed hard into him and nearly fell to the floor before righting herself in an awkward, wobbly dance.

She looked up at Alex. His eyes were wide and vacant, their normal dark brown now almost completely black. The blood had drained from his face, bleaching his skin to the color of bone. She had seen this look on him before, and it was never a good sign.

"Alex?" she whispered, lightly touching his arm. Although they had been literally on the run for several minutes now, he felt cold to her touch. "What's wrong?"

His next words turned her spine to ice.

"He's here."

Rachel forced back the initial shock of Alex's announcement. "Adam? How is that possible? We left him in Pine Haven! And how could he have gotten in here? This place is more secure than the Pentagon!"

"I don't know how he got here, I just know he's here," Alex answered. "And he's close."

Dr. Forrester caught up with them, his footfalls heavy with fatigue and his breath a gale force wind. He leaned against the wall and propped himself up with a hand on each knee. "Are we there?" he gasped loudly; each word separated by a forceful sucking of air.

As Rachel turned to answer him, Alex swiftly spun around and forcefully brought them both down to the floor. He gathered them under his protective embrace, shielding them as best as he could. In an instant, a tremendous explosion erupted, sending shock waves down the corridor and enveloping them in a thick cloud of dust and smoke.

As the echo of the blast faded down the hall and the smoke rose to the ceiling while the dust settled to the floor, Dr. Forrester risked poking his head out from under Alex's armpit. "What in sweet mercy was that?"

Alex groaned slightly as he lifted himself off the other two, a sharp pain running up his back. He could feel a slight trickle of blood traveling down his side and falling into his pants. When he went down, he felt something sharp graze his skin, but the injuries appeared to be superficial. As he stretched, he felt a few pin pricks along his back, but it quickly faded away.

He squinted through the flickering of the shattered ceiling lights and still swirling dust to see a wall of rock blocking the corridor. It was difficult, even with his eyes, to see that far ahead through the undulating lights and random sparking of broken electricals, but he couldn't see any gaps they might exploit to get through to the escape tunnel ahead. Even Rachel's slight form wasn't small enough to get through.

"That," he sighed, "was Adam. He's sealed the escape tunnel. There's no way through."

"Adam?" Forrester blurted, his voice laced with equal parts surprise and terror. "How do you know it's him?"

"I can sense him," Alex answered. "I can feel his hatred. His loathing. It's pretty hard to miss. He means for us to die here, even if he has to sacrifice himself to make it happen."

"That's insane!" Forrester exclaimed, panic pushing his voice up an octave.

"He's not exactly a pillar of mental stability," Alex shot back. "You, of all people, should know that."

"What do we do now?" Rachel interjected. "Is there another way out?"

"None that I know of," Alex answered, defeat creeping into his tone.

Forrester shrugged slightly. "Me neither."

"So, we just lay down here and wait to die?" Rachel asked. "We just give Adam what he wants?"

Her question hung in the air like dust for a moment before Alex's face lit up. With a snap of his fingers, he said, "Maybe not. There might be another way."

"How?" Forrester whined. He was now sitting on the floor with his face buried in his hands. "A complete lockdown is just that. Complete. This facility is sealed airtight. Not even a microbe could escape."

"It's just a shot in the dark, Doctor. No guarantees. But I'm not willing to just give up and wait to die." Alex extended his hand to the scientist. "Are you?"

Forrester looked up at him and sighed a heavy sigh before accepting Alex's outstretched hand. "You can be annoyingly upbeat. Has anyone ever told you that?"

"I haven't been accused of that lately," Alex replied as he checked his watch. "We only have about ten minutes. We need to move."

"Where?" Rachel asked.

"To find a fallen angel and see if we can't help her up," Alex replied, taking her hand and heading back down the corridor. "Watch for Adam. He'll be after us."

"How does he know?"

"He knew it as soon as the idea came to me. And he's none too happy about it, so we have to beat him to the great cavern. Come on!" Alex tugged at her, urging her along.

Forrester gasped, his breath catching in his throat as the weight of Alex's plan settled on him. "The great cavern? Fallen Angel? Good Lord, man, you can't be serious!"

By the time he finished the sentence, Alex and Rachel had already disappeared around the next bend, leaving Forrester alone with the echoing silence. Casting a quick glance around, he mustered his final ounces of stamina and set off in pursuit.

Behind them, a figure emerged from the undulating swirls of smoke and dust. It dragged something behind it like a dirty sack of laundry, which it dropped unceremoniously at the blocked tunnel entrance.

"You can run," Adam sneered, "but you can't hide. There's no escaping the inevitable. Isn't that right, Robert?"

He regarded the object he had just dropped, the broken and bloodied corpse of Robert Penders; his eyes wide open but unseeing, his mouth frozen in mid-scream. The rest of him was a charred and almost unrecognizable mass of human pulp being held together by a ten-thousand-dollar suit, the result of being caught in the explosion that had sealed off his private escape tunnel. Adam smiled wickedly at the irony of it. Robert Penders had always been a narcissistic egotist, but for him to die while trying to use an escape tunnel he'd had built solely for his own protection was pure poetry.

The only regret he had was that he wouldn't be able to kill Burke or Colonel Harriman. He had come upon Burke's body moments too late, finding him face down in one of the surgical suites, his head destroyed by a couple of bullets. He was surprised to find out that the mysterious Sleeper he'd heard rumors about for years not only turned out to be real, but that it had also been none other than Burke Darnell himself. All those years of chasing power and when he finally had *real* power, he choked in the finals. Adam chuckled quietly to himself at that.

As surprising as it had been to learn that Burke had been the Sleeper, Adam had been aghast to learn that it had been none other than Colonel William Harriman himself who had killed him. Harriman had always been the original rule-follower, completely dedicated to whatever cause he was attached to, unwavering in his commitment to upholding regulations. Adam wondered what would have made a man like that suddenly change sides. It was a pity he didn't have time to track down Harriman and get some answers. And to kill him. He would simply have to settle for killing Dr. Forrester, and then Rachel and Alex Carter. In that order. Alex Carter would be the last to die, but not before bearing witness to the destruction of everything he held dear. He had to experience the pain of his life being cruelly snatched away. The life he had stolen from Adam. He had to know the same pain Adam had experienced before he was finally granted death himself. A death Adam would happily give him.

With that thought warming him, Adam took off after them, leaving the unseeing corpse of Robert Penders where it lay.

64

Alex and Rachel raced out of the corridor and into the immense cavern that housed Fallen Angel. Slowing down to a strolling pace, Alex was momentarily stunned by the sheer magnitude of the cave, its size appearing much more impressive than during his previous encounter. It loomed larger and more foreboding, the feeling of its immensity made greater without the bustling activity of scientists and soldiers milling about and the cacophony that accompanied it. Except for the continuous hiss of air being circulated throughout the cave, along with the persistent hum of abandoned computers and electronic equipment, the vast space was completely still.

In the center of the chamber, its true size masked by the enormity of its surroundings, sat the silver elongated disk that was Fallen Angel. The ship looked almost forlorn; alone and rejected in its berth. Abandoned by its captain to captivity deep underground, away from the open vacuum of space that had been its home for so long. For a moment, Alex thought he could feel that crushing loneliness emanating from the ship. Like it was calling to him, yearning to be set free.

Set me free.

The crystalline chorus rang through his head again, just as it had before. Stunned, Alex stood frozen in disbelief. After they had discovered the body of the alien in the Project Gabriel lab, he had assumed the voice calling to him had been some spark of life from the creature held there. He hadn't heard it since then, when the creature appeared to have finally and truly died after transferring its energy to the baby. But now here it was again, stronger and more insistent than ever. It hadn't been the alien. That creature had called Rachel and the baby alone. Someone else now called him.

It was the ship.

Alex's head spun at the thought of it. The ship wasn't simply a vehicle. The ship itself was a sentient being. It had consciousness and thought. It had *feelings.* No matter what it appeared to be, it was a thinking and feeling creature in its own right.

And it had been imprisoned.

Next to him, Rachel was likewise entranced by the magnificence of Fallen Angel, absorbing every detail during her inaugural experience. She had seen the picture on Dr. Carlton's thumb drive, but seeing it now had completely stunned her. With eyes wide open in amazement, she stood in front of the majestic, shimmering metal ship, her jaw hanging loose in utter astonishment. In that moment, all thought of the impending danger from the cleansing protocols left her mind as she took in the ship's spectacle.

Behind them, Dr. Forrester emerged from the corridor, finally catching up. He held his chest and wheezed heavily as he sloughed his way to them, slumped over from exertion and anxiety. His heart was beating so forcefully in his chest that for a moment the doctor was afraid it would burst through as his lungs screamed for relief. With a heavy clang, he fell against the guardrail next to Alex.

"It was the ship," Alex whispered to himself.

"What was that, my boy?" Forrester gasped, using the rail to pull himself up to his full height. His heart rate had slowed a bit and it no longer felt like an animal fighting to get loose, and his lungs were finding an acceptable breathing pattern again. The pain in his leg muscles intensified, a fiery reminder that they were being pushed in ways they hadn't been in years. Or ever. Exercise had never been the scientist's strong point.

Alex didn't respond, his attention still focused solely on the ship. Forrester, having seen the vessel thousands of times over the years, had long since gotten over the captivating feelings of awe it often brought out in people and was, unlike his companions, acutely aware of the danger they were still in.

He gently grabbed Alex's shoulder and joggled him. "Alex? We have to hurry, son. We need to leave this place now. What was that you just said?"

Alex turned slowly to Forrester, his eyes still unfocused. "It was the ship all along. Doctor, I don't know how to say this, but that ship is alive! I thought it was the alien at first, but just now it reached out to me. It asked me to set it free! It was the ship talking to me all along!"

Forrester felt as if he'd been struck. He had always believed the ship possessed intelligence, but this exceeded his wildest expectations. If what Alex was saying was true, this was more than a simple means of conveyance. Beyond being a simple tool, it possessed the ability to travel through the universe, defying the limitations of its race. It was asking for help. It was pleading for its freedom. That would mean it was aware. It was not just an object; it held emotion and memory within it.

It was alive.

Taking hold of both shoulders, he twisted Alex around until their eyes met. "Are you absolutely certain? Beyond any doubt, do you know it is that vessel speaking to you right now?" He swept his arm out and pointed at the ship.

Alex nodded. "Yes, I am. I don't know how, but I know the ship is speaking to me." Turning his attention from Forrester, he focused on Rachel. "To us."

For the first time since entering the cavern, Rachel shifted her attention from the ship to the two men standing next to her. "I'm sorry," she replied, "but I don't hear anything."

"That's because it's not talking to you," Alex answered, reaching out and placing a gentle hand on her stomach. "It's talking to her."

Rachel covered his hand with her own. "How do you know?"

With a slight nod, Alex smiled and pointed towards the ship. "They told me."

Forrester stepped up to the couple. "Yes, yes, this is fine and all, and I am fascinated by the thought of that ship having true sentience, but for now, we have a bigger problem! This entire facility is about to blow sky high! Coming here was your idea, my boy. What's your plan?"

"The ship will take us away from here," Alex stated calmly.

Forrester chuffed. "No one has ever breached the skin of that thing! How are we supposed to get inside?"

"It'll let us in," Alex answered. "It responded to me once. That was before I knew what it wanted. That it needed my help. Now, I feel confident it'll open up for us."

For the second time in as many minutes, Dr. Forrester was dumbstruck. "You got inside? How? What did you see?"

"I never actually went inside," Alex explained. "It was Penders' experiment, to expose the ship to me. I touched it and my hand just... passed through, I guess. Like it knew me. Like it trusted me."

"Amazing," Forrester sighed. Suddenly, his eyes went wide as a realization set in. "Wait a moment," he continued, panic rising in his voice. "You have no idea what you did, how you did it, or whether you can do it again? And that is what you have staked all our lives on?"

"It's the right thing to do," Rachel said.

Forrester turned to her, his bug eyes wild. "And how do you know?"

"I simply do," she responded, gesturing towards her hand, entwined with Alex's, resting on her belly. "After everything that's happened, is it too much to ask to have a little faith?"

Forrester's panicked face softened at the calm and surety in Rachel's tone. Alex wasn't sure how or why, but he felt calmed as well just by hearing her. As if she had somehow reached out and touched his soul. Their relationship had always been strong, but he had never felt more connected to her than he did at that moment.

"Come on," he said, unable to repress a smile. "Let's get out of here."

With a grin mirroring his, she eagerly followed his lead, carefully descending the metal staircase that led to the cavern floor. With an exasperated sigh, Dr. Forrester begrudgingly followed.

As Alex approached the ship, the surrounding air seemed charged with an energy he couldn't explain. It was all around him, cascading over and through him, filling him with a sense of warmth and comfort. The closer he got to the metal disk, the stronger it felt. As he reached the underbelly he could feel it almost overwhelming him.

Love. It was love. The purest, strongest expression of love he had ever felt. Something had changed since the last time he was in the ship's presence. Since he had last interacted with it. It was as if the vessel had regained consciousness at his last touch and realized they were connected. That they were kin.

He found a spot where he could easily access the underbelly of the ship and reached up to touch the cold, metallic surface, just as he had done before. The surface thrummed with power; he could feel it as his hand got closer, each pulse coursing through him. His fingers brushed the surface.

"Ahhh..." Rachel cried, and fell to her knees. Alex pulled back his hand and raced to her, dropping to her side.

"What is it?" he asked, taking her arm and helping her back to her feet. She wobbled a bit as she stood, steadying herself against him. "Are you hurt?"

"No," she answered, pulling away from him as she regained her footing. "It was just this incredible feeling that came over me. More specifically, that came over me through the baby." She turned her face to him, tears streaming down her cheeks. "The ship is talking with her. I can hear them. Oh Alex, it's so beautiful. I've never heard anything like it before. There's no way to describe it."

Her face shifted in that moment, transforming from an expression of sheer joy and beauty to one of immediate concern. "I'm not sure how I know this, it's not like they're using words, but they want you to hurry. There's danger coming."

Alex moved away from her and refocused his attention on the ship. "Here goes," he said, once again reaching for the smooth metal surface. As before, the underside of the ship dissolved at his touch into an array of red, blue, and yellow light that swirled and danced around his fingertips. Behind him, he heard Rachel and Dr. Forrester gasp in unison as the lights flitted away from his hand and engulfed the surface.

"Amazing," Forrester uttered, his face lit up with child-like wonder. "Simply amazing."

"It's beautiful," Rachel whispered, as if afraid her voice might scatter the lights.

Filled with the enthusiasm of a child who had just learned a new trick on his bike, Alex couldn't contain his excitement. "Watch this!" he exclaimed, as he extended his arm into a swirling sea of lights, the gentle warmth of the glowing orbs brushing against his skin.

"You try it," he urged Rachel.

She stepped forward slowly, tentatively, past Alex until she found a place that would allow her to reach the skin of the ship. The lights swirled above her and danced excitedly, beckoning her to join them. She watched as they flittered and dashed like children at play. The lights near her had an electrifying excitement that was absent with Alex. It was dizzying to see, but more than that was the feeling that emanated from the tiny baby inside her. Her happiness mirrored that of the ship, as if both were overjoyed to finally be together.

"Beautiful," Rachel whispered.

"Go on," Alex said. "Touch the ship."

Rachel hesitated, a twinge of fear springing up in her as she thought of the way Alex's hand had disappeared into the storm of lights. With the lights above her almost in a frenzy, she was nervous about the effect they might have on her. At least she was, until a feeling of comfort came over her, emanating from her daughter. As small as she was, too small even for her mother to be showing she was there, the baby knew they would be safe. Knew that the ship meant them no harm and that it would protect them to the end of its existence, as it had been intended for.

Holding on to that feeling of calm confidence, Rachel reached out and made contact with the flitting lights. The instant she did, they stopped, frozen in place, buzzing with the vibration of a new presence. A familiar presence. A presence they had been waiting to experience for a long time. The vibrating lights built to a crescendo, the buzzing almost too loud to bear, before they exploded in a bright burst that engulfed the cavern in pure white light. The entire ship, previously a staid metal disk, then a showering of colored lights, was suddenly awash in cleansing light. It was as if the craft had suddenly come alive, throbbing and pulsating with renewed energy, casting a warm and inviting luminescence over them all.

"Oh my stars," whispered Dr. Forrester as he stared into the light. It was captivating, enthralling, drawing him into it with the promise of comfort and safety. As he stared into it, he felt the ship, the entity, staring back into him. He could almost hear it speaking to him, a gentle forgiveness for the harm inflicted during its years of captivity.

In that moment, he wept.

Rachel reached out to him. "It's okay, Doctor. They understand. Go ahead, touch it. They won't hurt you."

Forrester stepped toward her and took her hand, allowing himself to be drawn in closer to the ship. He shook uncontrollably, his body wracked with conflicting feelings of joy and guilt as he approached. Unlike Alex and Rachel, he was squinting against the light. It wasn't that it was too bright; it was more that he felt his sins were exposed in its glow. All the terrible things he had done, that he allowed to happen to this poor creature, were alight for all to see.

"You're not to blame," Rachel whispered. "They know that. They understand you were as much a captive as they were."

Dr. Forrester blinked against the brilliance and, while it didn't dim, it was much more comfortable for him to be in its presence. He looked at Rachel, who smiled a warm smile, and slowly lifted his arm to the glowing ship.

As soon as his fingertip came in contact with the pure light, a loud popping and hissing sound erupted and it instantly shifted back to the cold, hard metal he had always known it to be. A groan escaped from Rachel as she fell away, the white light dying around them. As Alex ran to catch her, the entire surface of the vessel became like chrome again.

"Rach! Are you all right?" Alex gently brought her to rest on the cavern floor. "What happened?"

She rubbed at her temples as if in the throes of a terrible migraine. "I don't know. Everything was fine, and then it was like the entire world exploded. It sounded like a chorus of screams in my head. Like a thousand children crying out in pain all at once. Oh God, it was terrifying!" She buried her head in his chest, hot tears soaking into his shirt.

Dr. Forrester's chin dropped to his chest. "It was me. I was the cause."

"No," Rachel answered. "They don't have any ill will towards you. I know it. I felt it."

"Perhaps," he replied, "but I also don't share its genetics. I'm not a part of it. You are, you and Alex. Alex because of what I made him, you because of the incredible child you're carrying that shares his gifts."

"What are you saying?" Alex asked. "That you can't enter the ship?"

Forrester was silent, his eyes large and mournful.

"No," Alex said, his voice rising.

Rachel said nothing, her face blank. Her eyes darted back and forth, as if she were seeing a problem none of them could. Without a word, she stood, turning her gaze back to the ship. "Are you certain?" she asked no one in particular. After a beat, she replied to the same disembodied voice. "I'll try."

Once again, she reached for the underbelly of the craft and touched the ship. There was no transformation to sparkling lights, no explosion of white light. The smooth metallic surface remained.

At first.

At her touch, the metal appeared to come alive, transforming and contorting as if it were liquid. The metal flowed like mercury, expanding outward and forming a ramp that ended right at Rachel's feet. At the other end was a darkened opening in the ship itself.

“There,” she stated, “that should do it.” She broke contact with the ship and, unlike earlier when the light disappeared, the ramp remained in place.

Alex was awestruck. "How did you...?" he stammered, his eyes widening as he gestured towards the unexpected entrance that had appeared on the once tightly sealed vessel.

“I had some help,” she replied, and winked at him.

A thousand questions ran through Alex’s head, but a glance at his watch showed they would have to wait. “You’re a miracle,” he said, cupping Rachel’s face in his hands and kissing her quickly on her forehead, “but we need to get moving!”

“But we don’t know what’s in there,” Dr. Forrester protested.

“Could it be any worse than what’s going to be out here in a few minutes?” Alex replied, grabbing him by the arm and shoving him to the now solid metal ramp.

“Yes, I... I see your point,” Forrester said as he stepped cautiously up to the base of the ramp. His foot hovered above the shiny surface for a second before he committed to making contact, the memory of his last encounter still fresh in his mind. He flinched slightly as he stepped on the spotless metal, but this time there was no light show. No buzzing or hissing or popping. No reaction from the ship to this previously unwanted visitor. Letting out a giddy little laugh, he tramped the rest of the way up the ramp and vanished into the darkness.

Alex looked at his watch. Two minutes remained before all hell broke loose and the facility came down around them. It was time to go. He stepped onto the ramp to follow Rachel and Dr. Forrester, but paused as a familiar buzzing stung the back of his neck, nagging at him to move away from the ship.

Without fully understanding why, Alex backed down the gleaming gangway to the floor of the cavern. The buzzing in his head increased in intensity and urgency, like an angry swarm of bees in his skull. There was something here with him. No, some*one*. Someone familiar.

As the realization hit him, it was already too late. In that same instant, Adam slammed into him, confirming the presence he had sensed moments earlier. The floor greeted Alex’s face with a painful impact. He skidded across the floor from the momentum of the attack, the heavy weight of Adam’s form centered atop him, pinning him to the ground. The left side of his face was torn and ravaged by the rough concrete beneath them, and he cried out as his world exploded in pain.

"That's what I want to hear," Adam yelled as he shoved Alex's head harder against the unforgiving floor. "I want you to scream, you son of a bitch! Scream!"

Alex felt his head being lifted from the floor, then immediately brought crashing down again against the unyielding surface. A slight, almost inaudible whimper escaped him as his world threatened to go black. All he could see was a blurred face hovering over him, a slavering smile pasted across it. And eyes. Deep blue, yet alive with a fiery anger. As his head was bounced off the concrete again, he fought against the encroaching oblivion, with a shock of agony being the only thing keeping him awake. He reached blindly for his attacker, grabbing at him and trying to pull him off, unable to get a firm grip.

"Not going to die easy, huh? We'll see about that."

Adam rummaged through his jacket pocket, searching for something. Alex's mind flashed through the lethal possibilities; a gun, a knife. Whatever he was reaching for, Alex knew he had to get out from under him before he found it. His only chance, a slim one, was being able to face Adam on even ground. Adam had him pinned down, making it impossible for him to twist away. He was completely immobilized. No matter how hard he tried, he couldn't twist his arm or leg for added leverage. With each struggle, Adam's pressure increased, making it harder and harder for him to draw in a breath. Already he could only draw quick, shallow gasps, his lungs unable to expand under the pressure Adam exerted. Around him the light was fading, the world once more turning dark. The explosions would start soon, he had maybe a minute. Maybe thirty seconds. He couldn't be sure. As the blackness enveloped him, he wondered if he would pass out before the flames shot up through the floor and consumed him.

As that morbid thought passed through his quickly fading conscious mind, Alex felt the weight on top of him suddenly give way. Inhaling sharply, he felt the rush of air fill his lungs, the sound of his breath ragged and uneven, as he greedily replenished his starved system with much-needed oxygen. With his consciousness restored, the darkness receded, and he pulled himself up, catching a glimpse of Dr. Forrester grappling with Adam, his arm constricting around Adam's throat.

They fell hard, but the doctor had somehow gained the topside advantage as he clung hard to Adam. Adam swiftly reached up and effortlessly flung the scientist aside, as if discarding a soiled garment into a laundry basket, extinguishing his short-lived advantage.

Alex's vision was still nothing but a dull red haze as his lungs struggled desperately to bring oxygen to his body. His breaths were coming hard and fast and he was afraid he might hyperventilate, leaving him unable to protect Rachel or help Dr. Forrester. There was no way the aging scientist could fight off Adam alone. He focused on his breathing, slowing each intake of air, expanding and deflating his lungs in an ever-slowing pattern. The process seemed to last an eternity, an eternity they didn't have, but in a few quick seconds his breath had normalized and his vision cleared.

A half dozen feet from him lay Dr. Forrester, his leg twisted up beneath him at an odd angle. Blood ran freely across the left side of his face from a deep gash in his forehead, oozing across the lens of his thick glasses. Adam stood directly above him, the same sinister sneer smeared across his face.

Forrester ignored the imminent threat and focused on Alex. "Run, my boy!" he yelled, waving his arms frantically as if he could somehow will Alex into action. "Get to the ship while you still can!"

With a flash of his arm, Adam struck the doctor, a loud crack resonating through the chamber. There was no doubt the hit had broken bones. "I think we've had enough of you and your interference, old man," Adam grunted.

"No!" Alex yelled as a sudden burst of rage-driven energy filled him. With a burst of energy, he flung himself at Adam, their bodies colliding and causing them to tumble to the ground in a heap. This time Adam took the brunt of the impact as his breath left him in a rush. As Adam gasped for air, Alex quickly pulled away from him, moving back just far enough to draw his arm back in a mass of potential energy. Releasing that energy, he brought his fist down squarely on Adam's nose, which exploded under the impact.

Blood and flesh crushed under Alex's fist as he drew back for another hit. As he repositioned himself to throw another punch, Adam pushed blindly against him and he tumbled back, landing on his tailbone as a jolt of pain shot up his spine. Pushing that aside, he scrambled to his feet as Adam cradled his devastated nose, trying to staunch the flow of blood running down his chest.

"You broke my nose!" Adam shrieked, his voice a shrill mix of anger and pain. "I'll kill you! You bastard!" He stood on unsteady feet and thrust his arm into his jacket pocket, producing what looked like a small pistol. Except this was tipped with a needle and, instead of bullets, it was loaded with a vial of swirling amber fluid.

Dr. Forrester's face drained of color, his body suddenly tensed with panic. He attempted to stand and reach Alex, but his leg, which had buckled beneath him, refused to cooperate, causing him to collapse onto his hind end. Unable to stand, he flailed his arms wildly, hoping to catch Alex's eye.

"Alex, get away from him! Don't let him inject you!"

Adam advanced on Alex, who reflexively stepped back, his foot catching on a small crease in the poured concrete floor of the cavern. In an instant, Alex went from standing to lying flat on his back, the sharp edges of the cavern's rock ceiling filling his vision. His head smacked hard on the floor and bright stars lit up his field of vision as tiny lightning bolts of agony coursed through him. He shook his head, clearing away the spots in his vision as blood spattered across the floor on either side of him. As he attempted to stand up, the relentless shots to his head finally took their toll. The room spun uncontrollably, causing his legs to give way beneath him. With his eyes squeezed shut, he pushed against the floor, feeling a wave of nausea wash over him. Swallowing hard, he continued to climb toward an upright position, making it solidly to his knees.

Without warning, Adam launched himself at him, his grip on Alex's throat intensifying, causing his lungs to struggle for air. Worse, he could feel Adam digging his thumb and fingers hard into either side of his neck, closing off his carotid artery. In a few seconds, Alex would either pass out from lack of oxygen to his body or lack of blood flow to his brain.

"I've been waiting for this since I first learned about you," Adam whispered, venom in his voice. Blood smeared his face and more flowed freely from his shattered nose, creating a crimson river that fell from his chin and onto his shirt in expanding blobs, forming an obscene Rorschach test. His lips curled back in a vicious snarl that was half smile and half sneer, revealing teeth stained a dark crimson like those of an animal that had just finished a hearty meal after the hunt.

Alex's stomach turned at the stale, coppery smell of Adam's breath and he tried to turn away, but he was held fast in the other man's inhumanly powerful grip. Grasping at his attacker's arm, Alex twisted his head enough to take in a single, meager breath. A breath he used to ask one simple question.

"Why?" The word was almost non-existent as he spoke, like a wisp in the wind.

Adam leaned in, the smell of blood and sweat and rage coming off him. "Because you were given everything. Everything that could have been mine. That *should* have been mine. Wife. Career. Home. Friends. *Everything*. While I had nothing. While I lived as a lapdog to Penders and the Eden Project, trotted out when they needed a mess cleaned up, and then caged again. I was a prisoner while you had the chance to live a life! A life that could have been mine. But they chose you. Someone gifted you that life. We had the same thoughts, the same impulses, the same urges, and yet they chose you over me. Why? Why you and not me?"

Gasping for air, Alex struggled as Adam's grip on his throat tightened. With each passing moment, Alex's world grew fainter, a consequence of the lack of oxygen and blood flow to his brain, as well as the repeated impacts to his head. In that world, where everything seemed dull and lifeless, the brightness of Adam's eyes stood out. Eyes that had seemed so cold before. Those eyes held a coldness that seemed to freeze Alex's soul. While discussing the unfairness of his life, his eyes betrayed a mixture of anger and sadness, flickering from side to side. They were still the hard and remorseless eyes of a killer, but something about them seemed different. There was passion behind those eyes now, passion that warmed the emotionless chill. Passion that focused his intention and fired his anger. Fueled his hatred.

Alex felt his anger. His hatred. It was impossible not to. And it was impossible to shut it out as a thousand icy daggers stabbed into his head and bored their way into his soul, cutting a swath that revealed all the pain and terror and regret of his past. They carved up his psyche, tearing through him with every trauma he'd ever had. Tears stung his eyes and bile rose to choke his throat as the reality of what Adam was saying tore him apart. It was true. Everything Adam was saying was true. They were the same. Underneath the veneer of the life he had forged for himself lay the heart and mind of a stone-cold killer. He couldn't escape that. No matter how far he ran, how desperately he tried to escape it, that was the fact.

He realized then there was one way to escape his destiny. Acceptance. He needed to accept the sins of his past and the inevitability of what he was. Just like he should accept the oblivion Adam was hastening him towards.

Above him, the fiery blue eyes of his only true kin fell away as he embraced the end of his existence. Blackness surrounded him as the choking sounds of his death faded from his ears and the warm comfort of nothingness wrapped around him. He floated in the dark and waited for the end.

Stop.

The word sliced through the comforting black, a gleaming beacon that drew his attention. It danced around him, more felt than heard, much like the shining chorus in his head from before. But there was something more to this. Something familiar. Something close to him.

Come back. Chimes sang out, and the darkness receded slightly from him.

Not bad man.

Needed.

Loved.

Father.

Father. The last word hit him like a shot of adrenaline as realization coursed through him. It was true that he had been created to be a monster, but he didn't have to become one. He had a choice. He had chosen to build a life. To find love. To build a family. He could choose to be different from Adam. He was loved. He was not a bad man. And his daughter needed him.

In that moment, he chose to live.

With a sudden surge of renewed strength, Alex again struck upward at the arm that held his throat in a death grip, driving his fist into the outside of Adam's elbow. The elbow gave way with a loud crack, accompanied by a sharp cry of pain and surprise. The crushing pressure on his throat lifted and Alex gasped hard, drawing in as much precious oxygen as he could, shaking off the daggers of ice from his mind.

"No!" he shouted, locking eyes with Adam. "I know who I am. What I am. And it's not you. Now get the hell away from me!"

He slapped his hands against Adam's chest and pushed, toppling him back. As soon as the weight of his assailant vanished, Alex quickly scrambled upright, steeling himself for the next attack.

The attack didn't come. Adam lay on the cavern floor, a foot away from him, his body convulsing uncontrollably. Alex stepped forward cautiously, watchful for any sign this was a trick, that he was being lured in. Adam didn't stop quivering, making no obvious attempts to stand and fight. As he moved closer, Alex understood why.

Adam's head twisted sharply at an odd angle, propped up by the small pickax that lay beneath it, most likely discarded and abandoned by one of the scientists during the evacuation ordered by Harriman. The blade of the instrument had pierced the back of his neck, very close to his spine by the look of it. The tip of the blade protruded from his throat, having gone straight through him. Blood flowed freely from the wound, pumping out in fountains with each beat of his heart, the flow becoming less forceful each time. It didn't take a doctor to deduce Adam was dying.

Alex fell to one knee, hovering over the man who had made it his singular mission to kill him and steal his life. A man whose entire existence had been predicated on violence and murder, acts he justified as merciful to those he killed. A man who had hurt him, his wife, his friends. Who had destroyed his past out of jealousy and revenge. As he stared now into those cold blue eyes, the eyes that had haunted his nightmares for as long as he could remember, he felt something stirring deep inside him.

Pity.

Like Alex, Adam had no choice in how he came into this world. Unlike Alex, he hadn't had any choice in how he lived after that point. He existed as he had been made. As he was trained. As he was used. He existed as a conscious entity, meticulously shaped into a weapon, and tragically coerced into perpetrating unspeakable horrors for those consumed by insatiable ambition and lacking any moral compass. His entire life was co-opted for their cause, and he followed them because he wasn't aware there might be another path for him to follow. That he could break the chains and disrupt the cycle of pain and anger and live a life of his choosing.

He was what he was, not by his choice. Choice had never been a part of his life, and Alex had to wonder what his life would have been like if it hadn't been a part of his, either. As much pain and sorrow as Adam had brought into his life, in that moment Alex couldn't bring himself to hate the man. He could only mourn the life he never had the chance to live.

He reached down and grabbed Adam's hand, which now shook only slightly. The fountains of blood that had erupted from his wound with each heartbeat were now mere trickles. Alex wrapped his fingers gently around the other man's hands, squeezing lightly, affirming his presence. Staring deep into Adam's eyes, he saw the deep cold melt as awareness slipped from him. Blood gurgled from his throat as he tried to speak, the words lost. His breathing became ragged and shallow as he struggled for each bit of air. Adam's grip tightened around Alex's hand as they locked eyes. The grip faded to nothing, his hand going limp as the light faded from his eyes, leaving behind nothing but emptiness.

A tear ran down Alex's face, startling him. "You're free now," he whispered, dropping Adam's hand to his now still chest. "Brother."

"Don't get too close!" Dr. Forrester suddenly cried out. "Don't let him draw you in!"

Alex wiped away the single tear on his cheek and stood, moving around Adam's body and making his way to the doctor. As he did, his foot hit something that skittered away with a metallic ring. He looked down to see the hypodermic gun Adam had taken from his coat, the amber fluid that had been so concerning to Dr. Forrester sloshing and swirling in the vial as it spun away from him. Following Forrester's warning, he cautiously reached down and grabbed it, making sure to avoid the needle.

"What is this?" Alex asked, holding the instrument out for the doctor to see.

A grimace crossed the scientist's face as he examined it. "A safeguard. It was designed to be used against the Eden Project's soldiers in the event they turned. It's a genetic destabilizer." He surveyed Adam's motionless form as he used the sleeve of his coat to blot the blood from his face. "I suppose I should have used it sooner."

"Or not at all," Alex answered, examining the fluid in the vial. He thought of Adam and all the methods that had been used to control him throughout his life. The pain he had endured. The imprisonment. Suddenly, the hypodermic gun felt hot and heavy in his hand. He kneeled and placed it on the floor, glad to be rid of it.

Alex pivoted to Dr. Forrester, still seated on the floor, with his leg twisted beneath him. "Can you stand?"

The scientist pushed against the floor, moving the other leg to give him some leverage. As he did, his wounded leg screamed in protest as something in his knee made a sickening grinding noise and he landed once more on his posterior.

"I don't think so," he stated, his face twisted with pain. He nodded his head toward the ship and the waiting ramp. "You should go. You have little time."

"No," Alex replied, "I can carry you."

Forrester waved him off. "Don't waste your time on me, my boy. You need to go. You need to live your life. This is somehow... fitting for me. To die like this."

"Don't be ridiculous," Alex said, slipping the doctor's arm over his shoulder and wrapping his arm around the man's waist, hoisting him up. "We'll go together. You still have some life left, Doc. Make good use of it."

Just as Forrester began to protest, the ground trembled violently. Alex managed to maintain his balance and support Forrester, just in time for a stronger and louder tremor to occur.

"The protocols!" Forrester cried. "They've started!"

"Let's go!" Alex shouted, as the cavern came apart around them. Shards of debris, shaken loose from the natural rock ceiling, crashed to the surrounding floor. Alex was amazed that they hadn't been crushed by the first volley. "Inside the ship! It's our only chance!"

Alex raced for the makeshift gangplank, dragging the doctor behind. Grunts and whimpers of pain from his hurt leg accompanied each step Forrester took, yet he still pushed himself forward. As falling boulders broke away from the ceiling, Alex looked upward, attempting to avoid being crushed. He skillfully sidestepped larger chunks and endured being pelted with smaller bits of debris. The metallic ramp gleamed like a lighthouse beacon signaling safety.

As Alex moved toward that beacon, he felt his ankle catch on something, his leg twisting and throwing him off balance. Forrester slipped out of his grasp and he fell hard to the cavern floor, his lip splitting open as his face impacted on the concrete. Warm, coppery liquid filled his mouth as dust and rocks continued to rain down from above. He tried to stand, but his leg was still snagged on something, keeping him down. A sizeable chunk of rock hit the ground and blew apart from the impact about four feet away, the shrapnel lancing painfully into him. Up ahead, the ramp gleamed, waiting.

To break free, he rolled and wriggled, feeling a surge of relief as he untangled himself. His relief quickly turned to fear as he came face to face with Adam, who had a vice-like grip on Alex's ankle and a menacing glare in his eyes. His face was ashen, his lips a pale blue. The wound in his throat bled anew, spilling out onto the floor beneath him as he struggled to keep Alex pinned.

"No," he gurgled, blood streaming from his mouth in rivers. "It can't end like this. You can't live! I won't let you!" He laughed a choked laugh, cut short by the blood welling up in his throat.

All the pity Alex may have felt for him evaporated in that instant, replaced by a desperate need to survive. He shifted his body to the side and kicked hard at Adam, hitting him squarely in the remnants of his shattered nose. Adam's head jerked back as blood and viscera were cast off, but he continued to laugh his maniacal, guttural laugh. The sound cut through Alex, chilling him. Adam's eyes, once cold and calculating, were now feral. Pure instinct had overtaken him. Instinct that drove him to kill his rival. He had accepted his death was imminent, but in that acceptance came the strength and will to make sure he took Alex to the grave with him.

Alex kicked at him again and again, obliterating even more of his already ruined face. But Adam held fast to him, his grip like an iron shackle. Another explosion rocked the cavern and Alex could feel the heat of it radiating through the floor. Soon, destruction would rip through the cavern, obliterating anyone and anything in it. Alex glanced toward the ship, hoping Rachel would have the sense to get herself and the baby to safety. His heart fell as he saw the gangplank still extended from the underbelly of the ship.

Overwhelmed by a renewed sense of desperation, he spun around to attack Adam once again. But as he did, he caught a fleeting glimpse of movement beside him. It was Dr. Forrester, his lab coat torn and his body bruised, who had been dragging himself across the floor and navigating through the wreckage of the crumbling ceiling to reach them. Extending his arm, he reached Adam's side, swiftly injecting the needle into Adam's neck with the hypodermic gun, and activating the trigger. The hypodermic gun emitted a hissing sound as the amber fluid drained from the vial, quickly seeping into Adam's body.

His ice-cold blue eyes, shrouded by the devastated meat of his face, went wide with shock. He released Alex's leg and grabbed at his neck where the doctor had injected him, turning his attention from Alex.

"No!" he screamed, the word muted as it rumbled from his destroyed throat. "Kill you!"

Forrester made no attempt to even try to avoid the attack as Adam launched at him, their bodies colliding with a loud thud. They rolled across the cavern floor in a heap, like a pair of worn rag dolls, rocks falling and bursting apart all around them. Dodging falling missiles of stone, Alex jumped to his feet and swiftly moved toward them. As soon as Forrester caught a glimpse of him, he waved his arm frantically.

"No! Get out! Now! While you still can!"

"I'll get you out," Alex yelled back, taking a step toward them. As he did, a piece of debris twice his size fell to the floor where he had been standing a second earlier.

"Go!" Forrester shouted. "Leave me!"

Dr. Forrester looked away from one creation and down into the face of another, which was now less of a face and more a mass of crushed flesh and splintered bone. But his eyes remained the same. The cold eyes of a predator that had finally found passion and purpose in death. Eyes that would never let him go. Eyes he would die staring into. It was a poetic end, he thought.

As Alex made his way towards the doctor, he encountered a wall of falling debris that blocked his path. Large chunks hit the floor with great impact, splitting off smaller pieces that cut into him like shrapnel expelled from a grenade. He was completely cut off from Forrester, with no time to circumvent the debris. He needed to get to the ship before his chance to board it was lost.

"I'm sorry, doctor," he whispered, the desperation clear in his trembling voice, then turned and bolted towards the ship.

As Dr. Forrester watched him go, a great sense of relief flooded over him. Although his life had come to an end, his most remarkable creation would endure. Endure and prosper. He would carry on the lessons learned and pass them down to a new generation of exceptional individuals, empowering them to use their talents for the betterment of the world. A wave of parental pride surged within him and he smiled.

Both surge and smile faded as he focused on Adam, who lay beside him. Adam, his child of sorrow, who had brought him nothing but anguish, fear, and disappointment. He loved Adam, certainly. He was still his child, after all. But that love was tainted by the deep feeling of shame Forrester felt for him. Adam had proven himself to be irredeemable, his end today a sense of relief for the doctor. There would be no more atrocities committed by him, and he could finally be at peace.

Adam was losing his fight with the genetic destabilizer. His body was breaking down, the sparks in his neural pathways fading. Every movement was a great effort as his body rebelled against him. Most of all, the cold light was gone from his eyes as the fire of his rage slowly died away to embers. His passion and hatred, fueled by his will and determination, would soon vanish entirely. All he was would be no more.

A moment of sadness consumed Dr. Forrester as he reflected on the unfortunate fate of his creation. His child. It would only last for that moment. With a surge of determination, Adam tapped into the deep well of his hatred and resentment, summoning a last surge of energy. Reaching for the doctor, he wrapped his hand around his creator's throat and squeezed, crushing it with a loud crackling sound. In that poignant moment, Dr. Elliot Forrester took his final breath, becoming the tragic casualty of his own invention.

Adam watched the doctor's life leave him. His death had been quiet and, despite the method of it, peaceful. He had died satisfied with his end. The fact sent waves of fury surging through Adam, who had desired more than just the demise of the scientist. He had wanted suffering. Regret. Pleading. Pain. There had been none of that. Forrester had simply slipped into the cold darkness of death as easily as if he had fallen asleep.

Another tremor rocked the cavern as the far wall exploded inward in a cascade of fire. In a matter of moments, the entire cavern would collapse in on them, swallowing them with fire and stone. With great effort, Adam turned his head to the silver ship. Alex was already vanishing up the gangplank and into its depths, but it was too late for them. There was nothing they could do to save themselves, any more than he could for himself.

Adam laid back his head and laughed a thick, gurgling laugh. He would be dead in minutes, but so would Alex and Rachel. Even though it had come at the cost of his own life, he'd had his revenge. He had been true to his word. He had made a solemn promise that if he couldn't attain the happiness they enjoyed, he would obliterate it. He had won, and there was nothing to do now but savor that victory as he waited for the end. Which he did. Until the enormous silver ship burst with white light, the energy shimmering across its surface as it lifted itself from the cavern floor and floated up toward the ceiling of the cavern.

His body was being unraveled by the genetic destabilizer Dr. Forrester had injected him with. The same one he had planned to use on Alex. Unable to move or even speak now, he silently cursed them as he watched the glimmering ship rise toward freedom, their escape the last thing he witnessed as the final explosion consumed him in a wave of fire.

Alex ducked under the ship as the cavern collapsed around him, momentarily safe from the rain of rock. Another tremor hit, throwing him off balance, and he watched as the far wall of the cavern disintegrated and fire swept across half the vast space. It consumed everything in its path, including where he had left Dr. Forrester and Adam. Watching the devastation, guilt and regret overwhelmed him.

His regret was short-lived as the reality of his own peril sank in. He raced onto the ship as the ramp behind him melted into mercury again, flowing up the walls of the entrance and sealing him inside. A sudden quiet surrounded him. Even the impact on the ship of the collapsing ceiling was gone. It was as if he had walked into another world.

The ship appeared to be changing, with calming patterns of light swirling around the inner walls in a hypnotic manner. Its configurations were continuously morphing as walls sprang up and vanished, the floor shifting beneath his feet as it moved him along. The wall directly in front of him evaporated into the floor, revealing a spacious chamber. Lights continued to flash and flicker throughout the ship's interior, mirroring the shifting and changing space around him. In all the changes, one constant stood out: a throne-like chair at the center of the chamber. Fighting his way forward against the ever-changing landscape, he approached the chair.

In it, Rachel remained motionless, her unblinking eyes fixed on the empty space before her. She had a serene expression on her face, as if lost in a pleasant memory. Still and silent, she didn't acknowledge his presence, her focus completely absorbed by something unseen.

Without warning, her eyes shifted rapidly, tracking something in the ether. In that moment her fingers came alive, moving with a frenzied energy. The movement wasn't random, Alex noticed, as they traced the same patterns in the air over and over. Beneath him, Alex could feel a slight rumble from the ship as the fluid motion of the interior rose to a frenetic pace. He hoped the rumbling was the ship powering up and not the sound of explosions ripping them apart.

Rachel twitched slightly, her eyes continuing to dart back and forth at a dizzying pace. It was unnerving to Alex, but he didn't dare touch her or interrupt her. The ship rocked violently beneath them once more and he wished he could see what was happening outside, even if only to see if they were going to escape or be burned by explosions and crushed under the weight of a mountain.

No sooner had he had the thought than the wall directly ahead of them suddenly vanished, revealing the outside of the ship. He realized he should have been amazed by that, but at this point it was just one more remarkable detail to add to the long roster of extraordinary things he had come across.

Through the new viewing portal he could see they were still in the cavern, still climbing to their escape, as boulders broke away and battered the hull. Massive tongues of flame leaped at them, trying to incinerate them with their touch. Eerily, it was all happening with the absence of any sound, as if the end of the world was unfolding in a deafening silence.

In the midst of the chaos, another explosion erupted, sending a terrifying wall of fire hurtling towards them. He felt his entire body instinctively tighten up, preparing for what seemed like the end. When no blast of heat or shattering impact overtook them, he opened his eyes and breathed in the cool, clean air of the ship's cabin. A heavy sigh of relief escaped him and he relaxed slightly while outside, the devastation continued.

Without warning, a sudden pain lanced through his skull, engulfing his entire body in agony. The pain shot through him, leaving no nerve untouched as a sound like a hundred thousand glass wind chimes shattering rang through him. Clutching his head, he was unable to stifle a scream as the world went black for a moment. He kept a tenuous grasp on consciousness as he reached out with his mind, searching for the source of the pain.

It was the ship. While they were safe inside, the ship was absorbing the damage of each strike of rock and fount of burning fire. While the punishment was not nearly as severe as what it regularly withstood from the rigors of space travel, it was still a sentient being who knew pain and fear. Plus, it was still weak from decades of imprisonment. The strain it was under had to be incredible.

Alex focused his thoughts and called out. *I'm here.*

The singing chime voice replied. *Hurt. Need escape. Help her.*

Rachel, he thought. I need to help Rachel.

The surrounding walls began to hum and shift again, louder and with a higher frequency than before, as the dancing lights raced and jumped through them. Something was about to happen; he could feel it. The ship, with Rachel's help, was about to make a final bid to escape.

As the ship moved, the flames outside changed pattern and accelerated, rising towards the ceiling, while another explosion from below caused further destruction to the cavern floor. Fire leaped through the jagged hole beneath them and lapped hungrily at the underside of the great ship, seemingly trying to pull it back down. Alex couldn't feel any heat through the walls of the ship, but he still felt a phantom residual of pain from his connection with the vessel.

Next to him, Rachel muttered something he couldn't understand as her eyes stopped their frantic dance and fixed on one location in the craggy rock ceiling. There was no exit he could see, but Rachel was undeterred as her fingers danced wildly once more and the craft moved upward through the rain of debris. Tearing his eyes from the destruction playing out before him, Alex glanced at his wife. Her face had changed from when he first found her in that chair. No longer a blank and distant stare, her brow was tightly furrowed and her eyes remained steadily fixed ahead of her. Her eyes were filled with blood, the capillaries swollen, and a small stream of blood flowed from each nostril and ear. Her fingers were moving so fast now that he could hardly track their movement as she guided the vessel forward through the destruction. Alex was fighting the urge to yank her from the chair before the blood vessels in her brain imploded from the stress, but he knew he couldn't. She had been chosen to pilot this ship, and she was their only hope of survival.

Help her.

The ship chimed a plea to him that sounded desperate, despite the inherent beauty of its voice, and it was enough to snap him back to the moment and into action. Stepping up next to her, he gently laid his hand on her arm, being careful to avoid the deft movements of her fingers. He felt the warmth of her under his hand, the smoothness of her skin. There was something else there, too. A slight tingle of energy in their touch, mingling and flowing between them.

Just as he had in the hospital with Babcock, Alex focused on the flow of energy inside his own body. He could feel it flowing through him like a river, feeding and strengthening him. Also like a river, he could redirect it. As he held onto Rachel's arm, he focused on the connection they shared, channeling his life force into her. He let it flow freely to her, and he could feel her hungrily accept it. He felt the tension in her body ease and her breathing became less labored as she sank back into the chair. Her fingers still danced frantically and her gaze remained steadily focused, but the intense strain had melted from her.

On the transparent wall ahead, the ceiling was looming ever closer. Alex desperately wanted to close his eyes against what he was certain would be them splattering themselves across the great cavern just seconds before being consumed by the final explosion. His eyes remained fixed on the scene in front of them, just like Rachel's, and he could only watch as the ship crashed into the jagged rock.

The great impact he was expecting didn't come. There was no shaking, no crushing, no rending of the skin of the great ship. There was nothing. It was as if the wall of rock had never been there at all, that it was a figment of his imagination. The wall that had been transparent a moment ago once more dissolved into a swarm of lights, closing them off from the world outside. He wondered if they had made it out and were now darting across the night sky, or if they were dead and waiting for the angels to come and claim them.

Realizing his hand was still locked on her arm, Alex released his grip from Rachel. Her arm dropped from his grip and fell against the side of the chair with a thump. She sat still and unmoving in the chair, red streaks of blood crossing her face and neck, soaking into her shirt in an ugly red blotch at her neck. Her eyes were closed and her head had fallen against the back of the chair, her body limp like a child's discarded doll.

"Rachel!" Alex screamed, grasping her shoulders and lightly shaking her. She shifted slightly as he did, but her eyes remained closed.

Safe.

It was the ship again, in his head. Stronger now, its tone lighter once more.

"What do you mean?" Alex yelled, panic rising in his voice.

Safe.

Alive.

Well.

The words, carried by the melodic tone of the ship's 'voice', calmed him. Rachel would be all right. She had saved them. It had come with a cost, but they were safe now thanks to her.

He kneeled by her side and placed his head gently in her lap, the rhythmic rise and fall of her chest with each breath and the warmth of her skin comfortable reminders that she was alive. Against all odds, they had survived.

As his body relaxed, Alex could feel fatigue taking hold. He couldn't remember the last time he'd had any real sleep, and he was tired. So tired. Tired of running. Tired of fighting.

A soft voice, different from that of the ship, whispered in his mind.

Rest.

Sleep.

Father.

He smiled as the tiny voice sang in his head, letting the peacefulness it brought draw his eyes closed. Slowly, he let the darkness envelope him and nestle him comfortably in its embrace.

His eyes opened to a vast, star-filled sky overhead. For the briefest of moments, Alex lay where he was and stared at the simple beauty of the twinkling lights above him, shining brightly against the deep black of the night. The scent of damp grass filled his nostrils, and he breathed deeply to take it in as crisp, cool night air filled his lungs. In response, he breathed out a deep, satisfied sigh.

The moment of peace fell away as the memory of their escape from the horror of Gabriel's Nest in a shining silver alien spacecraft crawled into his mind. Panic set in and supplanted the contentment and he sat up, frantically searching his surroundings. The glowing, shifting walls of the great ship were gone and a vast field surrounded him. The grass beneath him was damp with dew and it seeped into his clothes, bringing with it a sharp chill against his skin. In the distance, the horizon was fading from the black of night to the light purple of morning.

A low but satisfied groan rose from the grass beside him, and he turned to see Rachel lying next to him. The wetness of the grass permeated her clothes, and she shivered slightly as she pulled herself into a sitting position. Dried blood caked her ears and nostrils.

"Where are we?" she asked, shaking her head slightly as if trying to scatter the fog gathered there.

"I have no idea," Alex answered as he surveyed their surroundings. The light of the coming day was overtaking more of the sky, allowing him to make out some shapes, such as the silhouette of a house in the distance. As if in response to being noticed, two small rectangles of light appeared within the dark outline.

"How did we get here?" Rachel asked as she ran her fingers through tangled hair, flecks falling away as she pulled strands free from the dried blood that had ensnared them like insects in amber.

"You don't remember?" Alex asked as he pulled his overshirt off and wrapped it around her shoulders.

She pulled his shirt tight around her and shook her head. "The last thing I remember is running inside that silver spaceship. Everything else is a blank."

Out of nowhere, he was struck by her beauty and couldn't help but smile. After everything she had experienced, everything she had endured, she had faced it down and remained radiant.

"You saved us," he said, his voice flushed with affection and admiration. "You flew that ship out of there just in time, and I mean *just* in time, and you saved us."

To Alex's surprise, she chuckled. It wasn't the reaction he had expected.

"It might have seemed that way," she said, "but I don't think it was me."

Alex shifted slightly in the grass, turning to her. "What do you mean?"

She ran her hand lightly over her belly. "I think it was her. With a little help."

"Help?" Alex asked. "Help from who?"

"From that alien in the lab. I don't think he was completely... gone. I think a part of him was still alive. Alive and waiting for us. For her. When it gave up whatever it did, its life force or whatever, to the baby, I think that's what saved us." She rubbed lightly across her stomach.

Alex flashed back to the small voice he'd heard just before falling asleep on the ship. He had thought it was a dream, a hallucination running through his subconscious as he faded from awake to asleep, but he could have sworn the voice had called him 'father'.

He breathed another heavy sigh. It was becoming a habit for him. "So, it sounds like we still have some adventures ahead of us with this little one."

"Seems that way," she replied, smiling brightly.

The purple edge to the sky was vanishing into a light yellow as the sun emerged over the horizon. Standing, he held his hand out to Rachel. "Come on."

"Where are we going?" she asked, slipping her hand into his.

He pulled her to her feet and stood close to her, kissing her gently on her forehead. "I don't know yet, but we have to keep this little girl out of the hands of the Eden Project. Or anyone like them."

She rested her head against his chest. "Do you think they'll still come after us?"

"I don't think they're likely to give up because we slipped through their fingers once. If anything, they'll only be more driven now that they know what that little girl of ours is already capable of."

"Where do we go?" Rachel asked, her voice weary again. "How do we hide from something like that?"

Alex looked out at the sky, the singular black of night replaced by a series of oranges, yellows, and blues. With morning approaching, they had to keep moving.

He pulled Rachel's hand in close to his chest, just over his heart. "I don't know yet, but we will. Have faith."

"I love you, Alex Carter."

"I love you, too."

With that, they stood in silence and watched the sun come up, washing away the darkness and bringing with it the hope that came with a new day.

Epilogue

Ernest Babcock leaned back in the hard, worn swivel chair behind the scarred and pitted desk of the Chief of Police for the town of Pine Haven and, with a deeply satisfied smile, set his feet on top. He'd been waiting a long time to do that, and after a long and hard road, the right was finally his.

He lifted his coffee mug to his lips to take a drink, but a knock at the door stalled him. "Who is it?" he called out, dropping his feet back to the floor and pulling himself up to the desk, straightening his back in an effort to look as professional as possible. It was a tough thing to do at eight o'clock in the morning with a coffee stain already screaming out from the front of your shirt.

"Maggie," came the answer from behind the door.

Babcock sighed and resumed his previous position. "Come on in."

The door opened halfway and Maggie McCall slipped into his office, dressed sharply in an olive suit with her hair pulled tautly yet elegantly back from her face. She stood just on the other side of his desk, her hands resting behind her back.

"Morning, Maggie. What can I do for you today, Lieutenant?" Babcock asked, being sure to add emphasis to her new title and position as head of Investigations.

He risked taking a careful sip from his steaming mug. Not careful enough, apparently, as a droplet of coffee fell from the cup and barely missed his dark paisley tie, splattering onto his white shirt. Mumbling, he wiped at it with his hand, smearing it across his chest in a way that only accentuated it. "Guess I'll never bring any class to the job, huh?"

Maggie smiled a warm, friendly smile. "Why start now, after all these years?"

"Har, har, har," Babcock replied. "So, what brings you to my luxury accommodations this morning?"

Maggie took her hands from behind her back and in one of them was a wedge of polished wood about six inches long. A brass plate was affixed to one side, and she held it up so he could read it. "It just came in this morning. I thought I'd bring it by personally."

The plate read simply: Ernest Babcock, Chief. Babcock pushed away from his desk and stood, taking the nameplate from Maggie.

"I can't believe they put me in charge," he said, turning the piece of wood and metal over in his hands. He meant it sincerely. He was surprised to have made it to the rank of lieutenant, let alone chief. But in the last year, since he had last seen Alex and Rachel Carter, his life and career had taken some dramatic turns. Some of which he never would have expected in his wildest dreams.

"That's what a lot of the guys are saying, too," Maggie jabbed, although nothing could be further from the truth. Babcock's promotion had brought nothing but rave reviews from the rest of the Pine Haven Police Department. Ernest Babcock had earned the respect of the officers he served with long before he ever took the position of Chief, and they appreciated he was one of them. That he had been there for them and was ready to assist and defend them now. It was common consensus that there was no one better suited for the job than Ernie Babcock, coffee stains and all.

"That's not the only reason I stopped in, though," Maggie continued, her voice dropping back into her business tone. "I got another call from Hardawick this morning."

"The Homeland Security guy? What's that, the fourth call this week?" Babcock sighed, leaning his ample frame against his desk.

"Fifth," Maggie answered.

"How in the hell do they expect us to get anything done when we spend half our lives on the phone with them?" He set the nameplate on the edge of his desk, pushing back a small bit of the already considerable amount of clutter that had gathered there. "What did he want this time?"

Maggie shrugged. "The usual. Wants to talk about what you found in that farmhouse we raided after receiving your 'anonymous tip'. And he still wants to know who the tipster was."

"Whatever he wants to know about the stuff we found there is fine," Babcock replied, plopping back into his chair. "But as for who gave us the tip..."

Maggie held up her hand, cutting him off. "I know. That's none of his business."

"None of his *damned* business, Maggie," Babcock corrected her. "Adjectives are important. They can make or break a sentence."

"None of his *damned* business," she repeated. "Got it."

"Good to know I can count on you," Babcock replied, giving her a curt salute.

"Have you heard from him lately?" Maggie asked, changing the subject.

Babcock looked away from her. "Not in a while, no."

"Just wondering if they're okay," she said. "I think about them, wonder if they're alright. It's got to be tough on them, always on the run. Especially with a new baby."

"I'm sure they're fine," Babcock uttered, his voice low. "Wherever they are."

Maggie chuckled as she turned to leave. "Chief, remind me to invite you over for poker sometime. You are the world's worst goddam liar."

She slipped out of his office before he could reply, chuckling as she went. Try as he might, Babcock couldn't repress a smile. McCall had always been a crackerjack detective; he should have known better than to try to keep secrets from her.

He leaned back once more and was just getting comfortable when a light chirp sounded from the bottom drawer of his desk. Pulling the drawer open, he grabbed the compact flip-phone style cellular phone that was sitting atop a pile of papers. It was a burner phone he had picked up a while ago. The number on the caller ID screen was unfamiliar to him, but it didn't matter. There were only two people in the world who had that number.

He flipped the phone open, holding it to his ear. "Hello?"

"Hello, Ernie," came the familiar voice from the other end of the line.

Babcock breathed a sigh of relief he didn't realize had been gathering inside him. It was good to hear his voice, better that he sounded happy. "How you doin'?"

"About the same," the caller answered in what sounded like an audible shrug. "Things never change much around here. How's the family?"

"The usual," Babcock answered. "The kids are driving me insane, but in the most adorable way. Ang is doing well. She's constantly asking about you are your lovely wife, not to mention that baby girl of yours. How about you? Everyone okay? You doing all right so far?"

"We're settling in," answered the caller. "It's been a challenge, but I think we've finally found a place where we can be safe. It's a beautiful little town. I wish I could tell you where we are, but you know how these things work."

"I get it," Babcock replied, but it pained him not to know. After everything they had gone through together, he wished there was more he could do for them. "It's enough to know that the three of you are all right."

"Any more news about the Eden Project?" the caller asked, changing the subject.

"Nothing more than what you've seen online," Babcock replied. "The fallout from what happened has ruined PenTech. Their stock is completely worthless, and the company has filed for bankruptcy. Their shareholders are pissed and are demanding answers. So is the government, who are consistently shredding them in the congressional hearings. The piranhas are gathering to pick the corpse clean."

"Was it a good idea for you to go public with everything before calling Homeland Security?" the caller asked.

"Maybe not," Babcock chuckled, "but it sure has made meetings with Homeland more interesting. Besides, you know damned well that if that information hadn't been 'leaked' to the public first, the government would have snatched up all that data and tech and conveniently swept the story under the rug. Calling the newshounds first made it impossible to do that. And now I get to watch their faces turn six different shades of purple when they have to deal with me."

"Did you just say 'newshounds'? Were you born in the Great Depression?" the caller chided.

"Very funny and go fuck yourself," Babcock replied.

"In all seriousness, Ernie, are you safe? Are you sure they won't come after you?"

"They know I've got 'em by the short hairs," Babcock responded as he took a flawless sip from his mug. "With all the information floating around the internets about this thing, there's no way they can come at me. It's just too public and I am smack in the center of it. Anything happens to me, there's no way they can write it off as coincidence. I have to be dealt with. Consulted. Hell, even pandered to, if the mood strikes me. It infuriates them to have to kowtow to a small-town hick cop like me. They despise it. I'm having the time of my life."

"I'm sure you are," the caller laughed.

A few seconds of silence passed between them before the caller spoke again, his tone more serious. "I just want you to be safe. You and your family. You've risked enough already; I don't want anyone else getting hurt helping us."

"I'll be fine," Babcock assured him. "I have Maggie and Celeste to back me up in the department, and in case you aren't aware, my wife can take care of herself. I just wish you had some backup of your own."

"Oh, I think you might be surprised on that front," the caller replied. There was another brief pause. "I have to go. We can't stay on the line too long."

"I know," Babcock answered sullenly. Despite the fact that he had picked up a few anonymous pay-as-you-go 'burner phones' to facilitate their ability to stay in touch, Babcock was sure other parties were listening in on their conversations. That wasn't his biggest concern, as he had just explained, he was protected. He didn't want Homeland Security or any other organization that might be listening to be able to track the call back to its source, though. That would undo every precaution they had taken in the last year.

"Just do me a favor and hug that pretty wife of yours for me," he continued, trying to keep his tone upbeat. "And hug that baby girl. She's special, you know."

"I know," the caller answered. "And Ernie...?"

"Yeah?"

"Don't think I missed the fact that you said 'internets' a minute ago, grampa."

"Shut up," Babcock shot back.

"Just one more thing," the caller said, his voice quavering slightly.

"What is it this time, smart ass?"

"In case I haven't said it enough, thank you."

"For what?"

"For believing."

Before Babcock could reply the caller dropped off, the tiny screen on the phone showing the call had ended. He sat there for a long time staring at the phone, as if he could will the conversation back, before finally folding the phone closed and dropping it back into his desk drawer. He didn't know why, but this conversation seemed different from others they'd had in the past year. It had more of an air of finality to it. That the book was closing for good. He hated the thought, but there was nothing he could do. They were on their own, and he had to trust that they would be all right. They were tough, to be sure. After everything they'd been through, he knew he really didn't have to worry about them.

Yet he couldn't stop. Despite only knowing them briefly, he had established a deep bond with them. A strong link through their shared experiences. He had become emotionally invested in them, and the thought of never being able to see them again was heart-wrenching. That there was nothing he could do to protect them. He felt useless, and it was infuriating to him.

He couldn't just sit and dwell on it, that would drive him insane. He needed to talk to someone, someone who might understand what he was going through. After a few moments of thought, he picked up his desk phone and punched in a few numbers. Maggie answered after two rings.

"I need you to do something for me, Maggie."

"Sure thing, Chief. What do you need?"

"Call Celeste over at the hospital and tell her to get to the Bagel Stable. Then get your coat."

"Okay," Maggie answered. "Why?"

"I need to talk, so I'm taking the two of you out to breakfast. You have a problem with that?"

"Not at all," Maggie replied. "Be ready in a minute."

Hanging up the phone, Babcock stood up and picked up his coat from the back of his chair. While breakfast and conversation with Celeste and Maggie wouldn't help Alex and Rachel, at least it would make him feel a bit better. And that was a start.

The baby in the crib was sound asleep, her breathing light and rhythmic as her tiny chest expanded and fell with each breath. Her father peered at her as she slept, which had been his routine since she came into his life a few months ago. He looked forward to it every night.

A creaking of floorboards behind him alerted him to someone else in the room and he turned to see his wife standing just inside the doorway. He pressed a finger to his lips as she glided silently across the floor without another creak underfoot.

"Is she asleep?" she asked in a hushed tone, coming up beside him and wrapping her arms around his waist.

"Like an angel," he whispered back.

"She's beautiful, isn't she?"

"Just like her mom," he answered, slipping an arm around her shoulder as she leaned into him.

"Well, aren't you just a special kind of charmer?"

He smiled. "I've heard specialness runs in the family."

In the crib, the delicate form stirred, her tiny fingers stretching out. Her mouth curved slightly, as if forming a tiny smile.

"Look at that smile," her father said. "She knows we're here."

"It's just gas," her mother replied. "She's too little to smile yet."

"You don't really believe that, do you?"

"Of course not. I also don't want you getting all cocky with pride about your daughter, either."

"I do not get cocky."

"Yes, you do. And insufferable."

Rachel smiled at him and nestled in closer. Her smile was still the same warm smile Alex had always known, even though the face it was on now was slightly different. Her hair was colored a plain brown and cut to just above her shoulders, and it bounced with a bit of curl. The once vibrant green eyes were now concealed behind contacts, transforming their color into a subdued slate gray. It complimented the changes in him as he had grown out his hair to a reasonable length and added a touch of reddish blonde to it, along with the close-trimmed beard he now sported. Her face was different, but it was still the face of the woman he loved.

Her name was different now, too, as was his. When they had first come to the small seaside town in British Columbia they knew the life they had before was over. They would have to create something completely new. They had adopted the maiden name of Rachel's great-grandmother, Neal, as their last name and had built a life for themselves as Nick and Amanda Neal. The tiny community had welcomed them, and they quickly immersed themselves in the rhythm of life there. Accounts set up by Drs. Carlton and Forrester funded their new life, using assets siphoned from various PenTech sources and revealed to them by Dr. Carlton in a hidden file on the thumb drive left for them. Their financial security would allow them to fully devote themselves to raising their daughter and enjoying a tranquil life as a family.

Amanda took Nick by the arm and let him away from their daughter's crib. "Let's let her sleep for a while without us hovering over her, okay?"

"It'll be tough," Nick answered, "but I think I'm up to the challenge."

"She is beautiful, isn't she? Our little Faith?"

"That's what he we always said we needed, a little faith." Nick looked back to the crib where Faith lay, still deep in sleep. "Now we have her and I feel like there's nothing I can't do."

"Except beat me at *Jeopardy!*," Amanda said, looking at her watch. "But if you'd like to try, it's on in five minutes."

"You're on," Nick replied, smiling a warm, deep smile at her. "I love you."

"I love you, too," Amanda answered, "but I won't spot you any points."

The two of them carried their banter downstairs and away from the slumbering baby, who started to shiver and twitch. With a few soft noises, the kind babies often make when scared or nervous, her eyes opened to her darkening room. She searched as far as she could see, looking for something. Something special. Something she needed desperately.

She found it at last, across the room on her dresser. Her teddy bear, the one her father had brought to her the night she was born. The bear had slept in her crib with her every night of her life, but tonight her father had forgotten to put her bear in with her and she missed it terribly. So terribly. She needed her bear. Her friend.

As if in answer to the newborn's unspoken need, the bear rose gently from the dresser and floated through the air, coming to rest next to the little girl. With a satisfied grin (that her mother would no doubt have passed off as gas) little Faith Neal rolled back onto her side, closed her eyes and went back to sleep, dreaming of the silver disk that would someday take her to her cousins among the stars.

About the Author

The God Makers is Scott's first work to see publication. His passion for comic books and science fiction, fantasy, and horror novels labeled him as a nerd during his younger years; a reputation he has embraced with pride and carried into adulthood. He is especially fond of stories about ordinary people who find themselves in extraordinary circumstances, which is reflected in his work.

In addition to being a writer, he is also a skilled stage actor who has taken on the roles of Jean Valjean in *Les Miserables*, Dr. Jekyll/Mr. Hyde in *Jekyll & Hyde*, Max Bialystok in Mel Brooks' *The Producers*, Archibald Craven in *The Secret Garden*, Daddy Warbucks in *Annie*, Lord Farquaad in *Shrek*, and many more. His most significant theater collaboration happened in 1994 when he married his incredible wife, Jessica, whom he met backstage during a production of Gilbert and Sullivan's *The Mikado*.

He and Jessica live in New Hampshire with their dog, Scout, and cat, Boo Rad.

Made in the USA
Monee, IL
13 September 2024